For artists and creatives, who choose every day to put light and colour into the world despite it all.

Kiln Me Softly

Kiln Me Softly

B.B. WOODS

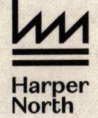

Harper
North

HarperNorth
Windmill Green
24 Mount Street
Manchester M2 3NX

A division of
HarperCollins*Publishers*
1 London Bridge Street
London SE1 9GF

www.harpercollins.co.uk

HarperCollins*Publishers*
Macken House,
39/40 Mayor Street Upper,
Dublin 1, D01 C9W8, Ireland

First published by HarperCollins*Publishers* Ltd 2025
1

A catalogue record for this book is available from the British Library.

ISBN: 978-0-00-875345-0

This novel is entirely a work of fiction. The names, characters and incidents portrayed
in it are the work of the author's imagination. Any resemblance to actual persons,
living or dead, events or localities is entirely coincidental.

Set in Bembo ST by Amnet.

Printed and bound in the UK using 100% Renewable Electricity by CPI Group
(UK) Ltd

This book contains FSC™ certified paper and other controlled
sources to ensure responsible forest management.

For more information visit: www.harpercollins.co.uk/green

Acknowledgements

Juniper and Aiden's story has been a pleasure and a privilege to write in so many ways, and it might not have existed if, while plotting the spicy woodcutter romance that would soon become *Kindling*, I didn't say to my editor, 'TikTok potters are also quite yummy.' Which is to say, thank you to artists who share their work in online spaces, giving us romance authors plenty of inspiration.

In all seriousness, I poured a lot of my heart into *Kiln*. It was quite strange to write this book at a time where, now more than ever, the value of human artists is at risk. It would feel wrong not to acknowledge that here. I am not a potter, but like Juniper, I adore art for everything that it represents: joy, passion, love, creativity. These are things that can't be taken away, things the world relies on to stay bright and alive, so whether you are someone who colours outside the lines on weekends, paints every single day, writes a few poems on your notes app every now and again, or studies art in the hopes it will lead somewhere like the characters in this book, I hope you know that it matters – especially in marginalised communities, especially when it's hard to get up in the morning, especially when you're wondering how you'll pay the rent. This book is for you and all the ones who came before. Our world would be grey without you.

Speaking of artists, I would like to thank the people who made this book happen. Clare and the Liverpool Literary Agency gang for still not being too fed up with my little panics and doubts. You make me all the prouder to be northern! To Daisy, for letting me write the pottery book of my dreams and for getting me this far. To Genevieve, for being so kind, warm, and welcoming when *Kiln* was transferred to your hands. To Laura for the edits, and to the rest of the team at HarperNorth, who have gotten my little kissing books into supermarkets and bookshops across the world! I'm still in awe of everything we've accomplished since publishing *Kindling* last autumn.

To my best friends, Ivy, Leah, and Mahlina, who let me ramble about the little people in my head and have taught me what love and found family means. I'm running out of ways to tell you how much I love you. Also to Fi and Beth, for being there even after so many years apart.

To the Swords & Sapphics Discord, for letting me bounce ideas and worries off you, and for being the kind community I always dreamed of building – Merlina, Lillian, Magnolia, Katherine (who helped me with the Medusa bit), Josie (whose company during sprints made sure I actually wrote the thing), and many more.

To author and reader friends who have supported me from being a little-known indie author to now: Rebecca Crunden, AKA Indie Book Spotlight; Jane, who is too supportive for words; Hayley Anderton, a generous and bright light in the indie community; and Bethany, AKA beths_bookblog, for the same reason. To Abbie and Stef, for sharing my books with anyone who will listen. Authors couldn't exist without support like yours, and I appreciate you endlessly.

To the writing group I was brave enough to join, Daisy and Belle. I have loved getting to know you.

To my family: no, you are not allowed to read this book either, but thank you for never discouraging me from choosing art the way Juniper's and Aiden's family do. To Enzo the dog, who shouts at me when I have been at my laptop for too long and loves me at my worst. To my old hamster Billy Bob, who inspired Cerberus.

Finally, and as always, I would like to thank the readers I've found along the way. The response to *Kindling* blew me away, and I received so many messages about how much of a comfort Harper, in all her bisexual plus-size glory, was to you. I see you, and you deserve your happily ever after, too – even if you're messy like Juniper, and even if you grind your teeth like Aiden.

Oh! And also thank you to *The Great Pottery Throw Down*, which is where most of my knowledge came from (sorry). Watching Keith Brymer Jones shed tears over ceramics is actually quite special.

1

Juniper was lost. Geographically, that was. Probably emotionally, too, but she wasn't thinking about that at the moment on account of the fact that it was the first day of her new and improved life – or would be if she could just find the building where all her hopes and dreams lay.

She swiped her sweaty curtain fringe from her eyes, nerves jangling as she looked around the grand college campus situated in the heart of London. RACA, the Royal Academy of Ceramic Arts, was a small university in comparison to most, but no less intimidating, especially to a northern lass who had spent the last couple of years away from education. She currently stood in Potter's Square, a paved open space surrounded by tall, modern blocks of classrooms on one side and a cluster of historic Georgian buildings on the other: a far cry from the industrial red bricks and Gothic architecture of Manchester. In front of her, the vast exhibition gallery gleamed like a temple, supported by elaborate pillars. Behind, the library was almost as grand, housing a turret clock that reminded her she was quite late.

Late, and officially out of her depth. Even the majestic bronze statue of Magdalene Wells – also known as one of the earliest pioneers of modern ceramic sculpting, so Juniper had researched – seemed to know it, narrowed eyes looking down haughtily at her.

'I know, Mags. I'm buggered,' she muttered, and took out her phone just to make sure the clock wasn't lying to her.

Okay, she was doubly buggered. Her workshop introduction had started five minutes ago. She cursed herself for taking that extra ten (okay, twenty) minutes in the shower this morning and ran to the first person she could find, who happened to be a short man with a very red, very wiry beard. He didn't seem all that happy when Juniper touched his arm, quick to put distance between them with a Magdalene-like cock of his head.

'Hello. Sorry!' Juniper blurted. 'First of all, do I have ketchup on my chin?' She'd eaten a bacon butty – sorry, *sandwich* now she was down south – on the way in and couldn't be certain.

He blinked, then said, 'No.'

'Are you just saying that to get rid of me?'

'Yes.' He made to continue on his way, leaving Juniper to dash after him. Despite being barely taller than her five-three height, his strides were surprisingly long and difficult to catch up to. She'd known Londoners wouldn't be quite as patient as the friendly northerners she was used to, but bloody hell.

'I just wanted to know where the Whiteread Building is?' she asked between trying to catch her breath. Powerwalking was not her strong suit, especially not with anxiety tightening her lungs.

'No idea,' he said as he reached a heavy black door on the left side of campus, the name of which read *Whiteread Building.*

Without deigning to glance her way, the red-haired stranger pushed through, leaving the door to swing shut in Juniper's mystified face. Not before she shouted, 'Arsehole!' loud enough to garner a few perplexed looks from passersby.

She flexed her fingers tighter around the straps of her black leather backpack, trying to ignore the heat crawling up her throat. She would *not* cry. Not even if she wanted to turn back and go home, where everything was familiar and people were at least a little bit nicer to her.

But also where she'd always felt aimless and out of place.

C'mon, Juni. You're here. You made it. Just go in.

She wiped her clammy palms on her jeans and followed the rude man inside before she had the chance to talk herself out of it. She'd be damned if some tweed-wearing ignoramus ruined this opportunity for her.

Juniper was hit by the smell of paint chemicals and earthy clay, a sign she was in the right building and enough to set her skin tingling with anticipation. Soon, she'd be able to call herself a real ceramicist, just like Mags.

All right, not *quite* like Mags, but she'd try her best.

The lobby was modern and bright, with a noticeboard spanning one wall. A cluster of posters were tacked to the cork, advertising upcoming events both on and off campus. A few loudly dressed students loitered around glass coffee tables and yellow couches with their laptops, the patchwork cushions making the space feel less like a college and more like a common room. The walls were just as eye-catching, painted a powdery shade of sky-blue that Juniper had been longing for all summer. A sign laid out workshop rooms, studio spaces, and classroom numbers on a map. Using her phone to quadruple-check she hadn't misread, she searched for WS2 and followed directions into a lift to get to the first floor.

Here we go, then, she thought as the lift clunked up one flight.

When the doors slid open, she headed down an echoey corridor filled with abstract paintings and pictures of sculptures, just like she'd imagined. She was surrounded by art, and she'd never felt more at home as she knocked on the door—

'*You?*' she blurted.

In her workshop room, the rude man stood in front of a PowerPoint presentation, shirt rolled up to the elbows and that same completely unimpressed expression on his face.

Lazily, he leaned against the corner of his desk. 'Glad you could *ketchup* to the rest of us.' And then, when Juniper only stared: 'Come on, that's quite funny for an arsehole like me.'

The smirk rising under his beard did nothing to quell Juniper's dismay… *or* her steadily growing embarrassment.

Mutters rippled through the students, who were now all staring at Juniper, likely wondering why the hell she'd interrupted their class to shout at their tutor.

'I, er…' Should she apologise? She didn't really want to, not to him. But if her timetable was correct, this was Christopher Curtis, one of RACA's most experienced professors, and she didn't fancy being on his bad side.

4

'Dig your hole later.' Christopher pointed to one of the only empty seats by the window. A collection of chairs had been arranged around the whiteboard, which was not what she'd hoped for. She was ready to get comfortable at one of the workstations laid out behind.

Dipping her head like a scolded puppy, Juniper went to her chair, trying to ignore the burn of a dozen pairs of eyes on her. She'd forgotten how demoralising education could be, or perhaps she'd expected better in an undergraduate course. She wasn't a kid anymore, and she'd had enough talent to earn her place here with a full tuition bursary to cover the expenses. Fine, she wasn't anything special, but didn't she deserve at least a little bit of respect as an adult who had come here to learn?

She plopped her bag down on the floor, intending to sit, but the student beside her chair was still staring. She snapped her head up, intending to ask if the dark-haired lad would rather take a picture instead, only the words didn't come out quite like that.

Instead, they were a sharp utterance that conveyed the dread, memories, disgust, rising inside her: 'You've got to be shitting me.'

Again, the room fell silent. Again, Juniper had trouble noticing, too busy wondering why the hell the seat beside her was currently occupied by somebody she'd assumed she'd never, ever see again.

Aiden Twatface Whittaker, the definition of wealthy white male privilege, and Juniper's greatest enemy.

He'd made her adolescence miserable, mainly because he'd tried half as hard as her in art class and still had their teacher wrapped around his finger, along with everyone else in that miserable little high school. It wasn't even the way he'd patronised her that had pissed her off, or the silly nicknames he and his mates had thought up to get under her skin. No, it was the way he'd walked around like he was owed something just by existing. Sure, he'd been a talented painter, but wouldn't anyone who had a father that worked as a renowned dealer in the industry be? Not to mention, he'd always bragged about having a private studio decked out at home. Juniper might have rivalled him if she'd had the same money, the same connections, but her parents were working-class, her school uniform and supplies all second-hand.

She wasn't surprised to find that he hadn't changed much, though his once-short hair had grown out to be a floppy, brushed back assortment of chestnut waves that ended in curls around his jawline. Of course, his pretty hazel eyes and chiselled features had done him favours, too, now made rugged by a hint of stubble. He'd grown into his square jaw, and his face and brawny body had filled out in a way that was both hard and soft, muscular and not, as though his scrawny arrogant arse hadn't already taken up enough space.

That obnoxious little smirk, always reserved just for Juniper, made its appearance, smarmier now thanks to the deepened dimple in his cheek and the asymmetry of his plump bottom lip versus his thin top one. He might have been one of those sculptures outside, carved by deft ancient hands. How Juniper would love to smash him up into pieces.

'Nice to see you again, too, Juni.' His gravelly voice – had it been that deep before? – sent a zap of goosebumps down

Juniper's arms, just like it used to. It didn't take much to make her skin crawl, but he'd always commanded a physical reaction with only a few words, an abject disgust she felt now more than ever.

What was he doing *here*? This was *her* dream. Her moment. Not *his*!

'Oh, my apologies. I thought we were done with this little performance,' Christopher said behind her, dragging her back to the present. For a moment, she'd been in Mrs. Park's classroom again, sent to the corner for being 'disruptive' while Aiden mimicked disappointed tuts, oozing cocky immaturity.

She would *not* let history repeat itself. He'd taken enough from her already.

With an unwavering glare at Aiden, she took her seat, willing the twist in her gut to ease. It didn't. His presence seared a hole through her layers of clothes, and she could still feel his scrutiny as Christopher began to speak.

'Well, now that we're all *finally* here and *finally* quiet, shall we begin?'

Christopher had only gotten two slides into his presentation when Aiden leaned towards her, a pen jiggling between his thumb and forefinger. 'Aren't you going to say hello to me properly, Juni?'

'*Per*,' she hissed out.

His dark brows dipped in confusion. 'Eh?'

'Juni*per*. Only my friends call me Juni.' Not that she had many of those lately. She'd been too busy working her arse off at a fast-food chain, trying to earn enough money to get here. Even with the bursary, and even living in dorms, London wasn't cheap.

'Ouch. Here I thought we were old chums.' His hot breath tickled her ear and she squirmed away, too aware that she'd yet to register a single thing Christopher had said about the course.

She at least pretended to engage, dragging her notebook from her backpack along with her pen. She'd hoped for prettier stationary, but settled on plain Poundland stuff after discovering textbooks were the biggest form of daylight robbery she'd ever seen.

'Last I heard, you were off to Elmington for a degree in snooty-prick-ology. If you ask me, you wouldn't have needed it. You're already excelling in your field.' Elmington School of Fine Arts was one of the leading art universities in Europe. Only one artist from each county was selected per course, their attempt to make things fair – only it wasn't. It hadn't surprised her one bit when, after receiving her own rejection letter, she'd opened Instagram to find old friends celebrating Aiden's acceptance. She'd unfollowed all of them, then spent the following two years trying to convince herself that she just had to be patient. That her time would come. That she didn't want to attend some elite school that favoured the rich anyway. And then, when she'd decided to give education a second chance with RACA, that everything would be different.

Only it wasn't, because *he* was here. A walking, smirking symbol of all the ways she fell short.

He snorted. 'You haven't changed a bit. Always so testy.'

Yes, I have. I wouldn't have gotten here otherwise, she wanted to reply, but rage had wired her jaw shut.

This was supposed to be her new life, and that meant no more of the things she'd struggled through in the past.

If Aiden Whittaker was anything, it was one big, neon-red reminder of everything she'd like to forget.

She shrank in her seat and ignored him until, finally, he returned his focus to Christopher's presentation. Meanwhile, hers remained on him.

Just like old times.

2

To at least *try* to convince her new professor that she wasn't a completely insolent loudmouth about to cause him a year's worth of problems, Juniper stayed behind after the class finished up and hoped she didn't appear too much like she had her tail between her legs. She stood by her statement, after all. He *had* been an arsehole to her, and she wasn't in the habit of letting people walk all over her.

Still, she didn't want the person who would be grading her work to hate her, either. She'd done that all through school, teachers mistaking her blunt nature and difficulty concentrating for disrespect and an unwillingness to learn. Just once, it would have been nice not to have those big rainclouds following her.

She remained in her seat while the others prepared to leave. Beside her, Aiden's waft of spiced, woodsy cologne was a welcome change from the Lynx deodorant of high school's past, but that was about the *only* thing she welcomed.

He glanced at her, eyes narrowing. His lashes were unfairly long; she'd forgotten that. Then again, everything about him was unfair. Smooth olive skin, high cheekbones. Why was he here? He'd never bothered with anything but painting before, would walk around school with acrylic staining his hands and white shirt. *She'd* been the sculptor, the one to venture out of the box, only to be told that, while 'ambitious', the darker undertones of her artwork just didn't quite 'land'.

Now, his fingernails were bitten down and stained by ink, though she hadn't seen him jot a single word. She allowed herself another glower, just as a treat, and then turned back to the front of the classroom. On the walls around the whiteboard, tools hung. She'd like to use one of the pointy ones on him if he got too close to her again.

'Are you really not going to talk to me, Juni?' When her scowl deepened, he added, '*Per*?' Puzzlement laced his voice. That was new. Usually, his confidence masked any of that. He had fooled the entire school into thinking he was the most knowledgeable, self-assured boy to exist.

'Nope,' was her curt reply.

He rubbed his jaw, then seemed to remember who he was. Unfazed once more, he shucked on his black denim jacket and said, ''Kay. If that's what you want.'

'It is.'

'Good.'

'*Very* good,' she bit out. Why was he still talking to her at all? She wanted to shoo him away as the classroom emptied, but thankfully, he seemed to get the message. *Un*thankfully, he slung on a shiny brown satchel that made him look more like a professor than the *actual* professor. Juniper couldn't help but take it as an insult, a show of his money, like he wanted to be sure to shove it in everyone's face.

Then again, most of the students here were well-dressed, with branded clothes and bags, some even designer. Like always, she was the outlier.

She was sure it wouldn't be long until Aiden started pointing it out.

For now, he just muttered, 'Yep. Still a nutter,' then disappeared into the corridor.

Christopher — he had told them to call him Chris, but Juniper didn't really feel like she deserved to, yet — had his back turned as he shut his laptop and packed up his work.

On shaky legs, Juniper stood and cleared her throat.

'No,' he said, pushing his round glasses up his nose.

She huffed in exasperation. 'You don't even know what I'm going to say!'

'And I don't particularly wish to.'

She deflated, realising that any hope of making things right was clearly a delusion. Did he treat all his students like this, or was she just that talented at making enemies out of authority figures?

She began to play with one of her dragon-shaped earrings nervously. As her first foray into sculpting, they looked more like worms, but she'd worn them today as a symbol of how far she'd come since discovering her love of clay. A good luck charm.

Fat lot of difference they'd made.

Since Christopher wasn't giving her the time of day, her defences began to rise like a hard slab of metal in her chest. 'Look, I get it. I made a bad first impression.' Which was a common habit of hers, but she didn't mention that. 'But so did you, really. You were quite rude, and very unwelcoming to a new student like myself!'

'Contrary to popular belief, Jupiter—'

'Juniper.'

He ignored her correction, finally whirling around on his brown brogues. '—I'm not here to be pleasant. I don't actually care about what happens outside this classroom. My problem is your disruptiveness within it. Whatever strange thing is going on with you and Alex—'

'Aiden.'

'—is to be left in the corridor. I'm sure you're used to being a quirky little Zoomer,' Juniper wrinkled her nose. What did that even mean? 'But in these walls, you're a student, and you're here to listen and learn.' He stepped forward. 'My advice to you, Jupiter, is to shush a bit.'

Juniper's face burned. How many times could this man humiliate her in one day?

Before she could respond, his mouth curled into a smile and he cupped one of his ears with his hand in a show of listening. 'That's what I like to hear. Quiet.' Then, he took his laptop bag and sauntered out of the classroom, not before calling over his shoulder: 'See you in throwing class!'

★

Juniper skulked out of the Whiteread Building, half-tempted to call her mum just to hear a friendly voice, but she already knew what she'd say: that she should come home, that she needed a stable job, not something that would only leave

13

her bankrupt and disheartened in the long run. Neither of her parents understood her love of art. Mum packaged orders in a textile factory and Dad was a truck driver. Juniper got it. They were steady jobs, they made ends meet, they were careers most people of their generation had been encouraged to chase, and with Juniper's recent ADHD diagnosis, they were certain a consistent nine-to-five job would benefit her. Of course, it usually did the opposite. Working fulltime over her gap years had left her in a burnout she was still recovering from.

Juniper didn't need monotonous eight-hour shifts. She needed passion. Otherwise, what was the point?

The point was that she'd never been humiliated like this, not even when a customer complained their burger was cold. Not because they'd been any kinder than Christopher, but because she didn't actually care about burgers. Her mistakes didn't matter by the end of the day. But art was such a big part of who she was, a reflection of her, and that reflection was currently cracked.

She slumped onto the first bench she found, wondering what the hell she was supposed to do now. Her next class wasn't until after lunch, and she didn't feel particularly inclined to go to it. Already, at least two people in the room were just waiting for her to mess up. But what was the alternative? Her dorm room was a tiny, dark little cupboard in the corner of the building, with only a hamster she wasn't technically allowed to have and a few pigeons on her sill for company.

She'd been naive to think that this could be a new beginning. It seemed that, no matter where she went, her shortcomings would always cling to her like a second skin. The harder she tried to shed them, the tighter they held on.

As she pulled out her phone to calm herself down, a voice startled her from above. 'You look like you need a friend.'

Juniper looked up and found a girl stood over her. Well, a woman. She supposed they were all adults now, a fact Juniper was still coming to terms with, and this one might have been a few years older than her. She recognised her from the workshop just now, though she'd been sitting on the other side of the room. With short, glossy black hair and an endearing overbite that poked through when she smiled, she was difficult to miss. But that wasn't the first time Juniper had seen her. They'd skirted around each other's boxes on moving-in day last weekend, exchanging timid smiles and muttered complaints of how narrow the corridors were. If memory served, she'd been passing in and out of the room opposite Juniper's. Juniper had intended to introduce herself once the chaos died down, but as soon as the boxes had hit her carpet, she'd dashed off for a couple of job interviews. When she'd gotten back, the common room had been filled with chatter she could only linger on the edge of, clearly having missed the most important bonding experiences, so she'd gone upstairs and kept to herself, eager for the comfort of pyjamas and quiet.

She shifted her bag off the bench, leaving room for her neighbour to sit, which she did in a flurry of beads and fringe. Her cardigan appeared handmade, a patchwork of earth-toned granny squares composing the body and sleeves, which immediately made her ten thousand percent cooler than Juniper and therefore, once again, out of place in her comfortable dark clothes.

She winced at the girl's question. 'Is my misery that obvious?'

The classmate pinched her fingers together, a dimple appearing on her left cheek. 'A smidge.' Then, she nudged Juniper as though they were already playful pals. 'I'm Tilly, by the way. I think I'm staying in the room across from you in Chaplin House?'

She spoke with a warm, Irish lilt, one that could easily trigger Juniper's pansexual panic if she focused on it too much. She loved accents, and Tilly was unfairly pretty in the unique sort of way that some people – silly people – might overlook.

'I thought I recognised you.' Juniper forced a smile, though her stomach was tight both from the terrible start to her day and the fact that she was absolutely awful at socialising with new people. Any moment now, she'd say the wrong thing and Tilly would think she was weird, not worth knowing.

'And you are…?'

Oh, yeah. This was the part where Juniper was supposed to say her name. 'Juniper! Or Juni. My friends call me Juni.'

Tilly raised her brows. 'Oh, I love that wee name! Your parents clearly knew you were going to be an artist.'

'Weirdly not. They would much rather me be… well, anything else.' Juni laughed, nervously playing with the sleeve of her jacket.

'Oh, no.' Tilly's features darkened, her brown eyes wide. 'You've had the "art doesn't make money" talk, too.'

'Yup.' Juniper popped the P, relaxing a little. Okay, she could do this. Tilly was nice, and clearly she got it. 'You too?'

A nod as Tilly crossed one flared jean-clad leg over the other, revealing a pair of fancy black platform boots that seemed to have been hand-painted with stars and crescent moons. 'I think they could have dealt with my struggling artist dreams if it didn't mean moving so far away from home. I assume you're from the north?'

'Manchester. And you, Ireland?'

'Aye, Dublin. Needed a change. I love my mam, but she's... a lot.' Tilly let out a serene sigh, as though they were soaking up sun on a beach rather than sitting on a cold, wooden bench in the middle of London.

Envy struck Juniper. She'd never been able to do that: just *enjoy* something. Everything came with struggle, whether it was too much noise and people or just her tendency to mess up.

'By the way,' Tilly continued, amusement dancing in her voice, 'how brutal is our new tutor? I am *not* looking forward to this afternoon.'

'Yeah.' Juniper squirmed. 'I accidentally might have called him an arsehole before I'd even gotten into the classroom, so we're not off to a good start.'

A choked laugh fell from Tilly. 'Bet he deserved it!'

'Oh, he absolutely did.' Juniper found herself snickering, too, suddenly very, very grateful that Tilly had come over. She'd envisioned spending the entire year alone, a bit like in high school after her best friend-slash-girlfriend had moved to Blackburn. She didn't mind being alone, was used to it, even, but the September sun felt a tad warmer with someone in her corner.

Tilly sat up straight, leaning closer so that Juniper could smell coffee on her breath and peachy perfume on her clothes. 'Hey, by the way, did you hear that weird noise last night? I couldn't sleep for hours!'

'Oh? I don't think so. What was it?' Juniper tilted her head, though her pulse started pounding in her ears. She might have an *inkling*...

'Sort of like a rattling whir. I don't know.'

Yes, Juniper had, in fact, heard a rattling whir, but to admit to it would mean revealing her very dark secret: that in order to combat her loneliness, and to save her pet from certain starvation at home, she had smuggled her beloved hamster, Cerberus, into halls despite the rule printed in bold in her contract that specified no pets were allowed in student accommodation.

She would have to take his hamster wheel out of his cage immediately.

'How bizarre,' she brushed off quickly, scratching the back of her neck as she searched for a way to change the subject. 'Hey, would you fancy a coffee or something? I need a boost.'

Tilly brightened once more, quick to hop up off the bench. 'Let's do it!'

See? Juniper thought. She wasn't so bad at this being-a-person business after all.

Hamsters, mean professors, and old classmates aside.

3

'Okay, people. Welcome to the throwing room,' Christopher announced on a sigh, as though already bored of his students' presence.

Aiden fought not to roll his eyes. He'd had a lot of different art teachers over the years: the encouraging Mrs. Parks, then his chaotically unprepared sixth-form teacher, Hassan, and up until January of this year, Jennifer at Elmington, whose stern attitude and dull lectures had at least partly contributed to him dropping out midway through the course.

None of them had ever been so utterly uninterested in their own career as Chris. Aiden had done his research. He knew that this tutor was one of the most experienced ceramics teachers in England and had looked forward to the top-class education. So why on earth didn't he give two shits about leaving a decent impression on his students?

He shared a flat look with one of his new classmates, a nineteen-year-old international student named Luc who probably already longed to return to France. They had already asked Aiden over an awkwardly quiet lunch in the library's small café if all British tutors were so 'dour'.

No. No, they weren't. Just his last two.

Not that it mattered, currently. He was more focused on the woman directly in front of him. Juniper seemed to have made a friend, too, and gained some of her old confidence, because she was no longer hunched in on herself as she exchanged whispers with the dark-haired, brightly dressed girl. When she listened to Christopher, her chin tilted high.

Aiden suppressed a smile. He'd been right earlier: she hadn't changed a bit in the fact that she was ever-changing. Some days, she'd been quiet and reserved. Others, fierce and quick to anger. Beyond that, she was even prettier than he remembered, complexion fair and quick to redden, with a triangular formation of beauty spots pointing from her jaw to her earlobe. Only now, her septum was pierced with a golden hoop and her dark eyeliner framed her amber-brown irises. Still as curious as a Munch painting, requiring a second, third, fourth look that usually came with a new interpretation each time, partly because of her beauty and partly because emotions seemed to pass over her face as constantly as trains whistling in and out of a busy station. The last time he'd seen her must have been at sixth-form college two years ago, but their paths had barely crossed in such a large building. They hadn't shared a classroom for much longer, not since high school.

'Excited to get your hands dirty, Hodge?' he couldn't help but remark when she began bouncing on the balls of her feet. One thing that remained consistent? Her restless energy. He'd forgotten that part of her, remembering her more as the bright-eyed teenager with wild brown-gold curls framing her face and an unwavering focus on her artwork. Sometimes she hadn't heard the bell ring at the end of class and Mrs. Parks had snapped at her to go to lunch with the others. But then he'd seen her in other lessons: doodling in English Lit, tapping her knuckles against the desk in Spanish, a vacancy glazing her round, pretty features.

Maybe that was why he'd always tried to engage with her: he liked challenges. It had never worked, though. The only thing she ever seemed to keep close was a paintbrush, and his friends had loved to tease her for being so different. For not fitting in. She'd been dubbed one of the weirdos, a loner, someone his mates stayed clear of, but then, they'd never been good judges of character.

Now, he was settling into old habits, and he couldn't help himself. She'd tugged him in with her fierce attitude and unreasonable hatred. Why *did* she hate him?

At his question, she sent a glare over her shoulder. 'Oh, good. You're still here.'

'I don't plan on going anywhere.' He leaned closer, feeling a heavy heat where her shoulder brushed his chest. 'Y'know, there's something I just don't get.'

'How to take a hint?' she snapped.

Beside her, her friend stifled a laugh. He almost did, too. He didn't mind giving her an opportunity to bite at his expense. He quite liked to be on the receiving end of it. It had been a long time since he'd been treated like a human rather than a prop made to be moulded to everybody else's standards. She didn't handle him with subtle, light touches like the others. She poked and prodded, and he felt it with every word.

Before he could respond, Chris sent a sharp gaze their way, and Aiden clamped his mouth closed as he leaned away from Juniper. He'd rather not get on his bad side, if the way he'd treated her this morning was anything to go by. No, he could do without failing a second time.

The professor continued to explain the principles of the workshop with lazy gestures towards the different equipment and facilities, which Aiden only now paid attention to.

He'd spent enough time practising in pottery studios over the summer to know his way around. Each of them would have their own wheel and desk space, the likes of which were set up in two rows of eight. Drawers and cupboards of tools filled the worktop areas along the back wall, and adjacent was the drying room. The kiln process went way over his head, but he was certain he'd learn on the job, as he always did.

'Eek,' Juniper's friend let out quietly, drawing closer to be heard. 'It's like *The Great Pottery Throw Down*.'

Aiden had never watched it, so he wouldn't know. Luc, too, only offered a confused glance. With an emerald-green buzzcut and a bright pink jumper, they were one of the more noticeable students in the class, aside from Juniper, although much quieter when it came to conversation.

'Is it just me,' they said now in Aiden's ear, 'or is Juniper's meanness quite badass?'

'Just you,' Aiden lied, and judging by the sniff she emitted, he was certain Juniper had heard. He was afraid to say that Juniper wasn't only badass, but also more gorgeous than ever. She'd always been chubby – one of the other reasons their classmates had teased her, which he'd thought absurd – but to him her body was a perfect combination of delicate arches and supple curves. She wore black dungarees over a striped T-shirt that tapered in at the waist, accentuating her devastating fullness, especially at her hips.

'Why doesn't she like you, anyway?' asked Luc.

Aiden raised a brow. 'Think it's just a hobby of hers. To not like people, I mean. We were in the same year at school.' Otherwise, he had no clue. Sure, they'd never been the best of friends. He'd been… popular, and she'd been… well, not. A few of his mates thought they were clever for picking on outcasts like her, so he could see how being associated with them might have been an issue. But they were adults now. Holding a grudge for something he barely even remembered was ridiculous. And besides, she'd never been fazed by the things most teenagers were, had never fought to fit in the way most people did. The way *he* did. Between that and her talent, he'd been glad to share a few lessons with her, her presence leaving him curious and maybe a little bit fond.

'Ohhh, so you already know each other,' deduced Luc with a hint of curiosity.

'Yup.' As much as he wanted to drop the subject and let her harbour her inexplicable bitterness to avoid any confrontation, a gnawing feeling had stretched inside him all morning. He wanted to know why. Sort of deserved to know, really, if they were going to be spending a lot of time together over the coming three years.

'Anyway, I'm bored of talking now.' Chris clapped his hands together, breaking Aiden out of his thoughts. 'The best way to learn is to just do it. Be warned: the pottery wheel isn't for the faint of heart. Some of you will go home and cry into your pillow tonight, and that is the beauty of it.' He flashed a grin that seemed to be aimed at Juniper. 'It weeds out the weak.'

A sharp pain shot through Aiden's big toe when Juniper shifted back. The heavy soles of her Doc Marten's weren't for the faint of heart, either, and he gritted his teeth, catching her elbow in an effort to stop her squashing the rest of his foot. '*Ow.*'

He heard her breath catch, and then her foot lurched away, thank god. Still, from the way she whirled to free her elbow, tearing it from his grasp like his skin was made of stinging nettles, he suspected he wasn't about to get an apology.

'Beginning to think Marten was *not* a doctor,' he said, rolling the feeling back into his toe. 'Those things are lethal.'

'You shouldn't leave your feet under them, then.' She blinked innocently, and then turned her back on him, her long, choppy waves whipping him in the face before she sauntered to one of the desks with the rest of their scattering classmates.

Luc whistled under their breath, 'You're in trouble,' and then left him hovering alone at the edge of the classroom.

Yeah, it seemed he was. He just didn't quite know why.

4

Of course Aiden chose the desk in front of her. Juniper took out her fraying patience on her apron tie, yanking the knot until it cut into her stomach. Even his *voice* annoyed her, all dry and husky as he drawled out little quips he probably thought were hilarious.

Well, they weren't. They were obnoxious, just like everything else about him.

'So, you two clearly know each other,' Tilly commented from the desk adjacent to her. Unlike Juniper's second-hand grey apron, already stained with paint from its previous owner, Tilly donned a gorgeous canvas covering that resembled Monet's water lilies, shades of swirling light and dark blues broken up by vivid sap greens.

Most of the others had clearly invested in something fun, too, the university's spares hung at the back of the workshop untouched. In a sea of colour, Juniper was a drab rock.

In front of her, Aiden dipped his head into the loops of a pristine indigo apron embroidered with a crown logo on the front pocket. *Likely bought by Daddy or one of his artist friends*, she presumed sourly.

His grey T-shirt rode up against his tie and her eyes snagged on a strip of tanned flesh. Something tingly and unwanted flared through her, especially when his shoulders bunched to make the knot. As charming as his broad, muscular shoulders were, she preferred the hair-dusted, fleshy curve of his waist, proof that he hadn't been perfectly chiselled out of stone after all, but rather—

Nope. Nope, she preferred none of it, because it was Aiden, and besides, she was far too busy answering her new friend's question to pay attention to those things.

If she could remember what the question had been.

'Sorry, what did you say?' she said, breaking away from her ogling-slash-glowering. Mostly glowering.

Tilly's smirk was dry, suspicious, which did nothing to slow Juniper's pulse. 'I said you two clearly know each other.'

'Unfortunately. From high school. And sixth form.' The glowering recommenced.

'What a coincidence you both ended up here!' Tilly was already unearthing her heap of clay from the plastic wrap, though Christopher hadn't instructed them to yet. He sat at the desk positioned at the front of the classroom, looking bored as a gangly dark-haired boy who also lived in Chaplin House grilled him about which famous potters he'd met, spurred on by an overly expressive friend on the desk adjacent. Even so, the lass was more diverse than she'd expected: the lads were outnumbered, and a few mature students were dotted around, too. It made Juniper feel better about her delayed entry into undergraduate studies.

'Coincidence. Curse. Same difference.' Juniper shrugged, trying to loosen the knot around the waist as she perched on her stool. Maybe she'd been a little too aggressive with her apron tie, and now she was struggling to breathe.

'I can hear you,' Aiden muttered without turning around.

'Well, that's a shame. I certainly wasn't trying to make my dislike for you abundantly clear.' She directed the sarcastic retort at his fumbling fingers, which still hadn't tied a knot properly.

See, not so good at everything after all. Ha!

Tilly snorted. Juniper enjoyed watching him struggle for a few more moments, until Christopher finally decided to teach them something.

'Right, I'm bored now, gang, so we're going to do what we actually came here to do. Pottery.' He began tearing the wrap from his clay and then threw it down on his desk with a thud. 'Here we have some stoneware clay: the easiest to work with, since you are clearly inexperienced beginners and, despite what you may think, I'm not trying to break your spirits just yet. That will happen later, when we start using porcelain. Can anybody enlighten me on where we start with this?'

Aiden's hand shot straight up, because of course it did.

Much to Juniper's enjoyment, Christopher folded his arms impatiently. 'Not in high school anymore, Alex. No need for the raised hand business.'

Aiden's arm lowered slowly, and the tips of his ears turned red. Finally, her luck was turning.

He still answered the question right, leading to a display of wedging from Christopher. His palms dug into the clay in a way that made it look easy, though Juniper knew it wasn't. 'Why are we doing this?'

'To get out the bubbles!' Juniper was quick to shout out her own knowledge, gained from the few classes she'd taken over the last year and also perhaps *The Great Pottery Throw Down*, which she was binge-watching for research purposes. Since she hadn't been able to afford *many* classes in throwing rooms, she'd learned a lot from TV shows and online tutorials, and most of her experience was in hand-built sculptures and accessories.

Now that she was here, it was all beginning to feel real, and she itched to get started like her favourite contestants… although she also felt slightly daunted. After all, she didn't have a supportive mentor to aid her, and she was sure Aiden was just waiting for her to screw up.

'And to smooth out the clay,' added Aiden, stealing her limelight and proving her right.

'Right again, Alex,' Christopher said.

She bit the inside of her cheek to keep from insulting Aiden – or Christopher – again. Was she bloody invisible?

Didn't matter, because she was finally allowed to touch the clay as Christopher guided them through a few different wedging techniques. Determination gripped her muscles as she kneaded. She'd show them that she had more talent in her pinkie finger than Aiden Whittaker had in his whole sickeningly athletic body.

She'd missed the feeling of something smooth and strong in her hands and took to the exercises quickly, having already mastered a few before. In fact, as she pounded the clay into submission, arms already aching, she imagined it was Aiden's face and found it even more effective.

Christopher raised a brow as he sauntered past Juniper's desk. 'Interestingly aggressive approach, Jupiter. Have you considered taking up boxing?'

Juniper suppressed a grin. If she didn't know any better, she'd think it was a compliment, or at least a roundabout way of one.

'Okay, gang, let's move on. Cut your clay, give it a weigh, and then it's time to… thray.'

Some of the students chuckled at his attempt at a rhyme, though Christopher's face remained as indifferent as ever.

'I think boxing would be a good idea, Hodge,' Aiden commented once their tutor had returned to the front, turning to her only as he moved his clay onto the wheel. 'Seems like you need a release for all that pent-up anger.'

'I'm not angry.' She threw her own clay onto the wheel, adjusting her stool to make sure she wasn't stooping too low to reach it. 'And stop calling me that.'

With her last name being Hodgson, and having been rather podgy – something she still was but now liked about herself – many of her high school classmates had taken to calling her *Hodge Podge*. She couldn't remember if Aiden had been one of them, or if he'd always used the shortened down version, but it still felt too much like the old taunt. They may not have been in high school anymore, but she hated the reminder of who she'd been there. A joke. An outcast. Alone.

'You could've fooled me.' Oblivious, he kept his body angled towards her, which only enraged her more. Couldn't he at least mind his own bloody business? 'You need to wipe down your wheel first. Clay won't stick if it's too dry.'

Nope. Nope, he could not.

'I know how to throw, thank you very much.' She had, after all, done this a grand total of three times.

Still, he might have been just a *teensy* bit right, so she used a sponge to dampen the wheel before repositioning her clay. Again, the corner of his mouth tugged smugly.

When she noticed Tilly watching them, she pondered aloud, 'How much damage do you think the wire cutters might do if one was to, say, strangle someone with them?'

Of course, it probably wasn't wise to joke about violent acts with a friend she'd quite like to keep, so she was grateful when Tilly's eyes sparked with amusement instead of concern. 'I'd be interested to find out myself. I do, after all, support women's wrongs.'

Aiden reared back. 'I feel bullied. What did I ever do to you?'

Tilly shrugged. 'I'm sure you did *something* to deserve it.'

You have no idea. Juniper didn't want to think about it anymore, or ever again, which was difficult considering he was barely a foot away. Still, she tried to focus on centring her clay on the wheel, stomping down on the foot pedal to turn it.

'Shit!' she hissed when the clay began to spin a little too wildly.

'Go easy on the pedal, Hodge,' Aiden advised. Yes, she was definitely interested in finding an answer to her wire cutter question.

'Ah, yes,' Tilly murmured just loud enough for Juniper to hear. 'Definitely deserves it.'

Well, at least Tilly didn't think she was bonkers. She lightened her pressure on the pedal, no mean feat considering ire had locked every bone in her body.

'I'm sure some of you obnoxiously talented folks would love to show off your throwing skills,' said Christopher, 'but for the sake of this being an introduction workshop, let's start with the basics. A cylindrical vase. Follow my lead.'

He worked effortlessly, drawing the clay into a cone shape before encouraging it back down into a smooth lump. From there, it seemed to happen by magic. One moment, it was nothing. The next, Christopher was using the pressure of his thumbs to drag up a smooth barrel, offering a few tips and tricks as he did.

He might have been an awful tutor, but he was a great potter.

Eager to get stuck in, Juniper worked her pedal, finally getting the clay a little more centred. The classroom soon dissolved into a whirl of creation, each student engrossed in their own project. She wished she could master the same concentration, but her gaze kept falling to Aiden.

Like Christopher, he commanded the clay with effortless grace and was already well on his way to a cylinder. His big hands looked as though they should have been heavy, incompetent, but instead, his fingers drifted nimbly over his work, biceps flexing as he leaned closer to the wheel with his thick thighs parted at either side.

Something tight coiled in Juniper's core, unexpected and completely unwelcome. She pressed her own thighs together, squirming on her stool to try to encourage the feeling away. She didn't. The clay caked his skin, spattering his veiny forearms, where more dark hair reminded her that he wasn't that boy from school anymore. He was a man, sturdy and confident and—

Looking at her. He was looking at her, looking at him. She raked her focus quickly back to her clay, the wheel shuddering as a result of her unsteady feet.

'Enjoying the view?' he remarked, voice rough with knowing.

The sound sunk right through her, vibrations gathering in the same place that already throbbed. 'You have clay in your hair. It's gross.'

It wasn't a lie. Those with long hair, like the woman two rows in who had introduced herself as Nomi over lunch, had tied it up to avoid mess, and while Aiden's didn't quite reach his shoulders, he dipped close enough to the wheel for it to splatter. She pulled the spare lavender-coloured scrunchie from her bag and pinged it at his face like a slingshot.

He caught it with a smirk, but then raked his dirty fingers through his waves just to irk her even more, which it did. The scrunchie ended up on his wrist, and she lamented at the fact she might never get it back. He didn't deserve her scrunchies.

'Maybe you should focus on your own work,' he said. 'A little erotic, don't you think?'

She frowned, and then realised she hadn't made a cylinder at all, but rather something much thinner and taller. Something much, much more phallic.

'Very mature,' she grumbled.

Aiden cleared the laugh from his throat and went back to his perfect little vase, but, to her surprise, tied his hair up in a way that should have looked ridiculous yet didn't. Only the back was long enough to stay put, wisps escaping to frame his jaw.

Juniper allowed herself a final moment to watch – hatefully, of course – then worked desperately to fix her phallic vase, using water to better mould the clay and trying to remember Christopher's advice. *Soft touch. Keep your hands connected.*

'I did it!' she announced finally, perhaps a little too loudly, but was too excited to care.

Everybody looked at her as she lifted her arms up in triumph… and slumped them back down again, perfectly mirroring her vase's untimely collapse. It was painful to watch the slow fold of her cylinder, clay becoming curved and distorted as it fell in on itself.

'I didn't do it,' she whispered.

And while she tried to hold back tears, Aiden laughed. So did the rest of the class, but it was his that hurt most. Always his.

5

Aiden felt just a sliver of guilt when Juniper dashed out of the classroom as soon as they were dismissed. He didn't get it. She wasn't the first person to screw up throwing. His first attempt had resembled a wonky version of the Gherkin skyscraper, but the people in his class had laughed – with him, not at him. That was the point, wasn't it?

He'd spent all day subjected to her anger, and as he threw his apron into his bag and tugged on his jacket, he wondered just what he'd done to deserve all this bullshit.

Fuck this. He bounded after her without saying goodbye to Luc, glad to find her in the lift at the bottom of the corridor.

'Hold it a minute,' he demanded, and then rolled his eyes when she pressed the *close* button. The doors sliced over her dejected form, leaving a dull pang inside him.

Double fuck this. She couldn't treat him like that in class and then ignore him altogether outside of it.

She would talk to him. He would make sure of it.

He rushed to the stairwell and skipped down the spiral steps two at a time, coming out in the building's entranceway just in time to see her step outside.

Gritting his teeth, he followed, the warm humidity of late summer leaving a light sheen of sweat on his face as he jogged over, stopping her in her path.

She tutted, making to turn around, but his fingers looped around her wrist to keep her there. He let go quickly, palms smarting against the contact. Other than when she'd trodden on his toes, it might have been the first time he'd ever really touched her. It shouldn't have mattered, but it did, somehow.

'Do you want to tell me what's going on?' he asked, breathless.

'Why can't you just leave me alone?' Juniper tilted her face stubbornly, but her glare wasn't quite as fierce anymore. Her mascara was smudged, eyes watery and dark as ink. She'd smeared clay on her cheek, and her hair was falling out of its ponytail to curl around her oval face. He resisted the urge to fix both problems, knowing that even if she'd let him touch her, she was better off left messy.

'I could ask you the same thing. I don't get what's happening here!'

She scoffed. '*Nothing* is happening here. I just didn't come all the way to London to share a classroom with the same moron I did in high school, okay?'

'Well, believe it or not, I didn't come here just to piss you off.' She had the nerve to imply *he* was arrogant? Aiden couldn't help that they'd wound up in the same place at the same time. God, he hadn't even thought of Juniper since sixth form. All right, maybe sometimes, when scrolling through Instagram or looking through old Facebook memories. With that disarming presence, she was hard to forget.

'Why *did* you come here?' she shot out, her knuckles turning white around the badge-covered strap of her backpack. He recognised a few logos there – bands he quite enjoyed himself: Sleep Token, Linkin Park, and then an LGBTQ+ flag badge and Van Gogh's *Starry Night*, which he thought was a little too obvious for an art student, but everybody had their tastes. Some of them he remembered seeing on her old school blazer, which had resulted in plenty of detentions. Not that she'd ever cared about those.

He pursed his lips, without an answer. At least, one he could stand to give her. 'I don't owe you an explanation, just like you don't owe me one.'

'What about Elmington?' she pried.

The back of his neck began to prickle. The last thing he wanted was to think of his last stint at university and the way it had seemed to tear everything apart. Nine months down the line and his dad still hadn't spoken to him. He didn't know if he should be glad about it.

'Wasn't for me,' he replied. It wasn't a lie, but there was far more to it than that. Things he wasn't sure he could ever admit to another person, let alone someone who was looking for more reasons to unravel him.

Juniper's scoff dripped with twice as much venom this time. 'Right, that world-renowned uni, where most artists in the UK would die for a chance to even be considered, just *wasn't for you*. Do you understand how ridiculous that sounds?'

His hands began to shake, and he curled them into his pockets roughly. 'RACA isn't that much easier to get into.'

'Yeah, and unlike you, I'm not going to throw this opportunity away, so just stop with all...' She motioned vaguely towards him, and he felt her eyes drag over his body like sharp fingernails. Felt his gut and something a little further south react in response, because he liked it when she looked at him. It was far better than when she ignored him altogether. That just made him feel cold and restless and *wanting*. Her attention felt rare, valuable, and he liked being valued – even if it came in the form of scorn. '*This*,' she finished after a beat too long.

'I would consider it if I knew what *all this* was.' He arched his brows. 'You've had a problem with me since you barrelled so gracefully into the classroom.'

'And *you've* enjoyed it!'

'I'm not going to deny that.' He pinched his smile between his fingers. Maybe it made him terrible, but he liked to see her riled up and red-faced. It left wrinkles at either side of her nose, and she kept biting her lip in a way that made their heart-shaped plumpness hard to ignore. It helped that she was much shorter than him, that he had to look down to see it. What she lacked in height, she made up for in temper.

'Stop!' she repeated harshly.

'Then tell me what the problem is!' He rubbed his thumb across his brow roughly. 'Jesus, Juni, I know we weren't really mates, but I was actually...'

When he trailed off, she demanded, 'Actually what?'

'Well, it wasn't that unpleasant to see a familiar face here.' He shrugged, dipping his head to hide his embarrassment.

That seemed to make her falter. She took a step back, forehead crinkling a little like her collapsed clay creation. 'You really have no idea, do you?' she muttered quietly.

'That is what I've been trying to tell you, yes.'

Somehow, his cluelessness only seemed to anger her more. Her lip curled, and she ripped her gaze away so he could no longer meet her eyes. Her ponytail swung with the rest of her, a shaggy mix of copper and gold. He'd always liked watching her curls when he'd sat behind her in art: untethered to the rest of her, moving even when she didn't. They'd snuck his way into some of his coursework paintings in subtle ways: a flicker of red in brown soil, pale gold highlights in the dark.

'I just don't like you, okay?' she said finally.

'You don't *know* me,' he fixed, and now it was his turn to get annoyed. 'Jesus, are you still the same person you were at seventeen? Because I'm not.'

Another waver of her resolve. For a moment, he thought he'd gotten through to her, but then her features shuttered again and she was somewhere he couldn't reach.

'The things I don't like about you aren't things that seem to have changed,' she decided flatly.

'Or maybe you're just bitter that you mucked up your first day and you need someone to blame,' he suggested.

He knew it was the wrong thing to say immediately. Her chin wobbled, and she recoiled just a little bit further.

'See?' she whispered. 'Still the same twatface.'

She turned on her heel, leaving him to stew in the smell of her: leather and something rich, sweet, like chocolate and cherries. He watched her stomp over the grass, ignoring the path entirely, and wondered why, even at a distance, she could still pull his focus along with her.

That rope holding him hostage finally snapped when she turned at the library and disappeared, and he rubbed the place where he felt it most, his lower ribcage. Exhausted, he could only shake his head, his jaw so tight that he was surprised it didn't stay locked there. He convinced himself to stop thinking about her and headed the other way.

A friendly face at least greeted him when he neared the exhibition gallery. Sat by the steps, Luc winced, making it clear they'd witnessed the whole thing.

'May I give you some advice?' they asked as they fell into step, the two of them heading towards the great arched doorway. When Aiden had mentioned his plans to visit earlier, Luc had invited themself, a fact that Aiden was both uncomfortable and glad about. Uncomfortable, because he hadn't had many friends around since dropping out of Elmington, and he'd gotten too used to his own company in recent months. Glad, because he wanted to change that. He'd liked himself most in high school, when he'd been surrounded by people who paid attention to him. When he'd been so busy enjoying their company that he hadn't stopped to think about the future and the things he wasn't supposed to want.

If he could fit in here, it could be considered proof that he hadn't made the wrong decision.

'Please,' he said, the word echoing as they entered the large gallery. It was a miniature museum, dozens of sculptures housed within protective glass cases, descriptions and information about the students who had created them beneath. He waited for that usual ease to come, the one that made him feel at home in places where art was displayed. Galleries had basically been his second home growing up, his father always dragging him around the country on work trips as an art dealer. He'd probably been introduced to Monet before the Teletubbies.

It didn't come this time. Just more of that shuddery coldness, the one he'd felt at Elmington. The one that told him he wasn't supposed to be here. It left a knot in his belly, one he tried hard to ignore as he began to admire the work. While he was glad to dive into pottery, he wanted to get to know its history better, hopefully prepare for a job his father would approve of on the business side of things.

Luc squatted down to read an inscription about a piece inspired by the London skyline, then finally offered some insight. 'Just be quiet. Sometimes, it's very okay to be quiet.'

Aiden paused, brows knitting together. 'What do you mean? I'm not loud, am I?'

'Well, how do I say this? You react to her a lot.'

The tips of his ears began to burn. Did he? He was trying to react a normal amount, but she was just… 'She's a lot to react to!'

Luc hummed, adjusting their necklace. It was their initial, *L*, on a golden chain, and Aiden wondered who it had been gifted by, if anyone. 'I will be honest. Sitting in a room with the two of you is like sitting in a kiln. And when one cracks, the other does. You see?'

'Not at all.' That was a lie. He could see past the terrible pottery metaphors to what Luc meant. All day, he and Juniper had been back and forth, like a tennis match he hadn't even noticed he'd been playing. But how was that his fault? She'd started it. He'd been just fine before she'd scuttled in, all breathless and angry at *everything*.

Luc sighed. 'Men.'

'Oh, come on. She kept attacking me. What was I supposed to do?'

'Did you two ever have sex?' Luc questioned bluntly.

Aiden spluttered on thin air. '*What*? No!'

'You act like you did.'

'No. No, definitely not.' And he certainly wasn't going to think about her like that now. Legs wrapped around his waist while she used that mouth for more than just insults. Nope. He was not thinking about what it would be like to see all of her, touch her—

No.

Jesus, what was wrong with him?

It was the pottery, he decided. All that hand motion mixed with her barbed words was basically like foreplay.

Luc was right. He needed to stop engaging. If Juniper wanted to hate him, she could, but he'd tried to make it right and she'd shut him down. From now on, she'd have to start arguing with herself – something he wouldn't put past her after today.

Besides, he wasn't here for *that*. He was here to fall back in love with art, and not just the paintings hung in the National Gallery. He wanted to *make* something. Something important, something that would prove both to himself and to his father that he didn't have to follow the same path to be worth something.

He would forget Juniper altogether.

6

'Juni!'

Juniper wiped her tears with the sleeve of her jumper at the sound of her name floating down the corridor of Chaplin House. She knew it was silly to get emotional over one terrible penis-shaped creation, but she was so sick of failing.

Maybe you're just bitter that you mucked up your first day and you need someone to blame.

Aiden's words crooned over and over again in her ears. What if he was right? What if some of her hatred towards him was only born from her own insecurities?

What if coming here, believing she could be successful, was a mistake?

She swallowed the lump in her throat and turned to find Tilly ambling to catch up with her. Concern was etched on her brow, which only made Juniper feel more embarrassed. Day one, and she'd already revealed herself as the weakest link in the classroom. The two lads at the front had asserted themselves as strong potters, vying for Christopher's attention during the whole lesson, and one of the mature students sitting behind Luc, Diane, had known more than the rest of the class combined.

'Hi.' She sniffled and forced a smile, but it did nothing to wipe away Tilly's frown.

'Are you okay? I saw you bouling the head off Aiden outside, and you looked pretty upset. Also, you walk too fast.' Tilly leaned against the pale blue walls for support, hunching to catch her breath.

Juniper softened. A near-stranger had chased her across campus just to make sure she was all right? It made her feel even sillier. Even more pathetic.

'It's stupid, really,' she waved off. 'Thanks for checking on me, though.'

'Are you sure? It doesn't seem stupid.'

Juniper huffed. She supposed it might feel good to get it off her chest, and Tilly had been kind to her. At least this way, she wouldn't think the worst.

Planting her bag down, Juniper sat cross-legged, leaning against a dorm room door for support. Tilly laid out her cardigan and then did the same so they were face-to-face, knees almost touching in the narrow hallway. The residential building wasn't so unpleasant, if she ignored the overpowering stench of carpet cleaner and burnt toast coming from a shared kitchen – whose countertops were already dusted with crumbs and sink was piled high with dishes. After daring to peek her head in this morning, Juniper had resolved to get her own appliances as soon as she could afford them. She was due to start her trial shift at Caffè Verde, a coffee shop on the corner of busy Regent Street, in a couple of hours, and hoped working part-time there would keep her afloat. If she could manage not to cock up another thing, that was.

'C'mon.' Tilly nudged Juniper's calf with her burgundy ankle boots. 'Spill the beans.'

'His dad is a well-off art dealer, so he's only ever known wealth and success,' Juniper explained, flicking a piece of carpet fluff from her dungarees. 'He was always the golden boy at school, always treated like a saint because everyone wanted to be on his good side.' And it was already happening again. The two lads at the front of the classroom, who she'd learned were called Amir and Tom, had been quick to try to befriend Aiden after seeing his honed throwing skills. 'All of my teen years, I watched him get handed all of the opportunities that I had to work twice as hard for, and he didn't even bat an eye. He thinks he's entitled to it just because of who he is and where he comes from. It just… it really rubs me the wrong way. *He* rubs me the wrong way.' She bit her tongue to keep from saying the other thing, the thing that aggravated her most. It would sound just like he'd said: like she was blaming him for her own failures. It was just difficult not to feel as though people like him took things from people like her. That their privilege relied on her lack of it. Especially after being rejected from Elmington.

Tilly leaned forward, wide-eyed. 'Wait, what's his last name again?'

'Whittaker.'

'As in…'

'Jonathan Whittaker, yes.' Just his name filled Juniper's mouth with acid. As much as she hated Aiden, she hated his father more. She'd only had the displeasure of seeing him in person once, but it was enough to cement everything she'd already known: that the Whittakers were a selfish, conceited family who believed money and talent were interchangeable. They wriggled their way into any space in the art world they could find, ensuring people like Juniper would never get a second glance.

'Wowzer,' Tilly mouthed. 'Well, I guess it makes sense he got special treatment. Jonathan Whittaker is a pretty big deal.'

'Believe me, I know.' The memory of his cardboard-straight tailored suit and oily demeanour made her feel sick. 'I'm sure I'm supposed to be the bigger person, but he made me feel so small in high school. He got all of the best opportunities from our teachers, always the main event in any showcase while the rest of us were just there to fill spaces on the wall. Between that and his arrogance, it's hard to let go of. I wanted a spot here so badly. I would have given everything for it. It was supposed to be something new and wonderful, and instead it's just like it used to be again. Like, no matter how hard I try, I can't grow beyond that version of myself.'

Sympathy tugged on Tilly's features, enough to make Juniper comfortable. She'd never been good at holding it all in, one of the reasons why people didn't always want to be around her. She was too much, too emotional, too sensitive, too angry, too loud, too honest. Too everything.

Tilly didn't seem to think that of her. In fact, she put her jewellery-embellished hand over Juniper's. 'It's shite you had to feel that way. But I reckon it can still be new and wonderful.'

Juniper hummed, unconvinced.

'It can!' insisted Tilly. 'You just have to ignore him and focus on you. Easier said than done, I know, but look at where we are!'

Juniper did, and wasn't all that impressed. 'Is that a piece of spaghetti on the wall?' she asked, squinting at the thin, curly shape behind Tilly's head.

Tilly covered Juni's eyes quickly, more of that peach smell on her wrist. 'Okay, well, don't look at that. What I mean to say is that we're going to live our best fecking lives here, and we're going to start this weekend.'

'What's this weekend?'

'A party. That lad who looks like Timotheé Chevrolet with a man bun invited me. I forget his name, but it's at his house off campus. One of the fancy streets, so we can steal all his liquor without feeling bad about it.'

'Timotheé *Chalamet*,' Juniper corrected on a laugh. 'I suppose that's why Christopher was calling him Timmy.'

'Aye. That's the one. So, what d'you say?'

She fidgeted, deliberating. Tom, who did look like Timotheé Chalamet, radiated the same air of snobbery as Aiden, having tried to steal Christopher's attention through the whole workshop. Besides, she wasn't really a party girl. They were too loud and warm and social. It didn't take much time for her social battery to drain, and even less for her to get overstimulated by too many sensory experiences at once. 'I don't know. Parties aren't my favourite thing.'

'Mine, either, but what better way to forget about a man than to get blind drunk and snog someone's face off?' Tilly winked. 'Besides, I need a wingwoman. How good is your gaydar?'

'Terrible when I try to approach women. Excellent when it's on behalf of someone else.' She'd been convinced that the last girl she'd dated, a colleague, was looking for friendship until she'd initiated foreplay in the middle of a *Barbie* screening. Then again, that was probably less about her gaydar and more about her ability to believe that someone might be interested in her.

'Good. There are a few people in our class I'm trying to fathom.' Tilly stood, then offered out her hand to help up Juniper. 'Luc is cute.'

Juniper wrinkled her nose. 'Yeah, but they're hanging around with Aiden.' In fact, most of the class had ended up flocking towards him by the end of the workshop to praise his talents and make idle conversation, following Tom and Amir's leads. They'd probably worked out who he was after seeing his name on the register and hoped it might help them get a few connections in the industry. If Aiden had anything, it was connections.

'True.' They fell into step as they continued down the corridor towards their neighbouring doors. 'What about Nomi?'

'So beautiful it hurts,' Juniper answered immediately.

'Right?' Tilly's voice rose excitedly.

To be fair, she found most of the people in her class attractive, but she'd been too focused on Aiden to really notice.

Maybe Tilly was right. Maybe it was time to put herself out there. That was what everybody else did at uni, wasn't it?

'Wait!' Tilly halted suddenly, putting her hand out to make sure Juniper did the same. With a shush, she motioned to her ear, which was as decorated as the rest of her. 'That's the noise I heard last night!'

Uh oh. Juniper tried to school her features into something resembling confusion, but her cheeks began to flame. 'I don't hear anything.'

'That whir!' Tilly tilted her head, following it towards the end of the corridor, where their rooms faced one another.

Please, stop there, Juniper begged silently.

She had no such luck. Tilly pressed her ear to Juniper's door and gasped. 'It's coming from your room!'

'No. No, it can't be.' Shaking her head, Juniper nudged Tilly out of the way to shield her door, and hopefully drown out some of the noise.

But it was too late. Tilly narrowed her eyes, hands falling to her hips. 'You're hiding something in there. What is it? A motorbike? A really powerful vibrator?' She gasped. 'A time machine?'

Juniper wished. She would go back in time and redo this entire day to set things right. The powerful vibrator wouldn't have been unwelcome, either. 'No! I'm not Doctor Who!'

'Then what is it?' Tilly grabbed her hand, shaking it like a kid begging for sweets. 'Tell me! I love secrets!'

Defeated, Juniper checked the hall was quiet, and then said, 'Promise you won't tell anyone?'

Excitement gleamed in Tilly's round eyes. 'Promise!'

Juniper unlocked her door to let Tilly in first and hoped she wasn't judging all the mess. Yesterday's clothes hadn't made it to her laundry hamper, instead spilling over her desk chair. A dozen wires were already tangled up by the bed made for devices that were probably out of battery regardless. The books she'd checked out of the library in preparation for her studies were all over the floor instead of the bare shelves. But the thing that would really get her in trouble lay on the desk: a cage housing a tiny, tan little Chinese striped hamster who was enjoying a run on his wheel.

Tilly squealed. 'No way! I thought pets weren't allowed in halls!'

'They're not, which is why you can't tell anyone.'

'Well, shite.' Tilly planted herself down on Juniper's desk chair to get a closer look at Cerberus and his beady black eyes. 'He's so cute.' A frown. 'But you know they could kick you out if they found him?'

'I know.' Juniper winced. 'But I couldn't leave him at home. My parents would absolutely forget to feed him.'

'Fair.' She shrugged as though that was that, poking her finger through the wires of the cage. 'What's his name?'

'Cerberus. After—'

'The hound of Hades! I love it.' Tilly grinned, and so did Juniper. She was soon finding that she didn't have to explain herself to Tilly, not like she did with other people, and it grounded her in a way she hadn't felt for a while. Even at home, her parents didn't really understand her. Mum had wanted to name the hamster Bob. Dad had wanted to name him Hamster.

Maybe this place could be her home if she just gave it another chance. So what if it was dark and Aiden-filled? There were things she could love about it, too.

Starting with this.

7

By Friday, Aiden had become almost as excellent at ignoring Juniper as he was at throwing. Sort of. Her jabs had been replaced with the silent treatment, which was just fine with him, or so he told himself. Besides, he didn't need a familiar face from back home. All of the faces that greeted him as he walked into the workshop that morning were friendly.

He cast Amir and Timmy – or was it Tommy? – a wave, which turned into fist bumps, on his way to his seat, stifling a groan when Amir said, 'Morning, Whittaker.'

Everybody now knew his last name, and he'd already received a few questions about his dad. As much as he wanted to believe these people wanted to be his friend, it wouldn't be the first time he'd been used for the sake of his connections. Most of the students he'd befriended at Elmington had been shallow, difficult to talk to unless it was about the industry and his father's career.

But what did it matter? Luc was genuine enough, and a few of the girls had enjoyed a bit of flirting here and there. He was just glad to be on the course, glad to be out of the cage his dad had created for him – even if it felt like he'd just hopped from one set of bars to another sometimes. He clearly enjoyed torturing himself, because the sight of Juniper's empty stool pressed into his periphery even when he tried to focus on the conversation happening in front of him.

'Are you going to Tom's party tomorrow night?' Luc shuddered as though the thought alone was enough to break their spirit. Okay, so it was neither Timmy *nor* Tommy.

'Well, it *would* be good to get to know everyone a bit better.' Aiden had been contemplating it only because his other option was to sit in his flat alone and wonder who he was without anything to do. It was a light week as far as work went, so reading wouldn't keep him busy for long. Besides, he and Tom lived on the same street, and he couldn't think of anything sadder than sitting in, listening to people have fun from a few doors down.

'Why? Not a party person?' he couldn't help but tease when he saw Luc's withering look.

'Not in this country. Drunk British people are terrifying. And most of your alcoholic beverages taste like urine. But I don't want to be the odd one out.'

'Well, you don't have to drink. And we don't have to stop for long, if you don't want.' Aiden wasn't sure he'd enjoy it much, anyway. Tom was a little too into the fresher's week spirit, coming to class hungover and smelling like a whisky factory most mornings. Aiden got it. He'd been the same when he'd gotten his first taste of freedom at Elmington, but partying had swiftly snowballed into an escape, a remedy for his deteriorating wellbeing, when studying had started.

'Right, gang,' Chris said by way of greeting as he strutted into the classroom. 'Shush up.'

It had become his way of saying hello, now. Aiden had warmed to him, day by day, even with his harsh remarks and constant deadpan attitude. He liked feeling challenged, like he really had to work to impress someone.

Maybe that was why he'd been hooked on Juni, too.

In the past.

As though summoned, she burst through the door behind Chris, her curls poking in all directions and sweat beading on her brow. 'Sorry we're late!'

The *we* was for Tilly, who stumbled in behind Juniper, equally as flustered.

'*Again.*' Chris folded his arms over his chest, rumpling his tweed blazer. 'What was it this time? Another goose blocking the path?'

'No.' Juniper's glare swooped over to the front of the classroom, where Amir chewed the lid of his pen. '*Somebody* set fire to the microwave last night. We were up until three while the inspectors sorted it.'

'Nobody told me that Pot Noodles are flammable!' Amir defended, mischief dancing in his eyes.

'Anything is flammable if you cook it for several hours,' Tilly said.

Amir made a *pfft*. 'I'll make up for it. Promise.' And then he winked at Juniper. 'I'm very good at apologising, y'know.'

Without invitation, Aiden's fist bunched on his thighs, clenching tighter still when Amir winked and Juniper's lips curled in a half smirk. Was he *flirting* with her?

Of course he was. Amir flirted with everyone. Nomi had already warned him to back off or else face the wrath of her boyfriend. And yet it didn't quell the tightness in his stomach, because she had smiled back. At *Amir*. She'd never smiled at Aiden like that.

'Glad to know that some of our best future ceramicists are absolutely useless as human beings.' Chris glanced at his watch to emphasise his dismay. 'With your permission, may I start teaching?'

The room fell silent, but a steady thrum settled in Aiden when Juniper took her seat behind him. This was the worst part. When they sat in the workshop and she was *there*. He couldn't see her, but she could see him. Her presence was like winter fog thickening the air with ice, and he felt it all over him. Was she watching him, or was his tingling body just paranoid?

All right, maybe he wasn't *that* excellent at ignoring her. But he was excellent at pretending, so he did that now, bracing his elbows against the desk to focus on the whiteboard. Chris set up a presentation that was titled: *Term 1 Coursework*.

A chorus of groans filled the room.

Chris put a hand on his chest. 'I know, I know. It's terrible that we expect you to actually do some work at this university. Thoughts and prayers are with you all.' He clicked the next slide with an abrupt jab of his finger on the keyboard. 'In my opinion, the best way to improve your pottery is to understand what it means in every context. The way to start that is by looking around the room. Talking to each other. A foreign concept for you Zoomers, I know. So, this term's coursework will make up thirty-five percent of this year's final grade, and because I really enjoy being mean, it's going to be a collaborative experience.'

Aiden didn't like where this was going. He might have enjoyed socialising, but collaborating was a different story. It never ended up fair. His work could be dragged down by a less adept student, or worse, he could have someone like overly eager Diane badgering him night and day.

A few other people must have felt the same, because the room grew considerably gloomier, and so did the groans. He was tempted to look over his shoulder just to see Juniper's reaction. She gave him the impression that she wasn't all that good at working with other people, either.

'Since we have a nice even fourteen of you this year, you'll be divided into groups of two to bring this project to life,' Chris continued. 'It'll cover everything from an initial research paper to a final exhibition, where you'll be expected to present your work to the rest of us over in the gallery.'

Aiden could only hope that they were allowed to choose their partners. It was Luc or no one.

'What I'm hoping is that you can marry' – Aiden didn't like the smashing together of hands Chris did to convey the word *marry* – 'two individual ideas to create something that reveals who you are, together and apart.'

He went on to show them some examples, none of which Aiden really got. Previous students had combined football-themed pottery with Ancient Rome. The Wild West with Halloween. Animals whose body parts had been mismatched so that there was a horse with a fish head, a shark with a tabby cat's orange legs. Was he missing something?

'You'll be expected to use a decent range of techniques and materials for this, and most of this work will be done outside of teaching hours, so if you're a slacker, I'm certain I'll be able to tell.' Chris gave a few pointed looks to the lads at the front of the room.

'Do we get to decide who we work with?' Tom asked. Next to him, Amir was crossing his fingers, much like Aiden wanted to. Suddenly, this course felt like it was going to be a lot harder than expected.

'Ha!' Chris erupted. 'Absolutely not, you sweet, naive boy. No.' – He grabbed a terracotta bowl from his desk and began to shake it, revealing half a dozen white slips of paper inside – 'we'll let the Bowl of Doom decide your fates. Take your pick, Timmy.'

Shit.

The bowl was offered to Tom, who reached in with trepidation to pick out a name. When he opened it, he asked, 'Who's Laura?'

'I assume that would be me.' At the back of the class, Lauren lifted her hand. In her thirties, she was one of the quieter ones, with fine blonde hair and sparkling eyes.

'There we go. Our first pair! Congratulations. Next.' The bowl was passed to Amir, who unfortunately got Luc. There went that hope, then. As the bowl got closer, Aiden's knee began to bounce up and down. Juniper hadn't been picked yet, but there was no way—

'Alex. Your turn,' Chris said, shaking the bowl in front of his face.

Aiden wiped his sweaty palms on his jeans and reached in. There were only three people who hadn't been matched yet:

Tilly, Owen, the sandy-haired guy who sat behind her, and Juniper.

Please be Owen, he prayed, but his pounding heart must have known before the rest of him, because when he unfolded the paper to read the smudged ink, his worst fears were confirmed.

'Jupiter.'

'No. You're messing with me!' Juniper rushed around the table to snatch the paper from Aiden's hands, and her proximity made him bristle with tension.

Her nostrils flared when she read the name. Her name. Well, almost. She looked up at Chris, ignoring Aiden entirely. 'Well, this doesn't count because Jupiter is not my name.'

'Nice try, but there's a reason we call it the Bowl of Doom.' Chris tore said bowl away, motioning between Tilly and Owen. 'That means Tammy and Olly are our final pair. Congratulations. I hope you will all be very happy together.'

Aiden finally mustered the courage to look at Juniper. If she was icy before, she was an arctic blizzard now.

'Somehow,' he mumbled, 'I doubt that very much.

8

Juniper massaged her temples, her muscles turning rigid when Aiden spun on his stool to face her. She'd spent the last hour of class trying to morph reality into something she could handle with the powers of her mind, and when that hadn't worked, she unlocked her phone under the table and Googled how to build that time machine Tilly had mentioned. Since she'd failed horribly at trying to build a simple bowl on the throwing wheel, *again*, quantum physics wasn't exactly much help either.

Which meant that she was stuck with Aiden.

'So,' he began as she used a cloth to wipe the clay off her hands. Her knuckles and her biceps were aching. Meanwhile, Aiden had made the work look easy as ever. His perfectly sculpted bowl was currently in the drying room, ready for the kiln on Monday. A place Juniper hadn't yet needed to visit. All of her clay ended up back in its bag to be dried out and reused by somebody who was probably more capable than her.

'So,' she repeated flatly, and hoped he sensed the warning in it. It was half *don't fuck me around for the sake of my own sanity*, and half *please don't let me fail this bloody module*.

'Jupiter,' he said with a straight face.

She narrowed her eyes. 'Alex.'

His lips twitched. She tried not to let hers do the same. This wasn't funny. It was tragic – and just plain cruel of the universe, or the Bowl of Doom, or Christopher. Whoever had done this had a sick sense of humour. Talented or not, there was no way in hell she could rely on Aiden Whittaker to get her a decent grade. He would probably laze about, leave all the hard bits to her because he'd never had to work for a single thing in his life. Or maybe he'd sabotage her just to piss her off, bribe Christopher to give him a decent grade and leave her at the bottom of the class. She wouldn't put any of it past him. He'd already proven himself to be sly and immoral, good at taking things he didn't deserve. And she was the only one who saw it, the only one who knew just what he'd done to get into Elmington.

'We should set a few dates each week to meet up,' he decided finally, his hands inching a little too close to hers on the desk. Clay caked his fingernails and clung to the hairs on his forearms, but what she really noticed was how big his hands were compared to her stubby little fingers. Always at an advantage, right down to his biology.

'I have a gap between lessons on Tuesday and Wednesday afternoons.' Spending them with him was the last thing she wanted, and her stiff voice conveyed it. Sitting behind him was bad enough. Now, she would have to work with him. *Marry* their ideas. She was certain that their ideas were completely *un*marriable, or at least destined for divorce.

Aiden pulled out his phone and unlocked it with a quick tap, his schedule lighting the screen and turning his face silver. It made his eyes greener, features harsher, and she marvelled at the unfairness of it all. To think someone so entitled could be so good-looking. Yet another thing she would have to take up with the universe.

'Hm. What time?' he asked. 'I have seminars from two.'

'That won't work then.'

'How about evenings?'

'I'm working.'

'*Every* evening?' His brows lifted, and she gritted her teeth.

'Yes, Aiden, every evening. Some of us need money.'

The muscle in his jaw feathered, but he went back to his schedule. 'Monday mornings?'

Juniper hesitated. The last thing she wanted was to start her week with *him*, but she did have some free time before lunch.

She sighed. 'Fine. How's ten?'

'Perfect.' She almost laughed at that word. Almost. 'We can meet at the library.' He locked his phone with a terse flick of his thumb, sliding it into the back pocket of his jeans. 'We should get started as soon as possible, really. Are you free now to grab a coffee and brainstorm some ideas?'

Juniper looked at the clock above the workshop's threshold. Unfortunately, she couldn't think of a single thing she could be doing. That, and he was right, as much as it pained her. She needed this project to work. She needed *everything* to work. Since she wasn't known for her ability to meet deadlines, she'd need all the time she could get.

'Fine.' She grabbed her bag. 'Let's go.'

★

She felt a little less vulnerable as they stepped into the campus café: it was a crowded, neutral spot beside the library rather than the place where everything she'd ever wanted in life balanced precariously on a workbench. She stopped in front of the counter and wondered when coffee had gotten so expensive. Her successful trial at Caffé Verde had proved that some people were willing to pay double digits for a cappuccino, but she'd expected as much on Regent Street. Weren't people here supposed to be struggling students, or was she the only charity case at RACA?

'You can put the purse away, Hodge. It's on me.' Aiden nudged her hand away from her backpack, skin pink and rough from throwing. She jolted away immediately, but a traitorous current of electricity still shot up her arm. She told herself it was more of that abject hatred, though it wasn't unpleasant so much as disarming.

'No, it really isn't.' The thought of him paying for anything of hers made her want to gag. The last thing she needed was to owe him, even if a few quid meant nothing to him. It meant enough to her. If they were going to do this, they'd do it on equal footing – if that was even possible.

Before he could protest, she walked up to the counter and ordered a cold brew, which probably wasn't wise given all the caffeine and sugar, but she needed something energising to get her through this. She heard Aiden ask for a latte beside her and was surprised he didn't request something fancier, like truffle syrup or those extortionate beans pooped out by Asian palm civets.

Once her drink was ready, she didn't bother to wait for him, heading over to a table by the tall window so that she at least had something other than him to look at. It was a grey day outside, like most in the UK, with only a few patches of blue breaking through the overcast sky. Still, it was warm enough that a few students congregated around Mags' statue, with more overcrowding benches or socialising on the steps of the gallery across the square. If she was alone, she might have taken a moment to really drink in her surroundings, to appreciate them. She'd longed to be one of those students lazing on the grass between classes, and now she could be.

But when Aiden sat opposite, chair dragging across mosaic tiles with a deafening screech, it was hard to appreciate anything at all. She sipped her iced coffee from an already soggy paper straw and waited for him to start.

'Any ideas on what themes you'd cover?' he asked, peeling off his khaki jacket, which brought out the green of his eyes to an obnoxious degree. Was it her, or did pretty-eyed people open their eyes a bit wider just to brag?

Not that *anything* about him was pretty.

With his muscular bare arms back on show in his white tee, it was all that much harder to concentrate.

Still, she perked up as her brain stuttered back into action. One thing Aiden couldn't ruin was her creativity, and she'd been preparing project ideas for months. It was a shame some of them would be wasted on *him*, but hopefully she'd be able to cross the themes over into other modules. 'Well, actually, yes. I'd like to explore mythology.'

'Right. Yeah. I remember you always liked history and all that stuff.'

The ice in Juniper's drink rattled against the cup, proof of her shock. He remembered her *that* well? She'd always thought him to be more interested in his dim-witted mates or that black sketchbook he'd carried around with him everywhere. 'You did, too, from what I recall. Probably because you sat right behind me, which meant you were always kicking my chair or making fun of my hair.'

He pinched his chin with a pensive tilt of his head. 'That doesn't sound like me.'

She rolled her eyes. He really did love pissing her off. Always had. Just as she was about to say as much, he continued, 'Besides, I liked your hair. Still do.'

She didn't know if she wanted to laugh or throw her coffee in his face. Aiden Whittaker was giving her a compliment, which meant something terrible must have been happening. Maybe she'd hopped dimensions, or he'd been cloned. More likely was that he was messing with her, but when she searched his face, she saw no taunts.

His sincerity was somehow far worse than the alternative, so she decided to ignore it entirely, sweeping her hair back and returning to the matter at hand. 'Anyway. Mythology. I'd like to focus specifically on creatures and monsters. The chimera and the Midgard serpent spring to mind.'

'Sounds good.' Aiden nodded, and then frowned. 'What are those?'

She bit back a smug grin. Finally, she knew something he didn't. 'The chimera is a hybrid that's part-lion, goat, and snake. She terrorised men in Greek mythology, a hobby I greatly respect.'

'Colour me shocked.'

She waited for him to mock her for the excitement she couldn't contain whenever she spoke about her interests, but it never came. Maybe he was saving it for later, getting to know more so he could really pack a punch.

She didn't particularly want to ask about *his* ideas, but when silence blanketed the table, broken only by tentative sips of coffee, she grew restless. 'And you? What grand ideas do you have?'

'Honestly, I don't know.' He leaned back in his chair, folding his arms over his chest in a way that made his T-shirt stretch across his thick shoulders. A tuft of dark hair peeked from the white collar, which she quickly looked away from.

'Well, don't overwhelm me with too much brainstorming,' she deadpanned, crossing one knee over the other.

He smirked, shaking his head. With half of his face cast in the watery noon light, the other caught in the golden glow of the café, his lashes cast thick shadows. Every part of him was another lump of coal to fuel her fire. He didn't deserve to be perfect, but he was, and maybe it was shallow, but she'd feel better if she could find some kind of external flaw to match all of his internal ones. Even the faint scar in his chin only served to pronounce his dimple better, offering an inviting rugged edge to his otherwise faultless features.

She'd almost forgotten she was waiting for an answer, and quickly dragged her attention to the window again when he spoke. 'I guess I like music.'

'Everybody likes music. What sort of music?'

A shrug. 'Anything really. Rock. Pop. Folk. Classical.'

'Okay…' She could work with that, maybe. She liked the first three genres herself. 'Do you play any instruments?'

'No.'

Or not. As she'd suspected, he didn't seem eager to talk about it, about anything – not like she was with mythology – and if he lacked the creativity to care, it was sure to reflect on their work. *Her* work. She could already see a million different ceramic sculptures floating in her mind, both with her monsters and his music, but it wasn't her job to do all of the heavy lifting. He owed her at least some enthusiasm.

'Again, calm down with all these wonderfully unique ideas,' she said in that same flat voice, then shifted in an effort to release some of her impatience. 'Give me something here. Christopher said it should be something personal. Something that shows who we are as individuals.'

'And together,' he added, despite it being the part she was quite happy to ignore. He leaned closer, resting his cheek on his hand and offering a wolfish grin. 'Who are we together, Hodge?'

He was trying to get under her skin. She could feel it. She wouldn't give him the satisfaction, even if the low, rumbled words tiptoed under her jumper and scuttled over her skin. 'Let's get this clear. We're *nothing* together, Whittaker. And if you don't know who you are, what you care about, I doubt we'll figure it out for the sake of this project.'

'You don't mince your words, do you?' He frowned into his latte, an absent finger tracing the rim of the mug. 'I know who I am, and I care about plenty.'

'Good. Then tell me, because I'm not doing all the work here.' She stretched out her legs determinedly, and then regretted it when her toe brushed Aiden's shin.

He nudged her back with a softer sole. 'Playing footsie with me now? I can't keep up with you, Juni.'

'Shut up. It was an accident.' She tore away roughly enough that her chair scraped back with her, which only seemed to entertain him more. Had she mentioned recently that she hated him? A lot? 'Look, I've got better things to be doing, so if you're not taking this seriously—'

'Art,' he drawled, interrupting her. 'Art is the thing I know most about. Happy?'

'Art.' She frowned. It made sense, had been the first thing she'd assumed he'd come up with, yet she didn't sense any sincerity in his voice. Like he wouldn't choose it at all if there was another option. Like it was something that haunted rather than inspired. 'Y'know, knowing the most about it doesn't mean much – only that you grew up with an art dealer for a dad and the means to pursue the same path. That's not the same as loving something.'

He splayed his hands out in a sudden, rough gesture. 'Well, then, what do you want from me?'

I want you to be honest with me. The thought came without reason, without want, and she tried to shove it down quickly.

It wasn't true. She didn't want *anything* from Aiden, especially not his honesty. All she wanted was a decent amount of effort on this project so that she could prove to everybody she deserved a place here, that she could be a decent potter like the rest of them.

She sipped more of her drink, the bitterness matching her mood. 'I'm only saying you don't sound very passionate, but whatever. If that's what you want to do, fine. Maybe we can find some paintings of mythological creatures or something, combine the two.'

'I could name a few.'

'Wonderful. You really are the fount of all knowledge, then.' Her tone was dry, sardonic, something she never could seem to control around him.

For once, it didn't seem to amuse him. 'Look, we're going to have to spend a lot of time together for this project, so can we just quit it with the snide remarks?'

'I'm not *snide*.'

'You're *something*,' he retorted.

'And what's that supposed to mean?' Her voice rose, causing a few students around them to look her way. She shrank back in her seat, feeling scolded. Feeling sick of this already.

Aiden blinked, his gaze lingering on her for longer than was comfortable. 'You know, you're going to need my help far more than I'll need yours,' he decided finally.

She scoffed so hard that she almost choked on her own saliva. *The fucking nerve of this lad.* 'Get off your high horse. I don't need shit from you.'

'No? Because you've been struggling on the wheel all week. If that's anything to go off, our exhibition will be nothing more than a few questionably shaped lumps of clay.'

'I made *one* accidental penis! One!' She held a finger up for emphasis, wishing she could poke it right in his eye. 'I'm trying, and that's more than I can say for you! You're just perfect at everything, aren't you? And if you're not, who cares? You're Aiden Whittaker. You can get away with it. You can get away with anything, and you'll *never* have to try.'

'I'm trying *now*,' he muttered, deep tone dripping with something Juniper couldn't decipher.

She paused. On the table, his fingers were furled into his palms, and a splash of red coloured his cheeks. Had she actually affected him?

A shred of guilt fluttered in her chest, but it soon dissolved. Maybe she *was* a little snide, but he was worse. He would always be worse after what he did.

She was over this. Over him. At least for today. She stood up, drink in hand and fatigue on her shoulders despite the caffeine humming through her. 'Let's just do some research over the weekend then try again on Monday. We're not getting anywhere with this.'

'No shit,' he spat out.

When she stormed out of the café, she was just proud that her iced coffee remained intact, rather than dunked on his head and staining his white tee. She could imagine it, brown fabric clinging to his pecs and tongue jutting out to catch the droplets. The shock as his lips parted, hair flopping into his eyes.

She'd expected to feel the heat in her chest at the fantasy, but it bloomed further south, an invisible string tugging between her gut and her core. *Stop. Just stop.*

But it felt pointless to even try. She was learning that nothing she did would snuff out this thing with Aiden, whether it was anger or something more. He was unavoidable – inevitable, it sometimes felt like.

Still, she couldn't let him win.

Not like he had last time.

9

Energetic pop music was already blaring when Aiden and Luc turned onto Cartwright Gardens, strobe lights flashing from Tom's house and painting the rain-slick path green and purple so that nobody could mistake which house the party was taking place at.

'Yikes. Is everybody at RACA rich?' Luc asked. In the end, Aiden had managed to convince them to come, although they'd complained about it the whole walk here. Luc lived on campus, and since they didn't know their way around London, Aiden had met up with them beforehand to grab pizza. A far cry from student accommodation, the houses along this street bore elegant Georgian facades with creamy white panelling on the ground floor and brown brick above. The black arched doors were flanked by lanterns on either side, and potted plants with pink petals and lush green leaves draped from the first-floor balconies. Aiden didn't dare admit that, thanks to his maternal aunt owning some of the most sought-after properties in the area, he rented the ground floor flat a few doors down at number 47.

Instead, he answered cautiously, 'Not everybody.'

A mangled noise of amusement left Luc's throat, and they nudged him with a sharp elbow as the two of them continued down the crescent-shaped lane. 'Just you and Tom?'

He didn't exactly know how to reply to that. Money wasn't something he'd ever had to give thought to, which he knew was a mark of his privilege, but it also meant he wasn't sure how to react when people brought it up. Sometimes, he preferred how Juniper handled it: bluntly, without skirting around their differences. He didn't mind being the rich arsehole as long as he knew it. It would be far worse to be judged as only that, or have friends reduce him to it behind his back, which had happened often at Elmington.

Juniper. He could only assume she'd be here tonight, ready and waiting with some more insults up her sleeve. Maybe he liked that about her, too, even if they were becoming a little too personal for his liking. She was the only person who didn't feign niceties to get close to Aiden. The only person whose intentions were abundantly clear – even if they were to murder him in his sleep.

'Have you and Amir decided what your project will be?' he asked Luc, absently tearing a leaf from its branch through the wrought iron fencing. His fingers never resisted that drive to keep busy. Without a paintbrush or a lump of clay, they were destructive, forever tearing at paper or wearing down the etchings of his thumb ring, or else picking at calluses on his hands until the skin bled.

'Avoiding the subject.' Luc tutted, but was gracious enough to move on. 'No, we are meeting on Tuesday. How about you and Juniper?' They waggled their brows. 'I am imagining your exhibition to be rather angry and erotic.'

He let out a 'Ha!', though his stomach burned at the words. Angry and erotic weren't too far from the truth, at least for him. Those venomous scoffs she loved to give him made his cock twitch, her glare pierced right into his flesh. It probably made him a masochist.

She was testing his patience now, though. If they had to do this project together, he wouldn't sit and take all the insults much longer. The way she presumed all sorts of terrible things about him, the way she implied that he didn't *try*…

Yes, definitely erotic, and also definitely angry. He just didn't know how to change her opinion of him, nor what he'd done to deserve it.

Luckily, the noise of the party was enough to make him forget as they passed through the gate of the liveliest house. They skipped up the low steps, and eagerness hummed through Aiden. Eagerness, and something with a far more serrated edge. Something that left him stopping for just a moment. The last party he'd gone to had been at Elmington, and he'd been miserable in a sea of people who couldn't see it, didn't care enough to, at least not until he'd gotten bladdered enough to puke all over the carpet mid-panic attack. What if he lost himself again here?

'Are you okay?' Luc asked, blotting the dark lipstick from their mouth and leaving it to stain the pads of their fingers.

Aiden nodded. Swallowed. It wouldn't be like that again. He didn't drink to forget anymore. He was finally where he wanted to be, not caught pursuing a degree just to make his dad proud. There was no one else to let down but himself, and that made him freer than ever. 'Yep. All good.'

He didn't bother knocking on the door, instead heading straight into a hallway crammed with people. The bitter smell of beer and mingling aftershaves hit him like a wave, and he found himself high-fiving and shaking hands with people he'd never seen before in his life.

And then his name was yelled over the electronic beat of the music: 'Fuck yeah, Whittaker!'

Tom stood on the stairs, pumping his arms as though he'd known Aiden for years rather than days.

'Yikes,' Luc whispered again, and tactfully disappeared into the first door, which Aiden assumed was the living room.

Since he'd been spotted, he smiled and waited for an already stumbling Tom to make it down the stairs.

'All right, Timmy Tom?' Aiden teased. Chris's nicknames for them all seemed to be sticking. Aiden was sometimes referred to as *Al* by the lads as a tribute to his new name, Alex.

Tom's grin was hazy, just like his eyes, as he slapped Aiden on the back. 'Glad you're here, mate. Let's get you a drink.' Much to Aiden's mortification, he began to shout to the party-goers: 'Move, everybody. Son of art royalty coming through!'

Maybe it wasn't so different after all. Aiden kept his head down, face blazing, as Tom guided them through the crowd now ogling him and into a large kitchen. Drink bottles were lined up on every surface, and groups congregated around countertops to chat and take pictures.

'What can I get you, mate? Beer? Lager? Whisky?' Tom was already riffling through his collection, clearly eager to impress. At least, Aiden could only assume that's what it was after the scene he'd just caused. It wouldn't be the first time somebody had sucked up a little too hard.

'Beer's fine.'

'Only the best for you.' He picked up one of the more expensive brands, removing the cap with his teeth. 'Listen, I've been meaning to talk to you. One of my mates is at Elmington—'

Aiden's heart stopped, the world slowing down around him as though everyone was wading through tar, including him. Tom's words were drowned out by the alarm bells in his ears, but he imagined the possibilities: *And he said you had a nervous breakdown and walked out in the middle of an exam. And he heard you stopped getting out of bed to go to your lectures. And he was wondering why the fuck you'd turned your whole life into something barely recognisable.*

'Whoa,' Tom said with his mouth around his own beer. 'Am I out of line? Sorry, Al…'

Dizzy, Aiden tried to tune back into the conversation. Tried to look like he was a normal person, not that broken shell he'd become last year.

'Sorry, I missed that. What did you say about your mate?' He leaned closer, feigning interest even as the bottle in his hands began to quiver.

In his ear, Tom shouted over the dance music: 'He was wondering if you could put in a good word with your dad about that apprenticeship he's running. Dead interested in the dealer business he is!'

'Right.' Aiden might have felt relieved if the question didn't make him feel so numb. This was why he hadn't wanted people to know who he was. There was always someone who needed something, usually from his dad, which left him as nothing more than pawn, a go-between. 'I think the position has already been filled, but I'll see what I can do.'

It was a lie. He wasn't even talking to his dad right now – or, rather, his dad wasn't talking to him. Not after he'd turned down that apprenticeship himself, among a few others. He'd gleaned from shameless social media stalking that Jonathan had hired someone else over the summer, a young lad not too dissimilar in looks from Aiden. Probably a nice replacement now the heir to the business had been unofficially disowned.

'You're a top bloke!' Tom said, clinking their bottles together. 'Cheers, mate.'

'Cheers,' Aiden said, and then, when Tom got pulled into another conversation, muttered, 'I'm not your mate.'

He leaned against the kitchen table, trying to gather his composure. It would have been easier if, at the same moment, his eyes didn't drift around the room and inevitably land on Juniper's. His first instinct was to straighten, reassemble his composure before she caught a chink in his armour. Hers was to look away, as always, which at least gave him the opportunity to admire her form in the bright lights. Her hair was down, curls slightly more organised, and her face glittered with more makeup than usual. Her eyeliner tapered into a point beyond the smoky corners of her eyes and velvety cherry-red lipstick accentuated her plump mouth. She wore a black leather skirt that didn't leave much to the imagination, pleats draped over irresistibly wild hips and ending midway down her overwhelmingly curvy thighs. Her mesh top was just as generous – *too* generous. Something lurched inside Aiden at the sight of her cleavage, and kept lurching when he noticed a tattoo curling around her shoulder like vines.

Fuck.

He was so enchanted by her that he hadn't even noticed who she talked to, not until she laughed straight from her belly when her friend whispered in her ear.

No, not just a friend. Amir.

Why was it that *he* was the only person she couldn't stand? The only one who couldn't make her laugh like that? The only one she didn't even want to look at.

The room seemed to expand, leaving him a lonely dot floating at the centre of it, and he couldn't help but imagine what it would feel like if his lips got as close to her as Amir's were, hovering just above the soft hinge of her jaw.

'Staring isn't cool, man.' Luc's black-painted fingernails were suddenly clicking in Aiden's face, and he tore away quickly.

'Not staring. Just observing. That's what artists do, isn't it?' He handed Luc a drink, but they nudged it back to the table.

'No thanks. Smells like piss, just as I'd feared.'

Aiden didn't care. He was going to need something stronger than the beer he currently sipped to get through tonight. Maybe he would fall into old habits, after all. He gestured with his head to the living room. 'What's it like in there? Any better than out here?'

'If you like David Guetta, which you shouldn't.' Luc grimaced. 'Why are we here again? To see if you can exchange dissing for kissing with your high school nemesis over there?'

Aiden's brow furrowed. 'Am I supposed to know what that means?'

Luc's sigh was withering. 'Why don't you just go over to her?'

'Why would I want to?' he snapped, and then regretted it. Luc was about the only friend he'd made, or at least the only one who seemed to see him as more than just a Whittaker. It wasn't their fault that everybody else in this room, bar one very fiery classmate, had already decided he was only worth what his surname could offer.

Luc seemed oblivious to his frayed temper, only shrugging. 'That, dear friend, is a mystery to me. But it beats ogling her from the other side of the room, does it not?'

Frustration bubbled in Aiden at the prospect of another terse conversation with her. He already felt on the edge of his limit after the conversation with Tom, though he'd hoped to be stronger than that. Hoped he was finally recovering. 'I can't get through to her. It's pointless.'

'Her drink is running low,' they noted. 'Get her another one.'

He looked over again. Amir had disappeared and Juniper now chatted with Tilly, back pressed against the wall as she nursed an empty bottle of cider with a pink label that he assumed made it berry-flavoured.

A Strongbow-flavoured olive branch…

It wasn't the worst idea in the world

10

'I just don't know why he has to be *there* all the time,' Juniper groused, getting comfortable on one of the leather couches in the living room. The music was giving her a headache. Or maybe it was the cider. Or maybe it was Aiden's presence.

Beside her, Tilly sprawled onto the arm, cuddling a beige pillow to her chest. It had taken her back to see just how differently they were living compared to her more well-off classmates. Unlike Juniper, who only had a view of scaffolding around a derelict building at the back of campus, the residents of Cartwright Gardens had the pleasure of tall sycamore trees to look out at. It didn't seem fair, somehow. Juniper had a bed and a desk chair. Tom had *rooms*. Furniture. Space. A home.

And an Aiden, currently. An Aiden Juniper was sick of seeing. An Aiden Tilly was probably very sick of hearing about, but she couldn't help it. Her tongue was loose from the alcohol, and god, she was pissed off.

'Because he's in our class,' her friend said now, and then pouted. 'You know who's not in our class? Lesbians. No lesbians for Tilly.'

She looked gorgeous tonight, dark skin warmed by a rich purple lipstick and golden eye shadow. Juniper had helped pick out her outfit, a velvet burgundy halter top and flared matching trousers that she would never have been able to pull off herself. In return, Tilly had done her makeup, a fierce smoky eye that made her feel more herself than ever.

'You deserve all the lesbians. What about her?' Quick to take on her wingwoman duties, Juniper pointed over the crowded living room at a short-haired woman playing a game of spin the bottle with Tom and his friends.

Tilly clucked her tongue. 'You pointed at her an hour ago!'

'Did I?'

She nodded. 'She's Tom's sister. I can't date somebody related to him!'

Since Tom was currently trying touch his chin with his tongue, and almost succeeding, it was a valid point. Juniper huffed and sat back, wishing somebody would turn the music down. Or stop the strobe lights from circling the room. Or, at the very least, remove her least favourite person from the premises.

Just as she kicked her legs over the side of the couch's arm in an attempt to get more comfortable, the heel of her boot collided with a passerby. Right in the groin. They let out a moan of pain, and she sprang to her feet with the intention of apologising – until she realised that the groin in question belonged to Aiden.

He hunched over, hands outstretched in an attempt not to spill the drinks he held: a beer and the same cider she'd been guzzling. 'Your shoes are fucking lethal, Hodge. What was *that* for?'

'You tell me. You hit my foot!'

'Fine. I will give Tom's sister another chance,' decided Tilly.

Juniper gasped in horror. After all of the efforts she'd put into her wingwoman duties, this was how she was treated? But it was too late. Aiden watched Tilly go, slowly rising as the pain eased from his face. His very, very handsome face. Juni must have drunk more than she'd thought, because he looked better than ever, his hair falling over his forehead in brown waves and a black T-shirt, half-covered by an open corduroy shirt, stretched over his thick chest.

'Drunk already?' His eyes sparkled with mischief.

'Tipsy,' she corrected, shimmying the hem of her skirt down her thighs when his eyes lowered to her outfit. She'd known it was too short, damn thing. 'And not in the mood.'

She nudged past him to leave only to find that, through the kitchen, where she'd hoped to get some air, the courtyard was lit up with the orange glow of a dozen rowdy smokers. One of them had decided to take his top off and swing it around his head while singing Tina Turner.

Honestly, she was ready to go home, but she didn't want Tilly to realise that she was a party pooper so soon into their friendship. She went back into the corridor and wobbled her way up the stairs, her head feeling less like cotton wool as she grew further from the noise. The intention was to lock herself in the bathroom, but there was a queue of people, so she slipped into the first bedroom she found, which was cloaked in darkness and, best of all, quiet.

'Okay, Juni. Take a breath. It's just a party,' she whispered to herself as she perched on the thick double mattress. She left the room unlit, eyes still dancing with red dots left behind by the strobe lights, but she could make out a surprisingly tidy room. The streetlights outside reflected on something silver in the shadowy corner, catching her eye. When she realised what it was, she let out something akin to a growl.

A bloody throwing wheel. Tom had his own. Of course he did. She dragged her finger along the cold metal surface as envy spiked through her. If she wanted to practice throwing, she had to wait until workshop hours or stay behind after class, something she didn't much feel like doing after the mess she'd made this week.

'Hiding?' The gruff voice behind her caused her to jump. She spun around already knowing, somehow, who she'd find, but still aggravated by his silhouette nonetheless. Aiden's features became visible as he let the door swing shut behind him.

'Are you just following me around now?' she questioned impatiently. What did she have to do to have a moment to herself? A moment away from him and his stupid smirk?

He set the drinks down on the desk, where a laptop was half-concealed by notebooks left open, scrawled handwriting inside.

'I was trying to offer you a drink. If you didn't avoid me like the plague, you would have seen that downstairs.' He held out the cider, strawberry and lime.

She squinted at the bottle. Did it bring him joy to keep his enemies hydrated, or was it just some gentlemanly act to charm her into submission? 'What's the catch? Did you poison it?'

He snorted. 'If anyone's doing the poisoning, it's you.'

He had a point, but he hadn't exactly been happy with her after their meet-up at the café. She was beginning to suspect that she needed him to hate her as much as she did him, just to even the ground between them. Unfortunately, it seemed they were forever going to be on different hills, hers rocky, his paved smooth.

Begrudgingly, she took the drink and sipped, letting the fizz take her mind off the utterly terrible time she was having. 'If this is you trying to be friends, you'll have to do better than a drink that was already free.'

'What about…' He stuck his tongue out as he reached into the back pocket of his jeans – at least, she hoped that's where he produced the packet from. 'Mini Cheddars?'

She brightened, and then felt like she was betraying herself – but she was hungry, and she loved cheese-flavoured carbo-hydrates, and Tom was a terrible host who had only put out a few trays of food that had already been gone when Juniper had shimmied into the kitchen. 'Where did you find them?'

'Weird thing happened. They just fell out of Tom's cupboards right into my hands.'

Her laugh surprised even her, and she covered her mouth quickly to stop it. But when she reached for the orange packet, he tore it out of reach, leaving her to stand on her tiptoes desperately.

He waggled his finger. 'Not until you call a truce. C'mon, Hodge. Be my friend. Or at least a civil acquaintance.'

Using snacks as leverage only made him eviller. She crossed her arms over her chest, glowering from under her lashes. '*No.*'

Currently, he was not her least favourite person in this house, but she would never let herself forget all the reasons why he was terrible and untrustworthy.

She wouldn't be fooled by him the way everyone else was. She was better than that.

'Fine.' He shrugged and ripped open the packet. 'More for me.'

The smell of salty cheddar flooded the room as he threw a disc up into the air and just about caught it in his mouth, not without a little help from his nose. Her stomach grumbled, and she was certain that he heard it when his smile spread wide enough to make his cheeks dimple. The light outside glinted off his canines, making him look half-beast. 'C'mon, Hodge. I'm trying here.'

'No, you're not. You're tormenting me. And with my greatest love: *snacks*.'

'I'm giving you a chance to put this little grudge behind you. You only have to say please.'

She rolled her eyes. *Little grudge.* She wished it was little. These days, it took up all the space in her life, including that meant for pottery. She might have gotten everything she wanted, but it was two years later than planned thanks to him. 'I wouldn't beg you for anything, Whittaker, and I certainly won't play your games. You're so used to getting what you want, aren't you?'

'Maybe.' He licked the salt from his lips with his usual confidence, leaving them pink and difficult to look away from.

'Well, you can't get me.' She ripped the bag from his hands, her breath falling heavier. She didn't know why, didn't want to, so she shoved a cracker into her mouth. It was as tasty and cheesy as she knew it would be. 'People like you and me' – she sprayed out crumbs – 'we're not supposed to be friends.'

'That's bullshit and you know it,' he replied. 'What does that even mean, *people like you and me*? We're not different bloody species.'

They might as well have been. She didn't have the energy to spell it out, so she turned her back on him to look out of the window. It was nice to see London in the dark. With only lights and outlines to paint the cityscape, it didn't feel as big and daunting as in the day. She might actually have a place in this version of it, might be able to blend in with the shadows until she felt like she belonged.

The warmth of Aiden's body grazed her back. She shivered.

'Are you just going to stay up here in the dark, then?' he asked, voice barely above a whisper.

'Depends if you're staying here, too. If you couldn't tell, I was actually trying to get away from everyone. Especially you.'

'Or you could just have fun, Juni,' he suggested drily. 'Y'know, like most people came here to do.'

'You didn't look like you were having that much fun, yourself, but then, it doesn't surprise me that you're a hypocrite as well as a snob.' She put down the Cheddars finally, whirling to face him, to tell him that having fun was easier said than done, but when she realised how close he was, the air whooshed from her lungs, the words catching in her throat.

She leaned back against the windowsill, the cold pane of glass an extra, confusing sensation in an already teeming swarm of them. As a fat woman of fairly average height, it wasn't often that she felt small, dainty, but he towered over her like the Shard over the city, and she had to look up at him to really see him.

She gulped despite herself, her body pleading for friction, for something, as though she didn't already feel more than enough. She could feel him there, pressing on her skin, even without him touching her. Her nipples tightened in her bra, heat burning in her core.

She shouldn't have wanted him. She shouldn't have wanted anybody when she was trying to combat sensory overload, but especially not him. It was the drink, she told herself, though she felt more sober than ever. It had to be the drink.

'It doesn't need to be like this between us,' he said finally. 'I don't want it to be.'

'Why does it matter?' Her throat was dry, hoarse, and everything inside her clenched when his eyes scratched over her again, this time darkening to a near-black. She itched to know the answer, to know why he kept trying, to know why he was looking at her like he wanted to rip her clothes off.

And to know why she liked it.

'I care about doing this project right,' he said. 'I care about not spending every waking hour fighting with you for the rest of the school year.'

'Not everything in life is convenient.' She tried to sneer, but her body was incapable of listening to her, especially when he closed the gap between them with a final step.

His toes nudged against hers, and he reached to brush a stray curl from her eye. 'And you, Juniper Hodgson, are the least convenient person I know.'

Her lips parted. He was touching her, and she should have hated it, but instead, she could only try not to melt into him completely. When he leaned in to kiss her, she failed even at that.

His lips explored her tentatively, as though waiting for her to pull away. Nobody had kissed her like that before. She was too awkward, too forthright. People either treated her like the rough, abrupt woman she was, leaving nothing to the imagination, or were too put off to bother at all.

'See? Not so hard to let go of all that anger, is it?' he murmured against her lips, thumb tilting her chin so delicately she barely felt it. 'All that fighting. You should have just told me you wanted me.'

She shook her head. 'I don't want you.' The lie cracked in her throat, but she refused to admit that she was hopelessly attracted to the man she despised.

'Then tell me to stop.' His fingers curled at the nape of her neck, and she felt the touch bolt down her spine like lightning.

She couldn't. With her thighs pressed tightly together, she couldn't imagine him walking away now. She wanted to be touched, wanted to feel, for once, like she was a human. Like everybody else.

The hot breath fanning over her face centred her, put her back down on solid ground, but it also made her aware of every sensation she'd ever felt. Every tickle of hair on her scalp, every pinprick of heat. It pooled between her legs, scraped against her ribs, as the scent of that same cologne she'd been wrapped in all week mingled with mint and beer and salt.

What would he taste like?

What would he kiss her like, if he really, truly knew she wanted it?

The urge to find out drove her lips back to his. She kissed him furiously, viciously, letting all of her spite bleed together with desire until she wasn't sure how to tell the two apart. It didn't matter, all of it fuelling her actions: fingers curling into his shirt, teeth nipping down on his bottom lip.

He moaned, and she wondered if that meant he was at her mercy. If he might be the one to beg *her* for something. If only she could pull away for long enough to find out, but it was impossible when his heavy hands floated to her lower back, his stomach pressing against hers.

'Fuck, Juni, I want…' His words were jumbled and incomplete, fingers digging deep into the soft flesh around her hips.

She wanted, more now than before, and she didn't have to ask when his mouth began to map her neck, collarbones, chest. He kissed her through the mesh of her shirt as though he couldn't wait to devour her, as though no amount of layers could stop him, and she leaned back, body sparking in response. She could only grip onto the windowsill, gasping when he frantically nudged her skirt up to her hips to reveal the simple black underwear beneath. She was certain he'd find the fabric damp, but was too turned on, too furious, too *everything*, to feel embarrassed.

'D'you know how gorgeous you are? Just the thought of touching you makes me hard,' he confessed as his finger traced over the lace edge around her groin.

'Then touch me,' she pleaded, knotting her fingers in his hair. Her hips rocked, desperate to meet him, and there she found he was right. He was hard, the outline of his length tautening his denim jeans.

She couldn't resist teasing him, dragging her palm up with just enough pressure to make him hiss. She jolted as his finger brushed her folds. 'Do you want my fingers or my tongue?'

'Both,' she admitted, because she was nothing if not honest. It was clear there was no turning back now, and she was too hazy with want to find a reason to want to.

'So impolite. Aren't you going to say please?' he asked, running his hands up her stomach to squeeze her breasts.

She shook her head, though her spine arched of its own accord. 'Aren't you going to hurry up before I change my mind?'

His chuckle vibrated through her, and he finally slipped a hand beyond her waistband. He was as good at teasing her as she was him, swirling a finger around her warm, wet heat – everywhere but the spot she needed him most.

'Aiden,' she whispered, teeth gritting. 'If you don't get on with it, I'll do it myself.'

Another laugh, this one deep and sensual. 'Well, we can't have that.'

He sunk a finger inside her, and only then did his thumb finally toy with her swollen clit. She cried out when the cold metal of his ring sent unexpected darts of pleasure through her, and he covered her mouth with his free hand. 'Shh. Don't want people hearing you, do we?'

She couldn't give a flying fuck about people hearing her in her present state, hips grinding as she sought more of him, more pressure, more pleasure. She used him as her anchor, wrapping her arms around his sturdy shoulders and letting her nails scratch over his skin as he worked her in all the right places.

'Fuck, Juniper,' he cursed, parting her legs with his own when she tried to squeeze around him. Lowering to his knees, he draped a leg over his shoulder to allow him deeper access. His head tilted up to her, eyes gleaming as though he was looking up at something divine. Awed, almost, but that couldn't be right. Still, he suckled on the marks and freckles patterning her inner thighs until she was terrified he wouldn't have time to use his tongue, terrified she was already too close.

But then he rolled her underwear to her knees, tongue lapping a slow strip between her folds. 'Like this?'

Juniper nodded, fingers curling in his hair as she closed her eyes.

'I need you to say it, Juni. Tell me if this is okay. That you're okay.'

It surprised her, this sudden cautiousness, enough that she felt less like she was dangling on the edge of the cliff and more like he was about to catch her as she stepped off a low ledge. She was safe. She could say no and he'd step away. Only she didn't want to. 'Yes. Yes, it's more than okay.'

He inserted his fingers again, beckoning against her G-spot. She bit down on her bottom lip to keep from crying out, yanking at his hair until he matched her force both with his fingers and his tongue. Right as her climax approached, dragged closer by the sounds of his frantic mouth against her wet pussy, a rustle outside left her jolting.

She nudged him away with her foot, losing her own balance in the process in an effort to pull down her skirt.

Just in time, because the door swung open to reveal Luc in the hallway, blinking slowly. 'Gross,' they said with perfect nonchalance, and then shut the door again.

'*Shit*, Aiden.' Juniper tugged her underwear up, wincing when it hit her wet, pulsating core, before rearranging her crumpled skirt.

On the floor, Aiden looked like he'd just woken from a dream, dazed as a deer in headlights. His stubble was slick with Juniper's juices, which almost left her changing her mind and letting him ravish her again, but fuck, this wasn't her. She didn't have sex in a near-stranger's bedroom at a house party – with Aiden Twatface Whittaker of all people. What had Luc seen? Too much, probably, considering her knickers had been tangled around her bloody ankles.

She felt empty without Aiden's fingers inside her. Empty, unsatisfied, and maddened, but the humiliation overpowered even her writhing ache for release. She tried not to look at him as she assigned her boobs back to her admittedly flimsy bra, not even when he stood to touch her wrist.

'Juni…'

'This shouldn't have happened. It didn't happen, okay?'

'Well, I think it did.'

'Nope! Didn't happen.' She rushed out of the room before he could argue further, refusing to allow reality to set in.

Even if, when she got home later that night, the ghost of his mouth still lingered in all the wrong places, and she found her fingers much less satisfying than his.

11

Aiden watched the rain patter against the windows of the library, the dreary bruised sky matching his mood perfectly. He'd been both dreading and anticipating this meeting with Juniper since he'd woken up to go for a run at the crack of dawn this morning, only it looked like he'd been stood up. Between that and still having no idea of what to focus on for his part of the collaboration piece, that familiar black cloud was hovering just over his head again.

It didn't help that he'd been left high and dry on Saturday night. One minute, Juniper had been his. The next, she'd been distant as ever, leaving him alone with a hard on that no amount of cold showers could have fixed. By the time he'd gone back downstairs, she and Tilly had gone, and Luc had been eager to disappear, too.

Aiden didn't know what he was doing. Of all the people at that party, why was she the only one he'd wanted?

And why didn't she want him at all?

She had, momentarily. But like her moods, it had been fleeting. So fleeting it barely felt real, especially now that she was obviously avoiding him.

He slammed his laptop shut, giving up on waiting. It had been half an hour, and she couldn't blame fire alarms or geese this time. She was wasting his time. And she had the gall to say it was him who wasn't trying.

Just as he began to pack up, the heavy thuds of boots disrupted the tranquillity. Juniper dashed out of the lift and straight towards Aiden.

A little too late.

He sat back down, throwing his bag on the floor again. 'What time d'you call this, Hodge?'

'I know. I'm late.' She blew out a tired breath and slumped into the chair opposite, laying out her belongings on the table.

'That's okay. I accept your apology.' He leaned lazily back in his chair, tugging on the ends of his rain-knotted hair. If she could act indifferent, so could he.

And yet it still stung when she refused to acknowledge his words, focusing on getting her notebook and pen ready. 'So, did you properly decide on your theme, yet?'

'That's it? Nothing about how our little sexcapade was cut short this weekend?'

Juniper shushed him with a tight hand around his mouth, glancing around as though worried someone would overhear despite the fact that they were in a quieter corner of the massive library. It reminded him of the one at Elmington, stacked with more textbooks than any ceramicist surely needed, with a domed roof that might have poured in daylight if there was any to be found. The shelves and stair railings were all elegant dark mahogany, the storeys marked by balconies on each floor that spanned the perimeter of the building.

It was because of that that he didn't like it much. It felt too big, too ostentatious, a place he might lose himself in again. He wondered if there would ever be a place where that risk didn't seem possible; maybe he was too easy to lose, too fragile, and he was just waiting for everyone to find out.

Including Juniper, who at least glared at him like he wasn't made of glass. 'Don't say sexcapade!'

'Well, how would you describe it?' he invited with a wide, smarmy grin. He could play her game if he had to. Besides, for all her complaints about his arrogance, she'd seemed to like it just fine when he was tasting her. And, fuck, had she tasted perfect.

'A mistake,' she said brusquely. 'A very, very big mistake. One that won't happen again.'

He tried to rub away the disappointment in his sternum, hoping that his mask remained in place. 'I recall you enjoying yourself quite a lot. Besides, I don't see what's wrong with two friends—'

'We're not friends!' she blurted, brows connecting into a perfect zig zag.

So it had *all* been pointless. The olive branch, the trying, the everything. It was for the best, probably. Did he honestly want to be hung up on a handful like her, someone who hated his guts and never filtered her unkind words?

The thought didn't quell the ache, nor the exhilaration that still plagued him from having his hands on her, his mouth on her. He hadn't felt alive like that in a long time – and not just alive, but *known*. For a moment, he'd been sure she'd seen him for who he really was, not who she wanted him to be: the enemy.

He'd been wrong, clearly. She'd just wanted him for a good time, like everybody else, and now she was back to kicking him away like he was dirt on her shoe.

He swallowed the bitter taste in his mouth and opened his laptop. 'Fine. In that case, next time you're going to be late, warn me. Don't like having my time wasted.' He unlocked his phone, opened the contacts list, and threw it in her general direction. 'Going to need your number.'

'I didn't *know* I was going to be late.' Her tone was cutting, but it bounced straight off his carefully built walls. She typed in her number, then sent a text to herself to make sure she had his, too.

'You never do,' he remarked. 'Another pattern I've noticed about you.'

'Oh, so now that sex is out of the question, you're going to be pissy with me?'

'I'm going to be pissy with you because that's how you are with me,' he retorted. 'And because I've been waiting here for the last half an hour. Are we doing this project or not?'

She hunched her shoulders, elbows planted on the desk. 'Fine. What's the plan?'

'I'm going with art,' he said, flicking his laptop around to show her the images of paintings that he'd collected. 'I found these pieces over the weekend. I think our research paper can be about the representation of human nature in mythology, and how that's translated on canvas.' He didn't give her time to really look at the paintings, instead flicking to the slides. 'My pieces will focus on classical compositions where the canvas is replaced by clay.'

He could only take her silence as surprise, especially when she nodded slowly. 'Okay. And our joint pieces?'

'We can combine that with elements of mythological sculptures, I'm sure.'

'Sculpting is my strong suit,' she admitted, worrying on her bottom lip.

'Here.' He pulled his sketchbook out of his bag without much enthusiasm, turning it to the first page, where his messy graphite lines and colouring pencils blossomed across the thick white paper.

Her brows disappeared into her messy fringe. 'You drew these?'

In an effort to try to forget Juniper, he'd spent the rest of the weekend doodling potential ideas for their pieces, with sketches of everything from earthenware to tiles. In truth, he wasn't well-acquainted enough with pottery to know which would work best yet, but he assumed Chris's lessons would soon provide some ideas.

He smirked. 'Are you surprised that I'm actually good at the subject I'm studying?'

When her expression darkened, he knew he'd made a mistake. 'Unlike me, you mean?'

'No, that's not what I meant at all.' He had every faith that Juniper would pick up her throwing skills soon.

She didn't seem to believe him, scratching the edges of her pencil as she stared out at the blurred lights of campus. 'They're good ideas. Better than anything I've come up with yet.'

'Juni…' Something was wrong, something beyond her struggles with the wheel. He'd never seen her like this before, like she wasn't even here.

But then she snapped back to attention, checking her phone with newfound energy. 'I have to leave early.'

'You only just got here!' His voice rose, and this time, he was unable to control it.

To her credit, she offered him a guilty grimace. 'I know, but work threw a shift at me out of nowhere.'

'What about throwing class?'

She was already packing up, eyes cast down. A clump of mascara spotted the space below her lashes, and he fought the urge to wipe it away. 'I'll catch up.'

He didn't like it. Not at all. She was already behind, and now she was skipping their workshops?

But he knew better than to point it out, so he only said, 'I'll cover for you with Chris, then.'

'No need. I don't need your help.' She slung her bag over her shoulder and left without a goodbye.

Aiden gritted his teeth and kicked the leg of the chair she'd just been sitting in out of frustration. He couldn't bloody win with her, and she seemed to be intent on keeping it that way.

12

'Cold. Again.'

A mug was slammed down in front of Juniper on the marble countertop, foamy coffee splashing onto the surface she'd only just finished cleaning. Her fingernails bit into her rag at Gianna's condescending tone. The manager had been on her case all shift – rightly so, probably, because Juniper was terrible at her job. Between causing a milk explosion at the steamer, dropping several toasted paninis on the floor before they reached the table, and accidentally inputting the wrong numbers into the till, charging somebody ninety-eight pounds for a cup of tea, she would have been better off going home and giving up on everything.

In her defence, hard-faced Gianna was an even worse teacher than Christopher. Her dark hair was slicked back into a painfully tight bun, which only accentuated the prominent vein on her forehead. Every time Juniper messed up, she feared it might pop. With a narrow face, pointy chin, and icy blue eyes, she was terrifying. More so because she was able to switch to a different personality altogether around the customers, harsh Italian lilt turning dolce sotto when she was behind the counter. Juniper was all for strong, scary women – when they weren't shouting at her.

Throwing down her rag, she stretched out her stiff back and went to discard the ruined coffee under Gianna's watchful gaze. She should have been in class, but she was aware she had a lot of proving herself to do if she wanted to keep this job and Gianna wasn't the type of person who took no for an answer. She dreaded to think how much she was missing and could only hope this would be the first and last time she was called in to cover a shift unexpectedly.

So, she pasted a smile on her face and was extra careful as she remade the oat milk latte.

'Too slow,' Gianna barked out as first the coffee and then the milk was poured in. 'Faster next time.'

The older grey-haired woman whose coffee she had made a pig's ear of watched from behind a display of pastries, chin tilted in a haughty show of disapproval. She clearly expected the best, and currently, Juniper might have been the absolute worst in all of London.

It didn't help that she was still curled up in a little ball of self-loathing and regret since Tom's party. Seeing Aiden this morning had left her hollowed out and vulnerable, something she never liked to be, let alone with him. She'd let him get too close, and now everything was all tangled and confused. There was a cord between them, tightening evermore since they'd hooked up, and she wasn't sure what would happen if it snapped. She'd take scissors to it herself if she thought it might get rid of him, but he had a way of softening her with his patience and charm whenever she got close, and his tongue, eager and skilled, had also had an effect. A very, very big effect that she still felt between her legs now.

'Thank you for your patience,' Juni said as she set down the coffee on a saucer and added two extra amaretti biscuits for good measure. 'So sorry about that.'

'As you should be,' the customer declared before returning to her table by the leafy monstera plant in the corner. Caffè Verde stayed true to its name, with greenery all around. An accent wall of artificial roses drew customers to take selfies, and the hanging strings of pearls and sugar vines across the ceiling made her feel like she was in an elegant, fairy-tale greenhouse. Juniper would have loved it if not for the management, the air tasting fresh and cleaner than most places in the city even when mingling with the fog of hot coffee and spiced pastries.

'I think that you should stay behind for extra training tonight,' Gianna said. 'Let's go over everything one more time, yes?'

'Sounds good,' lied Juniper, wiping the sweat from her brow with the back of her hand. She was just about to go back to cleaning when another customer entered, announced by the tinkle of the bell above the door. The sounds of London's mid-afternoon pandemonium were a much-needed reminder that life existed outside of this place, that she would eventually be allowed to leave. It felt as though time stood still in here sometimes, like Gianna might hold her hostage forever.

An even more appreciated reminder appeared in the form of Tilly. Juniper waved at her friend, who bounced in with an enviable amount of spring in her step. 'Look at you, coffee queen! You look like you've been busy.'

'Not busy enough,' Gianna muttered, but then checked her rose-gold wristwatch. 'Take your break now. Back in fifteen.'

'Thank you.'

Juniper tore her striped moss-green apron off in lightning speed, then hopped around the counter to find a seat with Tilly. They settled at the island by the window, Juniper struggling to climb onto the tall stools. Regent Street was as manic as it had sounded, red buses honking at unbothered cyclists while shoppers wrestled with overflowing bags. She hated to even think it, but she missed Manchester. It might have been just as packed some days, but she lived just far enough outside of the city that she had plenty of peace and quiet at home. Until her dad came home from work and put on the football, at least.

'Your boss is terrifying.' Tilly cast a wary glance towards the front of the café.

'Tell me about it.' Juniper blew her fringe from her eyes only to find it was too sweaty to really move it. She'd gotten the haircut as another symbol of her new start, but like everything else, was proving difficult to maintain. 'She's not very happy with me. I'm crap at this.'

'You'll get the hang of it.' Tilly's words were the reassurance Juniper needed, although she wasn't certain they were true. She'd worked at her last place for long enough and had still served raw chips on a regular basis. It was just too difficult to balance all of the responsibilities, to keep track of each step in the task. Her brain was too noisy, too full, too quick to forget something and hurtle into distraction.

'How was class? What did I miss?' Juniper asked worriedly. She dreaded to think what she might have fallen behind on in only her second week.

Tilly's expression did nothing to calm her down this time. She nibbled on her lower lip as she pulled out a notebook from her bag, the spiral-bound cover patterned with illustrated frogs lazing on lily pads. 'We learned to glaze today. I made as many notes as I could. Feel free to go through them and copy them down.'

'Thank you so much.' Juniper flicked through the pages to find Tilly's neat, round writing clear and easy to read. 'I can't believe I'm already behind. Actually, that's a lie. I can.' At this point, it felt like it was written in her DNA. She didn't know if she could blame it on her ADHD, or if it was a fundamental flaw in her personality. Only knew that nothing ever seemed to go as planned – and even when it did, she had a knack for ruining it. She'd tried to fix it with planners and meditation and even medication, but none of it helped.

'I'd ask if you wanted to go over it properly tonight, but I have that job interview at Nando's and then I'm meeting up with Owen for the project.' Tilly winced.

'No, honestly, this is more than enough. Good luck with it! And see if you can steal some chicken.' She tried to force enthusiasm. She just wanted to cuddle Cerberus and crawl back into bed, but she didn't even have time to do that. 'I think I'll see if the workshop is still open after my shift. Get some more practice in.'

'Good idea. How did it go with Aiden this morning?'

Juniper rolled her eyes. She didn't want to think about him anymore, and yet she couldn't stop. She could still feel the graze of his stubble on her cheeks, the gentle exploration of his fingers between her legs, and it made her want to scream – in more than one type of frustration. He'd been so cold this morning, enough to make her wonder if she'd deserved it. He had, after all, left her on the brink of a rather wonderful orgasm. Men usually expected something in return.

Well, tough. She wasn't the giving type. Not with him. Besides, he'd taken far more than he'd given if they were to tally up their history. It would take more than his tongue, skilled as it was, to settle their debts. 'I'm pretending he doesn't exist.'

'Even though he—'

'Yes.'

'And even though you—'

'*Yes*,' Juni emphasised. 'It was a mistake. I don't know why or how it happened, but it won't ever again. From now on, things will be strictly professional between us.'

Tilly's smirk was filled with doubt. 'Aye, because one thing I've noticed about you, my dear friend, is that you are always very professional. *Especially* around him.'

Juniper glared, leaving Tilly to shrug innocently. She gave Juniper a placating pat on the shoulder as she stood up. 'Got to go, but movie night tonight?'

'I'll let you know. I'm already shattered.' Juniper yawned. As much as she loved having a friend to spend time with, and as wonderfully romantic as Tilly's taste in movies was, she needed time to shake off the day, recharge her batteries.

'Fifteen minutes are almost up,' Gianna warned somewhere behind her.

Tilly scuttled off, her figure a blurred blot of colour that soon disappeared into the bustle of the city.

Juniper didn't blame her. She looked at the clock on the wall and tried not to dread the next several hours of coffee disasters. She just hoped that she could lose herself in some creativity tonight.

13

'You must have had somewhere rather exciting to be yesterday, Jupiter,' Chris said as she walked into the workshop the following day. To Aiden's surprise, she wasn't late this morning. Just dishevelled, her hair piled up in a lopsided… something. It didn't qualify as a bun, since half of it had fallen out, but the intention was there.

After his first glance – accidental, of course, because he absolutely had not been watching the door to see if she'd make it to class – Aiden kept his head in his sketchbook, his fingers smudged grey from the graphite. He heard Jupiter falter on the threshold, then stutter out the same excuse that she'd given him in the library: an unexpected work shift. He wondered how on earth she planned to get through the year if she was dividing her time with working, and then decided it wasn't his problem. That little twinge of worry in his chest disagreed, but he played it off as his new normal anxiety. It came and went in waves, so much a part of his everyday rhythm now that it no longer surprised him, only made him uncomfortable, but his anti-depressants and daily jogs took the edge off that.

If only his doctor could prescribe something similar when it came to Juniper.

'Well, you can tell your boss that my classes are far more important, next time,' Chris said as he peered into his laptop. 'Your schedule is there for a reason. Keep to it or don't bother studying here at all.'

Juniper said nothing, only brushed past Aiden's desk to the seat behind him. He shivered against the cool air she carried with her, scented by a deep cherry perfume that had driven him mad, both at the party and before it. It was worse, now that he knew how it tasted: like almonds and bitterness. He was too aware of it, too aware of every fibre of her.

He decided that, before the lesson started, it was time to bite the bullet and swivelled around on his stool. From his pocket he produced a crumpled leaflet he'd seen in the library yesterday, plucked from the front desk on his way to class. He placed it on her desk, sliding it between her hands so that her lowered gaze would see it.

'What's this?'

'What does it look like, Hodge?' He couldn't keep the light teasing from his tone. 'An exhibition on myths and legends at the British Museum. It's only on this weekend.'

He might not have held her interest, but this certainly did. Immediately, her dull eyes brightened as she scanned the front page, then flicked through the images of exhibitions that detailed some of the displays. He felt a little bit proud to have cheered her up, but he convinced himself it was only because that was usually impossible. Anybody would have felt good about it. It was like getting a *yes* from Simon Cowell.

'It's free entry?' she asked.

'Yep. Figured it would help with our research paper — if you can stand to walk around a museum with me for an hour or two, that is.'

She hummed, an edge of weariness flattening her tone. The tip of her thumbnail flicked across the chipped purple nail polish on her index finger. 'I'm supposed to work, but I can try to leave early. *If* I can stand it.'

He rubbed his jaw if only to hide his smirk. 'It closes at eight, so let me know. If you can't make it, I'll send you a postcard from the gift shop.'

She slid the pamphlet away and muttered, 'Wonderful.'

The rest of their classmates filed in, a hungover Tom soon vying for Aiden's attention with a story about last night's antics. He'd been asked to go with them to a local club, but having made the mistake of partying too much once before, he'd politely declined in favour of venting to Luc about Juniper's bullshit behaviour. Since Luc had already walked in on them mid-sex, he figured he could tell them the rest, even if Luc pulled faces and complained it was *TMI* quite often. Other than that, they were pretty chill, and never made Aiden feel like a burden. They'd even opened up about their family in Paris, how they didn't know they were non-binary yet and London was their chance to truly be themself.

He'd never been able to talk to his friends at Elmington like that. They'd never gotten personal, their connection expressed in the form of dry taunts he was all too talented at joining in with. As much as Aiden wanted to fit in with the laddishness of it all, it only seemed to stave away anything meaningful, a fact that was proved when Aiden went through his darkest period alone.

He pushed off the desk, returning to his own, when Chris called for their attention with a loud, 'Hello!' through cupped hands. 'Oh, good. That invisibility spell didn't work after all. Now that I have your attention, let's cover a few things. Number one: group projects.' He indicated the number on his hand with a waggling index finger. 'By now, you should have settled on a topic and started your research. *How might I do this?* some of you may ask. Well, back in my day, we started with these things called books.' He picked up a gigantic copy of *Ceramics in Modern Times*, waving it around until it fell out of his hands and back onto the table with a thwack. 'Books look like this. You'll notice that they have been printed on paper and written by scholars, which, strangely enough, makes them much more reliable than Google.'

'What about Wikipedia?' Tom asked.

'Do not say the devil's name in a place of worship, Timmy,' Chris scolded. A few people laughed, Juniper included. The sound scuttled through him like vibrations across violin strings, left him wanting more. More, he'd likely never get.

'If you really want to impress me, and you should, you might consider going outside.' He motioned to the windows with a dramatic flourish. 'You see, some of the buildings out there are called museums. They have art and sculptures that may just help you on your way. And speaking of museums, I have bad news. While I'm not going to hold your hands and take you on cutesy little walks around the local galleries, which are more than accessible without my help, I do think it mandatory to visit the pottery capital of the UK during your studies. In January, I'm off to Stoke-on-Trent, and I would encourage you all to join me. Well, that's a lie. I don't really want you to. But I am doing it for your benefit, so I guess you're all welcome. You can sign up on your student app.'

'You mean, where they film *The Great Pottery Throw Down*?' Tilly asked excitedly.

'Yes. You may stand in the very room where many a reality TV show contestant has cried on camera. How exciting.'

Tilly wasn't the only one looking forward to it. Nomi was practically bouncing off her seat, and Amir held his hand up for a high five that never came from Tom.

'All of the deets, as the cool kids call them, will be sent via email closer to the time, but the university has arranged our stay, so you'll be glad to know that everything bar food, drink, and train tickets will be free.' Chris returned behind his work desk, where a wedge of clay sat ready and waiting. 'Now, moving on. Throwing isn't the only way to make things, and quite frankly, I'm alarmed at how many of you are utterly terrible at it, so today we shall be hand-building.'

'Yes!' Juniper shouted triumphantly, causing everyone to turn around. She sunk back down with a, 'Sorry.'

'Dear lord,' Chris muttered, and then went back to explaining by flicking through his PowerPoint. A display of ideas was shown, offering everything from mugs to delicate sculptures in all colours and sizes. 'This should be a project you'd like to include in your final portfolio at the end of the year, so I'm not going to tell you what to do here. All that's required is that you create something you yourself have use for – whether it's in your kitchen, living room, et cetera. You can use any of the techniques we've covered so far, and you will be glazing next week after a trip to the kiln, so don't fluff it up, otherwise you'll have to stay behind to catch up.'

No pressure, then. Aiden stretched out his fingers, eager to get to work. Only his imagination seemed to fail him as soon as he looked down at his clay. Without the safety of the throwing wheel at his disposal, it was entirely possible that he might, in fact, fluff this one up.

★

Ten minutes later, Aiden still had an untouched slab of clay and zero ideas. Around him, his classmates were busy creating their pieces, using both tools and their hands to form an array of shapes. Tilly's already resembled a bowl. Amir seemed to be making a dinner set.

In the end, he decided he'd better play it safe and used the mugs displayed on the board as his starting point. He could worry about making it stand out when it came to glazing, but for now, anything would do. He was more than capable of something this simple. He'd studied art his whole life, after all.

So why did his hands shake when he began to wedge the clay?

He needed a break, needed to stop overthinking. He turned around on his stool. Paused at the sight that awaited him.

Juniper seemed to be a million miles away from this class-room, where none of the worries he felt could touch her. Her tongue poked out as she concentrated – something that shouldn't have been hot, and yet somehow roused the creature in his gut, the one that answered only to her. As she coiled the clay around in layers, a delicate crease carved a triangle over the inner edges of her brows. The pads of Aiden's thumbs buzzed with the need to smooth it down like he would a crack in his clay. He hadn't seen her this engrossed since high school, and there was a serenity to it, a calm, that left him awed. His own art had given him that same security, once. Now, he was always worrying about the results, wondering if they would be enough to impress his father, his friends, his tutors, all of whom expected every piece he produced to be a masterpiece, because hadn't he held a paintbrush in his hand before he could even walk? Wasn't he supposed to be effortlessly talented at this after twenty years of being Jonathan Whittaker's son?

'You're staring at me,' Juniper murmured without breaking her focus. 'Stop it.'

'Can't.' Not a lie. 'What are you making?'

'A medieval torture device, just for you.'

His lips spread into a crooked grin. 'Kinky. I like it.'

'Do you like your head? Because if you keep distracting me, it won't be on your shoulders for much longer.'

'I seemed to remember that *you* liked my head quite a lot,' he quipped.

She slapped her hands to her knees and shot him daggers, and he relished the pink stains of incredulity on her cheeks. '*Aiden!*'

'What?' he asked, although he was beginning to think he'd made a grave mistake in bringing it up again. Bringing it up meant thinking about it, and thinking about it meant wanting it, and…

Fuck, he wanted it. *Her*. No matter how badly she treated him, how much she made her disgust for him known, he couldn't stop. Especially not now, with her fingers caked and eyes light, fervent. She may have been struggling, but she loved the craft, and that was sexy as hell. He found himself suddenly jealous of the clay. She touched it so gently, so lovingly, perhaps the only thing in the world that got to see her as her most tender, authentic self.

Proof she wasn't all barbs after all.

Across the aisle, Tilly choked on a laugh, having clearly overheard. He didn't doubt that she already knew about their little hook up and ached to wonder what Juniper must have said. She could call it a mistake, her biggest regret, but he'd heard her whimper and moan, felt her rock against his tongue for more, and knew that she'd been at his mercy for a fleeting moment in time. He'd made her feel good, and she clearly couldn't stand it.

His underwear pulled taut against his hardening cock, and he headed to the cupboards at the back of the room in an attempt to hide it, searching through tools in the hopes they might inspire him. Nothing.

He knew even before he saw her when Juniper joined him, the air thickening around him and the hair on his arms dancing on end. From his periphery, he watched her stand on her tiptoes to try to reach a box of fabrics, fingers barely brushing the shelf.

'Having trouble, Hodge?'

'Clearly not as much as you.' She looked pointedly down at his erection.

With his mind nothing more than a fuzzy haze of *her*, he didn't think when he moved behind her to grab the box she'd been reaching for. Her breath hitched when their bodies met, cock brushing the plump curve of her ass. He shuddered. Stepped away, unsure if he'd gone too far or not nearly far enough as held the box in front of her. Their hands met around the rim, and he didn't know if it was intention when she closed the distance between them. Not until she wiggled her hips, torturing him. He held his breath. Tried to remember where he was, and who he was with, even when his mind conjured images of her without the jeans on, without anything on. Would she take him like this, back to him? Or would it be her riding him?

She ripped the box from his hands, bringing him back to the present. Still, she didn't move away, shoulders rolling against his chest.

'What are you doing with these, anyway?' he asked, voice strained at the attempt to make idle conversation while white-hot desire devoured him.

'Why? Feeling uninspired?'

'I was.' He nudged one of her waves off her shoulder to whisper in her ear, 'not so much anymore.'

'So the rumours are true. Men really do think with their dicks.' She tore away from him without warning, leaving him cold – but still amused. As long as she was spitting out those little insults, giving him the time of day, teasing him by getting just a tad closer than was necessary, he couldn't help but be amused.

Besides, this was all the confirmation that he needed: he hadn't imagined the chemistry between them. This back and forth might as well have been their foreplay for all it did to convince him that he wanted her, more and more every day, and that at least a sliver of her felt the same. He didn't know what it was: the confidence, the honesty, the fieriness, or the fact all of those things were barely contained in the body of a gorgeous, short woman with curves no sculptor would ever do justice.

He thought that would be it, that their little fun was over again and she was back to ignoring him, but then she sighed and continued, 'I'm using them for texture, pressing them against the clay.' And then, pointing firmly at him: '*Don't* copy me.'

He lifted a brow, then two hands in mock surrender. He hadn't even considered textures, too hung up on the building of the thing. 'Wasn't going to. Promise.'

But he did envy her creativity. He could create textures on a canvas, but on clay? That wasn't something he was used to. He'd been too focused on throwing the perfect vessel, making sure every seam and curve was as smooth as he could make it.

Juniper swayed her hips as she returned to her desk, feeding his lust just a little.

Yep, he was definitely a little more creative now.

14

'No, Mum, I'm not coming home,' Juniper droned into her phone, biting down on her tongue to keep from saying something she'd regret. The campus was already mostly in darkness, but she was on her way to the workshop studio to practice throwing, a fact that Mum was revelling in as an excuse to tell her she was better off at home before she burned out.

The line crackled on the other end with what was no doubt a passive-aggressive huff, Mum's specialty. Juniper could imagine her now, sitting on the sofa watching her TV soaps, socked feet curled under her and short blonde-silver hair pushed back by reading glasses. Dad would be in his armchair, tapping away at the games on his phone and complaining about the ads, while the neighbour's cat, Nutmeg, looked in through the window.

The twinge of homesickness surprised her. That had just been her normal, the ordinariness she'd been fighting against all her life. But it was home, comfort, ease, and maybe just for a moment, she wouldn't have said no if offered a place on the couch again.

'I'm just saying that it doesn't sound very healthy for you, love,' Mum said in that all-knowing voice. She had a way of making even support sound like a scolding, like Juniper was one walking disappointment. No hopes, no talent, no ability to take care of herself. 'You know how overwhelmed you can get, and if classes aren't going well then you're throwing all this money down the drain for nothing.'

Juniper collapsed onto the nearest bench, staring at the silhouette of Mags. With only the dim light of a few lampposts to illuminate her, her stone head looked like it was sagging on her shoulders, casting a shadow onto her chin that made her seem lonely, tired.

As lonely and tired as Juniper felt. After another disastrous late shift, her bones ached and her hands were raw from pot washing, a task she'd been given because she was less likely to mess it up. Supposedly. A few plates and mugs hadn't survived her shift, but she'd promised Gianna that, once she was a master on the throwing wheel, she would replace them with Juniper Originals.

Naturally, Gianna wasn't all that sold on the idea.

But she was trying, and she had decided to continue to try tonight. With her sculpting work yesterday reminding her that she was capable of something, she was inspired to have another go at the wheel. Or, she had been before Mum's call.

She was right, a fact that Juniper hated most. The effects of studying fulltime while trying to keep down a job she was terrible at were already taking their toll. Maybe if she didn't drag such emotional weight, so many doubts, into everything she did, she might have been better at coping, but she only ever felt snowed under. She wasn't strong enough.

And whenever she was reminded that her mum believed it, too, it felt almost impossible not to let it bury her. 'It's not going down the drain,' she said now, trying to convince herself as much as Mum. 'It's going into my future. This is what I want to do. I just didn't think it would be so hard.'

'Well, life is hard,' Mum replied, a patronising edge to her voice. 'We can't always manage the things we want to. Part of being an adult is accepting your limits.'

As tears sprang to her eyes, Juniper tilted her head to the indigo sky. The crescent moon hid just behind the spire of the library, hazy from the surrounding clouds. She couldn't keep doing this. She needed to get through this year, and if Mum didn't believe she could, then maybe she just couldn't talk to her about all this anymore.

'I can manage,' she decided sharply, finally. 'I'm managing.'

'It doesn't sound like it.'

'That's because to you, everything I do is a failure,' she blurted, and then instantly regretted it. She loved her mum, truly, and knew she had Juniper's best interests at heart. It was just that she seemed to limit Juniper even more than she limited herself; even more than her neurodivergence did. Instead of encouraging her to try, even if something was more challenging for her than for others, she expected her to just… stop.

She expected *nothing* from her at all, and how was Juniper supposed to feel like anything but broken, insignificant, incapable, if that was how Mum saw her?

Mum took a sharp intake of breath, and Juniper heard Dad muttering, 'What bloody nonsense,' in the background.

'Well, that's just not true. Dear me, Juniper, you do talk some rubbish!' Mum exclaimed.

Juniper had nothing left to say. They didn't listen to her, or at least didn't hear her. 'I'm going to practice throwing before they lock up the workshop for the night. Speak soon.'

'Fine.' Mum's tight-lipped glower was practically audible in the terse word. 'N'night.'

'Night.'

Juniper hung up, chin wobbling as she wiped her cheeks. She wished there was someone who believed in her, someone who didn't just see her for all of her flaws.

Better yet, she wished Mum would call her back to apologise. Tell her that she was proud, that Juniper was doing a great job.

But that had never happened before, and it wouldn't now, so Juniper threw her phone in her bag and made her way to the workshop. She *would* be a good potter. She'd prove to everyone that she wasn't a joke or a failure.

She would.

★

Juniper's first port of call was the drying room to check on the piece that was due to go into the kiln tomorrow. After all her experimentations with jewellery, she needed something to hold all of her earrings and necklaces in, so she'd made a stand for their hand-building task.

She allowed herself a smile when she found her shelf, glad to find the clay hadn't collapsed. She'd surprised even herself with this one, sculpting Yggdrasil, the Norse tree of life, into

116

curling branches that would hold earrings and necklaces, upon a smooth plate for smaller accessories. With any luck, she'd be able to glaze it to show the different mythological realms in each segment and branch.

'You're here late.'

A voice from behind made her jump, and she tore away from her shelf. Aiden leaned against the doorframe, that permanent smirk on his face – the one that made him look happy to see her, but only so he could torment her.

She felt her guard rise, but the heat inside her, too. Seeing him react to her in class yesterday hadn't helped her forget about their little encounter. Though it brought her a satisfaction she'd never felt before to turn him on so visibly, it had also left her feeling restless, and no amount of orgasms alone under the covers of her single bed or in the shower of her ensuite would remedy it. Maybe she would have to invest in a toy with her next paycheck. She'd never dared to before, living with her parents, but something had to be done about all of... *this*. She needed to become self-sufficient, because she sure as hell wasn't turning to Aiden for pleasure again.

'Are you following me now?' she accused curtly.

He pushed off the frame to join her inside the drying room. 'No. I saw someone in here, figured I'd say hi.'

'Hi. Bye.' She gave him a wave, which he ignored completely in favour of bending to look at her project.

'Shit, Hodge. Is this one yours?'

Her stomach fluttered, certain he was about to tear apart the only decent thing she'd made since getting here. She took a subconscious step back. 'Yup. And?'

Silence ticked through the warm space as he assessed it more closely. She hadn't noticed before, but from the side, his nose was a perfectly straight line, raised just slightly at its peak. How completely predictable that he had no bad angles to speak of.

'Bloody hell,' he said finally, quietly. 'So *this* is how you got onto the course.'

When he reached to touch it, she slapped his hand away, afraid so much as a jostle could send the tree collapsing like her poor vase. He flinched back, shaking out his fingers with an, 'Ow. Sorry. It's just so detailed, so intricate. It almost looks real, even without glazing.'

'I'm not bad at everything,' she snapped. And then, with the phone call in the back of her mind: 'Just most things.'

She hoped it sounded like a joke, something he would inevitably bounce off so that they could resume their usual jabs, but his eyes snapped to her, dark brows bunching. 'That's not true, Juni.'

She tried desperately to change the subject before he saw the cracks in her. 'Why are *you* here?'

He gave half a shrug, a shadow flitting across his face for just a second. Maybe she wasn't the only one cracked tonight, because it penetrated his usual confidence, revealing something hidden beneath, but it was gone too quickly for Juniper to decipher it.

'I'm not getting anywhere on my sculpture. I keep changing my mind about it.' His attention was pulled back to her piece. 'Is it based on something, or is it just a creepy tree?'

Great. They were now in a 'changing the subject' tennis match. 'It's Yggdrasil, Norse tree of life,' she explained, because she would never pass up the opportunity to talk about her beloved interest in mythology. Not even with him. 'Each of the branches represent one of the nine realms. Asgard, Alfheim, Midgard…'

'Oh, you mean like in *Thor*. Love those movies.'

She raised a brow. 'Oh, god. Don't say your only knowledge of mythology is based on Marvel films.'

He dipped his head in what was clearly admission, at least having the decency to look embarrassed. 'They're good!'

'They're *fine*, but they don't exactly stay true to the original material.' A small grin tugged at the corner of her mouth, try as she may to conceal it, and he chuckled in response.

Her pulse pounded in her ears. She was suddenly very aware of the fact that they were alone together – and this time, not at a party, but in an empty drying room linked to an equally empty classroom. There was nobody here to keep her distracted, no way of escaping his intent focus.

And if he tried to touch her again, there would be nobody around to walk in on them. To stop it. She clearly couldn't rely on herself for such things.

'So, what is it with you and mythology? Why'd you love it so much?' he questioned.

The discomfort of the dry air did nothing to calm her down, so she went back into the classroom, perching on the nearest desk when he followed.

'Why'd you love art?' she returned, avoiding his question because she wasn't quite sure she knew the answer.

'You know, it doesn't always have to be tit for tat. We could just have a conversation.' His chest bunched as he folded his arms, biceps made thicker, more difficult to ignore, where the short sleeves of his grey shirt stretched around muscle. It was difficult to believe she'd been so close to him just a few nights ago. Difficult to believe that he wasn't just a memory better forgotten, but a real human, burly and overpowering and close enough to touch.

And also a twatface, she reminded herself, but somehow, it didn't feel as relevant as it used to.

'We could if I wanted to,' she sniped finally, because he'd clearly noticed she was watching and this was her only way of regaining control. Because who would she be to him if she let him close enough to kiss her again?

'What if *I* want to?' For once, he wasn't looking at her body or her lips or her glower. He was looking at *her*, his irises brown and murky under the dappled lighting. Dark enough to forget the green completely. Dark enough to swallow her whole.

She kicked her legs out like a child on a swing. Fine, she would play his game, but only because she was tired of being affected by him. She'd come here to practice throwing, not engage in more of… *this*.

'I like mythology because the real world is busy and confusing and I always feel like I'm trailing just behind it.' She didn't realise it was true until it fell from her – too easily. She crossed one leg over the other, picking at a frayed hole in her work leggings. 'I like to be lost in stories, especially ones that were created by people who came from a completely different society. They're a reminder that all the loneliness and pain and everything that makes us human has always existed, and that it can be turned into something magical, something that has a purpose.' She shook her head. She couldn't remember why she was still speaking, but wasn't that always the case? 'I don't know. Probably sounds silly.'

'No, not at all. In fact...' He raised his brows. 'Can I steal that answer for why I like art?'

She laughed in surprise, though regarded him with a little scepticism. She doubted that Aiden had ever felt lost the way she had. 'No. Get your own deep thoughts.'

He tossed his head back with a dramatic sigh. 'Fine. I guess it was like you said at the café the other day. Liking art has never really been a choice for me.'

'Yeah, figured.' She couldn't imagine a world where she was encouraged to make and learn about art rather than dissuaded from it. Her parents had never taken her to art lessons or bought her craft supplies, never even considered it. It wasn't part of their lives, and hadn't expected it to be part of hers.

'That's why I'm here,' he said. 'To make my own choice for once.'

That took her aback. It was why she was here, too, but acknowledging that would mean acknowledging that they had something in common. That he was a person beyond the privilege. 'And the choice is... to do the exact same thing you've been doing for twenty years?'

'Not quite. To people like my father, being a potter is a far cry from making it in the art industry. He wanted me to be like him, make money from other people's art instead of my own, or at least produce something worth selling. Somewhere along the way, I realised how exhausting it is to only see art for its monetary value. I forgot how to love it the way we did as kids.'

'Yeah. It can be easy to forget.' Hadn't she forgotten over the last few weeks? Art was becoming a chore, another responsibility she was barely hanging on to. The rest, she couldn't pretend to understand. He was still lucky to have that upbringing. Still, something held her back from dismissing him. The way his shine dulled when he talked about his dad, or perhaps it was just the delicate tranquillity in the workshop. She didn't want to shatter it. Not after the day she'd had.

Maybe, just tonight, she didn't have to hate him.

Aiden hummed, and the space between them became a little too tranquil. A little too intimate.

To escape it, she hopped off the desk and returned to her own, where she'd already measured out a lump of clay. She didn't know what she was aiming for with it. The cylinder she'd failed at last week would have been good enough. As she wedged her clay, she watched Aiden stare at his. And then, when she pretended to look down, at her. He'd moved to the opposite side of the desk seemingly just to do that. Probably to watch her fail again, she told herself, because the alternative would do nothing to help that self-sufficiency she was striving for.

Still, another question weighed on her as she kneaded the clay. 'Do you still paint?'

'Sometimes. Haven't really known where to start recently.' He planted his elbows on the desk, resting his forehead onto the paint-stained wood as though it could provide some answers.

Juniper would have loved to watch him suffer with the same cluelessness she often felt, but the answer to his problem seemed so obvious that she couldn't keep her mouth shut. 'So, make a paint palette and brush holder. One of the painters I watch on YouTube uses ceramic materials all the time. They look nice and work well.'

Aiden's eyes widened, and he lifted slowly. 'You know what, Juniper Hodgson? You're just a bit brilliant.'

'A lot brilliant. I expect full credit.' She tried to staunch the pride rising in her chest but, as much as she resented it, she was beginning to see why people flocked to him to feel important. Despite all of her hostility towards him, his soft smile and unnecessary gratitude had her feeling like she'd worked some sort of miracle. Like she wasn't so terrible at everything after all.

She liked the way he liked her. The way he watched her, responded to her, coaxed her into conversation regardless of whether it was frosty or thawing.

Unfortunately, tonight, she *was* thawing. Quickly.

15

It would take Aiden a while to master hand-building, he decided, but thanks to Juniper, he had an idea, and that was what mattered.

Not that he could focus on it much now. She was doing that thing again: concentrating, but in an unfairly sexy way that made him want her more than ever. Only, where all of that focus had helped her in their sculpting lesson yesterday, it now seemed to come as more of a hindrance as she operated the wheel. Her hands couldn't seem to find any steadiness as she centred her clay. Up until this point, she'd done everything right. He knew exactly what her problem was, especially when she took her foot off the pedal and grunted in frustration.

Wordlessly, Aiden set down the sponge he'd been using to smooth the edges of his slowly emerging palette, heading to the switches beside the whiteboard.

Juniper barely looked up, proof she was lost somewhere else. What was worse was that she looked close to tears. He didn't cope well with anyone crying, always unsure what to say or do, but witnessing her so disconnected from her usual self was more unsettling than ever.

He turned the lights off, blanketing the workshop in darkness.

'Aiden! What the chuff are you doing?' Juniper bellowed. As his eyes adjusted to the light, he found her again, one side radiating gold where the glow of the streetlamp outside hit her hair and skin. Even in darkness, the light flocked to her. Just like he did, hard as he tried to stop it.

'I'm helping you,' he answered simply.

'By making sure I can't *see*?'

'You're thinking too much about it.' He found his way to her desk, the corner jutting into his hip when he stopped in front of her wheel. 'You're not letting your body do the work because everything is getting lost in here.'

He tapped her temple gently, and didn't miss the shiver that travelled across her shoulders, first one, then the other. Where the light shone, he saw goosebumps on her arms. She might have affected him in ways he couldn't hide, but he stirred something in her, too, and her body was snitching on her.

As much as he wanted to focus on *that*, he wanted to help her more.

Yet she looked up at him stubbornly instead. 'Are you a therapist now, too?'

'Am I wrong?'

Silence. And then a sigh that meant he'd won. 'A lot of things get lost in there. That's just who I am.'

'It doesn't have to be. Throwing is about surrendering.' He grabbed a stool from the nearest table and slid it behind hers. 'It's a connection between the clay and your hands. When the brain comes in, the wheel gets overcrowded.'

'So you think I'm going to do a better job in the dark?' She scoffed. 'Are my *eyes* overcrowding the wheel, too?'

'Not just in the dark.' Aiden took a clean rag from the cupboard and sat down beside her, grinning when her spine stiffened. 'Do you trust me?'

'No.'

His chin brushed her shoulder as he leaned in close to whisper in her ear: 'Liar. Let me show you, Juni.'

'I told you. Only my friends call me that.'

'And I think I've gotten a little more acquainted with you than most of your friends.'

Her lip tucked itself beneath her two endearingly crooked top teeth. Already surrendering. He'd achieved the impossible, just like that.

'Arsehole,' she murmured without malice.

He snickered and then tied the rag around her eyes, handling her the way he would the clay: delicately, never pushing too hard. He knew just how fragile this moment was. Knew that tomorrow, she'd likely go back to hating him, and he might never get to touch her again.

As he tied the knot at the back of her head, he heard her breath grow thicker. 'This isn't going to work.'

'I don't think you know how much you're capable of.' He couldn't help but draw her hair out of her face, knuckles tracing across the sides of her neck as he guided the strands down her shoulders. Everything about her was beautiful, but especially now. She was bare tonight, barely any makeup, none of her usual acidity.

'Put your foot on the pedal,' he instructed, thumb brushing the side seam of her soft leggings. She did shakily, applying pressure. The wheel began to turn.

She was cautious as she centred the clay, none of that first day's overeagerness evident now. He kept her elbows braced against his stomach when they tried to poke out, which only caused another jagged breath to escape her.

'Feel?' he said when the clay began to rise into a cylinder. 'Just like that.'

'I don't know what I'm doing.'

'And yet you're doing it, anyway.' She was, thumbs moulding the inside of the vase to hollow out its walls.

'This is silly,' she groused.

'So be silly. There's no one here but me and you. What are you afraid of, Hodge?'

He imagined her eyes rolling behind the blindfold as she replied, 'I'm not afraid of anything, *Whittaker*.'

Yet she continued, letting her hands mould the clay into its new form. When it began to flare out of shape, he guided her into a more stable position, his palms sparking with electricity as first her, then the clay, listened. Answered.

This was why he loved pottery. Clay had a life, and all it needed was someone to coax it into being. There was nothing that could happen on this wheel that would ruin him the way Elmington had. No pressure, no expectations. It was the steadiest relationship he'd ever upheld, the only thing he could control when the world felt far beyond it.

Watching Juniper discover that was like watching magic happen. He felt her relax against his chest, felt her wrists fall slack as she followed wherever the clay took her.

She didn't need his help anymore, and yet he couldn't pull his hands away. Couldn't sever this sudden, overwhelming connection.

'Is it working?' she whispered.

He nestled his chin into her shoulder. 'You tell me.'

As she slowed the wheel, he couldn't help but lace their clay-slick fingers together, knees growing tighter around her hips. 'See? It's good not to think for a while.'

She hummed, wriggling back against him just like she had in class. His lips brushed her temple, finding friction where her skin met the blindfold, and he needed her. Fuck, he needed her, so much that he was already hard again.

'Sometimes, feeling is enough.' His attention fell to her earlobe, and he nibbled until she gasped, arching her neck. 'I can't stop thinking about you, Juni. I need more of you.'

'We can't,' she said.

'Why not?'

If there was a reason, she didn't give it, instead pursing her lips.

And then she guided their intertwined hands to her chest, brows furrowing on the edge of the rag as though she was making up her mind.

'We shouldn't,' she corrected.

'Says who?'

Again, nothing.

'At least let us finish what we started,' he begged. 'You were so close, weren't you?'

She nodded.

'Did you think of me when you finished yourself off after?' he asked.

She rutted her ass against his cock as though her body had already decided for her.

'Tell me,' Aiden urged. 'Please tell me.'

'Yes,' she whimpered. 'Fuck, Aiden, yes.'

'Do you want me to touch you like that now?'

Her nod became frantic, but it wasn't enough for him. If they were doing this, he needed to know she wouldn't regret it again in the morning. Needed to know it wasn't all him. 'Tell me what you want. I need to hear it, sweetheart.'

'I want you.' She dragged their linked hands to her breasts, squeezing them over her oversized T-shirt. 'I want you to fuck me like this. Blindfolded. I want to feel everything. I want to forget everything but you.'

He groaned hungrily and peeled their hands apart, slipping his under her shirt, her bra, to toy with her full tits. He hadn't spent enough time with them at the party, and he made up for that now. Her back arched against him as his thumb found her nipple, and he wished he could see her properly. He didn't dare tear away, though, afraid anything might drive them apart, just like then.

With his fingers slippery from the clay, she was moaning in seconds, grinding her ass harder against his erection until he was gritting his teeth.

'Please, Aiden. More.'

He grinned into her neck, smelling coffee and sweat and *her*. 'I thought you said you'd never beg me for anything.'

'Shut up,' she ground out, and he laughed.

'I love it when you tell me what to do. So fucking hot.' He dipped his hands beneath her waistband, cupping her heat above her underwear. Dampness seeped into the fabric as she bucked against him, finding friction in his palm. As much as he wanted to get her off like this, he wasn't sure he'd survive another minute without her touching him, too.

'Turn around,' he said into the nape of her neck. 'Let me see you properly.'

He stood, kicking his stool away so that it could no longer come between them, then did the same for hers. He guided her close with his hands on her hips, kissing her until she was all he knew. She was as rough as she was fiery, and he revelled in the idea that she might leave marks come tomorrow. He would need something to remember that this wasn't just a fantasy, a figment of his imagination.

To direct her, to see her putting all of her trust in him with that rag around her eyes, was exhilarating. He wanted to earn the honour, wanted to make her feel every type of pleasure possible, wanted to know her body inside out. He fingered the hem of her black jumper. 'Can I take this off?'

'Yes.'

Aiden rolled the soft material up slowly so as to drink in every new part of her. Every curve, every roll of her stomach, the peaks of her barely contained breasts in a black lace bra. He could finally see all of that tattoo: they weren't vines, but rose stems that curled around her shoulder and ended in flowers below her collarbone. Much more apt – she was all thorns meshed with silk petals, too.

'You're so fucking beautiful, Juniper,' he marvelled, letting the jumper fall to the floor.

She nibbled on her lower lip, reaching out a hand to trace the planes of his chest and stomach. 'I don't suppose you brought a condom with you?'

He snorted. 'To class? No, not this time.'

'I'm on the pill,' she admitted. 'And I'm safe. Had my last check-up before term started.'

'Me too. Checked after Elmington, haven't been with anyone since.'

She was already fumbling to unbutton his jeans. 'Good, because I don't want to wait anymore.'

'Are you sure?' He laced her hair through his fingers, gentle now. 'Because if you decide tomorrow that this was a mistake, I don't know if I could deal with it a second time. You drive me mad enough as it is, but this hot and cold will kill me.'

She traced the outline of his cock through his boxers in a way that made his knees weak. 'I'm sure. No more regrets. But it can't mean anything. No… feelings or anything.'

'Just sex. That works for me.' He was glad for the blindfold, afraid the lie was written all over his face. It didn't feel like *just* anything with her. But some of her was better than none of her, so he nudged her back towards the desk, bracing his hands on either side of her arms. 'You still want this on?' he asked, dragging a knuckle across the linen's edge.

Another nod, and then she was pulling his face down to kiss him again, this time palming him over his boxers until he was moaning her name. She knew exactly how to make him throb, using delicate fingers around his head, then squeezing lightly down his shaft. He tried to focus on her, massaging her clit with her underwear providing friction, then lapping his tongue against her bra when she finally freed his mouth.

Soon, she was tugging down her leggings and perched on the desk, legs splayed open just for him.

Fucking hell, those thighs were heaven. All of her was heaven. Just as he didn't know why she hated him, he didn't know what he'd done to deserve this part of her. This much of her.

He wiped his hands down on the nearest cloth to clear them of clay, then nudged her underwear to the side to touch her. When his fingers entered her, she clenched around him, and he almost came just imagining they were his cock.

'Are you ready for me, sweetheart?'

She freed his cock from his boxers, and then, when she gave permission, sunk into her until they both cried out.

16

Juniper had never felt anything like it, like him, before. He might have been desperate to keep her talking, but she didn't have to guide him. He already knew exactly how to make her feel toe-curlingly, stomach-clenchingly good, and it was only intensified by the blindfold, drowning out everything but his touch.

She gripped his arms just for something to hold onto when he asked if she was ready, afraid her grip on anything but the pleasure she felt was slipping. She could end up on the floor and she wouldn't know it as long as he was with her.

'I'm ready.' She peeled up her hips to show him, no longer in control of her need.

His breath tickled her neck, something she hadn't been expecting in her anticipation. It made her throb just as fiercely as his fingers inside her had. Not knowing where he was, where she might feel him next, set her skin alight.

The kiss he placed on her collarbone was another surprise. A more jarring one. Not because it was rough, heavy, like the way they'd been kissing just a few moments ago, but because it was feather-light. Delicate. Too delicate for what they were about to do.

Delicate enough to make her worry that this went beyond sex. Beyond anything she'd experienced before.

But it couldn't. It wouldn't. No matter what they did now, he was still him, and she still hated—

'Oh, fuck. Aiden.' She gasped when he sheathed himself inside her, his length spreading her thighs even further apart. She grappled for his shoulders to keep herself steady, hooking a thigh around his hip.

She heard him loose a strained breath and knew he was trying to go slow. For her sake or his, she wasn't sure.

'Is this okay?' he asked, voice vibrating against the shell of her ear.

She rolled, taking him deeper to show just how okay it was.

He uttered her name like a curse, like a prayer, like something in between the two.

'It's perfect,' she said when he still didn't move, unable to take the stillness much longer.

His stubble scraped against her cheek as he tugged her close, like he wanted their stomachs, chests, bodies, to meld into one.

And then he started thrusting, and she wanted it, too. Her lashes caught on the blindfold as her lids fluttered, a tight coil of bliss curling around her from the crown of her head to the tip of her toes. She couldn't remember the last time she'd felt this connected to her own body, so often caught floating around somewhere above it in the tangle of racing thoughts.

Her nails dragged over his skin, eliciting another guttural moan from him. 'You feel so good,' he whispered. 'So good for me, Juni.'

So vulnerable, she realised. She was in the dark, blindfolded: he could have done anything to her, with her. She'd never trusted much before, afraid people were laughing at her when her back was turned. He was the last person on earth she should have given her body to, and yet his lips roved her face, her nose, her forehead, and she'd never felt safer.

'Touch me again,' she begged, and he did, rolling her clit between trembling fingers, then creeping down to the place where their bodies met. She imagined the things she couldn't see, imagined watching him move in and out of her, and she gripped him harder.

She curled her fingers into his hair as her thighs began to quiver. Tugged just a little harder than would have been comfortable if she was with someone else, at least for the first time. But she was already getting to know what he liked: her, even in her fiercest moments. Even when she pushed him too hard, hated him more than was probably fair.

And like she'd hoped, it left him growling with insatiable hunger. He filled her faster, harder, her glutes stinging against the uncomfortable wooden surface now, but she liked the way the pain mingled with the pleasure. Liked that, for once, it wasn't too much for her to handle. She wasn't overwhelmed or afraid. It was just the two of them, tucked away somewhere where the rest of the world couldn't touch them, and she could control it if she wanted – only she didn't.

She almost didn't want it to end, but the promise of climax soared through her belly with this new pressure. 'I'm close.'

'Me, too.' His voice was sharpened by clenched teeth. 'Let me feel you come first, sweetheart. Please.' He returned to her clit, no longer so delicate.

She keened as her body shook with an orgasm that seemed endless, chasing every lick of it with reckless abandon.

'Just like that. So good, Juni,' he was saying, and then another gruff noise left his throat as he spilled into her. The warmth of his seed was almost enough to take him again, just to feel him, hear him, so wrapped up in this shared pleasure.

Instead, she leaned back on her elbows breathlessly, feeling spent and boneless. He pulled out at an agonisingly reluctant pace, and then the cold damp of a cloth sent another jolt through her body as he cleaned the stickiness from her skin.

She wasn't sure what to do now. She was in a fog she didn't want to emerge from, still tingling from what might have been the best orgasm of her life.

His knuckle mapped over the inside of her elbow, then over to her stomach, her cheek, before settling on the edge of her blindfold. 'Can I see you properly now?'

She nodded, though secretly she found it easier this way. If she couldn't see him, she didn't have to wonder why she wanted him, or why he wanted her.

The blindfold was lifted, and facing him didn't feel so terrifying when she saw the sweat glistening above his brow, his lips plump and swollen. His eyes were soft as honey as he took her in, and she had to look away when it left something in her sore. With what, she didn't know. Or, at least, didn't want to know.

He dipped to kiss her again, just once, lingering until she wished he would wrap his arms around her, keep her stable like he had before.

But that wasn't what they were doing here, so she didn't ask. Instead, she averted her gaze to the clay abandoned on the throwing wheel. She'd made an almost perfect cylinder, smooth clay gleaming tall and steady. 'Quite the teacher, aren't you, Whittaker? Do all your mentees get special treatment?'

He grinned, forehead knocking against hers. 'Just you, Hodge. Seems you have a habit of distracting me.'

And, surprisingly, she was quite okay with that – because he'd distracted her, too. From the phone call, from work, from all of her insecurities and doubts.

He didn't have to know it, but his lesson had worked. She had surrendered: to the clay and to him.

★

It was almost impossible for Juniper to keep the huge smile from her face that Friday. She had never carried anything as carefully as the jewellery holder on her return trip from the kiln. It had survived the firing process with only a tiny crack, one that would easily be fixable with a glaze.

The icky self-doubt from the last couple of days had been chased away. She'd done it. What's more, her vase was ready and waiting to go in, too, which would leave her with two – two! – fired pottery pieces to her name.

As she reached the workshop, she winced, wondering how she was going to push open the door without any free hands.

She turned around, trying to use her curves to her advantage, but the door didn't budge. The classroom was locked.

Before she could ponder why that might be, Christopher appeared down the corridor, his ginger hair a messy, wind-swept tuft on top of his head and his glasses slightly wonky. Juniper had soon learned that he wasn't a morning person, though nobody held it against him the way he did her.

When he saw her, he stopped short in the hallway, checking his wristwatch with a mystified expression. 'Is it the apocalypse? Is the world finally ending?'

'It's been ending for a while now, just very slowly,' she replied. 'Why is the workshop locked?'

He blinked. 'Because it's ten-to-nine, Jupiter. You're… early.'

Was she? She hadn't really looked at the time on her way out this morning, eager to see how Yggdrasil had fared in the kiln.

She would like to think her new enthusiasm came more from her own skills than the ones Aiden had taught her the other night, but she couldn't pretend as though his unique methods – and the part that had come after, literally – hadn't played a part. He'd been right about surrendering. Clay must have sensed her fear; when she let go, her hands moved with ease, the usually raucous world quietening to a hush. This new comfort in her own abilities had changed something in her.

And something in them. They'd already planned their research paper and began sketching ideas for their final exhibition. After the museum visit on Sunday, Juniper hoped they'd have everything they needed to make headway with this project. She'd fallen asleep with her nose stuck in a book about Ancient Greek ceramics last night, phone slipped between the pages midway through texting Aiden about her findings. And they'd already began their first piece, an amphora. While Aiden threw the perfect shape, she'd began sculpting her creatures.

Somehow, they actually did work well together. The knowledge she lacked, he made up for, and vice versa.

'Oh my lord.' Christopher covered his eyes suddenly. 'There's something on your face.'

'What?' Juniper frowned, almost dropping her piece at the worry that she'd left the stale chocolate croissant nabbed from work's leftovers on her chin. 'What is it?'

'It's…' Christopher peeked through his arm and exclaimed, 'A smile!'

A smile that was quick to leave her face at his terrible joke. She hadn't realised she'd been smiling, and she didn't intend to do it again. Not in front of Chris, and not in front of anyone. She didn't want people thinking it was all for Aiden. It certainly wasn't. Even if she had spilled the beans to Tilly because she was terrible at keeping secrets and some orgasms simply had to be discussed with friends.

'Well, I'm happy with my work,' she grumbled. 'Can you let me in before I drop it?'

She budged aside and he unlocked the classroom before motioning her in.

'Is it a tree?' he asked as she set it down on her desk. It brought her joy to see just a hint of approval on his face.

'The tree of life,' Juniper said. 'And a jewellery holder.'

'Not bad at all, Juniper.' He nodded. 'Let's just hope it holds up during the glazing.'

Juniper froze. Had he just called her by her real name instead of a planet?

She didn't want to jinx it, but she could only assume that she'd earned at least a modicum of his respect. It was difficult to keep from doing a happy dance when his back was turned, but more classmates were already filing in, and she was working on *not* smiling now.

She tried not to look towards the door, because she was also absolutely not eager to see Aiden. A few classmates complimented her, some eager to show off their own pieces. Luc had made a kitchen set to keep herbs and spices inside, the square pots smooth and sleek even without a glaze. As Tilly arrived, she revealed a yarn storage bowl that had turned out lovely.

By the time Aiden showed up, Chris was already delivering another lesson on glazing, running through the different methods, some of which Juniper had already tried either with her jewellery or the classes she'd paid for. She tried to listen closely nonetheless, but her eyes kept getting pulled to the work in Aiden's hands. He'd made the paint palette she'd come up with, along with holders and cups for water and brushes. It was almost annoying how good it looked, and she felt some of that familiar resentment rising to the surface again. She'd been wrong before about him trying. He coasted through life, but not through pottery, every detail of his work painstakingly thought out.

'Couldn't you have made just one mistake?' she whispered. 'It isn't fair that you do a decent job of everything.'

'That was almost a compliment,' he remarked as he took his seat, and then waggled his fingers. 'What can I say? I'm good with my hands. But you already know that, don't you, Juni?'

She glared and pretended to be more interested in Chris's teaching, though her body reacted as it always did, worse now since they'd had sex on this very table. It hadn't been the last time, either. Last night, he'd touched her in a quiet corner of the library, his shushes vibrating against her neck and his fingers rubbing her clit. The memories felt like someone else's. She'd never been very adventurous before, not unless the other person initiated it, and usually she was far too worried about being caught to enjoy it.

But with him, she got lost. Nothing else mattered bar his throaty little whispers and the heat between her legs.

At their interaction, Tilly's brows danced. Since she'd yet to find an eligible woman on campus, she claimed to be living vicariously through Juni.

Finally, Chris left them to explore the oxides and paints left out at the front of the classroom. Juniper already knew exactly what she wanted. Each branch would represent a different Norse realm with patterns and colours to signify the landscape, and the trunk would be a rough, textured bark in browns and coppers. The plate, sectioned by the tree's roots, would be painted in celestial blues and golds to form the cosmos.

So, collecting her colours, Juniper got comfortable on her stool and began working – very, very carefully. Her chronic clumsiness was always a worry, so she didn't dare lose concentration on her paintbrush.

Or, at least not all of it. Tilly soon began chatting, seeming well-practised in this part of the process. She had chosen a pomegranate-coloured powdered glaze that she was currently sieving into a bowl. 'So. How are you two getting on with the project? When you think about it, it isn't long until the research paper has to be submitted, and then it's exhibition time!'

Juniper remained quiet, letting Aiden reply.

He scratched his head with the end of his pencil. 'It's going surprisingly well. We've got our research planned out, and some of our pieces are coming together.'

'Hmm, not the only things coming together, I've heard.' Tilly gave a suggestive wink, and behind Juniper, Luc stifled a laugh.

Juniper hushed her as Aiden turned to glance at her in surprise. 'Are we that obvious, or are you telling people?'

'Both,' Tilly said.

'I'm not telling *people*,' Juniper corrected, planting her paintbrush on the paper towel beside her. 'Just person. One.' When his grin turned more shit-eating than ever, she added, 'And don't think it means something, because it doesn't. Friends tell each other things. You wouldn't know because you don't have any.'

'I have Luc.'

'Well, we're friends of convenience,' Luc said. 'But, yes, he did tell me, too.'

It shouldn't have meant anything. It *didn't* mean anything. But the rising swell in Juniper's chest begged to differ. She didn't know if it was gladness or panic. Both, probably. She was sure that she was one of many sexual conquests for Aiden, a fact she'd tried not to think too hard about, but clearly she was still worth talking about.

'I just hope you cleaned the desk,' Tilly muttered in the quiet.

Juniper blazed with embarrassment, made worse when Luc gasped. 'You did it on the *desk*? Gross. You didn't tell me that!'

'Shh!' Aiden and Juniper hissed at the same time.

'We were perfectly sanitary,' said Juni. Another reason she preferred private sexual encounters, but those would mean either inviting Aiden to her tiny room or going to his fancy flat, and neither of those felt appealing. Too intimate, and far too contrasting to one another. 'And we're not talking about this anymore.'

Aiden adjusted the collar of his flannel shirt and cleared his throat. 'Anyway, what about you, Tilly? Making progress with Owen?'

'A little. I think we're going to visit some museums for inspiration this weekend. Hey, you two should tag along!'

Juniper perked up. She liked the sound of a few extra people joining them this Sunday, both because it meant avoiding her chemistry with Aiden and spending more time with Tilly, who she truly was beginning to adore. She was much more understanding than Juniper's old friends when it came to Juniper's struggles, whether it was money or mood swings, and if Juniper was exhausted after a shift, she didn't feel obligated to talk in her company while they curled up with Cerberus to watch rom-coms.

She'd worried so much about being alone here, but she wasn't at all. In fact, she was less alone than she had been in a long time. Maybe even ever. It had been difficult to keep up with people back in Manchester. They'd never got her 'weirder' parts – her ability to always say the wrong thing and show up to plans at the wrong time. She hadn't dared open up about having ADHD and how, sometimes, it disabled her, afraid it would only divide them more. And then, when she'd started working, she'd been too burned out to even care about maintaining friendships, with the exception of her then colleague, now ex, the relationship of which had been brief and full of red flags.

'I'm working until two-thirty on Sunday, but we were actually going to head to the myths and legends exhibition at the British Museum afterwards. You should come! You too, Luc!'

'As a fifth wheel? No, thank you.' Luc slipped a chewing gum into their mouth. 'Besides, Amir and I are focusing on our two different cultures and their geography, so we've already been there, done that, got the feet blisters.'

'Well, if you change your mind, the invitation's there.' Truthfully, Juniper appreciated Luc's honesty. They weren't all that different to her, never caught appeasing someone with politeness just for the sake of it. If they didn't want to come, why should they pretend otherwise?

'I can't wait.' Tilly clapped her hands excitedly. Then, quieter, 'Me and Owen don't exactly have a lot in common, so I could use the buffer, honestly.'

'Well, I've got you.' Juniper smiled and headed back to her work, only then noticing that Aiden hadn't said a word as they'd been planning.

When he headed to the glaze station, she shuffled along to follow him, feigning interest in the spray guns. Meanwhile, he grabbed some colours for his palette, though he looked a bit lost amid all the different choices.

'Can't bear to be without me now, Hodge?' he quipped after a few awkward moments of silence.

'The opposite, actually, but you're acting all weird.'

His brows furrowed, and she couldn't tell if it was at the instructions for the oxides or her. 'No, I'm not. I just don't think I've grasped all this chemical stuff yet, and I haven't decided where to start with it all.'

'Well, I can help you with that. But I mean about the museum trip.'

'Oh.' His hands moved closer to hers on the table, pinkie fingers brushing barely enough to feel it. But she did, because it was him, and for whatever reason, her body had decided it liked him even when her brain didn't. Goosebumps skittered down her arms, and she found herself wishing it would just be the two of them again, throwing together in the darkness. 'Well, I'm not weird about that either.'

'Okay.' Juniper shrugged, though she still wasn't convinced. She plucked up a piece of gold leaf that she hadn't noticed before, thinking it would make a lovely effect on the tree's bark.

'Need me to inspire you again?' She nudged him lightly.

Strangely, his grin didn't trigger her usual annoyance. Instead, she noticed how pretty the shape of his lips were when they weren't pursed, and how his bottom front teeth faced away from each other just slightly. 'I'll never say no to that.'

'It can be arranged.' She gathered a few of the glaze powders, including a copper that she imagined would fire to make the same green as his eyes. 'This would be a nice colour mix for your palette. Just make sure to look at the labels instead of the colours, because they change when they're fired. You just do what Tilly's doing: mix and sieve.'

'Okay. Thank you.' He seemed taken aback by the advice. Because he was surprised she knew things, or surprised she was being nice?

Not daring to decide, she made to head back to her desk, but he took stopped her with a light hand on hers. 'I sort of hoped it would just be the two of us on Sunday,' he admitted, playing with the hem on her bell-sleeved jumper.

'Oh? Why?'

He shrugged. 'Maybe I'm selfish and want you all to myself.'

Her mouth turned dry at that. When she looked up at him, she expected his usual taunting expression or sultry smoulder, but instead, his forehead was still creased – as though having company genuinely bothered him.

She tried to lighten the mood. 'You don't think you've had more than enough of me for one week?'

He licked his lips, gaze fixed on hers. 'I don't think I'll ever get enough of you, sweetheart.'

Sweetheart. He wasn't supposed to call her that, not here, and yet her knees weakened at the sound of it in his husky throat.

Still, it didn't sit right. With the class moving around them, she stepped back. She'd been in relationships before where she'd had to sacrifice every minute of the day for the other

146

person, and there was no way Aiden could expect any more from her than she was already giving. She occupied her brain enough as it was. 'I don't do possessiveness, Whittaker.'

'It isn't about possessiveness.' Concern tugged at his words, and a sincerity that she was still getting used to hearing from anyone, let alone him. She couldn't remember him being so honest, so genuine, in high school. What if she'd remembered him wrong? Mashed the memories of his cat-calling mates with him?

It didn't matter. She remembered the other thing perfectly. Remembered how it had felt to walk out of Elmington already knowing the rejection letter was on its way.

'I just think you let me closer to you when no one else is around,' Aiden continued. He checked nobody was looking, then tugged her closer, her hip knocking against his. 'I've noticed that guard of yours doesn't only come up for me, y'know.'

That wasn't true. *Was* it?

Maybe. She was still learning to unmask, and whenever her true self slipped out, all bluntness and wit, not everybody seemed to like it. With Tilly, it was different, but in a room full of people, there was a constant pressure sitting just under her skin. Like she was always waiting to feel as small as she had in high school, as small as her parents sometimes made her feel. It didn't stop her from saying the wrong things, but it did leave her protecting herself with dry wit and 'cheek', as her mother would call it.

She'd enjoyed being vulnerable with him a few nights ago, but now, she only felt raw. She took a step back, wondering if maybe she'd made a mistake with this. Just sex didn't ever really exist, did it? The lines between physical and emotional intimacy always crossed, and if she did have a guard up, he seemed to have invaded it easier than she would have liked.

'You don't have to come if you don't want to,' she said finally, tersely.

He weighed her up for a moment, none of his usual amusement evident. 'I thought I'd made it obvious, Juni. I always want to come with you.'

She didn't know whether he was trying to be funny or not, his tone wispy and unsure.

'For the project,' she said, less of a question than a demand.

He nodded slowly. 'Of course. What else?'

There. She could relax.

Only she didn't, not even when she got back to her stool and began to paint again.

Strange how one person could make her feel both safe yet in a war zone.

She supposed it meant that Aiden was who he'd always been: perfectly infuriating and better avoided.

If only Juniper was good at following her own instincts.

17

It came as no surprise to Aiden when the group was left waiting for Juniper outside the British Museum. He'd considered picking her up from Caffé Verde himself, just to make sure she arrived in one piece, but after her reaction to his accidental show of… well, infatuation, the other day, thought it better not to. One wrong move was sure to send her running once and for all.

He didn't get it, though. They got along, no matter what she said. Their chemistry was off the charts, and the sex was like nothing he'd experienced before. What was it about him that made her want to keep him at arm's length? Why did he spend his days waiting for her to shove him away?

'Typical Juniper,' Tilly said when the silence got a bit too awkward. Beside her, Owen shifted from foot to foot, laces loose on his Adidas trainers. No wonder Tilly had needed a buffer. As nice as he seemed, conversation was stilted, awkward, and his attempts at humour often fell flat.

Now, Owen brightened, pushing his glasses up the crooked bridge of his nose. 'Did you know that, in ancient times, Juniper branches were used to ward off evil spirits?'

Aiden chuckled, slipping his hands into his coat pockets. An autumn chill had crept over London this week, though Tilly seemed not to feel it in her crocheted mustard vest.

'Something funny, Aiden?' asked Tilly, a challenge in her inky eyes.

'Well, I just thought it was ironic. Juniper seems to carry some traits of evil spirits herself.' Her hot–headedness was just one of them. Maybe he could do with something to ward her off – but he'd never want to, even if he was tiptoeing a steady descent into madness.

'Oi! I heard that!' a voice bellowed behind them. He turned to find Juniper hopping up the steps two at a time, her hair twisted into a messy braid that draped over one shoulder. She looked as she always did after a shift at the cafe: drained.

He could remedy that later, he was sure. A pattern had begun to emerge this week: the worse her time at work was, the hungrier she was for him. He was her distraction, a fact he might have had a problem with if she wasn't also his.

'Juniper, my dear,' Tilly said, checking the time on her phone, 'I love you and all of your terrible time-keeping skills, but the exhibition closes in two hours, so can we get a shifty on?'

'Sorry. Gianna was teaching me how to clean the coffee machine. Again.' She puffed out her cheeks as she reached them. At his side, Aiden's fingers flickered with the urge to brush the matted fringe from her eyes, then kiss her until she was capable of smiling again. 'Hi, Owen.'

Owen seemed pleased by her attention. 'Hello, Juniper.'

'No hello for me?' Aiden teased.

'Nope. Shall we go in, then?'

Tilly linked her arm through Juniper's and tapped the round peak of her nose. 'Less of the flirting, please. You're beginning to make me jealous.'

Falling into step beside Aiden, Owen frowned. 'Wasn't that the direct opposite of flirting, or am I just out of practice?'

'Oh, Owen.' Tilly patted his sandy hair, flattening the already fine strands. 'You have much to learn about these two.'

'She's in love with me, secretly,' Aiden supplied, coolly turning up the collar of his shirt. 'Her dislike for me is all an act.'

He'd been hoping for a reaction, and it was what he got. She turned around to send out a harmless kick to his shin. 'In your dreams, Whittaker.'

'That's right.' He winked. 'How did you know?'

It wasn't a lie. The thought of her found him at all hours of the day, whether it was in the darkness of his bedroom at night or when he was scribbling into his sketchbook on the tube. It was aggravating. Worse because he'd been trying to find some inspiration to paint again, but his brain was too full of her to fit in much else. They'd been getting more than just pottery done during their study sessions and after-hours workshops, too, though thankfully, it hadn't impacted their progress. Their first amphora was almost done, and they only had a few more paragraphs to write for their research paper.

Juniper's heatless scoff carried into the museum. The interior was exactly as he remembered: echoey, vast, the white stone

151

walls cold and uninviting. It had once been his favourite place to visit with his father when they travelled to London. Now, it was just another reminder of where he should have been. All the goals he'd abandoned, the people he'd disappointed.

He couldn't bring himself to regret causing those disappointments by dropping out of Elmington, not when Juniper's elbow brushed his as they stopped to look at the Myths and Legends Exhibition poster, which displayed an oil painting of a centaur. The details of light and shadow, colour values and varied brushstrokes, pulled him just as it always did, the beauty not lost on him. It must have taken months, if not years, of patience for the artist to pull together the bend of tawny fur against brown skin, not to mention the effeminate facial features that broke traditional expectations.

'I could spend days in this place,' Tilly confessed. 'Y'know, I never used to see people like me in paintings growing up. This… This is special.'

Juniper squeezed her hand in silent support, and Aiden's chest grew a little fuller. He hadn't had reason to think about it before, how few people of colour were framed on the walls of museums like this, but now it was impossible to ignore. He couldn't imagine what it must feel like to never see parts of himself in a place that supposedly existed to immerse people in culture.

'Did you know that this was the first public museum in Britain?' Owen rattled off, fiddling with a button on his shirt. 'It's been here since 1753.'

Juniper frowned at him, much the same way Aiden had when he'd first realised that Owen had a habit of listing a lot of facts. As interesting as it was, it was a stark change in subject, as though he was trying to gloss over Tilly's point.

'What themes are you two focusing on for your project again?' Juniper asked.

'Fashion and textiles for me,' Tilly said. 'Trains for Owen.'

'Oh. That will be an interesting mix.' She turned to Aiden, jabbing him in the side. His skin smarted as though she held a hot poker. 'In fact, I wish *you* had an interest in trains. Those would be fun to sculpt!'

'Well, I'm sorry to burden you with my boring art.' He couldn't help but squeeze her hip, where he'd learned she was ticklish. She yelped out, slapping him away, but the corner of her mouth rose in a half-concealed smile, and he knew he was doing something right. Helping her relax again after what had probably been a shitty day.

'Seriously, guys. I'll vom if you carry on,' Tilly said. 'Remind me why you're not actually dating again?'

'Because we don't like each other,' Juniper was quick to reply.

'*She* doesn't like *me*,' Aiden corrected. 'I'm indifferent.' He was surprised at how smoothly the lie fell from his mouth, though it didn't seem to convince anyone.

'Yeah, right.' Tilly ushered them towards the steps. 'Let's just head to the exhibition before you start ripping off each other's clothes, yeah?'

Owen scratched his head as though he couldn't understand any of it, which seemed fair. They followed the tall staircase up to the second floor, joining the lines of visitors that meandered into the several open exhibition rooms. Tilly and Juniper began chatting about something Aiden couldn't keep up with, leaving him and Owen to trail behind like lost puppies.

Owen took off his glasses, cleaning them with the corner of his sleeve. 'So, Aiden. Who is your favourite artist?'

He hated that question, mostly because his answer changed depending on where he was with his studies. His father had trained him to approach art critically, which meant that, for a while, it wasn't always something to enjoy or admire; rather, something to make money out of. If he was painting, it had to be perfect, too aware of all the mistakes that could cheapen a work. Then, at A-level, the theory side had become a requirement, packed full of essays and research that, at least back then, only felt like a way to restrict and dilute his practice.

Now, it wasn't either of those things. Sometimes, it wasn't anything at all to him. Sometimes, it was the reason for every terrible thing he'd ever felt.

'Well, I've always found William Blake's work fascinating,' seemed like a safe enough answer.

'Ah, yes. I'm a fan of his poetry, too.' Owen nodded, then eagerly bounced on the balls of his feet. 'I have to ask: what is the most famous painting your father has ever sold?'

Aiden's molars scraped together as they reached the final few steps. Another reason why he was so unsettled here: he couldn't enter a space like this without being reminded of his father, one way or another. 'I'm not sure. You'd have to ask him.'

'Have you ever gotten to work with him? I'm sure he's shown you the ropes,' Owen continued obliviously. 'What about the artists he works with? Have you met anyone famous?'

'A few times,' Aiden muttered vaguely. His lungs grew tight and he couldn't keep from feeling like he would always be trapped this way, no matter how far he tried to run.

His surroundings became a blur, heart pounding too quickly for his body to register anything else. Jesus, he hadn't had an anxiety attack in a while. Not like this. He stopped at the top of the steps, leaning against the railing for support and willing himself to calm down. *Breathe. Count to five. You're not in danger, for Christ's sake. You're fine.*

'Never mind artists.' Juniper stepped between them, suddenly much closer to Aiden. He tried to hold onto the threads of her voice, tangled around the loud, reverberating din of the museum. 'What's your favourite mythological monster?'

'Mermaids. I'm a simple woman,' Tilly said. 'Had a crush on Ariel from day dot.'

'Erm, I like dragons, I suppose,' Owen added, then cleared his throat.

'Very cliché, both of you.' Juniper gave them a disapproving tut. 'C'mon. let's educate you on the beauty of deadly serpent women.'

Tilly and Owen let her push them into the exhibition room. Once they'd headed inside, Juniper hung back, her focus sharp enough to whittle away at least some of his racing thoughts. 'Are you okay?'

He forced a smile, wiping his clammy palms over the back of his neck. He was fine. He was here. He could breathe again. 'Why? Worried about me, Hodge?'

'God, no,' she said, but the wrinkle in her facade didn't ease. Still, she let it drop, that usual stubbornness forgotten somewhere, and he'd never been more grateful for its absence. Whether she knew it or not, she was doing him a favour, letting him pretend everything was normal. Like his gut wasn't churning. Like he wasn't seconds away from sinking into panic.

Like he wasn't a complete and utter mess inside.

18

Aiden's interest in art could never measure up to Juniper's love of mythology. She led them around the space as confidently as a tour guide, pointing out the figures in every painting, tapestry, and ceramic piece. Most of it went over Aiden's head, not because he wasn't interested, but because it was difficult to focus on anything but the brightness in her eyes, the movement of her lips, and that snaking anxiety just beneath his surface.

For a moment, he wondered if he would fall short for this project. If the burden of his complex relationship with art would mean letting her down.

Stop. He mentally batted the thought away. He wasn't doing himself any favours, but it was difficult not to get trapped in the cycle of terrible thoughts once it had begun.

He was glad when Tilly and Owen went to check one of the other exhibits downstairs. Finally, it was just the two of them, and that meant he was safe from more questions, more reminders, of his dad.

After scrutinising a Grecian urn, trying to memorise the curves and rim so he might throw something similar for their project, he joined her at a painting that depicted demons and monsters of Japanese myth. 'Feeling inspired?'

She nodded without taking her eyes off the work. 'Very. You?'

He nodded without taking his eyes off her. 'Yeah, me too.'

He hadn't felt the urge to reach for a paintbrush in months, but with her side profile bathed in gold from the lights above, he could imagine some of the strokes he might make in whites and yellows, dissolving into coppers and browns where wispy strands of hair fell out of its braid. None of them would have been enough to capture her the way he'd like, but he'd give it his best shot.

And then he realised that he wasn't supposed to have those feelings for her. No wonder he'd had that burst of anxiety earlier. He was all over the place, letting himself care for a woman who clearly didn't want to care about him.

Just sex. That's what it was supposed to be.

And yet he didn't think it was. Not for him.

'I was thinking for our amphora, we could have Medusa and her snakes coiled around the base,' she said. 'I know she's one of the more common mythological figures, but I sort of love her. And I think it would mean playing about with different textures for the scales and stone.'

'Sounds like a great idea to me.' It was only then, with his chest free of pressure, that he realised something. 'You know, what I said the other day about wanting you all to myself? It was only partly true.'

She tipped her head: finally, he had interested her enough to get her attention. No mean feat in the middle of a gallery piled with things she loved. 'I do think that the more people are around you, the more guarded you are,' he continued. 'But I also think the same is true of me, and that's the real reason I wanted it to be just us.'

At first, he wondered if she'd heard him at all. She barely moved, barely blinked. And then she groaned. '*Aiden*.'

'What? What have I said wrong now?' He lifted his hands in a combination of surrender and exasperation.

'*Everything*.' She crossed her arms defiantly. 'You can't say something like that to me.'

'Why? It's true.' And she made him want to be truthful, even if it made him vulnerable. He wanted her to see that he wasn't just the cocky *twatface* he'd been in school, or the arsehole who was only good for sex. If that meant he was breaking their rules, so be it. But if she was going to hate him, she would have to hate all of him, and that meant knowing all of him first.

'Yeah, but you're not supposed to make me want to like you.'

His wide grin made his cheeks ache. 'So you *are* warming to me. Interesting. Very interesting.'

'I never said that.' She shook her head, moving to the next display: a set of animal head brooches from the Viking age.

'Sounded like that's what you said.' He rocked into her playfully, glad when he received a smile. A real one, unbridled and without any animosity.

'Wishful thinking again. You're just full of it, aren't you?'

Before he could retort, he heard his name uttered behind him. When he turned, dread shrouded him from all sides. The woman approaching in a neat black shirt and pencil skirt was familiar, though he hadn't thought of her for a long time.

'Well, what a pleasant surprise to see you here!' Sonya said with a bright, red-lipped smile. 'Is this a friend of yours? Girlfriend?'

'Just friend,' Juniper blurted at the same time Aiden introduced her stiffly: 'Juniper.' He was so dazed that he hadn't even thought to correct Sonya. Hadn't thought anything of the word at all. 'Good to see you, Sonya.'

'Are you enjoying the exhibition?' She huddled between the two of them as though just another visitor rather than one of the most talented curators in the museum.

Juniper clearly had no idea who she was, shuffling for some space with her lips pressed into a flat line.

'It's wonderful. Juniper is very passionate about mythology, so we couldn't miss it.' He didn't know where he was plucking the words from, body and mind stuck on autopilot. He had to be the old Aiden now, the impressive one who had plenty to say.

'That's great!' Sonya clasped her manicured hands in front of her. 'And how is your father doing at the moment? Well, I hope.'

'I believe so, yeah.' Aiden tensed, suffocated again. Everyone spoke as though he only had a right to be here because of his father. Like, without him, he served no purpose.

Everyone except Juniper.

'Good. We must admit, we were disappointed when you turned down the internship with us.' Sonya rubbed his shoulder gently. 'Will you be applying again this year? The deadline is soon!'

Ice pooled into his veins when he saw Juniper's reaction to her words: disbelief, quickly dissolving into disgust. He'd hoped she wouldn't bring it up, but of course he couldn't be so lucky. Of course his past was still there, waiting with jaws as sharp as the hellhound framed in front of him.

'Not this year,' he answered as politely as he could manage – which wasn't very polite at all, but Sonya didn't seem to notice.

'That's a shame. Just have your father give me a call if you change your mind.' She patted him once more, and then swayed elegantly from the room with a high-pitched click of her heels.

Juniper's silence was deafening. He dragged a hand through his knotted hair, finding them shaky again.

'She works here?' she asked, her voice dangerously low.

'Yes. She's a curator.'

Her nostrils flared. 'And you just… turned down an internship? For the British fucking Museum?'

'It was around the same time I dropped out of Elmington,' he explained, and then realised that it probably didn't sound any better. She couldn't understand, not really. To her, these differences between them were a rift they'd never be able to breach. He was certain a part of her liked that: that, if she could find no other excuse to hate him, there was this to fall back on.

Little did she know he hated himself for the same reasons.

'So you really just decided to throw every opportunity away, then,' she snarled. He looked around, glad to find the crowd thinning as closing time approached. 'It must be nice, to have the power to turn your nose up at chances like that, knowing another one will always come along.'

'It wasn't like that, Juni.'

'Then what was it like?' Her voice rose. 'Do you know how lucky you are to have these things handed to you on a plate?'

He squeezed his eyes closed. She sounded just like his dad. Just like everything he'd come here to avoid. 'Yes, I know.'

'God, I'll never understand you,' she whispered then. He could barely look at her, barely look at anything. 'I'm going to find Tilly. I'm ready to go home.'

'No, don't,' he pleaded, but she was already skirting around the ceramics displays to leave. Panic gripped him, and for a moment, he couldn't move at all. What was the point? He couldn't tell her the truth.

Could he?

It took him about five seconds to decide that he at least wanted to try. That, if nothing else, it would save their project. He'd worked hard to soften her, to get her to trust him, and he couldn't bear to go back to the way it had been before.

He hadn't minded her hating him so much then, but now he knew what it meant to taste her, feel her, be inside of her, tear down her defences. He knew how she sounded when she was on the verge of climax, knew how her voice was so much lighter, quieter, when she felt safe.

He raced to catch up, dragging her away from visitors' prying eyes with a hand around her arm. She soon fought him, slapping him away. 'Stop. Just leave me alone, Aiden, for once.'

'I wasn't well last year!' he blurted. He'd never said it out loud, never wanted to, but he'd do anything to stop her from looking at him like that. Like she had that first day of class. Like he wasn't worth anything to her, and she'd be glad if she never saw him again.

Behind him, an entryway was bathed in darkness. He used her surprise to his advantage, guiding her inside with his confession still hanging over their heads. The room held seats and a projector screen for visitors to view videos and documentaries, but the footage had clearly ended, because now all that flashed inside the frame were oil paintings along with soft piano music and the museum's logo floating from edge to edge.

When she said nothing, he forced himself to continue. 'I struggled at Elmington. I nearly failed the entire course.'

'Why?' Juniper interrogated.

'Because...' He trailed off, unable to say the truth even now. *Because I had a breakdown.*

With the exception of his doctor, nobody knew about it. His dad still thought he was a pathetic, uncommitted dropout who took his support for granted. A spoilt kid who hadn't lived up to his name. 'I just did, okay? Like I said, I wasn't well.'

It sounded weak even to him, but Juniper must have seen something else entirely, because she edged towards him with just a little less scorn. He wasn't sure who initiated it, but suddenly, their fingers were intertwining in the strip of light between them.

He stroked her knuckle with his thumb, a show of his appreciation. He'd never needed her touch quite as much as here, now. 'You always think the worst of me, don't you?'

She shrugged. 'Old habits.'

'I'm sure you'll hate to hear me say it, but I'm glad I dropped out. Glad I didn't take the internship. I never would have ended up at RACA, otherwise. Never would have ended up here with you.'

'Shut up.' Juniper scoffed, but it lacked her usual commitment. He'd gotten through to her, at least in part. He was learning that her defences weren't made of steel, but something more pliable, something that could be bent with the right amount of pressure. Something he would break down, eventually.

He decided to make a start now, leaning close. 'Make me.'

A fire ignited in her eyes, and she stood on her tiptoes, noses grazing first, then lips. He fought a gasp when she took his bottom lip between her teeth, the sharp twinge shooting straight down to his belly. 'I've been trying, but there's only one thing that seems to work.'

'And what might that be?' Aiden's voice trembled with anticipation, his erection pressing against her.

He was rewarded with Juniper's palm against his cock, caressing in agonisingly light strokes. 'I'm sure you know.'

He should have pulled away then, wary that anybody could walk in and find them, but the idea of sneaking around only excited him more. He wanted her so badly that the rest of the world didn't matter.

Her cold hands crept under the hem of his jumper, following the lines of his stomach up to his chest. When her thumb circled his nipple, he couldn't help but groan. He'd never been so loud with a woman before, never needed to, but she conjured all sorts of noises and sensations from him. She could unravel him with just a touch if she wanted.

And she grinned like she knew it as she unzipped his jeans, releasing his length from his boxers and swirling her thumb across his pink tip. With him speechless, she pushed him down to the nearest chair and lowered to her knees in a way that made his own buckle.

'I've never given someone a blow job before,' she admitted.

'You don't have to. You don't have to do anything you don't want to.' He drew circles over her arm, pretending he could be patient, controlled, even when her mouth was inches from his cock.

But it was in her nature to challenge him, so she did that now, tracing the inner seam of his thighs. Fuck, she was gorgeous, eyes big and bright and locked on his, framed by dark, fluttering lashes. Her lips were parted for him. Ready.

She took his cock in her hand and swiped her tongue across the head slowly. Aiden arched into her with a gasp. She felt better than his hands ever could. Than anyone ever could. The tears in his fabric stitched themselves up just slightly, the weight of his anxiety easing. He was himself again. 'Fuck, Juni. I needed this. You have no idea how much I needed it.'

His words only spurred her, and she welcomed more of him into her mouth. He couldn't keep from twirling her braid around his wrist, though he was intent to remain gentle with her. He'd meant what he said. He wanted her to be in control, just as she'd let him be in the workshop.

Nothing had ever felt so all-consuming as when he filled her mouth completely, hitting the back of her throat.

'You're doing so good, sweetheart.' With pleasure pulsating through every inch of him, it was an effort not to lose himself all over again. But he refused, not wanting to miss a moment of this: not a suckle, not a blink. She was too beautiful to look away from, and though she'd started wary, her pretty mouth seemed to know exactly what it was doing.

As she began to bob up and down his length, tongue lapping so that there wasn't a part of him left untouched, he couldn't keep his hips from rolling in time. It only seemed to turn her on more, her moan vibrating through him as she began to buck against thin air.

'Touch yourself, Juni,' he pleaded. 'Want you to feel good, too.'

She did, fingers disappearing into her leggings to play with her pussy, and fuck, he wasn't going to last. Not when her cheeks hollowed out and he slid further down her throat. His orgasm approached in a shuddering, dizzying tidal wave. 'Like that. Just like that.'

It felt like torture when she stopped, leaving him teetering on the brink of something earth-shattering. Her lips glistened as she said, 'Thought this was supposed to shut you up.'

His laugh was raw, fragmented. 'Can't when it feels this good.'

'You don't have to be gentle with me, Aiden. I'm not gentle with you.'

Exhilaration rushed through him, fist tightening around her plait. As she parted for him again, he rutted into her perfect mouth until he could no longer remember where he was. In the far, far distance, an announcement drifting over

at she was paying any notice, clearly, since she'd just given
m a blow job in a public place instead of ditching him like
e'd intended.

Instead of paying notice to her worry, he tugged her
wards another exhibition room by the hand. 'Let's make
e most of it. There's a gallery full of Chinese ceramics I
ink you'll love.'

'Aiden.' Juniper looked around hesitantly, but she didn't
ave time to voice her worries. He shushed her, pulling her
ehind the nearest pillar as the sound of clicking heels rico-
heted over marble floors. It was the curator from before who
ad asked Aiden about his internship, heading out of the
ythology exhibition room and down the steps. She didn't
iss the way Aiden's body stiffened against her, the way his
m curled tighter around her waist.

It took her too long to wonder why they were hiding
om one of the only people who might be able to let them
ut. 'We can't just stay here.' And yet she whispered it anyway,
nly pulling away so she could face him.

As tempting as the idea of sneaking around was, what if
ey got in trouble? Or worse, what if they remained locked
until morning? If she wasn't in her pyjamas in approximately
hour's time, she would cry. It had been another long day,
d the grime of her work shift still clung to her.

'C'mon, Juni. This is something we would have dreamed
in high school, isn't it?'

He was right, and she hated that he knew it. As a kid, she'd
ways imagined having a sleepover in a place like this, the

the speaker system, but the words were jumbled, rendered
meaningless in the wake of her.

'You're taking me so well, sweetheart.' Sweat beaded from
her hairline as she thrust both against him and herself, and
when her lids closed, so did his. 'I'm close. I'm so close. Fuck,
Juni. Stop before I—'

'I want you to,' she rasped. Her cheeks were flushed and
the sight of her finger circling her clit was sending him to
the edge faster and faster.

She let him sink back into her, and it only took a few
more heavy swirls of her tongue before he was spilling into
her mouth with lazy, desperate thrusts. His entire body
hummed with the pleasure of it, intensified when Juniper
came against her fingers with a cry.

Only when he'd ridden out every last bit of his climax did
she pull away, seed spilling down her chin. She swallowed,
dragging another awed curse from him as her plait slipped
through his fingers. He wanted to kiss her again, but he'd
tried that the last time and she'd been quick to walk away. It
was as though she only wanted him – or *wanted* to want him
– when they were fucking. As soon as it was over, she was
back to convincing the both of them that she hated him.

She didn't touch him like she hated him, though.

He readjusted himself and zipped up his jeans. When he
reached out his hand to help Juni off the floor, she took it.
Naively, he wondered if maybe this time was different. Now
that he'd shown her more of himself, couldn't she do the same?

Since wishful thinking was clearly in his nature, he dragged
her close, pulling her onto his lap. Their breaths were ragged

and hot as he cupped the back of her neck. 'Can I taste myself on you?'

She nodded, so he kissed her, salt and musk leaving him wishing they could have more time together. That these encounters wouldn't always end with her leaving.

19

'Where is everyone?' Juniper wondered as they st__ into the museum hall.

Where people had been passing between exhibiti__ the walkways and staircases before, it was now __ empty save for them. Her first feeling was panic__ Tilly with Owen alone, and she wouldn't be happ__ out her phone, which didn't make her feel any __ time said 8.25pm. Twenty-five minutes after closi__

She showed her screen to Aiden, aghast at h__ time had slipped away in the viewing room.

Instead of mirroring her worry, he snickered, only served to annoy her. She nudged him rough__ funny! We might be locked in!'

'Locked in a museum? Oh, no. How t__ deadpanned.

'Haven't you ever watched *Night at the M*__ planted her hands on her hips. 'I don't want to g__ a T-rex!'

His frown told her he clearly *hadn't* watched __ which was just another red flag on his long list o__ the speaker system, but the words were jumbled, rendered meaningless in the wake of her.

'You're taking me so well, sweetheart.' Sweat beaded from her hairline as she thrust both against him and herself, and when her lids closed, so did his. 'I'm close. I'm so close. Fuck, Juni. Stop before I—'

'I want you to,' she rasped. Her cheeks were flushed and the sight of her finger circling her clit was sending him to the edge faster and faster.

She let him sink back into her, and it only took a few more heavy swirls of her tongue before he was spilling into her mouth with lazy, desperate thrusts. His entire body hummed with the pleasure of it, intensified when Juniper came against her fingers with a cry.

Only when he'd ridden out every last bit of his climax did she pull away, seed spilling down her chin. She swallowed, dragging another awed curse from him as her plait slipped through his fingers. He wanted to kiss her again, but he'd tried that the last time and she'd been quick to walk away. It was as though she only wanted him – or *wanted* to want him – when they were fucking. As soon as it was over, she was back to convincing the both of them that she hated him.

She didn't touch him like she hated him, though.

He readjusted himself and zipped up his jeans. When he reached out his hand to help Juni off the floor, she took it. Naively, he wondered if maybe this time was different. Now that he'd shown her more of himself, couldn't she do the same?

Since wishful thinking was clearly in his nature, he dragged her close, pulling her onto his lap. Their breaths were ragged and hot as he cupped the back of her neck. 'Can I taste myself on you?'

She nodded, so he kissed her, salt and musk leaving him wishing they could have more time together. That these encounters wouldn't always end with her leaving.

19

'Where is everyone?' Juniper wondered as they stepped back into the museum hall.

Where people had been passing between exhibitions around the walkways and staircases before, it was now completely empty save for them. Her first feeling was panic: she'd left Tilly with Owen alone, and she wouldn't be happy. She took out her phone, which didn't make her feel any better. The time said 8.25pm. Twenty-five minutes after closing time.

She showed her screen to Aiden, aghast at how quickly time had slipped away in the viewing room.

Instead of mirroring her worry, he snickered, a fact that only served to annoy her. She nudged him roughly. 'This isn't funny! We might be locked in!'

'Locked in a museum? Oh, no. How terrible,' he deadpanned.

'Haven't you ever watched *Night at the Museum*?' She planted her hands on her hips. 'I don't want to get eaten by a T-rex!'

His frown told her he clearly *hadn't* watched the movie, which was just another red flag on his long list of them. Not that she was paying any notice, clearly, since she'd just given him a blow job in a public place instead of ditching him like she'd intended.

Instead of paying notice to her worry, he tugged her towards another exhibition room by the hand. 'Let's make the most of it. There's a gallery full of Chinese ceramics I think you'll love.'

'Aiden.' Juniper looked around hesitantly, but she didn't have time to voice her worries. He shushed her, pulling her behind the nearest pillar as the sound of clicking heels ricocheted over marble floors. It was the curator from before who had asked Aiden about his internship, heading out of the mythology exhibition room and down the steps. She didn't miss the way Aiden's body stiffened against her, the way his arm curled tighter around her waist.

It took her too long to wonder why they were hiding from one of the only people who might be able to let them out. 'We can't just stay here.' And yet she whispered it anyway, only pulling away so she could face him.

As tempting as the idea of sneaking around was, what if they got in trouble? Or worse, what if they remained locked in until morning? If she wasn't in her pyjamas in approximately an hour's time, she would cry. It had been another long day, and the grime of her work shift still clung to her.

'C'mon, Juni. This is something we would have dreamed of in high school, isn't it?'

He was right, and she hated that he knew it. As a kid, she'd always imagined having a sleepover in a place like this, the thickness of history wrapped around her in the eerie darkness. There was magic to be alone in a place that usually brimmed with people.

Or almost alone. The curator wasn't the only one still around. Below, two security guards conversed as they prepared to head home, and she heard the scuffle of more footsteps nearby. They could so easily get caught.

Then again, they could have gotten caught in the viewing room, too.

Her stomach swooped, the glittering mischief in Aiden's eyes difficult to say no to.

'Just for a little while.' He tugged her again. This time, she let him.

They ducked, creeping all the way to the other side of the museum with his hand in hers: a silent promise they'd be fine. She was starting to believe it. A thrill shot through her when he put his fingers to his lips again, and they listened as steps came and went not too far away. When it was safe, they dashed the last few inches towards the ceramics gallery, Juniper's heart racing – and then stopping altogether when they made it inside.

The displays were enchanting, and her fears fell away as soon as she soaked in the porcelain vessels hidden behind glass cases. She was awed by the intricacy of the patterns, finding each piece had been shaped different from the last. Everything from vases sculpted in 200AD to plates made this century were on display. She even found some mythological beings hand-painted on a set of china: dragons, phoenixes, foxes that could change shape.

'I can't imagine being talented enough to create something this good,' Juniper confessed. 'And they didn't even have the same tools we do. Can you imagine?'

She hadn't even realised that her hand was still in Aiden's, not until the pad of his thumb smoothed over the back of her hand lightly.

'They're fascinating,' he agreed. 'Makes me feel a bit silly about not knowing what to make in class. There are so many options I hadn't considered, so many vessels I didn't even know about.'

She stepped closer to him, for once, the ground even between them. If she could stay here, she would never feel lost with her clay again. And never lost with herself, either, because his presence kept her upright, steady.

A wave of emotion rolled over her: this was why she'd come here. To feel her love of art thrumming through her veins, and to educate herself so that, one day, she could create something just as beautiful.

With the world so quiet, she could finally focus on that. She often didn't even realise just how loud everything was until it stopped, but she'd been fighting through crowds at the exhibit earlier. Taking deep breaths when handbags dug into her side or families started discussing dinner plans too loudly. Aiden had been her escape, and she had a feeling she was his. Whatever he'd meant by not being well at Elmington last year seemed to haunt him beyond recognition, and all she'd wanted was to bring him back to the present.

She shouldn't have cared. She didn't want to. But her body had a mind of its own, and it was tied to his somehow. She would have to stop it, eventually, but Aiden was one of the only good things she'd stumbled across here. Whether she liked it or not, he'd made her a better potter, and their evolving project was proof.

Next term, she promised herself. She'd start fresh next term. Put some distance between them, focus on her studies.

'What's happening in that pretty, terrifying head of yours?' he asked, breaking the silence. 'I don't like it when you're quiet. I'm worried you're plotting my murder.'

She gave a small smile, shifting to view the next display. 'Nah. Too much work. I was just thinking about our project,' she lied.

'I think we're going to make something really fucking great, Hodge. You and me, we're good at that. Even if you hate to admit it.'

'Yeah.' She wasn't worried about the project in the slightest anymore. They'd found a way to mesh their interests together, and Aiden hadn't once made fun of her more outlandish ideas, even when his were much more traditional. A reflection of his upbringing. What she was worried about was her time-keeping skills. Her concentration. Balancing her studies with working. Mastering the throwing wheel. She always fell short on something, and maybe she was just waiting for him to realise that.

'Why did it bother you that Owen brought up your dad?' she blurted suddenly.

He paused, his grip on her hand loosening. Like in the viewing room, storm clouds rolled across his features. 'I hoped you hadn't noticed that.'

There was an unrest beneath his smooth surface that she couldn't quite read, and she didn't like it. Didn't like that, all along, she might have been wrong about him.

'I notice everything.' It was an attempt at a joke, but it didn't make him laugh.

He frowned at a plate marked in royal blues as though the porcelain had personally offended him. 'I just don't like to talk about my dad.'

'You don't get on?'

He shook his head. 'Not these days.'

'Why?'

'Y'know, you're the only person who doesn't give a shit about it.' He shoved his hands in pockets, the distance between them leaving her cold. 'Could we keep it that way?'

She shrugged, though really she was curious. Was Jonathan Whittaker not quite as wonderful as everyone thought? *Shocker*.

'If that's what you want.' She went back to focusing on the display, ignoring the gnaw of concern still lingering. 'You know, I think the penis I made on the throwing wheel would have been much more appreciated in Jingdezhen around 1506 AD. Some of these pieces are quite phallic.'

Aiden's laughter reverberated through the gallery, bouncing off the walls before landing somewhere deep in her core. She covered his mouth quickly, too aware that they might be found any moment. Her toes curled in her boots as she remembered how, not all that long ago, she'd elicited much different sounds from his throat. Both were aggravatingly sexy, but somehow, she almost preferred this. A near-empty museum, the clash of their present with the past. The two of them, alone, like they were the only ones left in the world.

He pulled her close as she lowered her hands, lips brushing the space between her brows as he whispered, 'Juniper Hodgson, you are something else.'

She made to kiss him, tracing the seam of his lips with her tongue only for a loud shout to cleave them apart. 'Oi! What are you two still doing here?'

They whipped around to find a uniformed security guard at the entrance, his middle-aged face wrinkled with distaste.

Aiden scratched the crown of his head. 'Oh, has the museum closed already? I wondered why it was so quiet.'

Clearly, the guard found no humour in it, jabbing a thumb across his shoulder. 'This is no place to frolic, you dirty pair. Get out. Now!'

They were escorted all the way out by the stern guard, the front entrance unlocked just for them. When they made it outside onto the stone steps, Juniper burst into laughter. Aiden braced her by the elbows as he cracked up, too.

'Is something funny?' someone said behind them.

Tilly stood on the path below, cars whizzing behind her. Her lips were pursed, expression stony.

'Oh, god. Tilly…'

'I don't even want to know what you two have been doing.'

Aiden winced. 'Time, er, got away from us. So much to see in there…'

'Uh-huh. You were supposed to be my Owen buffer!' she accused, dragging Juniper away from Aiden with a surprising amount of strength. 'You two are officially the worst, but I'll forgive you if you buy me pizza on the way home.'

Juniper linked arms with her and motioned for Aiden to follow. 'It's a deal.'

20

The next few weeks passed in a blur. Juniper felt as though she was dragging herself around, just trying to get through the day: work, class, repeat. The only escape was her project with Aiden. When they were in the workshop together, she could finally focus, sometimes so much so that they barely spoke as they sculpted and, later, painted together. He seemed not to mind, although she felt often his eyes on her, as though watching her work was the most interesting thing in the world to him.

She felt the same. Their stolen moments were the only time she felt alive, and she worried something was extremely wrong with that. She *loved* ceramics. She loved art. She even loved learning. But the rest of it wasn't nearly as wonderful as she'd imagined in her head. Theory essays and textbook pages seemed more difficult to wrap her head around than ever, if her brain would let her sit for long enough to engage with them before either getting preoccupied with something else or falling asleep from exhaustion. But with him, she had room to breathe. When she made a mistake with the clay, he was there to help her fix it, gentle words and touches pulling her out of her meltdowns just in time. A crack in the kiln wasn't the end of the world anymore, and he replied to her three a.m. panic texts almost immediately. She'd been completely, devastatingly wrong, thinking he would ruin her chances of a decent grade. If anything, he'd be the reason she passed at all.

Now, she sat in front of her cloth-covered exhibit, wondering if what lay beneath the cream fabric was enough to pass this first semester. It was their final day before Christmas break, and her fingers were pink and numb from the bitter cold outside. The exhibition centre teemed with nervous energy as her classmates prepared their own displays and presentations before Chris and guests arrive. Tilly and Owen were straightening out a sculpture of a train carriage, whose surface had been etched with fine lines to look like stitches knitted from yarn. Luc and Amir had a gorgeous set of home décor that merged the picturesque skyline of Paris with the mesmerising silhouette of Peshawar. It seemed as though everyone had managed to come together to make brilliant things.

Had she and Aiden? She'd thought so when they'd put the finishing touches on their work last night, smoothing the clay until Aiden had forced her away, but now, it was easy to doubt herself.

A takeaway cup of coffee was thrust in her face before she could quadruple-check that there were no cracks in their work, and while the roasted beans smelled even more delicious than the ones at Caffè Verde, she shoved it away. 'No thanks. I already need a nervous wee, and I can't guarantee I won't spew all over that ugly shirt you're wearing.'

Aiden looked down at the loud, clashing abstract prints of his shirt, mouth agape.

All right, it wasn't that ugly, but only because he was in it. She wouldn't say that, though. They may have been sleeping together for several weeks now, but she was still trying to keep this strictly non-romantic. At least when they weren't having sex.

'I was going for an artsy vibe!' He set the spare coffee down on the edge of a display platform and then sipped his own. She snatched the cup before it spilled all over their work.

'Because otherwise, how could anybody possible know that you're an artist?' she quipped.

'You and your monochromes are just jealous.' He sniffed, then took a step back to admire their hidden display. 'Why are you nervous, anyway? We've got this in the bag.'

She could only stare at him for a moment before pondering aloud, 'What must it be like to have enough talent and admirers to not doubt yourself constantly?'

'Quite nice, actually.' When she glowered, he smirked and pulled her closer, his warmth curling around her side. She was getting far too used to it, no longer questioning his show of affection in front of other people. 'C'mon, Juni. You're the most talented artist I know. It isn't about me being confident in myself. It's confidence in *us*. I've never been so proud of a piece as I am of ours. It's better than anything I could have done alone.'

She wasn't sure she could believe him, not when so much of her first-year grade relied on doing well today, but her stomach fluttered all the same. She was glad, in the end, that she'd been paired with him. If she was with someone else, someone she didn't gel with or understand, she probably *would* have thrown up by now. Or dropped out altogether. Tilly had had heaps of trouble trying to get Owen to listen to her ideas, and she'd heard a few of the others squabbling in a way that would put her and Aiden to shame.

'I'm going to stumble over my words in the presentation,' she warned. 'And then I'm going to swear. And then I'm going to cry.'

Aiden twirled her around, smoothing the frown from her forehead with the delicate pad of his thumb. It was smudged with colour: though he never showed her what he was working on, she'd seen him painting in his sketchbook a lot recently. Sometimes, he even stayed at Caffè Verde during her shift, watching the world pass outside the window from the corner booth. She wouldn't admit it, but his presence had helped. Her mistakes were happening less, though still often enough that Gianna scolded her at least once or twice a week, if not a day.

It was hard, sometimes, to see him experiencing the university life she'd hoped for. Getting spare time to create just for him, having room to breathe, his own home to return to every night. She still hadn't dared go there, afraid that seeing his lavish terraced flat would bring the resentment, which was burrowing down inside her, back to the surface.

'Juniper,' he said softly. He only ever used her full name when he really wanted her to listen, not that it ever worked. 'I've got your back, okay? If you stumble, I'll catch you.'

Something caught in her chest, a rusty latch on a door she thought she'd locked. She couldn't remember anybody ever saying that to her, ever telling her that they were here for her if she messed up — which she would. She always did.

It made her feel more vulnerable than taking her clothes off in front of him. She wasn't supposed to need help. She was independent, prepared to fight the doubts and the mistakes herself, because that made her strong. People could fault her less if they thought she was strong. The last thing she needed was to get too accustomed to having him near. Come tonight, their partnership would be over, and she had to be prepared for going it alone next term.

'You're right,' she said, trying to sound a little more confident than she felt, if only to let him know that she didn't need him to catch her. She could catch herself, thank you very much. Probably. 'It'll be fine. It's always fine.'

'Are your parents coming to see?'

'Nope.' She fidgeted with her necklace — a bright blue and gold crescent moon she'd made. She'd been preparing for that question, though not from him. Since the night in the museum, she'd learned to avoid any talk of parents, a fact that suited her just fine, since hers were still waiting for her to either drop out or get thrown out. Most of her other classmates had someone coming, whether it was family or friends. Tilly's sister had flown in from Dublin to see it before they both went back to Ireland for Christmas.

Juniper hadn't bothered to ask Mum, knowing she wouldn't be able to take the time off work even if she wanted to. Besides, if she was going to fail, she didn't need witnesses.

'How come? They must be proud of you. It's not every day your daughter has a hand in creating an exhibit, is it?'

She shrugged. 'I'll send them pictures. What about *you*? Shall I expect to be pestered by more than one Whittaker today?'

Aiden dipped his head behind his coffee, not quite masking his grimace well enough. 'No, you're safe today. I wouldn't be cruel enough to subject you to dear old Dad.'

'But he must be proud of you.' She mimicked his words, finding herself curious about what had happened between them. From what she'd seen, Jonathan had given Aiden everything. Money, talent, knowledge, status. She'd witnessed his slimy need for those things firsthand, had seen what he was capable of to ensure Aiden got everything he wanted. The memory still made her nauseous, and she'd spent plenty of time looking for signs of that cunning in Aiden, afraid he might take something far worse from her this time – to no avail. Maybe he truly had no idea what had happened that day at Elmington. How he'd got his place on the course. If that were so, she wouldn't be the one to tell him.

He scoffed. 'Yeah, no. Dad doesn't do proud.'

'Guess we do have something in common,' muttered Juniper.

She'd never been more grateful for Chris's entrance than now, his claps echoing through the gallery as he called for attention. Behind him, a crowd of frostbitten, winter hat-clad visitors was gathering outside the windows.

She jigged around, stomach cramping with nerves as Chris talked them through the morning. Her heart beat fast in her ears as she thought about just how much this display meant to her. It was her first real chance to prove that she deserved to be here just like everybody else. That her rocky start didn't define her. That she was capable of the same things everyone else was and her mum had been wrong to suggest otherwise.

'Breathe, Hodge.' Aiden's hand slipped into hers. 'You're okay.'

'Well, look at that. You've cured me,' she snapped. Still, she inhaled deeply and found it slowed the torrent of fears pelting her mind.

He chuckled as he always did, seeming to enjoy her even when she was at her worst. It was that more than anything he said that left her sinking into his warmth, even if made her feel just a tad weaker.

She wouldn't need him soon enough – so she told herself. She just had to get this over with, and then they would go back to being almost strangers.

Somehow, the thought didn't feel like much of a comfort.

21

Cruelly, Chris had saved Aiden and Juniper till second-to-last, which meant Aiden had spent the last two hours trying to find ways to calm Juniper while they watched other pairs show off their research and exhibits. It annoyed him more than it should have that he'd been unsuccessful. Why was she so hard to get through to? Why didn't she believe in them the way he did?

Now, he put a hand on the small of her back as they headed towards their display, still hidden beneath the cloth. Juniper tripped seemingly on nothing, and he steadied her before she ended up on the floor.

'Dear me. Haven't been drinking, have you, Jupiter?' Chris commented.

A few of the visitors laughed. *Not bloody helping.*

Aiden knew part of his unease was because he'd never seen Juniper so unlike herself, lacking the witty, unfiltered spark that usually oozed from her. He always wanted to take care of her, even when she was ruthless with her insults, but now especially, he didn't know what to do. He wasn't him if she wasn't her. They worked because they were opposite poles of the same magnet, and this was a side he was unfamiliar with.

'Okay, North Force. Tell us about your project,' said Chris, and then turned to the rest of the class with a smug grin. 'Because they're from the north, get it? I just made that up. How good is that?'

Aiden cleared his throat, getting his cue cards ready, but Chris lifted a hand to pause them. 'You start, Jupiter, if you will.'

Juniper blinked like a deer in headlights, her face a sickly shade of white. She took her time in glancing at her cue cards.

'Well, we've chosen to combine my love of mythology with Aiden's love of classical art.' Her words quivered, but she lifted her chin, and finally, he saw a glimpse of her usual stoicism. 'My interest is in mythological creatures, those supposedly considered monsters, and how, looking closer, it becomes clear that they're only defined from the hero's perspective. That, maybe, we wouldn't consider them monsters if the hero didn't.'

'How so?' Chris asked, looking genuinely intrigued now.

'Monsters are often solitary. Reactive, just like all of us. In the same way a hero chases a quest, the monsters of ancient myths are usually seeking an answer to their problems after a period of suffering. Either that, or they've been pushed to the edge of society, left to fend for themselves without the same community most people rely on. It's rare they display inherent evilness.' She looked to Aiden for reassurance, and he nodded, urging her to continue. 'Medusa is widely known to be the gorgon who turns people to stone, the one who Perseus 'bravely' beheads… but who decided she was a monster? The original stories don't focus on her origin, not at least until Ovid's version, and there's no proof that she hurt anybody prior to the tale. Therefore, we can assume that it was her nature alone that people rejected, something she had no control over. In Norse mythology, the Midgard Serpent was cast out of Asgard by Odin because of a prophecy that determined he and his siblings would cause problems for the gods. He was thrown into the ocean before he did anything wrong. Is it any wonder he became an enemy?'

Juniper took a breath, confidence tugging her posture a little taller. 'My pieces explore how monsters aren't born, but rather created by society, and how this also reflects in traditional art. With the aid of Aiden's classical art knowledge, we combine both ancient and modern ceramic techniques with painting styles, all of which were inspired by researching a range of art periods, to focus on representations of 'the Other' across history and how, in other people's stories, we could all be represented as monsters given the chance.'

Chris's brows rose over the frames of his glasses. Aiden didn't want to jinx it, but he seemed impressed, as did the others. As was he. He could have listened to Juniper talk all day about mythology, her intellect and passion radiating through every single word and expression. In fact, he was so busy admiring her that he barely noticed when the room fell silent.

'Are we boring you, Alex?' Chris asked, clicking his fingers to get Aiden's attention.

'Sorry.' Aiden shook his head and tried to pick up where Juniper had left off, which wasn't easy when he heard Luc say, 'He's whipped,' under their breath.

Beside Luc, Tilly muttered, 'Tell me about it.'

After a glare in their direction, Aiden went on to describe how he had studied paintings that represented mythological stories and reframed them to better reflect the truth behind the creatures involved, focusing on their perspective rather than those of the heroes. He passed the baton back to Juniper. During the lengthy explanation of their research, Juni did end up stumbling, but he meant what he'd said. He was there to catch her, help her get back on track.

Finally, it was time to reveal their exhibit. Chris orchestrated a drum roll, and Juniper and Aiden took either end of the cloth to unveil their project. Her lips were red from chewing them, fingers trembling. She still didn't know just how talented she was, but that was about to change.

A few sounds of wonderment echoed around the gallery as, finally, their pottery was revealed. Aiden was just as pleased every time he looked at it: they'd focused on common Greek vessels that Aiden had thrown on the wheel, though most of them jutted out with three-dimensional creatures built by Juni. His favourite was the amphora, with Medusa's snakes curling around the handles and her stony eyes closed to evoke the peace she'd never been given in traditional stories. It was his largest project to date and had left his arms aching for days, but he'd managed to throw the perfect the shape with her help. On a marriage vase, Aiden had painted a scene inspired by *The Great Wave*, only a Kraken emerged from the water to snake its tentacles around the bulbous bowl. A gold and grey kantharos took the shape of a harpy, the wings sculpted into handles and sinewy bird feet providing a solid base. The Midgard Serpent curled around its own tail instead of swallowing it, granted freedom around a jug that would once have been used to store oil. The three-headed Cerberus snarled out of their smallest piece. Finally, his pride and joy: a wine jug on which he'd painted coppers and rich indigo storm clouds to evoke Ragnarök, being watched from above, from the perspective of the gods, to show their corrupt authority. He'd used Rembrandt's landscapes as inspiration, following the brush strokes wherever they'd taken him to evoke chaos and destruction. It had been the first time in a while where he'd felt expressive in his art, allowed to paint imperfectly: because Juniper had convinced him to.

'Well, aren't these interesting?' Chris stepped forward to peer more closely through his glasses, his hands locked behind his back. 'Talk me through each one.'

They did, together, Aiden crediting Juniper for the gorgeous sculpting and she him for his throwing abilities.

'I must say, the finishes on these pieces are extremely clean.' Chris's stubby finger hovered over the seamless join of the amphora. 'I suppose that's what you get for having an exceptional teacher.'

A few people laughed, Aiden included. Juniper still looked like she was going to pass out.

'Very ambitious. Very ambitious indeed. Some of your technical skills could be improved here and there, but I'm very impressed by your creativity.'

As he jotted some notes and stepped aside for the others to admire the piece, Aiden finally nudging her playfully. 'See? Told you we'd be great.'

'Ambitious isn't a compliment,' she replied. 'It just means we've coloured outside the lines. Or, at least, I have.'

He frowned, half-convinced he'd missed everything Chris had just said. 'What are you talking about? He likes it! Everyone does!'

'Uh, yeah,' Tilly cut in, wrapping her arms around them both. Her height was somewhere in the middle of theirs, which meant she could reach his shoulders in a way Juniper would struggle to do. 'It's fecking epic. Are you kidding?'

'It doesn't fit in with the others,' Juni said. 'Tom and Amir were sniggering as though it was all just one big joke.'

'Take no notice. They don't get it. They're just used to more classical pieces.' Tilly squeezed Juniper's arm.

Aiden had to admit, he might have been laughing with them if he hadn't been the one to make it. There was a divide between artists who studied more classical forms and those who worked outside the box – but it was the latter he always admired more, one of the many reasons why Elmington hadn't challenged him much. There'd been twenty or so Toms in his class, all of them talented but complacent, just like Aiden had been raised to be.

'Fuck them. They don't know anything about decent art.' He was surprised at the anger in his own tone, surprised at how much he wanted to march over there and tell them both where to shove it. They'd upset his—

His what? Not his anything. She'd made that clear. And yet he still grew taut with the instinct to protect her, as though she could ever need his protection.

Since there was still one more presentation left, they fell back into their quiet, but Aiden still buzzed with annoyance. When he heard Amir and Tom tittering away, he parted from Juni and Tilly to join them. Unsurprisingly, they were making fun of Nomi and Tia's presentation now.

'Nice job, mate. Great exhibit,' Tom started, lifting his arm for a high five. Aiden left him hanging, tucking his hands under his armpits.

'Cheers. I heard you two had a lot to say about it.'

Tom and Amir exchanged a wide-eyed look, Amir saying, 'Oh, we were just saying how good it was. Though it could have been better if you were paired with someone who matched your style, I reckon.'

'And what's my style?' He leaned in close, feigning interest, though really, he already knew the answer. Whatever art his father bought.

'Y'know…' Tom's smile was dithering. 'Something a bit more refined.'

'Hm.' Aiden pretended to contemplate that, rocking on his heels in an effort to stay calm. 'Interesting.'

Tom scratched the back of his neck, scrambling for something to say. Meanwhile, Amir was slowly drifting away from them both. Wise choice.

'So, isn't your dad here today? Maybe he can buy our pieces after we get our grades.' A forced laugh. 'Though I heard he usually sticks to paintings, doesn't he?'

'Yeah, he does. *Refined* ones.' Aiden inched closer, and Tom had the sense to look intimidated. 'I'm sure you're used to putting people down, but next time you have something to say about Juniper's work, or mine, how about you come to me?'

Tom paled, scratching at his lobe. 'We didn't mean anything by it, mate. You know I have a lot of respect for you.'

'You have a lot of respect for my father,' Aiden snapped, his chest tightening. He was so sick of this, now more than ever. Like hell was he going to let them upset Juni, too. 'And like him, you think everyone's art should look the same, and that's why you'll end up washed up and disappointed in a few years' time, so you can shove your *refinement* up your arse. We're all here for the same reason. It takes some real insecurity to stand here and mock everybody else's work. Maybe that's something *you* can work on, yeah?'

He didn't give Tom time to reply, sauntering back to his friends.

From the looks on their faces, Tilly wide-eyed and Juniper wary, they'd clearly heard enough.

'Shite, now I kind of get why you fancy him,' Tilly said.

Aiden took it as quite the compliment, all things considered.

Juniper, however, narrowed her eyes. 'I don't need you defending my honour.'

'I wasn't. I was defending mine.' A lie, though it had felt good to finally set a boundary with someone like that. If nothing else, his connection to Juniper and even Tilly and Luc had taught him that he was more than just his father's son, and he deserved to pave his own bloody path.

He turned back to the presentation so that she would stop burning a hole right into his soul, only to be surprised when her pinkie finger scraped his. 'I can think of a lot of other things Tom should shove up his arse. Our Cerberus sculpture, for instance. All those spiky ears and sharp canines…'

He coughed to mask his laugh. 'I'd like to see that.'

He knew that it was her way of saying *thank you*, even if she didn't want to. He relaxed, finally, and so did she, their final exhibit glowing under the spotlight at their side. Fuck Tom, and fuck whatever Juni believed Chris had criticised. They'd made something beautiful, and he wouldn't let anyone take that from them.

22

See? Told you we aced it.

Aiden's text lit up Juniper's dark bedroom — the one she'd grown up in rather than her claustrophobic dorm. While she was home for Christmas, she was making the most of her constellation-patterned duvet and double bed, though the peace was set to end tomorrow when the extended family arrived for Christmas celebrations.

She begrudged moving, but the butterflies in her stomach, which had fluttered every time Aiden had texted her since the exhibit, made the decision for her, so she stretched onto her side to pull her phone from its charging dock. Opening her messages, she found an image accompanied the text.

A screenshot. Of their final grades for the semester.

Juniper shot up, clicking on the picture and zooming in. Her brows lifted at the sight of Aiden's full name at the top of the document.

Aiden James Whittaker? I thought your middle name would be something fancier than that, like Archibald or Herbert.

Jesus, thank god it isn't. I'm named after my granddad, who is actually the least fancy man I know.

She supposed that meant money hadn't been in his family for all that long. Either that, or the word 'fancy' was lost on him because it was something he'd always been.

He must have sensed her distraction, because a second text popped up. Read the bloody grade, Hodge.

She did, and then again when she was sure she'd gotten it wrong. Eighty-four marks. Out of a hundred. They'd bagged a top grade, somehow. Even after Juniper had been sure that Christopher's compliments were actually insults, because 'ambitious' before had always meant enthusiastic to the point of carelessness.

She squealed and opened her laptop, slung under her bed from watching Netflix the night before. In his cage, Cerberus emerged to see what all the fuss was about, his wet pink nose twitching through the bars. It seemed too good to be true, so she logged onto her own RACA account expecting to see a much lower score.

But Chris had given her eighty-four, too, along with some feedback: *Creative, well-thought-out exhibit with strong research and clear collaboration behind it. Technical skills need some polishing, as to be expected in the first term, but otherwise, thoroughly impressed by strength of piece.*

'I've only gone and done it, Cerberus!' she shouted, shutting her laptop to flail her arms around in a happy dance. 'We did it!'

We.

Juniper didn't know what to say, not without letting her growing fondness for Aiden bleed through. After nine weeks of working together, among other things, it was hard to pretend she still saw him as that intolerable rich kid whose success meant her failure. He was talented – talented enough to have earned his place at RACA with more than just money and status. And he was funny, quick to return her witty remarks in a way that broke her resolve with laughter. *And* he'd defended her with Tom. She hadn't wanted him to, needed him to, but he had. It hadn't felt as mortifying as she'd expected, to have someone fighting in her corner. In fact, it had turned her on, and the celebratory drinks afterwards had been spent trying not to crawl onto his lap.

Ugh. All of these feelings made her queasy.

With that in mind, she was only capable of sending a few exclamation points back to him. Maybe she owed him more – after all, he was the reason she'd grown comfortable on the throwing wheel – but she couldn't bring herself to say anything that would hint towards her inner turmoil.

She *couldn't* like him. It wasn't allowed.

I have an early Xmas present for you, came the next text from Aiden.

Juniper held her breath at another screenshot, this time with her favourite band's logo at the top. He'd bought two bloody tickets to see Sleep Token live next summer in London.

She didn't know what to do. What to say. She'd wanted to buy tickets herself, but she didn't have the money, and the arena tour had sold out in minutes. Her trembling thumb hit the call button, and she had no idea whether it was by accident or not. Her brain was too fuzzy and excited and confused.

Aiden picked up immediately. 'Hello, Juni.' She couldn't pretend that she hadn't missed the soft gravel of his voice saying her name. 'Knew I'd get your attention again somehow.'

'You can't get me concert tickets,' she blurted, knotting her fingers into the stars of her duvet until the fabric bunched.

'Well, I can. And I did.' He was so arrogant. And so, so difficult to hate.

'You don't even know if I like Sleep Token!'

A chuckle crackled in her ear. 'Sweetheart, you have their badge on your jacket and their lyrics on your lockscreen.'

She'd forgotten about that. Mostly because she hadn't worn said jacket since the end of summer, and she'd been meaning to change her phone's background.

He'd noticed? *And* remembered? Juniper was terrible at both of those skills, and couldn't comprehend why. Or how. Or… why. 'Are you that desperate to spend time with me that you're buying my affection, now?'

'Yep, you caught me. Though I didn't know you were capable of affection.' She could hear the smirk in his voice, but wished she could see it, too. Then again, she was glad not to be on a video call. Her pillow had fashioned her hair into a bird's nest, and her boobs didn't like to be contained by the vest top she was wearing.

'Why?' she blurted.

'After last term, is it so hard to believe that I like spending time with you? C'mon. You can't be that oblivious.'

She *was* that oblivious. They'd agreed that they were just two students forced to partner up, prone to accidental sex now and then. Sure, that sex was the best Juniper had ever had, and maybe they did have fun together even outside of it, but a part of her had suspected that she'd been more of a convenience for him. He could get anybody he wanted, and they no longer had an excuse to keep at it.

She wiped the sleep from her eyes as she tried to conjure a reply. Her mind was blank, heart doing all the talking with its thuds against her ribs.

'Still with me?' Aiden murmured after long moments of silence.

'Barely,' she admitted. 'I don't know what to say.'

'You could just say, *Thank you, Aiden. I'd love to see my favourite band with you.*'

She could say that, but it felt like admitting defeat. All this time she'd spent fighting her better instincts, fighting her feelings for him, trying to convince herself that their connection meant nothing... If she went back on that, what did it say about her? That her instincts were wrong? That she could push all of her standards and morals aside for a man if he was nice enough to her?

But maybe he's different now, an annoying voice in her head niggled. *Maybe you should let the past go.*

Even so, summer was months away. 'Isn't it a bit presumptuous of you, to plan so far ahead?' It was difficult to imagine him still liking her next week, never mind in six months' time.

'I'm committed to the cause,' he replied without missing a beat. Almost like he'd expected her to say it.

She took a deep breath. This was too much, too fast, and there would always be that siren in the back of her mind warning her not to get so close. He was still his father's son. Still capable of trampling all over her little life like he had two years ago. 'I'll think about it.'

Aiden hummed in amusement. 'Is it my turn to beg?'

The space between her thighs tingled. She imagined him in front of her, fingers roving her bare shoulders the way they always did, like he never got bored of exploring her skin. Maybe she was right. Maybe she should just give in. She couldn't imagine what it might be like to let him in in more ways than just physical. Would he like her, underneath all of the snark and barriers, or would he see her for what she really was: lost, afraid, bitter?

And what about him? Who would he be if she stopped finding all the bad in him? If she saw the good instead? She'd seen glimpses of it: in their project, in the way he respected her, listened to her, when they were together.

'It always was,' she said finally, softly. 'I told you I don't beg.'

'Liar. I've heard plenty of begging from you.'

'I hope you're not trying to initiate phone sex at' – she checked the time on her phone – 'ten o'clock in the morning.'

His laughter echoed down the line, making her smile, too. 'No, but I'm glad that's where your mind went.'

A knock sounded at her door, likely Mum letting her know she was heading out for a shift or groceries. Juniper grabbed her jumper from the corner of the bed and said to Aiden, 'I've got to go.'

'Of course you do.' He sounded as disappointed as she felt, enough that she wondered if he really did like spending time with her. She hadn't taken him seriously when he'd said it before, convinced he'd just wanted to have the freedom to touch her without prying eyes.

It was that that left her to quietly say, 'Thank you, Aiden. For the tickets.'

'Is that a yes, then?'

'It's a maybe.' She smiled into her hand. 'Have a good Christmas, okay?'

A pause. And then: 'You, too, Juni. Call me when you're home.'

The call cut off, but his words still floated in the air around her. *Home.* London wasn't home. For either of them. Yet he'd stayed, claiming that there was no reason for him to head up north for the holidays. Avoiding his dad, still?

At least it put some space between them. Juniper needed it to sort out her messy brain. Make a real decision about whether she'd be willing to give Aiden a fair chance, even if her heart had already tried to do it for her.

Another, louder knock sounded at the door, and she huffed. Juniper yanked her fleecy pyjama jumper on to contain her vest escapees. 'Come in!'

When Mum stepped in, Juniper smiled and re-opened her laptop to show her the news. 'Guess what? We got a high mark for the exhibit project!'

She didn't know what she'd expected. In an ideal world, maybe an apology for not believing in her, or a teary-eyed, *I'm proud of you, love.* Mum offered neither, instead giving a pleased, vague nod. 'Very good. This came in the post for you. Doesn't look very festive.'

She handed over a white envelope Juniper didn't like the look of with her name and address printed on the front. Juniper used her nail to peel the envelope open, groaning at the formal format. It was likely phone bills or...

'*What*?' The logo on the top, with clay letters shaped by illustrated hands, belonged to RACA, but she couldn't put the words together fast enough to add meaning.

Dear Miss Hodgson,

We regret to inform you that your bursary funding is due to be suspended. Due to unforeseen cuts in our college funding, the Royal Academy of Ceramic Arts is no longer able to cover your university fees for the summer term, which begins in April 2026.

Mum peered over her shoulder, the smell of her favourite jasmine laundry detergent clinging to her white knitted turtle-neck jumper. Her thin brows dug into a frown as Juniper reread the first two sentences over and over again.

'I don't understand. What do they mean, my bursary has been suspended?'

Mum took the letter, blue eyes scanning the rest of the text. 'It sounds like they've had some budget cuts and can't afford to keep you on.'

'But they said I'd been awarded it already,' Juniper said, her voice fragile and meek. 'The school year has already started. They can't just take it away...'

'These posh bloody schools can do anything they want, Juniper.' Mum clucked her tongue, setting the letter back in Juniper's lap. 'I told you something like this would happen.

It's never straightforward, especially not if you want to be an artist. They'll exploit you for all you're worth.'

An ache settled in Juniper's throat, eyes blurring as she looked at the letter a final time. They were taking away the only thing that could pay for her final term at RACA. The only thing that had allowed her to study there in the first place. Without it, she would have nothing come April.

'How am I going to pay for the rest of the year?' Juniper whispered.

Mum shook her head. As usual, the sympathy on her face was difficult to find, only visible at all because Juniper knew her inside and out. It was in the creases of her eyes, the thinness of her lips, but it was overshadowed by that neutral indifference. She'd always been hard to reach, and in some ways, Juniper was grateful for it. It meant she was difficult to faze, and if Mum wasn't upset, Juniper didn't need to be either. As a child, she knew something was bad when Mum reacted to it, and that meant rarely anything ever was.

It is what it is. It'll be fine. They were words used to offer comfort, but they felt more like dismissals as Juniper grew older. Now, she wished just once that Mum would be upset. That she would show some kind of empathy so that Juniper didn't feel like she was all on her own.

'Have you saved up much?' Mum asked.

'Not enough for this.' Living in London was even more expensive than Manchester, yet her paycheck barely reflected the difference. She'd have to work for years to earn this sort of money.

'What about a student loan?' Mum tried.

'You can't apply for them midway through the year.' She only received a small maintenance loan because both of her parents were working, as though that had any impact on Juniper's lack of funds. Her tuition fees weren't covered at all because of the bursary.

The bursary she would no longer have.

Hot tears rolled down her cheeks. It was like receiving that rejection letter from Elmington again, only this time, she'd had a taste of what she was losing, and that made it all the more painful. 'What am I going to do?'

Mum stared down at the beige carpet. 'What do you want to do?'

'I want to do what I've been doing! I want to study at RACA!' Her voice rose with an anger that didn't touch Mum.

She only shrugged, tugging at her earlobe. 'Why can't you drop out, try again next year?'

'They're not going to reissue a bursary they can't even afford to a dropout. I'll look like a time waster.' Juniper pressed her palms into her eyes. She couldn't believe it. How could they just take this from her? And why didn't Mum see how much it hurt?

'I don't know what to tell you, Jun. I did warn you this would be hard. You didn't want to hear it.'

Juniper turned away when Mum tried to pat her knee. She needed her to leave, now, so that she could process this without the unhelpful remarks. She was sure Mum thought she was offering sound advice, but she wasn't. She was saying *I told you so*. All that work Juniper had put into proving that she was more than just her burnout, more than her diagnosis, and it had been for nothing. Even if her funding hadn't been pulled, Mum hadn't cared about her high grade. Nothing was good enough. Nothing would ever be good enough.

'Do you want to help me buy a turkey? It's going to be mayhem in Tesco,' Mum said in the quiet.

Juniper choked on a sob. 'No, Mum, I don't want to help you buy a chuffing turkey!'

She wanted help to stay at RACA. She wanted faith that she could find a way to make it work. She wanted, for once, for somebody to take her seriously.

She just wanted one thing to be easy.

23

Aiden didn't have to look up to know when Juniper entered Caffé Verde. The energy in the coffee shop changed immediately, from the clatter by the door to the way his skin felt more settled around his bones. He dragged his eyes from the open page of his sketchbook to see Juniper apologising profusely to the old couple whose chair legs she'd tripped over on her way in.

She didn't see him at first, and he dared not distract her with that beady-eyed boss of hers around. In the end, he didn't need to. Gianna put her hands on her narrow, aproned hips and said, 'Your boyfriend is earlier for your shift than you.'

'I don't have a…' Juniper turned on her heel, then rolled her eyes at the sight of Aiden. Pink radiated from her nostrils, and her eyes were glassy: sick? She was peaky, too, dark circles under her eyes and her lips lacking their usual colour. 'Oh. Him. He's not mine.'

He was, actually. A couple of weeks apart over Christmas had proved that. He'd spent every second of the day wondering what he should text her next, how he could come up with something that would make sure she wouldn't forget about him while she was away. London wasn't quite London without her, and he'd found himself coming here to draw and read, just to feel like he was still a bit close to her.

'Why not? I'd quite like to be yours.' He flashed his teeth as though it was only a joke, though his chest burned with the truth of it. 'Happy New Year, Juni.'

Juniper scoffed and meandered behind the counter to put her apron on. He enjoyed watching the fabric tighten over her hips and wondered when she'd next let him touch her. It was different now. He'd sensed as soon as the exhibit was over that she was trying to put distance between them again, but it was too late. He knew her too well. Knew that her brain was full of creatures and music and colours, and he wanted to learn more about them all.

To avoid getting her in trouble, he went back to sketching, the Christmas lights that hadn't yet been taken down painting his graphite strokes golden. He hadn't fallen into a rhythm like this in months. Years, maybe. Lately, all he wanted was to make art and talk to her, which was probably pathetic for a twenty-year-old man, but… well, he was trying to not care what people thought about him these days.

'You cut your hair.' Her voice dragged him out of his reverie, and he let his fingers slacken around his pencil as he looked up. Juniper fiercely scrubbed at the table with a damp cloth, though he hadn't left any crumbs behind from his late breakfast of a blueberry scone.

He fingered his chopped curls soberly. The longest locks were only a few inches shorter, falling now by his lobes instead of the nape of his neck, so it surprised him that she'd noticed. 'My mum doesn't like when I grow it out. Figured I'd save myself a lecture over Christmas dinner.'

Juniper glanced over her shoulder to make sure her boss wasn't looking, then slunk onto the chair opposite. The café was quiet, the cold January blues staving off their usual customers. 'You have a mum?'

He snorted. 'We all do, Hodge. I think that's how it works.'

She looked as unimpressed as ever by his attempt at humour. 'You haven't mentioned her before. Thought you'd spent Christmas all lonely and Scrooge-ish.'

He shrugged. 'Nah. She travels a lot for work – has done since the divorce – but my aunt and grandma both live here in London, too, so I figured I'd join them this year. Hate to favour the southern side of my family, but they're easier to tolerate. I'm not *quite* an Ebenezer yet.' Although he was close after a few days spent with his family. Mum and Gran had been picking at him all Christmas about his future plans, what career one could actually have with a degree in ceramics, had he called his father recently, et cetera. It was better than being in Manchester with his dad – or, more likely, alone, because Jonathan's work came first and he still wasn't speaking to Aiden, anyway – but still. He'd had more than enough of his family until the next birthday, at least. 'How about you? How was your Christmas?'

'My cousin let Cerberus escape and we found him in my granddad's shoe. My grandma gave a monologue about why she just can't understand pronouns, all while using them seamlessly. My mum still doesn't understand why I'm studying ceramics when I could have a stable job. The usual.' She sniffled; definitely sick, or at least getting there.

'Who's Cerberus? Do you have a hellhound of your own you're not telling me about?'

'Sort of. He's my hamster.'

'Ah. Cute.' He planted his sketchbook on the table and leaned closer. 'My family doesn't get it, either. The ceramics.' But he was surprised that she had the same problems. As far as he knew, her parents didn't come from an art background. They should have been proud of her for breaking the mould.

'Were you waiting here for something, or are you just a fully-fledged stalker now?' Juniper's voice was unusually steely, even for her. He swallowed to think she might genuinely not want him here: not in her playful way that he could tease her about, but in a way that made all of his recent vulnerability sad and humiliating. He was trying to show her that he...

He didn't know, really. That he liked being with her. That she was his favourite thing about RACA. That, just because they weren't partners anymore, didn't mean he wanted all of this to stop.

'Honestly, I didn't think you'd be back so soon.' It was only the second of January; their classes didn't start until Monday. 'I like it here. It's a good place to think.'

'Think about what? Which Burberry coat you want to wear today?'

He tutted, though secretly, the insult stung. Didn't she see more than just his money by now? 'This is Superdry.' He tugged at the fur-lined hood of his parka. 'I'm not that posh. Yet.'

She took the napkin he'd used for his scone to blow her nose, and he narrowed his eyes. 'Are you getting a cold?'

'You're so observant.' Tucking the tissue away, she stood up, though her boss was still somewhere at the back of the café and nobody needed her at present.

'Well, are you going to be well enough for camping next week?' he pressed.

Her eyes widened, and she sat back down. 'What camping?'

'Didn't you get Chris's email?'

'I don't know. Maybe.' She shook her head as though it might dispel her confusion. 'Shit. What are we camping for?'

'To learn how to pit-fire with combustibles. You know, oldest firing method ever and all that?' He cocked his head, unsure whether to be amused or not by the way she leaned back in a daze. Unfortunately, he found her scattered brain quite endearing, though he could see her frustration bleed through sometimes. Like now, as she tugged on her hair.

'I need to start reading my emails,' she muttered to herself.

'Yeah, it might help. Look, I was going to head out to buy a tent later. I can wait until your shift is over if you want to come with?'

Slowly, she shook her head. 'No, it's fine. I'll sort it.' She was getting up again. He was disappointed again.

He took her hand, just like he used to, and hoped she'd let him. 'Well, what about this weekend? We could do something. Go to a museum or watch a movie.'

Juniper's puzzled expression surprised him, as though he was strange for even asking. Then, something shuttered over her features: that old barrier. It was back, but he no longer knew why. They'd become friends. They'd called over Christmas. He was *here*.

She opened her mouth, and then faltered as her gaze fell between his arms, to his sketchbook. The page was already coffee-stained, and a smudge of blueberry jam clung to the centre of the paper, but his drawing was clear enough that he was sure she could recognise it. He'd created his viewpoint from this table, shaded silhouettes sipping coffee and plants hanging from the ceiling. And at the centre of it, a curvy woman with her hair falling out of its ponytail, hunched to place a mug in front of someone.

Time seemed to slow, conversations quietening to nothing more than murmurs. He wanted her to like it. Wanted to see her eyes light up as she realised that he wasn't messing around anymore, that he liked her and wanted her and couldn't stop.

But that didn't happen. 'I'm working this weekend,' she said instead, and then turned away to go back to the counter.

He rubbed his face as humiliation rose in him. Clearly, he'd gotten it all wrong.

24

Juniper never thought she'd say it, but she missed sitting on those uncomfortable stools in the workshop. Anything would have been better than setting up camp on the muddy grounds behind the teacher car park on the coldest month of the year. It didn't help that, thanks to her snotty-nosed little cousins climbing over her all Christmas, she'd had caught some kind of flu. Mum had tried to blame it on Juniper being run-down, further proof she was incapable of surviving uni, but it was January. Everyone was ill. Tilly was blowing her nose in front of her right this very minute.

'If somebody were to fall in this pit and die,' Luc said, shivering with their hands in their pockets as the wind whipped their scarf over their shoulders, 'would we be allowed to go back inside?'

'I volunteer as tribute,' Juniper murmured. Since opening the letter from RACA, she hadn't had much zest for life. Apparently, she wasn't the only one to have her bursary suspended. When she'd gone to visit the student finance office first thing on Monday, she'd discovered from a chatty receptionist that the school's private funding – probably from some big, snobby investor who had realised art wasn't nearly as profitable as other business ventures – had been cut in half, which left them in a 'sticky spot'. Luc's bursary had been frozen, and Amir's, too, though neither of them were as distraught about it as her. Luc had a separate grant for being an international student, and Amir had claimed his family were loaning him the money to cover the rest of the school year.

Not like Juniper, who didn't have anything else to lean on. She'd worked until nine last night, preparing the café for the following morning, and with this cold bogging her down, she was close to breaking point. She and Tilly had at least ended up buying a shared two-person tent, and thank goodness, because Juniper might have been sleeping on the grass tonight otherwise.

At her words, she felt Aiden's heavy gaze press into her like thumbs against a bruise. He stood beside Luc and had done nothing but scrutinise her. She got it. She wasn't being fair, not after his Christmas gift, but she couldn't engage with him in the middle of this. He would pity her and her poorness or, worse, try to help her, and the last thing she needed was the one thing she'd always despised: Whittaker money.

No, she'd get through this on her own. If she kept picking up extra shifts, she'd probably be able to pay with the instalment plan the school had offered her. It might mean borrowing some cash from her parents and only leaving her room for work and class, but she'd manage. It would be easy enough to make a small fortune before April, right?

'That's the spirit! I can imagine they had just as much enthusiasm in ancient times,' Chris said on the other side of the pits, a comically oversized raincoat protecting him from head to toe. The sky was already darkening above them, daylight a thing of the past this far into winter. Juniper hated it. She wished she could bury herself in her duvet and never emerge.

A few murmurs of discontent proved Juniper and Luc weren't the only ones suffering.

She closed her burning eyes, laying her head against Tilly's shoulder, whose coat cooled her feverish skin just slightly.

Meanwhile, Christopher taught them about the origins of pit-firing, most of which they'd already learned in his lecture yesterday before they'd thrown their own designs on the wheel in preparation. Juniper's had been wonky thanks to her weak hands and pounding head, which still hadn't eased, but she'd managed to make a teapot. Keeping with the theme, she'd brought dried coffee and tea leaves pinched from the Caffè Verde's compostables bin to create colour variations in the fire, at least one less thing she had to pay for as part of her studies.

On another day, she would have been fascinated with the rich roots behind firing pottery this way, learning how different combustibles created unpredictable effects, but today, she was barely able to keep upright.

With eight dug pits available, one used by Christopher as demonstration, Tilly and Juniper shared theirs. Of course, Aiden and Luc took the one beside them, Aiden nudging Juniper lightly as she tried to figure out first steps. 'You okay, Hodge? You don't look well.'

She wondered if he'd ever stop trying, and worse, if she wanted him to. It seemed as though no amount of pushing him away changed things. Nothing on her surface mattered;

like this pit, he would always dig, and she didn't know if she was strong enough to withstand it for much longer.

'Fine. Never been better,' she murmured through chattering teeth, despite her body feeling like it was on fire.

Aiden's forehead scrunched, and he began peeling his arms from his sleeves, revealing a thick hoodie underneath. 'Here. Take my coat.'

'I'm fine—'

But it was already draped over her shoulders, and the weight of it soothed her sore limbs. The smell of him eased her, too: boyish aftershave and woodsy cologne that transported her right back to the stolen moments they'd spent together last term. It shouldn't have been a comfort, to feel like he was wrapped around her again, but she was tired. Feeling taken care of, in this moment, didn't feel quite as scary as getting through this week all alone as planned.

It wouldn't last. She wouldn't let it. But she sighed and put her arms in the sleeves with a 'Thanks' that seemed to satisfy him.

'So, are you two still boinking or what?' Tilly asked, motioning between them.

Aiden spluttered. 'Are we *what*?'

'They clearly are,' Luc commented, pulling materials from their bag: sandpaper and...

'Oh, god!' Tilly wrinkled her nose, leaning away from Luc with her coat sleeve covering her face. 'Is that horse shite wrapped in newspaper?'

Juniper had never been more grateful to have a blocked nose, but the sight of it still made her gag.

Luc shrugged and threw it into the pit. 'Manure is great for controlling heat.'

'Where did you even get it?' Aiden's lips trembled like he was trying hard not to laugh.

'Horse.'

'Aye, *obviously*!' Tilly shouted.

'It is cheaper than buying saw dust!' Luc defended quickly. Speaking of, Juniper had plenty of that to spare from Cerberus's supply, and she sprinkled it into the pit as she listened to the others joke about Luc and their manure. She wanted to join in, but felt like she was underwater, everything too far away to focus on. Finally, she placed her teapot in the pit and Christopher came around to light their materials. As they waited for the fire to smother the clay, RACA's kiln woman, a tall redhead named Annie, arrived bearing hot chocolate and marshmallows in polystyrene cups.

Aiden brought Juniper a drink over. She was too groggy to tell him that she could have gotten it herself, accepting it quietly. He sat on the ground beside her, closer than he needed to. With the fire burning behind, she watched the marshmallows and cream melt, feeling sick at the thought of drinking it.

'I think maybe you should go home, sweetheart,' he whispered.

Sweetheart. He'd only used to call her that during sex, and she didn't know what it meant that he was bringing it out in the open, away from their intimate corners.

'I'm fine.' She wiped her nose with a scrunched tissue that had been falling apart inside her pocket all day. The skin around her nostrils stung enough to make her wince.

He shook his head with a tut. 'Do you always have to be so bloody stubborn?'

'Yes.' She took a sip of hot chocolate just to spite him, but the sweetness left nausea swirling through her, so she was quick to pour it over her fire.

The flames sputtered in time with Aiden. 'Juni, you're not supposed to do that!'

She blinked. 'Why? It's already got a tonne of other crap in it. Coffee beans and hot chocolate basically make mocha.'

'Were the coffee beans at least dry?'

She shrugged. 'I don't know. They were old.'

Aiden pinched the bridge of his nose, and then, patiently uttered, 'Juniper. Moisture will make the clay crack.'

Shit. She hadn't even given it a thought, but she could hear the fire fizzing in anger now. Even her panic felt far away as she shot up to her feet, Aiden there to catch her when her jelly-like legs stumbled too close to the pit. Her poor, wonky teapot. It might have been terrible, but she'd been excited to see the results of the firing.

And... oh, god, Tilly's plates. They were in there, too. She'd ruined both of their projects.

'I need a fire extinguisher!' she declared.

'And this is why I oversee the fires,' Christopher said, and then sauntered over to her with his hot chocolate in hand. 'Whatever's the matter, Juniper?'

'I poured – *dropped* – my drink into the pit, completely by accident!'

'You did *what*?' Tilly broke away from the group to rush over, her eyes wide in alarm. 'My plates! My beautiful, beautiful plates!'

'I'm so sorry.' Juniper swallowed the lump of guilt in her throat. How had she been so careless? Why was it always her who made these silly, thoughtless mistakes? 'Can we save them? Please?'

'Dear me, this isn't an episode of *Clay's Anatomy*,' Chris said. 'No, we can't save them. We'll just have to see if they make it through the night.'

Tilly's face dropped. Crestfallen. Because of Juniper.

She sank back on weak knees, finding that Aiden's support was the only thing holding her up. His arms locked around her hips as he said, 'Chris, do I have permission to take a very ill Juniper home before she damages herself as well as the pots?'

Christopher squinted. 'I sensed you had the lurgy. Yes, go, before we all get it.' He waved her away.

'But my teapot—'

'Is probably broken. Like my plates.' Tilly didn't sound angry, just devastated. Somehow, that made it worse.

'Tilly, I'm so sorry,' Juniper whispered.

'I know. You're going through a lot. I just wish…' Tilly shook her head and closed her eyes. 'Never mind. Go home. Get some rest. I'll watch the pit and pray to the kiln goddesses for us both.'

'They might be fine,' Aiden provided, but he didn't sound sure.

Juniper hadn't been joking about falling into the pit before. She would have quite happily stepped in and let the fire ruin her like it was their pieces if she thought it might make things right. Tilly had worked hard on those plates, and she'd been so excited to see what would happen with her copper wiring and recycled yarn. She didn't deserve this. She'd been nothing but wonderful to Juniper.

'C'mon, Juni. Let's get you home.' Aiden nudged her, grabbing her backpack from Tilly and slinging it over his shoulder. Juniper didn't know what to say.

I'm sorry didn't feel like enough. She walked away from the fires feeling even worse than she had before.

25

'I'm a shitty friend,' Juniper murmured as they zig-zagged across campus. Well, Aiden zigged while she zagged, barely able to walk in a straight line. Her wan complexion broke up the darkness of the evening, and her breath fell from her in visible, jagged clouds that made Aiden anxious. He was sure it was just a cold, a virus at worst, but with the disaster of the pit-fire, he wasn't sure if she was completely okay – or, really, if she had been at all since she'd gotten back to London.

He didn't know how to help her, either, not when she kept tearing her arm away and snapping that she was fine.

'Don't say that,' he said, a little sterner than intended. 'It was an accident. We've all made mistakes like that.'

She scoffed. 'Yeah, right. Except you don't. Nobody else, either. It's always me who fucks everything up.'

He sighed, helping her up the steps as they reached Chaplin House. It had a more Victorian air compared to the rest of campus, with red brick walls and a chimney rising from the second storey. The door was a solid black arch, one Juniper struggled to open after scanning the ID on her lanyard, so he grabbed it for her quickly. 'Again, not true.'

Though he could admit, disaster did seem to follow her wherever she went. It was usually outweighed by other things, though: her humour, her rough edges and soft centre, her brilliant light. He couldn't quite describe it, which was probably why he sometimes tried to put it on paper instead. She wasn't necessarily warm or friendly like the people he'd dated before, but she didn't need to be. She was far more interesting, and far more frustrating, as she was. Far more beautiful, too, at least until she sneezed into her sleeve.

No, *his* sleeve, because she was still wearing his coat. It hung off her shoulders and fell past her wrists, making her look even smaller than he was used to, and for a moment, he could almost convince himself that it meant something. That, the way he was hers, she was also his.

'Remind me to burn that coat in the pit later.' He followed her up the steps to the first floor. As far as uni halls went, this place was pretty standard. He'd stayed in something similar at Elmington in an attempt to make friends, and the echoing, narrow corridors and tiny ensuites had driven him mad.

'Sorry,' she said, sounding more congested than ever. Her teeth still chattered. 'I'll wash it at the laundrette.'

'I was joking, Juni.' When she wouldn't look at him, he took her wrist and tugged her to face him. 'Oi.'

'What?' she groaned, all glassy-eyed and hoarse.

'It's okay to fuck up. Cut yourself some slack. Tilly will forgive you.'

'I wouldn't blame her if she didn't.' But he could tell her resolve had weakened by the way her eyes glistened as though she was about to cry. He hoped she didn't. He wouldn't know what to do, how to make it better, and he *wanted* to make it better.

She turned away from him and continued down the corridor, right to the end. 'You can go back to your pit-fire now, anyway.'

'No chance. Not until I know you're all right.'

She huffed, rooting for her keys, and then stopped dead at her door. A yellow sign had been tacked there with a hand-written note.

Please report to the accommodations office at your earliest convenience.

'Oh, god, no.'

'That's a bit ominous.' He ripped the sign off to get a closer look, but all he could find was a strange illustration of what might have been a dog or a horse. 'What's this supposed to be? Is someone messing around with you?'

'No. Maybe. I think that might be a hamster.' Her hands shook as she turned the key, and Aiden frowned.

'Why would someone draw a picture of a hamster?'

The door swung open, revealing a messy room strewn with clothes and textbooks on every available surface: navy carpet, the desk chair, the nightstands.

'Fuck!' Juniper trudged through her room, stopping at her surprisingly empty desk.

Alert, now, he scanned the room for some sign of an intruder.

'How the fuck has someone raided your room?' He nudged an empty packet of Space Raider crisps with his foot. 'And why did they leave their rubbish?'

'That's *my* rubbish. My room looked like this before, which is why you're not allowed in it. Get out!'

Well, that was a relief. Sort of. He didn't budge, instead saying, 'You know, I'm used to feeling quite confused around you, but you might have to fill me in this time.'

Defeated, she slumped onto a pile of library books stacked on her chair. 'They found my hamster.'

'Eh? Cerberus?' Juniper had treated him to a picture of the little guy the other day. The hamster looked more like a tiny dormouse, but saying so had got him into trouble.

Her head fell into her hands and she gave a muffled hum of confirmation.

'How did he even get here?'

She said something like, 'I'muggled'im'na'ty'it.'

'Pardon?'

She groaned and slapped her hands down on her thighs. 'I smuggled him in a tiny bit.'

'*What*? Pets aren't allowed in halls!'

'I know. That's why the smuggling part was necessary.' One of the books fell off the chair, and she made no move to pick it up, instead glaring at it like it was responsible for all of her woes.

Aiden could only shake his head in disbelief. 'Why on earth would you do that?'

'Because!' She waved in exasperation. 'My mum and dad wouldn't look after him properly, and living here is kind of miserable! I couldn't just leave him behind.'

'So now you're in trouble.' He would have laughed if tears weren't rolling down her cheeks. Instead, he perched on the edge of the bed, their knees clashing as he rolled the chair closer to him. It soon got caught on a pair of leggings. 'You never fail to surprise me. You really don't.'

'It's not funny.' She pressed her palms into her eyes, but he tore them away quickly, pulling her closer.

'I know. I'm not laughing. Yet. I might later, when we get Cerberus back.'

'How?' she whispered. 'They won't let him back into halls. They might kick me out for this. I'm already…' She bit her lip suddenly and turned away.

'Already what?'

'Nothing. Failing, probably.'

'Yeah, that top grade you got last semester is really the nail in the coffin,' he retorted sarcastically. And then he scanned the room as though he might find a solution to the problem under all the mess. He wasn't necessarily surprised by it – he wasn't the tidiest himself – but it did make him feel overwhelmed in such a small space. There was really only one thing he could think of, but that would require something he wasn't sure he wanted.

And yet he'd do anything to help her, knowing that she must've felt pretty fucking shitty to let him see her like this.

He wiped the tears from her flushed cheeks with the pad of his thumb. 'I'll take care of Cerberus. He can stay with me until you can sort something out.'

She scoffed. 'You hate him.'

'I don't hate him.'

'You said he looks like a rat!'

'A mouse. Mice are cute… to some people.' He winced. 'At least this way, you can come and see him anytime you want. He'll be close by.' *And* that would mean her seeing him, too. Not that that was on his mind. He definitely wasn't using Cerberus to win over his owner. That would be ridiculous and also selfish. And had he mentioned ridiculous?

She tilted her head, considering. The tears, at least, had stopped. 'Why?'

Because it hurts to see you sad. 'Because we can't have Cerberus going back to Manchester where nobody will look after him, can we?'

'I mean, why are you always so nice to me? I'm never nice to you.'

The question took him aback. He pressed his tongue against the roof of his mouth, searching for an answer that wouldn't give him and all his big, silly feelings for her away.

'I wouldn't say 'never'. Just not often,' he began softly. 'Besides, maybe I don't need you to be nice to me. Everybody else is only nice to me because they want something from me – or, usually, my dad. They use me because they think my name, my family, my money, can benefit them. I'd rather be around you. You don't use me. I know exactly where I stand with you. You see through all the bullshit, Juni.'

Her throat bobbed, and it took him a moment to realise that the sudden warmth in his hands belonged to her. For once, he hadn't been the one to reach out.

She looked down at their joined palms like she'd never seen them before, lids pink and lips chapped. Even like this, she was beautiful. Especially like this, because it was real. She wasn't hiding.

Finally, she could see him for what he was, and it felt like the chains around him had finally split.

'You'd really take care of Cerberus?' she asked quietly. 'You'd really do that for me?'

'I think you know I'd probably do anything for you. Within reason, so don't get any ideas.'

A laugh croaked from her, and the pressure in his chest eased. He'd done his job, made things right.

Somehow, it made him feel more accomplished than any degree or award.

★

From what Aiden could hear through the door, Juniper received a stern telling off from the inspections officer, but thankfully nothing more than a warning that this was her 'first strike.' With Cerberus's cage in his arms, they took a cab to his house, Juniper insisting that she oversaw the settling in before she left. Which left him here, on his doorstep, nervous in a way that felt silly because it was her first time visiting. He'd offered for her to come here after the museum trip, but it seemed as though Juniper had been trying not to cross that boundary, and he wouldn't force her.

He supposed he owed Cerberus a thank you, though it was difficult to appreciate the little ball of fluff when his sawdust smelled a bit like wee.

'Can you grab my keys?' he asked, turning to offer his back pocket.

She looked like she wanted to roll her eyes, and then must have remembered that he was doing her a favour and changed her mind. With her nose running in the cold night, she reached into his pocket, fingers lightly brushing his arse in a way that made him hold his breath. Not just because she was touching him, either, but because it felt like such a familiar gesture. They'd closed all of that distance she'd worked hard to put between them in one night, and this time, it wasn't because they were horny and swept away in a moment. It was because she was vulnerable, and he was helping her.

She slid the key into his lock wordlessly, opening the door into the dark hallway.

'After you,' he said when she hovered on the welcome mat. She stepped through, fidgety and hesitant. Why? Why, for once, couldn't she just *be* with him?

She eyed everything like it was her first time seeing someone's home, not that that was what this was. A home wasn't something he could ever recall having. His father's house was too big, big enough to feel like he might vanish among all the light and space, and this flat was just a place to put all his stuff in while he studied. A place to sleep and eat and shower.

He had tried to make it feel like his: his jackets were hung on the coat stand and a few of his favourite paintings added colour to the white walls, but they felt like a way of torturing himself with the life he was supposed to be living. Dad had gifted them to him because he'd wanted his son to appreciate art the way he did: for its beauty, yes, but also its monetary value. He wanted to give Aiden an eye for it so that he'd come to know how to sell, what, why, to who, and for what purpose, too.

When she paused, he took over, guiding her into the living room and flicking on the lights with his elbow. He wondered if she saw this place as he did: a bland, cold space that looked barely lived in, nothing like her room. At least mess was proof that she had a personality, interests. His were stacked on his coffee table. A few tubes of acrylic paint, a stained palette, and a pan of watercolours because he'd wanted to try a different medium if only to get away from the rules he'd lived by his whole life.

There was a low set of cupboards where he'd piled his textbooks, and he shoved them to one side to set Cerberus down. 'How's this? He'll get a bit of light from the window. Do hamsters need light?'

'It's better to keep him out of direct sunlight.'

'Why? Is he flammable?' It was only half a joke. Aiden knew nothing about caring for another creature. Dad had never let him have pets, probably for good reason: because Aiden was selfish and lazy and unreliable, at least to him. To Aiden, he was just trying to balance the weight of expectations he could barely meet.

Juniper's look was deadly, which quickly sobered him. 'He's nocturnal. He needs consistency. Nothing too bright, but light enough to give him a routine. Here should be fine.' She nudged the cage just slightly towards the books, where the corner was darker. Inside, Cerberus had disappeared into a little wooden hut.

'Does he always smell like that?' Aiden sniffed, then wrinkled his nose.

'Yes.'

Great. Thank goodness he didn't have many guests over. 'How often do I need to clean him?'

'Never. I don't need you letting him out and losing him.' She bent over to look for the hamster in his hut. 'I'll come by and take care of that.'

'Okay. Sounds good.' Aiden mimicked her, curiously wiggling his finger through the wire cage. Cerberus emerged, his tiny nose and long whiskers twitching as he came to see his new surroundings. He sniffed Aiden's finger, and then— 'Ow!'

'Oh, yeah. Sometimes, he bites.'

Aiden yanked his hand away, shaking off the sting. The thing had razor-sharp teeth for such a tiny animal. 'He's almost as violent as you.'

He almost won a smile with that. Almost. She sank back on her heels and finally looked at him. 'Thank you, Aiden. I don't know what I would have done with him otherwise. It really means a lot, that you'd take care of him.'

His heart stuttered with something warm and hopeful. 'Of course. Anything, Juni. Really.'

'I'll miss not having him in my room.' She slumped into the nearest seat on the couch, adding life to the cream furniture even with her dark clothes. Her hair, knotted from the wind, cascaded over one shoulder as she rubbed her eyes tiredly. 'Gets lonely in there, even with Tilly next door. Then again...' Sadness flickered on her features.

'Then again, what?'

She shook her head. 'Nothing.'

'You can talk to me, y'know.' He sat beside her, finger twirling through her hair softly. The smoky scent of the fire clung to her, to them both, along with the fresh damp of outside. She leaned into his touch, a revelation in itself.

'I can't.' It was whispered, but it still stabbed through him like needles. Her voice was thick, close to tears again.

'Why? Why can't you?'

'I'm just so sick of fucking everything up all the time. Even when I think I'm doing something right, it still all falls apart around me. And I can't keep blaming my ADHD for the fact that everything is such a fucking mess. And I can't keep blaming *you* for it, either, because it turns out you're actually not the devil's spawn after all, which is highly inconvenient, by the way.'

'Um, sorry, I think.' Aiden arched a brow, trying to piece it all together. He might have been offended, but he was more focused on the other thing.

ADHD. He supposed it made sense. At the exhibition, she'd gotten distracted by each new piece of art to the point of interrupting one sentence to start another, and it was no secret that she wasn't the best at managing her time. He couldn't remember knowing that about her in high school, but when he'd been researching his mental health problems, he'd read that symptoms manifested differently in women for all sorts of things, neurodivergence included. Perhaps focusing on her art and keeping that ferocity intact had been her way of masking.

'And also, I feel like shit,' she continued, words merging together in a rush now. 'My head hurts, and I can't feel my legs, and everything is just bad, Aiden. I think this has actually been the worst day of my life, and I'm only being a smidge dramatic about it. And you know what's fucked up?' Her eyes locked on his. 'You're the only one who makes me feel okay about it. *You*. It was never supposed to be you!'

It was everything he'd ever wanted to hear, but now he didn't know how to respond. Could only sit in silence, heart pounding, as he tried to resist kissing her until her tears stopped.

She threw her head down to her knees – then paused when she got close to the coffee table. He'd left his sketchbook there, open on the page she'd seen the other day. The page of her. It wasn't the only one, either. Beneath, he'd started painting the same figure, her, her back turned with a piece of art framed in front of her the way it had been at the museum. He'd wanted to remember that evening, the way she'd absorbed herself completely in it all. Problem was, he could never get her shape right. She wasn't someone who belonged on a page. She was too alive for it. A sculpture might have been better, but he wasn't sure he'd ever be talented enough for that.

'And you've been drawing me,' she said quietly after moments of suffocating silence. 'Why have you been drawing me?'

'I told you. I've been feeling inspired.'

She closed her eyes, sucked in a deep breath. 'Aiden, you're not my boyfriend.'

It hurt, but he'd been waiting for it. 'Do I need to be?'

'You're buying me concert tickets, and drawing me, and looking after my hamster, and taking me home when I'm sick.'

'And are those somehow defining factors of a relationship? Should I change my Facebook status to *it's complicated* or will that come during the inevitable custody battle for Cerberus?'

She slapped his chest playfully, then leaned back on the couch with her head twisted to look at him. Her lids were heavy, face still far paler than he liked. 'Stop.'

He leaned back, too, faces inches apart. 'No. I don't care what I am to you, Juniper, as long as I get to be something.'

Her mouth downturned as though it wasn't a suitable answer, and yet she didn't fight it. Didn't say anything.

He couldn't help but feather his fingers across her scalp gently, smiling when her lids fluttered shut. 'I've felt like you do now before. At Elmington.'

'When you weren't well.'

It wasn't a question, but he nodded anyway, though she wasn't looking at him. It was only right to be honest with her, now that she was being honest with him.

'I struggled there. With my mental health. I was miserable. Studying a course I didn't want to because I thought it would make my dad happy. Pretending to be friends with people who only cared about me because of my last name. I was so fucking alone, Juni. I didn't have anyone, and I was so depressed that I didn't even make it to class most days.' He dragged his ring up and down his thumb anxiously. 'It was like I couldn't get a full breath, couldn't keep going, even when I tried to force myself to. And I didn't know what was wrong with me, which made it scarier. I couldn't trust anything I knew anymore. Not my body, definitely not my mind. When I fell behind…' A thick swallow. 'My dad found out, and he said things like you're saying to yourself now. And it took me a long time to convince myself they weren't true. In fact, I'm still working on it. Even with therapy and medication and every coping mechanism under the sun, I can still feel it surfacing in me every now and again.'

Her hand found his chest, like she was trying to heal the part where it hurt most. He covered it with his own, feeling light-headed and strange – but free, somehow. He'd never told anybody but his therapist just how deep he'd sunk. But seeing the way Juniper was tonight, the way she beat herself up, he trusted her. Hoped maybe he could help her to feel less alone. Be the person he'd needed back then.

'I had no idea you went through something like that,' she admitted.

He shrugged. 'Didn't want you to. Didn't want anyone to.'

'When Owen was questioning you about your dad at the museum…'

'My anxiety isn't always predictable, but I feel worse when I'm around people who want to talk about my dad, who seem to have already put me in a box. I feel suffocated, like I'm back there, at Elmington, with people who don't really see me, and… it's terrifying. I never want to go back to that place.'

'I'm so sorry that you suffered that way.' She traced his jaw gently. 'But I see you, Aiden.'

He knew. He could feel it, like light flooding through areas that had only ever been in shadow before. He leaned forward to place a kiss on her forehead, glad when she sunk into him, head against his chest. 'You always have. Even my shitty parts.'

'Especially your shitty parts.' She pulled away, and he had to restrain himself from tugging her back. For once, he wished they could just stay slotted in place. 'You're going to catch my cold.'

'I don't care.'

'You will when you can't remember what it feels like to breathe through your nostrils.' She yawned, covering her mouth. 'I should go.'

'Or you could stay,' he suggested. 'You're exhausted, and I'm pretty sure I saw books all over your bed, whereas my bed is comfortable and bookless.'

'Show off.' But she didn't need telling twice, grabbing the fleecy throw from the back of his couch. 'I'm not staying in your bed, though.'

'Because I'm not your boyfriend?' he teased, helping her spread the blanket over her curled, clammy body.

She nodded, getting comfortable against him again. His arms curled around her waist on instinct, frightened she might disappear if he didn't hold on.

'But this couch is quite comfy,' she murmured finally.

It wasn't for him, the arm digging into his back and her thigh pinning his knee in an awkward position, but he didn't care.

As long as she was here and okay, he would endure the rest.

Even if he wasn't her bloody boyfriend.

26

Since Juniper still felt awful about the pit-firing disaster, she snuck into the cooling room and stole Tilly's cracked pottery during her free period that Friday. Tilly had another job interview at a vintage clothes shop she was desperate to get, so Juniper knew she wouldn't be caught.

By her, at least. She'd only just gotten comfortable on her usual stool in the workshop when Chris sauntered through the door whistling a tune that could have been 'The Wheels on the Bus' or 'Dancing Queen' by Abba. Or neither.

He stopped short at the sight of Juniper and her glue, quick to cover his mouth with his sleeve. 'Is it safe in here, or are you still contagious?'

'If I say I'm still ill, will you leave me alone?' She was still distracted by all things funding, made worse by the fact that she'd been too sick to work her last two shifts. Finally, the cold was shifting, but it had wiped her out good and proper. Enough that she'd fallen asleep at Aiden's again last night after cleaning Cerberus and making sure he was fed. She wasn't sure she could trust him to remember, but the hamster had seemed happy enough. Perhaps it

233

would be just another thing she was wrong about when it came to him.

'You're meaner than usual,' Chris pointed out, approaching her desk with narrowed eyes. 'I don't like it.'

'Well, lucky for you, you may not have to put up with me much longer.' The words slipped from her before she could stop them, just like the super glue from the nozzle, which she was currently using to fix Tilly's plates.

Above the thick frame of his glasses, his bushy brows pinched. 'You're not dropping out.' He said it like it was a fact; like Juniper couldn't possibly.

She supposed there was no harm in telling him. Perhaps he'd surprise her the way Aiden had and at least offer some advice. Maybe he knew about different, cheaper courses she could take next year, or better yet, perhaps he could have a word with the finance team.

Or maybe he would dance up and down with glee at the prospect of her leaving, and that would at least make it easier to say goodbye.

'I might not have a choice. They've frozen my bursary, and without it, I can't afford to stay for the final term. I've been taking as many extra work shifts as I can, but waitressing isn't exactly going to cover my tuition.'

'I heard about that. It was a shitty move to pull, even if the college is having money problems.' He shook his head, surprising her with his sour words. 'What? I do have some human empathy. Not a lot, but some.'

Maybe they were more alike than Juniper had realised, with their bluntness and dry sense of humour. Juniper shuddered to think it, but the feeling of missing something she hadn't yet lost left her gut sinking. This course was hard, and she wasn't sure she was cut out for it, but she'd wanted to try. She'd wanted to prove to her mum, to anyone who had ever mocked her or belittled her, that she was capable of the same achievements people like Aiden and Tom were. That people without money behind them could do the things they loved, too.

Now, it felt like her best days at RACA were already over, and all of them had involved Aiden and their project. Even at the exhibit, she hadn't been able to completely enjoy herself, and Mum hadn't cared about the brilliant grade she'd strived to achieve, just for her.

A small voice in her head wondered what the point was. Should she just cut her losses?

'Maybe it just wasn't meant to be.' She shrugged and went back to gluing, finding herself quite enjoying it. It was like doing a jigsaw puzzle, quieting her brain the way sculpting once had.

'I'm not sure I believe that. You may have cocked up the pit-firing, but you impressed me last term. And I don't say that lightly.'

She froze in surprise. She must have been pitiable if even Christopher was being nice to her.

'Besides.' He ran a finger over the broken pieces of her teapot, which would be much harder to fix. Much of it was in shards already, curved spout the only recognisable thing about it. 'The patterns on these are gorgeous. Your combustibles may have been a little too combustible, but both you and Tilly clearly thought about what effects you wanted to make here.'

'Not really. I just stole leftovers from the café I work in,' she admitted. He was right, though: the clay was iridescent as a rainbow in some places, and the coffee had left streaks of rustic browns and sunshine yellows.

'Oh, well then, I take it back. Leave this college immediately.' He smirked, and she couldn't help but do the same.

And then he snapped up quickly enough to make her jump, marching over to his desk drawer. He collected something from it, then returned, slipping a pamphlet across Juniper's workstation. 'I don't usually show this to first years, and the deadline isn't so far off, but this may be the only solution I can think of.'

'What is it?' Juniper picked up the pamphlet, which was titled The National Ceramics Contest and showed a picture of a gorgeous hourglass-shaped vase, where layering techniques had been used to scrape out different colours beneath the dark top surface. In rich midnight-blue, aquas, and pinks, it reminded her of a new galaxy leaking out of a black hole.

'It's been going for years. If I hadn't have won back in the day, I wouldn't be here now, either.'

That gave her pause. She'd assumed Chris wasn't too different to the majority of his students, with his posh accent and commanding confidence.

'The cash prize is twelve thousand. More, I believe, than a year's tuition. It also puts you on the map. My work ended up getting me a residency in Tuscany.'

Her mouth dropped open. That was *a lot* of money. It would certainly get her through the year, and imagining her work recognised by people up and down the country was a dream. Still, she flicked through the pages and knew there was no chance of her winning. Past participants had gone on to create homeware lines in major stores like Harrods, not to mention many had become award-winning artists with hundreds of credentials to their names. These pieces weren't *ambitious*: they were perfect, enough to make anybody want them in their house. Not like those creatures of hers, the ones Tom and Amir had laughed at.

'This is great, but I'm not sure I have any spare time to enter a competition I won't win.'

'Your optimism is so inspiring,' Chris deadpanned. 'I can't tell you what to do, Juniper, and I won't. You need to want this yourself. But I wouldn't show this to you if I didn't suspect you were capable. Your ideas are original, and you sculpt more confidently than most first years I've taught. There's plenty of room for improvement, but that's what this competition is for.' He jabbed his finger on the pamphlet. 'It's for people who want to be ceramicists. People who are driven to put their work out there even when it's terrifying. And those who do get rewarded. The only question is, are you one of those people? I thought you were when I met you. In fact, it's why I encouraged the dean to offer you that grant, and why I protested against them freezing student funding.'

Juniper was stunned. *Chris* had been the one to get her a place here? She'd assumed it was just somebody looking to fill their quota of northern women for the sake of statistics, just to make sure the university wasn't perceived as sexist or elitist. Then, she'd gotten here and discovered people like Tom, wealthy Londoners, were the minority. Was that his doing, too?

'The fact that you're gluing these pieces together when most people would have chucked them in the bin a long time ago tells me you have it in you.' He pushed up off the desk, looking at her over his glasses. 'And, to be completely honest, I'm not sure what you have to lose. But it's your choice.'

'What are the requirements?' she asked quietly.

He looked pleased as he flicked to one of the back pages of the pamphlet, where it listed the requirements as a cohesive collection of functional homeware pottery of between four to six pieces. Making five pieces with Aiden had taken her an entire term, and the deadline for this was marked at the beginning of March, less than two months from now.

'Easy peasy lemon squeezy,' Chris said.

'No, Christopher. Difficult difficult lemon difficult.' She took a deep breath and massaged her temples before finally coming to a decision. 'But I will try. I have to try.'

He was right, after all. What *did* she have to lose?

★

'Ta-dah!' Juniper was there to display the sort-of-fixed plates as soon as Tilly arrived after lunch that afternoon. Those words from the other day still weighed on Juniper: *'You're going through a lot. I just wish… Never mind.'*

238

Juniper knew what Tilly wished. That Juniper wasn't so clumsy and impulsive. But if she had to be those things, she at least wanted to make it right, and Tilly's face lit up like another dab of glue to smooth the cracks between them, too.

'You didn't!'

'Be careful with them because they're still wet. I got my thumb stuck to it for a while earlier.' She rubbed the part where her skin still stung from finally tearing it free.

Meanwhile, Aiden walked past them and snorted, though he looked impressed by her work. 'Juni and superglue. What a terrifying idea.'

'Well, hello, lover boy. I heard that you are now the proud father of a displaced wee hamster.' Tilly beamed, pinching Aiden's cheeks in a way that did, unfortunately, make him look very cute. But Juniper was more disgusted at the nickname, and the implication that she was now co-parenting.

'*No*. He's a babysitter. I am a single mother and will remain so.' Juniper dashed over to her desk before either of them could argue, returning to the teapot that still sat in shards. She'd already considered giving up on it. Thrice. But she'd worked her whole life to defy her brain's natural reflex, the one that made her want to abandon anything she wasn't immediately good at. Now more than ever, it felt important to do that.

She refused to go home at the end of term. Refused to let her parents see her fail the way they'd been waiting for her to since the beginning. She loved Manchester, but there was nothing there for her now.

'What's this?' Aiden swiped the National Ceramics Contest pamphlet before she had time to realise it was still on her desk, eyeing up the front cover.

She snatched it back quickly and shoved it in her bag. 'None of your beeswax.'

'Are you entering it?'

'*No*,' she lied, because if she didn't, she was afraid she'd have to tell him why.

He didn't look convinced, but he sat anyway, his stool an inch closer to her desk than it had been last term. 'If you are,' he said, 'I reckon you'll win.'

Juniper pressed her lips together, unsure how to respond. How did he always know exactly what to say? It wasn't fair. She was trying so hard to not fall for him, and one sentence could make her all… gooey. It was a completely different heat from last term, the first time she'd seen him on the throwing wheel. The desire was still there, but the edges had smoothed to make room for something else, something that kept evolving whenever she learned new things about him. Something she *couldn't* focus on right now.

'Right, gang,' Chris said from the front of the classroom when everyone was seated. 'Well done on pit-firing the other day. You should now have your pieces ready to finish off as you please. Try to do a good job, if you can. These aren't part of your final grade, but you can use them in your end-of-year portfolio if they don't end up a mess like Tom's.'

'Oi! It was meant to turn out like this,' Tom said, wielding his broken pot, and a few people laughed. At least she hadn't been the only one to screw up.

'Now, as you know, we have a trip planned to Stoke-on-Trent next weekend to see how the profeshes do it. That means professionals,' he explained when everybody looked baffled. 'God, get down with the kids.'

A few groans sounded that time. Rightly so.

Juniper's was for a different reason. She couldn't *afford* to go to Stoke-on-Trent. The train fare wasn't covered by the university, and a return ticket wasn't cheap. Not to mention, she would miss more work shifts and lose time she needed to spend on her project.

'Is this trip optional?' Juniper asked.

Aiden shot her a questioning look.

Christopher gasped. 'Absolutely not. You can't miss a visit to the pottery capital of the UK. Besides, we've already booked the hotel.'

Great. At this rate, she wouldn't be able to afford to stay at RACA for long enough to enter the ceramics contest at all.

'Are we going on the train?' Owen asked from the back of the classroom.

'Yes. You do not want to see me on a coach.' With a grimace, Chris smoothed down his blazer. 'Travel sick.'

He ran through the itinerary: a tour of Middleport Factory as well as a couple of other museums, plus some independent businesses the following day. Juniper mourned the version of her that would be excited for those things. Anxiety loomed too close to for that.

Once Chris left them to their own devices, it was only seconds before Aiden turned around to face her. 'Why don't you want to go to Stoke?'

Want to. As though *want* had anything to do with it. That question alone made her realise that he just didn't get it. He did what he wanted, when he wanted, because he could. Because he had money. Maybe they had more in common than she'd known, and maybe his honesty the other night had brought them closer, but their differences would always be there to throw them apart again.

That was why she lied. 'I do. Just… work shifts, and everything.'

'*Pfft*. Sack work. It'll be waiting for you when we get back.'

She didn't even have the energy to get angry at that, though a fresh spark of resentment made itself known. She wished she didn't have to feel it anymore. Wished they could just be wrapped up in their little bubble of banter and sex forever, without any reminders of their polar opposite lives. Even now, finally on common ground, she'd always be the one trailing behind. 'You have no idea, do you?'

'No idea of what?' A strand of his hair flopped over his forehead, making it almost impossible to remember why she'd been angry.

Was it worth it anymore? He was just confirming what she'd always known. Maybe he'd struggled at Elmington, and maybe he had issues with his father, but he still lived in his fancy flat, his future steady and certain. He had no idea that some people worked to survive. Some people were holding on by the skin of their teeth.

'Nothing. Never mind.'

He dipped his head, his knuckles feathering over hers on the table, breath sifting through the hair she was trying to use as a curtain between them. 'If you're worried about Cerberus, I can get someone to check in. I'm sure there's a hamster sitter somewhere in London.'

Ugh. It would have been easier if he wasn't so caring. Easier if he didn't know her well enough to see at least *some* of her worries.

And he didn't give up there, vying for a smile with another silly comment: 'If you're lucky, I'll let you have the window seat on the train.'

She forced one, because even when he pissed her off, she knew he was trying. Nobody had ever tried like that for her before.

So she would enjoy it until her time ran out.

27

'Hello. Earth to Aiden,' Luc boomed down their cupped hands, breaking Aiden out of his thoughts. He rubbed his tired eyes – bloody Cerberus had kept him up all night again on his wheel – and turned his attention from the pages he'd been staring at back to his friend.

'Sorry, what?' Absently, he jabbed his pen onto his page, clicking the nib up and down. The library hummed with life around them, a dozen students clustered around tables and hovering in book aisles. The semester was slowly picking up speed, and it showed everywhere on campus – including Aiden's classes. Apparently, there was a hell of a lot more to a pottery degree than just creating. The History of Ceramics module was kicking his arse, and his pit-fired gravy boat, inspired by his terribly dry Christmas dinner at Gran's, didn't even count towards the grade. Apparently, they'd just camped out for fun, and to learn the techniques, because an essay was required in three weeks' time about how pottery has developed since ancient times. He wasn't aware that it even had, really; that's what he liked about it. Painting was ever-changing, most styles reflective of the atmosphere and social commentaries of the time, easy to match to an era, but he could stare at a vase from thousands of years ago and not know if it had been made then or now. He could recognise the techniques that might have been used by fingers far more calloused and ancient than his.

Of course, that wasn't what he'd been thinking about before Luc's interruption, and Luc seemed to know it, too, because they raised a purple-dyed eyebrow. 'You're Juniper-dreaming again.'

'No, I'm not!' He was. Worrying about her. She was so busy with work, so distant even when she wasn't. He didn't know what he'd done this time. And that contest pamphlet in her bag had to mean something, didn't it? Was she afraid of telling him because he didn't think he'd support her? That could never be true.

'At least get better at lying about it.' Luc dropped their pencil into the fold of their book, silver nose ring winking at Aiden as they leaned into a spot of light streaming in from the ceiling.

Defeated, he slouched as well, kicking his legs out in an attempt to disappear beneath the table. 'I don't know what to do. I've never been this in my head about someone before.' He huffed. 'Have you ever felt like that? Like… I don't know.' He didn't have the words to describe all the feelings Juniper summoned in him, only that he was completely absorbed by her, and everything else came second. And when she didn't talk to him, when he felt something was wrong but couldn't reach her to find out what, he felt like he was caught in a whirlpool that never stopped spinning. Of course, his anxiety disorder didn't help, but he couldn't meditate away whatever the fuck she'd done to him, and his beta-blockers didn't seem to target any Juniper-related adrenaline, either.

It was too much. He knew it was. He just couldn't stop.

'No,' Luc answered honestly. 'I don't really experience romantic attraction, and honestly, watching you, I'm glad for it. You make it look exhausting. Who would ever want to fall in love?'

Aiden wrinkled his nose at that word, a defence mechanism that, once gone, left him feeling bare and unpleasant. 'It isn't love.'

He didn't sound convincing even to his own ears, and that made his grimace deepen. Shit. Maybe it was *a bit* love, or at least heading there. He'd been rapt by her since that first moment here. Maybe even before. He thought about her, worried about her, all day. He was enduring sleepless nights for the sake of her nocturnal hamster.

Luc cast him a pointed look, one that he wanted to hide from.

'Let's not go there,' he said.

'You started it,' they replied. 'I don't see why you can't just ask her to be your girlfriend. You've been *boinking*, as Tilly put it, for long enough.'

'I don't think she trusts me yet. Not completely.' And he didn't know how to change that. 'And stop saying boinking.'

'No. It's a good word.' Luc grinned. 'Have you given her a reason not to trust you, other than your general fuckboy appearance?'

'Oi! I'm not a fuckboy!'

'I didn't say you were. Only that you *look* like one.'

Aiden scraped his hair off his face as though that, somehow, would change Luc's mind. He attempted nonchalance, but then looked down at his brown lace-ups with concern. 'Is it the trainers? I knew I should have worn my Vans instead.'

'Yes, Vans would have changed everything,' Luc deadpanned.

'She's just always seen me as a rich arsehole.' When Luc opened their mouth, likely to agree, he jumped in: 'Yeah, all right, I guess I am, but it's sort of because that's who people want me to be. It's easier to meet their expectations. In fact, it used to get me friends. Shit friends, but friends.'

'But you must see that now, especially, she probably does not *want* to be with a rich arsehole.' Luc went back to scribbling down notes from their open book on Roman vessels. 'You are probably a walking reminder for her.'

Aiden halted. 'What do you mean? A reminder of what?'

'Of her own struggles.'

He paused. He hadn't known Juniper *was* struggling. That was why she had a job, wasn't it? To keep her afloat?

That pamphlet he'd seen on her desk yesterday flickered in his mind once more. The National Ceramics Competition. He'd researched it later, curious about why he hadn't heard of it himself, only to find it was a prestigious award judged by a renowned potter named Delia Melrose. It intended to boost the careers of new and lesser-known potters with a cash prize and the opportunities that followed. It seemed like a lot of extra work to put on herself in the middle of term, but now...

247

'Is Juniper struggling with money?'

'Oooooooooh, *merde*.' Luc cursed in their first language, paling slightly. 'I thought she would have told you. I did not say a thing, okay?'

'Luc, I need to know.'

They shook their head. 'It is not my business, Aiden.'

'Well it clearly is if she told you and not me!' His voice rose, heat blooming on his cheeks when a few pairs of eyes fell on him.

Luc chased away the stares before mumbling quietly, 'It wasn't that she told me and not you, okay? We both had the same problem.'

'What problem?' Luc hadn't mentioned anything, either. Did friends just not tell him things?

It stung, the idea that two of the most important people in his life hadn't wanted to talk to him about something. All right, fine, he *was* a rich arsehole and he looked like a fuckboy – he could handle that. But he was also understanding and eager to help his friends, and he'd sat here babbling about his feelings for Juniper while Luc kept their problems secret. What kind of shitty person did that make him?

Luc scratched their nose nervously, leaving the air between them uncomfortably quiet. 'RACA froze a few students' bursaries over Christmas. Budget cuts or something.'

Aiden didn't know what to say. He just couldn't stop wondering why they hadn't told him they were struggling. 'So, what does that mean for you all?'

'It means we have to pay tuition for our third term without aid. I'm just about able to do that with my international

248

funding, but I'm not sure if Juniper has a backup plan.' Luc's eyes turned pleading. 'Please do not tell her I told you, Aiden. It isn't my business to share, and if somebody spilled *my* financial status without permission, I would be furious.'

'Why didn't you tell me? Not about Juniper, about you. I thought…' He sniffed and cleared his throat, afraid he sounded childish. 'I thought we were friends, that's all.'

'We *are*.' Luc's own voice cracked. 'I just was not sure if you would want to hear about it. It was a moment of dread, and then it was over, and that was that. Not something you would need to worry about.'

He didn't believe Luc, not really. He knew why people didn't talk to him about money: because he had it. These people didn't trust him to empathise. To be a decent friend, a decent person. The people who supported him, who made this school year so much better than the last, wouldn't let him do the same.

Luc huffed. 'Please, not the sad puppy eyes.'

Aiden tried his best to rearrange his features, form a more neutral expression, but it wasn't easy. A wall divided him and the people around him. His side was wide open, allowing entrance to anyone he could find, but theirs remained locked up tight. This time, he couldn't blame it on shallow friends who only wanted to use him. It was *him* they had avoided, *him* they couldn't confide in.

After the other night, Juniper's confessions, he'd thought it had all been demolished, but it hadn't. It never would be.

'So, you're okay?' Aiden asked quietly.

Luc nodded. 'I'm fine. Honestly.'

'But Juniper isn't.'

'I don't think so.' Their mouth downturned with regret. 'But you can't force it from her, Aiden. She has to come to you.'

He scoffed. 'She never will.'

Luc was different. They had a clean slate. Aiden could build their trust in time. But Juniper had seen him before. She knew him at his worst.

How could he change that? How could he make her see that he was here for her?

'What will happen if she can't cover her tuition?' Part of him could guess. He couldn't imagine her taking on more work just because she wanted to. The contest was a last-ditch effort to afford the funding. And she'd asked Chris about the Stoke trip – were things so bad that she couldn't even afford the train tickets?

'I don't know. I think maybe…'

'What?' Aiden urged, bracing himself for the inevitable.

'I think she mentioned that perhaps she would have to drop out. Her job at the café won't exactly be enough to cover it all.'

Aiden cursed. She couldn't drop out. He'd seen how much she wanted this, how much she cared. She deserved her place here as much as everyone else. Certainly more than him.

An idea flitted in his mind, barely quickly enough to catch it, but he did, because he was desperate.

His dad. He'd written letters of recommendation for Aiden's friends before, back when Aiden still wanted to impress them, and he was connected to almost every art college dean in the country, either directly or through his colleagues.

If Juniper needed that funding, he might be able to get it.

There was just one tiny problem: it would mean that he would have to talk to Jonathan. That rarely ended well.

28

Middleport Pottery was even grander than it looked on TV. Juniper and Tilly marvelled at the tall chimney and round bottle kiln bringing the factory to life while students swarmed around them to take photographs. She felt a tiny bit more at home among the old brown bricks, or at least closer than she was in London. Even the canal behind them reminded her of Manchester's; grey and reflecting the colourful narrowboats on the water.

She sucked in a deep breath of frigid winter air in the hopes it would settle all of the mayhem inside her. No such luck. It grated on her, how she could always *feel* her thoughts like they were tangible things buzzing around her body, begging for her constant attention. Recently, none of those thoughts had been pleasant. She felt lost with her contest project, swamped with coursework essays she had no idea where to start with, and drained from work. This trip was less of a break and more of a thief, stealing precious time she needed to try to scrape together enough money to keep studying. Her bloody dad had paid for the train tickets, and not without grumbling down the phone about how lucky she was to be able to cadge off her parents; she wasn't sure she'd be able to put her pride aside again to ask him for anything more.

Warm skin grazed hers suddenly, and she snapped around to find Aiden at her side. He seemed to always be at her side: in class, on the train. Even his bloody hotel room was next to hers. She didn't know if it was the world still pushing them together at this point, or just him. As much as she liked his attention, it was growing more difficult by the day to keep her worries hidden, and the fact he kept looking at her like he knew something was wrong only made it worse.

'You look at home here, Hodge,' he said with a gentle poke.

Not nearly as at home as he did. Dressed in casual ripped jeans and a thick plaid shacket, he could have been heading in to work to guide visitors around the historical site. He was good at that: blending in. Or, at least, he would be if he wasn't one of the most handsome men she'd ever known.

'I think I'd die if I met Keith Brymer Jones here. I'd love to make him cry.' Tilly rubbed her arms with crocheted mittens to keep warm.

Juniper laughed at Aiden's concerned expression.

'With my pottery, obviously,' Tilly explained. 'When Keith cries, you know you've done a good job. God, haven't you ever watched *The Great Pottery Throw Down*?'

'Afraid not.'

'We'll fix that on my next Cerberus visit,' Juniper promised. She hated to think of her poor hamster all alone in Aiden's house, but apparently, he had a *friend* checking in. A friend who she'd already seen named on his phone as *Alfred Pet Sitter*. Either he had an interesting double-barrel surname or Aiden was paying him, which didn't sit right, but he insisted Alfred was just doing him a neighbourly favour and refused to let Juniper know more.

Soon, she wasn't sure she'd even be able to afford the hamster's sawdust. She was becoming his charity.

'You do know you're allowed to come around even for non-Cerberus related things.' Aiden's touch rested lightly on the small of her back, about the only sensation she'd felt recently that was actually enjoyable.

Still, she stepped away, glad when Tilly said, 'Stop right there. I don't need your raunchy sex lives being shoved in my face again.'

Juniper rolled her eyes. Tilly seemed to be just fine asking for the finer details when it was just the two of them. Juni linked her arm through Tilly's. 'We'll find you a pretty potter this weekend. I'll be the best wingwoman you've ever known.'

'I might be able to help. As you can tell, I'm decent at attracting the ladies.' Aiden gestured something akin to finger guns. Shudder. Juniper couldn't believe this was the man she was in lo—

Lust with. Yes, that.

She squared up to him, or tried to. Her shoulders barely met his even on her tiptoes, so it didn't have much effect, but she would let him know some other way that her wingwoman duties were not to be messed with. 'Any ladies attracted to you are *not* the type of ladies deserving of Tilly.'

'Well, that just feels like a self-burn,' Tilly commented, and Juniper realised she was probably right.

She sank back, a little embarrassed. 'Whatever. *I'm* the wingwoman.'

'Yes, good, that's exactly why I brought you all the way down to Stoke,' Chris butted in, casting a distasteful glare at each of them. Then, he addressed the whole class in a way that would put a megaphone to shame. 'Attention, gang! We have made it to the royal palace of pottery, the Taj Mahal of Stoke-on-Trent, the great temple of ceramicists' hopes and dreams!'

'Not to be dramatic, or anything,' Luc added dryly as they joined their formation of four.

Juniper chuckled, staring wistfully at the factory behind. She should have been that excited, too. Who was all these money worries making her become? Someone she barely recognised.

'This is Zoey.' Chris motioned to a short, blonde-haired woman who looked like she should have been one of the students, both because she was young and because she radiated the same confidence and class. Or maybe Juniper was just at a point where everybody seemed better-suited for her position at RACA than her. 'She shall be giving us the glorious tour today. Soak it all in, because you're guaranteed to learn a lot about how pottery factories like this operate.'

The tour guide, Zoey, beckoned them in. As the tour began, Juniper and Tilly drifted to the back of the class, where they could make comments about what they'd seen on their favourite pottery TV show in peace. Once Aiden and Luc were dragged into an example of how to extrude clay in one of the workshops, Tilly elbowed her gently.

'You're not yourself, babe. Are you sure you're doing okay?'

It wasn't the first time Tilly had asked, or even the fifth. Juniper had opened up to her about her frozen funding after mending her pit-fired plates, and Tilly had vowed to help her figure it out – but it was clear that was impossible, so after that, she'd vowed to help her with the contest instead. *We're going to be okay,* she'd insisted, as though Tilly had just at much at stake as Juniper. It was nice, not to be doing it alone, but at the end of the day, only one of them would be going home if everything fell apart.

'Just thinking about all the things I should be doing back in London,' Juniper admitted. 'The contest deadline isn't far off, and I still don't know what I'm doing.' She'd thrown a few vases that had turned out lovely, but not magnificent enough to win her any awards. Her next idea was hand-built bookends, but she had no idea what else to join them with. It felt like she'd used up all her best talents in the project with Aiden, though she'd admit she was holding herself back from her usual sculpted monsters, afraid they wouldn't be appreciated if the judge was anything like her classmates.

After the tour, she was only proved right. They wandered into the gift shop to find an infinite collection of sophisticated, gorgeous homeware pottery. Porcelain dinner sets swirled with blue patterns that reminded her of Grandma's old china plates; cake stands like the ones that customers of Caffé Verde enjoyed afternoon sandwiches on; teapots far smoother and more eye-catching than the one Juniper had shattered in the pit.

'Wowzer. These are fancy, eh?' Tilly went to touch a mug decorated with delicate pink florals and then thought better of it.

'Too fancy.' Way fancier than anything Juniper could create.

She wandered around the tables, holding her breath when she felt her backpack snag on the displays.

'I've got it!' someone shouted, thank god, and then the pottery she'd disrupted was caught in a set of sturdy hands.

Aiden's hands, of course. Clearly, he was an expert at fixing her messes, or at least wanted to be.

'Thank you.' Juniper put a hand on her chest in relief, but it seemed like proof that she just wasn't made to fit into spaces filled with delicate works of art. She turned around to joke as much only to almost knock off a toast rack on the opposite side of her.

He reached around her to catch that, too, one hand keeping her backpack away from any more disasters. His chest was flush against hers, grin inches away. It was as close as she'd let him get to her since the night she'd fallen asleep on his couch. 'How about I hold your backpack for you before the whole shop comes tumbling down?' he questioned.

'Whatever would I do without you?' she crooned sarcastically, earning her a laugh.

'I wonder the same thing all the time.'

She glared and squirmed away, though her entire stomach lurched with the need for him to be closer. God, she missed the smell of him, the taste of him, the way he moaned for her like nobody had before, and she him.

Maybe Tilly wasn't the only one yearning for connection. Problem was, Juniper already knew what she was missing, and it left her *aching*.

Something hard prodded her thigh, and she raised an eyebrow, glad to find nobody was looking. 'Happy to see me, Aiden?'

He dipped his head in amusement. 'Get your mind out of that filthy gutter, Hodge. It's a gift.'

Juniper groused, 'Look, I don't know what's with you and all these little shows of affection, but it needs to stop, okay? You're not my—'

'Boyfriend, I know. The gift isn't for you.' Aiden produced a paper bag from his pocket with a flourish. From it, he produced a marbled, ceramic toadstool with an arched doorway so tiny that only a mouse could fit.

Or a hamster.

'Cerberus's cage needs a little upgrade, don't you think?' he said.

She glowered frostily. 'Are you trying to out-parent me, Whittaker?'

'No.' His smirk said otherwise, so smug that his teeth poked through.

'I don't think he would like something this bright. His favourite colour is black,' she lied. His favourite colour was probably red, same as his wheel, and same as the top of the toadstool. It was adorable, and she wanted it immediately. She just wasn't sure why Aiden had been the one to buy it.

'I guess we'll have to let him decide for himself. Maybe he fancies a change.'

'I thought you didn't like Cerberus. Thought he was keeping you up all night.' Juniper crossed her arms over her chest, an accusation serrating her words.

'Which is why he needs a little place to rest his weary head.' Aiden tucked the toadstool back into its gift bag, chin tilted with pride.

Great. He was now better than her at taking care of her hamster. She had officially reached rock bottom.

29

Aiden hovered outside the cobbled stone walls of the Potter's Arms long after his classmates had headed in to celebrate their free evening in Stoke-on-Trent. The aptly themed pub spilled a buttery glow across the darkness as afternoon turned to evening. He should have been looking forward to heading in, getting warm, eating whatever delightfully rich, home-cooked meal he could smell emanating from within, but instead, he clenched his phone in tight fingers, frozen against an avalanche of anxiety.

He'd been waiting for it to rear its ugly head all day, that familiar jitter steadily growing since the train ride. It was a silly thing to trigger all this, a reply from his dad. One he'd expected, no less, after he'd reached out to ask for help on Juniper's behalf.

If you need my help, come home and see me like a man would, Aiden, Jonathan had written.

It was probably fair. Aiden didn't feel all that 'manly' when it came to his father, though Jonathan's regular intimidation tactics and general unapproachable demeanour seemed a deliberate attempt to make sure that stayed true. If *that* was manliness, Aiden wanted no part in it.

But he did want to help Juniper, so he could pretend. He would have to. Just as soon as he could feel his fingers and toes again, as soon as the world wasn't caving in on him.

He stepped out of the way of two patrons emerging from the pub, a huddled couple giggling about the paint on their cheeks. As well as food and drink, the wooden-framed chalk-board out front advertised pottery and painting sessions, something he might have loved to do with Juniper if it wasn't already part of their daily routine.

There were *too* many things he'd love to do with her. Things he knew he wouldn't get the chance to if she lost her place at RACA. He folded against the stone, trying to focus on the curling cloud of his breath in front of him, the way his knees still managed to hold him up. He wasn't dying, and this would pass. A mantra he'd told himself too many times before, and yet one his nervous system never seemed to believe.

'Aiden?' Luc's head popped out of the doorway, and then the rest of them. 'Are you okay? I saved a seat for you in there.'

Aiden nodded, though it felt like a lie. 'Thanks. I'll be in soon.'

They scrutinised him with careful eyes, then the phone in his hands. He felt like he'd been caught doing something wrong, probably because he was. He knew Juniper would never agree to his help, not in any way, shape, or form. She'd almost thrown a fit when he'd bought Cerberus that toadstool earlier, like she was afraid that somebody doing things for her, helping her, made her weak. In his eyes, it just made her cared for, and that was something he wanted her to be – even when she was a pain in the arse about it.

'I'm fine,' Aiden said when Luc remained unrelenting. 'Just give me a minute, yeah?'

As much as he wanted to tell them what was happening, he knew it wouldn't be fair to ask them to keep another secret. Besides, he was still trying to let go of their conversation the other day, the fact that Luc hadn't confided in him. Maybe Juniper wasn't the only one who didn't want to appear vulnerable.

'Aiden...' Luc twisted their nose ring as though deliberating something. 'You do know that I'm here for you, yes? I *am* your friend.'

Aiden's sinuses stung. He hadn't known that, not really. Luc was like Juniper: blasé, difficult to read. To hear it aloud meant more than Luc could know. 'Thank you,' he said gently. 'I hope you know it's reciprocated.'

'I do now.' Luc smiled. Aiden might have, too, if his phone wasn't burning a hole in his hand.

He tried to collect himself just long enough to say, 'I'll be in soon. Promise.'

'Okay. Sure.' At that, Luc headed back in, closing the door on the chatter and music within. Aiden bit the inside of his cheek and finally forced his digits into action.

Are you free tomorrow at noon?

They were supposed to be visiting a few businesses tomorrow, but he didn't have time to wait, and this saved a long train journey from London to Manchester.

He was surprised when the three dots popped up immediately, indicating that Jonathan was typing. It wasn't like him to respond – quickly, or at all.

See you then. Lunch at our usual spot.

They hadn't had a *usual spot* for years, but it would do Aiden no favours to point that out. He tucked his phone back into his pocket, already rehearsing what he would say. *The girl I'm infatuated with needs you to put in a good word so she can get her bursary back.* Jonathan wouldn't understand. He'd think it ridiculous.

But Aiden had to try.

He took another few minutes to collect himself, and then headed inside. The sight of Juniper laughing with Tilly over a colourful menu, dazzling and rosy-cheeked, was enough to cement that he was doing the right thing.

He could fix this.

★

'What about that white-haired lady over there?' Luc tipped their head towards a woman sitting on the other side of the pub, painting happily with a group of similarly aged women. *Elderly* women.

'Luc, that white-haired lady is about seventy,' Aiden retorted. After eating a hearty, gravy-soaked meal of bangers and mash, which Luc unsurprisingly hadn't enjoyed at all, they were back to helping Tilly find an eligible young bachelorette, mostly for lack of better things to do. His classmates had already caused the pub to descend into chaos, with Tom and Amir currently wailing a duet of 'Unchained Melody' into the karaoke microphone, much to the discomfort of the old ladies trying to enjoy their peaceful evening of arts and crafts.

KILN ME SOFTLY

Luc shrugged. 'Age gaps are popular these days.'

'I'm not against an older woman, but I'm not sure I'm emotionally ready for a grandmother,' Tilly said, rattling the ice around in her empty pint glass.

Juniper plucked a leftover chip from Aiden's plate and said, 'You're all terrible at this, which is why *I* am the only elected matchmaker here.'

Aiden clucked his tongue. 'If you're so good, why haven't you noticed the woman behind Owen over there?'

He gestured with his pint glass to a woman who looked to be in her late twenties, with glowy skin darker than Tilly's, a kind, red-lipped smile, and long black hair twists that reached far beyond her shoulders. She wore an eye-catching paisley-printed scarf around her neck and a tan coat that draped closer to the ground as she leaned her elbows on the bar to chat with a man. They didn't lean too close and had no visible chemistry bubbling between them, which Aiden found promising.

'Oh, she's stunning. Waaaay out of my league.' Tilly shrank back against the burgundy upholstery, prompting Juniper to tut.

'First of all, no. Second of all, I have my sights set else-where.' Juniper glared pointedly at Aiden, and then subtly jabbed her thumb over her shoulder. 'Autumnal goddess, nine o'clock.'

'That's not even close to nine o'clock,' Aiden said.

'That's because you're facing anticlockwise, obviously.'

He choked on his beer with a laugh that was half disbelief, half adoration. Still, Juniper was right. A gorgeous auburn-haired woman with their hair tied in space buns winced at

Tom and Amir's singing between scrolling on her phone. Her drink sat untouched on the table.

'And it looks like she's been stood up,' Juniper said. 'Perfect time for Tilly to swoop in and save the day.'

'Mine is better. She looks like she listens when people talk. Isn't glued to her phone screen.' Aiden didn't know why he was so desperate to help Tilly, only that he couldn't remember a time when he'd done something this normal. If he could prove he was a decent wingman, maybe they'd keep him around. Maybe he'd be better for more than just his money, and his friends would start seeing him as a real person.

Apparently, that wasn't to be, because Juniper rolled her eyes. 'If she looks so wonderful, why don't *you* go and talk to her?'

He nudged her foot under the table. 'Because I've set my sights elsewhere. No need to be jealous, Hodge. I'm all yours.'

'Vom,' Tilly said, pretending to retch. And then: 'Actually, it's cute and I want one. Not an Aiden. A Juniper, maybe.'

Juniper tapped Tilly's hair, leaving her thick curls to bounce against her shoulders. 'Trust me, you don't want a Juniper, but *I* will get you someone far better.'

Aiden gasped dramatically. 'I don't like any of what you just said.'

'Maybe you should get all this rivalry out of your system,' Luc suggested. 'Whoever gets their girl to talk to Tilly first wins.'

Tilly's brows lifted. 'Hm. I like it.'

Juniper jolted up in her seat. 'What do we win?'

'My eternal gratitude.'

'And ice cream,' Luc said, tapping a picture of a chocolate sundae printed on the pub's menu.

'Oh, you're on. There is nothing in this world that will stand between me and ice cream.' Juniper rose from her chair, towering over Aiden with a wicked grin on her face, her hands planted on the table at either side of her so that he had a perfect view of her cleavage. He was both intimidated and extremely turned on, eyes dragging down to her lips. He hadn't kissed them in so long. Too long.

'We'll soon see about that, Hodge.' He tapped her nose as he stood, his height a great advantage. She didn't back down from it, only redirecting her glower up instead of down. 'May the best wingperson win,' he decided, and then moved towards the bar to work his magic.

30

As Aiden slid onto the stool beside the woman he'd set his sights on, he locked eyes with Juniper across the bar. She was already talking to the autumnal goddess, as she'd phrased it, arms stretched against the back of the stranger's chair as though they'd known each other for years. When the woman looked at her phone, Juniper mouthed something that resembled, *I scream with wine*. He assumed it meant *ice cream is mine* and shook his head slowly, only then realising that the woman he'd come to chat with was staring at him, equal amounts disturbed and curious. Probably because he had stuck his face between her and her friend, having meant to say something before Juniper distracted him.

'May we help you?' asked the man.

Aiden stuttered his words for a moment. 'Well, possibly. Maybe. I was just wondering if my friend over there can buy you a drink?'

The man waved a hand. 'Sorry, mate. Not interested.'

'Not you, unfortunately.' With a sympathetic pat on the man's shoulder, he swivelled to the woman. 'You.'

She smirked, casting a glance over her shoulder to view their table. 'Well, that depends. Which friend are we talking about?'

'The woman currently chomping on ice…' Aiden winced. Tilly was gorgeous, but with her cheeks full like Cerberus's at mealtime and water dribbling down her chin, she wasn't exactly looking her best. 'Across from our green-haired friend.'

She hazarded a look at her friend, who shrugged and hopped off the stool. 'I was about to head off, so I'll leave you to it, I s'pose. Enjoy.'

And then it was just the two of them. Aiden slipped onto the abandoned stool and held out a hand, trying to work his practised charm. 'I'm Aiden, by the way. Sorry for interrupting, it's just sort of urgent.'

'Coco.' She narrowed her eyes, but shook his hand. 'Why urgent? Is she dying?'

'God, no! No, she's just terribly lonely.' He scratched his head. Again, probably not setting up a good impression of Tilly. 'In a very non-desperate way.'

Coco cleared her throat. 'Well, I'm not feeling all that into desperation myself, so…'

'Okay, I lied. It's me who's desperate.' He pointed to Juniper across the bar, who now had her back turned. 'I'm trying to out wingman my girl… my *friend*,' he corrected quickly, 'over there, and I made a very good argument about why you would be the perfect match for Tilly.'

'Hm.' Coco smirked. 'So, you're trying to impress your girl, in other words.'

He pinched his thumb and index together. 'A little bit. For a good cause, though.'

'Well, that is kinda cute.' She sighed and grabbed her drink from the bar, a tall, thin glass garnished with a slice of lime. 'Fine. You've caught me in a curious mood.'

Aiden jumped off the stool and then motioned politely for Coco to go ahead, silently cheering once her back was turned. However, it didn't last: he caught Juniper approaching with the redhead at exactly the same time, and he could do nothing short of pushing Coco into the table to win the battle – which, as a gentleman, he obviously did not consider doing. At all.

Juniper was quick to put her hands on her hips, blocking their path. 'Hello, Aiden. Who might this be?'

'I'm Coco?' She said it as though it was a question.

'Coco is very impressive at… the thing she does, which is…' Aiden realised he probably should have asked for some details before dragging her over here.

'I'm a small business owner,' Coco supplied.

'Well, my girl here is a waitress, like me!' Juniper beamed. 'You did say you wanted a Juniper, Tilly.'

'And what is your girl's name?' Aiden lifted his brows expectantly, enjoying the way Juniper grew flustered. 'Terrible wingwoman, really, not even asking her name. I'd never do such a thing.'

Tilly rolled her eyes and stood up. 'This was a big, big mistake.' She looked at both suitors. 'I'm so sorry. I don't know how I didn't predict that my friends would turn this into a disaster.'

'Yeah, I'm not really into this, so… bye.' The autumnal goddess marched off before anybody could stop her, and Aiden couldn't blame her. Still, a flare of something warm brightened inside him. *Friends.* Plural. He was one of them now.

'That means I've won.' He clapped like a giddy kid, then gave Coco a high-five, which was accepted reluctantly.

'I'm walking away now.' Tilly locked eyes with Coco, a small smile dimpling her face. 'Could I maybe buy you a drink to say sorry for all this?'

'Don't forget my sundae,' Aiden reminded, grinning when Juniper stuck his tongue out at him. As soon as their backs were turned, he flashed the shape of an L with his thumb and finger. 'Don't worry, sweetheart. I'll share with the loser.'

'You're intolerable. I can't stand you.' But she was trying not to laugh as she collapsed back down next to Luc. A stark contrast to the way she used to say it, chest puffed out and mouth twisted in disgust.

So, when Tilly slammed a chocolate sundae down onto the table soon after, he grabbed two extra spoons for her and Luc, and they all dipped into the ice cream. Luc took a few bites and then called it a night, claiming their social battery was officially drained. Aiden would have to make extra effort not to bother them back in their room tonight.

'And then there were two.' Aiden clanked his spoon against hers, forcing her away from the soft squares of fudge. 'Oi! Don't pinch the best pieces!'

It was too late. Juniper gathered a big heap of them, moaning smugly. He might have reprimanded her, but he was too busy watching her tongue swirl around the fudge-coated spoon.

She must have noticed, because one of her brows arched. 'Who's the loser now, Whittaker? Look at you, getting all hot and bothered over me licking a spoon.'

He rolled his eyes, twisting the stem of the bowl around so she had better access to the fudge. He'd meant what he'd said, that he'd do anything for her, even if he usually hated to share good food. 'You have to admit, I was good at that. Might drop out of RACA to pursue matchmaking duties full time.'

'It surprises me,' she said, then paused when instinct drove him to reach out. The pad of his thumb swiped gently at the sticky blob of chocolate on the corner of her mouth, lips parting as though she'd forgotten how it felt for him to touch her. Maybe she had. Maybe he wanted to fix that: but there was no chance tonight. He was sharing with Luc, she with Tilly.

So he showed her instead, bringing his thumb to his mouth and watching as her chest fluttered just a little big higher than the breath before.

'What surprises you?' he asked, sticky sweetness dissolving on his tongue.

'That it mattered so much to you. If you would have told me I was battling with Aiden Whittaker for the sake of our mutual friend's dating life in high school, I would have thrown a fit.'

'Oh, did you not like me back then, or something? I don't think you've mentioned it before,' he retorted sarcastically.

She chuckled, the sound light and melodic with just a hint of huskiness. It was the first time he'd heard it that way since before Christmas, and he hadn't realised how badly he'd missed it.

That was why he decided to offer her the truth, even if he didn't realise that was what it was until he said it aloud. 'This is the first time I've ever had the chance to actually have friends. *Proper* friends who don't give a shit about the superficial stuff. So, yeah, it matters.'

She propped her chin in her palms, eyes glittering. In the yellow light, she'd never looked so beautiful, irises a warm, whisky-brown and lips a deep pink from the cold sundae. He imagined this was their life, their every evening: coming to the pub and laughing, because she didn't hate him anymore, and because they cared about each other. He could see it, almost. Beyond the ever-growing line of hurdles, there were flashes of something better for them.

'Where d'you think Chris will take us tomorrow?' she mused.

And there it was. One of the many obstacles in his way. His stomach plummeted all over again at the thought of seeing his dad, but he tried not to let it show. 'I need to ask you a favour, actually.'

'Yeah? What kind of favour?'

'I need to head to Manchester for a few hours. Can you cover for me? Tell Chris I've got a migraine or something?'

'Okay.' A little divot formed between her brows, hands edging closer to his across the table. 'Am I allowed to ask why?'

'Dunno. Are you? You're not my girlfriend, after all, as you love to keep reminding me.'

She scoffed, making to lean away, but he caught her fingers on the scraped, lacquered wood. 'I've got to show my face for a lunch with my dad, otherwise I'll never hear the end of it.'

Concern remained etched in her, enough to make him fall for her again, again, again. She could keep lying to him, but she cared, and she was as bad as he was at concealing it these days. 'Will you be okay? Isn't he, like, awful?'

'Whatever gave you that impression?' His cheeks cracked with the force of his feigned smile.

She saw right through it, thumb gliding over his knuckles. 'Was he even there to support you when you were struggling?'

He was afraid that if he spoke, his voice would betray how much it hurt, so he only shook his head.

'You don't have to go. You don't have to do anything for him if you don't want to,' she said.

He wished that were true. He squeezed her hand, admitting, 'I sometimes hope one day it'll be different. That he'll accept me. I'm sure I'll stop torturing myself at some point, but I'm not quite ready to cut him off completely yet.'

'I get that.' She surprised him by bringing his hand to her mouth and kissing his knuckles, the coolness of her lips leaving him tingling. And then she mimicked biting him, causing him to laugh again. She was always good at that. 'I'll be here when you get back. Okay?'

'Okay.' He leaned closer, dragging her chair around, and her with it. Her breath caught in her throat as their foreheads knocked together. 'I've been wanting to kiss you all night. All year, really.'

She wrinkled her nose. 'A New Year's joke? Really?'

'Really.' His nose nestled against hers, lips inches apart, and he could already feel his cock stirring. 'I miss you, Juni.'

She kissed him for not nearly long enough, then replaced her lips with a finger. 'I can't.'

'You say that a lot.'

'Because it's true.' And yet her knees were still slotted between his, her breath fluttering on his lips. 'Kissing is never just kissing with you, and we don't exactly have much privacy here.'

'Never stopped us before.' He looked up, finding Tilly and Coco making out at the bar. 'Isn't stopping them, either.'

She giggled upon seeing them, then pecked his nose just once before finally opening the distance between them again. 'When we get back to London. Maybe. I'll consider it.'

Fine. He could wait for her.

It felt like something he'd been doing his whole life.

31

Juniper had stepped out into a crisp day, the sky bright enough she could almost convince herself she was in a good mood. As long as she didn't think too hard, she was, though she couldn't help but check her phone every five minutes in case Aiden texted. He hadn't told her too much about Jonathan, but enough for her to know he was a shitty parent. The mention of him always cast a shadow in their conversations, and she didn't want that for him. Nobody deserved it, but especially not him.

As Chris led the group down a shopping street in the city centre, Juniper turned her attention to Tilly.

'You got home awfully late last night.' She knew, because she'd gotten home around midnight and Tilly hadn't been there. She'd fallen asleep next to an empty bed, the sound of Aiden getting comfortable next door plaguing her through paper thin walls. She wasn't sure she'd be strong enough to resist if he asked her to kiss him a second time.

The beaming smile on Tilly's face was a dead giveaway for what had transpired between she and Coco. 'Well, let's just say your man did a decent job.'

Juniper tutted bitterly. That poor autumn goddess deserved better, though she'd admit Coco was equally as gorgeous and clearly had made her friend happy. 'Who knew Aiden had a fully functioning gaydar?'

'I know. Maybe you should keep him after all.'

She shrugged. 'Thinking about it.'

Tilly stopped in her tracks, then squealed, much to the alarm of their other classmates. Juniper shushed her, tugging her to one side.

'But I can't!' she added quickly.

That soon dulled her spirit. 'Juni, I love you, and I get you, but maybe you should let this money thing with him go. He has it, you don't. It doesn't make you Romeo and Juliet! Maybe he'd even be able to help you with your tuition fees.'

She could feel her face take on a life of its own, mirroring the iciness under her skin. Maybe the gap between she and Aiden was knitting shut, one thread at a time, but she couldn't make a life with somebody who took their privilege for granted. She just couldn't. She wanted to be understood, especially when it came to her struggles, and he had proved time and again that he couldn't provide that.

'I can't talk about it anymore.'

Tilly grabbed her shoulders. 'He makes you happy. I just want to see you happy.'

'You know what makes me happy?' Chris interrupted. 'Not having to hear about everybody's sad little love lives.' He stopped outside a brightly decorated shop front with a pink awning and painted pottery filling the window. Juniper was instantly pulled in by the pieces, enamoured by the abstract sculptures and vibrant glazes. Whoever had made these didn't cater to the same traditional styles as the potters of Middleport, nor the past contest entrants she'd researched.

She looked at the huge golden sign above the window and let out a *Ha*! 'Cococeramics! Wouldn't it be funny if her name was Coco, too? Or, even better, if it was—'

The shop's door swung open, and Tilly's jaw dropped. Juniper could do nothing but stifle her laughter behind a gloved hand as Coco waved at them all. 'Good morning, everyone! Thank you for coming today. I'm…'

She trailed off when her focus snagged on Tilly, whose face was now the colour of beetroot. She dipped her chin into her scarf in an attempt to hide, but judging by Coco's smirk, it was too late.

'I'm Coco,' she finished. 'I'm a local potter. I'd love for you to come inside.'

'I bet she said that to you last night as well,' Juniper jested.

'Very funny, but you know that's not how it works,' Tilly ground out.

'I know. Just had to. Didn't she tell you she was a potter?' whispered Juniper.

'We never quite got round to that, honestly. We were busy with… other things.'

Well, this was going to be interesting.

★

'Tilly, you might have snogged the most talented potter in Stoke-on-Trent,' Juniper decided as they drank in the vast, open shop space. There wasn't one corner without a splash of colour, every vessel and sculpture different from the last so that anybody could tell it had been formed by hand, the intentional imperfections making the pieces all the more special.

'We did a bit more than snog.' Tilly looked just as stunned. She kept at the back of the group as though Coco might forget she was there if she hid well enough.

To be fair, the others were vying for her attention, especially Tom. 'Looks like someone broke your jug,' he said, pointing to a gash that revealed layered pinks and blues beneath. Of course someone like him wouldn't get it. His work was neat, mono-chrome, perfect for people who valued style over substance.

As Coco politely explained the reason behind her choice, Juniper gravitated towards a selection on the back wall labelled *Pride*. Rainbows decorated each pot, some traditional colours and others matching LGBTQ+ flags. Juniper squatted to admire a pink, yellow, and blue plant pot, the colours of her pansexual flag. The glaze had been applied with a dripping method, blues smeared like a sunset melting into an ocean. She'd seen nothing so bold and bright since her studies at RACA had begun. Self-expression in professional pottery seemed to be much more contained, as though too much of it was considered something Other, a bit like her mythological monsters. A bit like her, if she was being honest. She'd never fit into academic spaces, not at high school and certainly not now, and her financial troubles only seemed to prove that to her.

But in this shop, she felt at home.

'I'm glad this collection has called to someone,' a voice said. Juniper straightened to find Coco at her side, a serene smile on her face. The others milled around the shop, Tom still murmuring something that was probably belittling about Coco's works. Tilly was tailing Christopher, using his short, broad form as an ineffective hiding spot.

'If I had a place of my own, and y'know, money, I think I'd have bought every single piece by now,' admitted Juniper.

Coco hummed. 'It only occurred to me a few years ago, when I was a vendor at the local Pride festival, that I was allowed to express this part of myself in my ceramics. That maybe people wanted – *needed* – to see it. We put a lot of ourselves in these flags, after all. Sometimes, they're the only places where we feel like we belong.'

Juniper's eyes prickled. She was lucky that her sexuality had never been a problem to the people around her, but she knew that wasn't the case for everyone. Before she'd learned about pansexuality, she'd spent a long time wondering why no other label seemed to fit her, why her sexuality didn't feel black and white, straight or gay, or even bi. And then that one word had clicked everything into place, providing her with an understanding of herself she might not have had otherwise.

'I'm really sorry about last night, by the way,' Juniper said to Coco sheepishly. Clearly, the autumnal goddess had been completely wrong for Tilly. This woman, on the other hand, might just be perfect. Damn Aiden and his wingman talents. 'I got a bit competitive.'

'I hadn't noticed.' Coco's lips twitched, and Juniper took it as forgiveness. Coco turned on her heel, scanning the store. When they both caught a wave of Tilly's crocheted scarf, she shook her head. 'Obviously, I didn't know you lot were students. No wingman today?'

'He's busy. With a migraine,' she added quickly when she felt Chris's presence close behind them.

'Ah, yes, a pesky migraine.' Chris's hands locked behind his back as he joined them at the Pride display. 'Stunning work, Coco. Thank you again for letting my uncultured scamps invade your space.'

'A pleasure. I don't think some of them quite like it, mind.'

'Well, some of them wouldn't understand stylistic intention if it whacked them in the face. Thankfully, Juniper here is not one of them.'

She raised her brows at the compliment. 'I'm not?'

'I think you would have liked her exhibit last month,' Chris insisted. 'A little darker than your pieces, Coco, but very illustrative. She's a talented sculptor, indeed.'

Juniper eyed him closely, checking for evidence of sickness or cloning. 'Who are you and what have you done with Chris?'

'Good question. I'm disturbed about it, myself. But these things need to be said. Occasionally.' He patted her head like she was a dog, which felt much more characteristic of him.

Coco laughed, her golden bracelets rattling as she folded her arms. 'Well, I'd love to see your work, Juniper. Have you considered your career plans?'

'I've barely considered my lunch plans,' Juniper admitted, overwhelmed at the prospect. Still, there had been a time before RACA when the idea of selling her jewellery and sculptures alone had brought her unbridled joy. Of course, people didn't go to the most prestigious ceramics college in the country just to learn how to sell things on Etsy. She should have been aiming higher now.

But then, why had Chris brought them here otherwise?

'How did you decide to do this?' she was eager to ask. 'Did you study ceramics first?'

Coco shook her head. 'Nope. It started as a hobby, purely for fun. My friend and I spent the summer before uni doing as many new things as we could, and one of our plans just happened to be throwing at the Potter's Arms around the corner. I fell in love with it immediately, ended up booking a few classes, and saved up through my business degree to get my own throwing wheel.'

Juniper was too awed to so much as blink – and too envious. Coco made the whole thing sound so easy, like pottery had just *found* her and decided to keep her.

'How long have you had your business?'

'Six years, now. I started out by selling on eBay and at local markets, anything I had the time to make, and when that took off, I took out a business loan and managed to get my first shop front. It was a tiny little building most people walked right past, but I managed to find my way here through blood, sweat and tears.'

So it wasn't just luck, then. Coco had worked hard to get here. It hadn't been handed to her the way it was for some.

A million thoughts clouded Juniper's brain. This was what she'd dreamed of, too, and she didn't need RACA to do it. But she did need something. The education, the practice, the workshop. A few lessons here and there wouldn't cut it, but she couldn't afford the tools and materials to learn any other way.

'You look deep in thought,' Coco noted. 'Is it a lot to take in?'

'I just find it difficult to know where my place is in ceramics sometimes,' Juniper admitted. 'I'm not sure I'd have the patience to build a business the way you have, but I'm not finding the academic route any easier, either.'

'I think it's natural for an artist to wonder which approach is best. There isn't always a right answer.' Coco's voice was soft. Understanding. 'You're allowed to take time to figure it out. By the sounds of it, you have a lot of talent.'

But not a lot of room to explore it. Not without her bursary, and certainly not when she was driving herself towards another burnout. All she could think about was the contrast between Middleport and here: the traditional versus the abstract. If she wanted to succeed in academia, and with that competition, it seemed as though she needed to fit into a box. Yet every instinct in her body screamed to break out of boxes, not crawl into them.

'Thank you for taking the time to talk to me,' Juniper said gratefully, avoiding Chris's assessing gaze. She drifted away to look around the rest of the shop, fidgeting with the hair tie on her wrist. She wasn't ready to confront the root of her inner conflict, not yet, telling herself that as much as she'd love a store like this one day, art school had been the dream she'd chased for years. She couldn't let it go, at least not without a fight.

A good potter would know how to do both surely: fit the mould, and break out of it. If she could do that for the contest, maybe she'd finally have the resources, the experience, to work out what kind of artist she truly was.

'Get her number,' she whispered in Tilly's ear as she returned to her by a rack of interestingly textured mugs. 'She's extremely great, and I want you to marry her.'

Tilly snorted, but her gaze still lingered towards where Coco conversed with Chris and, now, Luc. 'In the harsh light of day, she's even more out of my league than I thought.'

'Shut up. You're gorgeous, and she clearly thinks so. She keeps looking at you.'

To prove it, Coco's dark eyes drifted back towards Tilly, causing Tilly to duck and feign interest in a twisted mug handle.

Juniper tutted and decided it was time to reassume wing-woman duties. By the end of their visit, Coco had Tilly's number, neither of them having noticed Juniper slipping Tilly's contact details in Coco's pocket. Aiden might have picked the better suitor, but Juniper had made sure to keep them together. That *clearly* made her the better friend, and she couldn't wait to brag about it on the train home – once she heard back from Aiden.

She only hoped he was okay in Manchester.

32

Jonathan hadn't changed a bit since the last time Aiden had seen him. He sat at his usual restaurant table by the tall, arched windows, his flinty features carved deeper by the light of his laptop screen while Deansgate hurtled into the lunchtime rush hour behind him.

Aiden wrung the pins and needles from his hands, glad he hadn't yet been noticed. It allowed him a moment to get his bearings, remember who he was supposed to be, and how this was supposed to go. He wouldn't show weakness if he could help it, even if he felt it all over.

The soles of his trainers squeaked against the restaurant's glossy teak floorboards as he approached, finally alerting his father to his presence. With a disdainful glance, Jonathan shut his laptop and pushed it away to replace it with his cappuccino. As always, his dark hair was combed away from the harsh lines of his temples, revealing more threads of silver than before. He wore his usual pristine navy suit and tie, as though he was here for a client meeting rather than a chat with his son. He'd always been that way: businessman first, father when convenient, which was almost never.

Wordlessly, Aiden took the seat opposite, digging his elbows into the table. He didn't dare speak first, as though staying quiet would delay Jonathan's inevitable criticisms. He'd learned early on that there was even a wrong way to say hello if he was ill-tempered enough that day.

'You're late,' Jonathan stated finally.

Well, there went that hope. 'Am I?'

Hardly. It was barely two minutes past noon, according to the clock above the bar.

Jonathan pursed his thin lips. 'I'd imagine your mother has some things to say about your haircut, or lack thereof.'

Aiden scraped his waves back. He'd been letting it grow again, partly because he liked it long and partly because he knew Juniper did, too, but it was still not nearly as untamed as he'd kept it before Christmas.

'Trying something new.' He fiddled with the clasp on his wristwatch. Beneath the table, his knee bounced up and down.

'How adventurous you are these days.' Jonathan's tone was all sourness, punctuated by an audible slurp of his coffee.

Thankfully, he was saved by the approach of the server, who took their orders. He grimaced when Jonathan ordered a starter of roasted scallops; that meant he planned to stay, possibly for three torturous courses. Aiden picked the first thing he could find on the menu, a prawn salad, and requested a coffee. He should have asked questions, ordered something with more than two words just to keep putting this off, but the waiter was gone too soon and then the thick silence returned.

Jonathan was the one to break it. 'How was your Christmas?' He asked it in a way that showed he didn't actually want to know, his voice monotone and vacant.

'Fine. Yours?'

'Busy. I was in Edinburgh for work.'

'Of course.' Aiden couldn't remember the last Christmas his father had spent at home, which he was glad for. Childhood holidays, pre-divorce, had been filled with passive-aggressive micromanaging in the kitchen and meals eaten in silence. He'd never blamed Mum for leaving, though he resented that she hadn't taken him with her. 'How is work?'

'You might already know the answer to that if you weren't faffing around in ceramics.'

And there it was. Aiden's coffee was placed in front of him, another welcome reprieve that lasted not nearly long enough. He counted to five in his head, one breath in, one breath out, and when that did nothing to help, he went to ten. 'Not faffing, Father. Studying.'

'What does your mother think of it?'

She didn't think of it. The second Aiden had finished high school, he'd no longer been much of her concern. She checked in now and then out of what was probably a sense of obligation, but otherwise, they were strangers save for birthdays and Christmases. The lesser of two evils. 'She's fine with it.'

'Hm. Well, she's as bad as you when it comes to throwing good things away.' Jonathan raised a brow, green eyes turning translucent in the midday sun. He would have been handsome if he wasn't so miserable and stern, with a long, slightly upturned nose he'd passed on to Aiden and a similar square jaw. Aiden prayed he wasn't looking at a future version of himself. He had no idea when or why Jonathan had become this way. Whether it was because he begrudged being a father at all, or if he'd always had a heart full of spite. That steely presence had always made Aiden want to run the opposite way, even as a kid. As soon as his dad had gotten home from work, Aiden would disappear to his room, left to entertain himself until it was time to tread eggshells at the dinner table.

'I'm not sure she'd agree,' Aiden replied quietly, taking special care in stirring his coffee. It was brave, braver than he'd usually be, if the good thing Jonathan was referring to was himself. He must have been around Juniper for long enough to forget his filter, which might have been freeing if he wasn't here to save her future.

'So, what is it?' Jonathan leaned back, unbuttoning his blazer. 'What trouble have you gotten yourself into? Another college dropped out of, or another internship offer wasted?' Judgement seeped out of his every word, leaving Aiden's blood to broil beneath his skin.

'No, nothing like that.' His retort was strained as he fought to keep aloof, in control, two things he'd never really been. 'It's my friend who needs help. RACA have cut some bursary funds this year, and she's not able to keep studying without hers.'

'Oh, I see. A girl. How novel.' Jonathan tutted. 'And how is that anything to do with me?'

'I know you have contacts who work with RACA. They'd listen to you if you asked.' Aiden sounded so desperate, so pathetic, just as he'd dreaded, heat crawling up his neck like spider legs. 'It isn't fair, what they've done to her. I wouldn't ask if there was another way, but I know you could have them reconsider. In fact, you could fund a dozen bursaries yourself if you wanted to.'

'And yet I don't. Ceramics is hardly connected to my field of interest, and I can't say I'm eager to provide charity to that school, nor this struggling friend of yours.'

Aiden bowed his head, crumpling a napkin in his palm and tearing at the corners. 'For someone who claims to love art, you don't seem to know much about what it means to be an artist.'

Iron fingers gripped around his wrist suddenly, Jonathan hissing out, 'Don't try to manipulate me, Son. I paved my own way, worked for my own career. Your girlfriend should try doing the same.'

It wasn't a lie, but Jonathan seemed to have forgotten that he'd been working class once. He'd been the first Whittaker to earn a degree, the first to work in the arts sector, the first to own more than one car, one property. Both Aiden and his mother had been born into money, but his father hadn't – and yet he seemed to do everything in his power to make sure nobody knew that, Aiden included. Until it suited him, at least. Until he wanted to reinforce just how lucky Aiden was to have a hard-working father.

Aiden shook his head. 'She's hanging on by a thread. She's done everything she possibly can to keep her place at RACA, but she can't magic money out of thin air; *they* went back on their plan. That isn't her fault.' He tipped his chin, refusing to cower this time. For her. 'I'm not asking for your money, or your care, or anything that most people ask of their parents.

I know that I'm lucky to come from money, and I'm thankful for the doors you've opened for me. Now I'm trying to help someone who really, really deserves the same security. And all it would take is one conversation. You've done it before for colleagues and friends. It's far within your capabilities. If you need something in return, then ask me. I'm all ears.'

Slowly, Jonathan's fingers loosened, and Aiden let out a breath of relief, snatching his hands back.

'And what about in a year's time,' asked Jonathan, readjusting his cuffs, 'when you've moved onto the next pretty thing?'

'It isn't about my feelings for her,' he gritted out, though it was only half the truth. Of course he wouldn't go to these lengths for a stranger. But even if he'd never kissed her, never fallen for her, he was certain he would want to help her anyway. She was too talented, too good of a person, to not deserve it. He would have done it for Luc if they'd needed it. Tilly. Any of his classmates, bar perhaps Tom. 'I'm trying to make something right.'

Jonathan's eyes rolled as though he couldn't possibly believe Aiden. Bitterness flooded Aiden's tongue. The man sitting in front of him had no idea who he was. He had no idea why Aiden had dropped out of Elmington, or that he wasn't a fickle child anymore. Even when Juniper had seen the worst in him, it had never been to this extent.

He'd never felt more hated than when he was in front of Jonathan, not even by himself. And, fuck, he had hated himself plenty.

There must have been something in Aiden's gaze that called to Jonathan, because his resolve melted away, drip by drip, until the creases in his forehead finally smoothed. He adjusted his tie, scraping his tongue across his teeth. 'All right. I'll make a few calls. But you're correct in thinking that I expect something from you in return.'

Aiden scraped at the scab on the edge of his thumbnail, pink and peeling from months of picking. 'What?'

'You'll come back to work with me next summer,' Jonathan said. 'Remind our clientele that this is a family business. That I raised my son properly.'

It was ridiculous, and the thought alone left him nauseous, but…

But he had to. For Juniper. He could survive one more summer with his father, couldn't he? 'If that's what you want.'

'It should be what *you* want. This is your last chance to prove yourself, Aiden.' Jonathan's nostrils flared. 'If your venture into pottery, of all things, turns out to be just another failed whimsy of yours, I refuse to be embarrassed by you again. My support isn't unconditional, and it's *my* name you drag through the mud when you lark around in London.'

Aiden's tucked his fists under the table to hide his white knuckles, working to keep his breaths even. *My support isn't unconditional.* Wasn't it supposed to be? Wasn't that what family was?

Not his.

He would just have to take the win, even if it meant enduring this humiliation.

'I understand, Dad,' he uttered tightly, each word feeling like another serrated slice against his tongue. 'Thank you.'

He hoped to god it was all worth it.

33

'See? Told you he'd love it.' Juniper watched Aiden dust off
his hands, both delighted and slightly annoyed that he'd been
right about Cerberus's new toadstool home. Putting it in his
cage was the first thing they'd done upon arriving back in
London, and Cerberus had wriggled straight through the
ceramic arch to get comfortable inside.

His cage was spotless, food and water supply topped up
generously. Clearly, Alfred Pet Sitter was a very good *friend*.

She perched on the edge of Aiden's couch as an intense
wave of gratitude washed over her. Gratitude, and something
she didn't want to name, even if it was the strongest emotion
she'd ever felt: a thrum she couldn't tune out, reverberating
deep in the very pit of her. It was stronger when she looked
at him, saw his lopsided smile, mussed hair, and unshaven
jaw. Stronger still when she saw the way his throat bobbed
and his eyes faded, like he was holding back something
that hurt.

He'd been quiet on the train home; she could only assume
lunch with his dad hadn't gone well. Not wanting to bring
it up in front of their friends, she'd held his hand under the

table instead, and then went back to helping Luc with their crossword book.

But now they were alone, and she didn't know how else to be there for him than to simply ask what he needed.

'Do you want to talk about it?'

'About what?' He closed Cerberus's cage and looked anywhere but at her — until she pinched the hem of his hoodie and dragged him closer.

'About your dad. About what he did to make you sad.'

'I'm not sad, Juni.' He cupped her face as delicately as he might porcelain, clearing the errant wisps of hair from her face so he could see her better. 'How could I be sad when I've finally got you alone?'

The obvious attempt at distraction almost worked, especially when he kissed her with none of his usual hunger. A kiss that said *I don't want anything but this, here, now.*

She curled a leg around his waist, looping her arms around his neck. She shouldn't have been here, wasting precious time that might have been spent on her contest project, but god, she was exhausted, and the warm, spiced citrus scent of his living room suddenly felt like the safest place in the world. She was running out of reasons to push him away, worried Tilly had been right: their differences meant nothing when they were together like this. If he needed her, and she suspected he did, she would just have to stay.

'You can talk to me, Aiden,' she reminded him when he drew away. 'Was he shitty to you? Do you want me to fight him?'

'That, I would like to see.' He laughed, but it soon ebbed. 'I'm just coming to terms with the fact that nothing I do will make him love me. I went along with everything he asked of me for the first nineteen years of my life. It got me his approval, but not much more, and it made me miserable in the long run. Now, I'm doing something that feels right, that feels true to me, and all he sees is all the ways I've failed.'

She knew the feeling. Her own failures chased her around in everything she did, and they were currently nipping at her ankles. Sometimes, a person just needed to be told they were doing a good job, especially from their parents. She couldn't imagine a father not being proud of someone like Aiden. He poured more and more care into his art every day, and beyond that, he was a pillar for the people around him. Someone she was learning to trust, even if she was reluctant about it.

'Maybe he doesn't deserve to see you succeed, then,' she suggested gently. 'You shouldn't have to do anything to be loved by him. It's kind of what parents are supposed to do, without conditions attached.'

He hummed in uncertain agreement, forehead resting against hers. 'When did you get so wise?'

It was a good question. She'd never given herself the same grace she was offering him now, not when it came to her own problems. She tried to convince herself it was different for him: he dropped out of his art course because he was struggling, not because it was in his nature to fail the way it seemed to be in hers.

But then she thought of all the things she battled on a regular basis. The exhausting whir of brain chatter, the para-lysing inability to just get up and do things that needed to be done, the constant distractions where she could lose hours without realising it, the way everything she had to say and do felt urgent because otherwise she might forget about them altogether. The intensity of her emotions, and the over-whelming sensory experiences of everyday life. None of those were things she'd chosen. They were symptoms, and nobody had ever made room to just let them be there. She'd fought them every step of the way and still lost.

The only person who had never held them against her was him. In fact, he seemed to like her for all her mess.

When she didn't reply, he frowned and tapped her forehead. 'Where have you gone?'

She shook her head. 'I wish I knew.'

His hands lowered to her hips, sneaking under her jumper so that he could draw circles over skin. She sighed, eyes closing. Surrendering, just like he'd always wanted.

His lips found her jaw, her neck, and she leaned to grant him better access as her other leg wrapped around him. She twisted her fingers through his hair the way she knew he liked, and got the reaction she'd hoped for when he keened softly. It was like they'd never been apart. Her body remem-bered his after weeks away, and his hers.

'Take me to bed, Aiden,' she pleaded.

So he did, his strong arms lifting her off the couch as though she weighed nothing at all. He walked down the hallway without ever tearing his gaze away, each step sending another jolt of anticipation through her. It wasn't like the other times they'd done this, when they'd fallen into each other without any control. When their bodies had decided for them. This time, it was her deciding. There was no rush, no desperation, only a quiet knowing that left her feeling safer than ever with him.

Like hers, his bedroom floor was covered in clothes and art books, though they'd been pushed aside to corners. He laid her down on his sky-blue duvet, and she was quick to tear off his shirt. Maybe she was slightly desperate, after all, but it was difficult not to be when the light hit his chest, casting shadows across the planes of his soft middle. She'd never had time to appreciate it all before, but she did now, letting her finger drift from his sternum down to his belly button, where a strip of hair pointed to his already strained waistband.

'It's unfair, how beautiful you are,' she admitted.

He wrinkled his nose. 'Beautiful? Is that what I am now?'

A nod. ''Fraid so.'

'Well, it's a step up from intolerable, obnoxious arsehole.' He toyed with her jumper until she fought her way out of it, the two of them laughing when it left her hair mussed on top of her head. He tugged the tie from it, letting it fall freely around her shoulders with something like awe parting his lips. Dusky light kissed his high cheekbones, muddying his hazel eyes, and she wasn't sure she'd ever recover from him. From the way it felt to be seen by him. Like she was the centre of his universe, the gravity that kept him grounded. She'd never understand it; she'd done nothing to earn it, not really.

And yet he kissed her like she deserved every bit of it, starting with her lips then dipping down to the valley between her breasts. He tugged at the lace of her bra with his teeth, then carried on to peel her jeans down. She lifted her hips to let him, her walls clenching around nothing when his stubble scraped her inner thighs. His kisses followed the line of her stretch marks, some white from puberty and some more recent and pink. She'd never paid much attention to them before, but she propped herself up on her elbows and realised that they might have been beautiful to an artist like him. Added texture, expressive brushstrokes, the same way he often did with his clay.

'Do you have any idea what you do to me, Juni?' he asked, hoarse voice vibrating against her skin. 'I spend every hour of every day wishing I was yours.'

Her breath shook as she guided him back up with a finger under his chin, wondering if he truly meant it. Wondering if she felt the same. Knowing, deep down, she did.

'You are.' She unbuttoned his jeans and grazed the low jut of his stomach. 'You are mine.'

He stepped out of his jeans and then his boxers, completely bare. Her tongue swiped over her bottom lip at the sight of his length, hard and ready for her. His hips and thighs were as beautiful as the rest of him, the former as soft as his stomach and darkened by hair.

Unable to wait any longer, she tugged him back onto the bed and straddled his waist again. He unhooked her bra, fingers quicker and clumsier now, and she threw it somewhere behind her. His mouth was on her immediately, tongue lapping at her nipples and breasts spilling over his kneading fingers. It was better than anything they'd done before, skin clashing against skin, all of their past obstacles finally gone. She ground her hips against him, her covered clit finding friction against his cock, and she wondered what would happen if she let go of all the things holding her back. If she fell and let him catch her.

'There are condoms in my nightstand,' he rasped.

'I think we're past needing them, don't you?' After all, he'd filled her once before and she'd taken her contraception this morning, one of the few things she'd managed to uphold a routine with after years of avoiding heavy periods.

He grinned and nipped at the bunched, pink skin around her nipple, eliciting a whimper from her.

'I feel like I can't get you close enough,' he admitted, hands snaking to tug her closer by her arse cheeks. Her core hit his erection again, a taunt, a promise. 'I can feel every bit of distance, and it fucking hurts, Juniper. I need you closer.'

She felt it, too, her skin screaming whenever he drew back. 'Then get closer.'

She lifted to remove her underwear, running her hand over the length of his shaft to line him up before finally sinking onto him. She took him with as much restraint as she could muster, trying to feel every inch of him until their bodies were joined completely. His fingers flexed against her shoulder blades, breath hot and heavy on her collarbone. She almost didn't want to move, didn't want to put that distance between them again, but her core searched desperately for release.

She started slow, resting her head against his as she sought the place where it felt best, but then he tilted her chin and begged, 'Look at me. I want to see you. Never got to see you properly the first time.'

'I'd argue that it was me who couldn't see the first time.' And as pleasurable as that blindfold had been, it paled in comparison to this. It was another sensation altogether to lock eyes, to see whispers of pleasure write themselves over his face between the hoarse rattle of his laugh.

Her breaths grew more laboured as she rolled her hips deeper, harder, him swallowing her gasps into his mouth before he kissed her again.

'Tell me again,' he said. 'Tell me I'm yours.'

'You're mine. You're mine, Aiden.' And she was his, even if she couldn't say it yet. Her skin grew slick with sweat as she rode towards her climax at an alarmingly fast pace.

'I'm yours,' he whispered, over and over, helping her where he could. 'I'm yours.'

And then he was letting go of her hip to dip his hand between them, rolling his fingers over her clit until she was quivering. Her stomach swelled with heat as he ventured to the place where their bodies met and back again. Her ruts became unbridled, his cock hitting deeper with each one.

He must have been close, too, because he urged her onto her back without pulling out, still gripping her arse enough to bruise as he thrust into her. She tilted her hips against him, chasing those last few threads with searing fire in her belly as she watched his face contort with pleasure.

'Come for me, sweetheart,' he begged. 'I need you to come before me.'

She whined out as a bliss she'd never known before ravaged her, and then he was yelling with her, the two of them closer than ever before as their bodies rose and fell in tandem. He fucked her until her walls stopped shaking, until her thighs went slack with exhaustion and she could barely hold on, and then he collapsed against her, his forehead burning into her chest and his breaths fanning across her breasts.

'Fuck, Juni,' he muttered. 'I…'

His tongue formed an *L* sound, and her mouth suddenly went dry. For a moment, she was sure he was going to say the word she was most afraid of.

But he never finished his sentence, rolling his weight off her to catch his breath.

Still, the sentiment echoed in the spaces between them, enough to terrify her.

Because she knew.

And she did, too.

34

Meeting scheduled with funding director at
9 a.m. Wednesday to consider reinstating her
bursary. Tell your girlfriend not to be late.

Relief seeped through Aiden when he read the text message
from his dad. He'd never been more grateful for him, even
after the slew of verbal insults he'd been given that weekend
and the dread of another summer spent with him. Abandoning
the boiling kettle, he pushed off the kitchen counter and
padded barefoot down the hallway to share the news, only
sparing a moment to wonder how Juniper might take it.

It didn't matter. He'd gotten her a chance to stay, and he
couldn't wait to finally shove that weight off her chest and
help her breathe again.

'Juni?' As he slipped into the bedroom, he found her in
nothing more than his towel, the morning light of a new
week streaming through the half-open curtains and
bouncing off her damp skin. His stomach lurched, and his
cock, too – she'd told him he was beautiful, but no words
felt like enough to describe her, especially bare-faced and
barely covered.

She smiled, fingers sliding across his rumpled duvet as she fell back. 'I'm trying to get ready. I really, really am. I'm just' – a yawn – 'tired and hungry and I still haven't figured out what to do about this contest, and have I mentioned I'm tired?'

He smiled, convinced he could listen to her babble all day, especially when she was sprawled on his mattress, thighs kicking off the edge. 'Maybe you don't need to worry about the contest anymore.'

He inched forward, glad when she sat up again to straighten out her towel. It tried to come apart over her chest, causing her to pinch it together. 'What d'you mean?'

'Don't be mad, okay?'

She frowned as though she was already preparing herself to be just that. 'I'll be mad if I want to be mad. What are you going to tell me, Aiden?'

'I got you an interview with RACA's funding director. They're considering reinstating your bursary.'

'How do you know about my bursary?' Her voice was low. Dangerous. 'I never told you I had one, let alone that I lost it.'

He steeled himself against it, heart pounding. 'Luc let it slip, and I forced it out of them. But it doesn't matter, Juni, because this could make everything okay. You wouldn't have to work yourself to exhaustion anymore. You could take fewer shifts, forget about the contest entirely. You're going to be okay, now.'

Juniper's face crumpled in confusion. She shook her head, pushing herself off the bed and putting space between them, damp hair curling around the nape of her neck like the snakes she'd sculpted for Medusa.

'How long have you known?' she demanded.

'I don't know. Since last week. Does it matter?'

'It matters that you've gone behind my back!'

He grappled for the right thing to say, suddenly feeling like it didn't exist. 'Luc didn't mean to tell me, all right? But when I found out, I had to help you.'

'So, what, you did the one thing you apparently hate? You used your name, your privilege, to get me an interview?' She gasped, covering her mouth with trembling hands. 'That was why you saw your dad. Did you ask *him* to do this? To convince RACA to give me special treatment?'

White spots danced across his vision as panic set in. This wasn't how it was supposed to go. She was supposed to be glad, relieved. She was supposed to see how much she meant to him.

'I had to do something,' he uttered, trying to keep his voice soft even when it cracked. 'I couldn't see you so miserable, and you deserve that bursary.'

'I feel sick.' Juniper began searching the floor, snatching up her jeans and clumsily stepping into them. She yanked them up over sticky knees, breath heaving out of her as though it had taken every bit of energy. 'Did you get Luc an interview, too? Tell me you fucking did, Aiden.'

Aiden squeezed his eyes closed. Okay, maybe he did look like a piece of shit this way, but he had asked Luc in the hotel the night before, and they'd refused his help. They'd also warned him this might happen, but… 'Luc is fine without it. I asked Dad to consider putting his funds into RACA to help everyone who was affected, but he never would. This was all I could do. For you.'

'I can't believe it.' She found her jumper on the opposite side of the room. He tried to grab her, stop her, but she reared back like she couldn't stand the sight of him, let alone his touch. 'I can't believe that for a minute, I trusted you.'

'Juniper, I wasn't trying to hurt you, I was trying to bloody help you — and I have!'

'No.' Her laugh was bitter, cutting, and he flinched. 'No, you proved yourself to be the same person who took everything from me!'

Now, it was Aiden's turn to be confused. 'What are you talking about? What have I ever taken from you?'

'Oh, come on. You're not that dense!' Her voice was muffled by the jumper she thrust on over her towel, wonky and twisted so that the seam ran up her stomach instead of her side. She seemed not to care, throwing the towel on the bed. 'I wanted a place at Elmington, too. I applied for a combined fine arts and ceramic design course.' He couldn't remember seeing her on the day of the interviews, but then, he'd been swept up in all the peers who had wanted to be his friend, eager to ask him about his life. 'I was waiting outside the office for my mum to come and pick me up, and guess who I heard bribing the fucking dean?'

The colour leached from Aiden's face. *No…*

'Your dad. Since they only take on one artist from each county, needless to say, I didn't get a place on the course — but you did. Why would they choose the some thick, poor nobody like me when they had Whittaker money in their pocket? You pay your way through everything, and now you're doing the same for me! Who knew sleeping with a rich prick would get me some perks, right?' She was yelling now, angrier than he'd ever seen her. Aiden grabbed his dresser to support his weak legs, trying to take it all in – but he couldn't. He was far away from his body, looking at the destruction from miles above.

'I didn't know, Juni. I swear, I didn't.'

She scoffed. 'You will *never* know what it feels like to have to work for something. You'll never know what it feels like to be told no, not because you're not talented enough, but because you just don't belong. I don't want your help, Aiden. I don't want *anything* to do with you ever again.'

He didn't know what to say, what to do. All of that hatred he'd worked so hard to make disappear was back with a vengeance, and all because he'd wanted the best for her.

'Juniper, please.' He sounded pathetic even to his own ears as he tried to grab her hand, but she snatched it away.

'No,' she snarled. 'No, stuff your pleas and apologies, Aiden. I don't want them. I don't want this.'

I don't want you. It might not have been said, but he heard it all the same, and it felt like a crack forming all the way from his sternum to his gut. *I love you*, he wanted to shout, but he already knew she wouldn't want to hear it. Hadn't wanted to even before.

'You should give that interview to Luc, or someone else who needs it,' she muttered. 'And you should stay away from me, because we're done. We're really, really done.'

Her voice shuddered with the threat of tears, and that crack stretched farther, to the floor beneath his feet. Last night, he'd been falling for her. Now, he was falling *without* her, *because* of her, and his entire body felt the impact when he reached the bottom.

He thought he'd known pain before, but this… This might just be the thing that destroyed him.

She stormed away, down the hallway, and he watched from his bedroom as she kicked on her boots without even bothering to tie the laces.

And then she was gone, the only thing left of her the whistling remnants of his door slamming.

Aiden let out something between a bellow and a sob, throwing his phone as far away as he could get it so that he wouldn't have to see that text. It collided with the nearest wall, landing on the floor with a cracked, black screen.

Juniper was right. He'd done the thing he claimed to have despised, used his dad to win her over, to keep her here. And she was the one person in the world who would never be impressed with it, never ask him for anything.

He might just have destroyed the only real thing in his life. Lost the only person who had wanted him despite his upbringing rather than because of it.

No wonder she hated him. Without his privilege, what was he even capable of?

Nothing.

35

Juniper didn't have time to be heartbroken, or at least so she told herself. She ignored the hollowness that followed her around campus that day, desperate to get her contest piece done. She had two weeks left, not nearly enough, but she would do it. She would have to.

That was why she stayed in the workshop after class that afternoon, throwing like her life depended on it. Blisters were beginning to form on her fingertips, but she refused to stop.

'Juniper?' Tilly seemed to appear out of nowhere, standing uncertainly on the other side of Juniper's desk.

Juniper looked up just long enough to acknowledge her. She didn't want to talk about it. If she talked about it, she would have to feel it properly, and she was sick of feeling things. Especially for Aiden.

'Babe, you're crying. Stop.' Tilly nudged her gently away from the wheel, bending down so that Juniper was forced to look at her. She hadn't known she was crying, and wiped her cheeks with her clay-covered sleeve quickly. 'What the hell's going on? You weren't in class this morning, and now you're lining up a table of wonky vases.'

She glanced behind Juniper at the creations she'd made so far. Not one of them had turned out as intended. Some of them curved in because Juniper had tried to smash the clay in anger, others had almost been thrown across the classroom. Nothing she did was right, too much focus going into the memory of Aiden's hands on hers, guiding her, the first time she'd made something she was truly proud of.

'I just need to get things ready for the contest,' Juniper said. 'I need six pieces and I have none.'

'You need to tell me what's wrong. Has something happened? Is it your funding?' Tilly took Juniper's sore hands, urging her onto the floor so they were on the same level. Juniper let her only because she didn't feel the least bit in control of herself, the cold linoleum a welcome reprieve after hours hunched over the wheel.

She brought her knees to her chest, nails digging into her thighs in an effort to hold herself together. 'Aiden,' was about all she could choke out.

'Oh, shite,' Tilly whispered. 'What's the plonker done now?'

Juniper told her, the story pouring out in fragments: him getting her an interview, visiting his dad, how it all linked back to Elmington. How, just when she'd fallen for him completely, he'd reminded her of all the reasons why she hated him.

'Except you don't hate him, do you?'

Juniper glowered at her. 'I do now.'

She hated how clueless he was, how ignorant. She hated how he said her name like it was the only one that mattered. She hated how he touched her in places she'd never even paid attention to before, places where she couldn't scrub the ghost of him away, and how his light snores had sent her into a soundless sleep last night. She hated that he just didn't get it. That he never would.

She hated that she'd let him in knowing all of this, and now it had blown up in her face – just as she'd always predicted.

'I shouldn't even care.' She sniffled. 'I should be focusing on the competition, but I can't even do that right!'

'Heartbreak can be inconvenient that way.' Tilly wrapped an arm around Juniper's shoulder and tugged her close, resting her cheek against Juniper's head. 'I completely understand why you're upset. He went behind your back, took your problems into his hands, and that was really fecking shitty.'

'If you say *but*, there will be consequences.'

'*But*,' Tilly continued, 'he thought he was doing the best thing for you, and you deserve someone who cares for you that way. It's okay to be supported, Juni, financially and other-wise. Judging how sour he was on the train home yesterday, it wasn't easy for him, either. He didn't just call Daddy and ask him to fix everything, did he? He probably had to put a lot of pride and self-preservation aside to ask for his help.'

Juniper bit down on her wobbling lower lip, thinking of how upset Aiden had been yesterday. He'd subjected himself to his dad for her, faced his own pain to heal hers.

And he hadn't known about Elmington. She'd suspected it before, when it had never come up in conversation even after he'd spilled his struggles with his health, but today had confirmed it. The shock on his face, the way his voice had broken, the way he'd reacted to all of her insults like they'd been physical blows. She'd been so angry that the rest was a blur, but she couldn't scrub the image of him in that moment. The pain she'd caused.

'I told you there would be consequences,' she said, and then sobbed until her stomach ached.

Tilly soothed her with a gentle hand through her hair, the two of them crumpled in an empty workshop, surrounded by things that used to make Juniper feel alive but now only seemed to hurt her. A longing to go home hit her, but it wasn't an image of Manchester that accompanied it. It was Aiden's house, with Cerberus in his cage nearby and paints scattered over the coffee table. And him, settling on a part of her, any part of her, to trace shapes in her skin with his feather-light fingers, a hint of pencil shadow or acrylic under his nails.

'I don't even know how I'm going to get my hamster back!' she realised. 'I have nowhere to put him!'

'Now, hear me out, Juniper,' Tilly said. 'What if, right now, we just focus on you, and not the happy wee hamster napping obliviously in his cage in a flat where he's clearly cared for?'

She had a point. Juniper might not have trusted Aiden with her heart, but she trusted him with Cerberus. Still, she couldn't just let him live there forever.

'What am I going to do, Tilly?' she asked.

Tilly wiped Juniper's tears with soft hands and straightened up assertively. 'You're going to get this contest out of the way. You're going to win it. And then, you're going to talk to Aiden like an adult because you clearly love him, and he clearly loves you.'

'If he did, he won't anymore.' Not after all the things she'd said. And besides, how could they come back from this? How could *she*? They just weren't compatible. It had barely been a few months, and they'd exploded.

They weren't right for each other. They never had been and never would be. The best thing Juniper could do was accept it and move on.

'I highly doubt it,' Tilly said. 'I've seen you two all swoony and mad for each other.'

'Well, maybe swoony and mad isn't enough.' She used the table to climb back to her feet, hoping she didn't look as terrible as she felt. On the throwing wheel, her lump of clay sat, waiting, and it was time to prove to herself she could be a decent potter without him.

Through tears and exhaustion and some more uplifting words from Tilly, she tried again to make something worth submitting. Something that would help her forget all of this.

In the end, she managed to do just that.

★

Aiden barely made it to Manchester in one piece, but he couldn't spend another day sitting inside, wondering how he hadn't known that his father had bought his place at Elmington. As he reached Whittaker North offices, he realised that he hadn't planned at all what he might say, even after a four-hour train ride spent staring out the window. Everything about him felt empty, his mind included.

And yet the sight of his surname on the white sign outside summoned enough anger that he strutted inside without care, waltzing straight past the receptionist and into the lift. He'd spent many days here as a kid, told to paint quietly in the corner while Jonathan tended to his business, and then later, made to file his paperwork or assist him on gallery ventures. Jonathan had taught him everything about art, and yet hadn't believed him capable of earning his college place alone. How did that work? How little did he think of him, truly?

The long corridor he stepped out on made him feel small and young again, but it was overshadowed by the turmoil inside of him, so he marched to Jonathan's office the way his father would: like he owned it. He pushed through the oak door without knocking, finding his father behind his desk and his bewildered Aiden lookalike apprentice seated opposite.

Annoyance blazed over Jonathan's features at the sight of his son. 'Excuse me. We're in the middle of something here, Aiden—'

'It's going to have to wait. Did you buy my place at Elmington?'

The apprentice hopped out of his seat to excuse himself, leaving just the two of them to stare each other down. For once, Aiden wasn't the first to break away.

'Did you,' he repeated through his teeth, 'buy my place at Elmington?'

'I don't know what on earth has prompted this, Aiden, but storming in here without invitation when I'm in the middle of something is completely unacceptable.'

'For god's sake, just tell me!' Aiden shouted. 'Did you bribe the dean for my acceptance?'

Jonathan clasped his hands over his stomach, assessing Aiden for a moment before saying, 'Yes, I did.' His tone held no sign of shame or regret.

A tear rolled down Aiden's cheek. He didn't care, didn't wipe it away. Not this time. Fuck his pride, and fuck his manliness, and fuck everything his father had tried to mould him into. 'Why?'

'*Why*?' Even when sat, Jonathan still managed to look down his nose at his son. 'Why did I work hard to get you into one of the most prestigious art programmes in the country? Do you have any idea how lucky you are? My father worked himself into an early grave just to feed his family, and you're angry because I got you the best opportunities – opportunities you threw away without a second thought?'

So that was why dropping out had been so terrible for Jonathan. It wasn't just that he'd expected Aiden to follow in his footsteps; it was that Aiden's struggles had led to a waste of Jonathan's money. God forbid. 'You didn't think I might have gotten in anyway? Or did you really have so little faith in me? In the skills *you* taught me?'

'Grow up, Aiden.' Jonathan tutted. 'There isn't an artist on this planet who gets rewarded fairly for their talent. It's rarely about something so simple. Maybe if you weren't so bloody insecure, you could handle that, but you can't. You've always been naive.'

Aiden tugged on his hair for lack of anything else to take his frustration out on.

'And you've always been desperate to control me,' he decided finally. 'It isn't just that you paid for my place at Elmington. You can't stand that I'm at RACA because it wasn't your decision. I chose it for myself, and I didn't need your help to get there.'

'Yes, you're so independent now. That's why you came to me to ask for my help just a few days ago.'

Juniper was right about all of it. Whittaker money was toxic, used as a means to tread over everyone else on their way to the top. Aiden wanted no part in it anymore.

'I'll never be enough for you, will I?' he muttered. 'It's always about the money, the achievements, the success. Never about who I am.'

'And who are you, Aiden?' Jonathan stood from his desk, planting a fist on the wooden surface. 'Because all I see is an insecure little boy with no direction, no sense of self. If I'm such a terrible father, see if you can succeed without me. See how long it takes before the opportunities stop coming, how long it takes until you can no longer afford to muck around with Play-Doh like the child you are.'

Every word wedged the dagger deeper, and Aiden could do nothing but take it. His father had always been cruel, but never like this. What had he done to deserve this much hatred, other than try to break free?

If he wanted to change, to be the man Juniper deserved, it started today. Here. And the best thing he could do was cut away all the rot, find out who he was without it.

'I'm grateful for the opportunities I've gotten thanks to you, Dad, I really am.' It took every bit of energy Aiden had to keep his voice steady, his spine straight, but he managed. He'd already resigned himself to what would happen next, and there was something liberating in the fact that he'd never have to stand in this office and be belittled again. 'I'm grateful that I've never known what it is to struggle financially. But I'll never live up to whatever it is you want me to be, and I'm done trying. I *do* have direction, and it's somewhere far, far away from your disapproval. Those insecurities come from you, and they nearly broke me. So if you don't mind, I'll go back to mucking around like the child I am, and I think it's best we stay out of each other's way.'

'Until the next time you need my help. You still owe me, or have you conveniently forgotten our agreement?' Jonathan smirked, though Aiden caught a slight tremble as he perched on the edge of his desk. He wasn't used to being stood up to.

That was what gave him the strength to say, 'The agreement's done. She didn't go to the interview. I think I'll learn how to solve my problems without you from now on.'

With that, he walked away, letting the door fall shut behind him. His hands shook, throat ached, stomach churned, mind raced. An anxiety attack. Still, every step put more distance between them, and he was prepared never to close it again.

He couldn't figure out who he was if he was only ever told who he wasn't. He just wished it hadn't taken losing Juniper to finally find courage enough to realise it.

36

By the Thursday of that week, Juniper missed Cerberus terrible amounts. She was thankful she no longer had much time to mope around her tiny dorm room between classes and work, but the empty place on her desk still made her feel lonelier than ever. And not just because the hamster was gone.

All she saw of Aiden these days was his back in workshop classes, hunched with more tension than his toned shoulders usually carried. She spent every lesson with a lump in her throat, trying not to cry at the sight of him, and it made her feel ridiculous. He was just a boy she'd slept with. A boy she'd never even liked. A boy who had no understanding of what she was going through and tried to heal wounds with bank notes instead of stitches.

So why was it all so heavy? Why did she feel like her life in London had suddenly gotten a lot greyer and a lot smaller?

It was that question that had led her to Cartwright Gardens, though she'd been lingering around the greenery on the other side of the road for well over fifteen minutes now. She just wanted to see Cerberus before she headed to work. Make sure he was clean and fed, because that was her responsibility.

But she'd have to talk to him, and she didn't think she'd be able to. Not without giving her misery away – and her guilt. Despite her anger at him, she'd hurt him, too, and she didn't want that.

Get it together, Juni, she told herself, and finally crossed the road. She took a deep breath before unlocking the gate, but as soon as she stepped into the narrow front garden, she was hit by a complete lack of air, as though she'd stepped into a vacuum. She couldn't do this. Couldn't see him. It was too messy, and not the sort of messy she was used to. If he tried to talk to her, tried to—

'Bugger!'

The door rattled, handle twisting, and her first instinct was to run. Of course, her legs had already turned to jelly, so the best she could do was fall into a tangled deep green shrub of red berries, muddying her black work clothes in the process. The thin branches scraped her skin, and she let out an 'Ow!'

Aiden stepped out just in time to see the whole thing. His hair was a ruffled mess like he'd just rolled out of bed, olive skin a tad paler than before, but frown as disarmingly fond as always. 'Juniper… What on earth are you doing in my bush?'

She huffed and yanked herself up, ignoring his hand when he reached out to help. 'I'm here to see Cerberus. And to tell you that I'll take him home at the end of February for half-term, so he won't be your problem for much longer.' She'd wanted to sound detached, but the roiling emotions inside her made it impossible. Perhaps it was time to accept that she could be a lot of things for Aiden – angry, sad, humoured, elated, infatuated – but indifferent wasn't one of them. Never had been.

He scratched his unkempt stubble with his thumb slowly. 'Right. And how did you plan to get in if you're hiding from me?'

'I'm not hiding from you. I fell. Your flagstones are uneven.' A lie. His flagstones were perfect, just like all the others on this street. Just like him, with his silly face and voice and—

God, even his eyebrows. Thick dark, shapely. Simply not fair.

'Right.' Aiden twirled his keys around his finger. 'Well, I was just heading to the shops, but come on in.'

She was hoping he might just let her in then leave her to it, but he held the door open for her and followed her back into the hall. She gulped at the sight of his living room, the place she'd found comfort on her shittiest day, and beelined straight to Cerberus's cage so she wouldn't be tempted to see what paintings he'd been working on.

It turned out there was nothing for her to do. The hamster was clean, fed, watered. He didn't look like he'd missed her at all.

'I changed his bedding this morning,' Aiden said quietly. 'He's all taken care of, if that's what you're worried about. I wouldn't…'

'I know.' The thought had crossed her mind just once, that maybe Aiden wouldn't want to take care of him anymore, but she couldn't imagine a world where he was cruel. He'd never been cruel. Not like her. 'You don't have to do that. I can come and clean him. I should have been around earlier, I just…'

'I know,' he whispered, voice soft and inviting and all the things it had always been for her.

She clamped her lips together and unlocked the cage, glad when Cerberus dashed straight into her palm. Her smile was shaky as she placed a gentle kiss on his tiny, warm head, smoothing his tawny fur with a light finger. 'I missed you, little guy.'

Aiden shuffled behind her, and then said: 'Juni. Can't we talk about this?'

'I can't. I really, really can't right now.'

'I miss you,' he said. 'All the time. Not seeing you—'

'I can't.' Her voice wavered this time as she turned to face him, keeping Cerberus steady in her hand. 'I need to stay focused on the contest. The deadline is two weeks away. And I have work in twenty minutes. We will talk about it, just not yet. I can't afford to be a mess now, okay?'

His downturned mouth made her want to change her mind, apologise, say all the things she'd been thinking over the last few days. Tell him she missed him, too. But this thing with Aiden had always been an explosion waiting to happen, just like her teapot in the pit fire, and she didn't have the strength to wade through the debris just yet. To try to piece together something that would help them move on once and for all.

He nodded, fingers flexing at his sides. 'Well, you know where I am if you change your mind. And if I can help at all with this contest thing, I'm here.'

So you can have your dad bribe the judges? she thought, but knew it wasn't fair.

Her eyes welled with tears. She admired Cerberus a final time and then placed him back in his cage. 'Thanks for letting me in.'

'Of course. Anytime.'

She grabbed her bag from the floor and walked straight past, unable to look at him. She still saw the devastation from the corner of her eye, though. Still saw the way he bowed his head when she turned to say goodbye.

All of this self-preservation wasn't preserving her much at all, because her insides felt as raw as ever as she walked out of his door.

★

Her porcelain had cracked in the kiln. Hours and hours of work into her traditional china tea set, lost. It was only a few of the more delicate sugar bowls and milk jugs that had fared the worst, but when Annie pulled the set from the kiln late on Friday evening, Juniper still felt a hole open up inside her chest.

'Pesky porcelain.' Annie tutted, patting Juniper on the shoulder. 'At least your teapot survived this time. Gorgeous pattern, too, by the way. Very Nordic.'

It *was* a gorgeous pattern, and it hadn't been easy painting it with a steady hand, which made the crack all the more devastating. She would either have to douse the cups in superglue or start again.

God, she was tired of starting again.

Juniper took a deep breath, placing the fired ceramics into a crate so that she could take them upstairs, where she had

Chris waiting to offer input with bated breath. 'I don't know what I did wrong,' she admitted.

'Oh, I'm sure it wasn't anything you did.' Annie smiled sympathetically, her blue eyes softening. 'I always say clay is like an ex. Sometimes, it's just impossible to please. Nothing you do can change it.'

'Then what's the point?' Juniper's face heated when she saw how the question took Annie aback. Still, she couldn't stop wondering it. 'If you might fail every time you put something in the kiln, what's the point of any of it? How do you know how to get it right if the rules change every time?'

'Isn't it part of the fun, never knowing how it'll turn out?' Annie shrugged. 'It might end up in pieces, but it might just be the most beautiful thing you've ever created. To me, it looks like you've managed both. Don't be so hard on yourself for the broken bits, yeah?'

Her words might have been inspiring on another day, but Juniper's exhaustion had tugged her to a precipice, and she was one or two terrible experiences away from being thrown over the edge. She couldn't remember a time when she'd ever been this burnt out. Not at school, not in full-time work, not even last semester. There was always something to do, something to fix, something to make, and not enough time in the day to do it all. All of her earnings were being poured into her tuition fee savings, and she was barely able to afford lunch most days. And on top of that, she was hamsterless. And Aidenless. And it was her fault, partly.

She trudged back up to the workshop with heavy feet, setting her crate down in front of Chris on his desk. 'We have some casualties.'

'How unfortunate.' He plucked out a saucer that had made it out alive, and then her pride and joy, the three-tiered cake stand for afternoon tea, a typical British enjoyment she'd never been able to afford but liked the sound of. She had to admit, it had turned out well, with polished white broken up by her blue Nordic-inspired patterns. She'd tried to emulate the same elegance as what she'd seen in Middleport, hoping that if she wowed the judges with technical skills similar to those of professionals, she might have a chance at winning.

'This is certainly an improvement from your first piece here.' He hesitated, and her heart leapt into her throat. He didn't like it.

'What? What's wrong?'

'Nothing's wrong…'

She pointed an accusatory finger at him. 'Your face says otherwise.' Even now they were on a friendlier basis, it was easy to spot when Chris wasn't keen on someone's work. He fidgeted with his glasses, features pinching like he'd just bitten into a lemon. About as subtle as Juniper was, which was probably why they'd started out so rocky.

'This is just my face,' Chris tried to defend, but Juniper put her hands on her hips. He lifted his hand in surrender. 'All right. I know you've worked very hard on these, Juniper, but…'

'But?'

He winced as he examined one of the teacups that was still intact. 'But they're awfully boring. I never would have guessed they were yours. They show none of your usual creativity. Nothing to distinguish you from other potters.'

Juniper took a wounded step away from the table, pretending to be interested in her boots. 'So, I have no chance of winning the contest with this.' It wasn't a question.

Chris shook his head. 'No, I dare say you don't.'

She blinked the tears from her eyes. 'I thought that's what they would want. After seeing all the pottery in Middleport and some of the past winners…'

'Maybe, if the pieces felt sincere. Something the artist excelled in, knew inside out. But these look like copies. They're not telling me anything about you. Just what you're trying to emulate – a plain old afternoon tea set. Do you even like afternoon tea?'

'I didn't realise I had to like something to make it,' Juniper couldn't help but snap. 'Do you just make these rules as you go along?'

Chris set down her work and stood, draping his tartan scarf around his neck with an indecipherable expression. He looked at Juniper just once more to say: 'If you don't know by now that you're supposed to find enjoyment in your own work, I've severely failed you, and I'm sorry for that.' He checked his watch. 'It's late. How about you take the weekend to consider the next steps, and we can discuss this some more on Monday?'

Juniper nodded, afraid any answer she said aloud would be broken by a sob. She was glad when Chris left and she could let the tears flow freely.

How was it that even when she *tried* to do better, she still failed? It was the only thing she was good at: messing things up, doing the wrong thing, following the wrong path.

The cracked edges of her cups taunted her, and she had no idea what she was doing until she picked up the cake stand and threw it onto the floor with a venomous grunt. The teapot came next, producing an ear-splitting shatter, and then the cups and saucers. The sugar bowl, the milk jug. All of it ended up in fragments of painted blue and white on the floor, where it belonged. What was the point? She wasn't going to get anywhere in the contest with them. She wasn't going to become a potter at all. At this point, she was just tipping her money, her energy, her everything down a depressing, hair-clogged drain, watching it swirl and swirl and swirl before the current sucked it all up.

Maybe she should have let Aiden take care of her, even if the thought of buying her place here by sleeping with someone wealthy felt oily and disgusting.

Or maybe she should never have come here at all, just like her mum had said.

With a final sob, Juniper tossed the crate of broken pottery away, and then kicked it for good measure. Whatever love she'd felt for her craft was gone, and all she could do was lower to the ground and wonder why she would never be enough.

37

As Aiden entered the workshop, he faltered at the crunch beneath the soles of his trainers. He looked down and immediately began to panic. Somebody had dropped their intricately hand-painted porcelain, and now he was stepping all over it.

He hopped off quickly, bending down to try to salvage what he could. Who had left it here? Were they coming back for it? How much damage had been there already?

This was the last thing he'd needed after his shitty week. He'd come in here to have some alone time, a place to find his inspiration again after staring at blank canvases and untouched clay for hours on end. He was supposed to be working on his portfolio, but so far, he had nothing. Nothing to say, nothing to convey. It had been that way since the minute Juniper had left him, like she'd taken all of his ideas with her. All of *him* with her.

'Don't pick it up. Leave it.' A barely-there voice rasped from somewhere nearby, all too familiar, and his stomach tugged in response. Juniper, hiding from him again, only this time, it wasn't so obvious where.

Not until he treaded slowly around Chris's desk and found her underneath, her back pressed against the wall, one knee to her chest while she stared lifelessly at a ladder in her work leggings. Pink blotches smattered her face as though she'd been crying for a while, though her cheeks were dry now.

The anxiety he'd been trying to push down all week forced its way out at the sight. 'Juniper… What happened? Are you okay?'

She looked at him as though surprised to see him. 'Of course it's you.'

'Of course it's me," he repeated, gentle, because didn't it always seem like something was pulling them together? A love for the same thing, or their own raw chemistry, or maybe something else, but she was always there, wherever he went. And he would always be there for her, even if she didn't want him to be. 'Tell me what happened, sweetheart.'

'It doesn't matter.'

'It does. It matters a lot.' He knelt, unable to keep from placing a hand on her bent knee. She gazed at it like it didn't make sense for it to be there, and maybe it didn't, but he had to do something, show her some way, that he was here. 'If you don't want to talk to me, I can call Tilly.'

'No,' she croaked. 'No. She's working.'

'Then Luc, or your parents, anyone.'

She closed her eyes, tears spilling over, and he could do nothing but hold his breath and try not to stop them. 'My parents have been waiting for this to happen.'

'For what to happen?'

'For me to fuck everything up, like I always do.'

'You dropped a few pots. We can fix them. Make some more.'

A shake of her head. 'I didn't drop them. I threw them. Because they were shitty and boring, and half of them didn't survive the kiln.'

He eyed them. They didn't look shitty or boring to him. He'd assumed they'd been made by a third-year student; Chris had barely scratched the surface of some of the glazing techniques used, not to mention that they'd worked with porcelain, a delicate material Aiden had tried to stay clear of whenever he could help it.

He reached for the nearest piece, a cylinder with a hole in the centre which he assumed had been a spout. The blue patterning around the lip was as intricate as that he'd seen in Middleport, barely a wobble in the paintwork. Something most potters would kill to achieve. How did she still not see her own talent?

There was no way it deserved to stay in pieces. He picked up as many of the bigger parts as he could, careful not to scrape his palms on the rough edges.

'I told you to leave it,' she murmured. 'I'll throw them away. You don't have to clean up all my fucking messes, Aiden.'

'I'm not cleaning up,' he said. 'I'm recycling.'

She sighed. 'What are you talking about?'

'In places like Japan, repair is part of a pot's life cycle. You can piece things back together with gold or silver, make the cracks part of its beauty. Or you can replace the missing pieces with different ceramics and materials. This isn't a mess. This is just one step in the process.'

'Is this some terrible, cheesy metaphor about how beautiful pain can be and how all heartbreaks can be healed, and all that other toxic positivity nonsense?'

'I wasn't talking about hearts. I was talking about pottery.' He lifted a brow, unable to keep from smirking. 'But if the shoe fits.'

'It doesn't,' she snapped. 'My heart is fine.'

'So I see.' He began putting the gathered pieces on the nearest desk, ignoring her when she told him again to stop. She could despise him and his help all she wanted, but he wasn't letting her give up on a project that could be beautiful. Not if it was the difference between her staying at RACA or going home.

She let out something akin to a growl and tried to stop him with a nudge, but he turned his back to her and salvaged the remaining pieces.

'Aiden, stop it!' she repeated, louder now. 'It's over, okay? I have less than two weeks until the contest, and Chris pretty much said I have no chance of winning. Just give up! I have!'

He glared at her. 'No. Fuck what Chris said. If he doesn't know what you're capable of, that makes him a fool, not you. Not unless you believe him.'

'Why can't you just leave it be, for once?' she asked desperately. 'Why do you always have to try to help me?'

The answer was so obvious that he could hardly believe she was asking it. Then again, this was Juniper. Stubborn, defiant, independent Juniper. Juniper, who couldn't see what was right in front of her eyes. 'Because I'm in love with you!'

Aiden held his breath, waited for her to react. Her lids fluttered, mouth parted, but for once, she didn't have anything to argue with.

He hadn't meant to say it, but he didn't want to take it back. What was the point? It was true, and hadn't they always been honest with each other?

He used her silence to his advantage: 'I'm sure this is terrible news for you, and I'm sure it doesn't make you hate me any less, but I do. I love you. And I'm sorry for doing things wrong. I'm sorry for going behind your back and doing the same shit my father would have done. I'm sorry I've been ignorant when it comes to money and privilege. But I'm not sorry for wanting to help you, because that's what people are supposed to do for the ones they love. And I will *keep* doing it, because you deserve a place here, and you deserve to win that contest. You deserve *everything*, Juniper.'

Her silence dragged on for minutes, so long that he wasn't sure she was ever going to reply – and he didn't need her to, so he went back to the pottery on the desk and began trying to piece together the matching fragments.

'You love me. You're *in* love with me,' she said, as though trying to piece together something else entirely. Something that didn't fit: confirmation that she was absolutely not on the same page as him.

'Yes.' Despite the hurt, he tried to stay focused. At least that way, he could avoid the utter humiliation that would come with her inevitable rejection.

But she didn't reject him. Not directly, at least. She instead murmured an, 'Okay.' She blinked the bleariness from her eyes and then hovered over his shoulder to match up two more parts. 'That's actually part of the handle.'

In Juniper language, he knew that meant something like 'I will cooperate with you, despite my better judgement,' and could only hope it meant he wasn't a lost cause.

Or, at least, that she wasn't.

38

Juniper had lied before. Her heart was absolutely not fine. In fact, it beat so rapidly that she wondered if she should be watching out for symptoms of cardiac arrest.

He loved her. She'd never stooped this low before, been broken this completely, but he loved her. Even as she bent, teary-eyed, over the pieces of her tea set. His warmth radiated against her side as, together, they tried to match up the pattern, like a jigsaw puzzle that would never quite be right. And he loved her. What was she supposed to do with that?

He didn't seem to expect her to do anything, his attention narrowed completely on her pottery. She looked at the clock with heavy lids and wondered if this could wait, or if she even *wanted* to pick herself up and try again this time. Aiden had made it clear that quitting wasn't an option, but it wasn't his decision.

'We don't need to do this now,' she said finally. 'It's late, and things are weird, and…' Well, that was it really. She was completely overwhelmed and incapable of doing much, but he'd probably deduced that already, considering how he'd found her. She didn't even know how long she'd been hiding under Chris's desk, only that workshop hours had officially closed hours ago.

'If you want to go and get some rest, I can sort this out.'

'Aiden.' She rubbed her gritty eyes, pushing away from him to rest her top half over the desk. But for once, she couldn't think of a protest. Not one she hadn't already used, at least. Maybe she would just have to accept that she'd never really understand why he cared about her so much.

But she couldn't just let him do this for her with the words she'd spat at him still hanging in the air between them. He deserved better than that, especially after he'd peeled her up off the floor and confessed a truth she still wasn't prepared to face.

She put her hand over his, halting his work so he would listen. He looked up at her expectantly, sucking his gums as though bracing for the worst. She couldn't blame him for that. 'I'm sorry for what I said to you the other day. I was angry and hurt, and maybe a little bit embarrassed. But you've never done anything to hurt me, not intentionally. In fact, all you ever do is take care of me, and I don't think I deserve it.'

Tears glimmered on his waterline, Adam's apple working as he tried to curate a response. It was strange, how easily she could read him now. How she knew that he was probably battling between two options: a dry joke or the truth, just like her. How the tic of his jaw meant that something still bothered him. How the crease between his brows only ever seemed to smooth when he was asleep or inside of her.

'You had every right to be angry,' he decided. 'I don't blame you for any of it.'

'But I wasn't just angry. I was mean, and I said things that I knew would hurt you. Things I know aren't true.' She was too tired to stand anymore, so she grabbed the nearest chair and sat at the edge of the workbench with him. 'When I told you that I see you, I meant it. You're nothing like your dad, and even though you did the wrong thing, you did it because you thought it was right. I've spent the last few days trying to convince myself otherwise, that you really are horrible and I was right to hate you, but I can't, because it isn't true. You wouldn't be here otherwise. Bloody hell, I don't think anyone else would, either. I know I'm a lot to handle, especially when I'm this much of a mess.'

He placed his hand on top of hers, tracing the side of her thumb. That alone gave her a little more strength, a little more comfort. Maybe, tonight at least, she would just have to need him. Just have to let him be there for her. 'You keep me on my toes, Hodge, but you're not a lot to handle. Not at all. And I was telling the truth about Elmington. I had no idea my dad would do that. It…' He shook his head, voice growing thick. 'Finding that out really fucked me up. It made me realise that he'll never see me for what I am, and I'll never be enough.'

'Not for him, maybe, but that's his loss. You *are* enough, Aiden. You're more than enough. You're kinder and more talented than he'll ever be.'

Aiden sniffed, one last attempt to stop the tears, but they came anyway, and this time she was there to catch them. Seeing him so vulnerable left her shaken and unsure, and she wished more than anything she hadn't played a part in his hurt.

'I, er, went to Manchester to see him,' he admitted after clearing his throat, wiping his eyes. 'I told him I couldn't have anything to do with him anymore. I should never have gone to him for help. I should have distanced myself a long time ago. I guess some habits are just hard to break.'

'Well, it's never easy with parents. How did he take it?'

A shrug. 'The way he takes everything. Without much empathy or care. I'd rather lose him than end up like him, though. I wonder how many friends I'll have in a few years' time, when he's smeared my name through the dirt.'

'They wouldn't be friends worth having.' Juniper couldn't help but run her fingers through his hair. 'How did you even get him to agree to help, if he hates ceramics so much?'

Aiden lowered his eyes. 'Doesn't matter now.'

Juniper held her breath. If Aiden had been the one to pay for this unsolicited favour… 'Aiden.'

He rubbed his face roughly. 'He wanted me to work with him next summer.'

'And you were going to?' she sputtered.

A shrug. 'If it meant getting to keep you here, yeah.'

She didn't know what to say anymore. It was her who wasn't enough, not against him. Not when he'd nearly sacrificed his own wellbeing for her. It was difficult not to sound angry when she demanded, 'Don't ever do that again. Don't ever put yourself in a position where you have to suffer for someone else. Not for me, not for anyone.'

He tilted his head. 'What if I said you're worth it?'

'*Nothing* is worth that. Not after what you went through at Elmington. *Promise* me.'

He didn't, instead looking at her the way he had a few nights ago, when he'd almost told her that he loved her the first time. That wobbly smile was too intimate, too raw, and she wasn't sure she deserved it.

Luckily, annoyingly, he changed the subject. 'So. Let's fix this. You ready?'

'No,' she admitted. 'How, exactly, are we going to do it?'

'There are a few methods.' Aiden blinked away his tears and stood, heading towards the drawers of materials along the side wall. His silhouette was the same as it had been that first time they'd thrown together, tall and broad agains t the night outside the window. Only now, she could pinpoint all the things that made him him: the defiant curl, always sticking up on the crown of his head; the way one shoulder was always slightly higher than the other; the subtle arch of his spine from a life spent hunched over his paintings and pottery wheels. She'd been right. He *was* hers, because she saw him, because she knew him – sometimes better than she knew her own body, her own mind. 'It's called kintsugi. Think it translates to golden joinery. But it doesn't have to be gold. We can use whatever we can find.'

She tried to imagine how it would look, but it was difficult to see beyond all the broken parts. One thing was for sure: it wouldn't be boring if she could pull it off. 'Well, I do happen to know a place where there are a lot of broken ceramics.'

'Yeah?'

'Caffè Verde. Haven't you heard? I was recently promoted to the role of chief pot dropper.'

He laughed, and all she could think was how she wanted to hear it again and again and again. To know that she'd been the one to cause it felt like being granted a second chance.

'Well, I'm up for a little adventure if you are.'

'Since I happen to have closed up tonight' – she produced her golden key from the zip pocket of her bag – 'I don't see why not.'

It wasn't as though she had anything else to lose, except for him, and she was beginning to think that, this time, she might do anything it took to keep him.

★

'Nope!' Juniper told the security alarm when it tried to blare out at her. She dashed inside quickly to shut it off, inputting the numbers in the wrong sequence a few times until she remembered the combination.

It was the first time London had felt peaceful to her, and she wasn't sure if it had more to do with the ebbing evening or the fact that she had finally surrendered to her fears and insecurities. Either way, the floating dust motes and sepia shadows of Caffè Verde covered her like a blanket.

'Wow. It turns out I quite like it here without Gianna and the customers.' She examined a potted fern. 'Was that always there?'

'Yes,' Aiden answered, and then he was close again, passing headlights dancing across his face. Somehow, they always did seem to end up alone in the dark. She tried to keep her focus on the task at hand: broken pots. She hadn't been exaggerating about her clumsiness earlier, and only hoped the bins hadn't been taken out before she could salvage some of the pieces.

Thankfully, as she hopped without much grace over the counter and into the kitchen, she found the remnants of her earlier shift shining in against the bin liner. Aiden flicked on his phone torch, then his face crinkled. 'Are you really going to put your hands in that?'

It *was* a bit minging. The coffee beans and teabags went into the bin for compostables, as well as the food, but somebody had clearly forgotten and dropped in a slice of tomato. Not her. That she could remember. Cake wrappers and old rags cushioned the ceramics, too.

'This is a job for my Marigolds.' Juniper retrieved her trusty rubber gloves from the sink, now familiar enough that they slid right on, since Gianna often delegated her to washing up duty on account of her sour moods. Still, she could practically feel the cold, slimy tomato even through the yellow layers and hesitated. 'Or you could do it. You know, since you love me.'

'Only you would use that as a weapon.'

'It's hard not to. Nobody's ever loved me before, y'know. Got to make the most of it.'

He rolled his eyes, though he was smirking, and so was she. 'I highly doubt that's true.'

It was very, very true. Her few relationships hadn't lasted long enough for the *L* word to come up, and it was usually Juniper who was more tempted to drop the bomb, though always for the wrong people. That she was preserving it now, she knew, was because of how real it would make it to say it aloud. A reflection of how much she truly felt it.

And she did. 'I... I can't say it back yet,' she admitted.

'I didn't tell you so that you would say it back, you dope.' He held out his hands, beckoning with his fingers. 'Give me the bloody gloves.'

She did, with her hand still inside them. 'I just mean that until this contest is over, I won't be able to think straight.'

'I know. That's okay. But I sort of need the gloves without your hands in them.' He tried to tug the gloves off, but she curled her fingers. She really, really needed him to know what tonight had meant to her, even if she was rubbish at articulating it.

'Aiden.'

'Juniper,' he mimicked, then looked at her with some reluctance. 'I'm not asking you for anything, okay? And I can wait. Until after the competition, or until we finish first year. Until we graduate, if you want. But eventually, you and me... we're going to do this properly.'

'You don't think we're too different? Too incompatible?' In the dark, it was easier to voice her worries. They might have been the only two people to exist in the city at this time, for all the noise they heard outside, and there was a comfort in that she wanted to sink into. Even with the contest looming, and her future uncertain. Even after everything.

Aiden chewed on his cheek for a moment. 'No, I don't think that. When I'm with you, close to you, all the ways I've felt lost and wrong go away.'

She felt the same. Like she could be herself, even when she was at her worst.

She stepped closer without realising it, and his hand slipped from her gloves to her elbow as he cast her an inquisitive glance.

'Be honest,' he whispered, and she readied herself for a question she wasn't yet prepared for. 'Do I want to know where those gloves have been?'

Her laughter peeled through the kitchen, so loud she didn't hear anybody come in. Not until she saw the deformed shadow standing on the threshold. It looked like a person, only some sort of horn protruded from its head. Her amusement died out, and she hopped back, dragging Aiden with her in the fear that one of her mythological creatures had come to life. With the day she was having, it wouldn't have been all that surprising, but she didn't feel like getting eaten alive by a bipedal unicorn, or a—

'Gianna,' she breathed in relief when the figure stepped onto the kitchen tiles. Not a monster – or, not a *paranormal* monster – just her boss sporting a bun that tapered into a messy point on top of her head… and, on her feet, slippers shaped like horses, which were slightly disturbing. 'What are you doing here?'

'What am *I* doing here?' Gianna snapped. 'I got a notification that the security alarm went off.'

Oh. She looked at Aiden as though he might produce an excuse from thin air, but when he only grimaced, she knew she had to handle this on her own. Honesty was probably not the best policy, but it was better than any alternative theories Gianna came up with after seeing Juniper and her non-boyfriend in her kitchen, the former wearing rubber gloves. She wouldn't let her misconstrue this for some sort of cleaning kink.

'Well, we were just going to go through your bins.'

'Oh, of course you were. What a normal thing to do at eleven o'clock in the evening. Mind you, you never do it during your *shift*.'

'It's for a project!' Juniper blurted quickly. 'I needed some broken pottery, and remembered the mugs I broke earlier, may they rest in peace.'

Gianna looked at the sky as though seeking aid from the powers that be. Juniper wondered if she was about five seconds away from getting fired and could only be surprised that it hadn't happened sooner.

But her boss glanced at the two of them, crossing her arms over the big fluffy cloud on her pyjama jumper. 'I'm going to assume that you two are back together, and therefore you will come into work less mopey tomorrow morning. At eight o'clock.'

'But my shift doesn't start until...' One scowl from Gianna had Juniper shutting her mouth. 'Yes. Eight o'clock. In the morning. That's a time I am very good at being awake for. See you then.'

'Good.' She already had one foot out of the kitchen. 'Get your pottery and then get out. No shenanigans. And remember to lock up!' She shouted that last part, because she'd already reached the front door. Once she was outside and out of eyesight, Juniper's tension eased, though not completely.

'She's going to fire me one of these days, and I'll deserve it.'

'Or, she'll be scrambling to buy your pottery when you create something wonderful.' Aiden motioned to the bin again. 'Give me the gloves, Hodge. I'll be chivalrous, just for you.'

She smiled and did just that, an idea already forming in her mind as he plucked the pots from the waste. Gianna had her faults, but her taste in pottery was great, most of the mug designs unique in some way. The vivid greens that matched the houseplants might just save her.

All thanks to Aiden. Once again, he'd believed in her work more than she did, and now, hope was returning, along with a dozen ideas of what to do for her contest set.

None of them would Chris accuse of being boring, either. If he wanted her to express herself, she had plenty left to say.

39

The National Ceramics Contest was held in an exhibition centre in Mayfair, and Aiden had listened to Juniper's complaints about it being too posh the whole way there. With Tilly and Luc, they walked through the grand venue's doorway and into what most potters would consider a fairy tale. Half of the hall was dedicated to the contest entrants, where Aiden spotting the empty pedestal reserved for Juni straight away. The other half was full of merchants behind stalls, selling everything from crafting tools to handmade goods.

Juniper gasped and almost dropped her crate of pottery in the process, causing Aiden to steady her quickly. 'Coco's here!'

'*What?*' Tilly spun on her thick platform heel to look at a pink and white stall in the corner labelled *Cococeramics* in swirling gold calligraphy. On her table sat a vast array of creations, from colourful Pride mugs to abstract shapes and patterns that Aiden would have to take a closer look at, since he'd missed it in Stoke-on-Trent. 'Oh, shit. Shit. Okay, nobody panic.'

'Why are we panicking?' Aiden asked.

'They hooked up in Stoke thanks to your wingman expertise, and now I suspect Tilly is dealing with some feelings,' provided Luc, to which Juniper nodded along in agreement.

'Yeah, that about sums it up. Oh, and also, I want to be her when I grow up. Not because of the Tilly thing, no offence, Tilly, but because of the successful pottery business.'

'Ouch. Kick me while I'm down,' Tilly muttered, and then turned around right as Coco's eyes landed on the four of them. Aiden grinned and sent her a wave, rather proud that he'd helped get Tilly and Coco together, if only briefly. If Tilly's uncharacteristic shyness was anything to go by, that might change soon. She was clearly smitten.

That made two of them.

Juniper observed the entries, pale with what was obviously nerves. Aiden wished she had at least one hand free so that he could hold it, but the best he could do was take the big crate from her with a gentle tug. 'You've got this. Nobody else has designed a piece like yours.'

'That's because nobody else had a breakdown and smashed their work,' she replied. 'I'm out of my depth. These all look professional, and mine...'

'Is beautiful,' Tilly interrupted, urging Juniper towards the white display plinths. The empty one was sign-posted with her name, proof she belonged here as much as everyone else.

'It's okay if I lose, yeah?' She turned to him. 'I mean, I'll be fine going back to Manchester, working a job I hate, living with my parents again. Most twenty-somethings do that. Usually after they've gotten a degree, but I've never been much of a high-achiever, so—'

'Take a breath, sweetheart.' He placed the crate down on one of the wider surfaces and then cupped her face in his hands. For him, he preferred not to be touched when he was anxious, but the last week of getting these pots together had shown him plenty about how best to help her when she was spiralling. Touch, bad jokes, Cerberus visits, and reality TV. 'You're the most talented, capable woman I know, and if this doesn't work, we'll figure out another way. Together.'

'All of us,' Tilly said, nestling into their little support gathering. 'We love you, Juni, and we're here no matter what.'

'Wow. You are all so mushy these days,' Luc commented, but joined nevertheless.

'Even if I have to live in a cardboard box to stay at RACA?'

'Even if I have to build a bunker under my bed for you and Cerberus.' Tilly tugged Juniper's hair playfully. 'Besides, I just saw an entire display of phallic sculptures in the corner. You were just ahead of your time!'

Juniper choked on a laugh and hugged her tight. 'I love you. I love all of you.'

Aiden stepped back to let them have their moment, though not without a pang of envy. He wished she could say that so easily when it was just the two of them. Of course, he knew it was different. Friendship wasn't quite as complicated as what they shared, and he would never pressure her, but...

But he loved her, and he knew deep down she felt the same, and one of these days, they both deserved for it to come easier, especially after all they'd been through.

'Do you mind if you don't look at everything until the showing later? I sort of want it to be a nice little moment.'

The question was aimed more at him, and he relented after a curious glimpse at her work. He'd seen most of it already, though once she'd gotten the hang of yobitsugi, repairing her pots with the pieces she'd scavenged from Caffé Verde, she'd been insistent that she do some parts alone. Since the whole point was making it feel like hers again, he was more than happy to let her.

'Of course. How about I return to wingman duties? C'mon, Tilly.'

With a groan from Tilly, they left Juniper to set up alone, where he knew she was most comfortable even now. Besides, the stalls on the other side were a much-needed reminder of why he loved art so much, colours and forms calling to him. His inspiration was slowly coming back, but he had so much left to learn.

So much he hoped he and Juniper could discover together.

★

Waiting for Delia Melrose and her two fellow judges to assess each contest piece dragged on for hours, to the point where Aiden almost felt as unsettled as Juniper. They went to get some air in the nearby park when she started to get overwhelmed, and he distracted her with a blueberry muffin and spiced latte to keep them warm in the March frost. Despite all of the nerves, he had a feeling he might look back on it as his favourite day with her yet. All of her reservations with him were finally gone. She'd opened up like the early spring blossoms, finally letting him see all of her. Even her fears and self-criticisms. Even her fondness for him. If that meant they were better off this way, friends before lovers, he would take it. Of course he wanted all of her, but getting to be part of this day, part of her life, was better than the alternative. He'd always settle for whatever she was willing to give.

When they returned, Tilly shared the news that the winner was to be announced in fifteen minutes.

'Well, then, I suppose it's time for you to see my pieces properly. C'mon.' She took Aiden's hand and motioned for him, Tilly, and Luc to follow her back to her display. He'd already known that they were rich in colour and abstract in shape, but it was the information card in front that caught his eye now. Like the other contestants, Juniper had hand-written the title of her piece along with information about what it meant to her beneath.

Rebuilt

This work began as a traditional Nordic-patterned tea set made from porcelain that I destroyed in a moment of despair. I had tried too hard to design something I believed other people wanted to see, and had failed my own individuality and passion for the craft in the process. So, when I picked up the pieces, it became a symbol of so much more, and wouldn't have existed if I didn't have a network of people who have supported me through a difficult time. That's why, beyond fixing the cracks with the Japanese arts of kintsugi and yobitsugi, I incorporated pieces of them into my work. The rough, textured coils of my vessels represent yarn as a tribute to my best friend's passion for crochet. The flowing shapes and vibrant greens of my linked set of vases show a place a dear friend told me about once: a waterfall in France where they feel most at peace. The bookends, one a hamster and one a toadstool, are inspired by my own small pet, who has made my journey a less lonely one. And my bowl has been placed inside two sculpted pairs of overlapping clay hands as a symbol of my healing process. Putting myself back together has been a group effort, but I have found an intimate, supportive love to lean on through it all — even when I've been reluctant to let it in.

As Aiden tried to process the words, Luc ran a gentle finger over the red bridge that linked together a pair of vases. 'This looks just like Buttes Chaumont,' they whispered.

Juniper nodded with a wobbly smile. 'You told me in Stoke-on-Trent that it was the place you used to visit to escape the city, something that's hard to do here, so…'

'Juni.' Tears shimmered in Tilly's dark eyes as she admired the yarn-like textures of her candle holders. They'd been glazed in sunset yellows and oranges, mimicking the brightness Tilly radiated as well as the colours she wore most often. 'These are so beautiful.'

'You've been such a good friend to me, Till,' Juni replied. 'Even when I snotted all over your clothes and broke your plates.'

'I forgave you for that almost right away, you plonker.' Tilly hugged her, then went back to admiring Juniper's work.

She looked at Aiden expectantly, and he wished he could find something to say that would convey just how beautiful the hands moulding the bowl were. She'd even added a freckle of brown on one of the knuckles, just like his. It reminded him immediately of the first time they'd thrown together, hands intertwining so that he hadn't been able to tell which belonged to him and which belonged to her. That moment had changed so much between them.

'I couldn't think of a better way to tell you,' she said, dipping her chin nervously.

'Tell me what?'

'That I love you, too. That I couldn't have done any of this without you. That I'm sorry I'm stubborn and difficult and—'

He didn't ever want to hear her put herself down again, but especially not after what she'd just said, so he cut her off with his mouth on hers, kissing her softly. Their fingers laced together just like their clay hands, and he smiled to think there would always be a version of them entwined now. She'd made them a little part of pottery history.

When he pulled away, she was rosy and wide-eyed, the most vibrant piece of art in the room. 'Stubborn, yes, but not difficult. In fact, I find it pretty fucking easy to love you, Juni. And it's not just us who have put you back together. You did the same for me, too. I don't think I knew who I was until you showed me again. Everything that I lost during the hardest time of my life, I found again with you – and so much more.'

She rested her head against his thundering chest, arms snaking around his waist. Tilly and Luc had disappeared to let them have their moment, and even Coco had joined them, which meant the former had shrunk into her coat.

'Well, well, well,' came a voice behind them. Aiden turned with Juniper still at his side to find Chris beaming proudly. 'I had a feeling you might rustle something together in the end.'

Juniper's face darkened a hair, but she smiled back. 'Fancy seeing you here. Did you come to see my boring piece lose?'

Aiden squeezed her waist in reassurance, a reminder he was there if she needed him, though he knew she was more than capable of handling the tension herself.

'I came to see you what you're capable of when you're not trying to fit the mould,' said Chris.

Juniper hummed, but softened. 'You were right. That last piece wasn't me. I realised I'd rather lose with something I've put my heart and soul into than try to win by being like everyone else.'

'Everyone else is boring.' He inched forward, observing the display from a new angle. 'This is outstanding work. Your tutor must be great at his job.'

'Unfortunately, he is. Even if he's mean sometimes.'

'Perhaps he could learn to deliver criticism a little more gently.' He patted Juniper's shoulder. 'You've done RACA proud today, Juniper. Well done.'

The compliment clearly meant a lot to her, because that crinkle of worry at the corner of her mouth finally ironed itself out. Just in time, too. Delia, the grey-haired woman who had become familiar after watching her as a guest judge on *Throw Down* took to the stage, asking the contestants to gather around for the winner's announcement. Aiden's grip moved back to her hand as they inched closer to the small stage, his stomach fluttering with anticipation. She had to win. While there was some real talent in this room, he hadn't seen anybody pour their heart into this the way she had. Perhaps he was biased, but still.

'Every year,' said the judge, 'we see more and more talent emerge from this competition, and while that's wonderful, it also makes my job very difficult.'

Everybody laughed, minus Juniper, who was gripping Aiden's hand hard enough that he could feel his knuckles beginning to crunch together.

He gritted his teeth and whispered, 'I sort of need my hands, sweetheart. Y'know for pottery. And other things you seem to enjoy.'

'Sorry.' She let go, shifting on her feet. Her grown out fringe danced across her forehead as she blew out a long breath, and all he could do was draw soothing circles at the bottom of her spine as Delia continued.

'All of these pieces will remain on display for the next month,' she said, 'and while everybody has done such a wonderful job, it's time to announce the runners up, each of whom will win a brand-new throwing wheel and set of ceramic paints.'

Third and second place went to two worthy contestants, one of whom had made a collection much like Juniper's pre-smash, and the other a coffee set inspired by the seasons.

Juniper picked at the skin on her lip. 'They were way better than me. There's no way I have a chance.'

Aiden shook his head. 'I can't wait to say *I told you so* when you win.'

She elbowed him in the stomach. 'Stop. I'm trying not to get my hopes up. I've already practised my loser's clap.'

'And without further ado, the winning piece,' said Delia with a grand flourish. 'This year's top potter challenged us to remember why we created this competition in the first place, and, really, what it means to be an artist. Their work told a story, with their passion shining through every element and technique. Not only does their display catch your eye immediately, but it also conveys a vulnerability few of us are comfortable expressing. So, congratulations to Juniper Hodgson for your piece, titled *Rebuilt*. Please could you come up to the stage?'

From the back of the room, Aiden heard Tilly squeal in delight. He whirled around to congratulate her, overcome with pride, only to find her clapping with the rest of the crowd as though she hadn't heard her name at all.

'Juni… That's you.'

Her feigned smile dropped, applause slowing. 'Oh my god, that *is* me!'

She leaped into Aiden's arms, leaving them both stumbling, but he didn't care a bit. 'You did it, sweetheart,' he murmured in her ear. 'And guess what? I told you so.'

A mixture of a sob and a laugh fell from her, and then he was urging her up onto the stage to shake hands with the judges, where her pottery was in the process of being moved for everyone to see. She was handed a glossy ceramic plate that named her as the 2025 National Ceramics Contest winner and then was invited to say a few words.

Juniper stepped up to the microphone looking daunted, but her eyes met Aiden's across the sea of potters, and he saw relief take over, along with something else. Something that made him feel full, safe, home, for the first time in his life.

'Well, I really didn't ever think this would happen,' she admitted. 'Like, really. Just two months ago, I broke a teapot by pouring hot chocolate into the pit-fire.'

More laughter, his included.

'I entered this competition as a last resort. My college tuition bursary was suspended, and I needed money. Sorry if you're not supposed to admit that.' She looked down at the trophy plate in her hands, frowning. 'I'm not the most talented potter in the universe. Definitely not even in this room. But I started this journey because moulding clay made me feel like I was at home. I don't have control over many things, but I had control over what I could create. Eventually, at least. Throwing took a bit of patience. Anyway, I was going somewhere with this…' She rubbed her temple, and he tried to push slightly closer to the stage to let her know he was still here. 'I feel like I'm at the Oscars. I didn't plan a blooming speech.'

Finally, she looked up from her feet, this time her attention on the crowd. 'I suppose mostly, I just want to thank you all. Like my pieces, I was a little bit broken, but this has made me realise that it doesn't have to be permanent. That I can feel broken and still achieve the things I've always hoped to achieve. And I couldn't have realised that without the love that pottery has given me, not just for the craft, but for the people I've met. Aiden, Tilly, Luc… Even you, Chris. Not that I love you – sorry – but you *have* helped me along the way.'

'Erm, thanks,' Chris muttered somewhere nearby.

'Oh, and you, Coco!' She pointed to the other corner of the room, where Coco still manned her stall. 'Thanks to you, to all of you, I think I know what kind of artist I want to be. Because art doesn't have to be perfect. It just has to mean something true.' She began to well up, which meant that Aiden did, too. 'And this means the world to me.'

After a round of applause and more encouraging words from Delia, the ceremony came to an end. Aiden waited with open arms as Juniper stepped offstage and returned to him, award in hand. Instead of hugging him, she handed him the plate, panicked. 'I'm too clumsy to be responsible for this. Please, take it.'

'I'm so proud of you, babe!' Tilly said as she skipped over. 'And that speech was lovely. A bit unorganised, but lovely. Just like you.'

Juniper exclaimed, 'I still can't believe it. I won!'

'You won!' Luc agreed. 'And that means you can stay at RACA!'

'Oh, yeah!' Her smile wavered, especially when Chris returned to their group. 'Erm, yeah.'

'Well, don't sound too ecstatic,' Chris said.

'It's just that this has been a lot. Studying, working, living in a box-sized dorm.' She chewed on her lip. 'And RACA did something that was actually really unfair to me. To us.' She squeezed Luc's shoulder. 'I've learned a lot, and I'm grateful for that, but I'm… I'm not a student. Or, at least, I'm not RACA's definition of a student. If they can't provide stability for me after promising it, I don't think I can keep pushing myself to exhaustion just to make it work. That twelve-grand cash prize will cover the rest of this year, but then what? It'll just be the same problem, over and over, and I'm tired. It's sucking the love I had for art away, and that's scarier than being broke.'

Panic twinged through Aiden. 'So, what are you saying? You're going back to Manchester?'

As much as he wanted her to pursue whatever path felt right, the idea of not having her here was like a black hole stretching out in front of him.

But then she shook her head, and he relaxed. 'No. I don't think I belong there either, not right now. Before this, my goal was just to get my art into people's hands. Sell my earrings and whatnot. It didn't seem grand enough, but now it feels calm and right, something I'm able to handle. I've spent a lot of time trying to force myself to be like everyone else, and that's one of the reasons I wanted to study, but I'm *not* like everyone else. Things are so hard sometimes. I'm ready to work at my own pace, to my own needs, instead of everyone else's.'

She stepped towards Aiden, grazing his jaw gently. 'I'm staying in London, but not for RACA. For us. And for me. To figure out how to be an artist in a way that works for me.'

'Whatever you choose, I'm here,' he replied, meaning every word of it. Whether she was on his path or a completely different one, he had faith they would always meet somewhere in the middle. She had his heart, and they'd figure the rest out. More than anyone else, she deserved to be happy.

'Well, I can't pretend like I won't miss you, Jupiter.' Chris winked, but his mouth was pressed into a solemn line. 'With this award under your belt, you never know what opportunity might be around the corner. I have every faith you're going to be just fine.'

'Thank you, Chris. You really have taught me a lot, but I'm ready to learn in different ways now.'

Tilly pouted. 'So, we won't be dorm buddies anymore?'

'I mean, who knows? I could waste my prize fund on clothes and be homeless in a month.' She sighed, and for once, it was serene instead of panicked. Aiden hoped to hear it more often, especially when she leaned against him to look at her friends. Her family. 'But I don't think that'll happen. You guys showed me what I need to be happy, and I think I'm ready to stop fighting it now.'

Aiden planted a kiss in her hair, Tilly taking her hand, and they stayed that way until Delia approached with a friend to introduce herself to Juniper properly. Chris was right about the opportunity. Aiden heard all sorts of ideas being thrown out as they went to chat in a quieter space.

She was destined for something good. He was just lucky to be able to witness it all. And lucky that, like her, he was finding his own way forward without the strings of past problems holding him back.

Thank goodness he'd discovered a new kind of art, one worlds away from his father's ideas of it. Without pottery, he might never have gotten here. Might never have met the woman he loved and friends he could trust.

He'd never been more excited to see what the future held.

Epilogue

The evening was Juniper's new favourite time of day. As grateful as she was for the steady stream of customers and students who wended in and out of Juni's Pottery Studio, she loved a little moment of quiet spent in the last patch of sunlight by her throwing wheel. A moment to feel the peace she'd been searching a long time to find.

Her studio wasn't the biggest or prettiest in London, but she didn't mind. Wedged between a colourful fruit and veg market and a barber in Camden Town, plenty of people found her business, whether it was art lovers come to browse the work on sale or friendship groups eager to paint their own pots together. Really, the building seemed to find them rather than the other way around, as it had her not long after she'd returned from a week-long course in Limoges, France, offered to her by one of Delia's friends. Chris had been right: winning the contest had served her plenty of opportunities that had taught her more about pottery, and herself, than ever before, and she'd poured all of it into this place, where potters who may not have the chance otherwise could sit in on weekly free lessons and hone their skills. If she would have had a place like this in Manchester, she might never have put so much pressure on her work at RACA, and she wanted to provide that for other people. Alternatives to the rigorous studying she'd felt obligated to enrol in. A safe place for artists to just *be*.

'Oh, no!' A sudden cry filled her shop, and she dashed into the kiln room to find one of her favourite students, Carol, with a broken mug in her hands. 'It exploded in the kiln. Goshity gosh, I'm so terrible at this!'

She tutted at herself, shaking her head until her white bob bounced against her jaw. She was one of Juniper's eldest patrons, but had that same ageless twinkle in her eye when it came to creating things. With arthritis in her hands, Juniper had been trying to find new disability-friendly techniques to teach, but the kiln was clearly not always kind regardless, something she'd learned over the last year. No matter how skilled she was, there would always be unexpected problems. Only now, she knew how to move past them with patience and creativity.

'Oh, Carol.' Juniper sympathised, taking a closer look at the stoneware pieces, glazed lovely greens to resemble summer leaves. 'You're not terrible at all. This is lovely work!'

Carol looked at her like she'd grown too heads. 'But it's broken!'

'Some of my best pieces started out broken. How about next time you pop in, I'll show you how I put them back together? I promise, it'll be beautiful by the end, and it's lots of fun!'

'Really? I shouldn't just chuck it in the bin?'

Juniper smiled. 'You should never, ever chuck it in the bin.'

Carol hesitated, then set the pieces down on the side. 'Okay. If you say so. I'll see you tomorrow morning, then, love.'

'Sounds wonderful.' Juniper patted her arm gently, and then saw her on her way, the tinkle of the bell above the door signalling her final customer's departure. She sighed into the new silence and prepared herself for her least favourite task: cleaning. She hoped to hire people who might be able to help her with it eventually, but for now, her only employees were Aiden, who had found a passion for teaching weekend classes, and Tilly, who also used the space for her crochet group on a Tuesday night. They weren't far from finishing their second year at RACA, and Juniper loved hearing all about their classes, finding she didn't miss sitting at a desk all that much. Luc had returned to Paris to study when they weren't able to get a bursary for their second year, so they kept in contact with bi-weekly Zoom calls and had plans to meet up over summer.

The thought of her friends distracted her enough that she didn't even realise she was wiping paint from the tables until the damp cloth cooled her palm, always a little less overwhelmed with them in mind. Of course, there were still difficult days where she felt like her noisy little brain was winning the battle, days where she didn't want to get up, or open the shop, or talk to strangers. But they were far fewer since she'd finally been in a position to quit her part-time job at Caffè Verde a few months ago, making enough income here to support herself. Needless to say, Gianna had been delighted.

Which reminded her. She'd stayed in touch to commission some new mugs and plates for the café, and Juniper had been all too happy to accept, offering a discount for the ones she'd personally been responsible for breaking. Scratch cleaning: her fingers itched to throw.

After flipping the open sign to closed, Juniper picked up her phone to put on her favourite playlist, whose loud bass and rocky vocals probably wouldn't be soothing to others, but were to her. She got comfortable at the wheel with her clay, centring it with far more ease than she had a year ago. Now, it moulded to her hands like air, and she soon got into a rhythm with it. So much so that she didn't hear the door open, only felt two warm palms cover her eyes. She grinned, wobbling just slightly, but in tune enough with her craft that the clay soon steadied.

'I thought you were studying tonight,' she said.

Aiden placed a kiss in her hair by way of greeting as she took her foot off the pedal to look at him. He was more handsome than ever, clean-shaven, with his hair tucked into one of her scrunchies. Freedom looked sexy on him, and she'd never been more in love with him. After his dad had stopped funding Aiden's bank account, he'd taken over her job – yes, he was better at that, too – and was already planning for life after RACA. His work placement at an art school began in a couple of weeks, chosen when he'd realised that he wasn't only a brilliant teacher for her, but many of her customers.

'Missed you too much,' he confessed. 'And I can't trust you to remember to eat otherwise, so I brought takeout.'

Now he said it, she could smell the warm saltiness of ginger and soy sauce emanating from a white bag on the counter, bought from her favourite Chinese down the road. It was true she was usually too hyperfixated on work to remember her basic needs. Thankfully, between him and Tilly, who was now her and Cerberus's doting roommate after moving out of halls this semester, she was never left hungry for too long. Aiden still lived in Cartwright Gardens, his aunt offering an extra discount on rent when he'd told the family about Jonathan cutting him off, but he hadn't needed to take her up on that yet. He worked as hard as everyone else to make ends meet, even if he had savings to fall back on.

'Have I told you recently that I love you?' she said.

His lopsided smirk sent shivers through her, and he pulled up a stool to place another gentle kiss at the place where her apron straps met her bare shoulder. 'Yes, but I'll never complain about hearing it.'

She *tsk*ed. 'So vain.'

He turned his attention to the clay. 'What are you making?'

'Plates for Gianna.'

'Well, that's good, because I learned a new technique in class today.'

'Oh, yeah?' She arched her neck as he swept her hair away from her skin, heat coiling inside her when she saw the hunger in his eyes. He was often learning new techniques, but she rarely ended up finding out what they were. Every time was like the first time with them, still magnetised to each other to the point of frenzy.

Aiden hummed, fingers tracing a slow line down her arm before he bracketed her hands. She put her pressure on the foot pedal again, only half-focused on it as his body became hers. He guided her and the clay, letting it slope just so before, together, they made a start on the rim.

'I've been thinking,' he said.

'Oh, no.'

He laughed. 'We've been together for over a year, now.'

'And what a long, terrible year it's been,' she deadpanned.

'You know I love it when you're mean to me, sweetheart, but I am trying to have a serious conversation here.'

She raised her brow and let her foot off the pedal, turning to face him. He pulled her closer by the base of her back so that there was finally nothing between them.

'You're not sick of me, are you?' she questioned, and she was only half-joking. As much as her confidence had grown, and as much as she trusted in him, it still felt surreal to be this in love. She supposed that was why she'd spent so long shying away from it... or, more accurately, flying headfirst into combat with it. Good things hadn't always come easy for her, love especially. While her parents sometimes told her they were proud of her now, they still didn't really get it, or her, and choosing someone was a far different type of connection. One that she'd seen break a few times with Coco and Tilly, though they always made their way back to each other – with very loud makeup sex that Juniper didn't necessarily wish to listen to.

Aiden tutted. 'Don't be ridiculous. I could never be sick of you.'

'Okay. Then what?'

He cocked his head, playing absently with her hair. 'Well, I know your flat is starting to feel crowded with Coco visiting more often. And you spend at least half the week at my flat anyway. I was just wondering if maybe you'd think about moving in permanently.'

'You want me to move in with you?' she repeated, stunned. They'd both decided when they'd made things official that they'd take it slow while Juniper started her business and Aiden focused on his exams and coursework. As easy as it would be to rush into everything at once with him, she'd wanted to make sure she was standing on her own two feet first. Besides, she wasn't easy to live with, what with her attachment to any object she'd ever owned and her inability to find a place for it that wasn't the floor.

'I do. Only if you want to. No pressure. I know you're happy where you are right now, and I wouldn't ask you to change that if you didn't want to.' His hands lifted to her rib cage, tender and loving. 'It's just that I love you, and I know this is it for me. You're my favourite person, and I couldn't think of anything better than coming home to you – and Cerberus, loud as he is – every night.'

Juniper didn't know what to say. Emotion stuck in her throat, still surprised even now at just how honest he could be with her. That was something she was still working on, always deflecting with humour because being vulnerable was so scary.

'Are you sure?' she questioned. 'I'm very messy.'

'Well, this is news to me. Why didn't you say so earlier?'

'I take extra-long showers.'

'I know. My water bill reflects that.'

'I leave my shoes out for people to trip over.'

'Yep. My toe is permanently bruised from your Docs.' He took her face in his hands. 'And yet I love you anyway. See how it works?'

She did see, but that didn't mean she understood. Then again, there were things about Aiden that would annoy anybody else, but that she accepted as part of him. The fact he always managed to smudge paint around, from the corner of his sleeve hitting paper to it somehow ended up in her hair. The way he sometimes burped in time to the music they were listening to. The sound of his teeth grinding in his sleep, a symptom of his anxiety that never seemed to go away even when he was feeling well.

She could sit there and find another five hundred reasons why this was a bad idea, but for once, she didn't want to.

So she braced her arms around his neck and said, 'Yes, Aiden. I want to move in with you.'

His toothy grin dazzled her, and then he was kissing her, palms pressing into her breasts. He pulled her onto his lap, where his erection already strained. Unable to wait any longer, she sought friction against his denim-clad thigh. The plate-in-progress was left abandoned as she unzipped his jeans and let him feel the same pleasure while he whispered all of the things he loved about her, all of the things he couldn't wait to do with her.

'I love you, Aiden,' she breathed, climax just a little out of reach. As sturdy as his thigh was, it wasn't enough. Too many layers between them.

He kissed her neck, teasing her nipples, and her hips bucked harder, faster. He knew her body like it was his own, knew when she needed more, so he picked her up and laid her out on the nearest table with his hands pinning her wrists above her head. Outside, anybody might have seen him guide her legs over his shoulders and thrust into her until she unravelled, but she didn't care.

In her world, it was only him and the life they were sculpting together. The life that finally felt like hers, even on the difficult days – and it was their most beautiful piece yet.

For more unmissable reads,
sign up to the HarperNorth newsletter at
www.harpernorth.co.uk

or find us on Twitter at
@HarperNorthUK

**Harper
North**

Printed in Dunstable, United Kingdom

71046849R00037

About the Author

♥

Welcome to my wild, wicked world of *over-the-top, heart-pounding instalove*. I write fast-paced, **spicy age gap novellas** that don't waste time. They are just pure heat, obsession, and unapologetic desire from page one. If you're into dominant older heroes, eager younger heroines, and deliciously deviant themes like **breeding** and **lactation**, you're in the right place.

These days, all my stories revolve around one irresistible idea: **men who fall fast, fall hard, and never let go**. Think possessive, primal, borderline unhinged alphas who'd burn the world down for their girl. They're obsessed, they're intense, and yes, more than one has been lovingly described as a full-blown *caveman* by reviewers.

So whether you're here for the age gaps, the obsession, or the kind of heat that leaves scorch marks, you're in the right place. Get comfortable. It's about to get *feral*.

Find me online at https://allmylinks.com/willow-watkins

Chapter One

Jack

The restaurant is too warm, too loud, and far too crowded with people I have little interest in making small talk with. But my daughter's happiness means I tolerate it.

"Dad, you're going to love her," Grace gushes beside me as we walk towards the private dining room. Her fiancé, Aaron, is on her other side, hand tucked at her back like he never wants to let her go. It makes me strangely proud to see how much he adores her, even if the kid still looks like he's barely out of college.

"She's incredible," Grace continues, her eyes glowing. "She's worked so hard for me this past year. Honestly, this whole wedding? It's all her. Jenna's the reason everything is exactly what I've dreamed of ever since I was a little girl. She even arranged everything for the rehearsal dinner tonight. I don't know what I would have done without her."

I nod and hum politely, but I don't care much about flowers and place settings. But if this wedding planner has made my only daughter happy, then I'm grateful to her. Grace is all I've had ever since her mom

left me six years ago for a co-worker, so my daughter's happiness means the world to me.

The doors open and we step into the private room. A long table is dressed in white linen, crystal glasses catching the low golden light, bottles of wine already breathing. The bridal party is there, laughing too loud, full of nerves and champagne.

I let my attention drift, scanning faces, cataloguing exits, already thinking about when I can slip away for a bourbon at the bar.

And then she walks in.

My lungs seize. My blood turns molten.

She's... Christ. She's everything.

I've never seen her before, so I have to assume it's the wedding planner Grace hasn't been able to stop talking about. Her blonde hair is in a soft twist, and she's wearing a dress the color of cream that clings so damn sweetly to her curves. My heart hammers so hard in my chest I'm surprised Grace doesn't hear it.

I've never believed in instant anything. Not fate, not destiny, and definitely not love at first sight. But the moment that blonde beauty steps into the room, I know with a bone-deep certainty: *she's mine.*

Not mine someday. Not mine if circumstances align.

Mine now.

My daughter is still talking to Aaron beside me, completely oblivious to the chaos running through my mind and body right now. I barely hear her as Jenna moves across the room, greeting all the bridesmaids with soft hugs, and shakes hands with the groomsmen. She's polite and efficient; all professionalism until her eyes meet mine.

The world stutters.

Her smile falters, lips parting with surprise. A flush blooms high on her cheeks. And in that heartbeat of recognition, it's obvious she knows me the way I know her.

"Jenna!" Grace calls, tugging her over. My daughter's voice breaks the spell, but I can't unclench my jaw. My hands flex at my sides like they already ache to hold her, to pin her, to keep her where she belongs - beneath me, against me, with me always.

"Dad, this is Jenna Lane. Jenna, this is my father, Jack Westmore."

Her hand is small, delicate, when I take it. Soft as silk. I have to force myself not to crush it, not to yank her towards me like a starving man finally handed his first meal in years.

"It's a pleasure, sir," she says, her voice gentle, musical. She looks up at me through her lashes, and it's like she's pouring gasoline on my already burning chest.

"The pleasure's all mine," I rasp, and it's the truth. My voice comes out too low, too rough. Like I've already been inside her. Like I'm already ruined.

There's small talk. I couldn't repeat a word of it if you paid me. She's explaining something to Grace about table placements, meal choices, decor. All I can think about is the way her soft pink lips shape each word, how her throat moves when she swallows, the voluptuous swell of her breasts beneath that pretty dress. My body reacts with brutal speed, blood surging south until I'm hard as stone.

I can already taste her. Can already imagine how she'll sound when she cries my name, the way her breath will catch when I sink into her for the first time.

My daughter slips her hand into mine, tugging. "Dad, come on, it's time to sit down."

I let her lead me towards the table, but my eyes never leave Jenna. Not once. I glance back over my shoulder, and she's staring after me, her lips parted and her cheeks flushed, that luscious chest rising and falling too fast.

She feels it. I know she does.

Good.

Because there isn't a damn thing in this world that's going to stop me from making her mine.

We all take out seats at the long table. Crystal glasses clink, silverware shines, and the servers glide in and out with plates of food. Voices rise around me, full of laughter and nerves.

Grace leans towards Aaron, her eyes shining. "Can you believe the wedding is finally almost here?"

He picks up her hand from where it rests on the table and kisses the back of it. "I've been waiting for this day since the first time I saw you back in high school. I can't wait to put my ring on your finger at last."

One of the bridesmaids sighs, propping her chin on her hand. "You two are so disgustingly sweet. It's like watching a romance movie in real life."

Aaron's best man and best friend, Ryan, grins and raises his glass. "You should have seen them back when they first met. He used to write terrible poetry for her."

Grace laughs, cheeks turning pink.

"Don't tell people about that!" Aaron groans, but the table erupts in good-natured teasing.

I smile faintly, nod when appropriate, but my mind isn't on their chatter. My eyes are locked on Jenna.

She floats around the room like she's the one holding it all together. Soft words here, a reassuring touch there, always smiling, always attentive. She doesn't sit. She doesn't stop. She's making sure every detail is perfect, and I can't take my eyes off her.

Every step she takes, every tilt of her head, every time her lips curve into that sweet smile, my chest tightens. It's madness. I've known her for less than an hour, and I already know I'll never want another woman again.

She approaches our end of the table, leaning down to murmur something to Grace. Her scent, subtle and intoxicating, drifts over, and I grip the stem of my wineglass so I don't reach for her.

Ryan's gaze drops straight to her chest, and something hot and ugly spikes in me. He grins as if he's got a right to look at her that way. "Hi, gorgeous. Maybe you'll let me buy you a drink later?"

Jenna stiffens, though she covers it up with a polite smile. "That's kind, but I'm working tonight. I'll have to pass."

Anyone with half a brain can hear the edge in her voice, see the discomfort in her eyes. But Ryan just chuckles, leaning back with smug ease. "Playing hard to get, huh?"

She steps away before he can push further, retreating across the room.

Grace turns sharply to Ryan, frowning. "Knock it off. She's here for work, not to get hit on."

He shrugs, unbothered. "Relax. She liked it. Didn't you see how she blushed? Women just play coy because they like to be chased."

My jaw tightens until my teeth ache. I lean forward, my voice dropping into the kind of tone that men recognize, the kind that promises consequences. "She said no. Once. That's all it takes. Now leave her the fuck alone."

Ryan raises his brows, smirking like it's all a joke. "Fine. I'll back off. For now."

I hold his gaze until he looks away, his smirk faltering enough to tell me he heard the threat beneath my words.

Across the room, Jenna glances back. Her eyes find mine. She looks flustered, pink-cheeked, but there's something else there too. Heat. Longing. The same desperate pull that's ripping me apart.

I don't look away.

Because there's no chance in hell I'll let anyone else touch her. Not when I've finally found the woman meant to be mine. And not when she so clearly feels it too.

He plants a hand on the wall beside me, leaning in close enough that I can smell the stench of wine that clings to his breath. "Hey, gorgeous. You've been working so hard tonight. Why don't you let me buy you that drink now? You deserve some fun."

I take a step back, trying to keep my smile polite. "Thank you, but I really can't. I'm still working."

His grin widens, shark-like. "Come on. Just one drink. I bet you'd loosen up real nice."

My stomach twists. I try to glance past him towards the table, but he angles his body, blocking my way.

"I... I should check on Grace." My voice wavers, but I lift my chin, trying to look professional. Calm. Not like my heart is pounding with fear.

He lowers his voice, eyes raking over me in a way that makes my skin crawl. "I'd make it worth your while. Come on. Just one drink."

I freeze. My chest constricts.

And then... he's gone.

Yanked backwards so fast that he almost tumbles to the ground. A wall of muscle and fury steps between us.

Jack.

My whole body trembles as he looms in front of me, broad shoulders blocking out the room, his voice a growl that rattles my bones. "You think cornering women makes you a man? Get the fuck out of here, Ryan. Now."

Ryan gapes, color draining from his face. "I was just..."

"You were being a creep," Jack snaps. "And if you're not on your best behavior tomorrow, you'll be out of that wedding before you can blink. Am I fucking clear?"

Ryan mutters something under his breath, but the steel in Jack's glare has him backing away fast, his walk of shame dragging every eye in the room towards us.

And suddenly, all that attention lands squarely on me.

My cheeks burn. Embarrassment squeezes my throat. Before anyone can say anything, I bolt past the table, down the hall, fumbling for the first door I can find.

I lock it behind me, my chest heaving, tears stinging my eyes. The safety of the single-occupant bathroom won't last long, but at least it's something.

I lean back against the counter, pressing my hands over my face as the tears start to flow. My body shakes with humiliation and fear.

And then I feel it. A damp heat spreading across the bodice of my dress, and the telltale sting of letdown.

"Perfect," I whisper bitterly, blinking back tears. "Just perfect."

I grab some toilet paper and dab uselessly at the fabric, but there's no hiding the dark stains that are spreading across it. Not only did I cause a scene at the rehearsal dinner, but now I'm leaking like a damn faucet.

My boss is going to hear about this. I'm going to get fired. My career is going to be over before it's even begun. And I can't walk back out there, not like this. Everyone will see exactly what I've been hiding.

Tears blur my vision as I grip the sink. "Why now?" I choke; half a sob, half a curse.

A knock rattles the door. I jump, panic clawing at my throat.

"Occupied!" My voice comes out too high, too shaky, thick with the tears I'm trying to hold back.

There's silence for a moment, and then a voice I know instantly even though I've only heard it a few times. Deep, steady, commanding.

"Jenna. It's me."

Jack.

My knees weaken.

"I can hear you crying," he says softly, but there's an edge of steel under the gentleness. "Let me in."

"I... I can't."

"Jenna." My name is a growl, somehow rough and tender all at once. "Open the door. Now."

And I do. Because if anyone is going to see me like this, I'd rather it be him in private than an entire room full of people.

The door swings open, and he steps inside, filling the tiny space with his presence. He shuts it behind him, locking us in together, and then his eyes drop down to my dress.

Shock flickers across his face, but his voice is gentle. "First things first... are you okay? After what that asshole did?"

I swallow hard, ashamed. "I'm fine. Just... shaken. I think I've ruined everything."

"You didn't ruin a damn thing," he growls. "He did. You hear me? Ryan made a fool of himself. Not you. And it's Ryan that Grace and Aaron are mad at right now."

The conviction in his tone makes my chest ache. But when his gaze drifts lower, settling on the soaked fabric clinging to my breasts, humiliation surges all over again.

Embarrassment makes me blurt the words out before I can stop myself. "I'm lactating. It started when my brother and his husband adopted a baby girl. They worried she wouldn't thrive, so I... I induced, so I could donate my milk to them. I know it's strange. I know it's wrong, but..."

"Wrong?" His voice is sharp, incredulous. His eyes snap up to mine, blazing with something that makes my thighs clench. Hunger. Pure,

unfiltered hunger. "It's beautiful and selfless that you would do this for your niece. It's not even close to being wrong."

I can hardly breathe as he steps closer, his body heat surrounding me. I had expected disgust, but all I see is need. Even more than before. As if this is the missing piece he didn't know he was searching for.

"Does your niece still need the milk?" His voice is low, almost reverent.

I shake my head, shame heating my cheeks once more. "She hasn't needed it for the last few months."

His lips curve into a dark, satisfied smile. "Good. Then your milk is all for me now."

My breath hitches, my whole body trembling as his hand rises slowly and deliberately to catch the edge of my bodice.

"Jack..."

"Shhh," he murmurs softly. "Let me take care of you."

And as he gently peels the top of my dress down, baring me inch by inch to his gaze, my shame dissolves into raw, aching anticipation.

I've never wanted anything so badly in my life.

Chapter Three

Jack

The scent hits me first.

Warm, sweet, rich. Like nothing I've ever known and everything I've ever needed. It fills the tiny bathroom, winding around me until I can barely breathe for the ache of it. My cock throbs, my chest pounds, and I know in my gut I'll never get enough.

Then I see her.

As I pull her dress lower, her breasts spill free. Heavy and round, her dusky pink nipples peaked and tight, with droplets of milk beading on each of them. Her cheeks are blotchy from crying, her lips trembling, her eyes wide and shining as if she expects me to recoil.

Recoil?

I want to drop to my fucking knees.

She's dripping with life, with nourishment, with a sweetness meant for me alone. My body responds like it's been starving all these years, just waiting for her. My mouth waters. My palms itch. Every primitive, feral instinct inside me screams to take, to claim, to drink until I'm full and then still demand more.

"Christ, Jenna..." My voice comes out raw, reverent, nearly shaking with the force of what's tearing through me. "Do you have any idea what you're doing to me right now?"

I step closer, drawn in like gravity, and the scent grows stronger, wrapping chains around my sanity.

"I didn't think you would want me when you found out about this," she says, her voice little more than a breathless whisper.

I reach up and gently cup one heavy tit in my hand, the skin slick with her leaking cream. "All this sweetness, and you thought no man would want it? You thought wrong, babygirl. I want it all."

She gasps softly. I have no idea if it's from my words or my touch, but I need the desperate little sounds she makes more than I need air right now.

My thumb traces a slow circle around her nipple. I watch in awe as the bead of milk quivers, and then trickles down.

"You've been full for so long, haven't you?" I murmur, leaning in closer. "Needing someone to drain you dry. To relieve all this pressure and make you feel good."

She shudders, eyes falling closed, her breath catching on a whimper. "Yes."

My cock is a rod of iron in my pants, throbbing so hard it hurts. My voice comes out harsh with barely restrained lust. "Then let me, babygirl. Let me give you what you need."

I don't give her a chance to respond before I lift her up to sit on the edge of the counter and my mouth closes over her nipple. She moans softly, one of her hands moving to the back of my head as I draw the sensitive nub between my lips. The first taste is a shock of electricity straight to my spine. A groan tears out of me as the warm, creamy liquid hits my tongue, and I suckle harder, demanding more.

I don't just want it. I fucking need it.

Her milk is rich and sweet and so goddamn pure it makes my dick throb. My whole body thrums with every pull of my mouth. I can already feel her relax, sinking deeper into the bliss of my touch, and a primal surge of satisfaction rises in me.

Mine. She's mine.

"Oh, God..." Jenna whimpers. She's gripping the back of my head so tightly I can feel the sting of her fingernails against my scalp. But I love it. I want her to mark me up. To brand me, scar me, leave no question that we are meant to be together.

I growl around her nipple, lapping the droplets from her soft, silky skin. The sound is muffled, greedy, desperate.

Her fingers twist in my hair. "Please. Don't stop."

My cock surges, pulsing against the zipper of my slacks, but the need to taste her is too strong to deny. So I switch to her other nipple, flicking the taut peak with my tongue.

She whimpers again, arching her back and offering her creamy tit. And I drink. I draw her deep into my mouth, and she writhes on the countertop, panting, whimpering, her legs parting and squeezing around my hips.

She's dripping, the musky scent of her arousal mingling with the rich sweetness of her milk. My cock aches, the tip leaking as precum beads. My balls are drawn up tight, and the urge to plunge inside her is overwhelming.

God, she'd look perfect with her belly round, her tits leaking just like this, our baby growing inside her.

Fuck. Where did that come from?

But I can't shake the thought. It burrows into my brain, making itself at home, until I'm dizzy with the need to make it real.

To put my seed in her, again and again and again, until it takes root.

The thought sends another pulse of precum into my boxers, and my cock strains for release. But I can't do that here. She deserves better than a quick fuck in a tiny restaurant bathroom. She deserves to be worshipped and spoiled and fucked like the fertile goddess that she is.

But I can give her relief, at least.

I slide a hand between her thighs, cupping her pussy through the lace of her panties. The material is soaked, clinging to her folds, and I groan against her breast. "Is this for me, babygirl? Does feeding me with your tits make your pussy wet and needy?"

"Yes," she moans. Her nails dig into the back of my neck, urging me closer.

"Mmm," I murmur, sucking on her nipple as I rub her pussy through the panties. Her clit is swollen and desperate for my touch, and I'm drunk on the knowledge that her body craves mine just as much as I crave hers.

I slide two fingers past the sodden fabric, tracing the seam of her lips until she shudders. Then I press them inside, groaning at the feel of her pussy clamping around me.

Fuck.

I've never felt anything so perfect.

She whimpers, arching her hips to take my fingers deeper. I thrust, crooking them inside her as her inner walls flutter and clench. I find a rhythm, thrusting with my fingers and sucking on her breast. Her body arches and trembles, and soon she's coming, her cries ringing off the walls as she gushes over my hand.

She's perfect. Absolutely perfect.

When she's finally trembling and spent, her tits fully drained, I force myself to ease back. My lips are wet, my throat still working around the taste of her, my body half-wild with the need to keep going.

But she's shaking, flushed, overwhelmed, and she's mine to care for. Not just to devour.

"Easy, babygirl," I murmur, helping her tug the bodice of her dress back into place. She won't meet my eyes, but I tilt her chin up until she does. "No shame. Not with me. Never with me."

Her lashes flutter as I shrug out of my jacket and settle it around her shoulders, broad enough to hide every damp patch. She looks small in it. Small and breakable and fucking beautiful.

"I'm taking you home," I tell her, voice rough with need. "I'll get you bathed, cleaned up, taken care of. And then I can claim your pretty little cunt properly."

Panic sparks across her face. She shakes her head quickly. "I... I can't. If I leave now, it'll look bad. I'll get in trouble with my boss. But I can't go back out there when I'm such a mess either. What am I going to do, Jack?"

I grit my teeth, every instinct screaming at me to scoop her up in my arms and take her home anyway, but I force myself to relent. No matter how much I want her, I'm not going to do anything that might risk her job.

"Okay, here's what we'll do, Jenna. You go home, and I'll stay here to cover for you. I'll tell Grace you had to leave, that you were upset after what that bastard pulled, which isn't even a lie, really. She won't think less of you."

Relief softens her expression, and I press my hand to the small of her back, guiding her quietly through the corridors and out into the night air.

"Thank you for everything you've done for me tonight," she says, glancing up at me with a soft smile teasing the corners of her lips.

"No need to thank me, babygirl. For any of it. I will always take care of what's mine."

Her breath catches, and she pauses for a moment before continuing the short walk to her car. She fumbles for her keys, and before she can escape me entirely, I catch her wrist.

"I can't let you go without this," I rasp.

And then I kiss her.

It's not soft. It's not tentative. It's hunger and promise and possession, her sweet little gasp swallowed into my mouth as I claim her pretty lips for the first time. She wraps her arms around my neck as she kisses me back, swaying into me, and I nearly lose the battle with myself right there. But I let her go because I have to. For now.

"Tomorrow," I promise against her lips. "I'll see you tomorrow, Jenna."

She nods, dazed, before slipping into her car and driving away, my jacket still drowning her frame.

I watch until her taillights vanish, then turn back towards the restaurant, jaw clenched.

Grace is waiting for me when I return to the table, worry clouding her face. "Dad? Did you find Jenna? Where is she?"

"She was shaken up after what happened with Ryan," I tell her smoothly. "She needed to go home, but she'll be at the wedding tomorrow to take care of everything."

Grace's mouth tightens. "I still can't believe he acted like such a jerk. His behavior was completely unacceptable."

Aaron grimaces, running a hand through his hair. "I'll talk to him tonight. Make sure he keeps his distance from her tomorrow."

"See that you do," I bite out.

The night goes on, but I'm barely present. My daughter and her fiancé chatter, wine flows, laughter swells again.

But I can't bring myself to eat or drink anything else. Because I don't want to lose the taste of Jenna.

She's still sweet and warm on my tongue, clinging to my lips, flooding every thought until I'm aching with the need to have her back in my arms.

She's mine now. And no force on earth is going to take her from me.

Chapter Four

♥

Jenna

The vineyard is buzzing.

The air smells like roses and fresh-cut grass; the sun is high and warm, and I'm moving through it all with my clipboard in one hand and my headset clipped firmly in place.

I'm in wedding-planner mode. Locked in. Efficient. Focused.

Mostly.

"Bride's family to the left, and the groom's to the right," I coach one of the groomsmen as the first guests begin to arrive. He nods, straightening his tie as he heads off to usher people to their seats.

I do a quick visual scan of the ceremony space. Arches are draped with pale pink flowers, and the chairs are lined in perfect rows with linen bows fluttering in the breeze. Everything is exactly how I designed it. Exactly how Grace asked for it.

A smile tugs at my lips.

I did this. All of it.

I've been dreaming of running my own events for years, and today is my first real solo wedding under the company banner. No manager

breathing down my neck, no senior planner second-guessing me. Just me, and everything is running like a dream.

I make my way towards the main house, offering warm smiles and gentle nudges to guests who arrive looking a little confused. I check my phone. The hair and makeup team should be finishing up soon. Time to check on the bride.

Before I make it there, I spot Aaron pacing near the groom's suite, nervously smoothing his jacket sleeves.

I approach quietly. "Everything okay?"

He startles slightly, then laughs under his breath. "Yeah. I think so. Just... wedding day jitters, you know? I really want Grace to be happy today."

I nod. "That's completely normal. If you weren't nervous, I'd be worried. But you've got this, okay? Grace adores you. She's practically floating this morning."

His shoulders relax, tension easing from his face. "Thanks, Jenna. Honestly, you've made all of this so easy. I don't know how you do it."

I flash a quick smile. "That's a trade secret. If I told you, then I'd have to kill you."

He laughs and heads back inside, and I turn towards the bridal suite. But as I walk, the buzzing energy in my chest shifts. It's not nerves. Not excitement.

It's the knowledge that I'll be seeing Jack soon.

I haven't seen him since last night when he pulled me from the most embarrassing moment of my life, peeled down my dress and fed from my leaking breasts like he couldn't get enough... then kissed me like he already owned me.

My body reacts just from thinking about it.

A pulse of heat flares low in my belly. My breasts throb behind the boning of my dress, full and heavy again even though I pumped

everything I had before leaving the house this morning. It's too soon, but my body doesn't seem to care. It's as if he triggered something in me that I can't shut off.

Focus, Jenna. This is Grace's day. Not yours.

I square my shoulders, grip my clipboard tighter, and head towards the bridal suite with brisk, determined steps.

The suite hums with energy the moment I slip inside. Grace is perched in a chair by the window, glowing in a robe as two of her bridesmaids fuss over her. The makeup artist leans in close, dusting shimmer across Grace's cheekbones, while the hairstylist carefully pins the last curls into place.

It's a happy chaos, with laughter and music playing softly from someone's phone. The faint scent of hairspray and roses fills the air.

"Jenna!" Grace beams at me in the mirror, her eyes bright. "Tell me everything's on track out there."

"Everything is perfect," I assure her. "The florals arrived on time, the chairs are set, and guests are already being seated. The ceremony is going to be stunning."

She exhales in relief, her smile widening. "Of course it is. You've been amazing through all of this."

I smile, but guilt pricks sharply in my chest. If Grace knew what I'd done with her father last night, I doubt she would be so complimentary.

I check in briefly with the hairstylist, nodding approval at the polished updos, then glance at the makeup artist's work. Everything looks flawless. I murmur encouragements, smoothing nerves where I can, hiding the fact that I'm barely keeping my own in check.

And then the air shifts.

The door opens, and a new presence fills the suite.

Jack Westmore.

He stands framed in the doorway, tall and broad, tuxedo fitting him like it was made for him alone. The chatter around the room dips for a moment, the bridesmaids straightening instinctively. My heart stops for a brief second before it starts slamming against my ribs.

Memories hit me like a tidal wave. His mouth on my breasts, the rough velvet of his tongue, his fingers inside me until I shattered, the way he kissed me like he'd never let me go. My body reacts instantly, a rush of heat between my thighs, a heavy ache in my chest.

"Dad!" Grace lights up, jumping from her chair to hug him. "You look so handsome."

"You look beautiful, sweetheart," Jack says warmly, kissing her cheek before turning his attention to the rest of us.

And then his gaze lands on me.

I can't move.

"Jenna's made everything so beautiful," Grace gushes, tugging him a little closer. "I don't know what I would have done without her."

Jack's eyes never leave mine as he replies, his voice smooth, low. "Jenna does have an exquisite taste."

The bridesmaids murmur agreement, thinking he means the flowers, the colors, the decor. Grace grins at him, pleased.

But I know better.

I see it in the heat of his gaze, in the way his eyes linger far too long on my lips before dragging slowly down my body. He isn't talking about the wedding. He's talking about me. About last night. About the milk he tasted from my breasts like he was starving for it.

My breath stutters. My cheeks flame.

Grace is standing right there. Her bridesmaids too. But I can't look away from him. The electricity crackles between us, undeniable, dangerous.

And the guilt slices sharper than ever, because no matter how wrong it is, my body is screaming the truth.

I want him.

Grace steps back from her father and smooths her robe over her hips, her smile radiant with anticipation.

"Okay," she says, clapping her hands softly. "Time to get dressed."

The bridesmaids buzz to life again, laughter and excitement spilling into the room as they gather around the garment bag hanging from the full-length mirror in the corner. I nod, tucking my clipboard against my chest and moving towards the door.

"I'll give you all a few minutes," I say, my voice calmer than I feel. "I'll be right outside if you need anything."

Grace beams at me. Jack tells his daughter that he'll be right outside with me, waiting for her to be ready so he can walk her down the aisle. As he follows me out of the suite, I feel his eyes on me, and every inch of my skin burns under his gaze.

Once we're in the hallway, Jack leans against the far wall, arms folded across his chest, tux perfectly tailored, his expression unreadable. But his eyes... oh God, those eyes. They rake over me like I'm something he wants to unwrap and devour.

I clutch my clipboard tighter, trying not to shake.

"Have you seen Ryan yet today?" he asks, his voice tight.

The question surprises me, but I shake my head. "Not yet. I assume he's been in the groom's suite with Aaron."

He nods. "Okay. I just wanted to make sure he was behaving himself. I don't want him touching what's mine."

Mine.

His voice rumbles over the word, low and possessive, and my core clenches. My nipples are hard, pressing against my dress, and I can't

stop myself from remembering how his mouth felt on them, hot and greedy.

How his hands felt on my thighs, strong and confident.

How his fingers felt inside me, thick and skilled, taking me apart in a matter of seconds.

The silence stretches, the air around us brimming with tension. I should leave. I should go check something. Anything. But I don't move. Neither does he.

His gaze drops down to my chest, lingers. His eyes darken, and for one dizzy second, I think he might reach for me. I want him to.

But he doesn't move. There's too much risk. Too many doors nearby. Too many people who could walk past.

His voice drops even lower. "Later. I need to taste you again, baby-girl. It's all I can fucking think about."

I'm trembling now, my knees threatening to give way. My nipples throb, aching to be suckled, and there's no doubt in my mind that he knows exactly what he's doing to me.

He pushes away from the wall, adjusting his jacket sleeves. He's close enough that I can smell his aftershave, and I nearly melt into a puddle on the floor.

"Later," he says again, voice rough. "I'll find you."

"Okay," I whisper.

His jaw tightens, and for a moment, he looks almost pained. But then the door to the bridal suite opens, and he steps back, putting some distance between us.

The makeup artist and hairstylist slip out, giving me a warm smile as they pass between us, shattering the moment.

I take a deep breath, trying to get myself under control. I glance at the clipboard clutched in my hands. It's shaking slightly, and my mind feels fuzzy, overwhelmed.

Focus, Jenna.

I have a job to do. And I'm determined to do it well, even if the father of the bride is hell-bent on driving me wild.

***

The music swells, soft and romantic, carried on the breeze across the vineyard lawn.

I stand off to the side, half-hidden by a climbing rose trellis, watching everything unfold. But my heart is thudding too fast, and my legs feel shaky.

Because he's walking her down the aisle.

Jack Westmore, tall and commanding in his tux, his arm linked with Grace's as they move slowly between the rows of seated guests. He looks every inch the proud father, stoic and strong, a faint smile tugging at the corners of his mouth.

But his eyes...

His eyes find mine. Just for a second. Just long enough for heat to curl low in my belly and my breath to catch.

I look away. I have to.

Come on, Jenna, I think to myself. *Focus. You're here to do a job. You are not here to fall apart because the father of the bride makes your knees go weak with a single glance.*

Grace reaches the altar, beaming. Jack kisses her cheek, whispers something I can't hear, and steps aside.

Aaron's waiting for her, handsome in his tailored suit, eyes shining as he takes both of Grace's hands in his. The officiant welcomes everyone and begins the ceremony.

It's beautiful. Not even the sight of Ryan standing beside the groom could ruin this moment.

The vows are heartfelt. Grace's voice trembles when she talks about how Aaron has been her safe place since high school. He smiles as if he's the proudest man in the entire world.

The guests sniffle. Bridesmaids dab at their eyes. Cameras click softly in the background.

I should be listening. But all I can feel is the weight of Jack's gaze.

Every time I glance across the rows of guests to where he sits in the front row, he's watching me. Never looking away.

And I'm helpless against the way my body aches with the memory of his touch. I shift my weight, pressing my thighs together, trying to chase away the ache. But it only sharpens.

The officiant says, "Do you, Grace, take this man..." and I force myself to refocus.

Grace's voice is clear. "I do."

The words are repeated for the groom, and Aaron's voice is thick with emotion. "I do."

The officiant smiles. "Then, by the power vested in me..."

There's cheering before he even finishes the sentence. Grace and Aaron kiss beneath the floral arch, petals fluttering down around them. The guests erupt in applause.

It's perfect. Absolutely perfect.

I clap with everyone else, smiling through the sting in my eyes. Happy tears, mostly. A little pride.

And a lot of confusion.

Because as the newlyweds turn to face their guests, hand in hand, glowing with joy... my gaze finds Jack's again.

And the way he looks at me makes me forget how to breathe.

Chapter Five

Jenna

Grace and Aaron are wrapped up in each other, swaying in the middle of the dance floor like there's no one else in the world.

It's their first dance as husband and wife, and it's everything I imagined it would be. Slow, tender, and romantic. The kind of moment they will remember for the rest of their lives.

I stand at the edge of the room, fingers laced together in front of me while I sway a little myself in time with the ballad that the band is playing.

Everything has gone perfectly. Not a single delay or hiccup. The catering team I hired turned up on time, the food was flawless, and the table decorations had been stunning.

Even Ryan, the best man, has been shockingly well-behaved. Not a leer, not a comment, not even a passing glance in my direction all day.

I should be proud. Relieved. Euphoric, even.

But I'm not. Because the only thing I can think about is Jack.

All day long, I've felt him watching me. Across the vineyard during the ceremony. From his place at the head table during dinner. Silent and hungry, like he's barely leashed.

And I've been waiting.

Waiting for the moment he'd take me aside like he said he would. For him to touch me again. To feed from me the way he did last night, when he'd treated me like I was the only one in the world who could satisfy him.

The ache has been building since morning, low and slow and punishing. My breasts feel heavy, sensitive, the tight bodice of my dress doing nothing to ease the pressure. I'm full. So full that I'm growing desperate for relief.

I know he'll come. He has to. And when he does, I'll give him anything. Everything.

The song ends, and the newlyweds laugh as the crowd erupts in applause. The dance floor starts to fill with guests. Glasses clink. Music swells again.

And then I feel a presence at my back.

I don't have to look to know it's him.

Jack's hand brushes mine. Barely a touch, but it sends a bolt of heat through me so fast that I nearly gasp.

"Come with me," he murmurs, his voice a rumble in my ear.

I follow him without hesitation.

He leads me through the rear doors of the reception hall, down a short hallway lined with stone, and into a cool, dimly lit cellar tucked beneath the venue.

Wine barrels line the walls, the air thick with oak and something sweet and dark and earthy.

And we're all alone.

I barely have time to turn to face him before my back hits the nearest wall, the exposed brickwork cool against the skin on my back left exposed by my dress. His mouth crashes into mine, hot and possessive, and his hands are already tugging frantically at the top half of my dress.

I help him, reaching behind me for the zipper, and between the two of us, we have it loosened and peeled down to my waist in seconds. My breasts spring free, heavy and aching, and his mouth falls to them with a groan.

My head falls back, eyes closing. I whimper as his tongue swirls, and then moan as his teeth graze my nipples.

"I couldn't fucking wait any longer," he mutters, taking a nipple deep into his mouth and sucking hard. The pressure builds painfully behind my nipple for a moment, before the sweet relief of my letdown hits.

He grunts as the milk floods his mouth, and the sensation is so intense that it makes my knees weak. He's not even touching me between my legs, but the pleasure is already so good I think I might come from the sensation.

"Jack," I gasp, clinging to his shoulders.

He growls and wraps one hand around my breast, squeezing, massaging, coaxing more milk from my aching nipple.

"Give it to me," he mutters, his lips brushing against my dripping nipple, and then his mouth is on me again, feeding greedily.

He's rough this time. Desperate. It's nothing like last night, when he savored every drop. No, this is raw need. A craving that he's barely holding onto.

He moves to my other breast, taking it deep in his mouth and sucking, groaning.

"Oh God," I whimper, bringing my hands to the back of his head, my fingers running through his hair as I hold him against my breast. "That feels so good, Jack. I've been needing this so badly all day."

He pulls his mouth from my nipple with something that sounds like a pained groan, and he brings his lips to mine. He tastes sweet and

nutty, the taste of my milk coating his lips and tongue as he kisses me hard, deep, making me whimper.

"I've been needing it too, babygirl. Needing to fill my belly with your sweet cream," he rasps. "It's the only thing I can think about. How it's going to feel when I drink from you again."

I don't know why it drives me so crazy when he says things like that, but it does. My pussy is slick and aching, and I know the fabric of my underwear is probably soaked.

"And this milk is all mine, Jenna. I'm not going to share until my baby is here, taking all the nourishment they need from your gorgeous tits. But you'll still need to feed me too, babygirl. I don't think I'll ever be able to get enough of you."

His mouth latches back onto a nipple, and it takes me a moment to process his words through the haze of pleasure fogging my brain.

"Baby?" I ask, the word turning to a moan as he nips at the stiff peak in his mouth with his teeth.

"Damn right," he growls, sliding a hand up to rest on my flat stomach. "I can't wait to see you full and round. Watch these pretty tits swell and fill with even more milk. Watch my baby grow inside you."

I moan, the thought almost too much. It's filthy. And it's way too soon to be talking about babies.

But it's the hottest damn thing anyone has ever said to me.

His words have an effect on him too. He's hard, his erection pressing insistently into my hip. I'm so tempted to reach down and stroke him, to feel his thickness in my hand. But he's focused entirely on my breasts. He's kneading them roughly, sucking and licking and biting like he's ravenous for it. Like he can't get enough.

And I love it. The sensation is intense, the ache giving way to pleasure so strong I'm afraid I'm going to lose my mind.

"You're mine, Jenna," he says, his voice ragged. "And when I claim your needy little pussy with my seed, I'll make you come so fucking hard you won't ever want anyone but me. You'll forget all about your ex-boyfriends, too. You'll know that your cunt, and your womb, are mine. All fucking mine."

Oh, God.

I can't believe he's saying all of this, and I can't believe how much I want it. He's so dominant, and possessive, and demanding. And I crave it all.

"I am all yours, Jack. Nobody else has ever... ever been inside me."

My face flushes with embarrassment at my confession, but I need to tell him. I need to let him know that he's going to be my first. That I belong entirely to him.

"You're a virgin?" he asks, his tone incredulous, but the look in his eyes is pure, hungry lust. "Fuck, babygirl. I can't wait to get my cock in that tight little cunt. You'll be so snug and wet for me, won't you? Going to squeeze me so good. Going to take every drop of cum from my balls and keep it all safe in your womb, won't you?"

"Yes," I pant, and God, if he keeps talking like that, I might actually come just from his words.

"That's right," he growls. "Gonna pump you full. Get you so full of my cum that you're dripping. And then I'm going to plug you and keep every single drop where it belongs. Where it will take root and grow."

"Now?" I ask, the word slipping out before I can stop it.

Jack lets out a low groan. "I want to, babygirl. Fuck, I want that so badly. But when I breed you, I want to be able to take my time. I want you spread out and bare and begging for me. Begging me to put a baby in you. I'm going to stretch your virgin pussy with my cock, and then I'm going to flood your fertile little womb with my seed. Something

like that deserves to happen when we have time and privacy. Not a quickie in a wine cellar."

I let out a whining sound. Disappointment, arousal, frustration. They're all mingling together in my body, making me ache so much that I can barely stand it.

Jack chuckles, the sound warm and low, and then he's kissing me again, slow and deep and sweet.

"But you're in luck," he murmurs against my mouth, his voice rough. "There are plenty of things we can do in the meantime. And right now, there's something I need you to do for me, babygirl."

"What is it?"

"I need you to sit on the barrel over there and spread those gorgeous thighs for me."

I look around, noticing the small barrel a few feet away. I'm not sure what he has planned, but the idea of it makes my whole body tingle.

He helps me off the wall, supporting me as I wobble a little. My breasts are still bare, and the cool air feels good on my heated skin.

"Sit," he instructs, guiding me towards the barrel.

I do, and he kneels in front of me, his hands sliding up my thighs. His touch makes me shiver, and when his hands push the skirt of my dress up, my breath hitches.

He hooks his fingers around the sides of my thong and drags it down. I lift myself slightly, helping him, and when the scrap of lace has been pulled all the way down, I'm left completely bare.

His eyes remain locked on mine as he folds the fabric and slips it into the pocket of his tux.

"This is mine now," he says.

"Yes," I say simply. My voice is soft and shaky.

Jack's gaze drifts lower, down to my bare mound, and he lets out a groan. "Fuck, Jenna. You have the prettiest pussy. It's practically

begging for my mouth. My cock. Fuck, I can't wait to sink inside you and make you mine."

He's barely touched me, and yet I'm trembling. He's staring at my most intimate place like he's mesmerized, and the hunger in his eyes makes the ache between my legs that much more intense.

"Please," I whimper.

Jack's lips quirk in a smile, and he leans closer, his breath ghosting over my sensitive flesh.

"Don't worry, babygirl. I'm going to take care of you. Give you everything you need."

He presses a soft kiss against the top of my thigh, and I shiver. He does the same thing on the other side, and then he's moving closer and closer, until I can feel his breath against my center.

And then he's licking me, one long stroke from the bottom of my entrance all the way up, ending at the swollen nub above.

I cry out, the sensation so intense. My whole body jolts, and I grip the edges of the barrel.

Jack holds me open, his thumbs tracing the crease where my thighs meet my hips, and then his mouth is back, his tongue delving deep. He licks and sucks, his moans muffled as he devours me.

"Jack," I whimper, arching my back and grinding my pussy against his mouth. "Please."

He slides two fingers inside me, stretching my entrance, and I let out a long moan.

"That's right, babygirl. Let me hear you. Let me hear how good it feels."

His tongue flicks across my clit, and I nearly scream. The pleasure is so sharp, so intense, that it's almost painful.

"Oh, God. Yes, Jack, yes!"

His fingers pump in and out of my soaking wet channel, the rhythmic squelching sounds echoing through the cellar. He adds a third finger, stretching me even more, and the pressure is so perfect that it's driving me wild.

I'm rocking against his hand, meeting every thrust, and the orgasm building inside me is unlike anything I've ever felt. It's all-consuming, like a tidal wave looming on the horizon.

Jack curls his fingers, pressing up into the front wall of my channel, and his mouth closes around my clit, suckling the sensitive bundle of nerves with as much enthusiasm as he sucked the milk from my breasts.

The orgasm crashes into me. I shatter, crying out as waves of pleasure wash over me. Jack keeps sucking and thrusting his fingers, drawing out every second of bliss until I'm completely spent.

He presses a final kiss to the top of my mound, and then slowly withdraws his fingers, leaving me empty and throbbing.

"Good girl," he whispers. "You're so beautiful when you come, Jenna. Fucking breathtaking."

He rises, his mouth crashing into mine, and his hands roam all over my body, like he can't decide where he wants to touch me first.

His jacket is still on, his shirt perfectly pressed and tucked into his pants. He looks so composed, so elegant. And I'm a wreck. My dress is loose and gaping at the front, breasts bare and nipples red and raw. My pussy is wet and swollen, and my knees are trembling so hard that I can barely stay upright.

He doesn't seem to mind, though. His cock is hard and straining against his pants, and I can't resist reaching out, cupping the hard length through the material.

"Do you want me to...? I mean, can I...?"

I can't bring myself to say the words, but that doesn't stop me craving to please him as much as he's pleased me the last two evenings. He captures my wrist though, pulling my hand away with a groan.

"As much as I want that, babygirl, I'm not wasting my seed like that. It's all going inside you when I take you home after the wedding is over. We'll have the whole night, and all day tomorrow. And every night after that."

He says it with such certainty, like it's a given. Like he already knows that this will never end.

And I want that too. More than I've ever wanted anything in my life.

Chapter Six

♥

Jenna

Jack helps me sit up gently, his hands slow and careful as he pulls the straps of my dress back over my shoulders. His fingers linger against my skin, warm and reverent, like he can't quite bear to stop touching me.

I'm still shaking from the orgasm. My lips are swollen. My thighs are slick.

And my heart is a complete mess.

He adjusts the fabric, making sure it sits just right, then brushes a few strands of hair back from my face. His touch is tender, making my chest ache in a way that has nothing to do with milk.

Then he leans in, pressing a soft kiss to my lips.

"I have to go back," he murmurs, his forehead resting against mine. "Can't have the bride wondering where her father disappeared to."

I let out a shaky laugh, still breathless. "Right. That might be awkward."

His hand trails down my arm. "But don't think for one second that we're done, babygirl."

My breath hitches.

"When this reception is over," he says, voice low and full of promise, "I'm taking you home with me. I'm going to strip you bare. Spread you open. And make you mine in every way that counts."

Heat floods my cheeks. My legs. My core. I can't speak. I just nod, eyes wide, completely undone all over again.

He presses one last lingering kiss to my cheek, then turns and slips out of the cellar, his footsteps fading into the distance.

I stay where I am for a minute longer, swaying slightly, trying to collect myself. My whole body feels like it's still vibrating from the way he touched me. Licked me. Praised me.

God, what am I doing?

I straighten my dress, smooth down my skirt, and gather what's left of my dignity. It takes everything I have just to make my legs move towards the exit.

But when I push open the door, I walk right into Ryan.

"Oh," I gasp, stepping back instinctively.

He looks down at me with a smug little smirk, with a wine glass in one hand.

"Funny," he says, eyes narrowing. "Didn't I just see Jack Westmore come out of here a minute ago?"

My stomach twists.

"I... I don't know what you're talking about."

"Sure you don't." He lifts his glass to his lips and takes a slow sip, his eyes never leaving mine. "So what were you two doing in the cellar, sweetheart? Checking on the wine?"

I try to move past him. "Please let me through."

But he steps in front of me again, body angled just enough to block the hallway. Not touching me. But too close. Too smug.

"It must have been quite a tasting," he says with a pointed look down my body. "Did you give him a sample of something special?"

My face burns. "Leave me alone."

"I'm just saying," he continues, his tone maddeningly casual, "if Grace finds out you were messing around with her father during her wedding, she's not going to be thrilled."

"Stop."

"And when she tells your boss what happened? Oof." He grins. "Hope you've got a backup plan, sweetheart. You'll be out of a job before you have time to pack up your little clipboard."

Panic hits me full force.

I shake my head, swallowing hard. "Please... don't do this."

"Oh, I'm not going to do anything. As long as you do the smart thing." He leans in just slightly, voice dropping. "Tell Jack it's over. Tell him you're not interested. And then we can all move on with our lives."

I stare at him, heart pounding in my ears.

"Fine," I whisper. "I'll tell him."

Ryan straightens, smug satisfaction radiating from him. He nods once, like a man who thinks he's just won something.

And I barge past him, my shoulders shaking and my throat tight.

The corridor blurs as I walk quickly, needing to get away from his eyes, his voice, his stupid smug face. The sound of laughter and music filters through the walls, but none of it feels real.

All I can hear is the voice echoing in my head.

You'll be out of a job before you have time to pack up your little clipboard.

God, I can't lose this job. Not after everything I've worked for. Not after how hard I fought to prove I could do this.

But Jack...

My steps falter, and I brace a hand on the wall, sucking in a breath.

I want him. I want him so badly it hurts. He makes me feel more seen, more wanted, more accepted than anyone ever has. And the way he touches me, the way he drinks from me...

It's not just heat. It's not just lust.

It's *connection*.

And now I have to throw it all away.

I wipe my face and steel myself. I can do this. I need to just get it over with quickly. Like ripping off a band-aid.

When I step back into the reception hall, it feels louder than before. Guests are dancing. Champagne is flowing. Fairy lights twinkle across the ceiling, and everything looks like a dream.

And Jack is standing just to the side of the dance floor, his eyes scanning the crowd.

When his gaze lands on mine, something in his face softens. He straightens, his whole body tightening like he's preparing to come to me.

I cut across the room before he can move. I need to do this quickly. Cleanly.

He opens his mouth to speak, but I get there first. My voice is quiet. Barely audible over the music.

"I can't see you again."

Jack stills. His jaw ticks. "Excuse me?"

I swallow, avoiding his eyes. "It's over."

"No." The word is a growl, sharp and instant. "No, that's not what you were saying five minutes ago. Not after the way you..." He cuts himself off, breath heavy. "Tell me why, Jenna. What made you change your mind about us so quickly?"

I look over his shoulder. Ryan's there, leaning against the bar, watching us like a hawk. Jack's gaze follows mine.

My hands shake. "He threatened to tell Grace if I didn't end things with you. Said she'd be bound to go to my boss and complain about me fooling around with her father on her wedding day. And then I'd lose my job." My voice cracks on the final word, and tears sting my eyes.

Jack's expression changes in a heartbeat. The fire in his eyes is immediate and brutal.

He doesn't say anything at first, though. He just steps forward, cups the back of my head, and presses a kiss to my forehead.

"I'll handle it," he murmurs. "Don't worry, babygirl. I'm not going to let that fucker take you away from me."

And then he turns and walks away.

I don't move. I just watch as he weaves through the crowd, heading straight for Grace.

My stomach twists so hard I think I might be sick. I wonder if I should follow him, give her my side of the story, but I'm frozen in place.

I can't hear what he's saying to her. I can only see her face; how she frowns, then blinks. Her mouth moves, her brows pull together with confusion.

Then her expression shifts from one of shock to anger.

My knees go weak. She's going to be so mad at me. I've ruined everything. If I manage to keep my job after this, it will be a goddamn miracle.

Then Grace turns fast and storms across the reception hall like a hurricane in white satin, her veil floating behind her like a war banner.

But she's not moving towards me. It's Ryan who gets the full force of her wrath.

I watch in frozen horror as she rips into him without hesitation. With no concern about who's watching. Just pure fury. I still can't

hear what's being said over the music, but her hands gesture wildly, and she shoves at his shoulder while she yells.

Grace points to the exit, and Ryan tries to argue, but she's not hearing it.

And then Jack is there too.

He grabs Ryan by the lapels and yanks him close, his mouth right at the other man's ear, and judging by the look of fury on Jack's face, I think I'm pleased I can't hear what's being said right now.

Ryan's eyes widen. Jack shoves him hard once, and he stumbles backwards before scurrying off like the coward he is. He's red-faced and seething, but he doesn't look back.

I barely have time to process what I just witnessed before Grace turns, her veil fluttering softly behind her, and makes her way back towards me with Jack beside her.

She's... smiling.

Not tight-lipped. Not forced. But warm and easy and full of affection.

I have no idea what's happening.

"Jenna," she says gently, her eyes kind. "I'm so sorry Ryan has been such a jerk this weekend. Aaron spoke to him after the meal last night, and he promised to be on his best behavior today. But apparently he didn't mean it."

My lips part, but nothing comes out.

"I'm really glad Dad told me what Ryan was trying to pull tonight," she continues. My gaze flicks to Jack, who stands silently beside her, his eyes locked intently on me.

"You've done such an incredible job today," Grace says, stepping forward to take my hands in hers. "This was everything I ever dreamed of. And honestly... if my dad is going to fall for someone, I'm glad it's someone as sweet and utterly lovely as you, Jenna."

I blink hard, but the tears still gather. I can't believe this is happening, but I'm not about to argue with her. "I... thank you. That means so much to me."

She gives my hands a squeeze. "Aaron and I are heading out now. Honeymoon time." Her grin is full of sparkle. "But I'll be sending a very generous tip later, along with glowing compliments to your boss. You've earned it all. And then some."

I laugh, breathless with relief. "Safe travels. You both deserve all the happiness in the world."

Grace pulls me into a hug, and then Jack leans in to press a kiss to her forehead. She hugs him too, and then she and Aaron are gone, sent off with a flurry of cheers, clinking glasses, and bubbles being blown into the night air.

The reception is still going on behind us, minus the bride and groom now. But here, in this quiet little corner... it's just us.

Just me and Jack.

He turns to me, his eyes heavy with heat and something deeper. And the second his fingers close around mine, the world steadies. My heart races. My pulse thrums in anticipation.

"It's time to take my girl home," he says, his voice low and full of promise. "Time to make her mine."

Chapter Seven

Jack

My hands fumble with the keys like I'm seventeen and two seconds from blowing my load in my pants. God knows I'm hard enough for that to happen. Jenna stands just behind me, close enough that I can hear her shallow breaths and the way she shifts her weight from one foot to the other on the porch.

She wants this. I can feel it in her.

And fuck, I'm going to give it to her.

The second the lock clicks, I slam the door open and turn to her, taking in those flushed cheeks and that eager sparkle in her eyes.

I can't wait another goddamn second, so I grab her.

She gasps softly, but her arms fly around my shoulders at the same time her legs hook around my waist, like her body already knows what to do. Her chest presses against mine, and her breath is quick and warm against my neck.

I hold her like I've done this a thousand times. Like she belongs in my arms, against me, wrapped around me like this.

I kick the door shut behind us, and then I start to climb.

One step at a time, slow and steady, because I want her to feel it. Every flex of my muscles. Every shift of her weight in my grip. Every inch she rises towards the place where I'm going to finally ruin her sweet, untouched little body.

Her fingers dig into my shoulders as I reach the top.

"You're mine now," I growl, lips brushing her ear. "And when I'm done with you tonight, your womb will know it too."

She shivers. Whimpers. Tightens her grip around me.

I shoulder the bedroom door open and carry her inside, towards the bed I've dreamed of laying her in since the moment I saw her.

Then I set her down gently, slowly, letting her slide down my body inch by torturous inch until her feet hit the floor. I step back just enough to look at her. My sweet, blushing, beautiful girl.

Her eyes are wide, her lips parted. She's waiting for me. Waiting for my next move.

My heart fucking aches.

"I can't take my eyes off you," I tell her, voice rough and low. "Not for one second. You're the most beautiful thing I've ever seen, babygirl. Do you have any idea what you do to me?"

She shakes her head, cheeks flushing.

"Everything," I say. "You make me feel everything. Desire. Need. Protectiveness. Like I could fucking kill anyone who even looked at you wrong. Like I want to possess every inch of you. Keep you all to myself."

Her chest rises and falls, the swell of her breasts visible above the neckline of her pretty dress.

I reach behind her, pulling the zipper down. "I need you, Jenna. And I'm not going to hold back tonight. Are you ready for that?"

"Yes," she breathes, the word shaky and desperate.

"Good." I pull the straps of her dress down, letting the material fall and pool at her feet.

My gaze roams over her naked body, and my cock pulses in my pants. After I stole her panties earlier, she's left in nothing but her heels now that her dress is gone, and fuck if it isn't the sexiest thing I've ever seen.

"So beautiful," I growl. "Every single inch."

"And you," she says, hands trembling slightly as she reaches up to push my suit jacket off my shoulders. "I want to see you too, Jack."

She doesn't hesitate as she unfastens my shirt, and I let her.

Let her take her time, revealing my chest slowly, like a present being unwrapped. Her hands are small and soft and reverent, and when she slides her fingers beneath the material, touching me with her bare skin, my pulse kicks hard.

Her hands are hesitant as they drop lower, and when she reaches the waistband of my pants, she looks up at me with a questioning look in her eyes.

"Go on," I whisper.

Her touch is feather-light as she undoes the buckle. The zipper.

Then she's pushing my pants and boxers down, and my cock springs free. It's heavy and thick and leaking, and the way her breath catches when she sees it makes me even harder.

"Oh," she whispers. "It's... you're..."

"Big."

"Yes." She licks her lips, her cheeks darkening. "So big."

She reaches out, tentatively wrapping her hand around me, and I have to hold back a string of curse words. Her soft skin feels so fucking good around my shaft, and when she gives an experimental stroke, it takes everything in me not to lose control right then and there.

"Fuck," I hiss. "That feels so damn good, babygirl."

In an attempt to distract myself from her touch so I don't embarrass myself, I grab a handful of her hair and pull her closer, crushing my mouth against hers.

Her lips are eager and pliant, parting for me instantly, and the way she melts into my kiss is intoxicating. It's messy. Hungry.

And when her tongue meets mine, sliding against me in the filthiest fucking dance, it sends a rush of heat straight to my balls.

I break the kiss, breathing hard, and press my lips to her temple instead.

"Get on the bed."

She doesn't hesitate. In fact, she scrambles to obey, crawling backwards onto the mattress. She keeps her eyes on me the whole time, a flush spreading across her chest and neck.

She's so beautiful, so goddamn perfect, and the sight of her spread out on my bed in nothing more than her heels is almost more than I can bear.

I reach down, wrapping my hand around my dick and giving it a slow stroke.

"Tell me what you want, Jenna. Let me hear you say it."

"I want you," she says, voice breathy.

"Be more specific. Where do you want me?"

She pauses. Bites her lip. Then she moves her hands down, fingers trailing over her collarbone. Across her tits, teasing her nipples until they harden into stiff peaks. Over the soft curve of her stomach, and lower still, until she reaches the apex of her thighs.

Holy shit.

I watch in complete awe as she opens herself for me, showing me the most intimate part of her body. Her fingers are soft and slow as they explore her folds, and when they finally slide inside, she lets out a soft moan.

"I want you here, Jack. Inside me. And I want you to fill me with your cum. I want it all inside me so it can take root and grow. So that it'll become a baby. Our baby."

I've never moved so fast in my life.

Before I can even blink, I've kicked off my shoes and pants and boxers and grabbed her wrist, roughly pulling her hand away from what's mine.

Mine.

Her pussy is mine, and now it's time to fucking claim it.

She's breathing hard as she watches me crawl over her, caging her body beneath mine. She's so small and perfect, and when her thighs part to welcome me between them, my chest tightens.

"So good," I murmur. "Such a good girl."

I settle between her legs, propping myself up on one arm while I reach down to guide my cock to her entrance. Her slick little hole is wet and ready for me, and when the head nudges against her, I have to grit my teeth to keep from losing control.

I rub the crown of my dick through her folds, teasing her. Making her squirm.

And when I finally start to push inside, the feeling is indescribable.

She's so fucking tight. Too tight. Her virgin pussy is a hot, velvety vice, gripping me hard.

But I'm not stopping.

She whimpers and shifts beneath me, and her body yields, taking a little more. Then a little more.

She's making tiny noises, little pained sounds, but her hips shift and rock, like she's chasing the sensation.

"Shhh, babygirl," I croon. "It's alright. It'll get better soon."

"It hurts."

"I know. But you're taking it so well. Almost there."

I push forward again, and then her gasp turns into a moan as I finally sink all the way inside her.

"Good girl," I rasp. "You did it."

She's trembling now, her legs wrapped around me and her fingers digging into my biceps. "God, it's... so much."

"Your tight little pussy feels so good, babygirl. Made for me. Made to take my cock."

She's breathing fast, but she's relaxing around me. Growing used to the size. The fullness.

I move slowly, sliding out and then pushing back in. The drag of her walls against my shaft makes me lightheaded, and when her breathy whimpers turn into moans, I feel like a fucking god.

"That's it," I say, leaning down to nip her ear. "That's a good girl."

I start a rhythm, pumping into her with long, deep strokes. Each one is more perfect than the last, and her whimpers quickly turn into gasps.

"Yes. More. Please, Jack."

Jesus.

I give it to her. Thrusting into her over and over, hard enough to make her tits bounce. Hard enough to make the bed shake and groan beneath us. My free hand moves to her breasts, squeezing one tit roughly and groaning as a warm spray of milk hits my chest.

I do it again, soaking myself with her sweet cream while her pussy grips me and her moans echo off the walls.

"You're so fucking perfect," I tell her. "Look at you, taking my cock. Taking all of me. You're so good. Such a good girl. But I need to fill you now. Need to plant my seed inside you and get you pregnant."

She whines, high-pitched and needy. "Please. Please."

I thrust harder. Deeper. I'm grunting and cursing, and she's clawing at my arms, her heels digging into my back and her breath coming in ragged little pants.

Then I reach a hand down between us, my fingers searching for the little bud and rubbing it in firm circles.

"That's it," I growl. "That's it, babygirl. Come for me. Soak me. Make my cock slick. Let me breed you."

Her nails dig into my shoulders as her entire body tightens, and I feel the pulse of her orgasm. Her release, clenching and squeezing around my cock, like she's begging for my cum.

And then I can't hold back anymore.

The world goes hazy. My pulse roars in my ears, and all I can feel is the rush of my release as it shoots out of me, filling her, painting her insides. Coating her. Claiming her.

Mine.

Jenna cries out, clinging to me like her life depends on it, and the sound makes my head spin.

My hips stutter, and I thrust through my release, groaning and cursing and saying her name.

"That's it, babygirl," I grunt. "Take it all, Jenna. Take every fucking drop."

Then I collapse, holding her close and pressing my face into the crook of her neck. Her scent is all around me, and her hair is soft against my skin.

"I love you," I say, voice raw. "I love you so much, Jenna."

"I love you too," she whispers, her lips brushing my ear.

My heart aches and swells and pounds, and I tighten my arms around her.

We're a mess. Damp with sweat and slick with our release. But neither of us moves. We just stay there, tangled together in a warm

heap. I can't even bear to pull out of her, wanting to keep her plugged with my cock so my seed can't escape.

And as I bring my mouth to her nipple, taking it into my mouth and sucking until her sweet milk begins to flow, I know I'll never get enough of this.

Of her.

Forever isn't going to be anywhere near long enough.

Epilogue

Jack

My palms are sweaty and my heart is thundering as I rise to my feet at the front of the church, taking my cue from the way the music suddenly grows louder.

I turn to look down the aisle, waiting for my bride to appear.

I've already seen her dress, already kissed her swollen belly this morning, already tasted the honey-sweet milk she let down just for me before we left for the venue.

But nothing could have prepared me for this.

She steps into view, and I stop breathing.

Jenna Lane is walking down the aisle towards me, glowing like the sun, one hand cradling the soft curve of the belly I put there. My baby growing inside my bride. Her other hand holds a simple bouquet of ivory roses, and behind her, Grace trails along in her pale pink maid-of-honor gown, tears already gathering in her eyes.

But everyone else in the room fades to nothing.

I only see Jenna.

I see the woman I worship. The body I claimed. The future I've anchored myself to with every touch, every word, every drop of my seed she's taken inside her.

And somehow, between growing our baby and keeping me completely wrapped around her finger, she still plans weddings like it's her superpower. She's booked out months in advance, with clients demanding to work with her, and she makes every bride feel like royalty.

Mine.

The thought pulses through me like a war drum.

Mine. Mine. Mine.

And it's not just her soft mouth or her sweet curves or the way she melts when I call her my good girl.

It's this. This moment. That dress clinging to her swollen belly. Her cheeks flushed. Her eyes locked on mine.

She's proud. She's radiant. She's carrying my fucking baby. And I'm about to give her my last name too.

My throat tightens.

God, she's beautiful.

She's not nervous. Not even close. She floats down the aisle like she knows exactly who she belongs to. Like she wants everyone in this room to know what I've done to her. That I filled her up and bred her deep and kept her by my side ever since.

I curl my hands into fists, letting my nails dig into my palms to keep myself grounded. If I move right now, I'll run straight down that aisle and pull her into my arms.

I won't make it through this ceremony without thinking about what she tastes like. What her breasts feel like when they are full and heavy in my palms. How her voice goes high and breathy when I stroke her stomach and tell her I want to give her another baby the moment this one's born.

I should be thinking about vows and rings and holy matrimony.

But instead, all I can think is: *She's mine. And she'll never belong to anyone else.*

Not when I've marked her so deeply. Not when my baby is growing inside her. Not when I've claimed her in every possible way a man can.

And when she's finally standing in front of me, eyes wide and shining, her belly gently pressing against me as I take her hands in mine...

All I want to do is fall to my knees and worship.

Forever.

Contents

Copyright Page

Overflowing for the Father of the Bride

Willow Watkins

My pulse kicks up, my breath shortens, and warmth coils low in my belly. He doesn't even try to hide the way his eyes track me, heavy and hungry, like I'm the only thing in the room worth looking at. Like he could devour me whole.

It makes my knees weak.

It also makes my breasts ache.

I swallow hard and force myself to stand up straighter, folding my arms across my chest. I shouldn't be thinking about that. Not when my body is already heavy and full, the swell of my breasts pressing uncomfortably against the bodice of my dress.

The truth is shameful enough: I'm twenty-two and overflowing with milk.

It started eighteen months ago, when my brother and his husband adopted a baby and worried that formula wouldn't be enough. I offered to help, and took herbs and used a pump multiple times a day to induce lactation. I didn't tell anyone how much I secretly loved it. How soothing and natural it felt to be able to provide something so vital. How feminine it made me feel. And I definitely didn't tell anyone that now I can't seem to stop, even though little baby Anna doesn't need my milk anymore. That I don't want to stop.

But that's exactly why a man like Jack Westmore could never actually want me if he knew the truth. He's older, powerful, perfect in every devastating way. From what Grace has told me, he runs his own very successful business in finance, and he's paid for everything for her big day.

And I'm just... me. Too young. Too inexperienced. And far, far too full of milk.

I drag my eyes away from him, cheeks hot, and force myself to focus on my job.

Which is exactly when Ryan, the best man, steps into my path.

Enemies

Jenna

The evening has gone better than I dared hope.

Everyone's fed, everyone's laughing, and the table is littered with empty wine bottles and scattered napkins. Grace looks radiant, Aaron is beaming, and the bridesmaids are tipsy enough to giggle at anything. Relief floods through me.

Maybe I can do this. Maybe I really am cut out for wedding planning.

This is the first event I've handled completely on my own since joining the company, and I've been terrified of slipping up. But tonight feels smooth, joyful, exactly what a rehearsal dinner should be. If tomorrow goes half as well, my boss will have nothing to complain about.

I should be basking in that small victory. But I'm not.

Because every time I glance across the room, Jack Westmore is already watching me.

And every time I catch him, it's like my body betrays me all over again.

Contents

CONTENTS

Foreword

The invasion of Panama in 1989 by the United States caught the world—and a brutal dictator—by surprise. U.S. forces struck hard, struck fast, and rapidly achieved all their objectives with courage and professionalism. Operation Just Cause had been planned carefully and fully rehearsed. But the timing for execution, December 1989, had not been forecast by anyone. With essentially a "no-notice" requirement to launch, forces from all services carried out a prototypical forcible-entry parachute assault. U.S. contingency operations came of age. Many of these same units would soon be further tested during Operations Desert Shield and Desert Storm.

Lt. Gen. Edward M. Flanagan, Jr.'s *Battle for Panama* shows that Operation Just Cause was an intricate and hard-fought battle. As a career officer of impeccable credentials and a widely published military historian, General Flanagan brings a unique set of qualifications to this task. A former comrade-in-arms of many of the key participants, with access to the most recently released after-action reports, he has been able to write a uniquely perceptive account. It is an exciting read. It is about combat. It is about American soldiers, sailors, airmen, and marines compassionately and courageously accomplishing their missions. These men and women gave the citizens of Panama a chance to live and work and raise their families in a free country. It was a job well done!

Maxwell R. Thurman
General, USA (Ret.)
Washington, D.C.

Preface

"Just Cause" seemed particularly intriguing to me for one main reason. I retired from the Army in 1978, having served in combat in World War II, Korea, and Viet Nam. Some of my final years were in command positions, first of an infantry division and then of a Stateside Army. In the seventies, I must admit, the Army was not an organization of which one could be inordinately proud. We commanders suffered through some bleak times. But by the end of the eighties, the Army had regained a level of excellence with soldiers who were volunteers, soldiers who were bright, soldiers who had discipline, soldiers who were well trained, soldiers who were equipped with the most modern weapons and technology that the United States could find and buy, soldiers who were led by well-trained leaders. The Army "brass" was saying that this was "the best Army that the United States had ever fielded." And I was skeptical of such a statement. (The marines, sailors, and airmen served in equally superb units, according to their commanders.) Operation "Just Cause" had gone so well that I wanted to find out if all this were true.

Right after the completion of "Just Cause," I started to ask questions of other officers I knew at Fort Bragg. The more I learned about the operation, the more intrigued with it I became. I heard "Buck" Kernan give a briefing in Atlanta to the Airborne Association and learned of the part played by his Rangers. I talked at length to the G3's of the XVIII Airborne Corps and the 82nd Airborne Division. All of this exposure pointed to the fact that Just Cause was "well done." And when I learned of the part played by the administration, I knew it had to be a winner. The administration, from the president through the secretary of defense and the chairman of the Joint Chiefs, practiced the one principle of war that almost ensured success: Give a man a well-defined mission, give him sufficient tools with which to accomplish it, and then let him do it without "micromanaging" him.

And so after much research on the operation, many interviews, and scores of letters, I must reluctantly admit, as an "old" and undoubtly prejudiced soldier, that I can find nothing to dispute the claims of today's "brass."

This book does not try to philosophize about the basic moralilty of the operation. It does not try to determine the guilt of Manuel Noriega. It does not investigate the validity or value of the Panama Canal Treaty. It does seek simply to tell the military side of the operation—the decision, the planning, the deployments, the actions. And it does, overall, I hope, point out the competence of the "new military establishment."

Acknowledgments

Writing a book about a military operation involving over twenty-seven thousand troops assigned to many units home-based across the width and breadth of the United States, from Fort Lewis, Washington, and Fort Ord, California, to Fort Bragg, North Carolina, and Forth Benning, Georgia, and others permanently stationed in Panama requires the help, patience, and knowledge of many troops—officer and enlisted.

I am particularly grateful to the staff officers of XVIII Airborne Corps who spent time with me when I mentioned that I wanted to write a book about "Just Cause." The chief of staff at the time, MG Edison Scholes, and the G3, BG Tom Needham, provided the overview and many briefing notes and charts and reports. Lt. Col. David Huntoon, the corps planner, did yeoman service. Not only did he provide many of the details of the planning for the operation, but later he read the entire manuscript, made corrections and additions, and farmed out pertinent parts of the book to other officers in the 82nd Airborne Division and Special Operations Command who were directly involved in certain phases. Dr. Robert K. Wright, the former XVIII Airborne corps historian, answered many questions and provided maps, photos, PDF organization details, and after-action reports.

At the JCS level, Lt. Gen. Tom Kelly sent me pertinent information and called to give additional data and statistics. One of his assistants, Maj. Raymond Melnyk, sent briefing charts and notes and answered many questions.

In the 82nd Airborne Division, Col. Dan K. McNeill, the G-3 at the time, answered many questions and sent me briefing charts, chronologies, notes, and his own personal diary of the operation. Lt. Col. Gerald L. Behnke escorted me around the 82d Airborne Division and Pope Air Force Base and explained the functions of the various elements in the Personnel Holding Area near Pope. I interviewed Capt. Gary J. Ramsdell at length. Lt. Col. Harry Axson and his staff reviewed three chapters dealing with their battalion's operations and added details that only they could know about.

ACKNOWLEDGMENTS

Lt. Gen. (Maj. Gen. at the time) Wayne Downing, the commander of JSOC, spent over two hours answering my questions and telling me the details of his portion of the operation. His aide, Capt. Raymond A. Thomas, who had been the commander of A Company of the 3d Ranger Battalion, filled in many blanks in my knowledge of the Rangers' part in the operation.

Brig. Gen. (then Col.) William F. "Buck" Kernan was especially helpful. He had his Rangers write to me about their personal experiences and feelings. He also sent me charts, notes, after-action reports, and letters answering detailed questions. Maj. (then Capt.) Albert E. Dochnal read and corrected the section of the book dealing with his unit's part.

Capt. Stuart W. Bradin sat with me and explained in detail his unit's part in the Pacoro River Bridge action. Later, Maj. Kevin H. Higgins reviewed the action and added many important details.

Col. Michael G. Snell sent letters and after-action reports from all of his battalions. Lt. Col. B. R. Fitzgerald's report was especially detailed and helpful.

Lt. Col. W. J. Leszczynski took the time to write a letter explaining his battalion's part in the operation. The chief of public affairs of the 7th Division (L), Maj. L. D. Walker, sent me many newspaper clippings, handwritten journals, chronologies, and briefing notes without which I could not have reconstructed the important part played by the 7th Infantry Division (L). His successor, Maj. Steven R. Hill, answered a number of my questions. Capt. Lisa M. Kutschera, a 7th Division pilot, was especially helpful in writing to me about the details of her unit's part in Just Cause.

Lt. Col. J. W. Reed wrote a long letter describing his unit's action.

Col. C. E. Richardson, the USMC component commander, answered all my questions and went to some difficulty to discover the pertinent parts of his unit's action, particularly before he assumed command.

I know that there are others who gave me assistance, guidance, and help. To them, I am grateful. And I would be remiss if I did not thank Don McKeon, associate director of publishing at Brassey's, for his macro- and microguidance through the development of this book. His expertise made it far better than it would have been without it. I thank him and all the others who were so generous with their time, patience, and knowledge.

U.S. SOUTHERN COMMAND
JOINT TASK FORCE SOUTH
(HQ XVIII Airborne Corps)

Air Forces, Panama
Army Forces, Panama

Naval Forces, Panama
Marine Forces, Panama

TASK FORCE ATLANTIC

HQ/HQ Company, 3d Bde, 7th Inf Division	Fort Ord, Calif.
4/17 Inf	Fort Ord, Calif.
3/504 Inf (Abn)	Fort Bragg, N.C.
Battery B, 7/15 Field Artillery	Fort Ord, Calif.
Battery B, 2/62 Air Defense Artillery	Fort Ord, Calif.
Company C, 13th Engineer Bn	Fort Ord, Calif.
Company C, 7th Medical Bn	Fort Ord, Calif.
Company C, 707th Maintenance Bn	Fort Ord, Calif.
Company C, 7th Supply & Trans. Bn	Fort Ord, Calif.

TASK FORCE AVIATION (HQ Avn Bde, 7th Inf Division)

1/228 Avn	Panama
Task Force Hawk (HQ 3/123 Avn, 7th Inf Division)	
3/123 Avn (-)	Fort Ord, Calif.
Company E, 123 Avn (-)	Fort Ord, Calif.
Task Force Wolf (HQ 1/82 Avn, 82d Abn Division)	
1/82 Avn (-)	Fort Bragg, N.C.
Troop D, 1st Squadron, 17th Cavalry	Fort Bragg, N.C.
1/123 Aviation (-)	Fort Ord, Calif.

TASK FORCE SEMPER FI
(Marine Forces, Panama)

6th Marine Expeditionary Bn	Camp Lejeune, N.C.
Company K, 3/6 Marines	
Company I, 3/6 Marines	
Company D, 2d Light Armored Inf Bn (-)	
Dets. G and H, Bde Service Support Group 6	
1st Pltn, First Fleet Antiterrorist Security Team	Norfolk, Va.
Marine Corps Security Force Company	Panama
534th Military Police Company (Army)	Panama
536th Engineer Bn (Army)	Panama
Battery D, 320th Field Artillery (Army)	Panama
2/27 Inf (-) (Army)	Fort Ord, Calif.

TASK FORCE BAYONET

HQ/HQ Company, 193d Inf Brigade	Panama
5/87 Inf	Panama
1/508 Inf (Abn)	Panama
4/6 Inf (M), 5th Inf Division (M)	Fort Polk, La.
59th Engineer Company	Panama

519th MP Bn	Fort Meade, Md.
HQ/HQ Det., 519th MP Bn	Fort Meade, Md.
209th MP Company	Fort Meade, Md.
555th MP Company	Fort Lee, Va.
988th MP Company	Fort Benning, Ga.

JOINT SPECIAL OPERATIONS TASK FORCE

Task Force Red (HQ 75th Ranger Regt)	
HQ/HQ Company, 75th Rgr	Fort Benning, Ga.
1/75 Rgr	Hunter Army Afld, Ga.
2/75 Rgr	Fort Lewis, Wash.
3/75 Rgr	Fort Benning, Ga.
Task Force Green (Army Delta Force)	
Task Force Blue (Navy Special Mission Unit)	
7th SF Grp (-) (Arrived D+10)	Fort Bragg, N.C.
HQ/HQ Company, 7th SF Grp	
1/7 SF Grp (-)	
2/7 SF Grp	
Support Company, 7th SF Grp	
112th Signal Bn (-)	Fort Bragg, N.C.
528th Support Bn	Fort Bragg, N.C.
160th Aviation Grp (-)	Fort Campbell, Ky.
617th Aviation Detachment	Panama
Task Force Black (HQ 3/7 Special Forces Grp)	
3/7 SF Grp	Panama
Company A, 1/7 SF Grp	Fort Bragg, N.C.
Task Force White (HQ Nav. Spec. Warfare Grp 2)	
Teams 2, 4, Nav. Spec. War. Grp 2	Little Creek, Va.
Naval Special Warfare Unit 8	Panama
Special Boat Unit 26	Panama

ELEMENTS UNDER DIRECT CONTROL OF JTF-SOUTH

525th MI Bde (-)	Fort Bragg, N.C.
Company A, 319th MI Bn	
519th MI Bn (-)	
35th Signal Bde (-)	Fort Bragg, N.C.
1st Corps Support Command (-)	Fort Bragg, N.C.
44th Medical Bde	Fort Bragg, N.C.
5th Mobile Army Surgical Hospital	Fort Bragg, N.C.
32d Med. Supply & Optical Maint. Unit	Fort Bragg, N.C.
36th Medical Company (-)	Fort Bragg, N.C.
142d Medical Bn (-)	Panama
41st Support Group	Panama
193d Support Bn	
1097th Transportation Company	
46th Support Group (-)	Fort Bragg, N.C.
2d Support Center	Fort Bragg, N.C.
330th Transportation Center	
7th Transportation Bn	Fort Bragg, N.C.

Joint Task Force–South: Order of Battle

4th Psychological Operations Group (-)	Fort Bragg, N.C.
1st Psyop Bn	
90th Psyop Company	
94th Psyop Company	
96th Civil Affairs Bn	Fort Bragg, N.C.
1109th Signal Bde	Panama
154th Signal Bn	
1190th Signal Bn	
1st Battlefield Control Detachment (-)	Fort Bragg, N.C.
HQ/HQ Company, U.S. Army South	Panama
16th MP Bde	Fort Bragg, N.C.
503d MP Bn	Fort Bragg, N.C.
HQ/HQ Detachment, 503d MP Bn	
21st MP Company	
65th MP Company	
108th MP Company	
92d MP Bn	Panama
HQ/HQ Detachment, 92d MP Bn	
549th MP Company	
470th MI Bde	Panama
29th MI Bn	
746th MI Bn	
747th MI Bn	

NAVAL FORCES, PANAMA

Naval Security Group (Galeta Island)	Panama
Mine Division 127	Panama

AIR FORCES, PANAMA

830th Air Division	Panama
1st Special Operations Wing (AC-130)	Hurlburt Field, Fla.
24th Composite Wing	Panama
CORONET COVE (A-7D Air	
Nat'l Gd rotation)	
Det., 114th Tac. Fighter Grp	S.D. ANG
24th Tac. Air Support Squadron	
(OA-37)	Panama
61st Military Airlift Group	Panama
VOLANT OAK (C-130 rotation)	Various
310th Military Airlift Squadron	Panama
Det. 1, 480th Recon Tech. Group	
(FURTIVE BEAR)	Panama

ARMY FORCES, PANAMA (HQ XVIII Airborne Corps)

7th Infantry Division (LIGHT) (-)	Fort Ord, Calif.
HQ/HQ Company, 7th Inf Division	
7th MP Company (-)	

2d Squadron, 9th Cavalry (-)	
2d Bde, 7th Inf Division (-)	
HQ/HQ Company, 2d Bde	
5/21 Inf	
3/27 Inf	
6/8 Field Artillery	
Battery A, 2/62 Air Defense Artillery	
Company B, 13th Engineer Bn	
Company B, 7th Medical Bn	
Company B, 707th Maintenance Bn	
Company B, 7th Supply & Trans. Bn	
127th Signal Bn (-)	
13th Engineer Bn (-)	
107th MI Bn (-)	

TASK FORCE PACIFIC

82d Airborne Division (-)	Fort Bragg, N.C.
HQ/HQ Company, 82d Abn Division (-)	Fort Bragg, N.C.
1st Bde, 82d Abn Division (+)	Fort Bragg, N.C.
1/504 Inf (Abn)	
2/504 Inf (Abn)	
4/325 Inf (Abn) (-) (+)	
Company A, 3/505 Inf	
Battery A, 3/319 Field Artillery (-)	
Battery A, 3/4 Air Defense Artillery (-)	
Company C, 3/73 Armor	
Company A, 307th Engineer Bn	
Company A, 782d Maintenance Bn	
Company B, 307th Medical Bn	
Company A, 407th Supply & Service Bn	
Company A, 313th MI Bn	
Company B, 82d Signal Bn (-)	Fort Bragg, N.C.
82d MP Company (-)	Fort Bragg, N.C.
401st MP Company	Fort Hood, Texas
511th MP Company	Fort Drum, N.Y.
1st Bde, 7th Inf Division (Manchus)	Fort Ord, Calif.
HQ/HQ Company, 1st Bde	
1/9 Inf	
2/9 Inf	
3/9 Inf	
Company A, 13th Engineer Bn	
Company A, 707th Maintenance Bn	
Company A, 7th Medical Bn	
Company A, 7th Supply & Trans. Bn	

Joint Task Force–South: Order of Battle (continued)

Acronyms

AA	assembly area
AAR	after-action review
ALICE	all-purpose, lightweight, individual-carrier equipment
ANVIS	aviation night vision system (goggles)
AO	area of operations
AT-4	shoulder-fired antitank weapon
AWADS	all-weather air delivery system
BDU	battle-dress uniform
BSSG	brigade service support group
CCT	combat control team
CD bags	combat deployment bags
CIA	Compañia de Infanteria (Panama Defense Forces)
CDS	container delivery system
CRRC	combat rubber raiding crafts
DENI	Departmento Nacional de Investigaciónes
DIA	Defense Intelligence Agency
DNTT	Dirección Nacional de Transito Terrestre
DRB	division-ready brigade
EDRE	emergency deployment readiness exercise
EPW	enemy prisoner of war
ESIP	emergency supply issue point
FAP	Fuerza Aérea Panameña (Panamanian Air Force)
FARRP	forward area rearming and refueling point
FAST	forward area support team
FAST	fleet antiterrorist security team
FSO	fire support officer
HMMWV	high-mobility multiwheeled vehicle
HWBDU	hot-weather battle dress uniform

ACRONYMS

IAW	in accordance with
IFR	instrument flight regulations
IR tape	infrared tape
IV	intravenous
JOTC	jungle operations training center
JSOTF	joint special operations task force
LAI Bn	marine light armored infantry battalion
LAV	light assault vehicle
LAW	light antiarmor weapon
LCE	load-carrying equipment
LCM	landing craft medium
LD	line of departure
MARFORPM	Marine forces panama
MCSF	Marine Corps security force
MEB	Marine expeditionary brigade
METT-T	mission, enemy, troops, terrain, time
MOUT	military operations in urban terrain
MRE	meal ready to eat
MTT	mobile training team (Army Special Forces)
NCA	National Command Authority
NMCC	National Military Command Center (in the Pentagon)
NVG	night-vision goggles
ODA	Operational Detachment A (Special Forces A Team)
OPSEC	operational security
PCS	permanent change of station
PDF	Panama Defense Forces
PHA	personnel holding area
PPF	Panama Police Forces
PSYOPS HB team	psychological operations team
PVS-4	night scopes
PZ	pickup zone
REMAB	remote marshaling base
RGR	Ranger
RPG	rocket-propelled grenade
R&R	rest and recuperation
RSOP	reconnaissance, selection, occupation of position
RTO	radio-telephone operator
SALUTE	size, activity, location, unit, time, equipment
SATCOM	satellite communications
SAW	squad automatic weapon (machine gun)
SEAL	sea, air, land (U.S. Navy Special Forces)
SOCOM	Southern Command (General Thurman's headquarters)

SOLL	Special Operations Low-Level
SOP	standard operating procedures
TACP	tactical air control party
TA-50	Table of Allowance
TAW	tactical air wing
TEWTS	tactical exercise without troops
TOC	tactical operations center

I | BACKGROUND AND PREPARATIONS

1 | Noriega's Rise to Power

Panama. In years past, the name might have brought to one's mind a canal, weaving its circuitous way placidly through gouged-out mountains, thick jungles, and broad lakes. Perhaps one might think of a tropical country covered with a rain forest and geographically shaped like a huge "S" lying on its side, connecting Costa Rica and Colombia.

More recently, the name Panama might conjure up a different mental scenario—a picture of a slightly bewildered, unsmiling, dark-skinned, square-shouldered, five-foot-five man arrayed in a khaki uniform with the epaulets of a four-star general gracing his shoulders. Usually, in pre-December 1989 newspaper photos or on television, the man is surrounded by groups of sycophantic men, some in civilian clothes, some few in the khaki uniform of the Panama Defense Forces, the PDF. In the photos, one might also catch a glimpse of a few beautiful young ladies in the entourage. In the post-Christmas 1989 scenes, however, the man, still in uniform, but somewhat passive and befuddled, is surrounded by the agents of the U.S. Drug Enforcement Agency, and he is being led to a waiting U.S. C-130 airplane for transportation out of his country. His decline from the strutting, powerful dictator of a small, strategically important Latin American country to a subdued prisoner of the United States was swift and decisive.

Manuel Antonio Noriega Morena was born in 1934 in Terraplen, one of the poorer barrios of Panama City. His father had a Colombian background and worked as an accountant for small firms in the area. His mother was variously described as his father's "domestic" and as a cook and laundress. Noriega's dark complexion derived from his mixed blood of black, Indian, and Spanish—in simple terms, a Creole. By the time he was five, his parents had deserted him and he was reared as an orphan by a godmother.[1]

As a teenager, Noriega attended the Instituto Nacional, the premier high school in Panama. After graduation, he wanted to study medicine, but the

3

limited family finances would not permit it. Instead, after a few years' wait, he accepted a scholarship to Chorillos Military Academy in Lima, Peru. His half brother Luís Carlos, who was a minor official in the Panamanian embassy in Peru, arranged the scholarship.[2]

Noriega's career as a cadet in the military academy in Peru hardly lived up to another military academy's standards of "duty, honor, country." In the first place, he subtracted four years from his age to meet the age requirements to get into the academy. And then, during the summer of 1960, he and some fellow cadets went into town for a weekend designed to relieve them of the rigors and hardships of military academy life.

First they went to a bar, where Noriega quickly spent his small allowance on beer. Later in the evening, broke, he could not meet the price of a balky young prostitute who had already serviced two of his friends. Noriega's innate pride, his feeling of intellectual superiority, and his age—older than the other cadets—would not allow him to return to the academy without having shown his manhood in more than one way. So he took matters into his own hands—literally. Frederick Kempe, in *Divorcing the Dictator,* writes that "During the summer of 1960, an American intelligence agent, serving under diplomatic cover at the U.S. embassy in Lima, Peru, wired home a secret cable with some disturbing news. One of his more promising recent recruits, a young Panamanian cadet at Peru's Chorillos Military Academy, had been arrested for beating and raping a prostitute. She had nearly died. The recruit: Manuel Antonio Noriega." Noriega was able to ease himself out of the predicament with the police. His brutality and ability to evade the consequences thereof were beginning to become manifest.[3]

The U.S. embassy's intelligence agent had recruited Noriega, because of his high academic grades and self-confidence, to provide the U.S. Defense Intelligence Agency with data on leftist fellow students. Shortly thereafter, Noriega went on a modest monthly retainer with the agency.

On graduation and return to Panama in 1963, Noriega was commissioned a sublieutenant in the Panamanian National Guard and was posted to a military base at Colón. Here, as the fates and his luck would have it, he found the entry to his path to power. His commander at Colón was one Capt. Omar Torrijos, who, in a short time, found Noriega a kindred spirit and adopted him as one of his favorites.

Later, through the help of Torrijos and U.S. intelligence officers, Noriega received training at U.S. schools. In July of 1967 he attended a course on intelligence and counterintelligence at Fort Gulick, Canal Zone; in September of 1967 he attended a seven-week psychological operations course at the Special Warfare School at Fort Bragg, North Carolina; later that year he took a two-month course on military intelligence at the School of the Americas in Panama. By 1968 Noriega had been promoted to first lieutenant and reassigned to Chiriquí Province.

In that same year, a group of rebels of the army in Panama, called the "Combo" force, organized to resist the military realignment instituted by President Arnuflo Arias, who had been elected to the presidency on 12 May 1968 and who assumed the office on 1 October 1968. Noriega joined the rebels.

On 11 October 1968, a military coup led by Torrijos attacked the civilian government of Arias. During the coup, Lieutenant Noriega and part of the "Combo" force seized the radio and telephone centers in David, the provincial capital of Chiriquí, severing all communications with Panama City. The power struggle between the civilian structure and the military continued for a short time. In days, Torrijos emerged as the military's leading figure and the nation's strongman. The victorious junta that he headed named Col. José M. Pinilla as president and promised "economic and administrative reforms and elections by mid-1970 under a new constitution and electoral law." The reforms, of course, never happened. On the contrary, the coup introduced an era of military rule that survived until Noriega's downfall twenty-one years later.

Torrijos's grip on power, however, was not yet firmly established. In December of 1969, while he was on a trip to Mexico, three rightist colonels staged a countercoup and temporarily seized control of the government in Panama City. But Noriega, now a major and commanding a National Guard unit in Chiriquí, displayed his loyalty to the dictator with some fervor and imagination. Torrijos, aware of the coup attempt, radioed him that he would risk a night flight to Chiriquí. Unfortunately, the primitive airstrip at David had no landing lights. But that did not stop the resourceful Noriega. He assembled every available motor vehicle he could find, lined them up along the strip, and, at the sound of Torrijos's aircraft, ordered all headlights turned on. Torrijos made a safe landing, mustered Noriega's troops, and marched east to retake the capital and put down the rebellion. As a reward, Torrijos promoted Noriega to lieutenant colonel in 1970 and appointed him as chief of military intelligence. This post made him Torrijos's right-hand man and gave him great personal power over the people of Panama through control of the corrupt secret police. It also brought him into contact with the U.S. intelligence community—both the Central Intelligence Agency (CIA) and the Defense Intelligence Agency (DIA). With the promotion and assignment, Noriega's march to infamy had begun in earnest.[4]

During the 1970s, Torrijos wiped out political parties; abolished the independent newspapers, radio and television stations; and, as the commander of the armed forces, consolidated his hold on the nation.

Winston Robles was the editor of the opposition newspaper *La Prensa*. He said, "As opposed to what some people believe, we were under a dictatorship since 1968. The fact that we have had presidents does not mean anything. The thing here is we have an institutionalized dictatorship. Not the rule of one specific dictator, but the rule of whoever was in charge of the armed forces."

The ruthless dictatorship of Torrijos was only part of the problem of Panama, as viewed through the eyes of successive American administrations. Richard Nixon was deeply concerned with the war on drugs in the United States and elsewhere. In 1971 he told Congress that the war was a "national emergency" and that his drug agents had considerable evidence that Torrijos and his chief henchman, Noriega, had established a multimillion-dollar drug business in Panama through its embassies, consulates, and airports and through "custom offices in the Far East and the Americas."[5]

Nixon was also concerned about the spread of communism in Latin America

5

and the part Torrijos was playing in it. Torrijos had known Communists in his cabinet, he had links to Fidel Castro, and he was shifting to the left in governing Panama. In 1971, Castro's henchmen had apprehended the American crews of two Miami-based freighters. Castro stubbornly refused to release them directly to U.S. authorities. Nixon, notwithstanding his abhorrence of the Panama regime, felt called upon to request Torrijos to assist in obtaining the release of the crews. On behalf of the United States and keeping his options open, Torrijos sent Noriega to Havana; Noriega dutifully secured the release of the crews.[6]

But in spite of this assistance and the intelligence furnished by Noriega's G-2 agency, the Nixon administration was becoming increasingly concerned with persistent reports that Torrijos and Noriega were deeply involved in the Colombian drug trade. In 1971 the administration went so far as to propose "decisive action . . . for destroying or immobilizing the highest level of drug traffickers." It was clear from memos of the U.S. Bureau of Narcotics and Dangerous Drugs that "decisive action" could possibly include assassination and other measures to control Noriega and Torrijos, according to a Senate Intelligence Committee report that was confirmed by John Ingersoll, the director of the Bureau of Narcotics and Dangerous Drugs. The administration rejected the assassination proposal.

As chief of the "dreaded" Panama G-2 agency, Noriega was able to keep secret and detailed files on dissidents. He and his thugs often resorted to torture, intimidation, harassment, beatings, and sexual aberrations to maintain control of Torrijos's opposition. In a major sweep of the country in 1975, Noriega's G-2 agents rounded up selected businessmen and media executives who had been critical of the government, confiscated their properties, and shipped them out to Ecuador. In 1976 Noriega and his equally demonic underlings cracked down on the Union Patriótica Feminina, a women's organization opposed to the harsh rule of the Torrijos government. One of those imprisoned was Alma Robles, daughter of a former leader of the National Assembly. For days she was held incommunicado in a filthy cell while Noriega trumped up charges against her. Even some of the officials of the Torrijos government were ashamed of the treatment.[7]

During the 1970s, when he was still in charge of the Panamanian intelligence agency, Noriega was on the payroll of both the Defense Intelligence Agency and the Central Intelligence Agency. From the CIA, he received $110,000 per year. For that money, Noriega provided data on Latin American military establishments, Castro's Cuba, and the emerging guerrilla movements in the region, particularly in Nicaragua. He was a reliable and generally the sole source for that kind of intelligence. But he was also devious and dishonest and played the role of a double and triple agent. In 1976 the Army investigated the "Singing Sergeants" scandal, in which members of the 470th Military Intelligence Group who had been taping Panamanian officials, allegedly sold copies of the reels to Noriega, who in turn passed the information to Torrijos. Washington also suspected that Noriega sold some of the information to Castro's intelligence service, which also had him on its payroll. In 1977, after a number of briefings on Noriega that detailed his methods and the barbarity of his agency's harassment of Panamanians, CIA director Adm. Stansfield Turner severed the CIA's relationship with Noriega and his intelligence agency.

But by this time, Noriega was the most feared man in Panama. On 8 March 1978, in an interview with Sally Quinn of the *Washington Post,* Noriega told her, "I know that I have an image problem. Mine is a position that doesn't attract much sympathy. But somebody must do this job. And it's a normal position in all the armies of the world. In Panama there is only one force that has control. That's my job."[8]

By the late 1970s, the crimes of Torrijos and, by now his number-two man—Noriega—were becoming clear and documented by U.S. government agencies. They included links to Colombian drugs lords, secret ties to Castro, gun-running for terrorists and insurgents in Latin America, money laundering for the drug cartels, and use of Panamanian airports as transfer points for shipment of drugs to the United States. To audit the Colombian cartel's drug accounts in Panamanian banks, Noriega placed intelligence agents on the banks' staffs.

In spite of being off the CIA payroll for the time being, Noriega managed to maintain his ties to the United States by his usual fraudulent and oblique schemes: He provided reliable intelligence, available from no other source, on Latin American insurgencies, especially in Nicaragua once the Sandinistas had taken over in 1979; he informed the United States in 1979 about a two-thousand- to three-thousand-man Soviet combat brigade in Cuba; he arrested small-level drug traffickers and shipped some of them to the United States; at the request of the U.S. government, he hosted and protected the ousted shah of Iran from December 1979 until March 1980; but he kept intact his contacts with the huge Colombian drug bosses, from whom he drew millions of dollars in recompense.

By 1981, during the first Reagan administration, Noriega was back on the payroll of the CIA, at $185,000 per year.[9] Nineteen eighty-one was also the year when Torrijos was killed in a plane crash near Penonomé, in western Panama. His death initiated a long power struggle between civilian and military leaders, with the military eventually winning. General Dario Paredes, in charge of the National Guard, emerged as the strongman; his chief of staff was Noriega. By August of 1983, Noriega had outfoxed three senior officers and became the commander of the National Guard. He also promoted himself to general. Noriega was an admirer of Israel and its military, the Israeli Defense Forces. One of his first actions, allegedly at the suggestion of his Israeli adviser, Michael Harari, was to combine the National Guard with the small navy and air force into the Panamanian Defense Forces (the PDF), which eventually numbered some fifteen-thousand men.[10]

Noriega immediately set about gaining control of the country through a number of means. He modeled his internal political network after the "Cuban-and Nicaraguan-style neighborhood spy committees." He revitalized his sub-servient military force. He secured legislation putting the military in control of airports, ports, immigration, and customs. In due time, the PDF was in control and owned hotels, liquor stores, and newspapers. In the Colón Free Zone, the military had a "protection racket" that netted some $275 million per year by

7

charging a 1 percent tariff on exports. "Ghost employees" on the state payroll drew some $300 million annually.

Noriega may have had dealings with the top "brass" in the United States, but he was not admired—at least by one of the "brass." In the early 1980s, Oliver North had met with Noriega on a number of occasions in connection with the Iran-contra affair. In his book *Under Fire,* North makes clear his opinion of Noriega. "For me, one of the ugliest aspects of the whole Iran-contra affair was the way my meetings with Noriega were described in some quarters as though the two of us had some kind of an alliance. We didn't. Noriega was probably the single most despicable human being I ever had to deal with. After meeting with him, you just wanted to go home and take a shower."[11]

Gradually and finally, the military came to control the country totally. And, of course, Noriega controlled every aspect of the Panamanian Defense Forces. He organized and armed the "Dignity Battalions," "Digbats" (later called "dingbats" by U.S. forces involved in Just Cause)—bands of young, civilian-clad hoodlums who were intensely loyal to the dictator. The "Digbats" copied the Sandinista *turbas divinas,* who did the "regime's dirty work out of uniform." By 1985 Noriega was in total control of the nation.

In the early 1980s, Noriega fostered a number of schemes that put him in good graces with the United States. He began to assist the Reagan administration with the contra war against the Sandinistas. He permitted the Israelis to use Panama to funnel weapons to the contras. He had a fairly reliable intelligence network in Managua, whose reports he shared with the administration. And he sent arms to the contras.[12]

But under the thin layer of goodwill was a multitude of sins. He was still involved across half of the globe selling arms, intelligence, and even restricted U.S. technology to the Sandinistas, the Eastern bloc, the Cubans, the Colombians, and the opponents of the Israelis, and in running drugs for the Colombian drug cartel. An article in the 12 June 1986 issue of the *New York Times* reported that in the early 1980s Noriega had a personal stake in a drug-processing plant near the Colombian border from which he extracted millions of dollars. In addition, large drug profits, perhaps reaching half a billion dollars a year, were laundered through Panamanian banks and transferred to banks in the United States and other countries. In one deal with Eastern bloc countries, he reportedly made $3 million selling them secret U.S. technological data.[13]

At home, Noriega tightened his control. In the 1984 presidential election, Noriega's candidate was Nicolas Ardito Barletta, who holds a Ph.D. in economics from the University of Chicago, had been the minister of economic planning in the 1970s, and had served as vice president of the World Bank for Latin America and the Caribbean from 1978 to 1984. Dr. Barletta won a narrow victory over the former president, Arnuflo Arias, amid charges that Noriega's military had tampered with the ballot boxes. On 27 September 1985, Noriega forced Barletta from office, ostensibly because he did not approve of Barletta's handling of the economy. But in reality, it turned out later that Barletta was investigating the government's part in the brutal murder of Dr. Hugo Spadafora.

Spadafora had been a critic of Noriega since the two served together under

Torrijos. But in 1984, Spadafora went public with his criticism of Noriega's drug trafficking. Dr. Spadafora was last seen alive near the Costa Rican border, being dragged off a bus by Noriega's agents. He was found sometime later, decapitated and stuffed into a U.S. mailbag, inside the Costa Rican border.[14] A *New York Times* article cited DIA information that linked Noriega to the crime.

Barletta had been the first directly elected president of Panama since Torrijos's 1968 coup. The Reagan administration was deeply concerned with Noriega's flagrant actions to relieve Barletta, and in 1986 took two important steps: It cut aid to Panama by 85 percent, and it sent national security adviser John M. Poindexter to Panama City to warn Noriega to stay out of the drug business. As expected, Noriega paid no mind to Poindexter, denounced the administration for "meddling" in his internal affairs, denied all charges against him, and named Vice President Eric Arturo Delvalle to replace Barletta. Delvalle did not pursue the Spadafora investigation and was therefore no threat to Noriega.

For about a year, relations between Panama and the United States were at an apparent standoff. But in June of 1987, Col. Roberto Diaz Herrera, a former chief of staff to Noriega and who earlier had been forced into retirement, went on a public offensive. He charged that Noriega had manipulated the 1984 election, had planned and ordered the murder of Dr. Spadafora, and might even have had a part in the plane crash that killed Torrijos. Herrera admitted that he personally had bribed polling officials in the Barletta election and that he and other Panamanian military officers had become wealthy extracting exorbitant fees from Cubans desiring Panamanian visas.

Herrera's public denouncement of Noriega and his regime initiated a series of street demonstrations ("pot-bangers," they came to be called) and renewed public outcry for Noriega's ouster. A loose alliance of business, civic, and church leaders called the National Civil Crusade sprung up. Alfredo Maduro, president of the Panamanian Chamber of Commerce, said that "People wanted a change, were tired of this repressive one-man system and everything going to one little group of people. The system itself was getting more rotten. There was no law or justice."

As expected, Noriega damned the Crusaders as *rabi blancos,* literally "white butts," a term of derision for middle-class businessmen and professionals. *Rabi prietos*—"dark butts"—refers to the poor, who generally supported Noriega. But the Crusaders, nonetheless, bravely demonstrated daily. Noriega responded with speed and power: He dispatched his Dobermans—the riot police—who attacked the demonstrators with bird shot and clubs. He declared a national state of emergency, suspended the constitution, forbade public gatherings, shut down newspapers and radio stations, and arrested or shipped out of the country key opposition leaders. And to silence and punish Herrera, Noriega mounted a dawn raid with two helicopter gunships and some fifty of his Dobermans on Herrera's home. Herrera had anticipated the attack and had assembled a small company of supporters. But after a four-hour firefight, Noriega's men captured Herrera and forty-four of his supporters. Once in the hands of Noriega's thugs, and the recipient of untold "measures of persuasion," Herrera retracted his charges and confessed to "inciting antigovernment violence."[15]

9

But that did not quell the public uprisings. A group of business, Roman Catholic Church, and civic leaders plus numbers of students staged a successful two-day strike to protest the state of emergency and to force Noriega to return the government to civilian control. On 26 June 1987, the U.S. Senate passed a resolution calling on the Panamanian government to oust Noriega and to investigate the charges against him. In response, four days later Noriega lifted the state of emergency. But the result was not a return to calm and order in the streets. The lifting of the ban permitted some five-thousand Noriega supporters to attack the U.S. embassy, from which the Panamanian police had just minutes before withdrawn their guards. The mob stoned the embassy, painted anti-United States graffiti on the walls, and inflicted more than $100,000 in damage. The State Department closed the consular and library section to protest the action of the mob.

The attack on the embassy triggered a new U.S. approach to Panama. The Reagan administration halted all military and economic aid and indicated its strong desire to find a replacement for the Panamanian strongman. On 11 October 1987, Noriega complained to a reporter for the *Washington Post* that after years of cooperating with the CIA and other U.S. intelligence agencies, "When the Americans need something, they picture it very nicely and say you're a hero, but when they don't need you anymore, they forget you."

By the fall of 1987, Noriega's support—except for his bureaucracy and the military—was crumbling. The unrest in the nation caused depositors in Panama's banks to withdraw billions of dollars, with a resultant heavy strain on the national economy. Banking profits accounted for nearly 10 percent of Panama's gross national product. In July 1987 even Gen. Dario Paredes, a Noriega predecessor, spoke out. He supported the public charges of corruption in the government and asked Noriega to resign. Gabriel Lewis, who had been an ambassador to the United States and who had been asked by Noriega to help settle the crisis, took a different tack: He fled to Costa Rica before Noriega could arrest him and, from exile, launched a campaign to unseat the dictator.

But Noriega would not back down. He insisted that there was not "a shred of evidence" against him and adopted a slogan, "Not one step back." He even hinted that he might run for president in the 1989 elections. He railed against the United States, the Catholic Church, and the National Civil Crusade and expelled a few foreign correspondents. In the summer of 1987, he ordered the PDF routinely, and in violation of the 1977 treaties, to stop and check U.S. school buses and military and dependents' automobiles. But in December 1987, perhaps feeling the strength of his position, he permitted opposition newspapers and radio stations to reopen.

José I. Blandon was Noriega's consul general in New York. In an interview with the *New York Times* on 26 November 1988, Blandon said that he had drafted for Noriega's approval a plan that would have allowed Noriega and his leading associates to give up power without "fear of facing criminal prosecution either in Panama or the United States." Early in December, Noriega, after having first given preliminary approval to Brandon's plan, disapproved it and fired Brandon. Brandon did not go quietly. He threatened to publicize papers that would without doubt link Noriega to drug trafficking, money laundering,

10

and the murder of Dr. Spadafora if Noriega would not relinquish power. "Noriega can kill me," Blandon said in the *Times* interview, "that's the risk, but he can't kill what I know." The United States quickly put Blandon under its protection.[16]

In January 1988, Blandon testified before a Miami grand jury that was investigating drug charges against Noriega. While he was testifying in Miami, Stephen M. Kalish, a convicted American drug smuggler, was testifying in Washington, D.C., before a Senate committee investigating Noriega. Kalish admitted that in exchange for help in his own drug business in Panama, he had bribed Noriega with millions of dollars.

On 4 February 1988, two grand juries, in Miami and Tampa, returned indictments in which the U.S. Department of Justice charged Noriega with violations of U.S. racketeering and drug laws by providing protection to international drug traffickers in return for millions of dollars in payoffs, permitting the laundering of drug money through Panamanian banks, and authorizing the use of Panamanian ports and airports for the transfer of drugs.

Noriega continued to have difficulties at home, including, increasingly, the military. In March of 1988, President Delvalle, a Noriega appointee, turned against him, pledged to return the government to a democracy, and tried to oust Noriega by stripping him of command of the armed forces. For his efforts, the Army-dominated National Assembly fired Delvalle and replaced him with the former education minister, Manuel Solis Palma, a close associate of Noriega. The United States did not recognize Palma's credentials. "We had to either acquiesce in this act or call Noriega illegitimate and get into a direct confrontation with him," remembered Elliot Abrams, the assistant secretary of state for Latin America at the time. "So we sided with Delvalle, and Noriega began to teeter." In addition, the economic sanctions imposed by the United States were having a detrimental effect on Panama's economy.[17]

Shortly after Delvalle's ouster, the people of Panama began to express, with action, their resentment of Noriega's iron rule and their falling standard of living. Dissident teachers, dockworkers, electricians, and medical workers paralyzed Panama with a series of strikes. On the sixteenth of March, disgruntled officers of the PDF, led by Col. Leonidas Macias, head of the police force, staged a coup. But Noriega was still in command. His loyal forces put down the coup attempt with brutality, speed, and ease. Thereafter he banned demonstrations and "militarized a number of key public services." On the eighteenth of March, Noriega declared a "state of urgency."

"He played the multiple track system like a violinist," said Elliot Abrams in 1988. "He played us, he played the Latin Americans and the Organization of American States and the internal opposition by giving people the sense that they should play along. But it was not in his interest to leave, and he didn't leave for the most fundamental reason: He didn't want to. . . . The Panamanians who were on the fence came down on Noriega's side. And the opposition was becoming quite disturbed with us. Noriega was appearing more and more like a superman and we were tied in knots."

Noriega might have begun to "teeter" in late 1988, but he was far from falling off his self-constructed pedestal. In spite of all the pressure from the majority of

11

the population of Panama, organizing into opposition groups increasingly, and from the United States, Noriega clung to power through his control of the bureaucracy and the PDF. The bureaucracy was a "kleptocracy." Some press accounts state that about 20 percent of the national budget was paid to *botellas,* political appointees who were paid but never worked. Luís Martins, a spokesman for Endara, thinks that estimate is too low. The 160,000-person bureaucracy was filled, he said, "with people who were on the payroll but never showed up, a lot of suspect travel expenses—that sort of thing. But on a massive scale. The one thing about the Torrijos-Noriega military rule was the institutionalization of corruption at every level, top to bottom, from richest to poorest. It was a system that didn't function without it."

In addition to control of the bureaucracy, Noriega also completely controlled the PDF, a body whose tentacles spread through the entire anatomy of the country. The PDF dominated the government; the PDF was the police force; the PDF ran businesses and banks; the PDF was corrupt; the PDF repressed dissidence with barbarity.[18]

Noriega had bought himself a respite. The United States could not topple him. Abrams said that "An amazing thing happened in the six weeks following the firing of President Delvalle by Noriega; nothing."

But 1989 would prove to be a year in which Noriega reached the extremes of absolutism: On the one hand, he rose to the heights of illegal and flagrant use of raw power in dominating Panama; on the other, by the end of the year he had sunk to the depths of impotence as a hunted, deposed, terrified, powerless, cringing former despot.

2 | 1989: The Climactic Year

After Noriega and the PDF brutally suppressed the coup attempt by Colonel Macias in March 1988, Panama entered a fourteen-month period of relative calm. Noriega abetted that atmosphere by instituting new repressive measures and even hinting that his departure from power might be "negotiable."

Several developments, however, pointed to ripples of trouble beneath the pseudoplacidity of the country. On 13 January 1989, the Panamanian government reported that the Soviet Union and Panama had signed a trade agreement that would result in the first Soviet mission in Panama. In 1988, trade between the two countries was about $2 million—mostly, curiously, Soviet automobiles. On 16 January, Noriega opened his own bank in Panama City in what was reported to be a move "to expand his control over the economy and to launder drug money." On 2 March, the opposition's first major rally drew fifty thousand anti-Noriega demonstrators. On 3 March, the Panamanian traffic police stopped 21 Department of Defense school buses and ticketed the drivers for operating vehicles with U.S. Navy license plates. On 21 March, President Delvalle, who was still recognized by the United States as the legitimate president of Panama, announced that he had taken up permanent residence in Miami. On 5 April, Kurt Muse, a U.S. citizen, was arrested and charged with violating state security. Noriega suspected him of operating a clandestine communications network that interfered with PDF and police transmissions and even became sophisticated enough to override the state radio network and broadcast opposition messages to the Panamanian people. His rescue became of prime importance to the Bush administration. Muse was, apparently, no ordinary U.S. citizen playing communications games with his fellow Rotarians. Noriega had him incarcerated in Carcelo Modelo.

On 18 April the Panamanian government announced that U.S. citizens

13

henceforth would require visas to travel to Panama, presumably to keep U.S. observers out of Panama during the upcoming elections. On 22 April the U.S. Southern Command, the senior headquarters for all U.S. forces in Panama, announced that it planned to move its headquarters to the United States as part of the "phased withdrawal" of U.S. forces from Panama, a move dictated by the 1977 Panama treaties that required the United States to end its military presence in Panama by 1999. On 23 April U.S. officials announced that in 1988 the Senate Intelligence Committee had vetoed a covert plan that had been approved by then President Reagan to support a military coup by "dissident Panamanian military officers." The committee disapproved the plan because "it might have resulted in Noriega's assassination."

In May of 1989, the counterfeit tranquillity in Panama was shattered.

Noriega had scheduled a national election on 7 May 1989 to elect a new president, two vice presidents, 67 legislators, and 505 district representatives. Prior to the election, and in keeping with its normal means of repressive control, the Noriega-dominated hierarchy attempted to ensure the results of the election by padding the voter rosters; closing independent newspaper, radio, and TV outlets; and jimmying the electoral code.[1]

The voter turnout on 7 May was large, and the voting places calm. On one occasion during the day, a smiling, waving Noriega, dressed in dark trousers and brown jacket and wearing his military uniform cap with its gold-braided visor, led a procession of supporters down a main street of Panama City. Undoubtedly, Noriega, knowing that the election was fixed, thought of the procession as a victory parade even before the votes were counted. Clinging to his right arm was a young beauty queen with a large white sash, proclaiming her to be *reina curundu,* draped diagonally across her voluptuous body. On her right, in white formal shirt and dark trousers, was one of Noriega's candidates. On Noriega's left, arm in arm with him, was another young beauty. On her left were two more ladies. Following the entourage was an assortment of men and, a bit incongruously, one platinum-blond woman. Many large, varicolored flags backed up the whole procession and lent an air of benevolence and gaiety to the day.[2] (That Noriega was surrounded by beautiful young ladies on this occasion was no abnormality. Visitors to his office in the Comandancia were struck by the number and beauty of the young women who populated his outer office.)

Noriega's handpicked candidate for president was Carlos Duque, whose running mates were Aquilino Boyd, a former Panamanian ambassador to the United Nations, and Ramon Sieiro, Noriega's brother-in-law. Nepotism also played a part in Panamanian politics. The opposition candidate for president was Guillermo Endara, the nominee of the three-party Democratic Alliance of Civic Opposition (ADOC). His running mates were Ricardo Arias Calderon and Guillermo (Billy) Ford.

On election night, with very little to go on except the knowledge that the election had supposedly been fixed, Duque claimed victory. But Catholic Church leaders in Panama and foreign observers, including Jimmy Carter, a member of a Noriega-sanctioned international observer team representing the Council of Freely Elected Heads of Government, agreed that the opposition

14

candidate, Endara, had won by an overwhelming margin and that the Noriega regime was trying to steal the election.

The first public indication of the results of the election suggested strongly that Duque had been massively defeated. That realization triggered two reactions: On 8 May, the PDF, reasoning correctly that the vote-fixing had failed, raided vote-counting centers and delayed the start of the official count; and ten thousand people took to the streets of Panama City in support of Endara. In one attempt to break up demonstrations, the police opened fire; in the melee, a suspected government agent shot and killed a television cameraman.

Foreign journalists, opposition supporters, and other observers reported that the Noriega regime had substituted voting returns with fake records, had ordered repeated voting by the PDF, and had erased opposition names from the voting records. According to Arias, the number of people on the voting records was up 1.2 million or 29 percent from 1984, and the list contained 100,000 duplications.

On the eighth of May, Jimmy Carter charged that the government had made up fake tally sheets to give the vote to Duque. "The government has stolen the elections by fraud," he said in a statement released in Panama. "The Panamanian people have been robbed."[3]

On the ninth of May, the government began releasing the first election results that showed that Duque led his opponents; on 10 May, the government's three-member Electoral Tribunal said that Duque was ahead of Endara, 66 percent to 32 percent. Conversely, on 9 May, the ADOC released its figures, based on polling half the voting places, and gave Endara 68.6 percent and Duque 22.9 percent. The Catholic Church's sampling gave Endara 74 percent of the vote.

On that same day, after meeting with members of Jimmy Carter's group and an official U.S. observer team headed by Rep. John P. Murtha (D., Pa.), President Bush denounced the election and said that it was marked by "massive irregularities." "The opposition has won a clear-cut, overwhelming victory."

Shortly before midnight that night, Noriega reacted to the charges of fraud and vote-fixing with a simple device: He annuled the election retroactively, charging lack of tally sheets and foreign interference, "obstruction by foreigners," principally by the United States, who, he alleged, had furnished printing and advertising funds to the opposition candidates before the election.

On the tenth of May, Endara, Ford, Arias, and their supporters staged a motorcade through the streets of Panama City to protest the annulment. While TV cameras were filming the scene and newspaper photographers were flashing away, unkempt, rowdy hoodlums of the Dignity Battalions, armed with clubs and metal bars, roared into the motorcade and savagely beat the three actual winners of the election. Endara was cut in the head so severely that he required hospitalization. Reportedly he was beaten again when he returned to his vandalized office. In that second beating, the left side of his body was paralyzed and he had to return to the hospital. Ford was beaten and arrested but released the next day. The "Digbats" killed one of his bodyguards and wounded another with a bullet. Pictures of Ford with his arms raised shielding his bloody head

15

from blows by digbats brought home to Panamanians and the rest of the world the extent of the Noriega regime's brutality and corruption. Many opposition leaders, including Luís Martin, an aide to Endara, were beaten and spent time in jail after the May debacle.

The apparent lack of overt response by the United States to the obviously fraudulent election roused ire in the Panamanian people. "In 1989, when the Dignity Battalions beat up the three candidates," said Luís Martin, "and a lot of people, including myself, were in jail for a few months, there was beginning to be a strong, strong, anti-Americanism on the opposition side for not acting stronger. I'm very pro-American; I did all my schooling in the States. But it was getting very hard to be pro-American. Everybody was saying: 'My God, can't they get rid of the man? They made him, they should help us.' And I couldn't argue that."[4]

But there was response by the United States, albeit not particularly obvious to the people of Panama nor yet militantly aggressive. On the tenth of May, President Bush called several Latin American leaders to discuss with them the situation in Panama and to invite them to unite in opposing Noriega. He said that he discussed ways to remove Noriega from power and that he hoped that "regional diplomacy" would answer the crisis. On the eleventh of May, most nations in the area, with the obvious exceptions of Cuba and Nicaragua, strongly condemned Noriega and his government. President Bush recalled the U.S. ambassador, Arthur C. Davis. On the eleventh of May, President Bush ordered some two thousand additional troops to move to Panama within the following two to three weeks to protect American citizens and property.

To the U.S. military, the augmentation of troops in Panama was known as Operation Nimrod Dancer. A mechanized battalion from the 5th Infantry Division at Fort Polk, Louisiana, deployed to Panama and moved into an area across from Fort Clayton, near the western end of the zone. A brigade headquarters and one battalion from the 7th Infantry Division (Light) from Fort Ord, California, took up positions on the Atlantic side of the canal, near Colón. In April of 1988, the U.S. Marine Corps had moved some four hundred Marines to Panama and, a year later, deployed an additional Marine Corps company, equipped with light assault vehicles (LAV 25's), to Howard Air Force Base, on the western side of the canal and to the western entrance to the Bridge of the Americas.[5]

On the seventeenth of May, Noriega commented publicly for the first time on the results of the election. He flatly denied responsibility for the crimes and violence against Endara, Ford, and the other opposition candidates and denied having any voice in the annulment of the election. He attributed the violence to militants "on both sides" and strongly denounced U.S. "aggression" and "imperialism." He categorically rejected Bush's call that he resign, declaring it "an unacceptable intervention in Panama's affairs," and suggested that the United States was using the election uproar as a screen for abrogating the 1977 canal treaties.

The Bush administration was not standing idly by. For some years the Department of Defense had had contingency plans for moving additional troops into Panama to take control in various emergencies or within forty-eight hours of the election violence. In May 1989, Gen. Carl Stiner, the commanding general of the XVIII Airborne Corps, the command with the major responsibility for developing the contingency plans for any U.S. operations in Panama, sent a small planning staff to Panama to review its own plan for an assault into Panama. This initial advance group consisted of Maj. David H. Huntoon, Jr. (USMA, 1973), the corps planner responsible for the Panama plan, and two other officers, Maj. Mike Findlay (USMA, 1976) from the corps G-2 section and Maj. Ed Lesnow, USMC, fire support coordinator from the corps artillery. Major Huntoon had joined the corps staff in July 1988 and had taken over planning responsibility for the XVIII Airborne Corps' six contingency plans in Central and Latin America. The trio stayed for five weeks, monitoring Noriega's activities, coordinating their plans with both U.S. Southern Command and U.S. Army South, and working with the various elements that would eventually take part in Just Cause. The original group was replaced by another "planning cell," Stiner's "eyes and ears" in the area. From then until the execution of Just Cause, Stiner kept a "planning cell" in Panama.[6]

In an operation called "Blade Jewel," Southern Command returned some dependents to the United States and ordered servicemen and -women and their families living off-base in Panama to move onto military installations. At that time a total of 51,300 Americans lived in Panama, including 10,300 military troops. None of these actions, however, was sufficient to topple Noriega nor even to cause him a loss of power. There was a temporary reduction in harassment of U.S. personnel but, on the whole, Noriega forged blithely ahead, dominating events in Panama, secure in his mastery of Panama's military and, through it, the bureaucracy and the nation's business.[7]

But during the spring and summer of 1989 there were attempts by the Organization of American States (OAS) to arbitrate a settlement between the government and the opposition. From May until July, the OAS delegation, made up of three OAS foreign ministers—one each from Ecuador, Guatemala, and Trinidad and Tobago—made three trips to Panama to meet with members of the government and the opposition. On 24 May the delegation met with Noriega and opposition members and representatives of the Catholic Church. Endara, Ford, and Arias, in defiance of a government ban, marched in protest outside the hotel where the talks were being held. On 26 May Noriega again met with the delegates and said later that he would not talk to opposition leaders and that it was up to the political parties to settle the matter. On 11 June the delegation returned to Panama and met with Noriega in an effort to transfer power from him to the winners of the May election. The session was of no avail. One member of the OAS said that the meeting was "a disaster." On 14 July the delegation returned to Panama for another attempt at settling the crisis. The meeting began on 16 July and ended in bickering and failure. The government insisted that Noriega would not step down; the opposition demanded that the results of the May election be recognized; and Noriega's representatives, going on the usual offensive, said that the meeting should attack not Noriega but the aggression of the United States against Panama.

The mediators reported to the OAS on 19 July that the situation in Panama "is a crisis which affects government institutions, the economy of the country, and the Panamanian society. The Panamanian people continue to suffer from the virtual disruption of the government system, from a feeling of uncertainty and fear . . . and from violations of human rights."

On 23 August the OAS met for its fourth special session on the Panamanian crisis. At the meeting, the OAS mediators criticized the United States for its recent training exercises that had a "negative effect" on the talks with Noriega, for refusing to discuss the problems with the Panamanian government, and for its efforts to remove Noriega from power "with diplomatic and economic sanctions." At the end of the meeting on 24 August, the OAS issued a statement that reproached the United States for demanding "tough language calling on Noriega to step down" and appealed to both sides in Panama to work out a settlement by 1 September. On that same date, Panama's ruling party announced that it would install a provisional government on 1 September.

Shortly after the OAS meeting, President Bush said he would not abandon the struggle to oust Noriega and would consider further sanctions against Panama. On 31 August, at a special session of the OAS, U.S. Deputy Secretary of State Lawrence S. Eagleburger told the delegates that Noriega had a personal fortune of $200 million to $300 million and furnished details of alleged links between Noriega and the Medellín drug cartel in Colombia. He also made public a letter from Noriega to a London bank, dated 8 February 1988—three days after publication of U.S. indictments of drug charges against him—directing transfer of $14,936,426 to a Luxembourg bank.[8]

During 1988 and during the spring and summer of 1989, a number of incidents, some publicized and some little known for various reasons, escalated the tensions between Panama and the United States. When the U.S. Marines arrived in country during the buildup phase, SOUTHCOM assigned them the mission of protecting the Arraijan Tank Farm, about seven kilometers to the northwest of Howard Air Force Base and near the intersection of the Inter-American Highway and Highway 1, Carpetera Thatcher, that runs directly to the Bridge of the Americas. At the time, Col. J. J. Doyle was the commander of Marine Force, Panama. According to Col. C. E. Richardson, the commander of the Marines during Just Cause, Colonel Doyle and his Marines were involved in "one hell of a firefight with the PDF (??). I question the who because it was probably the PDF and Cubans."

The firefight was on the night of 12 April 1988. By then the Marines had been on duty guarding the tank farm about a week. That night the PDF and, according to some intelligence sources, members of the Cuban Spetznaz Special Forces—Cuban commandos—attacked the Marine outposts around the tank farm. The attack apparently started from an estate owned by a Cuban leftist, National Assembly member Rigoberto Paredes, next to the tank farm. One Marine said later that the attack was a "graduation exercise" for some PDF basic trainees. Later reports indicate that three Cubans were wounded in the attack and taken to a PDF hospital and registered under aliases. One died. The other two were allegedly put on a Cuban ship transiting the canal. ABC News, citing U.S. military intelligence sources, said that men dressed in dark uniforms were seen in a nearby town after the firefight carrying several wounded men and at least one PDF dead from a gunshot wound to the chest. The Marines

18

guarding the tank farm were from reinforced I Company, 3d Battalion, 4th Marine Regiment.

In an incident the night before, Cpl. Ricardo M. Villa Hermosa, twenty-five, a squad leader in Weapons Platoon, India Company, 3/4th Marines, was accidentally killed. One report had it that the Marines were guarding the tank farm when PDF were reported to be intruding. The Marines went out on a split patrol and one of them tripped a flare that went up, sounding like gunfire. One patrol fired on the other, and Villa Hermosa was killed, according to a Camp Lejeune public affairs release.[9]

On 18 May the U.S. Defense Department reported that there had been more than twelve hundred violations of the Panama Canal treaties in the past fifteen months, enumerating specific incidents of harassment of military personnel. On 18–19 May Panamanian security forces had detained seventeen members of the Panamanian company that provided security for the U.S. embassy. On 8 June a U.S. State Department representative disclosed that in recent months Nicaragua had sent planeloads of weapons to Panama in anticipation of possible U.S. military attack. On 8 August U.S. officials arrested twenty-nine armed Panamanians, including nine soldiers, in a restricted area during a U.S. military training exercise. Presumably in retaliation, the PDF on 9 August detained two U.S. soldiers. In reprisal, the United States sealed off Fort Amador, jointly occupied by the PDF and the U.S. military, where the two soldiers were being held. The United States lifted the seal after Panama agreed to release the two soldiers and the United States agreed to release two men seized during the 8 August arrest. In the succeeding days, similar arrests occurred. On 11 August Noriega took his gripes to the United Nations and, charging treaty violations, asked the United Nations to send observers. The United States, not to be outdone, held a "major contingency operation" in Panama City on 17 August.

In response to this increased effort by U.S. forces, the Noriega regime's controlled press tried to create a war hysteria and an anti-American response in the Panamanian populace. The newspaper *La Crítica* ran a front-page story protesting the U.S. maneuvers and claimed that they were linked to an impending invasion.

Noriega's opposition kept up its activities. On 3 August students at the University of Panama demonstrated against the government. When the police fired bird shot at the demonstrators, one student was killed. On the seventeenth of August Olimpo Saenz, publisher of the *Panamanian,* was arrested at his office and jailed for three months on charges of publishing false reports about the government. On August 29 the Panamanian police arrested five members of the opposition party near the Colombian border on charges of threating the national security.

In the face of continuing opposition from the OAS and notwithstanding the fact that many foreign countries had "recalled their ambassadors for consultation" to protest the bogus May elections, on 31 August Noriega's subservient Council of State nominated Francisco Rodriguez, fifty-one, former comptroller general of the treasury and a close crony of Noriega's, to the presidency of Panama. He was sworn in on 1 September to replace the outgoing Manuel Solis Palma. One of the opposition leaders, Ricardo Arias Calderon, said that the

19

Rodriguez appointment was "the equivalent of a coup d'état. . . . This becomes the seventh front man for General Noriega in seven years."

The Council of State, in naming Rodriguez, also said that it would consider a new election in six months provided U.S. economics and military pressure against Noriega ceased. It also dissolved the National Assembly and appointed a commission that would act as the legislature. Thus Noriega tightened the thumbscrews on Panama a few more turns.

On 1 September President Bush declared that the United States would not recognize the new government, would have no diplomatic relations with it, that Panama was, in effect, "without any legitimate government," and that the United States would tighten economic measures to withhold funds from the Panamanian regime. On the same day, the Bush administration announced that it would not accept any administrator of the Panama Canal (due to be selected by Panama and take the job in 1990) named by Noriega. On the fourth of September, the United States barred U.S. companies and U.S. government agencies from trading with companies owned by some 150 Panamanian officials that did business with the U.S. Southern Command military installations. On 12 September the Bush administration announced that it had reinforced a ban on sugar imports. And on 21 September the U.S. government put an additional fourteen Panamanian companies and individuals on a trade blacklist, prohibiting U.S. companies from dealing with them, establishing penalties of ten years' imprisonment and fines of $50,000 for violations.[10]

There was another authority with some power that wanted Noriega to "hang tough": the dons of the Medellín drug cartel of Colombia, who feared that a successor to Noriega might give the United States access to Panamanian bank records, their laundry slips. To emphasize their concern and, in effect, their dominance of Noriega, the lords of the cartel, gruesomely to the point, sent Noriega a miniature coffin, suggesting, rather macabrely, that the only way Noriega could leave Panama was in a life-size one.[11]

But time was beginning to run out for Noriega. Rumbles of unrest and deep discontent within the ranks of the PDF and even within the circle of the dictator's closest advisers were beginning to reach the intelligence "seismographs" of the CIA and the Department of Defense. U.S. Southern Command (USSOUTHCOM), the military headquarters in Panama, watched local developments with increased vigilance. None of the agencies keeping an eye on Panama had long to wait before the next major blip on the EKG tape monitoring the heartbeat of Panama.

3 | A Tightening Noose

In late summer of 1989, Gen. Maxwell R. Thurman, fifty-eight, who had been commissioned through ROTC at North Carolina State University in 1953, had been set to retire from the U.S. Army after finishing a two-year tour as the four-star commander of the Army's Training and Doctrine Command at Fort Monroe, Va., the command responsible for training the Army's officers and men and developing the doctrine with which it would fight its battles. This position, loaded with the heaviest of responsibility, was another in a series of top-level Army jobs that Max Thurman had held and mastered. From November of 1979 to July of 1981 he had run the Army's Recruiting Command and turned it around from a "dead end of the world for an Army officer," in the words of a retired officer who later worked for Max Thurman, to a dynamic, successful operation that asked recruits to "Be all that you can be" instead of pleading with them with the pathetic previous slogan, "Today's Army wants to join you," whatever that meant. "Be all you can be" was also Max Thurman's personal, lifetime philosophy.

After putting the Recruiting Command and, with it, the Army, on its feet in the period between the post-Viet Nam doldrums and the beginning of the Reagan massive buildup, General Thurman became the Army's deputy chief of staff for personnel in the Pentagon, a position that made him responsible for all of the Army's vast array of personnel problems. His success at that job prompted the Army's chief of staff, Gen. John Wickham, Jr., to promote Thurman to four stars and make him the Army's vice chief of staff. General Wickham, in an interview published in *Army Times,* said that he selected Max Thurman as his principal deputy because "he was a detail man" who could handle a wide number of issues. "You have to get into the detail to ensure that the policies will be carried out." Thurman was "instrumental in assuring that we were building solid programs for acquisition and modernization and particularly in the people area. It's one thing to be very brilliant and theoretical, but Max's greatest capability is that he can apply his brilliance in practical ways."

General Thurman, for all his rank and positions of great responsibility, is not without a sense of humor and an ability to deprecate himself. "See me?" he asked when discussing a new slogan for Army recruiting. "The Army's not like me. The Army doesn't wear glasses. The Army hasn't got thin little necks. The Army's great big and strong." But the bespectacled, thin dynamo, with the will and determination of a Patton but the physique and the durability of a long-distance runner, worked through each of his prestigious and responsible positions with a thirst for detail and knowledge, and with skill, dedication, perseverance, and long hours for which he was famous in the Army's top-level circles and especially with those who worked for and with him. He demanded logical results based on exhaustive study and expected his officers and other soldiers to work as hard and as loyally as he did. He never told his staff to work long hours; he just seemed to have an unspoken trust and confidence in his subordinates that they would feel as committed to a project as he was: He knew, intuitively, without having to preach, that they would "do their absolute best." If he felt that a subordinate did not, that person was shortly assigned elsewhere to a less exacting clime. Max Thurman did not countenance the faults expressed in the Peter Principle. Among the officers who worked for him he was known variously, and admiringly, as Mad Max, Maxatollah, and Emperor Maximilian.

In the words of another retired general, "He does not suffer fools gladly." He simply does not accept slipshod thinking or ill-prepared studies. One officer, Col. Bill Sweeney, who worked for Thurman when he was deputy chief of staff for personnel, said, "His management style was to meticulously check you out to see if you knew what you were talking about. And once he had confidence in you, he would give you all kinds of room to succeed. He chewed my ass out once a week, whether I needed it or not. It was rarely unwarranted and usually constructive on the whole. If you had anything at all wrong with what you were working on, he usually found it. It was a painful, demoralizing, depressing experience." Some who worked for Thurman gained from the experience. Others felt somewhat abused. "Half the Army will bad-mouth him to you," Sweeney said, "and the other half will praise him to the skies." But all of them remember that for all his feistiness, his intensity, and his high expectations from his officers and soldiers, he also had compassion. He took care of his troops, looked after them when they needed it, and gave credit when and where due. He could also recognize the worthlessness of even one of his own projects and cancel it the moment a staffer could tell him the facts of its faults and inapplicability.[1]

Max Thurman seems to have little time for nonsense and relaxation. He sleeps only a few hours a night and spends the extra time in the early-morning hours in and near his quarters reading, scanning two or three newspapers, and walking his two Shetland sheep dogs. Max Thurman had never married; he seemed to epitomize that type of officer, totally devoted to the Army, who is alleged to have declared, only partially in jest, that "If the Army wanted you to have a wife, it would have issued you one with your TA-50" (Table of Allowance—basic issue of clothing and equipment). His brother, retired Lt.

Gen. John R. (Roy) Thurman III, a West Pointer, Class of 1946, never married either. They seemed to carry on the bachelor tradition of the Palmer brothers, both of whom had risen to four-star rank and for whom the Thurman brothers worked as young officers. One of the Palmers, Charles D., did eventually marry as a three-star, much to the initial chagrin of his brother, Williston B. Palmer. "Charlie Dog" eventually sired a son, and "Willie B." later recanted and treated his nephew as a grandson.[2]

Retired general William DePuy, a close friend of Thurman's and no slouch himself where energy, vitality, dedication, and productivity are concerned, said of Max Thurman: "Wherever he is, there's sort of a little dust storm of activity. You know, staff officers coming and going, day and night, unusual hours, doing jobs that no other officer would ever ask anybody to do. He gets all these jobs he never had any contact with and does them very well." Gen. Carl Vuono, the Army chief of staff, said of General Thurman: "He epitomizes selfless service, applying every ounce of his will, intellect, and ability to the challenges at hand. From the success of the volunteer force, through the victory of Just Cause, to the ongoing counternarcotics campaign, his standards of excellence set the ultimate example for our Army."[3]

Gen. Frederick F. Woerner, Jr., fifty-seven, USMA Class of 1955, had been the commander in chief of the U.S. Southern Command since April of 1987. He had had long experience in a variety of assignments in Central and South America. From 1966 to 1969 he served with the U.S. Military Group in Guatemala; he was with the Uruguay Military Institute in 1969 and 1970; he was commanding general of the 193d Infantry Brigade in Panama from 1982 to 1986. General Woerner, who spoke Spanish fluently, was intimately familiar with Panama and the Panamanians.[4]

On 17 February 1989, in a speech to a regional business group in Panama, General Woerner said that the United States was "ill prepared" to deal with the Panama situation "because, as you well know, we have a vacuum in Washington in the absence of an appointment of an assistant secretary of state for Latin American affairs." President Bush in a follow-on news conference defended his record of appointments, pointing out that he had already named sixty-seven executive branch appointees compared with fifty-five for President Reagan at the same point in his first term.

On 20 July 1989, Secretary of Defense Cheney announced that General Woerner was to retire. Apparently his criticism of the U.S. policy in Panama had antagonized the Bush administration. He is reported also to have felt that a political solution rather than a military solution to the Noriega problem was a preferred course of action.[5] At about the same time, the secretary asked General Thurman to put off his retirement and take over command of U.S. Southern Command in Panama. Given General Thurman's penchant for challenge and responsibility, he accepted willingly.

On the last weekend in September 1989, two significant command changes in the hierarchy of the U.S. military occurred: General Colin L. Powell, fifty-two, a former national security adviser to President Reagan, assumed the military's number-one position, chairman of the Joint Chiefs of Staff; in Panama, General Thurman assumed command of the U.S. Southern Command. As events were to prove, the selections of the well-rounded, universally accepted, politically "savvy" Colin Powell as the nation's top military leader and of the "aggressive," totally dedicated, widely experienced Max Thurman as the U.S. military boss in Panama were singularly propitious.

Some three days after these changes at the top of the U.S. military structure, a small group of PDF officers in Panama sought to alter their own top-level command structure more radically: They staged a coup. It began with some confidence. At about 0700 hours on 3 October, a procession of military jeeps and trucks carrying standing, armed soldiers jammed into their cargo compartments raced up Avenue A in Panama City and came to a squealing, noisy halt near the Comandancia. Out of the trucks poured about a hundred armed PDF troops who joined another two hundred already in place inside and outside the building. One of the rebel units was the PDF 4th Company. Part of the rebels stormed inside; another group stationed themselves outside. Shortly, gunfire echoed both inside and outside the Comandancia. In about an hour and a half, the firing stopped; the Comandancia was in the hands of the rebels.

One observer, a prisoner of the regime, witnessed the attack from his cellblock in a prison overlooking the Comandancia. He saw a small red helicopter land near the Comandancia. Soon he saw PDF troops set up machine guns around the headquarters. At about 0830 he heard the shooting begin. After a short firefight he saw that the PDF soldiers seemed to be surrendering to other units that had laid siege to the building. And much to his surprise, he saw that some of the so-called Dobermans, Noriega's elite riot unit dressed in riot gear and wearing helmets and carrying truncheons, were among the rebel forces.

At about 1130, the rebel leaders broadcast a communiqué on national radio announcing that General Noriega had been captured, that he and his entire high command had been forced into retirement, and that new elections would be held. The rebels added that the coup was "strictly a military movement" and that "there is no politics involved." The rebels also captured a state radio station and a Noriega-controlled TV station.

The leader of the coup was apparently Maj. Moises Giroldi Vega, the thirty-eight-year-old commander of the Urraca battalion, which was in charge of the security of the Comandancia. That Giroldi was the leader of the coup was surprising because he had been a loyalist and had been key to putting down a previous coup attempt in March of 1988. In fact, Noriega was the godfather of one of Giroldi's children. Other leaders of the coup, both of whom had signed the communiqué, were Capt. Jesús George Balma, chief of the PDF Special Forces, and Capt. Edgardo Dandoval, chief of the company responsible for public order.

The apparent success of the coup was short-lived. At about 1000 hours, a few hours after the fighting started, the elite PDF Battalion 2000, a well-equipped and well-trained unit, with many of its members Cuban-trained, left its base at Fort Cimarron, near Torrijos/Tocumen Airport, about fifteen miles northeast of the Comandancia. Battalion 2000, with some two hundred to three hundred officers and men "on a good day," according to one U.S. officer, allegedly contained 90 percent of the PDF firepower—including 120mm mortars, rocket launchers, and armored personnel carriers. Once it arrived at the Comandancia,

24

Battalion 2000, led by Maj. Francisco Olechea, encircled and attacked the rebels with rifle fire, grenades, and mortars. "Heavy fighting" took place in the early afternoon but, by 1400 hours, the battle was about over. Battalion 2000 was gathering up the rebels outside; the ones inside surrendered after little additional fighting. The loyalists recaptured the radio and TV station that the rebels had seized earlier in the day. Ten rebel troops, including Major Giroldi, died during the coup attempt; eighteen loyal troops and five civilians were wounded.[6]

As it so happens in even the best-laid military combat plans, the 3 October coup ran into complications, unexpected and unplanned-for developments, and failed. Murphy's Law was in effect even in Panama. In the first place, in planning the coup, Giroldi had counted on the neutrality of Olechea and Battalion 2000. But Olechea reneged and decided to come to Noriega's rescue simply because Giroldi did not get word to him that Noriega had been captured early in the fighting. Loyalist commanders then pressured Olechea to act. Giroldi's widow, who escaped to Miami after the botched coup, called Olechea a "turncoat."

In the second place, the rebels had expected over a thousand members of the PDF to join the revolt. As it turned out, fewer than three hundred troops made the scene. Nor did the coup planners seem to care much about security and secrecy. The United States, and even an exile in Miami, knew about the attempt before it was launched. Noriega reputedly had wind of the plot, but not the exact time and date.

In the third place, the rebels apparently had very limited goals. The coup leaders were midlevel officers whose goals were not the overthrow of the government—they even offered to recognize Noriega's puppet president, Francisco Rodriguez—but redress for low pay and lack of promotions. According to a spokesman for the U.S. secretary of defense, Giroldi had "no program, no civilian connection, nothing we could latch onto."

In the fourth place, the rebel leader, Giroldi, after having cornered Noriega in his office, where he was protected by two loyal bodyguards armed with submachine guns, tried to reason with him and persuade him to retire instead of killing him or turning him over to the Americans. He never placed him under arrest.

How Noriega and his loyal supporters broke the rebels' hold on the Comandancia is not clear. Certainly, the arrival of Battalion 2000 at midday had a significant effect on assisting in quelling the rebellion. In addition, apparently Noriega radioed orders to loyalists outside the building to gather up the families of the rebel leaders and hold them as hostages. Another version holds that the rebels allowed Noriega to telephone his mistress, Vicky Amado, who in turn contacted loyal army leaders, who came to his rescue. A third version may have some credibility. In this scenario, Noriega, still under control by the rebel leaders, learns that the loyal units have the building surrounded. Then he faces an armed Giroldi and yells at him: "To be a commander, you have to have balls. You don't have balls." In the face of the tirade, Giroldi wilts and surrenders. There is even some speculation that at that point Noriega "explodes in rage and orders the immediate execution of several of the coup leaders" and personally kills Giroldi. Another version—and this is probably the most exact—holds that Noriega ordered the PDF to move the leaders of the coup to Tinajitis, site of the PDF Mortar School, where they were tortured for more information on the coup leaders and then executed. Two days later, Noriega said that he had negotiated his own freedom from his captors and that "he had talked them into laying down their arms."

Noriega's reaction to the coup was swift and retributive. On the evening of 3 October he appeared on national television and called the rebellion a further attempt by the United States to prevent the implementation of the 1977 Panama Canal treaties and to "install another government of sellouts." He said that the coup "was part of the continuing aggression and penetration of the PDF by the United States." He also admitted that he had had advance knowledge of the coup. He imposed a curfew that night, and the next day Panama City was apparently "calm." On the fourth, his government announced that ten rebel soldiers, including Giroldi, had died, twenty-one had been wounded, and that thirty-seven soldiers had been taken prisoner.

Surprisingly, some of the prisoners were of high rank and held responsible positions in the PDF. Their defection indicated high-level discontent with Noriega's regime. Among the prisoners were Col. Guillermo J. Wong, the head of military intelligence; Col. Julion Ow Young, a member of the general staff of the PDF, who supervised the hated "Dobermans"; Lt. Col. Armando Palacios Gondola, head of the agency that worked with the United States on joint military operations; and two members of the Strategic Military Council set up by Noriega after the failed 1988 coup as an alternative to the general staff of the PDF. One of Noriega's close confidants said, "This was no gringo plot. This came from the general's inner core." U.S. officials said that the 4th Company, which had sided with the rebels, was "purged," and that some of the coup leaders had been tortured and then executed.

On the fifth, Noriega called for a "crackdown" on the opposition, banned unauthorized assemblies, and urged government employees to turn in traitors. He also froze the salaries of civilian government employees, some of whom had reacted too rapidly to word that the coup had succeeded and had happily torn photos of Noriega from their office walls. Noriega cautioned the Panamanians that he might impose "emergency laws" and that, under the current circumstances, this was "no time to talk democracy." Summing up his philosophy of command, certainly no surprise to the browbeaten citizens of Panama, he said that there would be "clubs for the indecisive, bullets for enemies, and money for friends" during the current crisis.

In keeping with that philosophy, on the night of the fifth, armed PDF troops attacked the offices of the opposition coalition and seized about a dozen members of the Liberal Party, including Endara, who was released by the weekend and took refuge in the Vatican diplomatic mission. The Panamanian government admitted that seventy-seven opponents had been jailed and that many others had been "beaten up" on the streets.

Noriega had regained control after a very short fall from power. But in spite of—perhaps because of—the rapidity and brutality of his "crackdown" on the rebels and the opposition, he must have sensed that his ironclad control might

26

be cracking and that he could not know whence might come the next attempt. In a figurative sense, he had to look to his rear constantly. His daily change of sleeping quarters was an indication of his increasing paranoia.

The role of the United States in the 3 October rebellion might be described as one of studied, minor involvement almost to the point of detached passivity but nonetheless with great concern and interest, to and including the White House, in the outcome.

The U.S. administration was aware in advance that rebels were planning a coup. On Sunday, 1 October, Giroldi advised representatives of the CIA in Panama that a coup attempt was "imminent." In spite of the long connection between the PDF and U.S. intelligence agencies, this was apparently the first indication the United States had of the pending coup. Because of Giroldi's previous close ties to Noriega, however, U.S. officials were skeptical and suspected perhaps a Noriega "sting" operation, an attempt to draw the United States into committing itself prematurely, to the detriment of its relations with the rest of Latin American nations, who are always concerned about undue *yanqui* influence in the area. "Giroldi's a bastard, a sort of mini-Noriega," declared one Pentagon spokesman. "Warning signs went up. We feared a Noriega trap." The fact that both Generals Powell and Thurman had been in their posts only a couple of days added to the suspicion of a "sting." U.S. officials had learned to respect Noriega's deviousness, resiliency, and cunning.[7]

A change of command in the military establishment is a significant event—not only for the commanders involved but perhaps, more important, for the command itself. The staff and commanders are faced with a new leader whose policies, work methods, temperament, and personality are generally unknown. And the higher the level of the command, the more widespread is the impact of the new leader.

The change of command at SOUTHCOM on 30 September 1989 was such an event. General Woerner was leaving for retirement, and General Thurman was assuming command just days after he thought he was going to retire. The staff and commanders in SOUTHCOM had heard of the legendary Max Thurman and his penchant for long hours, hard work, and attention to detail and the fact that he expected the same dedication from his staff. The officers in SOUTHCOM were resigned to lost weekends and long workdays and work-nights.

After the change of command ceremony on Saturday, Max Thurman went to his office. His staff gave him a series of detailed briefings on all of the nations in his command area, with emphasis on the current situation in Panama. General Thurman was in his office the next day, Sunday, just as if it were any other workday. To him, it was. At about 2230, one of his staff officers reported to him that the CIA had had a report from the wife of one of the senior PDF officers that a coup was planned for the next day. At 0200 the next morning, two men from the CIA reported to General Thurman that the leader of the coup was Maj. Moises Giroldi, who, they added, had been instrumental in putting down a coup against Noriega in March of 1988. He had handed the coup leaders over to Noriega, who had had them tortured and imprisoned. To General Thurman, the details of the coup seemed ridiculously amateurish. He thought it benevolent after the CIA representatives told him that Giroldi simply wanted Noriega to retire.

General Thurman called Lt. Gen. Thomas W. Kelly, director of operations (J-3) on General Powell's JCS staff, at his home on a secure phone at about 0230 and gave him what details he knew. He said that the rebels wanted SOUTHCOM troops to assist by blocking two access roads into Panama City, one near the jointly occupied Fort Amador and the other at the Bridge of the Americas. The rebels reasoned that by blocking these roads they would prevent the loyal 5th and 7th PDF companies from getting into Panama City and the Comandancia in time to block the coup. The rebels wanted no other U.S. assistance. Thurman recommended that the United States stay out of it. The whole setup looked too suspicious from a number of angles.[8]

General Powell had just taken over chairmanship of the Joint Chiefs of Staff at midnight on the first of October. General Kelly woke him early on Monday morning, Powell's first day on duty, with the news from Panama. General Powell relayed the news to Secretary Cheney at his home and then headed for the Pentagon in the dark of an early Monday morning.

Later that morning, after a meeting in Secretary Cheney's office, the secretary, Generals Powell and Kelly, and Rear Adm. Edward D. Sheafer, the deputy director of the Defense Intelligence Agency for support of the JCS, headed for the White House. General Powell briefed the president on the developments and recommended that, due to the nature of the coup's plan and the doubts about the leader, the United States not get involved—at least for now. The rebels would "have to do it alone."

There was no coup on Monday. Giroldi's wife said that it would happen on Tuesday, the third.[9]

On Tuesday morning, General Thurman was up before dawn and in his office in Quarry Heights. At 0740 he had a report that there was shots fired in the vicinity of the Comandancia, about a mile from Quarry Heights. As soon as Max Thurman got word that the coup was under way, he called General Powell and relayed as much information as he had—which, at that point, was probably very little. General Powell asked about Noriega's whereabouts. General Thurman at that point could not give a definitive answer. Powell ordered the roadblocks into effect, and Thurman ordered his twelve thousand in-country troops to assume "Delta" alert, wherein troops in battle gear move to previously reconnoitered positions to protect and defend U.S. installations in the area. In the blocking positions, U.S. units from Fort Amador got in the way of the PDF 5th Infantry Company, which shared a portion of Fort Amador with the Americans. Other units from the U.S. Howard Air Force Base took up a position near the Bridge of the Americas to impede the 7th Infantry Company, which was some sixty miles to the southwest of Panama City. The PDF did not confront the Americans at either roadblock.

Fort Clayton is the main U.S. Army base in Panama and the headquarters of U.S. Army South's commander, Brig. Gen. (at that time) Marc A. Cisneros. Sometime late in the morning, two rebel lieutenants reported to the gate at Fort Clayton. The MPs took them to General Cisneros's office. General Cisneros was called "The *Simpático* Soldier" by *U.S. News & World Report* in its 30 July 1990 issue. He had spent four years in Panama, spoke fluent Spanish, frequently visited small towns in Panama, and spoke to the people in their native tongue. He called Noriega a "dime-store dictator." He was a hero to the Panamanians who knew him.[10]

The rebel lieutenants told General Cisneros that the coup had been successful and that Noriega was under arrest in the Comandancia. General Cisneros passed this information to General Thurman and up the chain to the Pentagon and the White House, who decided to tell the rebels that the United States "was prepared to lift this burden from their hands." The rebels turned down the offer, apparently in keeping with the very unambitious and dangerous goals they had set for themselves. The rebels never did want to turn over Noriega to the United States, even though a botched message from Panama read that the rebels "want" to turn over Noriega instead of the correct "won't" turn over Noriega.

On 8 October Secretary of State James A. Baker and Secretary of Defense Richard Cheney confirmed a report in the *Washington Post* that early on the afternoon of 3 October, General Powell had relayed authorization to General Thurman to remove Noriega to a U.S. military base if that could be done without an overt show of American force. But by the time Max Thurman received the authority, the coup had collapsed. Thurman had also been authorized two other options: the first was to receive Noriega if the rebels handed him over, and the second was to seize Noriega by overt military force—but only on the authority of the president.

The U.S. congressional reaction to the failed coup was typical: Some members of Congress praised the Bush administration for its caution in avoiding an all-out rush to aid the rebels, while other more combative and vociferous members, both Republicans and Democrats, deplored the fact that the administration let slip through its cautious hands a unique opportunity finally to bring Noriega to justice. Congressman Dave McCurdy (D., Okla.) said, "Yesterday makes Jimmy Carter look like a man of resolve. There's a resurgence of the wimp factor." And some editorials matched the botched handling of the coup to Kennedy's Bay of Pigs fiasco and Carter's Iran hostage rescue mission.

On 4 October Secretary Cheney said that the rebels "were clearly not of a mind to turn [Noriega] over to us. They were talking about having him retire in Panama. They were not willing to have him extradited to the United States." On that same day, Marlin Fitzwater, the White House spokesman, said that the United States had "traditionally stopped short of . . . military involvement" and that President Bush did not want to interfere in the affairs of a Latin American nation. Secretary Baker testified before the Senate Finance Committee and repeated that the United States retained the option of using force but that "if you're going to risk American lives, it's the president's view that you do so on your own timetable. You do so based on your own plans, at a time of maximum opportunity and advantage."

Those assertions from the administration did not assuage the belligerency of the likes of ultraconservative senator Jesse Helms (R., N.C.), the ranking Republican on the Senate Intelligence Committee. Apparently he and other members of that committee had been briefed by the CIA that the rebels held Noriega, that they wanted to turn him over to the United States, and that they had invited U.S. troops to fight their way into the Comandancia and capture Noriega. On 5 October, after it had become clear that the administration had done little to seize Noriega or to aid the rebels, Senator Helms called the Bush team a bunch of "Keystone Kops" who showed a "total lack of planning." In rebuttal, Secretary Cheney, well aware of the reluctance of the rebels to capture Noriega or to turn him over to the United States, called Senator Helms's version of the event "hogwash" and defended the decision to avoid an open battle with the PDF.

Congressman Les Aspin (D., Wis.) was bluntly positive: "We should go in and capture Noriega." He declared that we didn't need military intervention but just a "snatch. All I want is Noriega." Senator John Kerry (D., Mass.) surprisingly described the administration's timidity as "a black mark on our diplomacy and our values."

As a final put-down to Helms, the Senate on 5 October voted 74–25 against a Helms proposal that would have allowed the president to use armed force to seize Noriega, bring him to trial in the United States, and restore democracy to Panama.[11]

One result of the coup attempt was an 11 October meeting between senior administration officials and members of the Senate Intelligence Committee. President Bush called the meeting in an attempt to smooth the relations between the administration and the committee's chairman, Senator David Boren (D., Okla.). Present at the meeting were President Bush, national security adviser Gen. Brent Scowcroft, Senator Boren, and the committee's vice chairman, William S. Cohen (R., Me.). The group discussed new guidelines for intelligence operatives in Panama in the event of another coup. The guidelines would make clear what was and what was not permissible in the intelligence-gathering activities. One guideline would provide for U.S. military, diplomatic, and intelligence officials in Panama to engage in clearer and speedier communications with the potential coup leaders. A former CIA director said that "The first, the absolute first thing you do in this case [a coup attempt] is to put somebody with a radio next to him."

The administration also decided, after reviewing Scowcroft's analysis of the 3 October debacle, to convene automatically the Deputies Committee as a crisis-management body in future emergencies. The Deputies Committee, made up of the second-highest-ranking officers of the State and Defense departments, of the Joint Chiefs of Staff, and of the CIA, would monitor the flow of information feeding into the White House Situation Room and take appropriate action.

But the 3 October coup, a blundering, low-level, limited-objective failure, was not without other benefits to the United States—both to the civilian and military sides of the administration. When the dust of the coup had settled a bit, the Bush planners in the White House could understand even more clearly the vulnerability and tenuousness of Noriega's power. They also hoped that Noriega's brutality in putting down the rebellion might "fire up" the opposition and lead to another, more successful attempt to oust him. And the White House realized that Noriega's strength, the PDF, might be waning in view of the rank and number of PDF officers who were purged by Noriega in the aftermath of the coup.

The planners in the Pentagon and in USSOUTHCOM learned a great deal from the reaction of the various elements of the PDF. According to one of the planners of Just Cause, the intelligence and operations sections of USSOUTHCOM "watched Noriega move his forces around" and learned of the loyalty and strength of the 6th and 7th companies at Rio Hato, the 5th at Fort Amador, and Battalion 2000 at Fort Cimarron. They also identified those PDF officers who were Noriega supporters and those who might assist the United States in the future. These were some of the more obvious merits emerging from the coup. But underneath these results, the planning at USSOUTHCOM went on with increased intensity and tempo.[12]

4 | The Planning Phase

The worsening political situation in Panama sent waves of increased work loads through the planning staffs not only of the JCS and SOUTHCOM but also through the principal tactical command, the XVIII Airborne Corps at Fort Bragg, North Carolina. With each passing day it became clearer that the Bush administration might be required to take some decisive military action in its own national interest.

The XVIII Airborne Corps is the U.S. Army's primary command for quick-reaction contingency-type operations. The corps commander has under him a vast array of active Army units (with many U.S. Army Reserve and National Guard units subject to call-up to fill out the units needed for specific operations) that he can tailor to meet a wide variety of possible contingencies around the world. The divisions under the immediate command of the corps commander are the 82d Airborne Division, at Fort Bragg; the 101st Airborne Division (Air Assault), at Fort Campbell, Kentucky; the 10th Mountain Division (Light Infantry), at Fort Drum, New York; the 24th Infantry Division (Mechanized), at Fort Stewart, Georgia; and, for contingency planning, the 7th Infantry Division (Light), at Fort Ord, California. The corps also commands two separate maneuver brigades, the 197th Infantry Brigade (Mechanized) (now the 3d Brigade, 24th Mech Division), at Fort Benning, Georgia, and the 194th Armored Brigade, at Fort Knox, Kentucky. In addition, the corps commands ten separate combat support and combat service support brigades, including the 18th Aviation Brigade, the XVIII Airborne Corps Artillery, the 20th Engineer Brigade, the 525th Military Intelligence Brigade, the 16th Military Police Brigade, the 35th Signal Brigade, the 18th Personnel Group, the XVIII Corps Finance Group, the I Corps Support Command, and the Dragon Brigade, all at Fort Bragg. The entire command consists of some eighty-five thousand troops at posts scattered throughout the United States.

In August General Thurman had not yet taken over SOUTHCOM, but he made himself ready to do so in the interim. He flew into Fort Bragg to review both the Joint Special Operations Command (JSOC) and the XVIII Airborne Corps contingency plans for Panama. The staff discussed "Blue Spoon," a plan already in existence for military action by U.S. forces against the PDF. After the briefing, given by officers of the corps staff and the Joint Special Operations Command, General Thurman made some suggestions (he was not yet in the chain of command and therefore not in a position to issue directives) dealing with the size of the forces involved. He also expressed his personal view that enough force should be committed initially to overwhelm the opposition in every objective area. He pointed out that superior force and firepower save the lives of Americans as well as Panamanians. He also arranged for Maj. Gen. William A. Roosma, the XVIII Airborne Corps deputy commanding general, to visit Panama.[1]

In early September, General Roosma and a team of key commanders and staff officers from the corps flew to Panama to conduct a detailed reconnaissance of the area of operations and to meet with SOUTHCOM staff and the major commanders on the ground. Based on this reconnaissance and discussion, Lt. Gen. Carl Stiner, the XVIII Airborne Corps commander, raised to the highest level the priority of work for the corps staff on the Panama contingency plan. Col. Thomas H. Needham, the corps G-3, and Col. William H. Walters, the corps G-2, worked long hours with their staffs to revise the Blue Spoon plan, incorporating General Thurman's guidance. Colonel Needham set up a planning cell with LTC Tim McMahon, the corps director of plans, and Maj. David H. Huntoon, Jr., the corps principal planner for Panama, as the editor and author, respectively, of the new operations plan. The result was XVIII Airborne Corps Op Plan 90-2, which became the essential planning blueprint for Operation Just Cause. Although based on Blue Spoon, Op Plan 90-2 called for the rapid deployment and the simultaneous employment of overwhelming combat power—both from special operations forces and conventional forces. The planners knew that this unique combination would be effective but complex. But they also knew that they could make it work.[2]

After the failed 3 October coup, and once he was in command of SOUTHCOM, General Thurman wasted no time in accelerating the revision of the SOUTHCOM plan. His chief planner was BG William Hartzog, the J-3 for USSOUTHCOM. Thurman first gave his explicit guidance to the planners. They, in turn, set to work updating the plan and reconnoitering the entire area of operations.

On 9 October, at the request of General Thurman, General Stiner and his key staff, including Colonels Needham and Walters, flew to Panama for a contingency planning summit. Operational security was a major concern for the members of the team from Fort Bragg. They wore civilian clothes, flew in a special-mission (unmarked) aircraft, and scheduled their arrival at Howard Air Force Base in Panama during darkness. For three full days and nights, the two staffs huddled in the USSOUTHCOM Command Post at Quarry Heights, compared their plans, and ironed out operational and tactical details of potential PDF targets and U.S. responsibilities. XVIII Airborne Corps Op Plan 90-2 served as a baseline for this planning session. One salient feature emerged from the

33

conference: In any contingency, General Stiner would be in overall command of all U.S. combat forces, regardless of service, and including Special Operations Forces. Thurman recognized the all-important principle of "unity of command"—one man in charge of all forces—neglected in such operations as Grenada and the hostage mission in Iran, and insisted on its application in this operation.[3]

While his staff was working with the SOUTHCOM staff revising the plans, General Stiner went on a personal helicopter reconnaissance of the probable areas of operation with Col. Mike Snell, the commander of the 193d Infantry Brigade, stationed permanently in Panama. Snell was intimately familiar with Panama, its terrain, road networks, cities, and force deployments. Colonel Snell's headquarters was at Fort Clayton, directly in front of the Miraflores Locks of the Panama Canal. His brigade consisted of one airborne infantry battalion, the 1st of the 508th Airborne, at Fort Kobbe (south of Howard Air Force Base), and one light infantry battalion, the 5th of the 87th Infantry, at Fort Clayton. General Stiner's air reconnaissance helped him to round out his analysis of "METT-T"—the Army's acronym for mission, enemy, troops, terrain, and time—all elements that must be carefully studied to develop a workable operational plan. He looked carefully at the various locations he thought would be significant objectives in "taking down" the PDF, Noriega's backbone of power. These sites included, as a first priority, the Comandancia, Noriega's major military and political headquarters; then Tinajitas, the location of the PDF's 1st Rifle Company and its mortar school; Panama Viejo, where several PDF elements had moved following the 3 October coup; Fort Espinar, in the "old" Canal Zone, the location of the PDF 8th Company; and the key terrain features and road networks surrounding these principal PDF locations.

General Thurman, acting on guidance from the White House and the JCS, dictated that the continency plan for Panama must include the following objectives: Protect U.S. lives and key sites and facilities; capture and deliver Noriega to competent authority; neutralize the Panamanian Defense Forces; support the establishment of a United States–recognized government in Panama; and restructure the PDF.[4]

With these objectives in mind, General Stiner and the staffs of both USSOUTHCOM and the XVIII Airborne Corps decided that Joint Task Force South (the name of General Stiner's command in the operation) would have to neutralize or protect some twenty-seven major targets simultaneously, employing surprise and minimizing collateral (i.e., not mission-essential) damage. Additional major targets outside Panama City included Río Hato, some 70 miles southwest of Panama City and the location of the elite 6th PDF Mechanized Company and the 7th PDF Ranger Company (Machos des Montes—Men of the Mountains), key players in the Noriega countercoup battle on 3 October; Torrijos-Tocumen Airport, for use as a second aerial port of embarkation (in addition to the U.S. Howard Air Force Base) on the eastern side of the Panama Canal, from which U.S. forces could block the advance of the PDF Battalion 2000 at Fort Cimarron (this battalion had been another key force in the 3 October countercoup battle); Kurt Muse; and Noriega himself, known by now for his elusiveness, use of decoys (two cars each possibly containing Noriega going in opposite directions), and the strength of his personal security forces.

Lt. Gen. Carl W. Stiner, fifty-three, is a rangy six-footer from Tennessee who has lost none of his Tennessee drawl, twang, and sense of humor. He has a vibrant personality, a down-to-earth, direct approach to problems, and a frankness that is disarming and brooks no rationalizations or compromises. Passivity is not part of his makeup. He gets the facts, makes a decision, and gets on with the mission—whatever its nature. He graduated from Tennessee Polytechnical Institute with a B.S. in agriculture and was commissioned through the ROTC program. His career has been crammed with a variety of important command and staff assignments, ranging from commanding an infantry training brigade at Fort Benning, to project manager for training the Saudi Arabian National Guard, to chief of staff of the Rapid Deployment Joint Task Force at MacDill Air Force Base, to commander of the Joint Special Operations Command at Fort Bragg, to commander of the 82d Airborne Division. He is a Ranger and a master parachutist and obviously well qualified in "special" operations.[5]

In 1985 General Stiner was the commander of JSOC (Joint Special Operations Command). It was also in 1985 that four Palestinian terrorists took over the Italian cruise ship *Achille Lauro* when it was about thirty miles from Port Said. The terrorists rounded up about a hundred passengers in the ship's dining room and, using them as hostages, demanded the release of fifty Palestinian terrorists in Israeli jails. On 8 October 1985, off the coast of Syria, the terrorists murdered Leon Klinghoffer, a retired American who had suffered a stroke and was confined to a wheelchair.

Oliver North, in his role as chief planner for antiterrorism contingencies on the NSC, recommended to the president the deployment of a JSOC special antiterrorist team to try to nab the terrorists wherever they finally arrived. In the end, the terrorists boarded an Egyptian airliner after the *Achille Lauro* docked off Alexandria. North had already gotten President Reagan's approval to have the Navy force the plane to land in Sicily—but forbade the use of any force that would harm innocent people.

General Stiner and his team in two C-141's landed just after the Egyptian 737. Stiner's men quickly surrounded the 737, which was still "buttoned up" and had one engine running. The pilot refused to open the door or turn off the engine. "Then General Stiner," according to North in his book *Under Fire,* "had a portable stairway brought over. Stiner, one of the braver men on this planet, laid down his weapon, climbed the stairway, and opened the door. He was met by an Egyptian commando officer who pointed his submachine gun straight at the general.

" 'I don't want you,' Stiner said. 'I want them.' "

The commando lowered his weapon and turned over the terrorists to Stiner and his men.[6] That was not the end of the *Achille Lauro* hijacking, but it points out the part played by Stiner and the sort of dedicated special operations officer he is.

General Stiner's unique background as a commander and staff officer of both special operations and conventional forces proved to be remarkably significant for all the diverse units of Joint Task Force South. That experience meant that General Stiner was able to provide both a sound planning insight and strong, confident leadership of all his forces when the plan was executed. Just Cause was to prove one salient point: Special operations forces and conventional forces could be meshed and integrated into one cohesive, effective fighting command.

He made his "war-fighting philosophy" clear to his planners: Hit first; surprise the enemy; overwhelm him with heavy combat power; use the cover of night for surprise during the initial assault and the follow-on attack so that one's superior forces are on the objectives at dawn; and fight under favorable conditions. With that guidance, the corps planners returned to Fort Bragg on 11 October. During the next week they revised OpPlan 90-2. This revision specified new postcoup PDF targets, expanded certain specified tasks to subordinate units, and integrated the streamlined command and control of all joint war-fighting forces in Panama under the leadership of General Stiner.[7]

General Stiner also deployed forward to Fort Clayton a six-man planning staff cell as a command and control advance element. Its mission was to refine contingency planning and report to General Stiner as a "directed telescope" on PDF activity. General Stiner also placed twenty key commanders and staff at Fort Bragg on a two-hour recall alert, and sharply increased senior staff and command focus on Panama for a potential contingency crisis.

On 19 October General Stiner and his corps key staffers made another "civilian clothes" visit to Panama. This time Stiner had called for a meeting of the commanders and staffs of the major units that would be involved in the operation. These included Maj. Gen. James H. Johnson, Jr., commander of the 82d; his G-3, Lt. Col. Dan K. McNeill; and his chief of plans, Maj. Bill Caldwell; Brig. Gen. Robert L. Ord, assistant division commander of the 7th Infantry Division (Light); and the task force commanders and senior operational staff of U.S. forces in Panama—Army, Air Force, Navy, and Marine Corps—including Lt. Gen. Peter Kempf, commander of the 12th Air Force; Brig. Gen. Robin Tornow, commander of Howard Air Force Base in Panama; Rear Adm. Jerry G. Gnecknow; and Col. Charles Richardson, commander of the Marines in Panama. Stiner's purpose in calling this two-day meeting, held in the Simón Bolívar Conference Room at Fort Clayton, the home of the U.S. Army South's headquarters, was to present the plan to his war-fighting commanders and "put all of the details together."[8]

By mid-November Noriega's increased belligerency toward Americans and his arrogance toward the Bush administration were beginning to be more and more apparent. On 15 November General Stiner and his principal operational staff officers made a third planning and orientation trip to Panama. But this one took on the aspects of more than a planning conference. The team from Fort Bragg included Colonel Needham; Colonel Walters; Col. Bill Mason, the Corps signal officer; and Major Huntoon. They flew to Panama in the crew compartment of one of two C-5A Galaxy cargo planes. These giant aircraft also carried six AH-64 Apache Attack helicopters and three OH-58 Kiowa Scout helicopters, along with four M-551 Sheridan tanks. The two C-5A's arrived at Howard Air Force Base under cover of darkness on 15 and 16 November. The

36

helicopters and tanks were quickly unloaded and moved to covered locations—a blacked-out hangar. Three days later, key commanders and staff of the 82d Airborne Division and the 7th Infantry Division joined General Stiner at Fort Clayton for another contingency conference.

During this period, General Thurman had received information about potential terrorist attacks—sponsored by the PDF—against U.S. military installations throughout Panama. In response to these threats, the CINC activated Joint Task Force South (JTFSO), with General Stiner as commander, from 18 to 27 November. SOUTHCOM's alert status was also increased. Once this crisis receded, General Stiner returned to Fort Bragg, but the week of JTSFO command post training at Fort Clayton was to prove an excellent rehearsal for Operation Just Cause.[9]

While General Stiner was not in Panama planning, reconnoitering, and talking to and briefing subordinate commanders, he was visiting various major command headquarters in the United States, briefing the details of his plan. From mid-October to mid-November he made three trips to the Pentagon to brief the chairman of the Joint Chiefs and his staff. He briefed Admiral Frank Kelso, commander of the U.S. Atlantic Command, at his headquarters in Norfolk. Admiral Kelso was responsible for providing critical air cover for the D-day MAC airlift from CONUS bases to Panama. He visited Scott Air Force Base to brief the commander in chief of the Military Airlift Command (CINCMAC), Gen. Hansford T. Johnson. He sent Colonels Needham and Walters to brief the commanding general of the U.S. Army Forces Command, Gen. Edwin H. Burba, Jr., at his headquarters in Fort McPherson, Georgia. Stiner made certain that all major commands—Army, Navy, Air Force, and Marines—were in sync on the plan. This operation, Stiner assured himself, was not going to be another Grenada.[10]

At the end of November and in the first part of December, both conventional and special operations forces conducted rehearsals of their parts of OpPlan 90-2. These rehearsals were at Fort Bragg, at Eglin Air Force Base in Florida, in Panama, and at other locations in the southeastern United States. Operational security continued to be a major concern of all the commands. Rehearsals were done as parts of routine training exercises. Only a small number of senior commanders and staff in each unit knew about the link to the actual contingency plan.

General Thurman had scheduled a fourth planning conference, for 18 December. But by that time, Noriega had lost any composure he might have had. His paranoid ranting against the United States, his provocative acts against U.S. citizens and members of the U.S. military, and his seemingly out-of-control bouts of megalomania sealed his fate.

On 15 December, the 510-member, Noriega-appointed National Assembly of Representatives voted to raise his stature to head of government and "maximum leader of the struggle for national liberation" (apparently "liberation" from the dominance of the United States). At that same session, echoing Noriega's bellicosity and chest-thumping egotism, the National Assembly approved a resolution stating that "the Republic of Panama is declared to be in a state of war" with the United States as long as U.S. "aggression," in the form of economic sanctions imposed in 1988, continued. U.S. officials, with some logic but minimum reaction to such a declaration, concluded that Noriega had in fact declared war against the United States. But the pro-Noriega clique in Panama said, with self-serving logic, that it was simply a statement of the state of affairs brought about by the actions of the Bush administration.[11]

The next day, Saturday, the sixteenth of December, words of bombast gave way to acts of brutal harassment. Some PDF guards stopped a private car, a 1981 Chevrolet with Michigan license plates and carrying four off-duty, unarmed U.S. servicemen, at a roadblock outside PDF headquarters, the Comandancia, in the old section of Panama City. The PDF and a crowd of unruly civilians milled about the car. Panamanian soldiers tried to drag the U.S. officers from the car, but the Americans, apparently in some fear, attempted to drive away through the throng. The PDF opened fire with an AK-47 and mortally wounded one of the men in the car, Marine lieutenant Robert Paz, twenty-five, and wounded another officer in the ankle. Photos of the car after the incident showed at least three bullet holes in the car—two on the driver's side and one through the trunk. Later, the other men in the car explained that they had made a wrong turn and had gotten lost; the PDF counterclaimed that they were on an unauthorized reconnaissance.

Shortly after that incident, the PDF took into custody Lt. Adam J. Curtis, a Navy lieutenant, and his wife, Bonnie, who had been stopped at the same roadblock about a half hour earlier and had witnessed the shooting of Lieutenant Paz. The PDF blindfolded both of them with masking tape, held them in custody, interrogated them repeatedly, beat the officer brutally, kicked him in the groin and the head, and threatened to kill him if he did not give them information about his unit and his activities. The PDF threatened the officer's wife with sexual harassment—fondling her neck and the backs of her legs—and then cut her head when they slammed her against a wall to emphasize their point. She collapsed on the floor. When Lieutenant Curtis protested the treatment of his wife, the PDF interrogators shoved wads of paper into his mouth. One of them put a gun to Curtis's head and kicked him repeatedly in the groin. One of the soldiers told Bonnie that her husband would never again be able "to perform in bed." After four hours of interrogation and beatings, the PDF abruptly escorted the pair to an avenue that led back to the U.S. area and released them. Lieutenant Curtis and his wife made their way back to the U.S. Naval Station at about 0215.[12]

On Monday, 18 December, a U.S. lieutenant shot and wounded a PDF military policeman, Corp. Cesar Tejada, near a U.S. installation. As an isolated incident, the circumstances might make the officer appear culpable. But given the increased tension in Panama City and Noriega's threats to Americans, the circumstances take on an entirely different look. The officer was in his car leaving a laundry in the Curundu area of western Panama City about a mile from PDF Headquarters and near Southern Command headquarters at Quarry Heights. The uniformed PDF soldier approached the officer's car and signaled him to stop. Later the officer claimed that he had felt "threatened" by the corporal, who appeared to be reaching for his gun. The officer fired two shots at

38

the PDF soldier, wounding him, according to one account, in the leg and the arm. He fell to the ground, then got up and left the scene.

On that same day, at a news conference, President Bush called the killing of Lieutenant Paz an "enormous outrage and a matter of enormous concern to this president." He refused to answer questions about a possible military response, saying, "All presidents have options. But they don't discuss what they might be." He did say, in response to a question about his possible steps: "For one, I can tell you how strongly I feel about it, which I've just done, and two, review whatever options might be available, and three, not discuss what they might be."[13]

The Bush administration had initially taken little public notice of the Panamanian National Assembly's "state of war" declaration. At the news conference, President Bush said only that "I've taken note of his statement." White House spokesman Marlin Fitzwater said that the declaration "may have been a license for harassment and threats." One top administration official described the president as "deeply disturbed" by the events in Panama. Former assistant secretary of state Abrams said, "The scuttlebutt I hear is that the sexual abuse of the Navy officer's wife sent Bush up the wall."

Noriega's days of mostly unchallenged power were winding down. His sometimes strong, sometimes tenuous ties to the United States were loosening and unraveling at a rapid pace. The CIA had played along with him because he furnished intelligence on Central America and the Caribbean. And in the war on drugs, he seemed to assist the efforts of the United States. From time to time, in the words of U.S. customs commissioner William von Raab, "they [Noriega and company] would swing some poor slob out, in effect give him away to make us feel they're cooperating [in the drug war]." And occasionally, perhaps to penalize his drug traffickers who did not pay off, Noriega would assist the United States in seizing large amounts of drugs.

He cooperated in other ways. He permitted United States–supported Nicaraguan contra rebels to train on Coiba Island, off Panama. He even suggested to Col. Oliver North, during one of North's frequent visits to Panama in 1985, that he would assassinate Nicaraguan Sandinista leaders and carry out various forms of sabotage within the country. But in exchange, he wanted the Reagan administration to improve his image in the United States. But at the same time, the devious, double- and triple-dealing Noriega was allegedly running arms to the Sandinistas and to Communist rebels in Colombia and El Salvador and supplying U.S. intelligence to Castro.[14]

Noriega had set the stage for the final act in his Panamanian drama. The cast would be drawn, for the most part, from the military forces of the United States and his own PDF and Dignity Battalions. The actuality of his declaration of a state of war against the United States was about to come to pass.

* * *

The most important item of information for any combat commander, whether he be a sergeant commanding a squad in attack or a general in command of a theater, is, "What's my mission?" Once the commander knows the answer to that vital question, he can proceed with his planning. Then he gathers intelligence on the enemy to determine the objectives he must attack to accomplish his mission; he tailors his forces to seize the objectives with the greatest surprise and speed and to minimize casualties to his own troops; he plans the logistics flow to support the operation, always keeping in mind the wisdom of Murphy; and he sets up a chain of command so that an objective or group of objectives is assigned to one subordinate commander—the time-tested and proven principle of unity of command. As the old (September 1954) Department of the Army *FM 100-5, Field Service Regulations,* so succinctly puts it, unity of command "is best achieved by vesting a single commander with requisite authority." That means "one guy's in charge."

Such was the case with the operation that became known as Just Cause. The derivation of the mission of the forces in Just Cause started at the very top of the chain of command: the national command authority (NCA), the president's own top-level planners. The national objective in Panama was long-standing, brief, and broad: Restore democracy and remove Noriega. Those two national objectives translated into four military objectives: Protect U.S. citizens; defend the canal; restore democracy; and capture Noriega. Based on these objectives, the chairman of the Joint Chiefs of Staff had developed broad planning guidance to refine the operations order that had already been approved by the NCA. Some of the guidance: Use maximum surprise; unify the command structure; minimize collateral damage; use the minimum force necessary; plan no evacuation of noncombatants; and plan for postcombat operations to restore democracy in Panama.

The command relationship at the top level for the operation was streamlined and simple: It went from the president to the secretary of defense to the chairman of the Joint Chiefs of Staff to the commander in chief of the Southern Command to the commander of Joint Task Force South. More simply stated: from Bush to Cheney to Powell to Thurman to Stiner, the commander in the field. When the president decided on 17 December to implement the plan, many pre-H-hour actions started, one of the most important of which was the prepositioning of the tactical command and control element of JTF South in Panama prior to the start of the operation.

Once the chairman of the JCS had received the broad military objectives, he converted them into this mission for General Thurman: "Conduct joint offensive operations to neutralize the PDF and other combatants, as required, so as to protect US lives, property, and interests in Panama and to assure the full treaty rights accorded by international law and the U.S. Panama Canal treaties." (One must always wonder if General Westmoreland had had any such specific guidance for the conduct of the war in Vietnam.)

The JCS staff developed the basic concept for the operation into a threefold approach. Phase 1: Combat operations at the onset designed to neutralize and fix in place the PDF, capture Noriega, install a new government, and protect and defend U.S. citizens and key facilities. Phase 2: Stability operations to ensure law and order and begin the transition to support a newly installed government. Phase 3: Nation-building that supports the Endara government to include restructuring and training the new government. This phase would eventually be turned over to the Department of State and other interagency organizations as the U.S. government would assist with the economic and political rebuilding of Panama. These phases were intended to and in fact did overlap, with no clear breaks between them.[15]

In more specific terms, General Thurman's operational tasks, inherent in his mission, were these: Protect 30,000 U.S. citizens; defend 142 key facilities along the Panama Canal; neutralize the PDF, who were spread out in some 13 key objective areas; neutralize the nonuniformed, armed Dignity Battalion hoodlums, almost unidentifiable, as they mingled with other Panamanians on the streets, in vehicles of all sorts, and in various buildings; and find and capture the elusive Noriega—who moved on a random schedule and slept in a different house every night. General Thurman's basic strategy was simply stated but complex in execution: "Simultaneously attack the Panamanian combat forces in the Panama/Colón area and force their collapse." That strategy supported the execution of the other operational tasks.

Because SOUTHCOM is based in Panama and has been there in one form or another for over thirty years, its combat situation was unique: At the start of combat operations, it was already firmly established in what was to become "enemy territory" (but with insufficient combat forces to accomplish its assigned missions). Its intelligence division, therefore, had been able to gather and refine detailed information on the strength and location of the PDF and other targets of military and political value.

The threat, as General Thurman's G-2 saw it, was this: In general, the Panamanian Defense Force was primarily infantry. It was organized into 13 military zones with two battalions; ten independent companies; a cavalry squadron; a riot control company; special forces, including UESAT (Unidad Especial de Seguridad Antiterror); and commandos. The Air Force had thirty-eight fixed-wing aircraft and seventeen helicopters; the Navy had twelve vessels and a naval infantry company (similar to Marines).[16]

The PDF over the years had extended its tentacles to assume control of numerous facets of government. Although it was composed of nearly fifteen thousand people, approximately thirty-five hundred were members of combat units. The remainder were police forces, conservation officers and forest police, customs officials, and administrative personnel. Control by the PDF had spread far and wide. For example, the entire vehicular control system, from vehicle registration to transfer of titles, licensing, and traffic control, was in the hands of the PDF. It was an institution warped to support one man: Noriega. Graft and corruption ran rampant. Those who disagreed or did not support Noriega lost their jobs.

As the crisis developed, the threat of the Dignity Battalions also grew. Over an eighteen-month period, rudimentary basic military training had been conducted and the "Digbats" increasingly indoctrinated. Rumors of PDF plans to use Digbat members to take U.S. hostages circulated. Exposed PDF Plans "Genesis" and "Exodus" called for kidnapping of Americans and transporting them to the interior. In the event of an invasion, Operation "Montana" planned for the PDF to take to the mountains and conduct guerrilla warfare. If that happened, Digbats would be well positioned to provide recruits and auxiliary support.[17]

41

Battalion 2000 at Fort Cimarron, fifteen miles east of Panama City, was unique and "elite" for a very good reason: With the signing of the Carter-Torrijos treaty in 1979, the United States was committed to turning over the canal to Panamanian sovereignty in 1999. During the first eight years after the signing of the treaty, relations between Panama and the United States remained friendly. Approximately three thousand Americans lived on the Panamanian economy, and the United States assisted the PDF both in training and in design. During this eight-year period, the PDF developed a modern infantry battalion designed to take over the defense of the canal in the year 2000. The well-trained and highly motivated unit was named Battalion 2000 or "Battalion Dos Mil."

The bungled 3 October coup and the reaction to it by the various PDF units and their commanders gave the SOUTHCOM intelligence division valuable information. Battalion 2000, for example, was a key unit in aiding Noriega to put down the coup. It was, however, slow to react and to move into the city. The 1st Infantry Company was a two-hundred-man force at Tinajitas. It had always been a staunch supporter of Noriega and occupied a key piece of terrain just north of Panama City. The 2d Infantry Company had two hundred men at Torrijos-Tocumen Airport. It was historically loyal to Noriega but did not participate actively in the 3 October coup. The 5th Rifle Company was a three-hundred-man unit at Fort Amador. Most troops of the unit were Military Police, and the commander of the 5th Company was also the commander of the Balboa Police Station. The 5th Company did not support Noriega on 3 October, but it was still considered loyal to him. The 6th and 7th Rifle companies, together numbering some four hundred men, were based at Río Hato and were very loyal to Noriega. Key members of the units aided Noriega on 3 October. The SOUTHCOM G-2 considered these two companies to be the best fighting units in the PDF. The 8th Rifle Company was a 175-man force at Fort Espinar and, during the 3 October coup, moved into Panama City and assisted Noriega in putting down the threat. A PDF cavalry squadron of 150 men was at Panama Viejo. It was reconstituted after the coup and consisted primarily of UESAT personnel and remnants of the PDF considered loyal to Noriega.[18]

The Comandancia was the home of the 4th Infantry Company, commanded by Major Giroldi, the leader of the 3 October coup. Following the coup, Noriega disbanded the 4th Company and executed or jailed its leaders. At the time of Just Cause, the Comandancia was guarded by about 150 men from various companies, principally the 6th, 7th, and 8th, and many UESAT personnel—all of whom were extremely loyal to Noriega.

SOUTHCOM intelligence indicated that the above units would be the major pockets of resistance during the operation. The final piece in the threat mosaic was Noriega himself. All available intelligence assets were focused on tracking his whereabouts. But some intelligence experts feel that more could have been done to locate him.

Douglas Waller, writing in the 17 June issue of *Newsweek,* said:

> Special-Ops officers were frustrated that their Intelligence Support Activity, a supersecret Army spy unit, was not allowed to send agents into Panama to track Noriega before the invasion. If they had, these sources insist, Noriega

might have been captured the first night of Just Cause. The command had tried to ease what it claims are cumbersome procedures imposed by the CIA and other intelligence organizations, who review all covert spying operations. Before the invasion the command wanted to sneak agents into a Panama City warehouse to check out a tip that the drug cartel was storing five car bombs to assassinate Just Cause commander General Maxwell Thurman. But the command could never get interagency approval from Washington. CIA supporters say the agency had plenty of assets in Panama to collect the information, but the Southern Command kept the CIA station at arm's length because it considered the CIA too close to Noriega.[19]

The U.S. planners had what they needed for the operation. The commander at each level of command had his mission, and intelligence on the PDF and Noriega filtered through the chain; the force was ready.

One of the senior staff officers of the XVIII Airborne Corps wrote recently that

on the 17th of December, the key members of XVIII Airborne Corps staff were called into headquarters (the former brick and concrete pre–World War II post hospital), as we had been on a high state of readiness since the shooting incident and we had been notified by the Pentagon that possibility was high that the Operation Plan would be implemented soon. We requested and received permission to deploy a small element of Corps Assault CP under the guise of attending a previously scheduled conference on the Op Plan and possible CPX (Command Post Exercise). We flew in, arriving in AM of 18 December and began initial work on establishment of Corps/JTFSouth Command Post in the Emergency Operations Center (EOC) of US Army South. Only General Thurman and a few of his staff knew of pending operation in Panama at this time. Once the execute order was received at XVIII Airborne Corps on 18 December, General Stiner issued his orders to commanders located in Panama on 19 December. Orders to relevant commanders in CONUS were issued prior to his departure from Fort Bragg. Times for orders to be issued to subordinate units in Panama were established and occurred after units were assembled and sequestered from families/public. Because of the shooting incident and current situation, bases and units were on a high state of alert in Panama and assembly of units had become a common occurrence.[20]

Lt. Gen. Carl Stiner was General Thurman's "war fighter." As the commander in charge of all operations, he had under his command for Just Cause nearly the entire 7th Infantry Division (Light), one parachute brigade of the 82d Airborne Division, a mechanized battalion from the 5th Mech Division, a battalion-sized task force of Marines, the three battalions of the 75th Ranger Regiment, task forces of SEALs and Special Forces from Naval Special Warfare Group 2 and the Army's 7th Special Forces Group, and the in-place 193d Light Infantry Brigade. Air support came from the 830th Air Division, the 24th Composite Wing from Howard Air Force Base, and assets from the 1st Special Operations Wing from Hurlburt Air Force Base, Florida. Additional combat support and combat service support units, such as the 41st Area Support Group and 1109th Signal Brigade, provided general support to the entire operation. In all, Stiner's troops numbered over twenty-seven thousand soldiers, sailors, airmen, and marines.[21]

Stiner was faced with neutralizing the PDF, garrisoned throughout the entire country. Not every position could be attacked simultaneously. The majority of the critical command and control nodes and the majority of U.S. citizens and interests were in Panama City, however. SOUTHCOM planners thought of the old Canal Zone and Panama City as the center of the target—the bull's-eye. In October, the PDF demonstrated their capability to reinforce the Comandancia rapidly from Río Hato and Fort Cimarron. Those two locations fell into the nine ring and could only be ignored at the peril of the rest of the operation. The rest of the country fell into the four or five ring and could be handled at a later date.[22]

Stiner's plan of attack called for a number of simultaneous attacks at various locations around the country.

- Task Force Bayonet: Isolate the Comandancia in the barrio of Chorillo, about four hundred meters south of Ancon Hill and USSOUTHCOM headquarters; seize and secure the Curundu-Ancon Hill-Balboa areas; air assault into Fort Amador and neutralize the PDF's 5th Company garrisoned there.
- Task Force Semper Fi: block the western approaches to the city and secure the Bridge of the Americas.
- Task Force Atlantic: Isolate Colón; neutralize the PDF 8th Company and naval infantry company; protect Madden Dam; free a number of political prisoners at Gamboa, midway across the isthmus.
- Joint Special Operations Task Force: Parachute assault onto Río Hato; neutralize the PDF 6th and 7th companies; disable PDF patrol craft in Balboa Harbor and a TV tower at Cerro Azul; deny the use of Paitilla Airport; mount operations to capture Noriega or rescue American hostages, as required; parachute assault onto Torrijos-Tocumen Airport.
- Task Force Pacific: Parachute assault onto Torrijos-Tocumen and then air assault to Fort Cimarron, Tinajitas, and Panama Viejo.

After the accomplishment of his initial missions, Stiner had the ongoing task of restoring law and order in Panama City and the outlying parts of the country.[23]

By the 19th of December all commanders in the operation knew their individual missions. The units had rehearsed their parts. The small-unit commanders had reviewed the details with their troops and had gone over each soldier's part in the operation. Woven together, the small-unit missions made up the fabric of the plan. The entire success of the operation was totally dependent on the readiness, the training, the discipline, and the enthusiasm of the soldiers in the teams, squads, platoons, companies, and batteries. No military plan, no matter how grandiose, how thoroughly war-gamed, how detailed, how completely blessed by the chain of command, is worth more than the tabulated volume it is unless the troops at the "forward edge" are combat-ready professionals. This operation, which melded together special forces of the Army, Navy, Air Force, and Marines with conventional forces, was an exercise to test the professionalism of the troops, the planning excellence of the staffs at the higher levels, and new equipment that had never before been used in combat. On the evening of the nineteenth, all commands were on the alert; rehearsals, briefings, soul-searching, second-guessing, and rewriting plans were over.

Operation Just Cause was about to be launched.

5 | The Decision

Some 330 days into his administration, President George Bush was faced, for the first time, with a decision to commit American troops to battle—and with it the unavoidable combat deaths and wounded that would result. As he pondered the decision, he must have at least momentarily visualized and weighed the consequences of battle casualties not only to his own personal feelings but also to those of the American people. Inevitably, the TV cameras would record for the evening news scenes of body bags, flag-draped caskets, and wounded soldiers on stretchers being readied for air evacuation from the battle zone to hospitals in the States. The graphic, stifling, nightly TV coverage of the Vietnam war was not hidden in the past and lost to the American public's memory.

But Noriega's imperious conduct in Panama and his blatant, amateurish "nose-thumbing" at the United States had escalated U.S.-Panamanian relations to the "critical mass" stage. Negotiations, third-party emissaries, liaison visits from White House staffers, and empty public bantering were no longer viable courses of action for the president. By the seventeenth of December, the chairman of the Joint Chiefs of Staff, Gen. Colin L. Powell, was fully prepared to recommend a course of action that would answer the president's needs decisively.

Just Cause was the code name of the course of action that General Powell would recommend to the president. Just Cause was the contingency plan that finally evolved from a long series of plans that had been on the drawing boards of various headquarters for nearly two years. Contingency planning at the Joint Chiefs of Staff and at the headquarters of SOUTHCOM started in earnest after a U.S. federal court indicted Noriega in February 1988. At that time, the chairman of the Joint Chiefs of Staff, Admiral Crowe, issued, through his J-3, Lt. Gen. Thomas W. Kelly, a planning order, code-named "Elaborate Maze," to Gen. Frederick W. Woerner, Jr., then the commander in chief of the U.S.

46

Southern Command. Woerner's missions, according to the order, were to "protect U.S. lives and properties in Panama, assure full exercise of rights accorded by international law, and be prepared to conduct noncombat evacuation in a permissive or nonpermissive environment." After detailed examination of "Elaborate Maze" plans, both Crowe and Woerner found the plans wanting, because the plans did not consider and deal with the full panoply of possible contingencies.[1]

To accomplish the assigned missions, Woerner's staff at his headquarters in Quarry Heights, Panama, then produced a number of contingency plans, among them Post Time, Klondike Key, Blue Spoon, and Krystal Ball; collectively, these plans were known as Prayer Book. In April of 1988, Admiral Crowe approved, for "execution planning," the Prayer Book series of plans. Specifically, Blue Spoon would neutralize the PDF and other combatants as required; and Krystal Ball, changed later to Blind Logic because of operational security considerations, would stabilize the situation and restore law and order in Panama. In the original Blue Spoon plan, the equivalent of five brigades would deploy on a time-phased basis from the United States to bolster the U.S. forces already on the ground in Panama; a corps headquarters would accompany the brigades for "adequate command, control, and communications."[2]

On 8 November 1988, General Kelly called a Pentagon meeting of the members of his J-3 staff involved in contingency planning for Panama; the J-3 of SOUTHCOM, Brig. Gen. William W. Hartzog; and the director of operations of the Army's Forces Command, Maj. Gen. Jerry A. White. The group discussed "the adequacy of SOUTHCOM's plan to integrate XVIII Airborne Corps as the command and control element for Prayer Book." General Kelly decided that XVIII Airborne Corps would be the senior headquarters commanding all combat troops on the ground in Panama. From that time on, XVIII Airborne Corps headquarters was deeply involved in all phases of planning for the operation in Panama. The result of its planning was XVIII Airborne Corps Op Plan 90-2, the supporting plan for USSOUTHCOM Blue Spoon.

The election that Noriega negated in May of 1989 caused no significant changes in the Blue Spoon plans. But in the aftermath of the "stolen election," the JCS did ask General Woerner to review the "adequacy" of the Prayer Book series of plans.

What did cause a revision of SOUTHCOM's plans was the failed 3 October 1989 coup and the obvious lack of U.S. support for it. General Powell gave new guidance to General Thurman; each had just taken over his new duties. The chairman's guidance included "a need for a wider range of military options phased over time"; development of "a capability to respond on short notice to unforeseen contingencies in Panama"; integration of conventional and special operations forces; development of an operations order that "addresses increased levels of anti-U.S. activities to include active, hostile actions against U.S. lives, property, and/or interests"; and the assumption that the PDF will not be friendly. The new guidance obviously called for plans for the combat forces involved to go into Panama en masse and ready to fight for their objectives immediately. There would be no "gradual" buildup this time. General Powell's guidance thus included some time-honored and battle-tested

47

principles of war: mass, objective, surprise, command and control, offensive, unity of command. In nonmilitary parlance that meant "Hit 'em hard, where and when they don't expect it and are not ready; give one guy all he needs to do the job and let him do it; get in, win, and get out."

The result of this guidance was a revised Blue Spoon that differed from its predecessor of April 1988 in several major ways: The 82d Airborne Division and the 75th Ranger Regiment, because of their unique capability for "forced entry" by parachute, were added to the troop list; all forces, conventional/ unconventional, those already in place and those arriving after H-hour, would all be under the command of one individual—the commander of the headquarters formed specifically for this one operation, Joint Task Force South, Lieutenant General Stiner, commander of XVIII Airborne Corps; and, a significant tactical modification, the assault forces would strike their targets with maximum surprise, as "simultaneously" as possible, as opposed to the "time-phased flow of forces," a gradual buildup, called for in the old Blue Spoon. The new Blue Spoon also ordered the troops involved to "minimize collateral damage and use the minimum force necessary."

In early November, General Stiner and General Hartzog briefed the details of the new plans to the chairman. He approved the plans. On the seventh of November, the secretary authorized the augmentation of the existing forces in Panama.

Even though General Powell had been on the job as chairman of the Joint Chiefs of Staff for only a little over a month, he had kept close watch on the evolution of the plans, especially Blue Spoon. He was completely knowledgeable of the details of the plan through visits and briefings by Generals Thurman and Stiner and through his own J-3, General Kelly, who had been following the planning sequence from the time he assumed duties as the Joint Chiefs of Staff J-3 in March of 1988. Thus General Kelly was able to provide continuity between Admiral Crowe and General Powell.

The Joint Chiefs of Staff had followed in detail the buildup of the crisis in Panama precipitated by the PDF shooting of a car carrying four unarmed U.S. officers. Following are some of the entries in the J-3 chronolog, maintained in the Pentagon's Crisis Situation Room, just prior to the implementation of Just Cause:[3]

TIME   CHRONOLOG ENTRY
Saturday, 16 December 1989
2125   NMCC (National Military Command Center in the
        Pentagon) notified that four U.S. servicemen were involved
        in a shooting incident in Panama with PDF forces and that
        one serviceman was killed in the shooting.
2130   Phone call from BG Hartzog
        Lieutenant may die
        Heading out for dinner
        Inadvertently entered checkpoint near La Comandancia
        Surrounded—asked for IDs

	Four servicemen felt threatened; attempted to flee the area and were shot at
	Lieutenant Paz in Gorgas Hospital
2149	CJCS notified
	Directed call to General Stiner, MAC (Military Airlift Command), and JSOTF (LTG Kelly, J-3, made the call)
2151	Lieutenant Paz confirmed dead by doctors at Gorgas Hospital
	Gunfire reported in La Comandancia
	Friendly actions:
	Quick-reaction force assembling at Quarry Heights and Fort Amador
	Personnel Movement Limitation Delta set by USSOUTHCOM
	Noriega's location requested by Joint Staff
	USSOUTHCOM starting to put birds in the air
	Occasional gunshots at La Comandancia (unconfirmed)
	Gunfire reported in different places
2202	Traffic open on Bridge of the Americas
2203	Latest information given to VCJCS and CJCS
2205	MAC notified
2210	JSOTF notified with a "heads up" for warning order
2224	BG Hartzog reported:
	Apache helicopters launched
	Situation confused
	Dignity Battalion of PDF lost control
	Helos report no activity; La Comandancia blacked out, traffic flowing
2318	CDR PDF 5th In Co asks for a meeting

Sunday, 17 December 1989

0110	Joint Staff J-3 call to BG Hartzog
	Treaty Affairs meeting
	Panamanians visibly shaken
	Claim it was an isolated incident
	PDF told not to load ammo
0220	Two U.S. MPs taken custody at Tocumen Airfield by PDF and later released
0530	Official PDF statements on TV (disinformation)
	A sedan with U.S. plates broke through two security checkpoints guarding the Comandancia
	As a result of this incident a one-year-old girl, another man, and a PDF soldier were wounded
0701	Critic recap:
	The shooting had earlier been blamed on the now defunct 4th Rifle Company and Doberman Company

49

0800	At 0215, a USN lieutenant and his wife reported into security at Rodman.
	Reported their detention and witness to Lieutenant Paz shooting.
0900	CJCS briefed
0940	JSOTF response posture good
0945	LTG Kelly phone conversation with MG Kellum, MAC, forty-eight-hour response time

Sandwiched between meetings at the Pentagon on 17 December was an informal but significant "get-together" of the four top members of the Joint Chiefs of Staff in the study of General Powell's Quarters No. 6 at Fort Myer. His house, the traditional home of the chairman, is in a row of senior officers' quarters along the eastern edge of Fort Myer on high ground facing a magnificent view of Washington. General Vuono, the Army chief of staff, lived down the street. Senior members of the Army staff lived in houses to the left and right of the chairman's.

General Powell asked the chiefs to meet him for coffee at 1130. He elected to have the meeting at home instead of the Pentagon to avoid alerting the media that "something might be up" if all of the chiefs arrived at about the same time at the Pentagon on a Sunday morning.

The chief of naval operations, Adm. Carl Trost; the Marine Corps commandant, Alfred M. Gray, Jr.; the Army chief of staff, Carl Vuono; and the Air Force chief of staff, Larry Welch, arrived promptly and were greeted warmly by the chairman. While sitting around in easy chairs in the study and drinking coffee, General Kelly briefed them for about ten minutes on the current situation in Panama, the killing of Lieutenant Paz, the harassment of the Curtises, and a summary of the Blue Spoon plan. The chiefs, who had been briefed on the plan within the past month, were familiar at least with its broad outline.

General Powell reported that he had met with the secretary and his staff earlier that morning and that they were in general agreement that Blue Spoon should be a "go." But, he said, he wanted the chiefs to know exactly what was going on and he wanted to have their personal views.

General Vuono was in general agreement with the plans, he said, and, although he recognized its complexities, he also realized that the troops were trained, ready, and able to accomplish the mission. He also recognized that the bulk of the forces were Army, under the command of an Army general, and he felt that added responsibility.

Admiral Trost, while generally supporting the plan, the timing, and the necessity, wondered if the plan wasn't a bit of "overkill" and if it were really necessary to parachute in all of the paratroopers. Perhaps the first echelons could be jumped into Río Hato and Torrijos/Tocumen to seize the airfields, and then follow-on echelons could be airlanded on the captured strips. Well, maybe, he mused, they all wanted the bronze "combat jump" star on their jump wings. But he strongly supported the operation.

General Welch spoke very seriously and listed a number of disadvantages of the operation, including adverse reactions by other Latin American nations, the possible unrecognized strength of the PDF, the "unfairness" of the fight, and the legitimacy of the threat to our own national interests. But even given these doubts, he recognized that "there was no other solution."

Gen. Al Gray, the bantam commandant of the Marine Corps, the "supreme Marine," held the floor for some time. He was, without a doubt, the top PAO (public affairs officer) of the Marine Corps. He said that the geography of Panama was ideal for a Marine invasion, that he had a Marine Expeditionary Unit (MEU) of several thousand Marines headed back from Hawaii, and that he could easily divert them to Panama and could take care of the whole problem by himself. He said that his Marines, trained, equipped, and supplied as they were, were a far more powerful force than the Rangers and the 82d who were going to parachute into the area, armed only with the equipment they were jumping with. Realizing, however, that this was an almost total Army operation, and aware of the need for speed and surprise, paratrooper prime attributes, he said that if the paratroopers got into trouble, his more heavily equipped Marines could be on call to bail them out. He also said that he could move some amphibious ships with Marines aboard off the Atlantic side of the canal just in case there were any problems elsewhere. General Powell finally said that he would "keep in mind" the commandant's suggestions and offers of help. General Powell knew that it would take the Marines a long time to get there.

After the chiefs had had their say, General Powell told them that he and General Kelly were on the way to the White House to brief the president and that he, Powell, would recommend going with Blue Spoon. He asked the chiefs again for their comments. They agreed that the execution of Blue Spoon was the legitimate and only course to follow.[4] The Joint Chiefs of Staff chronolog continues:

TIME	CHRONOLOG ENTRY
1215	BG Hartzog advises conditions were quiet.
1225	LTG Kelly briefed results of meeting with CJCS. Incident involving USN couple considered more provocative than shooting.
1230	BG White (CJCS Executive Aide to the Chairman), EA, reviews with LTG Kelly actions required prior to 1430 White House meeting. Highlighted copy of Noriega's speech declaring war on United States. Chronology of events showing escalation of incidents.
1300	LTG Kelly spoke with General Lindsay; reviewed situation and result of 1130 meeting with service chiefs.
1330	LTG Kelly and staff review Noriega's declaration of state of war.
1630	General Kelly returned and related that no decision was made regarding the situation. Possibly more NSC discussions tomorrow.

TIME	CHRONOLOG ENTRY
1700–1800	J-3 briefed J-3 staff on presidential decision. H-hour established. CAT to be formed o/a darkness Tuesday (19) Dec. CJCS contacted General Thurman, General Lindsay, General Johnson (commanding general of the Military Airlift Command), and General Burba (commanding general of FORSCOM, the Army's Forces Command). General Kelly called General Downing (Commander of the Joint Special Operations Task Force), LTG Stiner, BG Hartzog, BG Borling, and MG Kellum.

TIME	CHRONOLOG ENTRY
1715	J-3 called LTG Stiner President has authorized Blue Spoon. H-hour established. OPSEC to the maximum.
1826	J-3 phone call w/MG Downing. Rangers from Fort Lewis travel to Lawson tomorrow.

*   *   *

The president made the decision to go with Blue Spoon—or Just Cause[5]—under rather unusual circumstances considering that he was committing U.S. forces to combat. At the White House on Sunday afternoon, 17 December 1989, President Bush was playing host to a gathering of fifty close friends and family members at a Christmas party. The group sang Christmas carols, made small talk, and ate special delicacies; staffers escorted groups of children on the "ultimate" tour, a walk through the president's living quarters, excepting only the presidential bedroom. The calmness and graciousness of the president as he hosted the party belied the fact that he was well aware of the seriousness of the events that had transpired in Panama the day before.

As the Christmas party guests were leaving at about 1430, another group, far more somber, was arriving. The identity of the members of that group and the fact that they were calling at that time on a Sunday afternoon suggested that it was more than a casual visit to wish the president and his lady an early Merry Christmas. The group included General Powell; Secretary of Defense Dick Cheney; Secretary of State Baker; national security adviser Brent Scowcroft; General Tom Kelly; Bob Gates, Scowcroft's deputy; and White House spokesman Marlin Fitzwater. As inconspicuously as possible, the group headed for the elevator to the president's living quarters.

When the president arrived, General Powell briefed him on the plans for the operation in Panama. Throughout the briefing, President Bush asked him detailed questions about the plan: What kind of troops are involved? What kind of equipment do the paratroopers carry with them when they jump? Why are you taking out this target? How are you going to do it? How many helicopters are already there? What intelligence do you have on Noriega? Do you know where he is? Are you sending in enough troops? The president continued to ply General Powell with innumerable questions and to pry into all aspects of the

52

plan. Finally he was satisfied with its thoroughness and adequacy. And then, without reference to any of his half dozen or so top advisers who were at the briefing or even to ask their opinions of the plan, he said, without hesitancy, "Okay, let's do it."

Just Cause had just received the commander in chief's imprimatur. With those four words, the burden of proof shifted to troops already on alert—on the ground in Panama and scattered at bases around the United States. Their ability to react with speed and decisiveness reflected on their superb operational readiness—a gratuity from the buildup and changes engineered by the Reagan administration, resulting in the military's improved discipline, pride, top-notch training, and self-confidence. The post-Vietnam doldrums were over. The Just Cause troops were about to prove it.[6]

6 | Alerts

Col. William F. (Buck) Kernan had a problem—an OPSEC (operational security) problem he didn't know how to solve. It was Sunday afternoon, 17 December, and Colonel Kernan had just hung up the secure phone in his stuccoed, red-tile-roofed, pre–World War II quarters at Fort Benning, Georgia.

He remembers, "I had been in and out of the office (his headquarters at Fort Benning) the fifteenth and sixteenth of December responding to various phone calls and intelligence updates and was aware the situation was deteriorating, but I was at home when I was officially notified [by Maj. Gen. Wayne A. Downing, the commander of the Joint Special Operations Task Force]. I was called on the secure line at my home, given the order to execute, and immediately alerted all my battalion commanders and assembled the battle staff. Official notification was 171600R December (1600, 17 December, local time.)"[1]

Buck's problem that Sunday afternoon was his house guests, Brig. Gen. Jerry Bates and his wife, who were staying with the Kernans en route to the 7th Infantry Division at Fort Ord, where Jerry would serve as Maj. Gen. Carmen Cavezza's assistant division commander for operations. When General Downing learned that the Bateses were at Kernan's quarters, he cautioned Buck ". . . to keep the lid on this thing. You cannot tell Jerry anything—not even that I called." Downing, Bates, and Kernan had been close friends for years—ever since their duty together at Fort Lewis in the 2d Ranger Battalion. Bates would quickly piece together what was happening if he got wind of a secure phone call between Kernan and Downing on a Sunday afternoon.

So Kernan went downstairs and casually endured a maddening thirty minutes of idle conversation before he could gracefully slip out to the "office." It worked—or at least Jerry Bates was perceptive enough not to press Buck for details when he returned home that evening.

That same afternoon, Lt. Col. Alan H. Maestas, commander of the 2d Ranger

Battalion of the 75th, was unwinding in his quarters at Fort Lewis, Washington, home of the 2d Battalion. He and the battalion had just returned to Fort Lewis that same day after a week-long training exercise near Eglin Air Force Base, Florida. The exercise involved the entire regiment and was a "warm-up" rehearsal for the regiment's role in Just Cause. Gen. James J. Lindsay, the commander in chief of the U.S. Special Operations Command at MacDill Air Force Base in Florida, had, using two auxiliary runways at Eglin, duplicated, as nearly as possible, the mission and conditions that the regiment would find on its actual operation in Panama. After the exercise, during the "hot wash" session—latest military terminology for a critique or after-action review—at Hurlbut, General Lindsay and General Downing pointed out to the commanders of the regiment and other special forces involved in the rehearsal the "rights and wrongs" and then said that the situation in Panama was in a "state of flux"; that the actual operation would be a "go—anywhere in the next six to eight months"; and that the regiment must maintain a standby, increased state of readiness. His cautions were on the mark.

On Sunday afternoon, Colonel Maestas got a call from his executive officer, a very relaxed Maj. Clyde M. Newman, who said that he would be right over to show off his newly discovered two-liter beer container. "He arrived," Colonel Maestas remembers, "and Newman and Maestas went to the kitchen to draw beer from the container (pony keg). Two glasses were drawn and, as a second glass is drawn, the phone in the kitchen rings. The call is from Maj. Ken Stauss, regimental executive officer, for Colonel Maestas. Stauss and Maestas have known each other since 1977, when both were in the 2d Ranger Battalion. . . . Stauss asks Maestas if he is on secure phone. The answer is no, so Maestas and Newman depart 2391 Sixth Street (Maestas's home address) in Newman's Ford Bronco for the battalion area. En route Maestas finishes drinking his glass of beer. Newman's beer is half full when both arrive at Bn area. Maestas calls Stauss from the office on a secure phone and is told by Colonel Kernan that the Op Plan has been ordered executed on 200600Z December 90. Maestas tells staff duty NCO to initiate immediate recall of Bn. Maestas and Newman decide to return to their respective quarters to pick up ID tags, wallets, and clean T-shirts. Clean T-shirts important because battalion had just returned that same day from . . . an exercise on the East Coast.

"As Newman and Maestas left the parking lot, Newman picked up his glass with beer and emptied the contents of the beer out the window. Maestas remarked, 'You should have finished that beer. It won't be long before you regret throwing it away.'

"In the days to follow, in the Panama heat particularly in AO Diaz, Newman often remembered about the beer he had thrown away."[2]

Sgt. Andrew Spano was a squad leader in A Company, 2d Battalion of the 75th Rangers. He remembers the details of the call-up quite clearly. "It was Sunday evening, 17 December 89, at approximately 2015 when we got the alert notification," he wrote recently. "As soon as I got the notification, I called my fiancée and told her that I got called in and I would call her as soon as I got the chance. Although most of us heard on the news that the PDF had shot and killed that Marine lieutenant and beat up that soldier and his wife, it was hard to believe that we would be called to go anywhere, because battalion was going on "block leave" (all men in the battalion take leave at the same time so that only one battalion at a time is "down") in two days. Many of us were looking forward to this leave, especially three of us in 2d Platoon, because we were supposed to get married during this leave. When I got to the company, everyone was busy drawing weapons or doing other things, but everyone seemed pretty calm and orderly. As the night went on, we still weren't quite sure of what was going on.

"The next day came and the word came down that we were going to Panama. . . . I thought to myself that this couldn't be happening, I've got a wedding to be in in two weeks. As the day went on, we got the operations orders and we knew what our mission was. As you walked through the barracks, nobody was really saying much. It's funny how we train to go to combat every day, but no one ever really believes that you'll go. It hit me like a sledgehammer in the chest. One time during that day all of us squad leaders were in the platoon CP with the platoon sergeant, who happens to be a veteran of Operation Urgent Fury. He said to us, 'The first time you go to combat, it's easy cause you do everything by instinct. The second time you go, it's hard because you know what to expect.' As I sat in one of my men's room, I thought about the men in my squad. It's hard not to think about how it's possible that maybe someone won't be coming back. I sat there and wrote a letter to my fiancée, who was back in Massachusetts. I wanted her to know what I was feeling. Any one of us would be a liar if we said we weren't scared. The rest of the day was pretty much the same, yet sitting around and waiting, the waiting was the killer."[3]

Another soldier, Private First Class Bunch, 1st Platoon of B Company of the 2d of the 75th, recounted the days leading up to the Ranger regiment's deployment. On the fourteenth of December, he wrote, "The Ranger battalion deployed on one of the biggest operations in years. . . . The mission was 2d and 3d battalions were to parachute into Florida and secure the airfield, and assault and destroy all enemy personnel in buildings and on the airfield. I don't remember the times and dates the mission actually took place but we jumped in and secured the airfield in twelve minutes then assaulted the buildings and basically kicked ass. While doing all of this, generals and SOCOM and people up higher were watching to see how well the supposed 'elite force of the United States Army' did the job. They were very impressed, so impressed one of the four stars said it was the best he'd seen in his military career.

"On the sixteenth of December, we came back from Florida to Georgia by bus. Then we got on a plane late night 0100–0200 on the seventeenth of Dec. Got to Fort Lewis early morning on the seventeenth. Unpalletized and got our shit squared away by noon, then we were cut loose for the day. All the next two weeks were half days and four-day weekends. The perfect Christmas vacation— or so we thought. I went home for eight hours. The best eight hours I've ever had in a long time. I spent time with my newlywed wife, ate what was going to be a good meal, and slept a couple of hours. The news was on and they were talking about the situation in Panama. They declared war on the U.S.A. I was talking about going down there and stomping ass. Michele didn't share my opinion. No more than five minutes later the phone rang and we were alerted. I knew why, and I'm sure Michele did also. She isn't stupid. On the way to the battalion, I tried to ease her mind by saying I had no idea why we were alerted, when I knew, 'cause we just practiced the mission in Florida which was set up like the Panamanian military post. I told her everything would be fine, but I didn't believe that myself.

"Later that night all I heard through the barracks was echoes of war. Higher tried to cover by saying we were going to Fort Bliss, Texas, but we knew it was just smoke being blown up our asses. We repallitized, packed our rucksacks (again) and our CD bags (combat deployment), then drew weapons and went to sleep.

"We woke about 0545 and made ready for the day ahead. Then we got in cattle trucks and went to McChord Air Force Base again. Got on a C-141 and almost immediately took off (unusual). I began to notice a few things like the crew chiefs on the bird were wearing sidearms, and when we asked where we were going, he said, 'The East Coast is all I can say.' It began to really dawn on me what was about to happen but my mind was still thinking 'training.' We landed four hours later at Lawson Army (Airfield) in Georgia. Everything was fine, no one was jumping out the ass screaming or yelling. We went to our tents and unpacked. The day went well. The sergeants were being unusually nice, and we were treated better than we have in all my time in service. The day went well and night fell and so did the cold. We worked out the fireguard watch and got in the rack. Then the news came—we were going to Panama. Everyone got up, oiled their weapons, fixed their LCE (device for carrying combat gear), and dumped all unnecessary shit from the rucksack. All I took was a poncho, poncho liner, two-quart canteen, a PVS-4 (night scope), and an IV. I was set, then the operations order (how to) came in. They had pictures, maps, number of troops, location of antiaircraft guns—everything.

"Here's what was to happen. Second and 3d battalions were to jump into Rio Hato, Panama. Second Battalion was to take the south and 3rd the north. First Platoon (my platoon) was to assemble at point 'Buck' about one click down the southern end of the runway and two or so clicks from Noriega's home, which was supposed to be taken out by another unit. Once enough of us assembled we were to assault Objective 'Cat' with approximately 150 enemy troops. First Platoon had the building to the left and 3rd Platoon had the buildings to the right. After that we were to go on to Objective 'Lion' and 150 troops also."[4]

In Panama, Col. Michael G. Snell, the commander of the 193d Infantry Brigade (Light), permanently stationed in Panama, had been following the details of the planning for the operation for many months at his command post at Fort Clayton. It came as no surprise to him when, on the seventeenth of December, General Thurman's headquarters alerted him to carry out his preplanned and rehearsed missions. He received the execute message at 1800 on the nineteenth.

On the seventeenth of December, General Stiner called into the corps headquarters the key members of his staff. "The headquarters had been on a high state of readiness since the shooting incident," remembered General Scholes, the corps chief of staff, "and we had been notified by the Pentagon that possibility was high that the Operation Plan would be implemented soon. We requested and received permission to deploy a small element of the corps assault CP under the guise of attending previously scheduled conference on the Op Plan and possible CPX Command Post Exercise. We flew in, arriving on AM of the eighteenth, and began initial work on establishment of Corps/JTFSouth Command Post in Emergency Operations Center of U.S. Army South. Only General Thurman and a few of his staff knew of the pending operation in Panama at this time. Once the "execute order" was received at XVIII Corps on 18 December, General Stiner and remaining, previously identified staff members deployed to Panama. General Stiner issued his orders to cdrs. located in Panama on 19 December. Orders to relevant commanders in CONUS were issued prior to his departure from Fort Bragg. Times for orders to be issued to subordinates within Panama were established and occurred after units were assembled and sequestered from families/public. Because of shooting incident and arrest situation, bases and units were on a high state of alert in Panama and assembly of units had become a common occurrence."[5]

In more detail, what happened at Fort Bragg was this: General Stiner received the execute message in a phone call from General Kelly at 1800 on Sunday evening. In anticipation of that message, General Stiner had already sent Gen. Ed Scholes, his chief of staff, who had recently assumed the position after having served as assistant division commander of the 82d under Generals Stiner and Johnson, and a small advance party from his headquarters to Panama late on Sunday night via a C-141 from Pope Air Force Base, adjacent to Fort Bragg. The task of this advanced C-2 (command and control) element was to organize a small joint command post to handle a multitude of details before H-hour.

Later, General Stiner, his G-3, Col. Tom Needham, other key members of the corps staff, and an advanced command post group from the 82d took off from Pope in two C-20s. At 1930 on Monday evening they landed at Howard Air Force Base. (The corps staff did not get into their BDUs—battle dress—until Tuesday night.) The group moved to Fort Clayton, the command post of U.S. Army South, headed by Maj. Gen. Marc Cisneros, and joined the corps joint tactical operations center (JTOC) in General Cisneros' emergency operations center. Fort Clayton—unlike Fort Amador, for example, which is jointly occupied by U.S. and Panamanian forces and dependents—is totally occupied by U.S. forces. General Cisneros became the deputy commander of Joint Task Force South and integrated his staff with General Stiner's for the duration of the operation. The advanced group from the 82d moved into Building 200 (the 193d Brigade's headquarters) at Fort Clayton to prepare for the arrival of the remainder of the 82d staff.

Sunday night, General Stiner alerted Maj. Gen. James H. Johnson, Jr., commanding general of the 82d Airborne Division, that the operation was a "go." At 0900 on Monday, the eighteenth, the XVIII Airborne Corps G-3, Col. Tom Needham, under the guise of a routine EDRE (emergency deployment readiness exercise), gave the 82d Airborne Division G-3, Lt. Col. Dan McNeill, a no-notice order to execute Corps Op Plan 2-90. This order initiated the division's eighteen-hour planning and alert procedure, a routine through which the division units had moved many times in the past.[6]

At 1100 on the eighteenth, as scheduled in the division's SOP (standard operating procedure), the N+2 briefing was held in the division headquarters operations center. Col. Jack Nix was the commander of the division's 1st Brigade, the DRB (division-ready brigade) for that period. Present at the N+2 briefing were Colonel Nix and commanders of other selected division elements who would support the 1st Brigade on the operation. "Due to OPSEC (operational security) concerns, only brigade-level commanders were briefed that this no-notice EDRE was actually a cover for the execution of Op Plan 2-90" (the division referred to the plan as 2-90), reported the division's historical summary.

At 1400 hours the division assault command post moved to the PHA (personnel holding area) and continued planning and preparation for the EDRE. At about 1500, Colonel Needham alerted Colonel McNeill in the PHA to begin preparing for combat operations in Panama in accordance with the division's Op Plan 2-90. And at 1500, Brigadier General Kinzer, the assistant division commander of the 82d, and thirteen members of the division staff airlanded at Howard Air Force Base, moved to Building 200 at Clayton, and linked up with the first element of the division staff that had arrived two days earlier.

When Colonel Nix first received the alert for an EDRE, he moved his first battalion to the PHA. In the next four hours Nix alerted and moved two more battalions to the PHA. One was from his 1st Brigade; the other was the 4th of the 325th from another brigade in the 82d. The 1st Brigade's 3rd Battalion, the 3d of the 504th, had already deployed to Panama on 10 December under the guise of jungle training.[7]

The troops in the 82d had been to the PHA many times before for alerts of varying degrees of seriousness. The procedure and the route were always the same. Cargo trucks or trucks pulling eighty-passenger, aluminum-sided trailers pulled up behind their barracks along Ardennes Road and parked. The troopers, fully combat-loaded, filed out of their barracks and loaded up for the two-mile ride to the PHA. The convoy wound down Gruber Road, then turned on Butner and made a left on Gorham. Then it ran along a dirt road past rifle ranges to the PHA, a collection of six massive, canvas-covered Quonset huts, each capable of holding about two hundred men and their gear. The huts were furnished with double-deck bunks for a possible overnight stay. In addition to the troop Quonsets, the PHA had three big, canvas-covered buildings for administration and housing of the staffs. The PHA could hold about two battalions. For Just Cause, the 4th Battalion of the 325th Infantry staged through the nearby corps marshaling area.

The PHA also held an issue point where the troops drew ammunition, mosquito nets for the bunks, and rations. In the case of Just Cause, where the 82d troopers might possibly parachute onto the concrete runways of Torrijos/Tocumen Airport, the paratroopers were also issued knee and elbow pads. The PHA held another area of some importance to infantrymen: a range where they could zero their personal weapons.[8]

Colonel Nix's DRB, a reinforced parachute infantry-heavy brigade, consisted not only of his own two battalions, the 1st and 2d of the 504, but also was augmented by the 4th Battalion of the 325th, C Company of the 3d of the 505, C Company of the 3d of the 73d Armor, the 3d Battalion of the 319th Field Artillery, A Battery of the 3d Battalion of the 4th Air Defense Artillery, A Company of the 307th Engineer Battalion, a platoon from the 82d Military Police Company, a FAST (forward-area support team), and a TACP (tactical air control party).

In the PHA, rigging of heavy-drop items (artillery pieces, vehicles, Sheridan tanks, ammunition loads, and supplies) continued throughout the day to prepare twenty-eight C-141 heavy-drop aircraft for "forward staging at Charleston Air Force Base in South Carolina." The twenty-eight C-141s moved to Charleston Air Force Base prior to the departure of the parachute assault planes from Pope Air Force Base.

On the nineteenth, Colonel Nix and the DRB continued rehearsals in the PHA while the outload support personnel finished the rigging and loading of the heavy-drop platforms. At 1100, Joint Task Force South (the XVIII Airborne Corps in Panama) notified the 82d to execute Joint Task Force South's Op Plan 90-2, with D-day/H-hour as 20 Dec 890100. The three specific objectives in the plan for the 82d (now Task Force Pacific) were the UESAT/Cav Squadron at Panama Viejo (Objective One); the 1st Infantry Company (Tigers) at Tinajitas (Objective Two); and Battalion 2000 at Fort Cimarron (Objective Three). In addition, after successfully "taking down" these objectives, "the 82d was to move into Panama City and to neutralize the Dignity Battalions, specifically the Rosa Elena Landecho (REL) Battalion, staging at Tocumen; the Venceremos Battalion, staging at Panama Viejo; and the San Miguel el Archangel Battalion, staging at 11MZ Headquarters in the San Miguelito District."[9]

When word came to load aircraft, the troops marched from the PHA to Green Ramp adjacent to the Pope Air Force Base runways. The troops were loaded down with all of their personal gear for the jump, some eighty pounds' worth. At Green Ramp were parked the aircraft for the jump, and here the troops drew their main and reserve parachutes. Then the jumpmasters lined up the troops in order of exit from the planes over the drop zones and waited for the command to load up.

The 7th Infantry Division (Light) at Fort Ord has an alert procedure like the 82d's. Twenty-four hours a day, seven days a week, the division's three brigades are designated, on a rotational basis, DRB (division-ready brigade) 1, DRB 2, or DRB 3. The DRB 1's three battalions are designated DRF 1, 2, or 3. The DRF 1 Battalion must have all deployable soldiers assembled within two hours of N-hour, combat-loaded and combat-ready. The DRF 2 battalion must be ready to move in four hours and the DRF 3 battalion in six hours.

The 7th's alert sequence started at X-hour (0900) on Monday, the eighteenth, with a "crisis action team" briefing and an increase of readiness of the 2d Brigade, its DRB 1. Five hours later, an "outload support" meeting was held to plan transportation to the airfields and schedule units onto the aircraft. At 0749 on Tuesday, the nineteenth, the division commander, Maj. Gen. Carmen J. Cavezza, received an "execute order" for Just Cause from the Joint Chiefs of

Staff. N-hour, the time that General Cavezza set for starting the alert procedure, was 0900 that same morning, just seventy-one minutes later. At 1100, General Cavezza met with his staff and with Col. Linwood Burney, commander of the 2d Brigade. At 1930 that evening, the 5th Battalion of the 21st Infantry, the DRF 1 Battalion, commanded by Lt. Col. Robert Cronin, with 32 officers, a warrant officer, and 483 enlisted men, left Fort Ord by bus for Travis Air Force Base.[10]

One observer reported that "long convoys of olive-colored military vehicles snaked along Highway 1 and State Route 156 starting at about 10:00 P.M. Tuesday and then onto U.S. 101 on the way to Travis Air Force Base, 175 miles north of Fort Ord.

"By early morning, about two dozen buses loaded with soldiers arrived at Travis. Reporters said they heard jet noise as aircraft were moved at the base, but Travis was enveloped in heavy fog, and no planes had taken off as early as this morning."[11]

Another report held that

> Just past midnight, the troops and weapons began arriving at Travis, just outside Fairfield. Trucks covered with tarps but bearing "explosives" signs clearly on the sides, moved through the dense fog into the rear gate of the base. The first trucks bore Navy insignia and were likely carrying arms from the nearby Concord Naval Weapons Station.
>
> Convoys containing as many as a dozen trucks each arrived regularly throughout the night. One group contained at least five cannons being towed behind jeeps, in addition to buses full of troops. Many of the soldiers, wearing camouflage clothing—some with their faces painted—waved and smiled at the press assembled to record their arrival.
>
> At Travis the troops were to board transports for the seven-hour flight to Panama.
>
> The Light Fighters, whose nicknames include "Masters of the Night," carry mostly small arms, mortars, and M-16 automatic rifles on their backs. The boast: that Night Fighters can arrive combat-ready for action anywhere within 18 hours.[12]

In Panama, JTFSOUTH, General Stiner's command, had established its assault command post in the Emergency Operations Center (EOC) of U.S. Army South at Fort Clayton. The Assault CP had communications established back to the JCS in the Pentagon, with a hot line to General Tom Kelly in the JCS operations center, General Downing's command, and the U.S. embassy. It had, of course, communications to all of the major subordinate commands in the task force. Once the operation was under way, General Thurman and his J-3, General Hartzog, moved into the crowded assault CP on a full-time basis. Thurman stayed there with General Stiner through the initial assaults and through the phases of the operation that were most crucial. The small EOC was so crowded with communications gear, operational maps, and computers that General Thurman slept—catnapped is the better term—on a cot between a computer and a desk.[13]

The chain of command was working to perfection. On Sunday evening the president made the decision to implement Just Cause. Fifty-four hours later, the operation was under way. The rehearsals, the planning, the practice alerts, and the rumors were things of the past. The commander in chief had committed his military forces to combat.

7 | Initial Deployments

The troops stationed in Panama either on a permanent- or a temporary-duty basis were well aware that "something was up" on the nineteenth of December. They had heard of and read about the murder of Lt. Robert Paz and the harassment of the Curtises on the sixteenth—the culmination of a long series of incidents in which the PDF had harassed Americans, military and civilian. The troops knew that events were rapidly cresting to a climax—or, in their words, "The shit was about to hit the fan."

On orders from General Thurman, the commanders in-country ratcheted up the level of their readiness postures so that by the nineteenth, all U.S. troops stationed in Panama were in or within two hours of their barracks areas. The commanders had their missions, they had rehearsed their operations so often and over such a widespread area that, as planned, the PDF may have become numb to them. By the nineteenth, they were ready to operate.[1]

One of General Stiner's subordinate commanders for the operation was Maj. Gen. Wayne A. Downing, forty-nine, West Point Class of 1962. General Downing, stationed at Fort Bragg, was designated the commander of the Joint Special Operations Task Force (JSOTF), reporting directly to General Stiner. Some of General Downing's Just Cause units were already in-country; some he brought with him from the States about forty-eight hours before H-hour; and some, the entire 75th Ranger Regiment, came in by parachute at H-hour.

General Downing's military background is filled with airborne, Ranger, and special operations assignments, both in combat in Viet Nam and in the States. During his two tours in Viet Nam, totaling over two years, he served with the 173d Airborne Brigade, commanded a company in the 14th Infantry, and was a battalion and brigade S-3 in the 25th Infantry Division. In the States he commanded the 2d Battalion of the 75th Rangers and later activated and commanded the 75th Ranger Regiment. Between those Ranger assignments, he commanded an armored infantry brigade in Europe.

He is a fair-haired, youngish-looking, obviously physically fit officer who has an intensity, experience, drive, and charisma that make him uniquely well suited to his current assignment—commander of and contingency planner for all Army special operations forces. He knows the "special operations business" from a variety of command and staff levels.

On Saturday night, 16 December, at about 2200, he was in his quarters in the "generals' loop" near the Officers' Club at Fort Bragg. General Kelly, the JCS J-3, called him on his secure line and alerted him to the possibility that Just Cause might be a "go." Later, he and General Stiner talked continually through the night. He remembers the sequence of events thereafter this way: "I went in to work Sunday morning and I ended up not coming home. My wife, Cindy, had pressed my suit. I told her I needed it pressed to go to Washington the following day. She got up Monday morning and my suit was still hanging there. She was puzzled as to how I got to Washington without that suit. We left like we do—quietly, without fanfare or good-byes. Cindy didn't know what was going on until she got up Wednesday morning and turned on the TV and heard that we had invaded Panama." And that's how the spouses of many of the officers and soldiers who deployed on Just Cause found out where their mates were when they failed to report home on Tuesday evening.

General Downing stayed in his office all day Sunday. At about 1300, Lt. Gen. Tom Kelly called and told him, "It's on." Kelly called him back at about 1700 and told him, "You're going. What time do you want H-hour and what time do you want the aircraft?" General Downing gave him the information and got ready to depart.

At about 0100 on Monday morning, General Downing, some additional Special Forces and Navy SEALs, a total of about 450 men, left Pope Air Force Base and Norfolk Naval Air Station in C-141s and C-130s and landed at Howard Air Force Base in Panama some six hours later. General Downing set up his command post at Howard. His total force, the Joint Special Operations Task Force, totaled about forty-four hundred and was composed of elements of almost all existing special operations, psychological operations, and civil affairs units from the Army, Air Force, and Navy. The largest component, and the principal assault force in the JSOTF, was the entire 75th Ranger Regiment, dubbed Task Force Red for Just Cause. Supporting this task force were Air Force gunships and combat controllers from the Air Force's 1st Special Operations Wing and Army loudspeaker teams.

Another part of his command and another strike force was Task Force White, composed of five sea-air-land (SEAL) platoons from Naval Special Warfare Group 2, based at Little Creek, Virginia. On the nineteenth, General Downing brought with him four SEAL platoons to join a fifth, which was on a permanent rotation to Southern Command. Successors to the "frogmen" of World War II, the SEAL, assisted by the protection and speed of patrol boats, were assigned a broad array of maritime operations in the vicinity of the canal.

One of the units of JSOTF permanently stationed in Panama was the 3d Battalion of the 7th Special Forces Group, commanded by Lt. Col. Roy R. Trumbull. This unit, assisted by helicopters from the Army's 160th Aviation Regiment, was Task Force Black. For eighteen months the 3d of the 7th had had an additional Special Forces company, on a rotational basis, from the parent group at Fort Bragg attached to it because of the crisis. Trumbull's base of operations was Fort Davis on the Atlantic side of the canal, about four miles due south of Colón, near the Gatun Locks. Its primary responsibility, "eyes on targets," devolved into reconnoitering several target areas and PDF garrisons prior to H-hour. Because of the locations of some targets in and around the built-up areas, and the possibility of compromise of the reconnaissance teams, the 7th was not able to overwatch every target.

Another Task Force Black mission was the protection of the opposition leaders who had been duly elected in the May 1989 elections but never installed by the Noriega regime. One of the primary objectives of Just Cause, of course, was the capture of Noriega and his major subordinates. It was critical, therefore, that the legitimate leaders be ready to assume political power immediately, once Noriega had been dethroned. The key leaders of the opposition, President Guillermo Endara, and Vice Presidents Guillermo Ford and Ricardo Arias Calderon, obviously needed guarding, but an overt show of U.S. military protection before H-hour would certainly alert Noriega to the pending operation. The Green Berets of Task Force Black were well qualified to provide the security, but General Thurman himself solved the problem of guarding the trio while at the same time causing no alarm bells to ring in the Comandancia.

General Thurman quietly invited the three men to dine with him at his quarters at Quarry Heights on the evening of the nineteenth. In addition to providing them with dinner, General Thurman also briefed them on the upcoming operation and arranged to have them sworn into office at his headquarters by a Panamanian judge well before H-hour. The United States immediately recognized the Endara government as the legitimate political leadership of Panama.

Another of the missions assigned to Task Force Black was blocking the Pan American Highway at the Pacora River Bridge, about 30 miles east of Panama City. The bridge was important because its seizure would prevent the movement of Battalion 2000 from its barracks at Fort Cimarron to the Torrijos/Tocumen Airport complex at Panama City, the site of the drop zone for the paratroopers slated to arrive at H-hour, 0100, in the dark of the morning of the twentieth.

Colonel Trumbull assigned the blocking mission to Maj. Kevin Higgins, who commanded A Company of the 3d Battalion of the 7th Special Forces Group. Each company of the group had six A teams of twelve men each, generally led by two officers (or one officer and a warrant officer) and ten noncommissioned officers, all experts in one or more specialties: weapons, communications, operations, intelligence, medicine, survival, demolitions-engineering, and airborne operations.

General Downing had two additional Task Forces in his Joint Special Operations Task Force: Green and Blue. These forces, specially trained for this type of mission, had several challenging missions, which included the difficult task of capturing the elusive Noriega and his key inner circle. Diligent intelligence efforts traced Noriega from place to place and greatly narrowed the possible hideouts. Prior to the operation, the SOUTHCOM intelligence operators felt that they had Noriega's hideouts spotted about 80 percent of the time. Commencing at H-hour, Task Forces Green and Blue, supported by AH-6 helicopter gunships, UH-60 Black Hawk transport helicopters, and AC-130 gunships, applied constant pressure on Noriega's entourage and key cronies and tracked them relentlessly.[2]

Col. Michael G. Snell commanded the 193d Infantry Brigade (Light), which was permanently stationed in Panama and with its headquarters at Fort Clayton. When the 4th Battalion of the 6th Infantry, organic to the 5th Infantry Division (Mechanized) at Fort Polk, Louisiana, and the 519th Military Police Battalion from Fort Meade, Maryland, arrived in Panama during the Nimrod Dancer buildup after the grossly fraudulent May 1989 national elections, they were assigned to the 193d. For Operation Just Cause, Colonel Snell then had under his command, Task Force Bayonet, four rather diverse battalions: the 4th of the 6th, a mechanized infantry battalion from the 5th Infantry Division (Mechanized) at Fort Polk, Louisiana; the 5th of the 87th (stationed at Fort Clayton and a full-time part of the 193d); the 1st Battalion of the 508th Airborne Infantry, also a regular battalion in the 193d, a parachute infantry battalion, normally stationed at Fort Kobbe, on the west side of the canal near Howard Air Force Base; and the 519th Military Police Battalion, which had five military police companies, only one of which was organic to the 519th, under its control. Also part of his task force was the 59th Engineer Company, under the command of Capt. José A. Echevarria and normally stationed at Fort Clayton, on the east side of the canal; and D Battery of the 320th Field Artillery Battalion, under the command of Capt. Felipe S. Ibarra, stationed at Fort Kobbe.

TF Bayonet had been conducting contingency planning for defensive and offensive operations in Panama for over twenty months—or since the abortive March 1988 coup attempt. The operational plan for the 193d had steadily evolved until it was well tuned. According to Colonel Snell, "The 3 October '89 coup resulted in dramatic modifications of Op Plans, generally from passive defense to offense. . . . Being forward deployed (on the ground in Panama), the TF was able to conduct TEWTS (tactical exercises without troops) and tactical exercises (with suitable deception measures) at or near all objectives. While the troops were unaware of the real purpose of the exercises, they repeatedly rehearsed each defensive action and assault. . . . Each battalion and company produced a battle book detailing every aspect of their mission and plan. The result of this effort was a detailed, tested plan that was fully understood by the chain of command and that the troops had unwittingly rehearsed on several occasions."

Colonel Snell's principal objective was the Comandancia. But he also had seven other objectives, including the 5th CIA (which has nothing to do with the well-known U.S. Central Intelligence Agency but is an abbreviation for the 5th—or Quinta Compañia de Infanteria) stationed at Fort Amador; the Balboa and Ancón DENI (Departmento Nacional de Investigaciónes), police agencies; the Ancón DNTT (Dirección Nacional de Tránsito Terrestre), road patrols; the PDF Engineer Compound; Pier 18, Balboa Harbor; and the PDF Dog Compound. With that array of missions, Colonel Snell's few days after D-day promised to be exciting, and, if successful, rewarding.

For the operation, Colonel Snell divided his command into three task forces: TF Gator, under the control of Lt. Col. James W. Reed, the CO of the 4/6, consisting of two mech infantry companies, an airborne company, a platoon of M551 Sheridans, and a Marine Corps LAV (light assault vehicle) platoon; TF Wildcat, under the command of Lt. Col. William H. Huff III, the CO of 5/87, containing one mech infantry company and three infantry companies; TF Red Devil, under the command of Lt. Col. Billy R. Fitzgerald, commanding officer of the 1/508, comprised of two airborne companies and one mechanized company, the latter an ad hoc arrangement. The 519th MP Battalion attached several platoons to each of the task forces. And the 59th Engineer Company added platoons to Task Forces Wildcat and Red Devil.

At 1800 on Tuesday the nineteenth, Colonel Snell had a call from SOUTHCOM headquarters: "The operation is a 'go.' " He now had seven hours to complete marshaling, finish planning and "troop leading procedures" below company level (units below company had not yet been briefed that all of the rehearsing they had done was "for real"), and move his units to their lines of departure for an H-hour initiation of the operation.[3]

Marine Forces Panama became an integral part of Task Force South for Operation Just Cause and, for the operation, were appropriately christened Task Force Semper Fi. Its commander was Col. Charles E. Richardson, the commander of Marine Forces Panama at the time of the operation. The Marines were based at the U.S. Naval Station, Panama Canal—more popularly referred to as Rodman Naval Station. In addition to his command element, Colonel Richardson's Marine forces included K Company of the 3d Battalion, 6th Marines; D Company of the 2d Light Armored Infantry Battalion; MCSF Company, from the Marine Corps Security Force; a FAST platoon, from the Fleet Antiterrorist Security Team; a detachment from BSSG-6, Brigade Service Support Group 6; and, attached from the Army, the 536th Engineer Battalion and the 534th Military Police Company.

During normal times—or what were purported to be normal times in Panama before 20 December—the units in Marine Forces Panama rotated to and from the States every 90 days; the majority of the command element rotated every 179 days. The Marine units on the day of the Just Cause operation had arrived during October 1989. Colonel Richardson wrote, "I was fortunate the Marines in Panama on 20 December 1989 had been in country for almost two months. They knew the terrain and respected the people's desire for freedom."[4]

While the Marines were in Panama on rotation, they trained extensively in possible combat situations. One after-action report states, "By having maintained a high-paced training tempo, the Marines of MARFORPM [Marine Forces Panama] were extremely well prepared for the hostilities that were initiated on 20 December 1989.

"Of significant importance in preparing for combat were the Contingency Readiness Exercises, the Fire Support Coordination Exercises, the Freedom of

Movement Operations, the roadblock classes, and the numerous sand-table discussions. As stated by General Thurman, 'During the tense period before 'Just Cause' the Marines spearheaded the efforts to assert our treaty rights. . . .'"

In actuality, the Marines practiced in realistic combat situations, particularly with their LAVs (light assault vehicles). A LAV is a lightly armored, eight-wheeled vehicle capable of swimming, an important characteristic in Panama, land of the "big canal." LAVs are armed with various weapons depending on their mission. Of one practice mission, Capt. Stephen J. Linder, commander of Company A of the 2d LAI Battalion, wrote:

> On 28 May, Operation Big Show demonstrated several unique capabilities of our LAVs—maneuverability, firepower, swimming, and reliable communications. Assault and security elements swam the Panama Canal from west to east, landed on the Panama Canal shore, and maneuvered into position to help secure Fort Amador, a joint U.S./Panamanian base. It was executed flawlessly. The swim of the canal caught the PDF by surprise, and confusion was the order of the day in their response.
> On 9 June an armed reconnaissance on the fringes of the Empire Range area was conducted to capitalize on civilian contacts that had been established earlier.
> Our next mission was a night swim of the Panama Canal to conduct surreptitious reinforcement of Quarry Heights, the Southern Command's headquarters compound. The intent was to demonstrate to the PDF that keeping tabs on Marine LAVs would be a full-time job.[5]

Company D of the 2d LAI Battalion, commanded by Capt. Gerald H. Gaskins, arrived in Panama in the latter part of October 1989. The company carried on its training with the same intensity as its predecessor, B Company. On 22 November, Captain Gaskins led his company on a short exercise, theoretically to familiarize his men with their area of operations. After the operation, called Rough Rider, Captain Gaskins wrote:

> The route would take us through four major towns: Nuevo Emperador, Nuevo Guarre, Vista Allegre, and Arraijan.
> Two U.S. Army officers from the Treaty Affairs Section, JTF, joined the company to approach roadblock agitators and negotiate. Also, JTF sent a psyops armored HMMWV (in military jargon the Hum-V, the successor to the renowned and seemingly irreplaceable jeep) to inform the Panamanians of our "goodwill" intentions and an OH-58 to screen our movement. Company D executed Rough Rider with twelve LAVs, three HMMWVs, and its Scout Platoon.
> Nuevo Emperador gave us our first sight of a Panamanian town and a warm reception with smiles and enthusiastic waves. In Nuevo Guarre we made a left turn on Thatcher Highway, which leads directly back to Rodman Naval Station. As we approached Vista Allegre, the lead element reported people

gathered on Thatcher Highway waving a large Panamanian flag and several banners. The deliberate roadblock had been set, undetected by our air observer. (We later discovered that the Panamanians used the helo flyover as an indicator for our movement.)

The lead platoon set in seventy-five meters from the roadblock, while the rear element immediately set in the counterblock. The crowd of agitators was isolated to our front. When the officers of Treaty Affairs approached the agitators, a shouting match erupted and excited the crowd. I informed MarFor Panama of the situation and requested permission to give a five-minute warning. My request was granted immediately. At four minutes, I told Treaty Affairs to stop talking and board the HMMWV. All LAV drivers "buttoned up," and gunners manned their weapons to prepare for coaxial machine-gun engagements. Vehicle commanders and scouts remained exposed to monitor the crowd. The agitators realized what our intentions were, and several vehicles were hit by rocks. The company formation collapsed into a single file except for the rear element, which blocked traffic until every vehicle was through. One Panamanian rammed an LAV-L with a pickup truck, puncturing the right front tire. As the LAV-L continued forward, a Panamanian female agitator tried to block our movement with her body. She fell backward, feet in the air, flipping over another roadblock vehicle. The agitators were shocked, and began beating our vehicles with their fists, flagpoles, and anything else they could wield as the column moved forward. On the other side of the roadblock was another crowd, this one friendly, cheering at what we had done. We moved away from the roadblock to change the flat tire and get a damage assessment of the LAVs. Five minutes later we were on the move.

D Company, 2d LAI, was about ready.[6]

On 3 October, K Company, 3d Battalion, 6th Marines, under the command of Capt. Don Kline, arrived in Panama on its rotation. Lt. Kenneth M. DeTreux, a platoon leader in K Company, 3/6, wrote after Just Cause: "For three months, Kilo took part in security operations in the Arraijan Tank Farm and carried out a rigid training schedule in order to be ready for an emergency situation that might arise in that troubled country. Beginning on 19 December, the hard work and training truly paid off."[7]

"To best understand the Marine Corps' mission in Just Cause," wrote Colonel Richardson recently, "one must first have an understanding of their preinvolvement. In December 1989, Marine Forces Panama had been in the country for nearly two years. Their mission: 'to protect American lives and property.' Actually, Marine Corps' involvement in Panama dates back as far as 1905, when Marines were initially sent 'to protect American lives and property.'

"Marine Forces Panama was at a strength of approximately seven hundred and was the advance element of the 6th Marine Expeditionary Brigade. The 6th MEB has a mission in the contingency plan for the defense of the Panama Canal, known as Blue Spoon. Within thirty-six hours after notification, the 6th MEB would arrive in Panama and absorb Marine Forces Panama and be ready for combat operations. Prior to the brigade's arrival, Marine Forces Panama's mission was the protection of Howard Air Force Base, the Panama Naval

Station, Arraijan Tank Farm, the Pacific Ammunition Supply Point, and the Bridge of the Americas. This, however, was soon to change.

"On 3 October 1989, several PDF officers attempted, and failed, in a coup to oust Gen. Manuel Antonio Noriega. With the final shots still echoing in the air, Lt. Gen. Carl Stiner and his primary staff from XVIII Airborne Corps arrived in Panama to begin planning a new operation. The result of numerous planning sessions that spanned from Lt. Gen. Stiner's first trip to Panama until H-hour was Op Plan 90-2, which was ultimately called Operation Just Cause. Blue Spoon was shelved and along with it the plan to introduce additional Marine forces into the theater.

"Marine Forces Panama was initially represented (at General Stiner's planning sessions in Panama) by my operations officer, Lt. Col. Michael Franks, and myself. Because of the operational security requirements, only one other Marine, Maj. Bron Madrigan (the JTF South/Panama liaison officer), was involved in the planning.

"After the initial concept of the plan was delivered, it was apparent that the follow-on Marine forces were not included. This and the expansion of the Marine forces mission caused me to query Lieutenant General Stiner about the changes. In my reasoning I stated that my mission had now changed from defensive to offensive, that my area of responsibility had expanded to over six hundred square miles. Lieutenant Colonel Franks and I continually attempted to get at least one additional Marine battalion included in the initial flow of forces into Panama. Lieutenant General Stiner decided that there would be no more additional Marine forces in Panama but agreed to provide me a battalion from the 82d Airborne Division no later that H+36. In subsequent planning sessions, Lieutenant General Stiner promised a battalion from the 7th Infantry Division (L) after realizing the potential heavy involvement of the 82d Airborne Division. The 7th ID(L) battalion, 2/27, was chopped OpCon to Task Force Semper Fi at H+57. Additional forces included OpCon of the 536th Engineer Battalion and 534th Military Police Company. (These were attached by H+1.)

"... there was little similarity between Blue Spoon and OpPlan 90-2. Blue Spoon was basically a defensive plan that had offensive execution only in response to given situations. OpPlan 90-2 had as its focus the ousting of General Noriega, neutralization of the PDF, the reestablishment of the rightful democratic government of Panama, and in doing so, the protection of U.S. citizens and U.S. property. The supporting plan for Marine Forces Panama was named Ghostbusters.

"Additional taskings for Task Force Semper Fi that were in the execution order but not in the OpPlan were: The seizing of the port of Vaca Monte, and the neutralization or destruction of all PDF in zone and the seizing of PDF facilities. This mission also included the capture of key Dignity Battalion members in the AOR (area of operations). The superb intelligence obtained by Task Force Semper Fi's S-2 resulted in the capture of a number of important Dignity Battalion members and PDF officers that had gone to ground."[8]

By the twentieth of December, Marine Forces Panama were trained in the skills they would need for the operation, were well acquainted with the vagaries of their AO and the people therein, and were eager to move out on their

70

missions. Captain Gaskins said that "At 0800 on 19 December . . . Colonel Richardson told me he wanted a complete maintenance standdown. I called my platoon commanders and staff together and informed them that until further notice all training had been canceled, and the appointed place of duty would be the company maintenance ramp. All Marines would perform maintenance on all combat-essential equipment as if 'their lives depended on it.' By 1800 on 19 December, all equipment was 100 percent ready." So were the Marines.

Given the administration's "hands off" policy, the intense and pertinent training, the detailed rehearsals, the thorough staff planning, the mix of the forces selected for the operation, the insistence on unity of command, and the specifics of the mission—by any reckoning, the operation should be a winner.[9]

II | COMBAT

8 | The Attacks Begin

The initial attacks of Operation Just Cause were launched by in-country forces.

Maj. Kevin M. Higgins commanded A Company of the 3d Battalion of the 7th Special Forces Group, normally based at Fort Davis on the Atlantic side of the canal, near Gatun. Six A Teams, each with twelve Special Forces troopers, made up A Company. Lt. Col. Roy R. Trumble commanded the 3d of the 7th. He was on his third tour in Panama and had held every possible officer position within the 3d of the 7th. His battalion was part of Task Force Black, a unit in General Downing's Joint Special Operations Task Force, commanded by Col. Jake Jacobelly, the in-country commander of Special Operations Command South (SOCSOUTH), a joint force. Normally he worked directly for the SOUTHCOM commander, General Thurman.

"The groundwork for 7th Special Forces group success in Just Cause and Promote Liberty (a follow-on, in-country, "nation-building" mission after the completion of Just Cause) was laid in the decade prior," wrote Major Higgins recently. "There were some Vietnam veterans in the 3/7, but the men of the 3/7 SFG(A) were products of the 1980s Reagan Latin American policy. It was 3/7 that executed FID program in Central America to counter Sandinista/Cuban initiatives. It was 3/7 that spearheaded the counternarcotics efforts in the source Andean countries. It was 3/7 that participated in countless joint exercises and personnel exchanges in the region. In part, this was due to the fact that SOUTHCOM could easily get their hands on 3/7, the small SF MTTs could easily and economically hitchhike to their destinations on aircraft transiting through Howard AF Base to South and Central America. The Bn Commanders, LTC Scruggs, LTC Stankovich, LTC Froberg, and finally LTC Trumble aggressively pursued mission opportunities. What eventually evolved was a very heavy work load of back-to-back 179-day real-world deployments. The men loved it. Only the most dedicated were attracted to the unit. And it was these

75

most dedicated soldiers that kept coming back to 3/7, Panama for additional tours or just simply stayed on. The result was an impressive collection of highly motivated/trained, culturally aware Spanish-speakers, intimately familiar with the Latin American military mind. This foundation was responsible for the unit's success in Just Cause/Promote Liberty."

On the eighteenth of December, after he had received a preliminary alert, Colonel Trumble moved his forward operating base (FOB) and all available SF personnel, about half of his battalion, some nine A teams, to a hangar at Albrook Air Force Base, just north of Balboa on the Pacific end of the canal. A company's and Higgins's final mission at the bridge (one of his original missions had been simply to reconnoiter the Pacora River Bridge with four men) was to secure the Pacora River Bridge and deny it to the enemy, particularly the elite and well-trained PDF Battalion 2000, whose barracks were at Fort Cimarron, about twenty miles to the northeast of Panama City. Battalion 2000 had three companies: one armor, one airborne, and one air assault. Blocking the bridge, about eight miles to the east of Torrijos/Tocumen Airport, would prevent Battalion 2000 and other PDF units from moving troops, ammunition, and weapons along Highway 1 (locally called the Panamerican or Pan-A Highway) to reinforce the 240 soldiers of the PDF at Torrijos/Tocumen, around which were the drop zones for the 75th Rangers and the 82d Airborne units arriving later.

In the original plan, the 3/7 had been assigned approximately twelve different four-man reconnaissance missions. "On 18 December," wrote Major Higgins, "only four were selected for execution on H-hour:

"Tinajitas Recon. A four-man team was dropped off at the back gate of Fort Clayton at 19 1900 December and moved cross country on foot to place 'eyes on target' on the Tinajitas PDF *cuartel*. They were in position by 20 0100 Dec.

"Cimarron *Cuartel*. At 19 2100 December, a four-man team was placed by UH-60 five kms. outside of Cimarron *cuartel* to report PDF movement.

"Cerro Azul TV2 Antenna. An eighteen-man team was deployed at 20 0100 December to capture and temporarily disable Noriega's primary media contact with the Panamanian people. . . .

"Pacora Bridge.

"The remaining planned missions were not executed mainly because they became irrelevant when the decision was made to do a massive invasion."[1]

Capt. Stuart W. Bradin, Citadel '84, was the commander of ODA (Operational Detachment A) 775 in A Company 3/7. He is the prototype of a Green Beret captain—handsome, with well-muscled arms and chest, slender waist, strong legs. "He is one of the best," said Major Higgins. Bradin could run ten miles carrying full combat gear. In conversation, he is straightforward, positive, and gives the impression of total commitment to and understanding of the nuances of his Special Forces job. In the three months just prior to Just Cause, he had traveled at some length.

On the thirteenth of September, Captain Bradin had completed a Spanish course at the Defense Language Institute and reported for duty to the 3d of the 7th at Fort Davis, Panama. On the third of October, after he received word of the botched coup attempt ("Pot Banger No. 5, the Green Berets called it), Higgins gave Bradin a mission packet for the old Blue Spoon plan. His mission:

On order, reconnoiter Torrijos/Tocumen Airport and the Pacora River Bridge with four men from ODA 775. But on the seventh of October, Bradin left Panama for Peru with eighteen men on a counternarcotics mission; he returned to Fort Davis on the seventh of December.

It was on the eighteenth of December, in the hangar at Albrook, that Major Higgins received his new orders from Colonel Trumble: Forget the original reconnaissance missions. Instead, take and hold the Pacora River Bridge, some twenty miles northeast of Albrook. "The Pacora was changed from a four-man recon to a 'seize and deny access' on 18 December," wrote Major Higgins. "The Rangers were supposed to drop on Tocumen and then move to seize Pacora, but the planners realized that would be too late to stop the Bn 2000."

For the assignment, Major Higgins initially had two UH-60 Black Hawk helicopters, the only two left from other H-hour missions. Because the 617th's MH60s had internal fuel bladders for increased range, each helicopter could carry only eight men. Thus Higgins could plan to insert only sixteen men for the operation, including Captain Bradin and his A Team. Higgins's troops came from four different A teams, including three captains, and, according to Higgins, "that's why LTC Trumble felt it was that the major went to control the operation."

In the isolation of the hangar, Major Higgins planned and briefed the operation in detail. Higgins assigned Captain Bradin and four of his men to hold the left flank of the far side of the bridge. He assigned other detailed missions to other teams in A Company. At 2000 hours on the night of the nineteenth, less than five hours to H-hour, Major Higgins briefed his teams a final time. Shortly thereafter, while he was inspecting his men, Higgins received word that he had an additional Black Hawk from the 228th Aviation Battalion for the mission. His executive officer, Captain Glover, quickly assigned eight more men to the teams and adjusted the loading plans. Higgins and his men were obviously flexible and well trained.

Higgins began loading his two A teams, twenty-four men, into the three Black Hawks at 0010 on the twentieth. During the loading, they were fired on from an area outside the fence around Albrook Air Force Base.

"With intermittent gunfire crackling," wrote Major Higgins, "and six UH60s cranked, the SOCSOUTH J-3 informed me that an eight-vehicle convoy had just departed Cimarron *cuartel* headed toward Tocumen, and H-hour was moved up fifteen minutes and we were to depart immediately. I told the men to load. I boarded the lead helicopter, put on the headset, and before I could brief the pilot, the pilot informed me that we couldn't land on the NE edge of the bridge as planned. With the additional third helicopter we would have to land on the SW edge of the bridge, 180 degrees out! After that news, I then brought the pilot up to date on the situation. He was unaware of the firing alongside the LZ, change in H-hour, and the PDF convoy. We immediately lifted off. In the air he briefed the other pilots and likewise the SF men on these new developments. The pilots made the immediate decision to scrap the flight plan and make a beeline for the bridge, a risk since at H-hour the airspace would be crowded."

Fifteen minutes later, at 0045, the three Black Hawks were approaching the

Pacora River Bridge. "From the helicopters we saw the lights of the eight-vehicle convoy (two jeeps and six 2½-ton trucks), headlights fifty meters apart, winding like a snake, way off in the distance, about two miles off," remembers Major Higgins. "The pilots went right up the road, straight toward the convoy, looking frantically for the bridge. We reached the bridge simultaneously with the convoy. The pilots had to do a buttonhook over the top of the convoy to get us into the LZ. All the SF men had seen the convoy prior to landing, so when we hit the ground, no explanation was needed. In retrospect, we were fortunate to land on the SW of the bridge and not the NE as planned. The NE would have put us in a hand-to-hand combat situation and we would never have been able to use the standoff of the AC-130."

The troops, each with a full load of combat gear, unloaded and deployed "on the double" into three security elements on both sides of the road on the west side of the bridge. They had to run about 100 meters through tall elephant grass and weeds and then climb up a steep, thirty-five-foot embankment, along the top of which ran the road leading to the bridge. Meanwhile, the PDF convoy had moved to within a hundred meters of the other side of the bridge. Higgins said later that he and his men "arrived moments before the enemy convoy began to cross the bridge."

Once on the embankment, Higgins organized his men into a hasty ambush, using antitank weapons and grenade launchers. To fire at the convoy, Sfc. Danny MacDonald, followed by Captain McNamara and Staff Sergeant Roman, armed with LAWs, climbed to the top of the embankment and stood in the middle of the road to fire directly across the bridge. Captain Bradin remembers seeing Sergeant First Class MacDonald fire a LAW at the lead 2½-ton truck. His missile went harmlessly through the truck's tarp, but the driver screeched to a halt, blocking the movement of the convoy. The drivers of the other trucks did not turn off their headlights and thus provided targets in the black of the night.

One of the NCOs who had been on the bridge said later: "I was carrying a SAW [squad automatic weapon]. We immediately set up our weapons on the west side of the bridge facing the oncoming convoy. As I set up my SAW, I could see several vehicles of the convoy coming down the road toward the bridge. Our mission was not only to stop the convoy but to deny movement over the bridge in either direction. As the convoy neared the bridge, we fired two AT-4 antitank rounds and three LAW rounds and several bursts of light machine gun fire at it, stopping the convoy in its tracks."

Major Higgins set up a small company command post southwest of the bridge near the embankment. With him was E-7 Eckloff, a member of an Air Force CCT (combat control team). Eckloff, covered by Master Sergeant Daly, set up his SATCOM (satellite communications) dish on the extreme flank of the position, on the edge of the firing area, to give the best possible firing data to an AC-130 when it came on station. He established communications with an AC-130 Specter, and it was overhead in half an hour, making left-hand circles around the bridge. With his night-vision devices, the Specter pilot could clearly see the stalled convoy. Eckloff radioed the pilot that "All west of the bridge are friendly." Given the marginal safety limits, the pilot asked: "Do you accept friendly casualties?" Higgins told Eckloff to reply affirmatively. Then the Specter, still circling in left-hand turns, began to fire.

The Specter has a devastating array of firepower: 20mm cannon, 7.62mm Gatling guns, and a 105mm howitzer that fires from the door. The Specter can lay down seventeen thousand rounds of ammunition a minute in a formidable, ruinous stream of shells and bullets.

The PDF soldiers scrambled out of the trucks and took up firing positions on the far side of the river. They fired their AK-47s and began moving toward the Special Forces position. The Green Berets returned fire with their M-16s, M-203 grenade launchers, and LAWs. The AC-130 continued to report to Eckloff on enemy movements and provided infrared illumination to increase the utility of the Special Forces' night-vision gear. Higgins said that the "AC-130 had to go off station for a few minutes at 0200. At that point, some PDF decided to come across the bridge. They gave me a scare, because they were carrying a mortar and wearing gas masks." Higgins's men took out the PDF trying to cross the bridge. A number of the PDF in desperation jumped off the side of the bridge.

"The AC-130 reported to us that he saw the PDF dismounting the vehicles and moving to both flanks (the riverbed)," wrote Major Higgins. "I assumed the PDF were following an infantry SOP. When you receive fire from the front, dismount and move to flank the enemy. In addition to firing lengthwise along the convoy, I had the AC-130 fire up and down the riverbed to thwart any counterattack. Likewise, we periodically directed SAW and M-203 fire into the riverbed tree line. I don't recall receiving any incoming PDF fire, although I never did query the men on that during the AAR [after-action review]."

As the firefight continued, Higgins's men spotted several vehicles in the distance moving toward the bridge from the opposite direction, threatening his men from both sides. "I thought this was a PDF relief column," remembers Higgins, "but in retrospect it was probably PDF fleeing from the scene at Tocumen to try to reach 'safety' at Cimarron." Higgins told his flank security force to fire tracers over them. The AC-130 continued to circle the area.

Col. Jake Jacobelly had been monitoring his command net since midnight. He learned from the traffic that the AC-130, which had been on station for some time and had helped disperse the PDF convoy, was running out of fuel. "I called the Air Force to request another AC-130 be expeditiously tasked to move to the area before the initial aircraft would have to leave," he remembered. "The result was continuous AC-130 coverage for the soldier on the ground. The Air Force's response proved that joint operations and interservice coordination worked well. We didn't need a credit card this time to complete the mission." (During the joint operation in Grenada, communications between the Army units on the ground and the Navy offshore required the Army sometimes to use commercial phones to call their headquarters at Fort Bragg. The messages were then relayed via satellite to the Navy commander, who passed the requests on to the air controllers aboard the aircraft carriers.)

In the meantime, SSG Roman had heard some movement under the bridge. He threw several grenades underneath it. The noise stopped. By 0300, the situation began to stabilize. Major Higgins sent out a small patrol to verify that none of the PDF had made it across the bridge. At 0500, a PDF corporal on a bicycle was captured trying to cross the bridge. "The corporal seemed to have no idea of what had taken place," Higgins said. "He was visiting his girlfriend that night out in the countryside. He thought the convoy had parked to take a rest for the night."

At dawn, about 0600, a quick-reaction force (QRF) from A Company of the 1st Battalion of the 7th Special Forces Group arrived by helicopter. The QRF and Major Higgins's team made a sweep of the destroyed convoy. They found eight of the PDF dead on the bridge. Special Forces medics treated the wounded PDF soldiers that they found. Perez's men captured several PDF hiding in a house off the road. Another Special Forces team collected weapons and munitions to be moved out of the area. Higgins established local security around the bridge and set up checkpoints to inspect vehicles for enemy soldiers and weapons.[2]

Another team processed and interrogated prisoners. The interrogation revealed that there had been some fifty-six soldiers from Battalion 2000's heavy-weapons company in the convoy. (Higgins said that he had seen reports that as many as two hundred were in the convoy and that Chepo Hospital, 15 kilometers east, treated more than thirty patients that night.) They were led by the company's executive officer and were armed with 81mm mortars, 90mm recoilless weapons, and .30-caliber and MAG-58 machine guns. According to the executive officer, the company was on the way into Panama City to put down "some sort of a civil disturbance" and he had "lost control" of the company after the fighting started. He also said that a large portion of Battalion 2000 had passed over the bridge the previous evening at 2200 and were presumably on the way to Tocumen and scattered throughout the city.

At about 1545, a scout platoon from the 82d Airborne Division, on the way to Fort Cimarron, linked up with Higgins and his men—none of whom had been wounded or killed. From Fort Cimarron, a 2½-ton truck flying a white flag came to pick up the PDF dead and wounded. A few of the PDF did escape and later ran into the Rangers and the 82d Airborne units at Tocumen. At 1730 Higgins, his twenty-four Green Berets, and twenty POWs were helicoptered by three CH-53s back to Albrook Air Force Base—mission accomplished.

Shortly after midnight, other Special Forces units had conducted special reconnaissance of Fort Cimarron to report on other movements of Battalion 2000 and of the Tinajitas compound, where PDF mortar capabilities were a concern. According to a postaction report from Gen. James Lindsay's U.S. Special Operations Command,

> Task Force Black also assisted our Psychological Operations effort by temporarily disabling the primary Panamanian television station's transmissions. No longer do our forces plant explosives and knock over an antenna tower. In this mission, a Special Forces A Team, with appropriate technical assistance, "fast-roped" (rappeled rapidly down a rope from a helicopter hovering above the site) into the station compound (at Cerro Azul) and removed a critical electronic module (of TV Channel 2's transmission facility) that disabled the

TV. This prevented the opposition from using this media to support their cause and allowed our EC-130 Volant Solo aircraft to broadcast supportive themes to the Panamanian populace. This method also allows us to restore normal station operations much sooner.

The Volant Solo broadcast information to the Panamanian people to remain inside and not to resist the U.S. forces whose goal was to capture Noriega.[3]

The two technicians who accompanied the Special Forces had never fast-roped before. After a very hurried five-minute explanation of the technique, they fast-roped with the team into the compound. One observer from the U.S. Southern Command remarked, "The experience must have been somewhat to their liking, since it took nine days for their unit to pry them away from the Special Forces."

"An additional force that can only be mentioned in passing is Task Force Blue and Task Force Green," wrote one of the Special Operations Command's officers. "These forces, supported by quick-reaction helicopters and AC-130 gunships, had the difficult task of capturing the elusive Noriega. Our intelligence efforts greatly narrowed the possibilities for his location and allowed this force to apply pressure to him commencing at H-hour. This pressure never let up, with our force systematically pursuing each substantive lead. This effectively denied Noriega a place to hide and prevented his escape from Panama."[4]

A later report from U.S. Special Operations Command on the peregrinations of the desperate Noriega reported,

> Pre-H-hour intelligence showed Noriega to be in Colón on 19 December 89, but his precise location on the evening of 19 December, both prior to and after H-hour, was not known. Subsequent analysis and sources reveal Noriega left Colón in the early evening of 19 December. He drove to the Cerimi Military Recreation Center Hotel at Tocumen Airfield for a rendezvous with a prostitute. While at this location, he barely escaped capture by TF Red at H-hour. He departed in such a hurry that he left his shoes and uniform at the site. They were later returned to him to wear for his surrender. Allegedly, it is the same uniform he wears at the trial. Noriega traveled to several houses of close supporters in urban Panama City on 20 December 89. He spent 21 through 24 December 89 in hiding at a house on the outskirts of Panama City, his efforts to move thwarted by search operations.

Noriega's days were numbered; the countdown was under way.

9 | Task Force White

Task Force White was the U.S. Navy's contribution to Just Cause. Naval Special Warfare Group 2 (NSWG-2), a part of U.S. Special Operations Command, is based at Little Creek, Virginia. NSWG 2 normally had one SEAL platoon on rotation to Panama. For Just Cause, SEAL Team 4, under Cmdr. Tom McGrath, deployed four more platoons to the operation aboard the C-141s that General Downing brought to Panama on the eighteenth of December. TF White, a total of some 707 sailors, also included special boat units and a countermine division.

The SEALs are the Navy's elite commandos. They are carefully selected for brains, brawn, and dedication, and they undergo an arduous training program at Coronado, California. Included in the program are long hours swimming in the cold Pacific Ocean, many nights running long and difficult obstacle courses, and lengthy instruction on weapons and marksmanship. The training is so difficult and backbreaking that two thirds of the recruits flunked the course in 1988.

Task Force White had three major missions in Operation Just Cause: Deny the PDF the use of their patrol boats in Balboa Harbor; deny Noriega the use of his personal jet at Paitilla Airport; and isolate PDF forces at Flamenco Island.[1]

Balboa Harbor, just inside the Pacific Ocean entrance to the canal, normally berths large PDF patrol boats. But Task Unit Whiskey's target just after midnight of the twentieth of December was Noriega's yacht, the *Presidente Porras*, a craft that he could use to escape from Panama.

The on-scene commander of Task Unit Whiskey, made up of two dive pairs and a fire support team, was Cmdr. Norman J. Carley. At 2300 on the night of 19 December, Carley led his two teams in two CRRCs (combat rubber raiding craft) from Rodman Naval Station on the Pacific end of the canal and across the canal from Balboa Harbor toward his target docked at Pier 18 in Balboa Harbor. Each dive pair was equipped with an MK-138 Mod 1 haversack armed with a MCS-1 clock and a MK-39 safety and arming device with a MK-96 detonator. In simple language, these were explosive devices to disable the *Presidente Porras*. The four-man fire support team, armed with .50-caliber machine guns, 60mm mortars, and MK-19 40mm machine guns, was in position at Rodman and within range of the underwater swimming teams' target. Another element of TU Whiskey was a group of six SEALs in two patrol boats, led by Lt. j.g. Martin L. Strong, standing by as a contingency surface force in the event that the underwater swimmers were "compromised."

Because of unexpected boat traffic in the harbor, Carley's two boats had to take a circuitous route to the point where he would insert the divers, and because H-hour had been moved up fifteen minutes, to 0045, Carley had to insert the teams closer to the target than he had planned. Unfortunately, one of the CRRCs had motor trouble while traveling at slow speed to avoid leaving a telltale wake. Carley went on with the first boat and concealed the team at a mangrove tree line north of the target area, Pier 18 at Balboa Harbor, until it was time to insert the divers. Then, at 2330, the first CRRC, with coxswain Hospitalman Chief George P. Riley and HT-3 Christoper J. Kinney aboard, maneuvered to a point about 150 meters from Pier 18, and Carley inserted the first team. Then, with CRRC 1, he returned to CRRC 2, whose coxswain was IS-3 Scott L. Neudecker, and towed it to the insertion point. In five minutes the second team was underwater near Pier 18. Carley towed the second boat back to Rodman for a new motor.

The four swimmers dove on a compass bearing to Pier 18 and surfaced underneath it. Then each team moved independently underneath the pier toward shore, alternating above and below the surface. The *Presidente Porras* was tied to a floating dock near shore. Near the end of the pier, the swimmers dove and began an approach that would bring them under the target. Swim pair 2, ET-1 Randy L. Beausoleil and PH-2 Christopher J. Dye, arrived at the target at 0011, made a positive identification, and attached the twenty-pound haversack to the port propeller shaft and armed the system. Swim pair 1, Lt. Edward L. Coughlin and EN-3 Timothy K. Eppley, swam under the target at 0014 and attached its haversack to the starboard propeller shaft, armed the system, and tied detonating cord leads between the charges to ensure dual priming. Both pairs finished their jobs in less than two minutes.

But it was not a completely easy task. As Coughlin and Eppley were finishing the arming sequence, the target boat's engines started. Coughlin and Eppley finished their job and swam rapidly to the concealment of Pier 17. Beausoleil and Dye joined them under the pier. Just as they got there, they felt the blast of underwater detonations nearby. They swam behind pier pilings for protection. Shortly thereafter, four more detonations bounced them in the water. The men, alternating on the surface and beneath it to conserve oxygen, moved along Pier 17 to their preplanned extraction point. They had set the timers to explode beneath the *Presidente Porras* in forty-five minutes. They were still under Pier 17 when their charges detonated at 0100, precisely on time, disabling the target ship. Following the detonation, most of the ships in the harbor began churning their propellers as an antiswimmer measure. Shortly thereafter, the divers left Pier 17 and headed on a course that brought them close to the main channel of the canal, where a large-draft ship sailed overhead and forced the divers to a depth of forty-five feet. After ten minutes at that depth, they swam up to their normal operating depth of twenty feet and headed for Pier 6, their preplanned extraction point.

At 0045, Commander Carley led the two CRRCs from Rodman and headed for Pier 6. They arrived at the seaward end of the pier fifteen minutes later and floated quietly under the pier. While waiting for the dive teams, Carley and his CRRC crews heard firefights overhead near the pier and saw tracer rounds flash overhead. Nonetheless, they stayed in place. Because the swim teams were late, Carley began to worry about them and sent CRRC 2 to the next pier downcurrent to see if the divers had missed the first extraction point. CRRC 2 returned without the divers.

At 0200, Coughlin and Eppley arrived at Pier 6; five minutes later, Beausoleil and Dye surfaced near the pier. The dive pairs were equipped with MX-300 radios in watertight bags, but they had been unable to communicate with each other or with Carley because the many obstructions and vessels in the harbor interfered with their transmissions. Carley immediately loaded the dive teams into the two CRRCs and set out for Rodman Naval Station. Once they had cleared the Balboa side of the canal, Carley lit an infrared strobe to facilitate recognition at Rodman and radioed TF White that TU Whiskey was returning to base. At 0220—three hours, twenty minutes after they had left Rodman—the teams beached their boats back at Rodman, their mission accomplished. It was one of the rare incidents in battle where a unit takes off on a combat mission from its peacetime base and returns after accomplishing its task. It was also the first time since World War II that underwater swimmers attacked a docked enemy vessel.[2]

*   *   *

Paitilla Airport, a private airfield in the southwestern corner of downtown Panama City, almost abuts the shore of the Pacific Ocean. The airport was frequently used by Noriega, who maintained an executive-type Learjet at Paitilla. Noriega's staff also used the field and the jet for other clandestine purposes, including drug-related operations. It fell to the SEALs to "deny the use of the jet and the airfield for a possible escape" by Noriega.

At 0045, the new H-hour, Task Unit Papa, three SEAL platoons, a total of ninety-two men led by Cmdr. Tom McGrath, landed from rubber raiding boats along the beach at Paitilla. Earlier, in camouflage fatigues and jungle boots and carrying rucksacks and weapons, they had loaded up in combat rubber raiding crafts (CRRCs) on the dark beach of Rodman Naval Station on the west side of the canal, hooked onto the back of a Navy patrol boat, and were towed across the canal in the black of the night. Then, two miles offshore, the patrol boat turned them loose. For a short time the boats remained tied together on the ocean, but when word came to move up H-hour by fifteen minutes, McGrath ordered the boats to head immediately for Paitilla.

Lt. John Patrick Connors and Lt. Mike Phillips were SEAL platoon commanders. They had served together in the Persian Gulf and for four months of jungle training in Brazil. Both were superbly fit physically and extremely well qualified in the skills of a SEAL. (One requirement for SEAL qualification was an underwater swim of seven miles at night from one point to another with navigation by compass.) Connors, twenty-five, from Boston and a Boston Marathon runner, also spoke fluent Spanish. "John had a strong sense of patriotism," said his best friend, John Sheehan. "He was the kind of character who is full of life and lives it to the fullest." Before the operation, Connors was undergoing treatment for a skin disease he had contracted from a sandfly bite in Brazil. But he so much wanted to be on the operation that he faked a release from the hospital by telling his doctor at Walter Reed that he had "an emergency in his family." Connors joined his platoon the day before it moved from Little Creek.

As soon as the rubber boats beached on the hard mud of the beach at Paitilla at 0045, the SEALs unloaded and spread out in a security perimeter. The grass was low and afforded little concealment. The SEALs could see people moving under the control tower's lights, but the area of the field near them, the south side, was apparently deserted. Five minutes later, two platoons moved north on the western side of the field and one platoon and the mortar section moved north on the eastern side. They moved as they had been taught and as they had trained: One squad moved forward at a crouch, while another squad knelt in position and covered the other's advance. In the distance they could see tracers in the sky and hear the rumble of artillery and tank guns as other Just Cause forces attacked the Comandancia and parts of Fort Amador.

Phillips's platoon raced across the open strip to the PDF hangar that housed Noriega's Learjet. But an M-60 gunner in the first squad of Phillips's platoon identified and took under fire the armed guards in the adjacent Aero Perla hangar at the same time that Phillips ordered his men to disable the Learjet in the PDF hangar. The guards in both the Aero Perla hangar and the PDF hangar opened fire simultaneously with their AK-47's at the first squad at the edge of the parking ramp only thirty meters away. The fire was devastating: The Panamanians killed one man in the squad and wounded seven others. Phillips raced forward with the rest of his platoon, firing as they approached. When he saw the extent of his first squad's casualties, he called immediately for MEDEVAC. Phillips recognized that the Specter gunship on station overhead could not fire into the hangars without endangering his men. But he knew that he would need help to suppress the PDF in the hangar with heavy fire so that he could evacuate his wounded.

So did Commander McGrath. He immediately ordered the 2d and 3d platoons to reinforce and assist Phillips's platoon. Phillips had already spread out his other two squads and took both hangars under fire. In a few minutes, Connors and his platoon arrived. Connors spread out his men and led them, firing as they moved forward toward the hangars. Phillips remembered later that Connors showed no fear as he moved across the parking area from which the PDF bullets ricocheted off the hard surface and sparked all around Connors and his advancing men.

As Connors moved forward in the lead of his platoon, PDF bullets hammered against his web equipment and his ammo pouches. But he slowed only briefly. He ran forward firing his M-16 as he charged the hangar and the PDF guards. The PDF increased their fire at this new threat. The hangar was of cinder block,

85

and the SEALs' small arms had little effect unless they caught a PDF firing from a window.

Connors decided to use his grenade launcher, slung under his M-16. He knelt on one knee and loaded a grenade. At that moment, the PDF opened fire with a machine gun and blasted Connors in the chest. Phillips ran to Connors and dragged him out of line of the PDF fire. Other SEALs carried Connors to the MEDEVAC triage point. The medics cut away his uniform and webgear and tried to resuscitate him, but it was too late.

By now the 2d Squad of the 2d Platoon maneuvered forward to reinforce the 2d Squad of the 1st Platoon and took the hangars under fire. Then the 2d Squad of the 3d Platoon reinforced the 1st Platoon. Together the 2d and 3d platoons suppressed the enemy fire in both hangars with rockets, grenades, and machine guns. On the scene, Commander McGrath consolidated his three platoons into one perimeter.

Lieutenant Phillips went back to the triage point as soon as the perimeter was secure. There he found the medics working feverishly with the wounded. But he also found Torpedoman's Mate 2d Cl. Isaac Rodriguez, twenty-four, of Missouri City, Texas, mortally wounded and, lying in the grass, three dead SEALs: Connors; Boatswain's Mate 1st Cl. Christopher Tilghman, thirty, of Kailua, Hawaii; and Engineer Chief Donald McFaul, thirty-two, of San Diego.

By 0117, all enemy fire was suppressed; the Learjet was disabled; and, at 0330, Paitilla Airport was secure.[3]

The Navy awarded Lt. John Patrick Connors the Silver Star posthumously.

In another part of the city, just three miles from Paitilla Airport, a pre-H-hour strike was under way. It had been carefully planned and meticulously rehearsed by the Army's Delta Force, a unit trained and equipped for rescues under hostile conditions. The White House and General Powell were watching this one very intently. The man the Delta Force was going to try to rescue was a special case.

10 | The Rescue of Kurt Muse

On the nineteenth of December 1989, Kurt Muse was locked up in Modelo Prison, across the street from Noriega's headquarters, La Comandancia. But Muse was no ordinary jailbird. And his release was just moments away. Nor was that ordinary.

"The CIA was deeply concerned about Muse and wanted to avoid a repeat of the 1984 kidnapping and subsequent murder of their station chief in Beirut, William Buckley," wrote Bob Woodward in *The Commanders*. "In that episode, the agency's inability to locate and rescue one of its own had made it appear weak. So CIA director William H. Webster pressed Cheney to have the military draw up a rescue plan for Muse that would be ready for execution on short notice."

Maj. Gen. Gary Luck was the commander of the Joint Special Operations Command (JSOC) during the planning phase for Just Cause. At 1000 on the sixteenth of October, General Luck met with General Powell in his Pentagon office and gave him two thirty-minute briefings. In the first, Luck outlined his capabilities: Deploy anywhere in the world on short notice with a force of about 300 trained specialists, including helicopters, Delta troopers, a SEAL team, intelligence teams, special communicators armed with very sophisticated equipment, and medics. These men, tailored to a mission's requirements, could rescue Americans or other hostages. For operations in Panama, all he needed at any time—around the clock—was four hours to assemble his force and five hours to fly there. In the second briefing, Luck detailed Operation Acid Gambit, a plan to snatch Muse from Modelo Prison.

In this briefing, Luck had aerial photos of Modelo, a detailed, three-dimensional model of the prison with walls that flapped down to show the details of the interior, intricate maps of the neighborhood, and the location of guard posts, doors, stairs, and Muse's room. Luck outlined how the rescue would take place, minute by minute. He stated confidently that Muse would be out of his cell and on a helicopter on the roof nine minutes after the assault began.

Later, Luck's Special Forces actually rehearsed the Muse rescue plan in an isolated Florida area using a three-quarter-size mock-up of the prison. The rehearsal took place near the area where, in 1970, Col. Bull Simons had built a mock-up of the North Vietnamese Son Tay prison camp prior to the raid to rescue American POWs. In that case the raid was successful except for one major point: The North Vietnamese had moved the POWs just before the Green Beret raiders descended on the camp.[1]

Kurt Muse was born in Phoenix, Arizona, in 1950. Soon after his birth, his parents, both American citizens, moved to Panama, where the senior Muse went into the graphic-arts business. Kurt had one brother and one sister, and the three of them attended grade school in Panama. Kurt became so fluent in Spanish that his parents, to improve his English, enrolled him in Balboa High School in the United States–administered Canal Zone. All the "Army brats"— the children of the U.S. Army troops permanently stationed in Panama— attended Balboa High School. There Kurt met his future bride, the queen of the junior-senior prom, Anne Castoro. After high school, where Muse had been voted the "best all-around" and most friendly student, he went on to the University of Texas at El Paso and later served as an air defense artillery officer in the U.S. Army. Thereafter, he returned to Panama with his wife.

By the early 1980s, Kurt's father had expanded the business to include three quick-print shops, a graphic-arts distribution company, and stores that sold supplies to engineers, artists, and architects. There was enough of the family business to provide comfortable livelihoods for the entire Muse family. By this time Kurt and Anne had two children, Kimberly and Erik.

True to his classmates' appraisal of him, Kurt was an outgoing man, a personable gentleman. He was a golfer, a sailor, a "four-wheeler," and very active in the Panama City Rotary Club. He was the first baseman on the Rotary Club's softball team and, one year, the chairman of the Central American convention for Rotary International, a job requiring a great expenditure of time and polished skill at management and organization. He was also on the Salvation Army's local advisory board. The Muse family had retained its American citizenship, but because of his fluency in Spanish and his business and Rotary connections, Kurt was integrated into and accepted in Panamanian society.

In spite of Noriega's increasingly tight stranglehold on Panama, Muse stayed out of politics until 1987. "Noriega was bleeding the country dry," he said later. "He was sapping its morals—it was becoming an immoral place, with institutionalized graft. And the kids were starting to emulate their parents." And the Muse family business was beginning to feel the effects of the free-wheeling crimes of the digbats. They had burned down one of the quick-print shops because, they had thought, mistakenly, that it was printing anti-Noriega propaganda. Noriega's drug indictments in the United States in 1988 and the obvious, blatant evidence of widespread corruption in the government caused Muse a great deal of concern about the threat to the well-being of the only country he really knew: Panama.

In his spare time, Muse enjoyed monitoring PDF communications on a very simple Radio Shack police scanner that he owned and operated, even though possession of such a scanner was forbidden by Noriega's entrenched autocrats. But Muse was amused by the PDF's awkward and heavy-handed attempts to control the increasing number of demonstrations against the powers that were. "The whole country was in an uproar," he said later. "Every other street corner had burning tires on it." Another Rotarian shared Muse's interest in eavesdropping on the PDF, the police. The other Rotarian was a computer specialist. "He and I found each other doing the same thing," he remembered. "We began pooling our resources and assigned different frequencies to each other."

One day in the fall of 1987, Muse attended the opening of a Salvation Army school for the blind in Panama City. Agents of the PDF were also on hand in an obviously blatant attempt to show the people that the dictatorship of Noriega was somehow benevolent and "people-caring." At the dedication, Muse met another Rotarian and suggested to him, as they watched the PDF strut around officiously, bellowing orders into their hand-held radios, that it would be "nice if we could actually get into their communications and talk to those sons of bitches."

Muse's friend owned a small communications company and told Muse that it was a lot easier than he might imagine. He said that there were other Rotarians who were also listening in to the PDF network and that somehow they ought to form a clandestine group to monitor the PDF communications. A couple of weeks later, the five Rotary listeners were a loosely organized but dedicated group.

The Rotarians started out as a bunch of amateurs armed only with police scanners. "We simply grabbed blocks of frequency and scanned them to find communications," Muse said later. In time they managed to isolate PDF channels, interpret the PDF codes, and utilize their own two-way radios, which they had bought in Miami, to communicate with each other, actually using the PDF's own codes. They became increasingly proficient at interpreting the language of the PDF network, given the fact that the soldiers communicated in militarese and code. In flipping through the frequencies, the Rotarians happened upon the cellular-telephone channels used by the PDF and government hierarchy. They listened, for example, to officials talking intimately to their girlfriends. On these and other channels they heard drug dealers making connections, military officials actually telling a newspaper that the lead editorial for the next day was en route, and a Colombian drug dealer asking that police be removed from a shopping center so that a transfer could be made in the parking lot. Shortly they heard a command go out to the police in the area to attend an emergency meeting someplace away from the shopping center.

Muse stored much of the information in his Apple II GS computer in his den at home. But the Rotarians were still passive eavesdroppers and not involved in any overt activities. That was soon to pass.

On Saturday morning, 27 February 1988, Muse and his four fellow Rotarians were meeting to mull over the preceding weeks' events. They had their scanner turned on while they talked. At one point they heard a startling PDF transmission—an order to arrest the legal president of the country, Eric Arturo

Delvalle, and Vice President Roderick Esquivel. Esquivel was a doctor and a fellow Rotarian. Immediately, Muse and some of his compatriots raced to Esquivel's office ahead of the PDF, packed him into the back of their car, and sped off past the PDF. Esquivel was safe but then went underground.

From that date on, the group became more bold, innovative, and successful. With some more sophisticated equipment that Muse bought and smuggled into Panama City, the group found to their amazement and delight that they could override the signal from Radio Nacional. They called it "nuking." And they also realized that if they could "nuke" the Radio Nacional transmitter, they might also be able to broadcast their own messages while the government station's broadcasts were off the air. They tried it, with some apprehension, when Noriega himself was about to make a statement. When the announcer said, "And here is General Noriega . . . ," Muse and his friends punched the transmit button and all Panama heard: "We interrupt this program to bring you a message from free and democratic Panamanians, a message to their oppressors. . . ." The message lasted three minutes.

Later Muse said, "Our hearts were racing. There we are, listening to our message being broadcast all over the nation, realizing that all of the agencies in the country are going apeshit. Not knowing when a helicopter gunship was going to appear on the horizon, not knowing if troops were going to storm the house. I mean, it was a major emotional event." For the time being, the group of conspirators, flushed with their initial success, hid their equipment and departed the apartment that they had leased under a false name.

But, with success, the horizon opened, and the amateur communicators became more audacious and inventive. They bought timers and tape recorders from Radio Shack and set up a studio in a vacant apartment. The mechanism worked automatically with the timers so no Rotarian need be present and therefore could not be caught. They "nuked" talk shows and music programs with one-minute broadcasts as often as seven times an hour. One talk show emcee was so frustrated by the interruptions that he offered, on the air, to sell his tormentors radio time if they would stop. They reported on antigovernment demonstrations and broadcast public-service announcements and statements from Noriega's chief opposition group, the National Civic Crusade. And with new equipment bought in the States, they could now communicate directly with the PDF, even though, of course, the PDF did not know the origin of the interruptive communications. The Rotarians often urged the troops to revolt. They sent confusing orders to the PDF during protest demonstrations. And they ridiculed and harassed Noriega's elite riot unit, the Dobermans, calling them cowards and flunkies. Muse proved it one day when he contacted a Doberman officer on his portable radio and told him to look up at the apartment building near where he stood. Muse then told him that he could see him (he could not) and he had a thirty-power scope aimed "right down your running lights" and, "if he was brave," he would do something about it. A friend of Muse's on the scene told Muse that the Dobermans in the area scrambled in a hurry and slid under trucks and hid behind bushes.

The U.S. CIA and the U.S. Southern Command knew who was behind the anti-Noriega radio operation that was causing so much heartburn and difficulty for the Noriega regime. Early in 1989, Vice President Esquivel gave Muse and his team, now six in number, a sophisticated new transmitter. Muse suspected that the transmitter came from the CIA because of its sophistication. Later they received a second radio transmitter and a television transmitter. By now they were calling themselves "Radio Voz de la Libertad" and were broadcasting at 91.5 on the FM channel, with no program longer than fifteen minutes. For their radio broadcast times, they selected periods when traffic was heaviest so they could reach the largest number of people, and the heavy traffic would hinder the PDF from trying to find Muse's transmitter.

But the PDF, using direction finders and better-trained experts, and possibly with some help from the Cubans, began to close in on the locations of the transmitters. From nearby apartments, the Rotarian conspirators could actually watch the PDF, in unmarked cars or taxis, surreptitiously scout the area where they thought the transmitters were housed. In one raid, the PDF ransacked Apartment 10A in a building and stormed adjacent apartments. But the transmitter was in Apartment 10A in a building across the street. The government finally went so far as to announce that it would pay thousands of dollars for clues leading to the arrest of the illegal broadcasters. A few days later, the Rotarians, camouflaged as beachgoers, smuggled their equipment in several drink coolers out of the apartment within sight of PDF guards.

In the spring of 1989, the broadcasts were continuing even more boldly, some going so far as to encourage the PDF to vote for the opposition. Encouraged by their continued successes, Muse and a cohort went to Miami to investigate some new equipment. But on the way back through customs at Torrijos/Tocumen Airport, Muse found that his days of freedom were over. He handed his passport to an immigration official, who passed it routinely to a member of Panama's G-2 unit. At about the same time, Muse saw a sign taped to the booth's glass window that startled him. It read: "Kurt Muse. American citizen. Arrest him on sight."

The G-2 agent checked the passport, then a book, then the sign on the booth, and left. He returned with four civilian-garbed security men. They asked Muse to come with them for a "routine" check. The security men hustled Muse into a van with darkened windows and took him to a PDF substation managed by one Major Miranda, a short, dark man who sat behind his desk and tapped on it with his riding crop. Three PDF officers stood behind Miranda.

"We know you're a big spy," Miranda said. He examined Muse's passport, asked him a lot of questions about his travels, and wanted to know if he had been spying for the Americans in Nicaragua. Muse had reasonable answers for each of the questions. Then Miranda ordered Muse into a truck, and they took him to his home.

Muse lived in a two-story, Spanish-style home. His wife was in Miami, his son was visiting a friend, and only his fifteen-year-old daughter, Kimberly, was at home. Muse ran up the steps ahead of the guards. Kimberly met him and asked about his trip. Muse hugged her and told her in a low voice that he was being arrested. "These people are here to take me to jail. I want you to leave. Now."

Later, Kimberly said: "I could hear his heart beating. It was the first time I'd ever seen my dad scared. You'd never think he could be afraid of anything."

Kimberly ran out past the PDF but fell on the pavement and skinned her knees. Two PDF caught her and pulled her back to the house. But Miranda let her go. She quickly went to a pay phone and called her mother in Miami, her grandparents who lived in the neighborhood, and her brother.

Meanwhile, the PDF ransacked the house and jammed everything they thought was important, including all the papers from Muse's desk, into canvas bags. They also confiscated Muse's weapons, a Glock pistol and a carbine, and several boxes of ammunition.

Muse thought that he had been arrested because of the illegal broadcasts and the interference with the PDF communications. What he didn't know was that Miranda didn't know of these activities. What trapped him was that the wife of a man who made broadcast tapes for the radio transmissions had told the PDF only that Muse was "involved in seditious activity." But the guns in Muse's house made Miranda think that he had captured a terrorist. Miranda then directed searches of Muse's office downtown and his parents' home.

Fortunately, word of Muse's arrest spread rapidly to his fellow Rotarians. That night, twenty-six people, the Rotarians and their families, sought asylum in the United States–controlled Panama Canal Zone. They were granted asylum by some perplexed U.S. officers who were unaware at the time of the Rotarians' exploits.

At about 0100 the next morning, the PDF took Muse to the headquarters of the DENI (Departmento Nacional de Investigación), the Panamanian FBI. For the next two and a half days, a series of interrogators fired question after question at him. If he nodded, one of the investigators would tap him on the head with a pencil or pen. They fed him and permitted him to go to the bathroom but not to shower, shave, or change his clothes. If they left, they'd turn on a "boom box" behind his ear. Finally, exhausted, he began to mix up his answers. When they showed him yet another apartment key that he had trouble passing off, he finally confessed. "I'm Radio Libertad," he told them. "In that apartment you're going to find a transmitter."

Muse was finally allowed a couple of hours of sleep. Later he underwent more intensive interrogation and harassment by the DENI. In a few days, the government held a press conference to display publicly its "Yankee spy." Later he was taken to the office of the DENI chief, Lt. Col. Nivaldo Madrinan. Inside the office were ten people, three of whom were Americans. Because Muse's wife, Anne, was a teacher in the Canal Zone, Muse was technically a U.S. dependent and entitled to some protection as outlined in the Panama Canal Treaty of 1978. One of the Americans read Muse his rights and asked him if he understood them. "Inside I'm laughing and crying," he remembered later. "I'm screaming silently that I have no rights, that that pig over there, a PDF colonel, is going to issue me my rights. He's going to kill me if he wants. I belong to him." But he said that he understood his rights.

The three Americans would be Muse's contact with the outside world for the next nine months. One was an Air Force physician, Lt. Col. Jim Ruffer. Another was Lt. Col. Robert Perry of the Army. A third was a U.S.-Panamanian lawyer, Dr. Marcus Ostrander. They met with him every other day throughout his incarceration. Muse remembers that they were most supportive and that Perry "went the whole nine yards for me, never gave up." Ruffer "became my confidant, shrink, doctor, everything."

In a few days, the DENI moved Muse to a facility in the San Felipe district of Panama City. All day long, Muse was guarded by a man with a shotgun. He watched while the DENI thugs booked and interrogated suspects. On one occasion, the PDF brought in a Colombian for booking. Apparently he was uncooperative. Two PDF men smashed him in the face and ricocheted him off the walls. They put him in handcuffs, with one arm behind his back and the other over his shoulder. They kicked him in the groin and on his back and sides until he bled. "They beat this guy mercilessly," recalled Muse. They stood on his face with their boots, mashing it the way you would mash out a cigarette. They hit him across the back with a crowbar. It was horrible, horrible. I was certain he was going to die. I just sat there praying, 'Have mercy on this guy.' "

"Hey, shouldn't we get the gringo out of here?" one of the PDF asked the officer in charge of the beating.

"Leave the gringo here," he said. "He should know what could happen to him."

Later, Muse was moved to another police substation for additional interrogation. When the police were satisfied—they told him that the Noriega crowd was "Happy with his cooperation"—they moved him to Modelo Prison. His cell was on the second floor of the prison, an eight- by twelve-foot room with an adjoining bathroom. The U.S. embassy had meals brought to him twice a day.

The PDF confined Muse to his cell for the first four months except for visits to the hospital for physical exams by Colonel Ruffer, always in the presence of PDF officers. Ruffer and Muse managed to develop a code, based on whether he was wearing socks, to alert Ruffer that Muse needed to see someone. Muse was permitted to have one book per day, and he and Colonel Ruffer developed a signal to let Ruffer know that Muse had hidden a message in the spine of the returned book. One message actually got to President Bush. "Only military force could solve the problem of Panama," he wrote. In response, President Bush wrote to Muse's wife and children, now residing in the Washington, D.C., area, and invited them to visit the White House after his release.

During his nine months in prison, Muse watched the beatings of other prisoners, particularly after the 7 May elections, in which the opposition defeated Noriega's candidate and that Noriega annulled. One hundred fifty antigovernment protesters were jailed after the election and were, at one time, lined up along a wall, four at a time, and beaten with hoses. They "just beat the bejesus out of them," Muse recalled.

The short-lived coup attempt of 3 October had disastrous results for the rebels. Muse watched a lot of the action from his prison window across the street from La Comandancia. At 0830, some troops set up machine guns around the headquarters building, and a short firefight started. To Muse, it seemed that the troops who had moved in toward the building were winning. A small red helicopter had landed outside the headquarters earlier. Then at 1000, forces loyal to Noriega arrived in armored vehicles and attacked the building. The rebels inside the building returned the fire. But by 1330, the coup had fizzled. Muse heard some shots from inside La Comandancia and assumed that the rebels inside were being murdered. That afternoon, the PDF replaced the prison guards, and about 150 rebels were brought into the prison. Every night for weeks, Muse heard the sounds of beatings as the PDF clubbed the rebel officers with fists, hoses, and clubs. Once the interrogators arrived, "the torture would begin," Muse remembered. "The sound of a man being tortured is indescribable."

After the 3 October attempt to overthrow Noriega, Muse noticed a change in the atmosphere in the prison. New guard posts on the roof and in the halls were manned. There was a new guard at a desk at the end of hall. Through one of the rebel officers, using hand signals, Muse learned that an American officer had been killed on 16 December. On Tuesday, 19 December, he watched the PDF soldiers reinforce the sandbags around La Comandancia. He realized that something drastic was about to take place in Panama. To make matters far worse, the guard at the desk in the corridor told him, in answer to Muse's pointed question, that "Yes," he would kill him if anything happened. That evening, Muse drifted off into a troubled sleep.

He was awakened at 0045 on the twentieth by the sound of machine-gun fire. He grabbed a metal bed brace that he had kept concealed. The guard, however, woke some PDF officers and yelled at them, "Something's happening!" Muse thought that "World War III broke loose outside."

He heard the sound of the AC-130 firing its 105mm gun at the Comandancia and saw the black hole in the building where it had hit. He heard machine guns firing on the ground and from the air. The lights went out in the prison. He heard a loud explosion close by, a blast that sent debris into his cell. Then there were two more explosions followed by machine-gun fire. He could hear men shouting and running. The halls were black with smoke. Then, said Muse, "this apparition comes to my cell door. The guy looks like Darth Vader. He's wearing a funny-looking helmet, funny-looking goggles, funny-looking uniform, and had a funny-looking weapon." Muse did not know it at the time, but the soldier he saw shining a light into his cell was a Delta Force commando.

"Moose!" he yelled. "You okay?"

"Yo," Muse shouted back.

"Stay down. I'm going to blow the door!"

With that, after a blast, the Delta trooper was in the cell. "We're going to take you out. We're going to the roof. We have a chopper. You're going to get in the middle. Do you understand?"

"You got it," said Muse.

Muse could hear the sound of the battle outside and see the flashes of explosions reflected on his cell walls. The Delta trooper put a flak vest and a helmet on Muse and led him out into the corridor through the smoke. They climbed up a flight of stairs and emerged onto the roof. There was a small Hughes D-500 Bumblebee helicopter, with its rotor turning, on the roof. Other Delta troopers in the same black outfits surrounded the helicopter.

At 0111 on the twentieth, Powell and Cheney were in the Pentagon's Crisis Situation Room listening to a loudspeaker broadcasting reports from Thurman's SOUTHCOM. The word was that the Delta team was on the roof of the prison. At 0113 came the message that Muse was out of prison and on the roof.[2]

Muse described the scene. "There are helicopter gunships unloading on the Comandancia. Smoke. Fire. Tracers going down, tracers going sideways, tracers coming toward us."

The Delta troopers loaded Muse into the helicopter with a soldier on each side of him. Three more troopers climbed onto the pods on either side of the helicopter. Just as the chopper lifted off the roof, it was hit by fire from the ground. The chopper flew off the top of the building and landed on the street between the prison and the Comandancia. The chopper could not lift off, but it could lumber down the street a few feet off the ground. He drove it as "though it were a car," Muse thought. The pilot veered into a parking lot and tried to take off again. It got to about thirty feet in the air when it was hit again by fire, this time from PDF around the Comandancia. The chopper fell and landed sideways on its left pod, injuring three men who had been hanging onto the pod.

At about 0130, SOUTHCOM reported that the helicopter carrying Muse and the Delta team had crashed and that all of the troops, including Muse, might be dead. Powell was clearly disappointed. One mission given by the president—rescue Muse—apparently had ended in disaster.

At the crash site, the leader of the Delta team ordered his men to evacuate the helicopter. Muse had lost his helmet and was stunned but unhurt. One of the rescuers had taken a bullet that went through his leg and up toward his chest. One of the Delta team was knocked down by the whirling rotor blade as the helicopter fell on its side.

The rest of the team placed the wounded between a building and a Jeep Wagoneer parked next to it and took up a defensive position. In spite of their wounds, the casualties insisted on helping man the position. Muse, who knew the area well, told the Delta troopers that a likely attack would come from the direction of the Comandancia. One of the Delta men held up an infrared strobe light. A few minutes later a Black Hawk helicopter flew overhead and rocked from side to side to acknowledge their position. In a few minutes, Muse heard tracked vehicles coming toward them. "It had to be the cavalry," thought Muse. "Obviously they were Plan B, waiting to pick us up if something happened."

The Delta team loaded the wounded, Muse, and themselves aboard the first armored personnel carrier, and the driver radioed his unit commander that "We have the PC." The carrier headed back up the street between Modelo Prison and the Comandancia, back toward the Canal Zone. As they lumbered down the street, Muse could see "flames everywhere," fires set by the digbats. The whole district seemed to be on fire. Muse could barely make out Panamanians on the balconies of their apartments waving white handkerchiefs, flags, and towels and banging pots and pans.

When they got to Balboa High School, they unloaded the personnel carrier, and the U.S. medics took charge. After the wounded were readied for a flight, they boarded a helicopter and landed at Howard Air Force Base next to a MASH unit. A doctor examined Muse and found him in good health, save for some bruises. Muse got permission from a somewhat reluctant colonel with

Delta Force to see his wounded rescuers. One, the man with the chest wound, was in intensive care. For the first time, Muse could see the faces of the Delta men who saved him. "These guys were beat to hell," he said later. "Blankets over them, IVs, stitches, clotted blood, casts. They really looked bad. But they were all smiling."

"You guys are the meanest and ugliest fuckers I've met in my life. But I love you. You guys saved my life and I'm eternally, eternally grateful. . . . So long, guys."

At 0220, SOUTHCOM notified the Crisis Room that Muse was safe and out. Powell called CIA director Webster and told him, "Just wanted you to know we got your man out and he's safe." Cheney called the White House. Earlier he had talked to Gen. Brent Scowcroft. But after the first call, all calls from Cheney went directly to the president. This time Cheney had the good news: "Muse was out and safe," and Delta Force had done its job in less time than their rehearsals.

After Muse came out of the ward where the injured Delta men were in beds, he ran into the Delta colonel again. The colonel told him, "I want to thank you for talking to my troops. My guys train for a lot of missions. They train long and hard, and they never get to do many of them. But for this one they trained long and they trained hard and they got to do it."

At about noontime, Muse boarded a private jet and flew to Miami still dressed in his bloody prison garb: a T-shirt, torn Levi's, worn tennis shoes. After going through customs, aided by the pilots, he was escorted to a man and woman in civilian clothes. After a lunch and a beer in a Denny's restaurant, he was flown to Dulles International Airport near Washington, D.C., where he met his wife and children in a private terminal. Muse's nightmare was over. A few days later, he and his family's meeting with President Bush climaxed his release from Modelo.[3]

Kurt Muse had obviously not been an ordinary prisoner.

11 | The Comandancia

"The 3 October '89 coup resulted in dramatic modification of OpPlans; generally from passive defense to offense," wrote Col. Mike Snell after the operation was over. And to his Panama-based 193d Infantry Brigade fell the extremely important missions of (1) defending Ancon Hill, where several U.S. installations, including U.S. Southern Command headquarters and the U.S. Gorgas General Hospital, are located, and (2) attacking and neutralizing some of the most significant targets in Panama: La Comandancia, Noriega's headquarters, the Panamanian "Pentagon," a Priority One target and less than a thousand meters from the peak of Ancon Hill; 5th Compañía de Infantería barracks at Fort Amador; the Balboa and Ancon DENI stations; the Ancon DNTT; the PDF Engineer Compound; Pier 18, Balboa Harbor; and the PDF Dog Compound, a mission that would later take on more than passing interest to feminists and women's rights advocates throughout the country.

As Colonel Snell put it, his mission was

> to protect U.S. lives and property, defend the Panama Canal, and neutralize the PDF. TF Bayonet's area of operations varied throughout Operation Just Cause as forces were assigned and reassigned within the Joint Task Force. The focus of TF Bayonet's operations remained fairly constant and included the east bank of the Panama Canal, from Paraiso in the north to the causeway islands in the south, the bulk of which was former Canal Zone territory. In addition, TF Bayonet focused on the Santa Anna, Chorillo and San Felipe sections of Panama City, with other sections coming temporarily under the TF's control.

On 16 November 1989, four M551A1 Sheridan tanks from the 3d Platoon of C Company of the 3d Battalion, 73d Armor and six Apache helicopters, all from the 82d Airborne Division, landed in C-5 aircraft, under cover of darkness, at

Howard Air Force Base on the west side of the canal. Later, covered with canvas tarps on tank transport trailers, the Sheridans were moved to a nearby bivouac area on the west bank, at Camp Rousseau. The tank crews then stashed the Sheridans under GP medium tents to camouflage them as sleeping tents until D-day. Just prior to H-hour, the tank crews threw off the tents and drove their tanks to overwatch positions on Ancon Hill.

To carry out his missions, mostly in urban areas in and around Panama City, Colonel Snell had a formidable task force of some three thousand soldiers and Marines formed into fifteen company-size units plus the platoon of M551 Sheridan tanks from the 82d Airborne Division and one platoon of Light Armored Vehicles (LAVs) from the Marine Corps' Panama augmentation forces.[1]

One of Snell's three task forces was Lt. Col. James W. Reed's TF Gator, made up predominantly of the 4th Battalion, 6th Infantry, a battalion from the 5th Infantry Division (Mechanized) stationed at Fort Polk, Louisiana. The 4th of the 6th had been in Panama since September, when it replaced its sister battalion, the 5th of the 6th, that had been in Panama since May, when President Bush ordered a buildup of forces, called Nimrod Dancer, to counteract the increasing acts of violence and intimidation instigated by Noriega on U.S. forces, dependents, and citizens.

Prior to the beginning of hostilities, TF 4/6 was "Routinely dispersed to several locations around Panama City," according to Colonel Reed. "Our base camp was Camp Gator, a tent city immediately adjacent to Rodman Naval Station on the west side of the canal (near the Pacific end), at which we deployed one infantry company for maintenance and services. The TF's support elements were deployed at Camp Gator also. Another infantry company was also on the west side of the canal at Empire Range, which permitted them to conduct live-fire training. Two other infantry companies were deployed on the east side of the canal: a quick-reaction force located at Corozal, about two kilometers south of Fort Clayton, and a second company to reinforce the reaction force, if required, which we kept loggered in the Corundu housing area. It was highly classified at the time, but we also kept a platoon of M-551 Sheridan tanks from the 82d Airborne Division under wraps at Camp Gator. . . .

"It was our habit to rotate the infantry companies among these four locations every seven to eight days to provide each the opportunity to conduct various types of training or maintenance. This dispersal of the task force was always problematic, since each company had a unique mission under the Op Plan, and synchronization of their movements was dependent upon their starting points as they moved toward the LD (line of departure). . . .

"As we were alerted on the night of 16 December, our initial actions were to relocate the two infantry companies at Camp Gator and Empire Range to Fort Clayton on the east side of the canal (the platoon of Sheridans remained under wraps at Camp Gator). We did this as a precaution in case either of the two routes across the canal—the Bridge of the Americas or the swing bridge in the vicinity of Fort Clayton—might be denied to us. We also effected task organization with the other elements of the 193d Brigade and awaited further instructions."

Colonel Reed had been in command of "The Regulars" only since 1 December, when he took over command of the battalion from Lt. Col. William Steiger in a change-of-command ceremony at Camp Gator. Colonel Reed had previously been a Pentagon staff officer in the Directorate of Strategy, Plans, and Policy in the office of the deputy chief of staff for Operations. His metamorphosis from staffer to commander in combat was not only swift but also total.

As Colonel Reed wrote later: "My predecessor, Lt. Col. William Steiger, clearly preferred to stay in command and see the mission through to completion, and I know that the question of whether to change command in December was discussed among the senior leadership in the theater. The fact that the transition occurred so efficiently and that the battalion performed so well in combat is, I think, a remarkable tribute both to the high standards of training and discipline which Bill Steiger had instilled in the 'Regulars' as well as to the caliber of officer and NCO leadership common throughout the battalion."[2]

Task Force Gator had two mechanized companies from the 4th of the 6th, Company B, with three platoons, and Company D, with four platoons and a platoon of Engineers from the 59th Engineer Company (Combat); Capt. Timothy J. Flynn's C Company, 1/508th Airborne Infantry Battalion, permanently stationed at Fort Kobbe in Panama; two platoons of military police; a Psyops loudspeaker team; the Sheridans, under Capt. Kevin Hammond; and the platoon of Marine LAVs under Lt. Brian Colebaugh. For the operation, Colonel Reed formed the Sheridans and LAVs into Team Armor under Captain Hammond.

Colonel Snell tasked TF Gator with the main attack—the Comandancia—not only of his command but also conceivably of the entire operation, because of its significance—it was, after all, Noriega's command and control center for the country. Colonel Reed's mission statement read: "At H-hour, D-day, TF 4-6 Infantry (TF Gator) conducts offensive operations to protect U.S. lives and property, and vital Panama Canal facilities by isolating, seizing, and securing the Comandancia/Carcel Modelo complex and neutralizing PDF forces."

The Comandancia was not a single Pentagon-type structure but a compound of fifteen separate buildings, including the barracks of two PDF companies numbering some three hundred soldiers at any one time, located in the El Chorillo district of Panama City, in a two-square-block enclosure along Avenida A. The Comandancia complex was along the shoreline of Punta Mala, less than eight hundred yards across the water from the north end of Fort Amador. It was so close to Fort Amador that before the initiation of Just Cause, soldiers from the 1st Bn of the 508th, armed with telescopes, pulled three-hour guard tours sitting in a shelter, just off one of the fairways of the Fort Amador golf course, keeping tabs on the activities of the PDF around the Comandancia.

Snell's second task force was Task Force Wildcat, based around Lt. Col. William H. Huff III's 5th of the 87th Infantry, a permanent part of the 193d stationed normally at Fort Clayton, on the east bank of the canal, about four miles northwest of Panama City. Huff had three of his own infantry companies plus Capt. Isadore Bower's A Company of the 4th of the 6th, one of Reed's mechanized infantry companies. Snell assigned Huff four objectives: the PDF Engineer Compound, the Ancon DNTT, and the Ancon and Balboa DENIs.

Snell's third task force was Task Force Black Devil, built around Lt. Col. Billie R. Fitzgerald's 1/508 Airborne Infantry Battalion. Colonel Fitzgerald had three of his own airborne companies plus, on an ad hoc basis, Capt. Don Tower's C Company of the 4th of the 6th, two platoons of which were retained by Colonel Snell as the brigade reserve. Fitzgerald's mission was to "isolate and fix the 5th CIA (a military police company), seize and secure PDF facilities, and neutralize all PDF forces at Fort Amador. On order, relocate noncombatants at Fort Amador and La Boca housing areas. Conduct communications linkup with forces at Flamenco Island. Be prepared to seize and secure causeway islands and conduct follow-on missions." In short, air assault into Fort Amador, jointly occupied by the PDF and the U.S. forces, and clear the area of the PDF.

Because his command, the 193d Infantry Brigade (Light), was permanently stationed in Panama, Colonel Snell was faced with the proverbial "good news-bad news" situation. The good news was that he and his men were intimately familiar with the terrain over which they might fight; they had had ample time to develop plans for and to rehearse, without compromise, their phases of the operation; they were knowledgeable about the potential enemy, his habits, and his capabilities, and, according to Colonel Snell, "Brigade CP remained at peacetime location on Fort Clayton." The bad news, as Colonel Snell put it, was that "to my knowledge, Just Cause is the first time since Korea, possibly the first time since the opening stages of World War II, where family members of U.S. servicemen have been in the middle of a combat environment." Having U.S. families in the combat area obviously necessitated the careful and adequate use of forces to protect them and certainly caused some consternation by the U.S. soldiers who left their families behind as they themselves went off to battle—an incongruous situation, reminiscent, perhaps, of Johnny Rebs going off to fight the Yankees on terrain of the South.

"The execution of H-hour assaults entailed a complex movement of fourteen companies (one company was held in reserve) over two routes and the air assault of a battalion (-), all having to be completed within a thirty-minute period," wrote one of Colonel Snell's staff officers later. "The deployment began at 2345 hours as two MP companies administratively crossed the swing bridge to the east bank, securing the bridge as they went. The first unit actually moving toward the assault objectives was TF Gator, which was assigned the Comandancia. At 0030 hours, the MP platoon scheduled to secure Balboa Harbor was fired on by PDF elements."

Task Force Gator, with its mix of mech infantry in their armored personnel carriers, paratroopers, Sheridan tanks, and a platoon of Marines in LAVs, was a force well tailored for its mission of isolating and neutralizing the Comandancia in downtown Panama City. A spokesman for U.S. Southern Command said, "Although not normally used in urban terrain, the tracks were selected for their shock action and firepower as the headquarters for the PDF (La Comandancia) was expected to be a tough nut to crack."

The expectation was correct. Sfc. Anthony Marteen of D Company, 4/6, said that his men were under fire practically from the time they rolled out of the gates at Fort Clayton, about three miles from La Comandancia.

Col. Robert Coffey, commander of the 2d Brigade of the 5th Division, and Brig. Gen. Michael S. Davison, Jr., 5th Division assistant division commander for maneuvers, "happened" to be in Panama when the operation began, apparently "checking" on the training of the 4th of the 6th. From Ancon Hill near Southern Command headquarters, they watched the beginning of the 4/6th assault toward the Comandancia. Colonel Coffey said that the amount of small-arms and mortar fire that the "Regulars" of the 4/6th faced was "tremendous. It's been twenty years since I've been shot at in anger, but it was as much as I've ever seen in any combat situation. It was a tough mission. I think it was the toughest mission in Panama." He went on to add, "The PDF had AK-47's, rocket-propelled grenades (RPGs), and hand grenades."[3]

At an intelligence briefing at 2000 hours on the night of 19 December, the troops of Task Force Gator had been informed that the PDF was much more prepared than the JTF South had at first anticipated. The briefing officer told them that they could expect up to three hundred of Noriega's handpicked soldiers to be inside the compound. And the troops were also told that the PDF may have been warned that a U.S. attack was imminent. According to Colonel Coffey, "The PDF were somewhat more prepared than in normal times. They had established roadblocks using large civilian trucks, POVs. They had sandbags in emplacements around the built-up area of the city surrounding the headquarters. And we could see people who were well armed walking about. The vast majority were in civilian clothes carrying weapons. . . . The enemy were in the streets, they were in the balconies, they were in the windows, they were on tops of roofs. They had two very large high-rise buildings about sixteen stories high and the soldiers were receiving intense fire out of those buildings. . . . They fired not only small-arms fire and mortar fire but also RPGs, which are extremely dangerous and will take out our APCs. Two Company D tracks were hit by RPGs."

By 0015, all units of Task Force Bayonet were crossing their lines of departure (LD). "The LD for TF 4-6 Infantry was Fourth of July Avenue, which ran adjacent to the Comandancia complex," wrote Colonel Reed after the battle. "It was essential that our movement times from our various starting points to the LD be precise, since the task force LD time was closely synchronized with various activities of General Downing's JSOTF. (For the first phase of the operations, TF Gator was under the command of General Downing and his Joint Special Operations Task Force headquarters.) As we approached the LD, B/4-6, commanded by CPT Joe Goss, and D/4-6, commanded by Capt. Mike Etheridge, were both in the lead, moving on parallel axes through the heart of Panama City, and were to cross the LD precisely at 200045 Dec 89 (and, I'm proud to say, both companies hit the LD right on the mark). B/4-6 initiated movement from Corozal; D/4-6 from Fort Clayton; and their movement times to the LD were about 21 and 24 minutes, respectively, as I recall. In order to ensure that they were fully in synch, B/4-6 paused briefly at Quarry Heights and D/4-6 paused briefly at Balboa High School—we had timed the movements to the LD down to the second.

"Movement of all elements was in column formation, although, again, B/4-6 and D/4-6 moved on separate axes. About two hours prior to LD time, Team Armor pulled their Sheridans out from under their tents and prepared to move. Team Armor moved via the Swing Bridge behind D/4-6 into their overwatch position on the east side of Quarry Heights.

"C/1-508 (Abn) infiltrated in trucks behind the lead heavy teams and moved dismounted into an attack position just across Fourth of July Avenue. . . . Fire support was provided by two AC-130 gunships in orbit over the complex.

"Our basic concept," Colonel Reed continued, "was to establish a cordon around the roughly two-square-block area and firmly control all routes of ingress and egress. B/4-6 was to secure the northern one half of the complex with three infantry platoons; D/4-6 was to secure the southern one half with four infantry platoons. Team Armor provided overwatch from the east side of Quarry Heights (Ancon Hill). C/1-508 (Abn) moved dismounted into their attack position and awaited orders to begin clearing operations within the complex. A tight cordon was established by emplacing squad and section-sized blocking positions ringing the Comandancia complex. PDF soldiers who were willing to lay down their arms and surrender were invited to do so on a prerecorded message that was broadcast at LD time by our psyops HB team located on Ancon Hill. A safe route of egress was designated in the message; about six truckloads of captive PDF soldiers were evacuated by Task Force Gator throughout the night.

"Both lead infantry companies encountered heavy resistance as they crossed the LD. Substantial PDF obstacles (cars and trucks that had been parked to block the road) obstructed their route into the Comandancia complex, and soldiers were subjected to heavy volume of direct fire as they attempted to fight through or around these obstacles. Obstacles on both routes were cleared in a manner of minutes, generally by pushing our way through with our tracks.

"As soldiers attempted to move into their blocking positions, they received heavy volumes of machine-gun fire from PDF soldiers fighting from the multistory buildings above them. Many, if not most, of the PDF soldiers were dressed in civilian clothes, and many of them fought from the civilian apartment buildings which ringed the area. I recall being impressed by the fire discipline of our soldiers as they fired upon only those personnel who were actively engaging us. Fighting in built-up areas really tests small-unit leaders. I have said before that once the battle for the Comandancia was joined, it truly was a story of junior leaders taking charge, doing what had to be done, and controlling their people."[4]

Colonel Reed's mech units continued to move forward. As the tracks rolled across the four-lane street that separated the neighborhood near the PDF headquarters and the old Canal Zone, the companies came under heavy small-arms and rocket fire. "Hot and heavy," Colonel Reed described it. Barricades, narrow streets, and rooftop snipers hampered the movement of the APCs. "Bright red artillery shells arched over the city," one observer noted.

The shells filled the air over the old area of Panama City known as Chorillo. At about the same time, a bright orange glow appeared at the foot of Ancon Hill, where Noriega's barracks are located. Where usually the bay was lit with the steady soft glow of street and dock lights, now there were the trails of the bright red shells, reflected on the water. . . . Black smoke was seen rising from near the airport, illuminated by the lights of the city. Oddly, traffic in the city appeared normal for a weekday night for at least the first hour and a half of the attack. . . . Throughout the long night, machine-gun bursts and explosions continued sporadically. Two hours after the attack began, the area where Noriega's headquarters are located was bathed in a bright orange glow. . . . Flames forty and fifty feet high were visible from two miles away and bright orange and black smoke illuminated the city. Always the sound of aircraft droned overhead. Eerily, they were never seen—their navigation lights were turned off. . . . On the street below, the occasional pedestrian continued life as if it were normal.[5]

In a desperate move to slow down the American advance, PDF and Dignity Battalion troops set fire to the surrounding barrio. Many a U.S. newspaper or TV report coming out of Panama showed the flaming destruction of the barrio and attributed it to "collateral" damage done by U.S. gunships, tanks, and other fires. Panamanians, including local priests, who opposed Noriega knew the cause of the destruction and disputed the "collateral fire" accusations.

As the tracks made their way down the narrow, apartment-lined streets, sniper bullets from rifles and machine guns bounced off the skin of the tracks. An AC-130 circled overhead and, as directed by an Air Force controller in a command track, provided overhead fire support. Helicopter gunships cleared PDF fighting positions on the roof of an adjoining high-rise. And, according to a Southern Command staff officer, "In a desperate bid to stop the Americans, PDF and Dignity Battalion members set fire to the surrounding barrio. Although the smoke obscured the sights of the overwatching tanks, the attacking ground element moved on relentlessly. In one of the lead platoons (from D Company of 4/6), twenty-six of twenty-nine infantrymen were wounded. Luckily for the men, most of their wounds were on their arms and legs. Afterward they swore by the flak vests they had been wearing. Well prior to daylight, the mission (of surrounding the Comandancia compound) was accomplished. As the Barrio Chorillo continued to burn, TF Gator kept vigil in their blocking positions."

About an hour and a half after his company crossed the LD, Captain Goss reported that his company had secured the sector around the complex but that he had had one man killed. He was Cpl. Ivan Pérez, twenty-two, a track commander in the lead platoon of Captain Goss's company. Pérez's platoon leader, Lt. Harold Powers, was in the lead APC as the platoon tracks, in a single-file column, met one of the PDF roadblocks near the Comandancia. Powers attempted, with great difficulty, to drive his track through the block— under heavy machine-gun fire. Pérez saw Powers's predicament. His track was right behind Powers's. Pérez pulled his track out of the column to a position where he could better support his platoon leader as the platoon attempted to breach the obstacle. Pérez's track, with Pérez manning the .50-caliber machine gun on his track, came under heavy PDF fire. He did not move his track back even though he was exposed to the PDF fire as he stood in the track commander's open hatch. The heaviest fire was coming from the Comandancia prison yard behind two dump trucks and from the top of a building forty-five yards to Perez's left. Pérez saw the muzzle flashes overhead and opened fire with his machine gun. The return fire ricocheted off the track's aluminum skin. One round hit Pérez in the back of the head. His body slid down through the gun mount and fell against the knees of Sgt. Dave Blair, the squad leader. Sgt. Blair drove the track out of the line of fire and raced the short distance back to the top of Quarry Heights, where the medics pulled Pérez out of the track. He died shortly thereafter. Barry took Pérez's place in the TC hatch and roared back down the hill to continue the fighting. Corporal Pérez was awarded the Silver Star posthumously.[6]

In moving up to the Comandancia area, one of D Company's APCs was disabled by an RPG. Pvt. 2 Louis O. Miller, eighteen, volunteered to try to retrieve the track and the men still inside. When he reached it, Miller came under fire from PDF 40mm grenade launchers. Despite the barrage of grenades, he kept at the task and was able to bring the APC and its crew to safety. Later, at a company breakfast on Christmas Day, Secretary Cheney awarded him the Bronze Star with "V" device for his heroism. From then on, his first sergeant, William D. John, called him "Killer Miller."

Sergeant First Class Marteen, D Company, 4/6, remembers that the road-blocks around the Comandancia were covered by rocket-propelled grenades. Atop the roof of a PDF stronghold was a sniper position that menaced the U.S. soldiers as they advanced. "We took out the position with an AT-4 (shoulder-fired missile)," Marteen said. Knocking out the snipers was the job of .50-caliber gunner Sgt. John Skipworth. He was proficient at his job and "He's probably the reason our platoon made it," said Marteen.[7]

Within an hour after crossing the line of departure, Task Force Gator had secured the area around the Comandancia. "At this point," according to Colonel Coffey, "the battle became one of individual squads dealing with snipers and other people in the streets. It was dark, one o'clock in the morning. People were running around with small-arms weapons, AK-47's, RPGs, hand grenades, throwing them out at our soldiers. Despite this, soldiers were able to maintain their discipline and courage, reduce their area of responsibility, and isolate and secure the Comandancia area."

Captain Goss and his B/4-6 had secured the northern part of the area around the Comandancia by about 0200. D Company required about three hours after the start of the operation to secure its southern part of the area because "several pockets of determined PDF resistance remained. In its area, D/4-6 had sustained some twenty casualties, many from indirect fire," Colonel Reed reported. There is also a strong possibility that many of D Company's casualties were caused by a Specter gunship firing at the Comandancia but hitting short and into the tracks and on troops who had dismounted. But there was so much indirect fire in the area, both from the PDF mortars and RPGs, that it was difficult to determine the source.

One of the heroes of D/4-6th's fight around the Comandancia complex was SPC Roderick Ringstaff, a medic with the 2d Platoon of D Company. He was seriously wounded in his right arm and left foot by indirect fire during the platoon's attack. He refused to be evacuated from the area and, in the midst of continued intense indirect fire, Ringstaff began rounding up and administering first aid to five other wounded men in his platoon. According to a citation recommending him for a Silver Star, "Even as he neared exhaustion and still under devastating fire, Specialist Ringstaff dragged a severely wounded soldier to the medical evacuation vehicle. Although he physically collapsed at this point due to his own extensive wounds, he continued to provide words of encouragement and moral support to the other wounded soldiers of D Company." Only after all the wounded of D Company were evacuated did Ringstaff permit himself to be taken out.

Later he said, "You got to keep your adrenaline going, because if you just lay there, you're history. You've got to keep moving. It was very intense. To be frank, I was really scared but we pulled through and did what we had to do." The wounded he saw had mostly shrapnel wounds. "Guys with shrapnel in their legs, shoulders—basically limb injuries because the flak vest we had on protected us pretty good."

Colonel Reed said that Spc. Roderick Ringstaff is a great example of the kind of soldier we have in today's Army and that "he is about as modest and self-effacing a young man as you could ever meet, a great soldier." Gen. Carl E. Vuono, the Army chief of staff, personally awarded Ringstaff the Silver Star.[8]

A group of AH-6 helicopters had the mission of suppressing the snipers and other weapons positions on the top of the sixteen-story apartment buildings that overlooked the streets along which Task Force Gator was approaching the Comandancia. The lead helicopter was flown by Capt. George Kunkel and Chief WO Fred Horsley. As their helicopter crested Ancon Hill and neared their release point, they were greeted with heavy ground fire. Nonetheless, they flew on and, aware of the rules of engagement to use only the minimum force necessary, they used only their miniguns and no missiles to fire on the PDF troops on the roofs of the apartments. After a run along the rooftops, Kunkel turned his AH-6 to fire on the Comandancia itself.

On their run-in approach, Horsley noticed that Kunkel was having trouble pulling the helicopter out of its gun run. He grabbed the controls to assist. Despite their combined efforts, the helicopter did not respond, and it continued in a dive toward the ground. With no response from the collective and limited response from the cyclic, they tried to aim the helicopter toward an open spot to their right. The helicopter, in level flight, slammed into the ground, skidded across an open courtyard, slid into a concrete pillar, and caught fire. Horsley could not get out his side of the plane because he was blocked by a wall and by debris that entangled his flight vest and uniform. He struggled free and scrambled out Kunkel's side and joined him outside, forward of the fire.

The two men made a hasty and non-Fort Leavenworth-type "estimate of the situation." They were uninjured, they had no helicopter, they were in definitely unfriendly territory, they knew that there was an AC-130 Specter gunship overhead ready to lay waste enemy troops in the Comandancia (with themselves directly in the line of fire), they did not know exactly where they were, and they knew that they had to get out of the area "right now." Their first step was to

105

move to the dark shadows of a building away from the heavy firing they had seen on their way to the unscheduled touchdown. They used their PRC-90 radios unsuccessfully to contact the friendlies and darted around the courtyard to avoid the PDF who were in the area and to try to find out where they were.

Their first attempt to escape by trying to scale a wall in the corner of the compound was frustrated by enemy fire from several locations and from the AC-130. In the next few minutes, fire inside the wall decreased as fire from the 4/6th outside the wall increased in tempo.

At about 0215, a lull in the firing prompted Kunkel and Horsley to make another try to get out. With some haste but with caution, they made their way between some buildings and reached a wall topped by a single roll of concertina wire. After a hasty conference, they decided that one of them should scale the wall, unarmed, and approach the "friendlies," shouting the password "Bulldog."

Before they could carry out their "battle plan," Horsley heard a movement in some nearby bushes. He turned to shoot, but held fire as an unarmed, arms-raised PDF soldier scampered out of the bushes. In broken English he explained that everyone who had not been killed had run away and that he himself wanted to surrender and go back to the American lines with them. Horsley said, "Okay, but wait here."

Kunkel, operating in the dark by peering through the one operational tube of his night-vision goggles, threw his flak jacket on the concertina wire on top of the wall and climbed over it. Once on the street, he moved along the sidewalk, hugging the wall, looking for friendly troops. He finally found some infantrymen who recognized that he was an American and not a PDF emerging from the compound. The Americans permitted him to return for Horsley and the Panamanian soldier. As Horsley was helping the Panamanian over the wall, the AC-130 Specter opened fire on the area of the compound. Horsley vaulted over the wall and clung to the underside. After the AC-130 finished its firing run, the two aviators pulled their prisoner over the wall and raced toward the friendly position.

They spent the next three hours in the command track, an armored personnel carrier, of D Company of the 4th of the 6th. Later, when the fighting near the Comandancia had slowed, the aviators made their way back to Balboa High School, where they contacted their unit.[9]

But La Comandancia itself was still not cleared; that part of the operation would require additional forces and a few more hours.

*   *   *

From Task Force South's assault CP at Fort Clayton, General Thurman had been keeping the Pentagon's NMCC informed of developing events on an almost minute-by-minute basis:

- At 2330 on the nineteenth, he reported that Noriega might be in Colón.
- At 0029, he reported gunfire at Fort Amador, Albrook, and the Bridge of the Americas.

106

- At 0039, he reported that Endara had been sworn in as president of Panama.
- At 0057, he reported gunfire on the Atlantic side of the canal.
- At 0100, he reported that he had moved his alert status to DEFCON 1, the highest state of readiness.
- At 0130, he reported that the Rangers had dropped at Río Hato and that the Bridge of the Americas was secure.
- At 0240, General Thurman called General Powell and told him that the Comandancia was in flames.
- At 0249, he reported that Noriega was still on the loose. General Powell was clearly miffed that one of the main objectives of the operation had not yet been accomplished.

Secretary Cheney had in turn kept the White House informed of all of the developments as he received them. The president asked questions but stayed out of micromanagement of the operation. In Panama the fighting went on.

*   *   *

By the evening of D-day, the Comandancia had still not been "taken down." After surrounding the complex in the early-morning hours of the twentieth, Colonel Reed, commander of the 4th Battalion of the 6th Infantry, and originally a part of General Downing's Joint Special Operations Task Force, received a message from Colonel Snell, the task force commander, that he was "chopped back" to Task Force Bayonet control and relieved from General Downing JSOTF. A portion of the battalion, including Maj. Jim Donivan, the battalion S-3, and six empty APCs driven by men of the 4th of the 6th, plus a couple of Sheridans from the 82d and two LAVs from the Marines, remained under the control of JSOTF. "This element would later provide transport and security for JSOTF," said Colonel Reed, "as they pursued General Noriega and eventually helped establish the cordon around the Papal Nunciature where Noriega took refuge."[10] Major Donivan's "tailored on the spot armor command" became known as the "Panzer Gruppe" in General Downing's headquarters.

General Downing gave Major Donivan and the "Panzer Gruppe" the mission of moving up Balboa Avenue from the Comandancia toward the U.S. embassy to relieve the Special Forces around the embassy early on the morning of the twentieth. General Downing expected to have the Panzer Gruppe under his control for only a few hours or, at most, a few days, but in reality he had it for eighteen days. Donivan and his small armored task force were able to respond to calls from JSOTF and move Special Forces troops to trouble spots throughout the city. Because Donivan had the armored vehicles, he was able to move almost at will through difficult, sniper-riddled streets to various objectives.[11]

Later in the morning of the twentieth, Colonel Snell returned to Reed's control his C Company, which had been Snell's brigade reserve. Reed also assumed control of C Company of the 3d Battalion of the 75th Rangers that had jumped into Tocumen. He got C Company of the Rangers for the specific purpose of clearing the Comandancia. According to Colonel Reed, "That was a mission which C/3-75 had trained specifically for for more than a year, and it was clear that they were better prepared for that tough mission than probably any other company in the Army at the time. Throughout the day, I used C/4-6 to reinforce the cordon around the complex while Team Armor and some Apache helicopters were used to fire into the buildings where we suspected that some PDF continued to hold out."[12]

Capt. Alfred E. Dochnal was the commander of C/3-75. At about 1000 on the morning of the twenty-first, he received orders detaching him from the 1st Battalion of the 75th at Torrijos/Tocumen Airport and placing him OPCON to Task Force Bayonet and further to Task Force Gator, Colonel Reed's command. From Torrijos, Dochnal moved his company by helicopter to Albrook Air Force Base, about two thousand meters to the northwest of the Comandancia and just to the north of Ancon Hill. Capt. Kevin O. Harris, the S-4 of 3-75, met Dochnal and led him to Colonel Snell's tactical CP. Colonel Reed's TAC CP was also in the same area. At the TAC CP, Dochnal got an update on the situation. "The warning order from the brigade," wrote Captain Dochnal later, "was to seize and clear Carcel Mondelo and La Comandancia before dark." Captain Dochnal and Lieutenant Pugmire reconnoitered the area and then, about 1400, Dochnal wrote a frag order for his platoons. The company moved forward to an assembly area about a block from the Comandancia. Dochnal gave the frag order to his platoon leaders from a spot overlooking the Carcel Mondelo and the Comandancia.

"After a quick recon," he wrote, "we moved out, with 1st Platoon moving to seize and clear Carcel Mondelo. Upon seizing Carcel Mondelo, we found U.S. troops in the *carcel* looking around the building. They are lucky . . . we might have killed them. I asked why they were in there. The response—they just walked into the area and started collecting weapons. I was livid at best over this weak excuse.

"The company continued to move to the gym across the street from La Comandancia. We used a breach charge to enter the gym. We quickly took up observation positions inside the gym looking at La Comandancia. The attack was slowed as we waited forty-five minutes for the AH-64's, the M-551's and the LAV 25mm to conduct pre-H-hour fires on La Comandancia to soften the target. After the fires were lifted, 2d Platoon commenced its attack on La Comandancia. Second Platoon M-203 gunners suppressed the second floor with 40mm, and Team Gold suppressed the third floor with snipers, covering the breach team's movement to the east gate and placing of their charges. Charges were set and executed. Second Platoon entered the east half and began clearing from the first floor to the third floor. Third Platoon moved through the breach to the main entrance and cleared the west half of the building. Three EPWs ran out the back of the building and were policed by C/1-508. The attack started at approximately 1550 and was over by 1700. We searched the building and found a substantial amount of evidence and weapons . . . we conducted a relief in place with C/1-508 at 1900."[13]

La Comandancia was at last cleared.

12 | Fort Amador and Balboa

A "PCS" (permanent change of assignment) to Panama had always been a choice Army assignment, particularly in the "old, brown-shoe, spit-and-polish" Army prior to World War II. For the officers and NCOs, the quarters were of the "permanent" variety, the flora and fauna were tropical and exotic, the weather was warm, and the atmosphere relaxed and congenial. Fort Amador, and the other permanent posts along the canal, had golf courses, tennis courts, swimming pools, officer and NCO clubs, yacht and sailing clubs, and a friendly city nearby. All of the old customs and courtesies of the service applied—frequent black-tie dinners for the officers, even at home, for example, were *de rigueur.* (In the "old" Army, young officers wore out their tuxedos before they wore out civilian suits.)

For the soldiers, it was hard training in the mornings, formal inspections in ranks at least weekly, frequent calls for formations all day long, KP for the lower ranks, nightly bed checks, well-coached athletic teams in many sports, buffed squad rooms in barracks, and meticulously laid-out uniforms in footlockers and clothes racks always. Officers wore pinks and greens or starched khakis—many of them changing their khakis twice a day in the heat of Panama. The troops usually wore khakis and leggins. Polo and golf were popular sports for the officers, and payday poker games a monthly event for the troops, some of whom, the privates, were trying to live on "$21 a day once a month." The unlucky poker players were broke for most of the month, but the company messes were available for three "squares" a day, and the commissaries and PXs were bargain-priced.[1]

Even after the war, soldiers still welcomed an assignment to Panama. As one sergeant stationed with the 508th put it, "As assignments go, you could do a lot worse." The better-than-adequate permanent quarters were still there, the climate was still the same, but, admittedly, in the 1980s, the political atmosphere was charged with Noriega-inspired harassment and stress. By December of 1989, the congeniality and affability between the American soldiers and the PDF were long gone. But in spite of the harassment of soldiers and their families, the disciplined American troops held their tempers. Many soldiers did, however, send their families home in view of the rising friction between the U.S. and Panamanian forces.

Fort Amador, in the days since the signing of the Panama Canal Treaty, had become a "joint" post in order to facilitate the eventual and final takeover of the protection of the canal by the PDF forces. One of the by-products of this arrangement was the movement of the PDF's 5th Compañía de Infanteria into former U.S. Army four-story permanent barracks and facilities that were located along the entire south side of the peninsula, directly across the golf course from the quarters occupied by American military families on the other side. In some places, the distance from the PDF facilities to the houses was as little as a hundred yards. Maj. Gen. Marc Cisneros, the commander of U.S. Army South, for example, lived in one of those sets of quarters directly across the fairway from the PDF barracks.

Fort Amador is on a peninsula that juts into the Pacific at the western end of the canal just a few thousand yards south of Ancon Hill and Quarry Heights. It is on the Panama City side of the canal and about four air miles from Fort Kobbe, permanent base of the 1/508th, which is on the west side of the canal in the same complex as the U.S. Howard Air Force Base.[2]

Colonel Snell had assigned Lt. Col. Billie R. Fitzgerald's 1st of the 508th Airborne Infantry Battalion, less C Company, plus A Company of the 4th of the 6th, a mechanized infantry company, the task of "securing" Fort Amador. Securing Fort Amador meant a number of missions: protecting U.S. lives, property, and vital Panama Canal facilities located there; isolating and "fixing" the 5th PDF Company (sometimes referred to as the 5th CIA or Quinta Compañía de Infanteria); seizing and securing PDF facilities and neutralizing all PDF forces at Fort Amador; relocating noncombatants from the housing areas at Fort Amador and the nearby La Boca housing area; conducting communications linkup with the forces at Flamenco Island, one of three small islands about three thousand meters southeast of the tip of Fort Amador, all connected by a causeway to Fort Amador's southeastern tip; and preparing to seize and secure the three "causeway" islands. The battalion's mission, in short, was to secure the American family housing areas and eliminate the threat of the 5th Rifle Company at H-hour.[3]

Colonel Fitzgerald had prepared his battalion extensively for his mission. He had held numerous readiness exercises in the past months on the battalion's specific mission, and every soldier had been trained in detail for his part in the operation. On the evening of 16 December, Colonel Fitzgerald mustered his battalion. He wrote that "The next seventy-two hours was used to improve the posture of our forces and begin troop leading procedures for contingency plans. I intensified the final planning/coordination and level of detail of command and staff briefings. Brigade informed us that we would have a minimum of six hours' and maximum of twenty-four hours' notification to execute the Op Order. It was clear that we could no longer expect seventy-two hours' notification, and we would not execute the Op Order from a contingency readiness exercise during daylight hours. The plan was further compounded by the fact that only those with top-secret clearances had access to the plan. The approval was given to brief platoon leaders/sergeants at H-7 and all soldiers at H-4." Troop leading time was thus at a minimum. At 1800 hours, Colonel Snell ordered Colonel Fitzgerald to execute his portion of Just Cause.

Colonel Fitzgerald's plan of attack was fairly simple. Part of his battalion, the Headquarters Company, would already be at Fort Amador. A and B companies would air assault from Fort Kobbe and land on LZ Ditch, a narrow stretch of land behind the Amador American housing area, on the northeastern side of the peninsula, and establish positions around the family housing area. Then, in a two-pronged attack, Capt. William R. Reagan would lead his A Company in an assault from the north end of the PDF compound, beginning with Building 1; Capt. Robert G. Zebrowski would lead his B Company in a simultaneous assault from the opposite end of the compound and begin clearing Building 46. Headquarters Company, under Capt. John H. Hort, Jr., would support the assault with teams of snipers, scouts, and antitank crews. For fire support, a howitzer crew was attached and under the supervision of the battalion fire support officer, 1st Lt. David Standridge.

Captain Hort had been in command of Headquarters Company only nine days when the operation began. He organized his company into four platoons— three combat scout platoons, and one mechanized antitank platoon from the 4th of the 6th. He had infiltrated his company into Fort Amador on the nineteenth and, according to the report of the 508th, "kept the appearance of our usual security missions conducted since the 3 October coup." That same evening, Colonel Fitzgerald and his S-2, Capt. Pedro Nuñez, also "infiltrated" into Fort Amador. At 0035 on the twentieth, Fitzgerald ordered the front gate of Fort Amador "shut down."[4]

At Fort Kobbe, "From 2100 to 2400," wrote Captain Reagan later, "there was a lot of scrambling around as additional ammunition continued to arrive from the S-4. Soldier loads and ammunition were being crossloaded up until after midnight, when the company finally moved out to the helicopters that were staged on Red Devil Field, right behind the company barracks. Takeoff time was slated for 0047 and platoons practiced loading and unloading the choppers several times. We flew with seats out of the Black Hawks, something we had never done before. We put approximately seventeen on each of our assigned seven Black Hawks. We had an eighth chopper that would fly with us as backup."

Shortly after midnight on the twentieth, Captain Reagan received a radio call from Colonel Fitzgerald that "hostilities had begun" and that he should lift off earlier than the 0047 time. According to Captain Reagan, "We relayed this to our pilots (Company A flew with 7th ID pilots). They requested (through their channels) to go early but were told to maintain our posture. We lifted as planned at 0047 and followed a route that took us south around the causeway islands and then into the high ground on the golf course. The choppers seemed to labor, and they flew close to the water. It seemed like the longest ride of our lives. Tracer rounds could be seen in the distance, and, as we approached Amador, it was quite apparent that the fight at La Comandancia had begun. As we banked for

111

the final approach to Amador, we could observe all the rounds impacting on the far shore. It was a comforting sight because it gave us faith that we did in fact possess superior firepower over the enemy. The LZ had been declared 'Hot' and the pilots relayed that to us. All soldiers could see the tracer rounds coming at the aircraft, although no aircraft were disabled by the rounds and no casualties were suffered."[5]

Colonel Fitzgerald wrote later that "The three greatest concerns of the battalion CO and the operations officer, Maj. Mike Dearborn, during the air assault were (a) that the fight on Amador would begin prior to the arrival of Alpha and Bravo companies and that HHC would be fighting overwhelming odds; (b) that a helicopter would be shot down during the overwater approach to Amador from AA fire from either the Comandancia or PDF positions on Fort Amador; and (c) that LZ Ditch would receive mortar fire resulting in casualties and delays in the mission—especially for Alpha Company and the sling loads that carried needed ammo and the 105mm howitzer."[6]

"The choppers landed as advertised at 0100," Captain Reagan continued. "They wasted no time in getting out of the AO. As soon as they hit, they were taking back off. Many soldiers loaded in the interior positions told of having to jump from as high as eight to ten feet to get off the departing birds. One soldier and three rucksacks were left on the second aircraft. The soldier later linked up with us, but we never recovered the lost equipment."[7]

One of the pilots who flew the troopers of the 1st of the 508th into Fort Amador was Lieutenant Kutschera of A Company of the 3d Battalion of the 123d Aviation Regiment of the 7th Division. After the operation, Lieutenant Kutschera wrote: "I spent Saturday, 16 December, qualifying on the 9mm range with the rest of A Company. That night, at about 2200, we were alerted in response to the shooting of a U.S. naval officer by PDF troops in Panama City. All that night I was one of three crews sitting in our aircraft ready to launch on fifteen minutes' notice, with the rest able to launch within an hour. Sunday afternoon we were backed off to a one-hour notice, and by Monday things seemed to be relaxing back to normal except the company was still on a one-hour string.

"On Tuesday morning, 19 December, the A Company commander, Captain Muir, briefed his platoon leaders and sergeants that 'Der Tag' ('The Day' in German and the code for Task Force Hawk's mission) had arrived. The seats were removed from the aircraft, and soldiers from the 1st Battalion, 508th Infantry, practiced loading and unloading aircraft loads of twenty. Shortly after dusk, all the helicopters were moved off the Howard Air Force Base airfield to make room for aircraft coming from the States to support the operation. The lights of the baseball field next to Task Force Hawk's barracks were shut off to conceal the Black Hawks that were now parked there.

"Phase one of 'Der Tag' consisted of an air assault of troops from 1-508 to secure Fort Amador from the adjacent PDF base at 0100 on 20 December. Seven Black Hawks from 1st Battalion, 228th Aviation Regiment and seven from A Company would insert troops on the golf course at Fort Amador. Then the seven aircraft from A Company would return to the PZ at Fort Kobbe and pick up seven HMMWV sling loads and take them to Fort Amador. Moderate

112

resistance was expected from the PDF compound, which had air defense weapons.

"In the briefings we received, Captain Muir, my company commander, and Lieutenant Colonel Borum, my battalion commander, stressed that we were to fly just as we did in training, doing everything by the checklist and SOP and maintaining disciplined formations. The only risk factor that would change on our brief sheet would be the possibility of little pieces of lead flying around.

"The rules of engagement were also stressed. We were not to return fire unless we were fired upon and could positively identify the hostile target. There would be civilians and their property in close proximity to all the LZs and routes and we were to keep casualties and collateral damage to a minimum.

"As I copied information at the briefing and prepared myself and my equipment for the mission, I couldn't help feeling that it all seemed unreal. I watch this kind of stuff in the movies. It doesn't happen to me. We were all so matter-of-fact and outwardly calm it seemed more like any other big lift at Fort Hunter-Liggett on JRTC. . . . Here was a chance to prove ourselves, to prove that all the money spent by the taxpayers and all the years we had spent in training were worth it.

"We took off as scheduled, with twenty troops and their equipment packed into each Hawk. Our route took us out over the ocean in a wide arc in order to provide secrecy as well as to minimize the chances anyone would have to shoot at us. As we turned back . . . and headed for Amador we could see the lights of Panama City on our right. We could also see one huge bright spot burning in the middle of it and tracers arced out over the water in our general direction a couple of times but didn't come very close. We were flying with infrared formation lights and were invisible in the darkness to anyone without night-vision devices.

"We landed our troops on the golf course and took off again without taking any hits. Some of the crews could see fire coming from the PDF camp to our left but no one in my aircraft saw any. We returned to Fort Kobbe for the HMMWVs and headed back to Amador. The aircraft were more spaced out now because of the time it takes to hook up a sling load. I could only see one or two aircraft some distance in front of us. Again, firing came from the vicinity of the Comandancia. I couldn't tell if it came close to any of the other aircraft but suddenly tracers went out from the aircraft in front of us and the firing stopped. We dropped off our load on the golf course, and again I didn't see any firing, and we went to Empire Range north of Fort Kobbe to refuel and lagger until the 82d was ready for us.

"We shut the aircraft down in a big circle with the door guns facing out and waited for the word to go. The mood was good as we waited and compared stories. We had just passed unscathed through our first combat assault. We had also made history, since I was the first U.S. woman to fly a combat assault and we had done the first NVG sling-load operation into a hot LZ. We were concerned, though, for the crew of an OH-58 that was reported missing and sobered by the fact that we probably wouldn't be so lucky next time." Lieutenant Kutschera's first name is Lisa. She also runs marathons and sky-dives.[8]

113

"The troops moved very quickly off the LZ and headed for the caddy shack at the back of the golf club house," continued Captain Reagan. "Here all the soldiers got rid of the B-7 flotation devices and cached them for recovery by support personnel later. First Platoon was first in movement and had the mission to breach the wire fence into the naval headquarters parking lot. We used wire cutters, which was time-consuming. We had decided not to use explosives to reduce damage and not to draw attention to ourselves. In retrospect, there was so much noise from the explosions at the Comandancia and from other fighting that we should have just had the engineer squad conduct a breach in the wire for us."

"By 1800 hours (on the 19th), I had all four combat platoons assembled on Fort Amador," writes Captain Hort, the commander of Headquarters Company, 1-508. "By 2130, all soldiers had been briefed and were now conducting troop leading procedures to include rehearsals. The adrenaline and motivation were pumping through each soldier at this time as they began to realize that this was not just another exercise. . . .

"At 0015 hours on the twentieth, the platoon leaders and I began hearing automatic fire coming someplace to the north off Fort Amador. Lieutenant Manauis and First Lieutenant Vinyard were still unloading TOW missiles when the battalion commander called and gave me a 'be prepared to move at any time' order. Three to four minutes later the battalion commander told me to execute the closing of the front gate. Lieutenant Manauis and Sergeant First Class Cagle moved the platoon approximately thirty seconds later toward the front gate of Amador.

"Upon Team Recon's (one of the scout platoons) arrival at the front gate, the two PDF guards controlling the front entrance were not listening to the surrender ultimatums being given to them by the two U.S. MPs at the scene. The PDF guards, seeing the additional soldiers from TM Recon, surrendered and turned over their weapons to Staff Sergeant Meadows, 1st Squad leader. Before Lieutenant Manauis could establish any type of roadblock, he received a report from his platoon sergeant, who established a security position approximately five hundred meters down the road that a bus full of PDF soldiers was moving toward his location at a high rate of speed with lights off. First Lieutenant Manauis, along with Staff Sergeant Estes, Private First Class Mountain, Private First Class May, and Specialist Kemp, opened fire with M16A2 rifles. Staff Sergeant Estes, in the standing position, shot and killed the PDF bus driver. The bus swerved, nearly missing the HMMWVs and soldiers and continued to move down the road past TM Recon. The entire incident lasted approximately three to four seconds. The bus, continuing to return fire, crashed into a large coconut tree approximately five hundred meters outside the gate of Fort Amador. From the firing by the PDF soldiers in the bus, the PDF guard that was detained was accidently shot and killed while trying to run back into the guard shack." In just a few minutes, the PDF in the bus "took off," leaving their weapons, equipment, and even their uniforms behind.

"With little time to prepare the position, First Lieutenant Manauis established a hasty roadblock utilizing his three HMMWVs and road jacks. At 0032, a PDF sedan with six soldiers attempted to breach the same roadblock. The sedan began firing at Sergeant First Class Cagle and Private First Class Brown, who immediately returned fire and reported another vehicle was headed in the direction of the front gate. Private First Class Mountain, watching the vehicle approach, shot the driver with three round bursts from his weapon. The driver, shot in the face, crashed into the back of one of the TM Recon roadblock vehicles. The soldiers in the sedan continued to fire at the U.S. soldiers (Specialist Kemp, Private First Class Mountain, First Lieutenant Manauis, Private First Class May, and Private First Class Smith), who returned a massive volume of fire into the sedan. Realizing that their escape was futile, they surrendered after losing three soldiers to M-16 fire.

"At H-hour, TM TOW (the antitank platoon) moved to the back gate of Fort Amador by the Officers' Club. First Lieutenant Vinyard along with First Sergeant Hinman, Staff Sergeant Corvino, and Staff Sergeant Ramirez detained the two PDF guards and began clearing quarters 152, 153, and 154." Quarters 152, better known as the "Witch House," was a PDF house, apparently set aside for Noriega's private use, in which the troops found a bucket of blood—unknown whether human or animal—voodoo artifacts, a brewery for making concoctions and potions, and a candle still burning. At a press conference later, General Thurman said that General Noriega's "voodoo practitioners . . . practiced rituals for Noriega's protection." The troops cleared the house with concussion grenades. Some of the soldiers in the area reported that there were smoldering cigarettes in ashtrays and women had left their purses, and they believed that they might have come close to capturing Noriega himself. All duplexes and buildings were reported secured and vacant at 0230 hours, with one maid and one infant found in Quarters 154.

"Along with TM TOW," continued Hort, "the mortar platoon began moving at H-hour house to house, warning residents that this was not an exercise and to seek cover in their houses near the U.S. side of Fort Amador. TM Mech (the scout platoon from A Company of the 4th of the 6th equipped with five M113A2s and three M901s) moved into position at H-hour and had the responsibility of securing the exit ramp on the Bridge of the Americas and providing fire support and demonstration fire at the PDF barracks and buildings. This was conducted throughout the night in hopes of convincing the PDF soldiers to surrender. First Lieutenant MacDaniel and his .50-caliber machine guns and AT4s opened fire on specific buildings throughout the night without return fire from the PDF."

Sgt. Kent Long was a squad leader in A Company of 1/508. After A Company landed on LZ Ditch, Long and his squad, well rehearsed in their phase of the operation, set about clearing their portion of the housing area and moved with the company to positions behind the naval headquarters to secure the north end of Fort Amador and prevent the PDF from reinforcing the areas already cleared. A Company had moved into positions to support the front gate, and Captain Reagan sent Sergeant Long to establish an OP to control the area in front of the naval headquarters at the north end of Fort Amador. Sergeant Long and his squad passed the night at the OP hearing sporadic gunfire in the area. At about 0630, Captain Reagan sent Sergeant Long's platoon to clear the PDF housing area outside the front gate. The platoon quickly cleared the houses and moved into position to assault the PDF barracks.

Meanwhile, the Psyop teams from the 1st Battalion of the 4th Psyop Group had been continuously broadcasting surrender terms in Spanish between firepower demonstrations by the 1/508th. Colonel Fitzgerald's concept was initially to place fire on unoccupied buildings, such as a mess hall, as a demonstration and then broadcast more surrender demands. Following each broadcast, Colonel Fitzgerald stepped up the firepower demonstration.

Attached to the battalion was a howitzer section from D Battery of the 320th Field Artillery Battalion. They had flown in on the second lift from Kobbe and were now in a position to fire on the PDF barracks. Colonel Fitzgerald decided that, before B Company began its clearing operation into three of the barracks buildings, he would have the artillery fire one round into each of Buildings 7, 8, and 9. At 0545, Sergeant Brown, the section chief, fired the three howitzer rounds. "The effect," according to one observer, "was dramatic. As B Company moved into position, several dozen PDF soldiers were moving behind the buildings, throwing their weapons into the rocks on the waterfront."

While B Company continued its operation to clear Buildings 8 and 9 from one end of the street, A Company was receiving fire from Buildings 2 and 3. Sergeant Long moved his men into position and at 1000 began systematically clearing Building 1. He did it without the usual procedure of throwing in fragmentation grenades in order to reduce the damage and cut down on needless casualties on both sides. Sergeant Long's men were somewhat tense but, as Sergeant Long said later, "Everyone was really professional. They understood we didn't want to just shoot and destroy everything in sight and worked hard at using only what was necessary."

As the day wore on, the tension and heat increased, but the paratroopers of A and B companies carried on the tedious task of clearing each PDF-occupied building room by room. The Psyop's loudspeaker teams preceded each assault, and in a few hours only a few snipers were left holding out in the last buildings.

To flush them out, Colonel Fitzgerald ordered two M113s from A Company of 4/6 to move up and assist in attacking the sniper positions. After several bursts from the M113's .50-caliber machine guns, the snipers were silent, and the Psyop teams succeeded in coaxing them out of their nests.

At Building 3, A and B companies linked up and secured the area. They proceeded to search each building room by room and put out local security. They were also able to dispatch teams to the American housing area to inform them that all was secure.

During the hours of darkness, the paratroopers had some difficulty in identifying the "friendlies" from the PDF. One "After-Action Summary" from A Company reported,

> The calm professionalism demonstrated by the troops of the Moatengators was evidenced by the actions of Spc Sean Hebel, one of the company snipers. . . . There were a number of American servicemen assigned to the

Naval Station on Fort Amador who foolishly ventured into the action. One individual was an Hispanic Marine officer who left one of the Naval Station buildings dressed in battle dress trousers, jungle boots, and a green T-shirt while carrying a chrome-plated .45. Another naval lieutenant went outside to restart a generator dressed in khakis, which was incidentally the dress uniform of the PDF. Both of these officers could have easily been mistaken for enemy troops. Luckily, Specialist Hebel followed his rules of engagement by positively identifying his targets, thus preventing two incidents of fratricide.

Some of the PDF took unusual and imaginative measures to avoid identification and capture. Among other missions, Captain Reagan and his A Company were tasked to clear the Balboa Yacht Club, on the southwest side of the peninsula, behind the PDF barracks. "Sergeant Camp recalled the abnormally large number of waiters working at the club," wrote one of A Company's officers later. "Many of the PDF troops who had fled their barracks had attempted to disguise themselves as waiters. The dead giveaway was their combat boots. Prisoners were also retrieved from the boats anchored offshore. The men of A Company took 47 prisoners while clearing the Yacht Club."

Colonel Fitzgerald and his 1/508th paratroopers continued to clear Fort Amador all day on the twentieth. The resistance ended when the final twelve PDF were cornered (but not killed) in a shower of the gymnasium. "The fact that the paratrooper leaders and soldiers displayed this type of restraint," wrote Colonel Fitzgerald, "is once again a credit to the superb understanding of the USARO's CG, Major General Marc Cisnero's commander's intent. The 1-508 leaders and soldiers were still very much aware of the dangers and potential for danger when they coaxed the cornered PDF from the gym rather than choosing the easiest and safest way to negate their resistance."

At 1555, the troopers of Headquarters Company reverted to a time-tested task—police call of the battlefield. Finally, at 1749, Colonel Fitzgerald reported to Colonel Snell, "Fort Amador is secured." During the operation, the 1st Battalion of the 508th had captured more than 141 prisoners, 2,000 weapons, 2 V300 armored vehicles, and a ZPU4 AA gun. And because the battalion had been permanently stationed in Panama, it always had been subject to "unfair treatment by the Noriega government for years." With its neutralization of the PDF facilities at Fort Amador, part of what the 1/508th "suffered through the bad days of the Noriega regime" was finally redressed.

"Only when the final twelve PDF were cornered in a shower of the gymnasium did the resistance end," wrote a Southern Command staff officer later.

The resistance at 5th Company was indicative of the resistance of the PDF on many parts of the battlefield. In isolated places, professional, brave soldiers fought and fought hard despite abandonment by their leaders. Capt. Moises Cortizo, thirty-three (and a West Point graduate, Class of 1980), was the commander of the 5th Company. He had acted as Noriega's interpreter during Noriega's conference with Adm. John Poindexter in Panama in 1985. He

117

deserted his men early in the fight. Later he was seen hiding in a hospital in downtown Panama City before he ultimately surrendered.[9]

Fort Amador was now secure and back, totally, in U.S. hands.

* * *

"There's no jungle in downtown Panama City," said Capt. Bill Reagan, commanding officer of A Company of the 1/508th. In the days prior to Just Cause, the troops of the 193d Infantry Brigade went through an arduous series of MOUTSs (military operations in urban terrain) to prepare themselves for possible combat in the city.

Lt. Col. William H. Huff III was the commander of the 5th Battalion, 87th Infantry, a regular part of the 193d Infantry Brigade permanently stationed at Fort Clayton on the east side of the canal and about four miles northwest of the western exit of the canal.

In the weeks prior to Just Cause, the 5th of the 87th, plus other units that made up the 193d, had been engaged in around-the-clock security operations at U.S. installations in Panama and had kept a seven-day-a-week training schedule. Even at times when the troops were officially off-duty, they had remained on a two-hour "string." "That means," according to Capt. Don Currie, commander of C Company of 5/87th, "that if we get a call, we have to be equipped, loaded up, and out the door in two hours." Even though the two-hour "string" had been the norm since Panama's elections in 1989, troops had frequently been placed on one-hour or even thirty-minute strings during the anti-American demonstrations or other "potentially explosive activities."

The seven-day-a-week training schedule was rigorous and "exciting," according to some of the troops in 5/87th, in spite of the continual alerts prior to 20 December. In the weeks just prior to Just Cause, one example of training that was most beneficial was a month-long series of live-fire exercises that Huff had led his battalion through in a simulated urban environment. Colonel Huff said, "Jungle warfare used to be our big emphasis, but that was before the political situation in Panama changed. MOUTs weren't originally part of our wartime mission, but they are now."

Colonel Huff had started his MOUT training with squad-level defensive live-fire drills and then had advanced the troops to platoon-level operations. For Capt. Don Currie's company, the grand finale was a company offensive against a hastily built "enemy" camp. S Sgt. Jimmy Banks was a member of Currie's company. He was a "seasoned" infantryman, a veteran of Eleven Bravo, who had trained at Fort Benning, Fort Ord, in Hawaii, and Germany. "But nothing," he said, "approached the intensity of infantry operations in Panama."

"As C Company prepared for its mock assault against the 'enemy' camp," reported Donna Miles in *Soldiers,*

Banks crouched down behind a cluster of sawgrass and wiped raindrops from his eyes. He surveyed his rain-soaked platoon, each member locked and loaded and ready to move. Banks nodded toward the squad leaders, then watched as the troops bounded forward, one squad at a time, through the calf-deep mud. They splashed down behind the closest cover they could find, then returned fire on the enemy camp.

Despite the heavy M-16 and M-60 fire, the sound of the advancing company was muffled from behind by the ear-splintering roar of the 5th Battalion, 6th Infantry Regiment. An element of the 5th Division (Mechanized) from Fort Polk, Louisiana, the 5-6th was pulling a four-month rotation in Panama supporting the 193d "Lights." From their M-113 armored personnel carriers' support fire positions, the task force sprayed the target with .50-caliber machine-gun fire.

Covered by the barrage and the cloud of a smoke grenade, the 5-87th soldiers approached the enemy building. The first two soldiers to reach the doorway performed the entry procedure they'd been taught: Rock forward, backward, then forward into the building. When they crossed the threshold, they bellowed, "Entering the building!"

"We train them to enter in two-man teams and to yell out everything they're doing so everybody can hear it," said Capt. Bill Flynt, whose A Company of the 5th of the 87th conducted an identical operation on nearby Gallery Range. "When you're dealing with live ammo, it's critical that everyone knows what's happening. That's how you keep people from getting hurt."

Little did Flynt or anyone else realize that the following month the troops would apply the lessons in combat.[10]

At 0100 on the twentieth, Task Force Wildcat, Colonel Huff's 5th of the 87th plus A Company of the 4th of the 6th, crossed its line of departure outside the gate of Fort Clayton. Capt. Bill Flynt's A Company, the Jaguars, was headed for the PDF Engineer Battalion inside the Engineer Compound, a complex in the Curundu Heights area and just to the east of Albrook Air Force Base, about four miles from Fort Clayton. Capt. Mark Conley's B Company, the Junglecats, was headed for Balboa, just west of Quarry Heights and Ancon Hill, about five miles from Fort Clayton. Conley had the task of "seizing and securing" the PDF at the Balboa DENI (Departmento Nacional de Investigaciónes—police station) and neutralizing other PDF in the immediate area, securing Balboa, and protecting the integrated U.S., PDF and PCC (Panama Canal Commission) housing areas in Balboa Heights and Diablo Heights. Capt. Don Currie's C Company, the Panthers, was under orders to neutralize the PDF in the Ancon DENI and the Ancon DNTT (Dirección Nacional de Transito Terrestre—road police) and "prevent them from influencing the battle elsewhere." The Ancon Hill area was just to the east of Balboa. The U.S. Quarry Heights area and the U.S. Gorgas Hospital were just north of Ancon Hill.

Team Track, Capt. Isadore Bower's mechanized A Company of the 4th of the 6th, was attached to Task Force Wildcat and had the mission of blocking the main avenue of approach in Panama City and setting up roadblocks along Fourth of July Avenue so that PDF forces could not reinforce the Comandancia. Team Track's roadblocks tied in with Task Force Gator's left flank. TF Gator was the parent unit, the 4th of the 6th, of Team Track.

During the operation, the 59th Engineer Company, assigned to the 193d

Infantry Brigade and commanded by Capt. José Echevarria, provided direct combat engineer support to the various elements of Task Force Bayonet, 193d Brigade, by attaching separate platoons to each of the task forces in TF Bayonet.

The 519th MP Battalion, with headquarters at Fort Meade, Maryland, had been deployed just days prior to the start of the operation for a four-month tour of duty in Panama under Operation Nimrod Dancer. The 519th controlled five military police companies from various Stateside posts. Several of the MP platoons were subattached to the various units of TF Bayonet for the operation. The bulk of the battalion was responsible for rear-area security north of Erosivity Avenue and was also responsible for two H-hour targets, the PDF Dog Compound, and Balboa Harbor.

By 0100, all elements of Task Force Wildcat, including Team Track, had departed Fort Clayton by the SCN gate, a gate near a radio station and about four hundred yards from the main gate at Fort Clayton. The SCN gate was near the 5/87th barracks area and convenient to the highway into western Panama City, where its objectives were located. The Wildcats, a light infantry outfit, were mounted in trucks; Team Track was in its M113s.

En route to their objectives, the trucks of B and C companies of the 5th of the 87th were "ambushed" in the vicinity of the Albrook Air Force Base and Diablo Heights along Galliard Highway. The Panthers' convoy commander, Captain Conley, reported that he "received fire from a Chiva-Chiva bus and a PDF patrol." The Panthers "received automatic fire from the Albrook guard shack and Explonsa Building."

At 0126, A Company had reached the Engineer Compound and infiltrated into the area of some six buildings. The troopers of the company started clearing the buildings one by one, capturing PDF as they went along. They tried to "coax" the PDF out of the buildings with loudspeaker messages in Spanish and giving the PDF "countdowns." Sgt. Robert Judd of the 1st Platoon of the 59th Combat Engineer Company was with A Company. Captain Echevarria reported later that "The fighting was intense and the sappers [his engineers] fought aggressively as both engineers and infantry. The men of the 1st Squad showed their ingenuity by hot-wiring several cars and even a tractor to build a formidable defensive perimeter for the Jaguars of A Company." By 1240, Captain Flynt reported to Colonel Huff that the Engineer Compound was "cleared."

About forty minutes after the Junglecats left Fort Clayton via the SCN gate, they were in position at the Balboa DENI station, which had been the police station in the old Canal Zone. It stood opposite the YMCA, another old Canal Zone landmark. Nearby were the Christian Science building, the Marco Polo restaurant, and St. Mary's Hill. The DENI station was thus situated in a residential area, where, if the commander did not exercise care and caution, a great deal of "collateral damage" could occur.

At 0142, Captain Conley gave the DENI station PDF a five-minute warning and followed it with a "firepower demonstration." The PDF refused to surrender. Ten minutes later, Colonel Huff directed Conley to clear and secure the station. Conley gave the occupants of the station a final warning to surrender. No PDF appeared, so at 0335, Lieutenant Timotheus and his platoon assaulted the Balboa DENI. At 0359, the first building was cleared by Lieutenant Hampton and his platoon. By 0445, Captain Conley reported to Colonel Huff that the Balboa DENI was "cold." The assault on the buildings resulted in their complete destruction, but the company was so meticulous in its application of firepower that neither the YMCA nor the Christmas Nativity scene on the station lawn was touched. In the firefights in and around the station, one PDF was killed.

At 0050, Capt. Don Currie and his C Company Panthers left Fort Clayton via the SCN gate. After arriving at the Ancon DNTT building, the battalion S-3 requested his tactical operations center to phone the DNTT and persuade them to surrender. The DNTT refused. At 0300 the Panthers initiated an assault on the Ancon DENI station with the .50-caliber machine guns of A Company of the 4th of the 6th's M113's firing suppressive fire. Half an hour later, C Company prepared to enter the Ancon DENI and called for "fire for effect" on the Ancon DNTT. For the next four hours, the company worked on clearing the two station buildings. In the assault on the DNTT, Sergeant Dimoala and Private First Class Porter were wounded in an exchange of fire with the stubborn defenders of the stations. By 0802, the main building was cleared, and at 0853, Captain Currie reported to Colonel Huff that the DNTT was "cold."[11]

With that report, Captain Huff could report to Colonel Snell, "Mission accomplished."

13 | Task Force Atlantic

The Atlantic side of the canal—the Caribbean side—also had to be neutralized. It was one more phase in the multifaceted, simultaneously executed, zonewide campaign to paralyze the PDF and its operating facilities. The complexity of Just Cause, the extensive and meticulous planning, the depth of the staff work, the responsiveness and responsibility of the chain of command, and the demonstrated professionalism of the troops involved become apparent when one realizes that so many small operations, launched by a widely diverse mix of military units from all four services, from locations as far away as Fort Ord, California, Fort Lewis, Washington, Fort Bragg, North Carolina, and Hunter Army Airfield, Georgia, occurred at scattered in-country Panama sites at the same time.

Just Cause was not a classic military campaign in the sense that units were arrayed in the same general area and ready to attack at a predetermined H-hour along an enemy's more or less continuous defensive line. It was not a Desert Storm, a textbook war that was a perfectly developed and executed maneuver and attack against what was previously thought to be a formidable, dug-in enemy. Rather, Just Cause was a series of well-coordinated, relatively small-unit operations from a wide variety of in-country and Stateside commands against a diverse and many-pocketed enemy. It was an operation based on a contingency plan the likes of which the United States may possibly see more often in the wake of the almost miraculous success of Desert Storm with the attendant renewed worldwide respect for the determination and refusal of the U.S. government to compromise. With the collapse of the USSR, the United States remains the world's sole, formidable military power.

On the Atlantic side of the canal, U.S. forces had to isolate Colón, the canal's Caribbean port city; neutralize the PDF 8th Company in Colón at Fort Espinar and the PDF 1st Marine Infantry Company at the port of Coco Solo; capture

122

the PDF patrol boats at the port; protect the Madden Dam, which stores water used to raise and lower ships in the canal's locks; seize the electrical distribution center at Cerro Tigre; secure the vital Gatun Locks and the defense installations; free a number of Panamanian political prisoners, victims of the aborted March 1988 coup attempt, incarcerated in Renacer Prison at Gamboa, midway across the isthmus; establish roadblocks on the neck of Colón Peninsula and on Boyd-Roosevelt Highway; protect the Galeta Island facility; disable all multiengine aircraft on France Airfield; and protect the U.S. housing area at Gamboa.[1]

Colón, with a population of about sixty thousand, is a port city on Limón Bay on the Atlantic side of the canal and lies at the northern tip of a half-mile-long peninsula commonly referred to as the Colón Bottleneck. One-half mile to the east across another inlet is the town of Coco Solo. Situated on the bay's shore in Coco Solo is a former joint-use facility, two identical buildings running north to south. The northern building is Cristóbal Junior/Senior High School. The southern building housed the 1st Naval Infantry Company, a garment factory, and a Chinese restaurant known as the Noodle Shop. Two hundred yards to the west, behind the PDF building, was the docking area for the PDF's five patrol boats. Fifty yards to the east, across a stretch of green grass, was a U.S. housing area—a street with about two dozen homes, many unoccupied by the twentieth of December.

The accomplishment of the myriad tasks on the Atlantic side of the canal fell to the lot of Task Force Atlantic, whose headquarters was Col. Keith Kellogg's staff of the 3d Brigade of the 7th Infantry Division (Light). His principal units were Lt. Col. Lynn Moore's 3d Battalion of the 504th Infantry of the 82d Airborne Division and Lt. Col. Johnny Brooks's 4th Battalion, 17th Infantry of the 7th Infantry Division (Light).

The 3d of the 504th, from the 82d Airborne Division at Fort Bragg, had been in Panama since 10 December training, on a rotational cycle, at the Panama Jungle Operations Training Center (JOTC) at Fort Sherman, on the Caribbean. It was about to put its training into combat reality.[2]

The 4th of the 17th had been in Panama since 27 October 1989. On 15 October, the 3d Brigade of the 7th Infantry Division, as part of Operation Nimrod Sustain, had assumed responsibility for all U.S. forces in the vicinity of Colón from the 1st Brigade of the 7th and had become Task Force Atlantic. Before the operation, TF Atlantic was involved in intense mission analysis, planning, preparation, and rehearsals. Prior to the Just Cause campaign, the brigade rotated its battalions from Fort Ord through a three-week course at the JOTC. The 4th Battalion of the 17th Infantry had finished its three-week jungle training at the JTOC but had remained in Panama as part of the Nimrod Dancer buildup. The 4th of the 17th also conducted "Sand Flea" exercises primarily to exercise U.S. freedom of movement rights under the Panama Canal treaties and to rehearse contingency plans. The battalion ran "freedom of movement" convoys twice weekly from Fort Sherman to Fort Clayton or from Howard Air Force Base across the isthmus and back to Colón. In their rehearsals for the operation, generally speaking, the troops of the 4/17 had no idea they were rehearsing a specific wartime plan, yet they knew their jobs, their team tasks, and their individual squad objectives. Field training was never so closely related to the actual combat that would occur.

At H-hour on 20 December, the 7th Infantry Division (Light) had in Panama a battalion task force (the 4th of the 17th), the 3d Brigade's headquarters, and the two-hundred-man Task Force Hawk, made up of units from the 7th's Aviation Brigade. TF Hawk had originally been deployed to Panama by President Reagan about a year earlier. Starting on D-day, 20 December, Maj. Gen. Carmen J. Cavezza, the 7th Division's commander, would deploy another four thousand soldiers from Fort Ord to Howard Air Force Base and Torrijos/Tocumen Airport in just two days.

Before that buildup would occur, however, the 7th Division troops in Panama had tasks to perform under combat conditions. "Our missions were to eliminate the Panamanian Defense Forces and seal off the Colón area," reported Col. Johnny Brooks, commanding officer of the 4/17. "We had to neutralize the Panamanian Naval Infantry Battalion at Coco Solo, neutralize the 8th Infantry Company at Fort Espinar, block off the city of Colón from the rest of Panama, neutralize all aircraft on France Airfield, secure the Coco Solo Hospital, and establish roadblocks on the Trans-Isthmus Highway between Colón and Panama City."

As Colonel Brooks remembered, one of the 4/17th's big fights was the neutralization of the naval infantry at Coco Solo. Brooks had assigned that mission to Capt. Christopher Rizzo and his C Company. C Company had been garrisoned in an unused wing of Cristóbal High School and was therefore in the same area, just one building away from its target, the naval infantry. For the previous thirty-three days, after the completion of their stint at the JOTC, the company had been patrolling the Coco Solo area. According to one of Rizzo's men, "Each day we came face to face with our future enemy, the naval infantry soldiers, and had to ignore their sneers and degrading gestures." The U.S. soldiers may possibly have used more graphic words and hand language when talking about the naval infantry among themselves.[3]

In the days prior to Just Cause, Rizzo developed the details of his plan to knock out the naval infantry. His plan was relatively simple: Surround them, initiate the attack by firing a few rounds from rifle, Vulcans, antitank weapons, and machine guns, ask them to surrender via a broadcast from a Psyops loudspeaker, and, if they refused, up the ante.

To seal off the area, he planned to use one rifle platoon and some military police. In addition, he would assemble an infantry platoon in front of the barracks, a platoon armed with rifles, machine guns, 20mm Vulcans, and some antitank weapons. To cover the rear of the barracks, he would put another platoon, which also had the mission of capturing the PDF patrol boats. In reserve he had a fourth platoon to clear the barracks after the initial assault, if necessary.

Rizzo had about two hundred men included in his three rifle platoons, a rifle platoon from the 3d Battalion of the 504th, two Vulcans from the 2d Battalion, 62d Air Defense Artillery, a signal detachment from the 127th Signal Battalion, and a platoon from the 549th Military Police Company.

124

Rizzo charged Lieutenant Kirk and his 2d Platoon of C Company, "Hard Rock Charlie," to clear the barracks.

In the evening hours of the nineteenth, the men of C Company were either on guard duty or relaxing in their barracks, writing letters, videotaping messages to their families, or eating in the mess hall. Then the word came down the chain to Rizzo that H-hour would be 0100 on the twentieth. He alerted the company, assembled them, announced H-hour, went over the plans one last time, issued new call signs and frequencies, and ordered his platoon leaders to execute the plan they had rehearsed so diligently in the past weeks. The men of the company suited up for combat, put on Kevlar body armor, and applied more facial camouflage paint than they ever had before. Rizzo positioned two Vulcans from the 2d of the 62d Air Defense Artillery near the barracks as he had done every night for the past several months. Colonel Brooks came over and spoke to the company, the chaplain said a prayer, and the company was ready to take its part as one piece in the jigsaw puzzle of Just Cause. Rizzo had one more mission before he executed his plan: At about 0015, he awakened the eight American families who lived in the U.S. family housing area right across the areas from the PDF barracks and evacuated them to a neighbor's house one row of buildings away.

At about 0045, as the platoons were moving into their assault positions, they heard three shots fired from the vicinity of the center entrance to the Coco Solo barracks. The platoon en route to secure the dock answered with M-60 machine-gun fire, and Rizzo gave the order for the Vulcans to open fire on the barracks with a two-minute sustained fire of ten-round bursts. The rounds tore through the walls and dispersed the defenders but did not cause them to surrender. Kirk and his 2d Platoon were crossing the gap between the high school and the naval barracks. Then the platoon would enter the barracks through the Chinese restaurant and work its way through the building and into the PDF-occupied part of the barracks.

Sgt. Chance De-Wayne "Ranger" Brooks had been the leader of the 3d Squad in the 2d Platoon for only two weeks. But the rehearsals and the training in the past two weeks made him ready for his combat assignment. He positioned himself on the second floor of the building, where he could watch the 1st Squad, the spearhead of the operation, move across the gap and into the building. Brooks threw several grenades into the courtyard to suppress enemy fire while the 1st Squad entered the building. Sgt. David Rainer, a squad leader in the 1st Platoon, said later, "Everybody's blood was pumping and we all ran across the gap at Olympic-breaking speed."

By this time the naval infantry soldiers were alert and reacting to the movement of Rizzo's company. Gunfire was coming from all around the building, and tracer rounds flashed through the night air. Rainer remembered seeing tracer rounds fly past him and between his legs.

Cpl. Joseph Legaspi, a recent graduate of the Ranger School, had been in the unit only a matter of days. He was A Team leader in the 3d Squad. When the Vulcans opened up, Legaspi said, "The ground shook." He was eagerly awaiting the loudspeaker to ask the PDF to surrender. But, he recalled, things weren't that simple. Instead of surrendering, the PDF increased their small-arms fire from the building. But by this time the 2d Platoon had raced across the gap, were all in the building, and had begun their clearing operations.

The platoon went, first of all, through the area where the seventeen-member Chinese family lived in the garment factory, of which their restaurant was a part. Without firing a shot, the platoon managed to round up the family and get them safely out of the building.

To get into the PDF section of the barracks, Private Secor used some C-4 to blast open the locked door between the factory and the PDF living area. Rainer then raced through the blazing doorway into a blacked-out gymnasium and led his squad to a stairway on the other side. Meanwhile, the 2d Squad guarded the entrance and the Chinese family.

The PDF soldiers were still unwilling to surrender. Lieutenant Kirk "upped the ante." He asked for more fire from the Vulcans. "We hit the naval headquarters building at Coco Solo with our Vulcans set on direct-fire mode," said Lt. James Leary, a platoon leader with B Battery of the 2/62 Air Defense Artillery. "We did a number on that building and knocked out the PDF guys. We also hit and crippled a PDF patrol boat with a Vulcan. The boat was in the wrong place at the wrong time. . . . The Vulcan was a pivotal weapon during the invasion." The second blast of the Vulcans encouraged the PDF to yell their belated willingness to surrender. Before he accepted the surrender, Sergeant Rainer made certain that the platoon had cleared the entire building. Lieutenant Kirk led his platoon through the building from top to bottom, and when he was certain that the entire building was clear, he had Private First Class Davis, a Spanish linguist, take the surrender from Captain Jiminez, a young Panamanian who had been in command of the Coco Solo naval infantry for only ten hours. His experience as a company commander was somewhat brief, unrewarding, and bewildering.

It took the 2d Platoon about four hours to clear the PDF naval infantry barracks. The platoon suffered no casualties and captured twenty-seven of the PDF, only two of whom were wounded. Unfortunately, the fire started by the C-4 destroyed the living quarters of the Chinese family. But C Company quickly found other housing for them and helped the family recover their belongings from the building.[4]

"Hard Rock Charlie" was not yet finished with the Just Cause campaign. It assisted Colonel Brooks with the rest of the battalion's missions, one part of which was clearing the city of Colón. "The Buffalos," the nickname of the 4th of the 17th Infantry, cleared Colón on 22 December. Originally, Colonel Brooks thought that a sweep of Colón would be difficult because of the predicted resistance of the PDF and the Digbats. Such did not prove to be the case. "We began our sweep into Colón with mortars, LAWs, and small arms," said Company B's first sergeant, Larry Durham. "We didn't meet any resistance; instead, thousands of Panamanians came out of their homes cheering and applauding us. The crowds were so thick. It was amazing, unbelievable."

"Here, four hundred PDF soldiers surrendered to us," Colonel Brooks reported later. "We captured about sixteen hundred weapons, many of them brand-new, and some others were very old. After we captured Colón, many

Panamanians started waving white flags and cheering the Americans on. Most of the information that we received from the Panamanians was unreliable and false. We referred to these rumors as 'Vicky says messages,' named after General Noriega's girlfriend. The Panamanian people were pleased because we didn't destroy the city or kill innocent people." The battalion was able to keep the "collateral" damage at a minimum because of its careful planning and "measured application of combat power." Sergeant Rainer said, after the reception in Colón, "It felt like what he had seen in pictures of the liberation of Paris."

"The Coco Solo naval infantry, 8th Infantry Company, and blocking Colón missions were the most difficult ones for us," Colonel Brooks summed up after the battle. "We encountered pretty heavy resistance at all three places, especially at Fort Espinar. We received the most casualties at Fort Espinar, mostly from grenades and rocket-propelled grenades and some AK-47 rounds. Some of the wounded soldiers will need up to thirteen months of recovery time."[5]

After securing Colón, joint teams from the 4th of the 17th and the 7th Division's 7th MP Company patrolled the streets around the clock to prevent looting and maintain law and order. The 7th's MPs also worked with, helped to equip, and trained the newly formed Panamanian Public Forces in the Colón area. The MPs also provided the reorganized and redirected PDF with the vehicles and weapons they needed to transform themselves into a police force. The metamorphosis from a Noriega supporting force to a police department focused on law and order was under way.

14 | Madden Dam, Cerro Tigre, and Renacer Prison

On 10 December, the 3d Battalion of the 504th Infantry of the 82d Airborne Division had arrived in Panama to undergo three weeks of jungle training at the Jungle Operations Training Center at Fort Sherman on the Atlantic side of the canal. On that date, the troopers of the battalion were unaware that in ten days their training would suddenly become battle-realistic, that they would find themselves firing at live targets and getting shot at in return. Never before had the JOTC provided its students with such authentic combat conditions as a graduation exercise. The 3d of the 504th would graduate with honors. The battalion's attacks were part of 27 H-hour simultaneous assaults by the United States against PDF targets in Panama.

In the early weeks of December, as the atmosphere in Panama became charged with increasing tension between the United States and Noriega, Lt. Col. Lynn Moore, the commander of the 3d of the 504th, knew that his battalion would become part of the Just Cause operation. He had been briefed on the plan that made his battalion part of Col. Keith Kellogg's 3d Brigade of the 7th Infantry Division—Task Force Atlantic. Moore's mission, in the simplest of terms, was the responsibility for all enemy objectives along the canal between the outskirts of Colón and the outskirts of Panama City, a distance of some fifty miles. "Everything in between was our responsibility," said Colonel Moore. The rest of TF Atlantic was responsible for reducing PDF resistance in and around Colón itself.

Colonel Moore broke down his objective area into submissions and assigned them as follows: A Company, the town of Gamboa on the Panama Canal; B Company, Madden Dam and the electrical plant at Cierro Tigre; C Company, the prison at El Renacer near Gamboa; and three of his other platoons plus a platoon from his Headquarters Company and attached personnel, security missions at several locations. "Of the 632 people I brought in-country," Colonel Moore said, "every man, regardless of his military occupational specialty, was

128

fighting as infantry." Col. Jack Nix was the commander of the 1st Brigade of the 82d, of which the 3/504th was a part. "The best part," he said, "was these young paratroopers. Their training paid off; it reduced casualties."

At 0030 in the early black hours of the morning of the twentieth, a task force composed of the Panama-based 1st Battalion 228 Aviation Regiment, with UH-1Hs and CH-47Bs, and B Company of the 3/504th, reinforced, lifted off from Fort Sherman, thirteen kilometers southwest of Colón. Each Huey carried ten combat-loaded soldiers; the CH-47 carried fifty. The mission of the task force was to clear and secure the Madden Dam to prevent damage to the water control system for the canal. According to one report, "Flying the mixed aircraft formation took expert training and split-second timing. At 0045, the lead helicopter touched down at the dam with the CH-47s landing nearby in a clearing. A large volume of ground fire erupted, but darkness and speedy unloading resulted in no aircraft being hit. The entire flight was conducted under blackout conditions, with all aviators using night-vision goggles (NVGs). The surprise gave the infantry a significant tactical advantage during the ground action that followed." The troops quickly overcame the PDF guards, secured the dam site, and later cleared the logistical and electrical power site at Cierro Tigre.

About halfway across the isthmus, near the town of Gamboa, sits Renacer Prison, a makeshift collection of twenty or so cinder-block and wooden buildings with tin roofs. The prison yard, marked by a cyclone fence, measures about forty by seventy meters, inside of which were the two major buildings of the prison, the prisoner barracks and a recreation building. Most of the buildings were outside the fence. As prisons go, it was relatively small and decrepit. But because it supposedly held a few Americans and some of Noriega's political prisoners, many from the aborted October 1989 coup, it was a key target in the immediate U.S. scheme of things in the early hours of Just Cause.

The guard force, reconnoitered in the past weeks by U.S. patrols and operations around the prison under the Sand Flea scenario, numbered twenty to twenty-five. "Apparently such duty was not the high point of a PDF soldier's career," according to one report, "as the force included members of the elite Battalion 2000, who, because of various discipline infractions, were serving punishment as guards. Armament consisted of a variety of automatic rifles— mostly Communist AK-47's and a version of the U.S. M-16, the T-65. One machine gun was later found."

During the days prior to the assault, Capt. Derek Johnson, commanding officer of C Company, 3/504, led his teams through repeated rehearsals of the operation and trained them in building clearance, control of firing, and helicopter loading and rapid unloading. Johnson set up a mock-up of the prison using tapes to simulate its restricted dimensions. The forays near the prison, practicing the pending operation, caused Captain Johnson some concern. "I was more scared during Sand Flea than the actual attack," he said later. "After those operations and our rehearsals, we were comfortable with the actual mission." The rehearsals, however, were important and paid off: They lulled the PDF into a false sense of security because they saw the Americans so often; the troops could see their targets, the location, construction and size of the

129

buildings, the guard force habits, movements, and locations; and they demonstrated the determination of the United States to be present and move freely in its specified zone as guaranteed by the Panama Canal Treaty.[1]

The difficulty of seizing the prison and extracting the prisoners safely was compounded by the fact that the guards and the prisoners were intermixed in a very small area, and firing on the guards might endanger the prisoners. In addition, the prison was bounded on two sides by water and on the third by a jungle ridge. Colonel Moore and Captain Johnson knew that they must hit the prison quickly and precisely with surprise and an overwhelming force to protect the prisoners and knock out the guards.

The plan of attack called for a simultaneous air assault and amphibious landing at 0100 on the twentieth. For support and transportation, Captain Johnson had three Hueys from the 1st Battalion of the 228th Aviation, demolition elements from the 307th Engineer Battalion, two LCMs from the 1097th Transportation Company, and three MPs. Two Hueys, each carrying eleven paratroopers and whose pilots wore night-vision goggles, would land inside the cramped prison yard after flying over high-tension wires near the compound. The Huey door gunners were prepared to fire on preselected targets. Accompanying the Hueys was an AH-1 Cobra attack helicopter from the 7th Infantry Division, prepared to fire with precision rounds into the guards' barracks. On landing in the tight LZ, the assault force, part of 2d Lt. Christopher Oswalt's 2d Platoon, would search and secure the prisoners' barracks and the recreation building, the two major structures in the fenced-in area.

Simultaneously at H-hour, the remainder of the 2d Platoon, under Sergeant Niles, would land from an LCM on the canal side and provide fire support and security for the assault force. Sergeant Niles's men were armed with five M-60 machine guns and twenty AT-4 antitank weapons that could be used against sturdy buildings and any vehicles that might arrive, bringing in a reinforcing PDF unit.

Lt. Chuck Broadus's 3d Platoon of C Company was on the other LCM. Broadus's mission was to clear and secure the buildings in the prison area outside the chain link fence. In addition to those troops, also included in Johnson's command was one OH-58 scout helicopter, which carried a company sniper, and a third Huey, which carried ten scouts and would land outside the fence as reinforcement and to block any potential PDF relief force.

During the evening of 19 December, Colonel Moore received the "go" order to execute the missions. The weather was poor for night flying, with the cloud base at five hundred feet and little ambient light for optimum operation of the pilots' night-vision goggles. But the mission was "on." All elements of C Company, the helicopters, and the LCMs launched from Fort Sherman at precisely determined times to arrive on target at 0100.

Just prior to H-hour, two OH-58 observation helicopters flew down the canal and, when they came abreast of the guard positions near the prison, opened fire. Almost to the minute at H-hour, while the guards were momentarily distracted by the OH-58's, the two Hueys with the 2d Platoon's assault force aboard dropped inside the fence of the prison yard. They were met with a "hail of bullets" from the not totally distracted guards.

One observer said of the landing inside the prison fence, "It was a incredible display of airmanship. No one fired from the left side of the aircraft to prevent hitting the prisoners' barracks. On the right side of each helicopter the door gunner, two squad automatic weapons gunners, and a grenade launcher gunner all fired."

"Prison guards responded," remembered Chief Warrant Officer Michael Loats, the lead pilot. "How we never got hit, I don't know. All we saw were tracers in front, on the side, and behind us."

At the same time, the Huey with the scouts landed at the blocking position; the LCMs touched shore, and the fire support element raced off the boat's ramp; the Cobra flew in and shattered a guardpost with its 20mm Gatling gun; and a sniper with night-vision goggles was "picking off guards in a watchtower from his hovering OH-58 Kiowa chopper."

The floodlights in the yard shorted out, possibly due to a cable blowing across the power lines as the helicopters came in to land. Sergeant Coulter led his 1st Squad of the 2d Platoon to the main prisoner barracks and blew open a metal door. Specialist Reitveld was hit in the arm by a bullet or a grenade fragment. Sergeant Godfrey led his 3d Squad through the breached metal door into the interior of the building. They found the quick-thinking prisoners lying on the floor, covered with their mattresses. Sergeant Baker's 2d Squad, meanwhile, had entered and secured the recreation building, and Sergeant Niles had set up his five machine guns in a supporting-fire position outside the fence.

By this time and on schedule, Lt. Chuck Broadus had disembarked his 3d Platoon from the LCM after a two-hour ride from Fort Sherman. His force came under heavy fire within ten to fifteen meters of the boat dock and then had to move across a railroad track. "This was really a hairy, hairy mission," Lieutenant Broadus said later. "If the helicopters landed first, they would have been without support. If the boats landed first, it would have tipped our hand, and the helicopters would have come in under more fire. We called this San Juan Hill for a while. We had to come up quickly under fire."

Broadus quickly moved his men up toward the area where Sergeant Niles had set up his supporting machine guns. On the way, one of Broadus's troopers saw two PDF soldiers running between some buildings and notified Niles. Private First Class Watson, one of Niles's M-60 machine gunners, opened fire and killed both of the PDF.

One obstacle surprised Lieutenant Broadus and his platoon: a ten-foot chain link fence under the overhang of the office and headquarters buildings—part of the area Broadus was supposed to clear. Broadus tried grenades and a claymore mine to blow a hole in the wire, to no avail. "We tried to blow a hole in the fence but it was very thick," Broadus said later. Finally, "Pfcs. Derik Webster and Charles Ross, exposed to enemy fire, ran and cut a hole in the fence with their bayonets."

Sgt. Kevin Schleben led his squad into the blacked-out headquarters building, and they were met by a cloud of CS gas. They left the building, donned their protective masks, and went right back in to press the attack. As Sergeant Schleben moved through the building, he spotted a trail of blood on the floor and followed it back outside. Next to the building, behind an air-conditioning vent and within a few feet of other paratroopers who were unaware of them, Schleben spotted two PDF soldiers, one of whom was wounded. As the PDF soldiers swung their rifles toward Schleben, he fired first and killed them both. Later Lieutenant Broadus said, "They could have shot four or five of us. He [Sergeant Schleben] went between us and them. He could have taken our fire or their fire." "Just a job," Sergeant Schleben said when he heard Lieutenant Broadus's comments.

C Company's troopers had cleared almost all of the twenty or so buildings around the prison complex. Farther away, Sergeant Wilson led his squad up a jungle ridge to clear a couple of buildings still unsecured. One of the buildings was a duplex, apparently family quarters. The squad cleared one apartment in the duplex and then heard a woman cry, "Don't shoot!" The squad held its fire. A somewhat shaken PDF lieutenant, his wife, and his child, none of whom was injured, came out of the second apartment and surrendered to Sergeant Wilson and his men.

Later, Spc. Damian Benson, whose squad had cut down three of the PDF killed in the fight, said that he was really distressed that he almost shot the wife of a Panamanian lieutenant and her baby when they emerged from the duplex. "I came close to killing that woman and her baby," he said, shaking his head.

Sgt. Christopher Castillo said after the operation that they had worked hard on the plan to clear the prison buildings. He credited Spc. Felix Huamandiaz, fluent in Spanish and acting as a translator, for talking some of the PDF into surrendering.

By 0600 the prison was totally in U.S. hands. All prisoners—two American journalists, five political prisoners from the October coup, and fifty-seven other prisoners (actual criminals?)—were accounted for and unharmed. Of the PDF guards, five had been killed and twenty-two captured, six of whom had been wounded. The total U.S. casualties were four wounded.[2]

In a follow-on recap of the mission, one report said,

> During the assault on Renacer Prison, the soldiers of 3/504 PIR engaged targets with a multitude of weapons and encountered many unfamiliar obstacles. In addition to concertina wire, there were eight- and 10-foot-high chain link fences. There were steel doors and concrete walls along with iron bars and heavy-duty padlocks. Pressed for time and under heavy fire, soldiers used their organic weapons against these obstacles. They were sometimes dismayed by the results and often were required to try new tactics.

One of the prisoners rescued from Renacer Prison was a thirty-six-year-old Miami electrical engineer, Diego J. Jiminez, who had fled illegally from Cuba in 1973. In June of 1989, he was in Panama. "I went to the immigration office to get my wife and son out of Panama," he said later. "They pulled me out of line and said I was working for the CIA. I was just another civilian caught in the wrong placed at the wrong time."

The PDF incarcerated Jiminez in the bleak prison at Renacer. In an effort to break his will, the PDF taped his eyes shut for fifteen days. During that period, his captors beat him, drugged his coffee, put electrical shocks through his body, and pulled out his toenails with pliers. "I was isolated, without any rights," Jiminez said after his rescue on the twentieth of December.

Jiminez went to work immediately with a U.S. intelligence unit and succeeded in putting "the finger" on a number of his former captors. He said that after fifteen days of torture he would never forget their faces, once they took off the tapes over his eyes. "Now they're shaking," he said as he eyed his former guards. So far he has identified thirteen of his captors.

One of the officers in the intelligence unit said, "He's really helped us on several cases. Initially, he identified prison guards and interrogators. He also identified some criminals—thieves and drug dealers—among the released prisoners. They'll probably go back to jail."

Jiminez treasured most a telephone call to his mother. "They [his captors] told me she was dead," he added.[3]

The in-country troops, fighting isolated battles in and around the Canal Zone, may have thought they were fighting alone. But at other places in Panama, U.S. soldiers had parachuted onto various drop zones in the black, predawn hours and were attacking and securing other objectives.

15 | The Jump on Río Hato

Col. "Buck" Kernan, commanding officer of the 75th Ranger Regiment, was, as he remembers it, "In and out of the office [at Fort Benning] the 15th and 16th of December responding to various phone calls and intelligence updates and was aware the situation was deteriorating but I was at home when I was officially notified. I was called on the secure line at my home, given the order to execute, given the critical times, and immediately alerted all my battalion commanders (one at Benning, one at Fort Lewis, Washington, and one at Hunter Army Air Field, Georgia) and assembled the battle staff. Official notification was 172000R December."[1]

On Monday, the eighteenth, the 2d of the 75th flew from Fort Lewis to a REMAB (remote marshaling base) at Fort Benning to join the 3d Battalion, stationed at Benning. C Company of the 3/75 then moved by bus to join the 1/75 in its REMAB at Hunter. The 2/75 plus 3/75 minus C Company would attack Río Hato; the 1/75 plus C/3/75 would attack Torrijos/Tocumen Airport.

In the marshaling areas at Lawson Field at Benning and at Hunter Army Airfield on the nineteenth, the commanders down the line made final preparations for what would be, for the majority of the Rangers, a first combat jump. (For one young man, Capt. Raymond A. Thomas, West Point Class of 1980, this was a second combat jump. He had jumped into Grenada in October 1983.) Regardless of the circumstances and the intelligence estimates of the size and potential of the enemy, a trooper's first combat jump is an event seared in memory. And a jump at night, a seven-hour flight away, adds to the trepidation and concern in the minds of the paratroopers—no matter how well trained and disciplined they are. One's first jump at jump school is exciting; but one's first combat jump is "red-letter"—memorable. The prospect grabs one's attention —no matter how macho he considers himself.

On the apron near the aircraft to which he was assigned, each man checked his weapon, his rucksack, his squad or platoon gear. All of them realized that

134

this was not another training alert. "The night of 19 December," remembers Pfc. R. T. Anderson of B Company of 2/75, "people were nervous as to how the next night was going to be. They kept reconstructing their jobs in their heads to make sure nothing was to be left out. People prayed."

Lt. Kerry D. McCown, a platoon leader in C Company of the 2/75, wrote later, "On the evening of 19 December, just prior to loading the aircraft, we had a final manifest call over by the tents. We were freezing [he was at Lawson Field, Fort Benning, Georgia] and standing in slosh and mud. We [the officers] in the battalion had just received our final intel update and had received the very disturbing news that the Stealth bombers would not be dropping their two-thousand-pound bombs (at Río Hato), a report that brought confusion and anger to my ears with a taste suspicious of rotten politics [as it happened, the bombers did drop their bombs, but only to 'scare' the PDF]. Immediately following final manifest call, I knew I had to tell my platoon. It was then that I called them together, as did the other platoon leaders with their platoons. Attempting to control the emotion I was feeling, I informed my platoon of the news about the bombs. They looked at me rather shocked and there were questions of 'Why?' etc. I replied I didn't know and that we would just have to do the best we could. There was a silence when the air was broken by Staff Sergeant Shalala, one of my squad leaders. We were just about to leave and head for the birds when he yelled, 'It doesn't matter, men, it just doesn't matter. This is all you need!' With this gesture he held his weapon over his head, indicating the rifle was all we Rangers needed to accomplish the mission. The men yelled and we ran to catch up with the formation.

"That comment broke the ice and the fear. I will never forget it as long as I live. It was the only attitude we could have going into the unknown and he had said it perfectly."[2]

Some of the Rangers arrived at Benning not certain of their destination. Pfc. Richard Fox, B Company of 2/75 at Fort Lewis, remembered, "It was the seventeenth of December. We had just gotten off from a deployment to Florida. Everyone was out doing their postdeployment partying. Then came the call. It was around 1600 hours or so and I was one of the few people in the barracks. When everyone finally arrived at the barracks, they [the commanding officer] gave us a 'bunco' story that we were going to Fort Bliss, Texas.

"It was the morning of the eighteenth when we deployed to Grey Army Airfield [at Fort Lewis, Washington]. We were all standing around in this hangar full of jeeps when we noticed they were loaded to the hilt with live rounds. That's when everyone knew that we were going somewhere, but no one knew where, until that night. It was about midnight when they told us. Around 0230 I received the Op Order. Being in antitank, we were supposed to follow the platoon leader and blow apart a wall and any vehicle. But as you know, a plan is just an idea or format of what you are going to attempt to do.

"That morning we drew ammo, and I felt like a kid in a candy store. Then we got in chalk order and rigged for the jump."[3]

Specialist Steve Stadelman of 2/75 was also not entirely certain of the mission when he got to Fort Benning. "On the eighteenth of December," he wrote, "we were staying in a tent city at Lawson Field on Fort Benning. We had just been deployed there on short notice (alerted), and of course no one in the ranks of the privates knew what was going on, but it started looking very suspicious when I walked past a jeep fully loaded with ammunition, including antitank mines and LAWs.

"We received an Op Order that night and we were all shocked and surprised. After practicing and practicing for what seemed like forever, we were finally going to do it for real.

"On the nineteenth, we drew ammo early in the morning. As RTO (radio operator), I only drew three hundred rounds for my CAR-15, one LAW, and some smoke grenades. All I had in my rucksack was my radio, poncho and liner, spare socks, and my shaving kit. I think I was probably one of the lightest-loaded people to jump into Panama."

"Different soldiers have different missions, different weapons, and different loads to carry," according to the 75th Ranger Regiment's SOP (standard operating procedure). "Additionally, for some missions the company may need LAWs, demolitions, incendiary grenades, mines, etc.; however, not everyone needs to carry the same munitions, nor are the same numbers required for each mission. The fighting load is designed to distribute the munitions required by the entire company while at the same time compensating for the heavier loads carried by RTOs, medics, grenadiers, etc."[4] The SOP also prescribes

Uniform and equipment common to all: Rucksack; sling rope with 1/ snaplink, poncho, work gloves, 2 pr socks, shaving gear, 2 full 2 × quart canteens, 4 × MRE's (Meals, Ready to Eat), weapons cleaning kit, lightweight gortex top, headnet, insect repellant, E-tool, flashlight, air items, 2 × cravats, 2 × combat dressings, 1 abdominal dressing, PC. Uniform: K-pot, K-vest (for bike and jeep teams), HWBDUs, brown T-shirt, LCE per RSOP, protective masks, ID card, dog tags, jungle boots and socks, red chem light, and 1″ strip of IR tape on left upper arm and from right eye to left ear on Kevlar helmet. Elbow and knee pads are optional. Helmets will be covered IAW Regimental guidance for "rag head."[5]

"Based on an individual's duty position," wrote Colonel Kernan, "his rucksack and LCE (load-carrying equipment—used to distribute the weight of equipment on the pistol belt and wraps over the shoulders) would weigh between approximately 60 pounds and 100 pounds. Radio operators and mortarmen carried the heaviest loads, followed closely by medics and machine gunners and 90mm recoilless rifle crews. . . . The uniform and equipment breakout does not include special-purpose items (i.e., night-vision goggles, night scopes, and special operations equipment). Breaching teams also carried demolitions and cutting devices to breach obstacles/wire." In spite of reports to the contrary, the Rangers did wear their reserve parachutes. Colonel Kernan reasoned that even though a man with an emergency—a streamer or an inverted parachute— might not have time to pull his reserve at such a low altitude—five hundred feet drop height—he gained some confidence from the reserve and, in some circumstances, might possibly be able to use it.[6]

By the afternoon of the nineteenth, preparations for the 75th to drop on Río

Hato and Torrijos/Tocumen were complete. Before mounting the planes, the troopers had "loose-rigged" their equipment and their parachutes so that on the seven-hour flight to Panama the harnesses of their equipment would not be uncomfortable or so tight that they would numb their arms and legs. Nonetheless, for the sixty-four or so paratroopers jammed into the web seats along the bulkheads of the C-130's, and in two rows of canvas seats back to back down the center of the cargo compartment, "like sardines in a can," one trooper called it, the flight was not even close to "tourist" class on a commercial liner. The toilet facilities were somewhat primitive: A five-gallon water can passed up and down the aisles served the purpose.

One of the Rangers was somewhat skeptical of the use of the water cans as a makeshift portable latrine. "While on the C-130 ride to Panama," he wrote later, "we were told we'd have to use a five-gallon water can to urinate in. There I was an hour or two from the jump of my life and I wondered, 'Will these jugs ever be used again?' So I pulled out my trusty Swiss knife and etched the letters 'RGR' on the left side near the carrying handle. To this day whenever I see a five-gallon water can, I check for the coveted 'RGR.'"[7]

From Lawson, the 837 troopers of 2/75 and 3/75 minus C Company took off in thirteen C-130's with two C-130's carrying their heavy drop equipment—destination, Río Hato. From Hunter, 731 troopers from 1/75 and C/3/75 took off in four C-130's and seven C-141's, with five C-141's for their heavy drop—destination, Torrijos/Tocumen. The C-130's were from Col. Daniel E. Sowada's 317th TAW (Tactical Airlift Wing), based at Pope Air Force Base, and the 314th TAW from Little Rock Air Force Base, Arkansas.

These aircraft were not the first to depart the States for the operation. At 1650 on the nineteenth—eight hours, ten minutes prior to H-hour—five AC-130H's launched from Hurlburt Field, Florida. These aircraft, from Hurlburt's 1st Special Operations Wing, marked the first launch of the assault force of over 148 Special Operations Force missions that originated from the continental United States and transited through the "gap" between Cuba and the Yucatán peninsula en route to their targets and stations in Panama. Col. George A. Gray, the Air Force Special Operational Force commander in Panama, said that the flight to Panama was complicated because the unpressurized AC-130's are restricted to ten thousand feet and they do not have station-keeping equipment for IFR formation flying.

Other Army and Air Force planes were already on the ground before the operation took place. At Howard Air Force Base were two AC-130H aircraft and two SC-130A's. On 18 December, five Air Force MH-53J Pave Low helicopters from the 1st Special Operations Wing and three CH-47D helicopters from the Army's Task Force 160, based at Fort Campbell, Kentucky, and commanded by Col. Billy Miller, flew from Eglin Air Force Base, Florida, to Howard Air Force Base with HC-130 air refueling tankers. The rest of the 160th's aircraft—nine MH-6 helicopters, eleven AH-6 helicopter gunships, nineteen UH-60 Black Hawks, and two MH-47's—flew from Fort Campbell to Howard on the eighteenth and nineteenth in six Military Airlift Command C-5's.[8]

On the long flight to Panama, the Rangers had ample time to think about their personal situations. Lt. Tim Nye was a support platoon leader in the 2d of the

137

75th. He wrote later, "On the flight from Benning to Río Hato each Ranger was given almost seven hours to reflect on the course of his life. I, like every other Ranger in the battalion, was preoccupied with thoughts of the upcoming battle, what would happen, would I be afraid, would I perform, would I follow my instincts and training, and, of course, would I survive. My mind wandered to my old platoon, the 'Black Sheep,' in my opinion the finest fighting force in the battalion. I wanted to be with them, I wanted to lead them, I worried for them. I didn't worry about the men in the S-4 shop. I knew they'd be okay, partly because I knew our mission wasn't as dangerous and partly because I knew I could control my men to some degree.

"I thought of friends and family and special events in my life. My mind raced between my wife and my children and I felt guilty for thinking of them when I should have been focusing on the mission. Finally my mind rested on the date, December 19, 1989. The date was familiar. My grandmother's eightieth birthday. I had missed it. I knew she would be expecting a call. I knew my parents would be disappointed for my not calling her. I became very angry because now I had a new burden. I pictured my mother calling my wife, my wife not knowing for sure where I was, and my mother becoming emotional.

"As I stood up and hooked up, I kept thinking how I had wrecked my grandmother's birthday. As I exited I thought to myself,—'Oh, well, maybe I'll get a chance to make it up to her.'"[9]

Pfc. Leon Erickson was in the weapons squad of the 3d Platoon of B Company of the 2/75. "The lights [in the plane] were dim and we were all restless. We had just finished getting rigged and the aircraft's constant, unconsoling drone kept me awake contemplating my fate in the hours to come. We were aboard a C-130 flying into hostile country prepared to give our lives so that others might enjoy the many freedoms most Americans take for granted. Yet, we were going to war.

"We stood up six minutes to jump time. The doors were opened and the humid, tropic air of Panama quickly replaced the cool air conditioning. The time warnings came down and out the door we went. The bird was pitch black, not even a red light. I went out, did a poor exit, scared me a bit. Thought I was going to be towed. Chute opened. Saw and heard firefights on the ground. Some brave defenders were shooting us as we descended. Didn't have time to lower my ruck. Damn ruck twisted in the air. I was stuck on the ground, couldn't get out of my equipment for over a minute. Tracers were flying close by over my head in opposite directions for almost a minute. Never felt as relieved in my life as I did when I met up with a fellow Ranger and moved out to the AA [assembly area.]"[10]

"During the seven-hour C-130 flight into Río Hato, I found myself very mentally and physically exhausted," remembers Capt. John A. Davis. "The previous thirty-six hours had been a particularly stressful period of time because, as the 2d Ranger Battalion S-4, I was responsible for getting the unit (and all its mission equipment and ammunition) from home station to the REMAB at Fort Benning, coordinating for all supporting assets to feed, provide shelter and heat, transport, break down and issue ammunition, and provide aerial delivery equipment to the unit, all the while trying to get myself and my section prepared for the mission as well.

"The REMAB at Fort Benning was a 'tent city' located on Lawson Army Airfield, in the middle of a freezing rain. Since my battalion was alerted while at home station, it seemed like we were about twenty-four hours 'behind the power curve' compared to the rest of the Ranger regiment, which basically deployed on the mission from home station. Taking into account the weather, the crude living conditions at our REMAB, the intense and compressed time schedule, and the fact that our thirty-three pallets of ammunition arrived at Fort Benning on the last aircraft (a mere three hours remained for us to accomplish the time-consuming task of breaking it down and issuing it to our Rangers), the scene at Fort Benning during those precious hours prior to loading the mission aircraft were quite much like a nightmare running at fast-forward.

"Like so many other of the sixty-four fellow Rangers packed like sardines aboard that C-130, I tried to rest during the flight with very little success. We were rigged in our parachute harnesses the entire time, and comfort became a function of frequent minor body adjustments. Of course, the closer we approached H-hour, the tighter the knot grew in many a stomach. Word came over the radio that the Panamanians knew we were coming and positioned obstacles on the runway and V150 armored vehicles around the airfield. The knot grew tighter. Finally, the jumpmasters began their time warnings. It seemed that there was no turning back at this point, and for some strange reason, I think the stress level was reduced ever so slightly because at least we now knew that we were going to do it! . . . I'm sure that like so many others, those last few moments before jumping into the dark, tropical air were spent mentally rehearsing exactly how to get my weapon out of its container rapidly, extent my light antiarmor weapon, and get out of the parachute harness to fight off of the drop zone. It all happened very quickly from this point . . . green light, out the door, chute looks okay, the sound of antiaircraft fire and tracers on the ground, weapons ready to fire, parachutes and planes and tracers thick in the night sky, explosions nearby, find a buddy, then another, move quickly to the assembly area."[11]

"Everything was perfect," said Lieutenant Dichairo, weapons platoon leader in Charlie Company of 2/75. "There were sixty-nine men jam-packed into a C-130, one of many on its way to dethrone Noriega, burdened with their loads of ammunition and curiosity of combat. It was a thing of beauty to see the initiation of a combat mission. Everyone knew exactly what to do, where to go, and when to do it. There were no final plans or last-minute changes. The only thing left to do was wait and execute the mission. As we began the time warnings and jump commands (usually an adrenaline rush all by itself), I didn't see any fear on any Ranger's face. Just a bunch of American Airborne Rangers . . . on a one-way trip. . . . At twenty minutes out my RTO turned to me and told me that if he didn't 'make it,' I was to tell his wife that he loved her. I told him to do the same. What else could I say? We continued to close on our objective, Río Hato, when the troop doors finally opened and I felt the rush of hot, humid air. My eyes were locked onto the jump light and I could hear the humming of the device

139

I was standing next to that was designed to protect the aircraft from heat-seeking missiles. Everything was still perfect as the green light switched on, Rangers began exiting the C-130, and the sounds of machine-gun fire echoed from the drop zone below. . . ."[12]

Maj. Clyde M. Newman, executive officer of 2/75, found himself alone for a time after the drop. "After exiting the aircraft, I knew my stick was way north of the intended drop zone. I was having extreme difficulty in determining my exact location on the way down. Suddenly I saw a tree, a fence, a road, and highline wires—'Oh, shit, don't land on the road,' I told myself. I managed to miss the highline wire by two feet and the barbed-wire fence by one foot. I thought the worst was over, but suddenly remembered I had not seen anyone else in the air on the way down. Tracers and bullets were going off all around me. I now realized I was alone. What had gone wrong? I kept hearing the bullets whiz by as I was getting out of my harness. I looked to my right, 'Oh, s——, the dirt road,' What if a V-300 comes by now—I'm dead. I quickened my pace to get rid of the harness and ready myself for combat. Suddenly I heard a noise and could barely make out a silhouette of a person. Could it be the enemy? I froze, but the shadow kept coming toward me. What to do? Should I shoot or play dead? Neither. I challenged the intruder, 'Bulldog.' He replied, 'Bulldog.' I recognized the voice—it was my longtime friend and fellow Ranger Battalion XO from the 3d Ranger Battalion, Maj. Danny McKnight. I was a happy camper. God bless Ranger McKnight."[13]

Lt. Jeffrey A. Bouais's time in combat was short-lived. "It was twelve hours after TOT and here I was lying on a stretcher on a C-141 MEDEVAC flight heading for Fort Sam Houston, Texas," he wrote later. "It wasn't how I expected my first combat experience to end.

"The jump had gone well despite the tracers flying up at the aircraft. I didn't feel my fractured ankle until eight hours later. It is amazing what a little adrenaline will do to carry one through a situation. I made it to the mortar position. I was the weapons platoon leader, and started consolidating my people. We put the mortars into operation as the crew members arrived. We weren't used much that morning because it is hard to compete with the firepower of a Specter gunship. All I could do was sit back and hope my company was sweeping its objectives without taking casualties. The men around me were nervous yet displayed an unexpected composure, full of confidence. The sounds of the battle seemed to put each one in a unique type of trance. These Rangers wanted to fire their 60mm mortar rounds so badly. It hurt them to just sit there and pull rear security. When dawn came I tried to move around, but I couldn't put any weight on it. My mortar section leader, Staff Sergeant Nichols, carried me to the Bn. aid station. Halfway there he stumbled and without my ability to help the situation, we both went sprawling. This act hurt my ankle incredibly, but at the time I think my pride was the thing that was most affected. Here I was, in enemy territory, supposedly practicing stealth to avoid any further enemy contact, and I'm sprawled out on the airfield, with my section leader, totally helpless. We both laughed, of course, mostly to hide our embarrassment, but deep down we were both thinking, 'This is not what I expected combat to be like.'

"I was MEDEVACed and Staff Sergeant Nichols drove on and did an excellent job as acting platoon sergeant."[14]

Capt. William C. Doukas wondered about his abilities as the battalion surgeon of 2/75. "After exiting a C-130 into a tracer-filled sky," he remembered, "my biggest fear was not being killed, but taking care of wounded Rangers in an unfamiliar country with unfavorable conditions and supplies. I managed to make it to my assembly area near TOC 1 without getting shot, now burdened with the anxiety of receiving casualties. A part of me wanted to see no injuries, and a part of me wanted to see if all the training would pay off. So I lay prone in the TOC area planning the setup of the battalion aid station concerned about the nature and severity of injuries when the first one arrived limping on one leg, saying, 'Where is the goddamn TOC?' It was the battalion commander [Lt. Col. Alan H. Maestas]."[15]

*   *   *

During the planning stage before the operation, Colonel Kernan had, of course, laid out in detail the missions of each of his battalions at Río Hato and at Torrijos/Tocumen. Originally "Río Hato had not figured prominently in the original Blue Spoon operation order," according to an after-action report from U.S. Southern Command,

> but the quick response of the 6th and 7th Infantry companies to move to Noriega's aid during the October coup attempt indicated the base had to be attacked. With the targeting of the mech battalion [Task Force 4-6, the augmented 4th Battalion, 6th Infantry from the 5th Mechanized Division, Fort Polk, Louisiana] toward the Comandancia, a force of Rangers became available to target against Río Hato. The extreme loyalty displayed by the men of the two PDF infantry companies portended a tough fight. It was a good objective for the Rangers.[16]

The Río Hato airfield complex, a commercial and military facility, lies about sixty miles southwest of Panama City and is contiguous to the Gulf of Panama. The runway runs north-northwest from a point about a thousand yards inland from the gulf coast. Slightly to the west, between the shoreline and the southern tip of the runway, lie the barracks of the 6th and 7th PDF companies, the PDF headquarters, and the administrative areas. The NCO academy and the motor pool lie just to the west of the runway between the barracks of the 6th and 7th companies and the Pan-American Highway. The Pan-Americana Highway runs east and west at a right angle across the 4,380-foot-long Río Hato runway, cutting it almost in half. North of the highway on the west side was a suspected ammunition supply point; on the east side were *bohios,* recreational areas maintained by lightly armed PDF "caretakers."

Colonel Kernan elected to use five Ranger companies for the task of "taking down" Río Hato. He assigned Lt. Col. Alan Maestas and his 2/75 the mission of neutralizing the 6th and 7th PDF companies. He gave Lt. Col. Joseph F. Hunt and his 3/75(-) the mission of isolating the airfield, clearing the NCO academy, the camp headquarters, the communications center, motor pool, and the airfield operations complex and of severing the Pan-American Highway.

141

The PDF 6th Company, "Expeditionary," a mechanized infantry company, had about 220 men assigned; the PDF 7th Company, "Machos des Monte" ("Men of the Mountains"), an elite light infantry company, had some 200 men, all of whom were reportedly "fiercely loyal to Noriega." Both the 6th and 7th companies were so loyal and well trained that they were sometimes mistakenly thought to be part of Noriega's elite Battalion 2000. The 75th Rangers' intelligence officer, Maj. Richard Inokuchi, expected that as many as 250 students would be in the Military Institute (the NCO academy) barracks. He also estimated that the two companies, the 6th and the 7th, would be armed with at least forty-two machine guns, nine bazookas, four recoilless rifles, twenty-three mortars, nineteen vehicles, and three ZPUs. With these figures and the knowledge that the 6th and 7th companies were part of Noriega's "top-notch" forces, the 837 Rangers jumping on Río Hato knew that it would be more than a training exercise or a routine "pay" jump.[17]

During the preliminary planning, which involved among other tasks detailed study of aerial photos of the Río Hato airfield, Colonel Kernan recognized that his Rangers faced a "severe" threat at Río Hato: The barracks were very close to the drop zone, which was along the southwestern side of the airfield. And General Stiner had emphasized the "critical importance" of neutralizing Río Hato with minimum casualties. The solution: Bomb the barracks area prior to the drop, to keep the PDF away from the drop zone. How? Use the Air Force's new and previously untested-in-combat airplane, the F-117A. But where? Both General Downing and Col. "Buck" Kernan wanted to bomb the barracks to provide the Rangers jumping on Río Hato all the advantages possible. But General Stiner made the command decision to "offset" bomb an open area near the barracks but not the barracks themselves.

General Downing spoke positively about the need for bombing the barracks area. "Buck and I violently disagreed with General Stiner about the 'offset' bombing. We wanted to bomb the barracks. We argued with General Stiner about the psychological impact. From the Ranger point of view, these guys were going in there, jumping on top of that thing. I was more worried about that operation than any of them because . . . I was really afraid that they were going to set up the fifties. They had something like fifteen armored cars there with .50-calibers on them. They could have set them up on that airfield and that would really have gone bad for us. But they didn't. We achieved surprise. There's a psychological impact of jumping right on top of the enemy. You get a psych on a guy."[18]

General Stiner's decision was based on the need "to minimize collateral damage." According to Pentagon officials, who agreed with General Stiner, the purpose of the F-117A bombing operation was to "disorient, stun, and confuse" the PDF troops in Río Hato without hitting them. An Air Force official, speaking in general terms, said, "It was absolutely essential to hit that target. We needed that target to be PDF-free, and we needed to take it."

Precisely at 0100, two F-117A fighters flying from Nellis Air Force Base at Tonopah, Nevada, each dropped a two-thousand-pound bomb with time-delay fuses in a large open field near the airstrip and the barracks area at Río Hato. "Subsequent press reports," wrote Clayton H. Snedeker, the historian of the

Twenty-first Air Force, "indicated that one of the bombs missed its target by several hundred yards, much to the embarrassment of TAC and the USAF. That *faux pas* was compounded when Secretary Dick Cheney, operating from erroneous data, briefed the press that the F-117s had carried out their mission flawlessly."[19]

"Pentagon officials called the operation [the bombing by the F-117A's] a success," wrote John D. Morrocco in the 1 January 1990 edition of *Aviation Week & Space Technology*.

> An Air Force official said the noise of the explosions created considerable confusion among the Panamanian infantry who were seen "running around the area in their underwear" as the Rangers landed. . . . There were conflicting reports as to the rationale for employing the sophisticated aircraft, which cost nearly $50 million apiece, to conduct what appeared to be a simple operation. The F-117A was designed to penetrate radar and air defenses and perform single-aircraft attacks on high-priority targets behind enemy lines. An A-7 attack aircraft and AC-130 gunships provided air support for U.S. paratroopers and ground units attacking other military installations throughout the country during the invasion.
>
> An Air Force official said the Stealth fighters were used rather than other attack aircraft because of the uncertainties about Panamanian air defenses at Río Hato and what air support or warning might be made available to the Panamanians by Cuba. . . . According to a Panamanian pilot who routinely flies into Río Hato, as early as four months ago the only air defenses were a pair of aging small-caliber antiaircraft guns. But prior to the U.S. invasion, a Panama Defense Forces Boeing 727 transport had been making regular runs between Havana, Cuba, and Río Hato as well as Tocumen and David airfields in Panama. . . . Pentagon officials said, however, the F-117A's were used mainly because of their bombing accuracy, not their radar evasion capabilities. Defense Secretary Richard B. Cheney, who visited Río Hato on Dec. 25 and observed the craters left by the 2,000-lb. bombs, said, "The reason we used that particular weapon is because of its great accuracy."
>
> Defense Department officials said the United States needed such pinpoint accuracy to bomb a large field to create the maximum impact without destroying the barracks.[20]

One detects a tone of skepticism in the reports on the use of the F-117A on such an apparently "trivial" mission, reportedly missing its target by as much as 160 yards. The AC-130, for example, already in the area, is highly accurate with its 105mm door guns. Admittedly, a 105mm shell does not have the wallop nor the psychological impact of a two-thousand-pound bomb. The debate on the decision to use the F-117A in combat for the first time in Panama, dropping two-thousand-pound bombs inaccurately on an open field, will no doubt continue in aviation and military command circles. (The debate was over in 1991, given the F-117A's accuracy in Desert Shield and Desert Storm.) And, according to an Associated Press report, "The chief of the Tactical Air Command [Gen. Robert D. Russ] intensified training for Stealth fighter-bomber crews after learning that they had missed their targets in Panama, but did not pass the information on to the Pentagon, a spokesman said. . . . 'General Russ eventually knew that the aircraft had missed its targets, but not early on.' He said it was at least ten to fifteen days after the operation when the general found out. Russ 'made training decisions based on that information,' he said." The accuracy of and the rationale for using the F-117A on the Río Hato mission is subject to some debate; its deterrent effect on PDF soldiers in and around the nearby barracks is not.

Before the mission, the Air Force and Army commanders were deeply concerned about the location of the PDF's ZPUs, antiaircraft weapons. Through intelligence sources, the ZPUs "were positively located as the jump aircraft were being loaded," according to a 75th Regimental after-action report. "These locations were passed on to the USAF AC-130's for targeting as soon as the information was confirmed. The AC-130's reportedly received fire from these two confirmed operational positions; however, they were quickly snuffed. An additional six ZPUs were located in a small ammunition/weapons storage area on the north end of the runway."

Capt. Philip D. Colahan, gunship coordinator for the 75th, can attest to the accuracy of the AC-130. "While orbiting over Río Hato Airfield providing fire support for the airborne insertion," he wrote, "the AC-130 gunship came under direct fire from a ZSU-4 antiaircraft gun. After a minute or two of 'juking' about the sky, not unlike a bull trying to throw a cowboy, the pilot, Capt. Phil Lebrun, was overheard on the intercom to say, 'Boys, that's what's known as a PPPD—Piss-Poor Panamanian Decision.' Shortly thereafter, the ZSU was taken out of action by the gunship, which then prompted another member of the crew to remark, 'Well, that ought to get us membership in the VFW.' "[21]

Special Operations AC-130's and one Army Apache and two AH-6 helicopter gunships from the Army's 160th Task Force were orbiting at the Río Hato airfield before the drop and before the F-117A's arrived. The AC-130H can hit targets precisely with its 105mm howitzer or 40mm cannon while orbiting a target in a 30-degree bank turn at six thousand to ten thousand feet altitude. The plane uses a low-light-level television to aim and fire. Col. Billy Miller, commander of the 160th, explained that the AH-6 can move in on targets at night at low level using terrain masking. The helicopter has a low-level-noise signature. The pilot uses an Aviation Night Vision System 6 (ANVIS-6) goggle to fly low and spot targets.

A 160th Forward Area Rearming and Refueling Point (FARRP) team parachuted into Río Hato with the 75th to be ready to refuel and rearm the helicopters supporting the assault. Pallets containing ammunition, JP-5 fuel, and refueling equipment were also parachuted in. A second 160th FARRP arrived later in 160th Black Hawks, and a MC-130 Combat Talon arrived to provide a wet-wing refueling point.

For three minutes, starting at 0100 on the 20th, the AC-130 gunships and the AH-6's launched a preparatory firing on selected targets in the Río Hato complex. Then, at H-hour plus 3 minutes, 0103 hours, the lead C-130 flew in from the sea, on a flight course from south to north, and began dropping its paratroopers into the tropical blackness in an area along the western edge of the Río Hato runway. The remainder of the fifteen-plane C-130 serial, with aircraft in trail, followed at close intervals. After the troops made their exits, two C-130's heavy-dropped four pallets onto which had been lashed four jeeps and four motorcycles. For reconnaissance, the 75th had replaced the horse with the motorcycle.[22]

The first jumpers were from 2/75 because their targets were the barracks complex to the south, near the shoreline. Colonel Kernan's headquarters were to assemble about midfield, so his command and control team—some twenty-one men, including his S-2, Major Inokuchi, his operations officer, Major Scroggins, and a small security force—followed 2/75. Because 3/75's targets were to the north and its drop zone was across the Pan-American Highway to the north, that battalion was the last to exit.

Night landings by parachute can be relatively easy if the trooper is relaxed and lands on a level piece of ground. On the other hand, the landing can be fraught with some difficulty because, even on a full-moonlit night, the ground rushes up unexpectedly and with unseen hazards, especially if the jump is from five hundred feet above ground level—as it was at Río Hato. Pfc. John Price, a member of 2/75, was killed when his parachute malfunctioned.

Colonel Kernan found himself in some difficulty after jumping out of Plane 4 over Río Hato. Instead of landing in a smooth, often practiced PLF (parachute landing fall), he found himself suspended some ten feet off the ground, entangled in the fence surrounding the "Bull Ring." In addition, however, he had fallen through the power lines that provided electricity to some of the Río Hato buildings. Above his head, his parachute was in flames. Unintentionally, he had knocked out the power to the surrounding buildings—an unexpected advantage, as it turned out. In some haste, Colonel Kernan unloosened his harness and lowered himself to the ground.[23]

The drop at Río Hato was not without other difficulties. The PDF 6th and 7th companies apparently had been alerted to the jump and were out of their barracks and deployed onto and around the airfield. The Rangers began receiving fire from two ZPU-4's (12.7mm) and small arms mostly from the area near the south end of the runway. One Ranger was wounded by rifle fire before he hit the ground. True to General Downing's fears, thirteen of the fifteen C-130's received .50-caliber fire from the ground, but the pilots held a steady course in spite of the tracers rising toward them. General Downing said after drop: "They hit the right DZ. The 317th from here at Pope dropped the Rangers on target. They nailed that drop zone. That was as fine a jump as I have seen. . . . I went out the next morning. The chutes were still laying where the men left them so you could see exactly where they landed. They [the 317th] did a great job."[24]

After a seven-hour flight from the States and finding the precise location of a small drop zone in the dark without the use of Pathfinders already on the ground is no small navigational task. The C-130 crews were flown by SOLL II- and AWADS-qualified aircrews. SOLL stands for special operations low level, and the II means that the crews are capable of making blacked-out landings; AWADS stands for all-weather air delivery system and gives a pilot the ability to drop totally by instrumentation. In earlier days, combat jump planes were guided into the drop zones by radio-equipped pathfinders who had either jumped in earlier or had infiltrated cross-country, under cover of night, to the drop zone.

A few of the Rangers had more than ordinary difficulties on landing. S. Sgt. Richard J. Hoerner jumped from the twelfth C-130 over Río Hato. His jump was fairly routine until shortly after he hit the ground. "Upon making contact with the ground," he wrote later, "my parachute was still fully inflated due to the winds and I was sitting in the middle of a road. I popped one of my cable loop assemblies in an attempt to deflate my chute. I noticed an enemy vehicle coming down the road at a high rate of speed and coming straight at me. I then attempted to get my weapon (M-16) out of my M-1950 so I could engage the enemy. I couldn't unzip the zipper so I detached my M-1950 from my D-ring on my harness. At the same time the enemy on the vehicle [pickup truck] opened up at me with *full automatic AK-47 fire.* I rolled out of the way of the truck and it drove through my parachute. My chute got attached to the vehicle during the driver's attempt to kill me. The vehicle was going so fast it slammed me to my back and started to drag me down the road, going north near the cadet barracks. I was dragged for about a hundred feet before I could get control of my other cable loop assembly and pop it so I could fall free from the enemy truck. During the drag, I dropped my weapon, lost my Kevlar helmet, and ripped my LCE (load-carrying equipment) in half. I got up, recovered all my gear, and drove on to my platoon assembly area down at Obj Silver."[25]

General Downing was proved correct also in his estimate that the PDF had and would use armed and armored vehicles against the Rangers both in the air and on the drop zone. Some fifteen CG-150's, armored vehicles, were estimated to be located in the vicinity of the airfield. One Ranger remembered that "while trying to get out of my equipment, there was a vehicle going up and down the runway with an M-60 machine gun blazing; luckily, he was not accurate. Bullets were everywhere. A short while later two M-72 LAW rockets were fired toward the enemy vehicle and didn't miss."

The airfield control tower at Río Hato was near the center of the airstrip where Specialist Kristops of B Company, 2/75, landed. During his short descent to the drop zone, he could see several vehicles on the runway and in a nearby wood line firing on the descending troopers. After he got out of his parachute and "before moving out to link up with my fellow Ranger comrades," he wrote, "I engaged a vehicle with my M249 SAW, which was firing on our descending troops. The vehicle was quickly taken out by one of our men with a LAW.

"I quickly got my equipment together and proceeded toward the control tower. When I rounded the back side of the tower, I came across a fellow Ranger, Specialist Benchwall, who was tangled in some concertina wire and was receiving fire from the top floor of the tower. I shot up the top floor and quickly got him out of the wire. We moved to the right side of the tower where we came across a lieutenant who was injured. Specialist Benchwall was on the casualty evac team and took care of him. I linked up with Sergeant Brackenbury and we cleared the tower."[26]

After landing on the runway just outside the 7th Company's compound, Staff Sergeant Brackenbury joined up with three other members of his squad: Sergeant Rice, Sergeant Hadfield, and Specialist 4 Houlihan. The quartet started to move off toward the assembly area of B Company, 2/75. When they passed the control tower, they realized it had not yet been cleared. "They made a quick search of the surrounding area," Staff Sergeant Brackenbury wrote. "They noticed that the main entrance to the tower was locked, so Sergeant Rice shot it off. The small team then entered the tower with their weapons at the ready. They found a large stairway leading to the top of the tower. At the top of the stairs, they found a suspected member of the PDF speaking to them in a mixture of Spanish and English. After a series of threats by the Ranger team, the man surrendered. . . . Staff Sergeant Brackenbury and Sergeant Hadfield proceeded up the stairs, clearing each level. No other personnel were found. Sergeant Brackenbury ripped the phones out of the main control board and smashed a large window. He then placed three chem lights in the shattered frame, signaling that the tower was all clear. The team then left the tower and moved on with their prisoner to the assembly area to face even a larger objective."[27]

Capt. Steven G. Fogarty, S-2 of 2/75, regrets a prescient thought he had prior to the jump. "Prior to rigging," he wrote, "I walked over to Sergeant Nieman, the B Company senior medic who had been in my jumpmaster class a month before, and wished him good luck. I jokingly told him that he was the last person I wanted to see on the ground. He replied that if anything went wrong, he was the person I would have to see first. After breaking both ankles in the jump, I started to low-crawl off the drop zone. After crawling for several hundred meters, the Rangers moving south noticed me crawling. They walked up and asked: 'What the fuck are you crawling for?' I replied that I had both ankles broken. One of the Rangers moved to examine me and I realized that it was Sergeant Nieman. He put me on his shoulder and carried me to the airfield tower before he moved to his assembly area."[28]

After the jump, the Rangers gathered on the move toward their assembly areas. The troopers formed into their attack configuration, checked weapons and personnel, and made ready to move out toward their assigned objectives. Getting to Río Hato had not been easy; nor would its takedown be.

16 | Río Hato Takedown

Although the 317th TAW (Tactical Air Wing) dropped the paratroopers at Río Hato accurately, once on the ground the Rangers found some difficulty in assembling in the dark and moving on to their objectives, principally the barracks areas of the 6th and 7th companies, the Military Institute, and the administrative buildings around the airfield. The mission was not made easier when the Rangers found the PDF deployed both on the ground around the airfield and barracks and racing around the area in armored cars and other vehicles, firing indiscriminately, filling the air with red tracers.

First Sergeant Mattison of A Company, 3/75, discovered a couple of the vehicles as soon as he landed. He remembered that "There was sporadic automatic weapons fire coming from the vehicle as well as occasional small-arms fire going toward the vehicle from the airfield area. . . . While still in my harness and laying over my reserve parachute, I obtained my LAW from my M1950. I immediately put it into operation. While doing this, the vehicle pulled up in front of me and stopped. I completed putting my LAW into operation and engaged the truck. I was only about twenty-five meters from the truck when I hit it. . . . Moments later a Staff Sergeant Gibbons or Gibson from 75th RIP (Ranger Indoctrination Program at Fort Benning) linked up with me. We identified ourselves and I asked him if he had a LAW. He said 'Yes' and I told him to get it ready.

"While he was placing it into operation, a second vehicle came up the road at a high rate of speed. This second vehicle smashed into the rear of the truck I had previously engaged. There was a momentary pause and then the second vehicle shoved the truck off to the side of the road. I engaged the second vehicle with my rifle, firing about half of a magazine at it. The staff sergeant who linked up with me began to sight in his LAW. He missed and the second vehicle continued toward objective Green, which was only about 100 to 150 meters farther north. . . . All of this occurred at night and within the first appx. twenty minutes after TOT time. Later, after daylight, I went back to the truck and searched it.

"The entire side (right) and rear of the truck was badly damaged. The rear right side of the cab was badly damaged and some windows were blown or broken out. The cab of the truck had expended AK-47 brass in it. . . . The truck had an official vehicle tag on the rear and hung up on the rear of the truck and drive shaft was a parachute canopy." First Sergeant Mattison had knocked out the truck that had dragged Staff Sergeant Hoerner a hundred or so yards along a road just after the jump.[1]

Capt. Jonathan L. Beegle was the fire support officer (FSO) with C Company, 2/75. He found himself in hectic action shortly after he landed. "There I was on Río Hato, 20 December 1989," he recalled. "After maybe forty-five minutes of excitement—of jumping, getting out of the harness, linking up, moving to the assembly area—I was established at our company CP, wheeling and dealing on the radios, nonstop commo—with the gunship, the attack helicopters, the other FSO's, the FOs (forward observers)—it was hectic. And then to his everlasting credit, Lt. Jim Larsen, the executive officer, leaned over to me in the dark and waved a freshly opened can of Copenhagen underneath my nose. 'Wanna dip?', he asked. What a stud; instant gratification."[2]

The PDF vehicles that raced about the airfield and adjacent roads with machine guns blazing and with PDF soldiers in the back of pickup trucks firing at random through the blackness of the night caused the Rangers a great deal of concern, if not widespread injuries. One trooper reported that "While trying to get out of my equipment, there was a vehicle going up and down the runway with an M-60 machine gun blazing; luckily he was not accurate. Bullets were everywhere. A short while later, two M72 LAW rockets were fired toward the enemy vehicle; they didn't miss. Once up and out of the equipment, we collected up friendlies and gathered a fighting force, which finally moved to the assembly area. Once there we organized ourselves into our teams and moved to mission posture."

The 3d of the 75th had the mission of assaulting the camp headquarters, the communications center, NCO academy barracks, motor pool, and severing the Pan-American Highway. Capt. Raymond A. "Tony" Thomas, West Point '80, commanded Company A of 3/75. One of the objectives in the middle of his company sector was the main gate at Río Hato. He described the gate as "looking like a rook—a chess piece." On top of the gate was a .50-caliber-machine-gun position. Shortly after the drop, Thomas's executive officer, Lt. Loren Ramos; S. Sgt. Wayne Newberry, his fire support NCO; and Specialist Oler formed a three-man team to "take out" the gate. By firing and maneuvering, the team knocked out the gun and killed two of the defending PDF soldiers. In the process, an armored vehicle "came rolling through the gate and almost ran over Ramos as he went through the gate, the castle," Thomas remembered. "The wheeled vehicle, a B-150, ran out the gate and up toward Penonomé. We later found it abandoned."

In another part of his company sector, Captain Thomas found an "unidentified school building. It was not supposed to be occupied," he recalled later. "We had taken fire from this area when we first landed, so we proceeded against it with fairly good caution. The lead squad went in literally doing building clearing but turned it off on a moment's notice when they discovered unarmed noncombatants in there. The squad found 150 to 200 cadets all huddled in underneath their bunk beds. There were no KIAs as a result."[3]

B Company, 2/75, had the 2/75th's main effort: assaulting the military compound housing the 6th and 7th PDF companies. Capt. Joseph Anderson, B Company commander, assigned the mission to his 3d Platoon, with the specific instructions to "breach the east wall, assault the first building, establish a foothold, and continue to assault assigned buildings in sector," according to Capt. David B. Haight, the AS-4 of the 2/75. "They completed all assigned missions by 1700 hours on 20 December 1989 and then started the arduous task of clearing a housing area to the west that contained many PDF soldiers that had run from the compound. These soldiers were taken prisoner and sent to the rear."[4]

The assault on the building compound had been well rehearsed beforehand. The preparation paid off. "Once we assembled in the assembly area," one of the B Company, 2/75, Rangers wrote later, "weapons squad of 2d Platoon was designated support for the main assault on the objectives Cat and Lion (the barracks of the 6th and 7th companies) in Río Hato.

"We were to establish support position Banana not later than H+50 minutes. We were to have four M-60 MGs, one sniper, and a support team leader, assistant support team leader, for a total of fifteen pax [persons]. At H+30 we had everyone except for the support team leader. We started our movement to the objective. The jungle was incredible, thick, coupled with very heavy rucks made it a long two hundred or so meters. The terrain was up and down, very difficult, but we managed. During the initial movement we lost one MG crew. They went back to the assembly area and just after we reached the 9mm pistol range, just about the halfway point, we broke contact with guns two and three, which left me with one gun. I didn't find this out until we were occupying Banana. I looked at my watch and decided to go with what we had. The time was H+46 and I needed to be set up at H+50. There simply wasn't enough time to go back and find them so now my position consisted of one M-60 MG, one sniper, assistant support team leader: five out of fifteen. We had started to place sporadic fire on objective Cat. We received some enemy fire; however, we suppressed it with M-60 and sniper fire.

"It seemed like eternity but the assault force finally attacked and we went to a cyclic rate of fire with all weapons systems to cover their maneuver to the first building. Then we were ordered to shift our fires. Later we were told we had effective fires on the obj."[5]

The ability of the Rangers to proceed with their missions with only a portion of their assigned strength assembled is exemplified by the actions of some of the troopers as they attacked the barracks buildings and motor pool area of Río Hato. Sergeant Greene was in the 1st Platoon of A Company 3/75. After he landed, he stayed in "the prone position to avoid being hit in harness. . . . I got my weapon from the case (an M-16A2 rifle with Litton night sight attached)," he wrote later, "loaded a magazine into weapon. Looking through sight I observed a pickup truck west of my position with several personnel in the back firing on drop zone. I engaged them with my rifle fire to suppress or kill them. They were traveling south to north at a high rate of speed with headlights on. After I fired about thirty rounds at vehicle, it turned off its lights and continued to come to my position. I had to stop firing at it because of friendly personnel landing in between me and it. Shortly thereafter someone made a direct hit with a LAWs rocket—this stopping it. . . .

"I grabbed my ruck, as I was in front of Objective Green just east of it, and linking up with a Ranger from 2d Battalion began moving to my objective Silver [an area near the southern end of the runway], south about six hundred meters. We still had a lot of small-arms fire all around us but with no cover it was determined by myself to move out. Also, 2d Battalion had to assemble to Silver's south to stop mechanized threat of reinforcement onto drop zone.

"I made it to Objective Dog, where the enemy fire was so concentrated that I decided to ground my rucksack, after securing my second LAWs rocket, observed from the prone my objective still three hundred south. I found Sgt. D. Smith, 2d Platoon A Company 3/75 at his assembly chokepoint to the east of Dog [a barracks complex]. I could see no enemy through my scope on Silver so I took the 2d Battalion personnel and moved out skirting the runway to come into Silver from the northeast to southwest. However, as I was moving to my objective, I became engaged by a sniper on control tower before 2d Battalion cleared it. I did not engage due to the fact friendly Rangers were at the bottom of it. I crawled about twenty-five meters. When I was not taking fire, I moved on at a rush to the approx. vicinity of Silver's chokepoint assembly.

"I observed a Ranger coming south from north. I waited to challenge him. It was Sergeant Hine, 1st Platoon, A Company, 3/75. We made linkup and made a decision to locate the chokepoint at that time. I got a red chem. light bundle out and marked it with such.

"About four minutes after waiting for sufficient personnel to attempt to take objective I heard a vehicle coming at a high rate of speed from south to north. I threw up my Litton and observed a black BM-300 armored vehicle. I fired at it across Sergeant Hine's front. Told him to get down from the sitting position. I fired about ten more rounds at it. It stopped after about two hundred meters and began firing back onto objective drop zone, obviously assuming the fire was coming from drop zone. It fired about two hundred rounds, then left, still headed north. I later learned that Specter gunships blasted it with 40mm cannon fire.

"Having observed one armored vehicle go by Silver, Sergeant Hine and I decided to attempt to take objective (a fuel resupply-motor pool) with only the one 2d Battalion Ranger, Sergeant Hine, and myself. We moved by wedge to the fuel tank northeast of the motor pool. The reason we opted to attempt [takedown] of objective was due to the fact a secondary objective was to block any armor movement north from 6th and 7th company AO [area of operations] to reinforce drop zone or escape.

"We got into position to lob grenades onto row of parked vehicles then rush to clear. Then do the same to the long motor pool. However, by that time, the platoon leader with about five additional Rangers linked up with us. He took charge of assault and we moved across to take objective. Platoon leader opted not to frag vehicles or buildings due to possible secondary explosion, that is, fuel tanks. We cleared vehicles without incident. As I entered building on east end, I looked through my Litton and observed an enemy person attempting to stealthfully leave motor pool to the west. He was carrying what appeared to be an AK-47. He was wearing a white T-shirt. I centered the aim point of my scope and fired a single round into center mass of his back. He went down as my scope whited out. . . .

"By that time, all Rangers cleared to my position inside of building (west end). We observed a building, south (behind) main motor pool and a building across road to the west.

"Staff Sergeant Anta located himself to my right on a knee, where he fired a LAWs rocket into building west, then an M-203 HE round. Then he fired an M-203 HE round into building south. He took a fire team and cleared building south, a barracks-type building. He fragged into building using SOP [standard operating procedure] for clearing such. And he, along with Sergeant Griffin, captured a prisoner who escaped injury by cowering in concrete shower stall. Building was then secure.

"Sergeant Hine and myself were then instructed to go to building west and clear it. Bounding and running while platoon minus covered us from motor pool, we swung to right of it and came in from backside. I fragged an open bay-type room. No enemy presence. Sergeant Hine then went to front of building and fragged inside room through M-203 hole made in the wall by Staff Sergeant Anta earlier. Room was secure by lock on outside. We opted not to blow door because of no possible enemy personnel inside.

"We then went back to motor pool, where a defense vehicular ambush was established."[6]

A Company of 2/75 had the mission of clearing the barracks of the Military Institute. Spc. Michael M. Sonnenschein wrote about his part in the operation. "Alerted. Everything smooth. Don't really think president has the balls to go through with the mission. Nine-hour flight in the harness. Thirty minutes out jumpmaster from 2d Battalion recites Ranger creed. He's very nervous and bones it up. Bird is very crowded and it's hard to maintain good static line control. Two minutes out the word is passed. Bombs away! Loud and thunderous hoorahs!

"Jump out and immediately see tracers from enemy fire. Land on another inflated chute right in the middle of the airstrip. Weapon is put into action and fire on moving vehicles already drawing fire on the highway. Hear a fellow Ranger asking for a medic twenty-five meters away. Help him out and leave knife to cut any restricting material from his body. Later found out he had broken femur. B Company further assisted him when they cleared runway. Ran to the chokepoint hoping to make linkup with any fellow Rangers. Linkup with approximately five plus the lieutenant.

"We (Sergeants Smith, Hyde, Reynols) breach fence and head for first objective (Dog). Support is set in [McDougal] and just when we are ready to prep, a V-300 drives down the road behind us with the airstrip on the far side. It hits a vehicle already taken out with a LAW and slows down a bit. I get my LAW extended about five seconds too late as the V-300 continues toward objective Green. Later find out it was fired on by small-arms fire only, as it sped through Green and hung a left. The 60s prepped Dog and I moved a fire team-sized element (Smith, Hyde, Reynols, myself) up to a chain link fence to make a breach. The breach was successful and we moved up to commo building to clear barracks. Bars were on all the windows as we (myself, Smith, D.) moved around perimeter shooting out lights above that were illuminating us. Threw a grenade in one room causing power to cut off. The room was a dead end. Backup power source kicked in.

"Went back to support for demolitions that finally made it to Dog by someone in 2d Squad. Objective was obviously cold and the platoon leader was instructed not to blow door down and to move on the next objective (Steel). Supposed to be empty school buildings for future PDF officers. Moved over to objective Steel and stopped short to plan attack on buildings because we (Smith, C., Howle, Harrison, myself) approached from a different angle. Proceeded with one fire team (1st Squad) up to building and found three vehicles. Harrison cleared vehicles. I reported and [was] told to move on after check. Heard voices and what sounded like a weapon dropping on concrete. Enemy troops running through courtyard and going into doors. Smith, C., and Harrison fired two M-203 rounds through back wall. Call for a Spanish-speaking friendly back at the platoon hault. Enemy is warned to come out with hands up and no harm will come. Three times the warning was yelled. Smith, C., and I proceeded to clear the building 'hot.' Smith threw a frag in the first room, followed by Smith and Harrison spraying rounds to clear. The enemy was under the bunks and came flying up, yelling, with hands in the air. Eight enemy were injured. Quick thinking and reaction prevented students from getting killed. Holton and myself went into the room next to the first one. It was occupied, and students were hiding and yelling. We entered the room. One of the students spoke English and we used him to call out 159 others. We went from room to room escorting him and using him as lead man. All were put face down with hands on head in courtyard. Searched the entire building and [it] was cleared. One PDF instructor from the jungle surrendered to Staff Sergeant Friar and myself. He had dropped his weapon and was also detained in the courtyard. All prisoners taken in groups of twenty-five down to Silver. All injured patched up."[7]

Sgt. David R. Clifton, C Company, 2/75, was guilty of AWOL in reverse. On the drop at Río Hato, he injured his arm and was MEDEVACed to Howard Air Force Base. He saw two doctors, who informed him that "the nerve endings in his left arm were separated from the wrist down." The doctor gave him some medication and told him to wait.

About an hour later, he remembers, "a major and a captain came and got me. They started to escort me toward a C-5 that was being loaded with other wounded men. I turned and asked the captain where the plane was going; they told me it was headed for Texas and that I was going home. They then asked me for my weapon and gear. At this point I realized that I would be leaving my team

153

and platoon for good; this definitely did not appeal to me. I started slowing down and hesitating about giving up my gear. The captain left me to talk to another officer near the plane, and the major was talking to some other NCO.

"At this point, I decided it was time to get out of there. The area around the plane was crowded and fairly confusing, and it was dark, so I had little problem departing undetected. I made my way over to the operations center and found a Ranger officer. I told him I needed to get to Río Hato, and he started to ask me questions about where I had come from. I was the only person in the hangar in full combat gear. He told me to sit down and that he would see what he could do. I waited for about thirty minutes when I saw the medical corps major come into the hangar. I figured if he saw me I would be in big trouble, so I left the hangar. As I walked outside I saw an MH-53 starting to crank up. I walked up to the ramp and asked the crew chief where he was going. He replied, 'Río Hato, buddy.' I said, 'Great, that's where I need to be.' Nobody on the helicopter ever asked me a question. They landed at Río Hato the morning of the twenty-first and I got off. After catching another ride in a truck, I finally linked back up with my platoon. There was no way that I was going home while they were still there."[8]

Because the Rangers dropped into Río Hato by parachute and had few heavy drop planes available (the regiment had heavy-dropped only four jeeps and four motorcycles), they were short of vehicles for use in resupply and general transportation between units. With some ingenuity, a few of the Rangers solved at least part of the problem.

Lt. Brian M. Drinkwine was the executive officer of A Company of 2/75. "As morning came on 20 December 1989," he wrote later, "and the heat tab in the sky rose along with the humidity, we were soon to find that all but a few canteens of water had already been used during the night and we were dangerously low and needed resupply quickly to maintain combat-readiness. Through the resourcefulness of my two young buck sergeants, we located a water spigot near a trailer to fill canteens and they presented me with a resupply vehicle. The vehicle . . . was a brand-new cream-colored Mazda RX-7 equipped with sunroof, AC, and all the options, the ultimate resupply vehicle. We set about resupplying the forward platoons by shuttling five-gallon cans back and forth to the front. I drove with Sergeant Ghormley standing between the seats through the sunroof, M-60 machine gun posed at the ready to defend us as Sergeant Thornhill held on desperately to the water cans.

"As I drove across Río Hato compound on that historic morn, I pondered for a moment of great moments in history—General Washington crossing the Delaware in a rowboat; Napoleon riding into battle on his trusty steed; Rommel bounding across Africa in his desert half-track; and me cruising around Río Hato in my brand-new RX-7. I couldn't help but think that I had to go as far as combat to finally drive a new car instead of the rusty old jeep that I normally drive on a daily basis."[9]

The 2d Battalion had acquired another local vehicle, a red station wagon, for use as transportation among battalion headquarters, the companies, and regimental headquarters. The automobile had been abandoned near the NCO academy. Because of damage to the vehicle, however, it would move only in reverse. Capt. Edward B. Daly was the battalion's S-5. Out of necessity, he decided to drive the car as it was. According to one observer, Captain Daly "opened up the back hatch for better observation, put an orange VS-17 panel on the hood to identify the vehicle as 'friendly,' and knocked the glass windows out. He, Capt. Robert Bell, the signal officer, 1st Lt. David Morrison, the battalion S-2, and S. Sgt. James W. Redmore, fire support NCO, were tasked to search the kunda grass near the Río Hato airfield to find and recover lost communications equipment. They loaded into the vehicle and, driving in reverse with Captain Daly at the wheel looking over his shoulder as he drove, they headed off—in reverse—to the airfield. They stopped and First Lieutenant Morrison remained with the vehicle parked on the taxiway while the others went into the kunda grass.

"First Lieutenant Morrison was watching a parachute recovery detail on the airfield when a 'boom' was heard in the distance. A few seconds later, an explosion erupted about a hundred meters away from the work detail. First Lieutenant Morrison thought that a soldier had tripped a booby trap. He saw the Ranger fall to the ground. Then there was another 'boom' in the distance followed by another explosion. It was indirect fire. First Lieutenant Morrison yelled for the party to return. Once back in the vehicle, Captain Daly tried frantically to drive it forward. It wouldn't go. He then put it in reverse and raced off the airfield. Captain Bell and First Lieutenant Morrison were sitting 'point' in the back of the station wagon as the vehicle proceeded around the taxiway in reverse. Once off the airfield, they proceeded to the Ranger regimental head-quarters near the Pan American Highway to report the incident. When they drove up to the headquarters, Colonel Kernan, the Ranger regimental com-mander, happed to be outside and was laughing as they backed down the taxiway toward him. 'What ya doing, Daly?' Colonel Kernan said, laughing. Captain Daly replied, 'Oh, nothing much, sir, just driving the 'back' roads."

A few days later, one of the Rangers at the 2d Battalion CP checked the car out. He "disconnected the car's parking brake, and, according to Capt. Mike Newcomb, the battalion adjutant, "once again the car could be driven for-ward."[10]

At 0240, Lt. Col. Joseph F. Hunt, commander of 3/75, notified Colonel Kernan that his battalion had secured Objectives Dog and Steel, the NCO academy, and the motor pool north of the 6th and 7th company barracks area. At 0430, Lt. Col. Alan H. Maestas, commander of 2/75, reported to Colonel Kernan that he had secured Objective Cat, the barracks nearest the end of the Río Hato runway; at 0628, he reported that he had secured Objective Lion, the barracks next door. These objectives, the garrison of the 6th and 7th Rifle companies, were the main efforts in Río Hato and, with their neutralization, resistance thereafter was "very light and sporadic."

Even though the fighting at Río Hato was over in a relatively short time, the Rangers did not escape unscathed. One man was killed when his parachute malfunctioned, and thirty-five other Rangers were injured on the jump. Spc. Philip Lear was killed during the attack on the PDF barracks south of the airfield. And S. Sgt. Larry Barnard and Pfc. Roy Brown were killed while they were assaulting a sniper position halfway down the west side of the runway.

Some twenty-seven other Rangers were wounded in their attacks on the various PDF installations around the airfield. The PDF suffered 34 soldiers killed in the action; 278 PDF soldiers were taken prisoner.

One hour, fifty-three minutes after the Rangers jumped on Río Hato, the first U.S. aircraft, carrying company support items and command and control vehicles, landed on the runway. Río Hato was secure.[11]

17 | The Airport

At precisely 0100 hours on 20 December, the silence of the morning was shattered by the staccato fire of an AC-130 gunship firing at three .50-caliber machine guns and a ZPU-4 antiaircraft position in the compound of the PDF 2d Infantry Company at the PDF Tocumen Airport. The early-morning blackness was sliced through by the flashes of tracers from AH-6 attack helicopters firing at Tocumen's guard shack.

The Tocumen PDF military airport is part of the Torrijos International Airport complex. The runways of Torrijos and Tocumen are parallel but in prolongation of one another. The southwestern tip of Tocumen's runways is roughly adjacent to the northeastern tip of Torrijos' and about a half mile apart. The international terminal lies in this area between the two airfields. Torrijos/Tocumen (T/T) is about ten miles northeast of Panama City and connected to it by Highway 1, the Carretera-Pan American Highway. From T/T, the highway then moves fifteen or so miles to the east and northeast to the Fort Cimarron area and then swings in an arc to the southeast along the center spine of Panama, terminating at Yaviza, about forty miles from the border of Colombia.

Lt. Col. Robert W. Wagner was the commander of the 1st Battalion of the 75th Rangers, normally based at Hunter Army Airfield, Georgia. For the Torrijos/Tocumen phase of the operation, Colonel Kernan had attached to the 1st Battalion Capt. Alfred E. Dochnal's C Company of 3/75 Rangers that, on the 18th, had moved from Fort Benning to Hunter; combat control teams; elements of the 4th Psychological Operations Group, including loudspeaker teams; and two civil affairs teams from the 96th Civil Affairs Battalion. In precise, militarese language, Wagner's mission was to "conduct an airborne assault D-day H+0003 (200103R December 1989) to seize Omar Torrijos/Tocumen Airport and eliminate PDF in sector; to clear Tocumen Airport for airland operations; to be prepared to conduct battle-turnover to JTFSOUTH (Joint Task Force South, General Stiner's command); to be prepared to conduct follow-on combat operations as directed; and, on order, to redeploy to CONUS." In short, knock out T/T, take on some other missions, and return safely home.

Ready to thwart Colonel Wagner's plans to accomplish those missions were 200 soldiers of the PDF's 2d Rifle Company, 150 men of the FAP (Fuerza Aérea Panamena—Panamanian Air Force), and some 30 security guards at the airport. In today's modern military parlance, Colonel Wagner had certain "critical nodes" to neutralize, in this order of priority: the 2d Rifle Company barracks, the FAP barracks, the Torrijos/Tocumen terminal, the Ceremi Recreation Center (which, in the early-morning hours of the twentieth, would prove to be a far more important but more frustrating target than anyone had at first suspected), the Torrijos International Airport terminal, and FAP aircraft. He was also cautioned that within a forty-five-minute reaction time were 200 soldiers of Noriega's favorite battalion, Battalion 2000, armed with, among other weapons, twelve mortars and nine V-300's (lightly armored cars).

In his CP at Hunter before the operation, Colonel Wagner and his staff studied the maps and photos of the area; read and reread the intelligence data; developed a plan of attack; "ran it" by Colonel Kernan and General Downing; briefed the company commanders, including Dochnal, and checked and rechecked item after item. The company commanders, in turn, briefed their platoons in painstaking detail, including troop-leading procedures.[1]

At H + 55 minutes, five C-141's from Hunter Army Airfield heavy-dropped pallets loaded with twelve jeeps, twelve motorcycles, and two HMMWVs on the drop zone at Tocumen. Fifteen minutes later, Colonel Wagner and the 1st of the 75th jumped from seven C-141's on Tocumen Airport while Captain Dochnal led his C Company of 3/75 from four C-130's from Hunter onto the tarmac around Omar Torrijos International Airport. A total of 732 Rangers jumped onto the two-airfield complex. "The Air Force dropped the Rangers precisely on target," wrote one of the 75th Ranger staff officers. "Most Rangers landed within a few meters of where they had planned to land on imagery studied during the planning phases of the operation."[2]

On the ground, the troopers unbuckled their parachute and equipment harnesses, put on their rucksacks, readied their weapons, ran to their assembly areas, and prepared to accomplish their assigned missions. They knew that accomplishing their missions as rapidly as possible was important for two reasons: (1) They did not know the status of the motorized Battalion 2000, just fifteen miles away, and (2) a brigade from the 82d Airborne Division was due to parachute onto Tocumen forty-five minutes after their jump.

"Ranger fire control was remarkably disciplined," continued the Ranger staff officer, "as civilian (automobile) traffic continued well into the assault (one hour) with people using the perimeter road to escape the fighting. Ranger command and control elements were assembled in twenty to twenty-five minutes and operational in thirty to thirty-five minutes. In fact, an after-action comment made by many Rangers was that the assault went down by the numbers like the rehearsal they had conducted only one week earlier."[3]

The initial firing by the Specter gunship and the attack helicopters at H-hour on the twentieth was apparently Noriega's first indication that an attack on his country was under way. On the evening of the nineteenth, Noriega had left Colón, the port city on the Atlantic side of the canal, and had planned to spend the night with one of his female "companions" at Ceremi, a PDF military recreation center in the La Siesta Military Resort Hotel near the entrance to the Tocumen side of the airport complex.

"During this time (one to two hours before the drop) most PDF officers did not believe that the United States would actually initiate an invasion," a 75th Ranger after-action report concluded.

> though due to the killing of Marine lieutenant Paz on the sixteenth, the entire PDF was at a heightened state of alert. At 0100 an AC-130 gunship and two attack helicopters conducted preparatory fires on selected targets at the airfield. The PDF initially deployed two to four men in the ten known guard and machine-gun positions, a platoon-size element (approximately twenty-five militia men) of Dignity Battalion personnel (led by the 2d Rifle Company first sergeant) at Torrijos International Airport terminal and about thirty troops around the FAP area and military terminal. About thirty PDF and FAP soldiers tried to shoot down the two attack helicopters as they attacked the FAP communications and arms room buildings. The AC-130 fires destroyed the horseshoe-shaped 2d Rifle Company barracks. These prep fires had a significant effect on the PDF soldiers, causing the majority of the 2d Rifle Company and FAP defenders to run away. Three of the four machine-gun positions were suppressed by the attack helicopters.[4]

Noriega had received an earlier warning that U.S. aircraft were approaching, but, according to the after-action report,

> he did not regard the report as accurate. Once the planes roared overhead and the fighting started, he quickly fled his room (and concubine) and drove west toward the city on the road between Tocumen and Torrijos. Two PDF guards from the western gate of this road ran past him without their weapons. Approximately one kilometer to the west, the AC-130 destroyed a Dignity Battalion car at the entrance to Torrijos with a 105mm round. Noriega had his driver turn the lights off his car and escaped to the northeast into Tocumen. Noriega had come within three hundred meters of the advancing Rangers from C 3/75 and B 1/75.[5]

In his precipitate rush out of the rec center, Noriega left behind his briefcase, wallet, and uniform. No follow-up reports indicate with any certainty the disposition of his partner for the evening. Noriega's departure, although this time under pressure, was not unusual: For personal security reasons, he was in the habit of changing locales several times per night and had a number of luxuriously furnished and amply stocked beachhouses and mansions scattered around the isthmus for his exclusive and impulsive use. Other indications of his apparent paranoia were the facts that he had, in recent months, "taken to the bottle," occasionally drinking himself into a stupor, and that he refused to eat anything not prepared by the mother of his girlfriend Vicky Amado.

A number of PDF helicopter pilots were in a barracks near Tocumen at the time of the Rangers' jump. One of them, Raul Alberto Reyes, had heard the fires of the C-130 gunships. He looked out of the second-story window of one of Tocumen's BOQs into the darkness and saw, dimly, the Rangers parachuting quietly onto the tarmac. To no one in particular he said: "This does not look good." Goaded by that accurate summary of the situation, he and about forty of the pilots took off for the hills outside Tocumen. Five days later, on Christmas Day, the pilots came back into the airport complex and surrendered at Torrijos. While they were being interrogated, one of the American interpreters noted that Reyes spoke superb English. The interpreter asked him where he had acquired his unusual fluency. Reyes said, somewhat matter-of-factly, that he was a 1983 graduate of the U.S. Military Academy at West Point and that he had taken his flight training at Fort Rucker, Alabama.[6]

Captain Dochnal's mission was to isolate Objective Bear, the international airport terminal, eliminate enemy resistance, and prevent any interference with the follow-on operations. The troopers from Chalk numbers 13, 14, and 16, C-130's, landed on the runway of Torrijos International Airport while those from Chalk 15 landed in the kunda grass (elephant grass—ten feet high and razor-sharp) west of the runway, a minor deviation from the drop plan that slowed the company's assembly. Nonetheless, Dochnal regrouped his men and moved them quickly toward their assault objective.

Preliminary intelligence had estimated that there would be very few people in the terminal at 0100 hours. But, in fact, an international flight from Brazil had just landed. The passengers were in the process of off-loading and watched with some interest and trepidation as the parachuting men of C 3/75 landed all around their aircraft and the international terminal. The terminal shortly became fully operational, with almost four hundred civilians milling about the concourse. By this time the PDF and the airport security force were on general alert and patrolling in and around the area.

To "isolate" the international airport terminal, Dochnal had decided to move in on it from three sides: the 1st Platoon from the west, the 2d Platoon from the south, and the 3d Platoon from the north, with the weapons platoon setting up to support the three rifle platoons from a position on the infield a hundred meters east of the terminal. The plan was sound, but its execution was fraught with some difficulties—not totally unexpected.

About fifteen minutes after the jump, Lt. Mike Franck had assembled two squads from his 1st Platoon at a chokepoint south of the terminal. The 3d Squad joined up shortly thereafter. Franck's plan was to move to "battle position two," the entrance to Omar Torrijos International Airport. En route, the platoon moved to one of its preliminary objectives, a building used as a restaurant, south of the terminal. Franck assigned the 1st Squad the mission of clearing the building. The squad scaled a chain link fence surrounding the building and moved up next to one of the restaurant doors. The squad leader could see that there were only civilians inside. He called for one of his bilingual, Spanish-speaking men to tell the workers inside to open the doors and surrender and no one would be hurt. The workers followed the instructions. The squad members detained and "flexcuffed" eighteen civilian "detainees." (A "flexcuff" is a ⅜-inch plastic cord device about 24 inches long, one end of which passes through a metal device on the other end. When the knot is pulled tight around a person's wrists, it cannot be undone except by cutting. Flexcuffs are used instead of handcuffs when a number of people need to be temporarily incapacitated.) The squad then systematically cleared the building without fire or casualties.

Lieutenant Franck left his 3d Squad to secure the restaurant. He moved the 2d Squad, under Sergeant First Class Beam, toward the entrance to the international airport. To get there, the squad had to cut through two chain link fences. Once through, the squad found a guard shack, near the terminal entrance, with PDF soldiers' bodies strewn about. Fire from the Specter and the AH-60's had killed them. The 2d Squad cleared the guard shack and so marked it. Meanwhile, Lieutenant Franck and his 3d Squad moved to the west side of the main terminal and set up an observation post to "overwatch the terminal and its parking lot."

Captain Dochnal then ordered the 1st Platoon to enter the main terminal and establish an EPW (enemy prisoner of war) collection point on the second floor. The 1st Squad collected the original eighteen detainees plus thirty more from the Avis rental car facility and moved them to the civilian detainee point. The 2d and 3d squads also escorted another forty civilians to the EPW point. Lieutenant Franck's platoon controlled all of the civilians and EPWs found at the airport. Eventually the platoon gathered some 398 civilians and 21 EPWs.

Lt. J. Kashouty and his 2d Platoon had more than its share of difficulties— some unusual. One Ranger remembered that "On 20 December 89 at approximately 0200 hours, the 3d Squad proceeded to move across to the airport concourse. There was an Eastern airliner parked with the tailgate down that had had the lights on earlier. Sergeant Anderson, my squad leader, sent me, the Bravo Team leader, into the airliner to clear it. I took Private First Class Lopez with me and we went up the tailgate to clear the inside of the jet, which was pitch black inside. The front side door was closed and the airliner was empty. The 3d Squad then proceeded to go into the bottom floor of the concourse. We didn't find any personnel on the bottom floor so we proceeded to the main terminal."

The 2d Platoon entered the terminal from the south, with one squad going to each of the three floors. On the third floor, the 1st Squad came under fire. The squad chased the PDF soldiers into the airport security office, where they began to burn papers. The 3d Squad leader ordered the PDF soldiers to surrender. But the PDF were still belligerent. They responded to the order to surrender by firing at the 3d Squad Rangers. Then one of the Rangers from the 3d Squad threw in a grenade and waited for the PDF to acknowledge that they had had enough. That did not happen. When the office began to burn, the squad entered the room and tried to put out the fire. Fortunately, the sprinkler system came on and contained the fire. The squad then cleared the rest of the third floor.

On the first floor, after moving to the main terminal, Sergeant Anderson split his squad into two teams. The Bravo team leader recalled that "Sergeant Anderson took Alpha Team to the left and I took Bravo Team to the right. All the doors we checked were locked and we were told not to bust or blow them down. I moved down a hallway and found some steel double doors that were unlocked. I opened one of them and moved inside. It was dark but the PDF must have heard the door open because they started firing at me. My first reaction was to get low and return fire but some women started screaming in English not to shoot. I went back out the door and found Sergeant Anderson and told him of the situation. Sergeant Anderson sent the Psyop man to the hallway with me and then called the platoon leader to tell him of the situation. The Psyop man tried to talk them out but the PDF said they would kill the hostages if we came in. Sergeant Anderson left me and Private First Class Lopez and the Psyop man there while he took Alpha Team to clear the rest of the floor. Sergeant Anderson also was trying to find another entrance to the baggage claim area. I found out that there were at least two American female hostages and an infant baby among the hostages. The Psyop man told me that there were only one or two men holding the hostages. He asked me if I could go inside and take out the PDF guys and I told him that I probably could. I crept up on three of the PDF in the darkness but couldn't fire at them because I didn't see the hostages. . . ."

The electric power in the terminal had been cut off when Staff Sergeant Borja of the 3d Platoon had thrown a grenade into the power shack.

Once he became aware of the situation, Lieutenant Kashouty quickly had his squads isolate the area and sent for Captain Dochnal. When he arrived, Kashouty briefed him and told him that the airport security manager, a colonel in the security forces, anti-Noriega and very "pro-American," was willing to help to secure the release of the hostages. All Kashouty knew was that there were at least two American women detained by an unknown number of PDF in civilian clothes. One PDF soldier leaned out the door and fired in the direction of Sergeant Smith. He had gotten Sergeant Smith's attention. Smith jumped over the customs inspection counter and landed on top of one armed PDF soldier hiding behind the counter. Sergeant Smith quickly subdued that soldier without a fight.

To find out what was happening in the room, Sgt. Brad Beauchamp took off all of his equipment except his night vision goggles and, carrying a CAR-15, very quietly went into the blacked-out office. He could see the hostages and the PDF, but they could not see him. Beauchamp estimated that there were at least twelve PDF holding two American young ladies and one woman, apparently a Panamanian, with a baby. The American ladies were bilingual and kept screaming at the Rangers to leave the area so they would not be killed.

Beauchamp backed out of the room, and the security colonel tried to negotiate with the ringleaders of the PDF. Captain Dochnal used Specialist 4 Pagan, a Spanish-speaking Ranger, to ensure that there was no trickery in the shouted negotiations. After two hours of shouting back and forth, Dochnal lost his patience. He told the security officer to tell the PDF holding the hostages that if they didn't come out now, he would have them killed. That broke the ice, and the PDF put down their weapons and walked out. Dochnal's men discovered that the ringleader of the group was a Cuban, Bernardo Magesta, who had a diplomatic passport. The leader of the PDF was 1st Sgt. Luis A. Santos of the PDF 2d Rifle Company. In all, there were twelve PDF and

Magesta in the room with the hostages. The surrender of this group meant that the terminal was now completely cleared and secure.

Previously, on the north side of the airport, moving toward the terminal, the 3d Platoon, under Lt. Mark Gibbons, seized a fire station, where it captured about fifteen firemen. Then, as the platoon approached the terminal, two PDF soldiers in the terminal fired at the platoon through a glass window. The platoon rushed into the terminal and isolated the PDF in the latrine. What followed thereafter was, according to General Downing, who spoke later to one of the sergeants involved, "close quarters combat."[7]

Sergeant Reeves and Private First Class Farber followed the PDF into the men's room. One of the PDF in the first stall to the left of the door fired and hit Sergeant Reeves with three rounds. He fell to the floor, wounded. The PDF soldier stepped over Sergeant Reeves's body and started to "finish him off." Farber tried to fire, but his weapon malfunctioned. The two PDF soldiers moved to the far end of the latrine around the bank of washstands. Farber got out of the room and reported to Specialist Eubanks. Then Eubanks, Private First Class Kelley, and Sergeant Thorland went back into the latrine after throwing in two grenades that were ineffective because the blast went out the windows and destroyed only the porcelain sinks. Eubanks and Thorland pulled security while Kelley extracted Reeves. While Kelley was pulling Sergeant Reeves out of the door of the latrine, one of the PDF soldiers at the far end of the latrine shot Kelley three times in the back of the head with an FAL, a Belgian rifle similar to the M-16. But Kelley's Kevlar helmet saved him, and he was not injured. Outside the door, Reeves gave a "salute report" as Sergeant Thorland gave him first aid. Specialist Eubanks and Private First Class Kelley went back into the latrine and crouched down inside, Eubanks on the right and Kelley to the left front. Eubanks tried to fire his SAW, but the barrel dropped off because the locking lever was not fastened. He dropped his weapon and grabbed Sergeant Reeves's M-16 off the floor. One PDF soldier peeked out from behind the last stall at the far end of the latrine. That was all that Eubanks needed. With one accurately aimed round, Eubanks shot the man in the neck. Eubanks moved toward the wounded soldier to "secure" him. When he got near him, another PDF soldier leaped from a stall and wrestled Eubanks for his weapon. Eubanks backed him up against the wall.

According to General Downing, "They got into a fistfight. This private [Private First Class Kelley] who had been in the battalion nine months is trying to help his fire team leader. He backs up, leans over his shoulder, and shoots the PDF guy in the head at point-blank range. Simultaneously, another enemy soldier entered into the action. Private First Class Kelley kicked the PDF soldier through the window, and he lands right at the feet of another Ranger (Private First Class McKinney) lying out there in the prone position behind his M-16. He had no idea that the fight in the men's room had been going on." The PDF soldier who landed near McKinney attempted to draw a pistol; Private First Class McKinney killed him with the M-16.[8]

Two and a half hours after the jump at Torrijos/Tocumen, the terminal and the airports were neutralized. In the terminal, the Rangers separated the detainees and the prisoners and flexcuffed the EPWs. The Rangers guarded the

163

EPWs closely and simply had the detainees sit down in the terminal and "remain calm." After a few hours, some ten children, ages six months to ten years, became hungry. The Rangers arranged with the restaurant manager for food and paid for it with their own funds.

In the assault on the terminal, Captain Dochnal's company had killed five PDF soldiers and had collected 21 prisoners and 398 civilian detainees. No civilians had been killed or injured. With the surrender of the PDF holding the hostages, Captain Dochnal and his C Company of the 3d Battalion, 75th Rangers, had completed their mission—Objective Bear had been neutralized.

While Captain Dochnal and his company were clearing out the international airport terminal at Torrijos, Colonel Wagner and his 1/75 were operating along the flanks of the Tocumen runway. The PDF had fired very few shots at the jump planes or the Rangers in the air, but once on the ground and getting out of their harnesses, some ten or twelve PDF defending the old Tocumen military terminal "placed accurate fire onto the 1/75."

Colonel Wagner's main objectives at Tocumen were Tiger, the housing area of the FAP assigned to the airfield, and Pig, the old Tocumen multistoried military terminal and the H-shaped barracks of the 2d Rifle Company. Tiger and Pig were both at the northeastern end of the runway. The 75th's after-action report states,

> A small amount of rifle and light machine gun (squad size) came from objective Tiger (FAP area), the north end of military runway (northwest of Objective Tiger), numerous fleeing vehicles and Objective Pig. . . . Two PDF soldiers fired their rifles (AK-47's and M-16's) from the military fire house south of Objective Pig. Approximately ten to twelve PDF defended the . . . old Tocumen military terminal. . . . Neither runway was blocked. During the initial minutes of the assault, several cars and light trucks escaped to the northwest into the town of Tocumen (which bordered the west flank of the Tocumen runway). The PDF soldiers in the cars were firing pistols and rifles at the Rangers as they descended on the north end of the runway. One truck tried to escape to the south along the taxiway and ran into the bulk of C Company 1/75. During the ensuing firefight, Pfc. James Markwell, a medic, was killed in front of the military terminal, the only American fatality at TT2. Four PDF machine-gun positions (three MAG-58's and one .50-caliber) were found abandoned with their ammo belts fed into the machine guns.

At 0208, the first planes carrying the 82d Airborne Division troopers arrived over Torrijos/Tocumen and began dropping the paratroopers just to the east of the intended drop zones.

Just after 0245, Captain Allyn and his C Company of 1/75 had isolated Objective Pig. The PDF were not firing from it, but some remained in the building. Some 82d Airborne Division soldiers were, by this time, moving between buildings. At 0612 Captain Allyn reported that Pig was clear and that two PDF had been killed and ten captured.

At 0255 Captain Ritter and his A Company of 1/75 had isolated Objective Tiger against light resistance. In the firefight to take the area, two PDF were killed and twenty-four captured. At 0520 Colonel Wagner confirmed that the Tocumen runway was clear.

At 0300 the 75th made a radio linkup with the 82d on the 82d's command FM net.[9]

Captain Mathey and his B Company of 1/75 had had the mission of isolating Objective Hawk, a gasoline dump just to the east of the military terminal. At 0515 he reported that he had isolated the area against very light resistance—some sporadic rifle fire at his company while it was en route to the area. Mathey elected not to assault the objective because there were "numerous Panamanian civilians in the area and no PDF or resistance coming from it."

"At 0458," reported the 75th's journal, "the second 82d drop occurs. Air Force still dropped paratroopers too far east into the swamp."

At 0612 the regimental journal reported that all Torrijos/Tocumen objectives had been secured and all battle positions occupied with no further resistance. At 0650 Captain Dochnal reported that the hostage situation in the terminal had been resolved with the surrender of the last PDF defenders in the terminal.

Again from the journal, "0800—82d Abn third pass drops (Air Force places them on the runway this time.)" The journal continues:

- 0745—JSOTF CDR orders 1 Co of Rangers to be attached to TF Gator to clear La Comandancia. RCO radios DCO Frago (Fragmentary Order) for C Co 3/75 to conduct the mission.
- 0900—Ranger liaison officer to 82d Abn conducts linkup with Team Gold [75th's executive officer in command of forces at Torrijos/Tocumen] at Torrijos International Airport.
- 1000—82d Abn MPs and CA [civil affairs] elements take charge of POWs and civilian detainees.
- 1030—82d personnel begin to relieve C Co 3/75 from security positions on perimeter around Torrijos IAP.
- 1100—1/75 BPs around perimeter of Tocumen report Panamanian civilians beginning to come out of homes and talk to Rangers. Most seem friendly and anti-Noriega.
- 1115—82d elements in PZ posture for follow-on air assaults into Tinijitas and Cimarron.
- 1130—82d troops begin to expand perimeter around Torrijos IAP.
- 1200—C141's and C5A's begin to land at both TT2 airfields bringing in follow-on 82d Abn and 7th ID forces.
- 1330—C Co 3/75 is picked up by two CH-47's and one HH-53. They are lifted to Fort Amador for their mission to clear La Comandancia.[10]

In the operation at Torrijos/Tocumen, the 75th Rangers suffered 1 man killed in action and 5 wounded. Of the 750 Rangers who jumped on the international airport, 19 were injured in the jump. The PDF lost 13 men killed in action and 4 PDF officers, and 50 men were held as prisoners of war. Some 376 civilians were detained during the operation.

At Torrijos/Tocumen, the Rangers rounded up 384 rifles (mostly M-16's and

T-55's), 3 .50-caliber machine guns, 10 light machine guns, 5 75mm recoilless rifles, 110 pistols, 1 4.2″ mortar, 150 CS grenades, 1 million rounds of 7.62-caliber rounds, 12 Huey helicopters, and 13 fixed-wing aircraft.

With the collection of the weapons and ammunition, the Torrijos/Tocumen phase of Operation Just Cause was over. At 1000 on the twenty-first, A Company of 1/75 was airlifted by two CH-47's into Paitilla Airfield to relieve the SEALs who had seized it the night before. And on the afternoon of the twenty-first, to emphasize that Torrijos/Tocumen was in U.S. hands, several anti-Noriega Panamanians reported to the Rangers patrolling the area the location of weapons caches of the Dignity Battalions and PDF personnel.

18 | Task Force Pacific

On the afternoon and evening of Tuesday, 19 December, the weather at Fort Bragg and the adjacent Pope Air Force Base was North Carolina "winter miserable." The temperature was about thirty degrees, with the wind-chill factor much lower, the clouds hung low and dark, and a wind-blasted icy sleet storm covered the roads and land with a slick patina of ice. In the words of Col. G. A. Crocker, the 82d Airborne Division's chief of staff, "It was the worst North Carolina ice storm in fifty years." The aircraft parked at Green Ramp at Pope, ready to load the troopers of the 82d, were also being covered with a thickening layer of ice. And, unfortunately, Pope Air Force Base, in theoretically "mild" North Carolina, had few "deicers" available.[1]

By 2055 that evening, the ice problem was so bad that Gen. James Johnson, the 82d's commanding general, called General Stiner in Panama and requested that he delay H-hour by one hour so that the deicers could have more time to do their work. At 2208 word came back to Pope that General Johnson's request was denied—in effect, said General Stiner, do everything possible to take off as planned. The wing commander at Pope, Col. Daniel "Stump" Sawada, then recommended to General Johnson that the ten aircraft he thought he could deice on time depart on schedule and that the ten remaining depart as soon as they were deiced to catch up with the first aircraft en route to Panama.

Capt. Gary J. Ramsdell, twenty-eight, West Point '84, commanded C Company of the 2d of the 504th, part of Col. Jack Nix's (DRB) Division Ready Brigade on the eighteenth of December. The commander of the 2d of the 504th was Lt. Col. Harry Axson, a large "bear" of a man and, like so many large men, with a jovial sense of humor, an outgoing personality, and a self-confidence to match his physique. His figure was much like that of a four-star general who would win so much acclaim internationally in the United States' next war— Gen. "Stormin' Norman" Schwarzkopf. Admittedly, Axson was taller and less stocky than the commander of all the Allied forces in the Persian Gulf.

At 0915 on the eighteenth, Colonel Axson called his company commanders to his battalion headquarters and announced to them that N-hour was 0900. "Just another EDRE," thought Captain Ramsdell. EDREs (emergency deployment readiness exercises) were a way of life for the "always ready" 82d. In "normal" times, the division commander ordered a surprise EDRE for some unit in the division about every month. Thus Ramsdell and his company had taken part in one every six months or so as part of a one- or two-battalion jump into Fort Stewart, Georgia, for example, or Avon Park, Florida, Camp Mackall, North Carolina, or on one of the spacious drop zones at Fort Bragg itself. The EDRE tested a parachute unit's ability to deploy in eighteen hours from barracks to "wheels up" on the first aircraft taking off from Pope.[2]

"At 1100 hours, the N+2 brief was held at division headquarters for the division-ready brigade and other selected division elements," according to the division's historical summary.

Due to OPSEC (operational security) considerations, only brigade-level commanders were briefed that this no-notice EDRE was actually a cover for the execution of OPLAN 2-90.

At 1400 hours, the Division Assault CP (command post) occupied the PHA and continued planning and preparation for the EDRE. At approximately 1500 hours, the division assault CP was alerted to begin preparing for combat operations in Panama IAW 82d Div OPLAN 2-90. The DRB occupied the PHA and conducted rehearsals IAW the OPLAN. Rigging of HD (Heavy Drop) items continued throughout the day in order to prepare the 28 C-141 HD package for forward staging at Charleston AFB, SC.[3]

After the 0915 meeting with his battalion commander, Ramsdell went back to his company CP in the barracks area, alerted his men, went through a long checklist for an EDRE, and, by 1300, had moved his company in 2½-ton trucks from its barracks to the PHA. His men drew ammunition, extra water containers, mosquito repellent, sunscreen, and other necessities from the corps marshaling area, test-fired their weapons, and drew rations—MREs (meals ready to eat). (After months living on MREs in Saudi Arabia, some of these same 82d troopers, deployed there a few days after Saddam's rape of Kuwait, referred to MREs as "meals rejected by Ethiopians" or by even less flattering and more graphic terms.)

Ramsdell and the company spent the rest of the day reviewing troop leading procedures and rehearsing various phases of the operation. But even after he arrived at the PHA, he was still under the impression that this EDRE might just be another training exercise. "When we arrived at the PHA," he wrote later, "you could see mounds of live ammunition that were being prepared for issue. On a normal EDRE, we were issued blank ammunition only, so this was a positive indicator that it was a real operation. However, I do not think we truly believed it was the 'real thing' until an hour before drop time, when the message was passed from one end of the aircraft to the other that the Rangers had jumped and were encountering light resistance. Up until that time, I felt that the weather or diplomats would intervene and cancel the jump."[4]

By 1400 hours the entire 2d Battalion of the 504th Infantry was assembled in the PHA. At 1500 hours, Maj. Jon Chase, S-3 of the 2-504 PIR, assembled the battalion's "Orders Group A" and published the battalion warning order. At this time, everyone in the chain of command knew they were locked into the PHA and that this "EDRE" was the real thing. The warning order established the mission for the battalion: "TF 2-504 conducts airborne assault commencing 200145 to achieve PZ posture on Tocumen Airfield NLT 200245 DEC 89, conducts air assault to isolate, neutralize and, if necessary, destroy enemy forces vic OBJECTIVE AXE and HAMMER" (Panama Viejo)."

Major Chase also published the battalion's timetable for Phase I (alert, marshal, and deploy) of the operation:

TIME	CHRONOLOG ENTRY
2100	Brigade-level communications exercise
2230	CG backbrief
2400	Jumpmaster briefing
0100	Battalion operations order
0600	Air assault air mission commander's briefing
0800	Trial manifest/sustained airborne training
0900	ESIP (equipment and supply issue point) procedures
1330	Final manifest
1500	Move to Green Ramp
1600	Parachute issue (planeside)
1640	Rig/JMPI
1800	Load time
1845	Station time
1900	Takeoff
0145	Drop time[5]

On Monday night at 1900, Colonel Nix issued his brigade order in one of the Quonset tents at the PHA. Present for the briefing were about seventy-five officers and men, including the division commander, his principal staff officers, Nix's staff, his battalion commanders, and all the members of their staffs. Colonel Nix repeated in detail the brigade's plans, procedures, and sequence of operations to accomplish the brigade's missions: 2/504 to Panama Viejo; 1/504 to Tinajitas; 4/325 to Fort Cimarron. General Johnson was the last man to speak; he gave a "pep talk," outlining the importance of the mission, the U.S. president's concern about the operation, and the capability of the 82d Airborne Division. The entire briefing, including intelligence estimates and other details of the pending operation, took about 2½ hours.

At 2300 hours, Colonel Axson gave his battalion operations order backbrief to Brig. Gen. Richard Timmons, the assistant division commander for support. He was followed by Lt. Col. Richard Marable, commanding officer of the 1-504 PIR, and Lt. Col. John Vines, commanding officer of the 4-325 AIR.

At 0100 on Tuesday morning, in a continuing process of passing orders down the chain of command, Colonel Axson issued his order to his company commanders and his staff in one of the PHA Quonsets. The other two battalion commanders did the same. Axson's discussion of his mission—the neutralization of the PDF at Panama Viejo—took about an hour. Axson detailed his plan of attack; after jumping into Torrijos and assembling, loading up in helicopters at Torrijos, flying to two LZs near their objective, the barracks at Panama Viejo, landing, and then isolating the barracks, with B and C 2-504 landing on the same LZ, BOBCAT, to the north and the rest of the battalion from the west ON LZ LION. B and C companies would have the mission of isolating to the north. Axson pointed out to his battalion officers that he wanted to accomplish the mission "through the measured application of overwhelming force and not the immediate application of full firepower indiscriminately." After cordoning off the area, Axson said that he would then give the PDF a chance to surrender through broadcasts in Spanish by the 6th Psyops Group's loudspeaker teams.[6]

Ramsdell got back to his company in the PHA at about 0330 and, at 0530, issued his company order to his platoon leaders. At 0630 the men of C 2-504 ate breakfast; at 0730, Ramsdell ran his company through a trial manifest. The 82d SOP required that companies avoid putting "all of their eggs in one basket." Thus Ramsdell's 120-man company was scattered among twenty "birds," six men to a "bird." This procedure prevented the loss of an entire unit if one of the "birds" were shot down, aborted in flight, or otherwise did not make it to the DZ. Each C-141 carried 120 jumpers. (By contrast, the C-47's of World War II fame carried only about 20 jumpers for parachute operations.)

Ramsdell's company worked on the manifests until about 1000. After that the company went to the ESIP (emergency supply issue point) and drew a basic load of ammunition. Soldiers who normally complained about the amount of ammunition issued for a "practice" EDRE could not get enough of it on this occasion. By making changes on the ESIP records, a practice discouraged by their NCOs and officers, soldiers could draw more than the basic load. Soldiers were also required to jump with an additional one hundred rounds of .50-caliber ammunition for D Company's gun-mounted HMMWVs.

From 1000 until 1300, the platoon leaders went through the plan at platoon and squad level, outlined the PZ (pickup zone) posture, and went through basic squad battle drills—drills they had practiced endlessly in the past so the men of the squads could perform their battle maneuvers in the dark or in any kind of inclement weather.

By 1400 the men of C Company were in final manifest formation in an area next to the PHA. They were more than delighted to be out of the PHA and ready to get on with their mission. The accommodations at the PHA were not exactly of Hilton or Marriott standard. Some of the heaters in the tents did not work, some of the latrines were stopped up, and the ammunition supply points did not have all of the types of ammunition for all of their weapons. To add to their misery, soldiers had to stand in long lines in the sleet to get their gamma globulin shots. Finally, due to the temperature in Panama, Colonel Axson issued the order to start taking off the cold-weather gear prior to chuting up and loading the aircraft. There would be no time to remove clothes once they hit the drop zone. The temperature in Panama was expected to be eighty-one degrees.

170

This was not the most popular order that the soldiers received, but the paratroopers did it quickly, quietly, and without complaining.[7]

They went through prejump training and thereafter ate a sack lunch. Jumpmasters, meanwhile, had gone to Green Ramp to inspect their aircraft. The sleet storm continued unabated until the very end of final manifest call, when it seemed to pause for just a moment. At that moment, Major Chase assembled the 2-504 troopers on his aircraft and had them look across the huge area being used for final manifest procedures. He told them to "take a close look at what it looks like to have twenty-two hundred paratroopers assembled and ready to jump into the history books. . . ." It was an awesome sight, Major Chase decided.

Colonel Axson decided to walk from the PHA to Green Ramp by chalk. Although the trip was only about a quarter mile, it turned into a journey. Laden with over a hundred pounds of equipment, the troopers proceeded quickly and quietly down the muddy road leading to Pope Air Force Base. At the gate was Lieutenant Colonel James Grazioplane, the commander of the 82d's armor battalion. With his battalion dropping only a company of tanks, he was not going to jump and take a parachute away from a "shooter." "Nonetheless, he was there to heighten the excitement and warm the soul," wrote one of Colonel Axson's staff officers.

Between 1730 and 1800, the men loaded the planes for an originally scheduled takeoff time of 1900 hours. They carried on board their rucksacks, each weighing eighty pounds or more and stuffed with an assortment of extra gear, claymore mines, special ammunition, and plenty of water. They stored the "rucks" under their pull-down canvas seats and "loose-rigged" their parachutes.[8]

Because of the storm and the requirement to deice, the takeoff was delayed 2½ hours. The troopers remained aboard. It was going to be a long delay followed by a very long flight. Many of the men dozed. They had had little sleep in the last thirty-six hours. "In the PHA (18 December 89)," Ramsdell remembered, "the leaders averaged about one hour of sleep and the soldiers averaged about three hours. On Tuesday night (19 December 89), very few soldiers got any rest. The first night we spent In Panama (20 December 89), we averaged about three hours of sleep, but this was accomplished by being up an hour and then sleeping an hour, and so on." Ramsdell's and Axson's actions in the time frame after the alert and prior to the jump were typical of those of the other company and battalion commanders in Jack Nix's brigade.

At 2130, after an all-out effort by the Air Force ground crews to deice the planes, the first C-141 rolled down the runway at Pope. General Johnson was aboard it; so was Captain Ramsdell. At 2230, General Johnson sent a report to General Stiner: "Eight (8) Pax a/c (passenger aircraft) are up (chalks 1-6, 9, 10); all heavy equipment a/c are up. All Bn and Bde Cdrs are airborne. The lift of eight will make the original TOT of 0145. The remaining 12 a/c will attempt to link-up en route to make the scheduled TOT; if no link-up occurs, they will drop on arrival."[9]

"At 2228, Chalks 7 and 8 departed Pope AFB. At 2327, direct communication was established between COMJTFSO (Stiner) and COMTF PACIFIC (Johnson)," reported the division's historical summary.

The C-141's carrying the heavy-drop loads that had staged through Charleston Air Force Base, South Carolina, had not been affected by the Pope–Fort Bragg ice storm. Consequently, twenty-eight C141's carrying heavy-drop equipment and three C-141's carrying CDS (containerized delivery system) bundles arrived over Torrijos International Airport at 0145, right on schedule, and dropped their loads. This drop of heavy equipment and bundles marked the commencement of the 82d Airborne Division's combat operations in Just Cause.

The heavy drop included seventy-two Hummvees (M998), eight Sheridan tanks (the M551), four M102 105mm howitzers, two M1038s, two supply platforms, and seventy-four CDS bundles. This equipment was for the three infantry battalions of the 1st Brigade plus A Company of the 3d of the 505th PIR, C Company of the 3d of the 73d Armor, C Battery of the 3d Battalion 319th Field Artillery, A Company 307th Engineer Battalion, and elements from the 3-4 ADA Battalion, 313th MI Battalion, 82d Signal Battalion, a Psyops team, and the 82d Military Police Company. The 3-504 PIR, a battalion of the 1st Brigade, was already in Panama at the Jungle Operations Training Center (JOTC). It was attached to a brigade in the 7th Infantry Division commanded by Col. Keith Kellog, a former commander of the 1-504 PIR, 1st Brigade, 82d Airborne Division.

Much of the heavy-drop equipment landed off the designated DZ. One M551 Sheridan tank was heavily damaged when its parachutes apparently failed to inflate properly. It landed in an almost inaccessible area, very difficult to reach with a recovery vehicle. General Johnson decided to blow it up so no part of it could be salvaged by the PDF. A second Sheridan was also damaged on landing, but a recovery vehicle carried it to Tocumen Airport, where the Sheridan mechanics cannibalized it for spare parts for other Sheridans, the HMMWV belonging to the S-3, 2-504 PIR (nicknamed "Gunther" by the battalion's assault command post) suffered a cracked frame during its heavy drop onto the airfield. "Ironically," said Colonel Axson, "it survived the entire operation and enjoyed the best communications ever off its vehicle-mounted radios."[10]

Captain Ramsdell said that the five-hour, forty-one-minute flight from Pope to Torrijos was "not rough." The planes' doors remained closed until three minutes out—effectively cutting out the thirty-degree weather from Pope at the start of the flight. Aloft, General Johnson had communication through a VHF Tactical Satellite with, among others, General Stiner at Fort Clayton, General Downing at Howard, an AWACS plane, and the Rangers at Tocumen. A follow-on report claimed that "En route communications were superb. The division commander was able to communicate with all aircraft en route to the objective."

The drop zone, Torrijos/Tocumen Airport, consisted of two colocated airfields, Tocumen, the civilian airfield, and Torrijos, the military airfield. The serial of C-141's carrying the first elements of the 82d flew over Panama, out into the Pacific, and then turned back and came over Torrijos Airport on a northeast heading from the Pacific side of the isthmus.

At about two hours before jump time, the jumpmasters alerted the jumpers, who put on their rucksacks and tightened their parachute harnesses. They had worn their reserves throughout the entire flight. At three minutes out, the air crews opened the jump doors, the 80-degree warmth of Panama blasted into the planes, and the jumpmasters began their prejump safety checks followed by the jump sequence: "Stand up and hook up, check equipment, and stand by."

On the first plane, General Johnson was the first man in the sixty-man stick, jumping out the right door; Captain Ramsdell was number eight, going out the left door. At 0211, and from an altitude of five hundred feet at a jump speed of 135 knots, the green light came on and General Johnson led his men into the warm, humid, clear night air of Panama. Behind him, paratroopers leapt out of both doors of the plane. The exits were fast—jumpers exited at double time, ignoring the 82d Airborne Division's SOP of one-second intervals between jumpers because the troopers had been briefed that it would be "one pass and one pass only." Second Lieutenant Helms, who jumpmastored one flight, said, "Jumpers were so close that the fronts of the jumpers' reserves were actually touching the pack tray of the paratrooper in front of him." The Air Force loadmaster on the aircraft with 2d Lt. Maurice Heisig, B/2-504, told the troops as they were getting ready to jump, "The Rangers have not secured the drop zone yet . . . the DZ is hot. . . . Good luck." Their target, the DZ along the eastern edge of the Torrijos runway, was approximately three miles long and "could be characterized as muddy and having high grass," said one of the jumpers later in what turned out to be an understated appraisal of the DZ terrain.

Once his chute opened, Captain Ramsdell had a brief look at tracers streaking through the black sky and saw firing on the ground about six hundred meters from where he was going to hit the ground. He and his stick of paratroopers landed about fifteen hundred meters to the right side of the Torrijos runway in kunna grass that was fifteen feet tall. The paratroopers, laden as they were with their parachute harnesses, rucksacks, and weapons containers—altogether weighing over 140 pounds—wrestled to untangle themselves from their chutes and other gear in the thick grass and then struggled to "load and lock" (put their weapons into operation) and then don their rucksacks before they were ready to move to their assembly areas. Captain Ramsdell said that because the kunna grass was so thick he felt that he was walking—or struggling to walk—two feet above the ground. It took him almost an hour and a half from the time he landed to move the five hundred or so meters to his battalion assembly area that was also the PZ (helicopter pickup zone) on the west side of the Torrijos runway. The assembly areas for the various units were marked by twenty-foot poles with four- by four-foot banners on top, color-coded for easy identification. These markers were referred to as "Stiner aids." The assembly areas were also marked with "chem lights," which, when bent and shaken, glowed like neon. The assembly area of 4/325 was at the northeast corner of the Torrijos main runway, the 1/504's was in the middle, and 2/504's was at the southwest end.[11]

One soldier, a radio operator, remembered most clearly the "elephant" or kunna grass that ran up to the edge of the runway. He said that he had jumped with the heaviest load he had ever carried—including two radios, his personal

173

rucksack loaded with ammunition, extra clothes and food, a base station antenna, and his M-16 rifle. He landed about seventy-fve meters off the runway. "It was so bad that I could only take three steps and then fall down," he said after the jump. "And in the dark, I couldn't tell if the man only three feet away was a good guy or a bad guy, so I would lay very still until he went away."

"I was the number-one jumper on the sixth aircraft," wrote Capt. Steve Phelps later. "During the jump, I made my first tree landing about a half mile from the 2-504 assembly point. My PFL [parachute landing fall] was broken by another chute spread across the top of the tree. I slid off of that chute and became stuck in the tree. I jettisoned my equipment and later could not locate my rucksack due to the denseness of the underbrush. Later, Capt. Robert Krueger, the commander of Headquarters Company, 2-504, informed me that along with my rucksack a dead Ranger soldier was found in the same tree I landed in. When he told me that, I felt extremely lucky to have walked away from that landing."[12]

Relatively few men were injured on the jump, but typical of those who were was Sgt. Berry B. Kelly, a squad leader with B Company of the 1st Battalion of the 504th. He said that "his parachute collapsed when a fellow parachuter stole my air. [To steal air means a parachuter glided directly beneath another parachuter.] My chute collapsed about 150 feet off the ground and I kinda burned in." He tore some ligaments in his ankle when he landed on the concrete runway.

Behind General Johnson's plane were seven more C-141's in the first flight echeloned from side to side in their flight path rather than flying one directly behind the other. During the parachute drop, the PDF did not use any defensive antiaircraft weapons. The ZPU-4's reportedly at the airfield were never fired. However, the enemy did engage the C-141's with a considerable amount of small-arms fire. The C-141's received dozens of small-arms hits in the aircraft fuselage while flying over the airfield. "Enemy forces on the airfield consisted mainly of stragglers and security forces that had occupied the international terminal and taken civilians located there as hostages," reported the division historical summary.[13]

Several of the aircraft flew right (east) of the drop zone center line and put entire planeloads of paratroopers and equipment east of the DZ and into an adjacent swamp and sawgrass. A postoperation Joint "MAC/Army Hotwash," a review of the operation, stated,

> The crews were not briefed on the swamp. . . . DZs should be at least 800M wide for management/dispersion factors. . . . This DZ was 600M wide. . . ."Effective" DZ (right of active) was 400M wide × 500 long. . . . Crews were flying into a "black hole"; simply couldn't see features on the ground. . . . Featureless run-in after breaking land. . . . None of the crews have ever dropped at 500' AGL and do not have a sense of timing/time warnings. . . . Bottom line: Crews not trained for this.[14]

However, Colonel Axson, in an after-action briefing to the division commander, said, "When twenty Air Force C-141 crews can fly five hours without communications, in total darkness and drop two thousand paratroopers in a soft swamp only eight hundred meters off the target, the airfield runway, who is going to complain? The crews did an outstanding job."[15]

The troopers who landed east of the runway, in the swamp, did not complain at all. Rather, as trained, they linked up into small groups, some as small as two or three. The 2-504 Battalion S-3, for example, linked up with an NCO from the 2-504 Scout Platoon, who jumped from another aircraft but landed in the swamp within two hundred meters of Major Chase. They made their way to the airfield using only a general compass heading, used their bayonets to cut a hole through the chain link fence surrounding the airfield, found a 2-504 50-caliber HMMWV from D Company, derigged it, and drove to the assembly area. "Actions like this were not uncommon as the troopers displayed great poise and discipline while moving over unfamiliar terrain, at night with an unconfirmed enemy situation," wrote one of Colonel Axson's staff officers later.

Second Lt. Paul Helms, platoon leader 3/B/2-504, and Sgt. Robert Chappuis, platoon sergeant 1/B/2-504, failed to make linkup at the battalion assembly area along with approximately five other B/2-504 soldiers due to an early green light. "The green light came on just as the C-141 cleared the ocean," wrote Captain Phelps. "Helms, who was the jumpmaster of the aircraft, tried to hold the jumpers up, having recognized that the green light was early. Nonetheless, due to the forward momentum caused by the paratroopers pushing forward toward the door once they saw the green light, Helms could not hold them up. As he tried, he was pulled out the door with them. Among these soldiers was a battalion commander who was the number-one jumper. Lieutenant Helms landed approximately two thousand meters short of the leading edge of the DZ and had to negotiate a thousand meters of coastal mangrove swamp, a creek twenty meters wide, and then a thousand meters of kunna grass to make the drop zone."[16]

Because of the abnormal, foul weather at Pope and the inadequate deicing equipment, the follow-on air package from Pope was forced to fly to Panama in five serials. The first eight arrived over the DZ at 0211, twenty-six minutes late; two more came over at 0350; three arrived at 0400; two more dropped at 0455; and the final five dropped their paratroopers at 0515. In all, 2,176 82d Airborne Division paratroopers made the jump; 30 men sustained jump injuries for a parachute jump injury rate of 1.38 percent—an excellent rate compared to an average 4 percent injury rate for similar peacetime parachute operations. During the heavy-equipment drop, one Sheridan drifted under another and "stole the air" of the higher tank, causing it to fall more rapidly than normal. But in spite of that problem, almost all of the airdropped equipment functioned normally once it had been recovered. And, according to Colonel Crocker, "All air crews performed with complete professionalism. Heavy-equipment drop is rated at 90 percent by the Military Airlift Command Scoring System." The total delay of 3½ hours from the scheduled H-hour to the time of the last drop naturally caused a delay in the ongoing combat operations of Task Force Pacific.[17]

On the ground, the paratroopers, faced with the sudden heat and humidity and the thick, entangling kunna grass, found the task of assembling quickly almost impossible. Captain Ramsdell's PZ time was 0300, but it was not until 0430 that he had assembled about 70 percent of his company; 90 percent of the 2/504 was assembled between 0530 and 0600. At 0615, the commander of the 1/504, Lt. Col. Renard Marable, reported to the Division Assault CP that his battalion was in PZ posture. As soon as he assembled enough of his company, Ramsdell organized his men into "chalks" for loading on the Black Hawk helicopters when they arrived. He set up security around his company area, checked out his men and their equipment, and waited for the helicopters.

At 0440, the division assault Cp, consisting of General Johnson and scaled-down G-2 and G-3 contingents, formed on the center west side of the Torrijos runway. Twenty minutes later, General Johnson reported to General Stiner, that he had made a linkup with the Rangers at 0500. (General Johnson assumed operational control of 1/75th Rangers at 0600.) He was now about ready to move out to attack his three assigned objectives.[18]

*   *   *

During these hours of darkness, the troopers of the 82d continued to ready their weapons, get out of their parachutes, don their gear, and struggle through the head-high, thick kunna grass toward their assembly areas.

By 0438, Colonel Nix decided that he was about ready to launch his three battalions in separate air assaults on Panama Viejo, Tinajitas, and Fort Cimarron. He requested the division assault CP to bring forward the command and control aircraft for the three air assaults.

By 0650, the runway at Torrijos had been cleared of men and equipment, and the lift and assault helicopters had arrived. The 2-504 PIR began to load immediately. Of the twenty Black Hawks that were planned to lift the 2-504 assault forces in one lift, one nine arrived initially, forming a first lift, with eight reported to be following in ten minutes. Although the troopers had rehearsed extensively in loading twenty to twenty-five troopers on each aircraft, the loss of these aircraft meant some sixty to a hundred fighters might not make it to the battle for Viejo. Major Chase decided to scrap the battalion's air assault "bump plan" SOP and packed the Black Hawks with as many troopers as possible. Several Black Hawks landed in Panama Viejo with as many as thirty combat loaded soldiers crammed aboard.

Colonel Axson's assault plan on the Panama Viejo barracks was to air-assault into two LZs—Bobcat, a "six-shipper" just to the north of the objective and covered with grass higher than the heads of the troopers, and Lion, a "four-shipper" on the south side along the shoreline. These forces would then seal off the Panama Viejo area with Capt. Paul Defleuri's A Company and Captain Ramsdell's C Company. Captain Phelps's B Company would be assigned as task force reserve, rear security for the assault forces as well as protection of the battalion's mortars and command post and finally linking up with D Company just to the north of the objective. Capt. Gregory Sawyer's D Company (−), which was traveling overland to Viejo, consisted of four, .50-caliber-mounted HMMWV's, two M551 Sheridan tanks, the remainder of the battalion's mortar platoon in one HMMWV, the battalion commander's HMMWV for command and control, and one cargo HMMWV carrying ammunition and medical resupply items. Intelligence did not report that

176

Bobcat was covered with ten-foot-high kunna grass nor that some of Lion was a muddy quagmire that could not support the weight of a Black Hawk.

Colonel Axson planned the use of a measured application of force to isolate, then neutralize, and, if necessary, destroy the forces at Panama Viejo. His rifle companies would isolate the enemy at Viejo while Colonel Axson issued his surrender ultimatum through task force interpreters and Psyops loudspeaker teams. Major Chase lettered each of the buildings in the Viejo complex and passed this sketch along with his operational graphics to the company commanders and through both the Army and Air Force fire support networks to facilitate fire support and command and control. The intent was to isolate the barracks complex and attempt to talk the PDF into surrendering while the D Company convoy and support element made their way to Viejo. If the PDF refused Colonel Axson's demands, he had the ability to continue tightening the screw until his demands were met. Colonel Axson expected to take Panama Viejo by noon on the twentieth of December.[19]

Panama Viejo, on the eastern side of Panama City, was a town established in the 1500s, was later burned by pirates, and then was rebuilt of stone in the 1600s. Now, many of the buildings had been reduced to piles of stone. The ruins stand on a scenic point of land looking out across the Bay of Panama. The ruins were the location of a PDF barracks and special operations (UESAT—Unidad Especial de Seguridad Antiterror) training center occupied normally by about 350 soldiers, 180 of whom were from the 1st Cavalry Squadron, a unit that provided guards for Noriega's residences and troops for ceremonies. In the compound, the squadron had a stable in which Captain Ramsdell counted 76 horses. Some of these horses were on the Panamanian Olympic Team. The remaining 170 soldiers were members of UESAT, Noriega's antiterrorist troops. UESAT, highly trained and dedicated soldiers, were originally stationed on Flamenco Island. During the October coup attempt, when Noriega realized that the troops at Flamenco were too remote to come to his aid rapidly, he moved them to Panama Viejo.

These forces were armed with a wide variety of weapons, including Uzi submachine guns with night sights, antitank missiles, sniper rifles, an automatic grenade launcher, and "state-of-the-art body armor." One room of the main barracks was stocked with explosives. On the roof of the barracks, a .50-caliber machine gun was mounted; on the shoreline sat a ZPU-4, an armored vehicle equipped with a four-barrel antiaircraft gun aimed over the water.[20]

After the Fort Amador operation, Lt. Lisa Kutschera and all eleven helicopters of A Company, 3/123d Aviation Regiment, had loggered in Empire Range north of Fort Kobbe to refuel and wait until the 82d troopers had landed, assembled, and were ready to move out to their first three objectives. It was a short wait until they got word to lift off for the pickup point at Tocumen.

"The sun was coming up over the horizon as we flew our approach to Tocumen Airport, the PZ," wrote Lieutenant Kutschera recently. "My aircraft was one of the last in the flight and I watched as some of the open parachutes scattered on the runway became airborne on the rotor wash of the first helicopters, creating a hazard for all the aircraft behind. Luckily, none of them got entangled in rotor blades or ingested by engines."

The first mission was an air assault by 2-504 into Panama Viejo. "The stiff resistance expected at Panama Viejo didn't materialize on the first lift," continued Lieutenant Kutschera. "Some of the crews heard small-arms fire and my door gunner said he heard some as we were departing the LZ, but no firers could be identified and none of the aircraft was hit. The second load of troops we picked up at the PZ wanted to go into Panama Viejo also, rather than to Tinajitas as per our mission brief. On the second trip in, we took more fire and two aircraft were disabled and had to shut down after returning to the PZ.

"One of these was flown by Pilot in Command (PIC) CW2 Debra Mann, who hadn't flown on the first assault into Amador and had linked up with us at the lagger site. Her aircraft had taken three hits, the most serious of which was in the tail rotor intermediate gearbox. The round went completely through the gearbox, leaving entry and exit 'wounds.' Most of the oil drained out of the gearbox, and if the gears had seized at the altitude we were flying at, they probably would have crashed because helicopters don't fly well at all without a tail rotor. Sikorsky helicopters must know what they're doing, because they made it all the way back to the PZ, where the oil spraying out of the gearbox caught the crew chief's attention and they shut down to check it out."[21]

The flight route, south from Torrijos, was out over the ocean and then back to the north from the southeast to the northwest and took about ten to fifteen minutes. Colonel Nix used one UH-60 for command and control. The flight route took the aircraft out of small-arms range but also carried the troopers along a route that was completely observable from the complex of buildings at Panama Viejo. At about 0645, the first lift of troopers from 2-504 touched down in LZ Lion, carrying men from A Company, the scout platoon of Lt. James J. Johnson (the division commander's son), the Psyops team, and Colonel Axson's assault command post. As part of the first lift, five Black Hawks continued on to LZ Bobcat, carrying troopers from the scout platoon, C Company, and a battalion command and control element led by the Battalion S-3, Major Chase.[22]

One of the Black Hawk pilots making his approach to LZ Lion spotted a fully operational 23mm antiaircraft gun on the road just off the beach. As the Black Hawk approached, the gunner dismounted and ran. "Fortunately for us," the pilot said later. "If he had stayed with the gun and engaged us, it could have been a nightmare."

Despite the fire covering the LZs and the air immediately above them, the two overwatching Cobras from the 7th Infantry Division (L) and an Apache from the 1st Battalion, 228th Aviation Regiment, held their fire unless they found a specific and clearly obvious enemy target.

Captain Ramsdell remembered that about five seconds from touchdown on LZ Bobcat, he heard rifle and automatic-weapons fire. Several of his soldiers said that an air defense artillery gun along the road north of the barracks had fired at least three shots and then apparently and fortunately jammed as the Black Hawks were landing. The proximity of the firing made him accelerate the unloading of his troops. The PDF covered LZ Bobcat with automatic fire from AK-47's, assault rifles, and pistols. In the tall grass, Ramsdell's troops had a hard time finding each other, let alone the enemy.[23]

Sgt. Michael Alexander of C Company was finally able to locate some of the PDF. He called for a grenade launcher and fired several rounds. The PDF were not silenced; they returned fire directly at him. In spite of the PDF rounds coming directly at him, Alexander directed the fire of a machine gun that shortly neutralized the PDF position and permitted C Company to move off Bobcat. Gen. Carl Vuono, the Army chief of staff at the time, later awarded Alexander a Bronze Star for valor for his actions at LZ Bobcat.[24]

LZ Lion would prove to be an even more difficult landing zone than Bobcat, but for a different reason. The helicopters that touched down near the beach were on solid ground. But the troops in the Black Hawks that landed farther out, toward the water, had great difficulty. The mud flats looked firm from the air, but as the men jumped out of the helicopters, some sank up to their armpits in what turned out to be soft, oozing muck. Seeing the problem, several Black Hawk pilots, in spite of the small-arms fire covering the LZ, hovered their ships just over the mud so that the troopers could grab the landing gear and be lifted free. Spc. Hector Martinez, B/2-504, who speaks Spanish, was a grenadier on the operation. He said that Panamanian civilians formed a human chain and used ropes to haul other men out of the mud.[25] He said that the civilians kept asking him why it had taken the Americans so long to arrive. "The first thing they told me was," he said, " 'We were waiting for you a year ago.' " Later Martinez said, because of his language ability, "We did a lot of going house to house, looking for tips. I got tired of speaking Spanish."

Within fifteen minutes, the second lift was on the ground. This time the remainder of A Company along with an element from the battalion's communications platoon led by Lt. Scott Geiger were set down in the mud just off LZ Lion. At the same time, the remainder of C Company, and troopers from the battalion mortar platoon led by Lt. Chris Miller, and part of B Company arrived at LZ Bobcat. During the first lift, Colonel Nix determined that the 2-504 would be completely lifted out of Torrijos before the 1-504 would board the aircraft for its flight to Tinajitas. This decision allowed the remainder of B Company to move into the objective area using four more Black Hawks on a third lift. Unfortunately, these aircraft landed the troopers from B Company on LZ Lion.

With the landings of the eighteen helicopters, Colonel Axson had on the ground about five hundred troopers from his battalion task force. Unfortunately, this distribution of troops between the two LZs was not exactly as planned. "The lift of the A/C which took soldiers of B/2-504 into LZ Lion should have gone into Bobcat," wrote Captain Phelps. "So as it turned out, I had my company split between the two LZs. I positioned my mortars and XO between the two LZs (S Sgt. John Negre—mortar section leader, and 1st Lt. Byron Echols—XO) in order to relay communications between Bobcat and Lion and to support with indirect fire if need be. Although the B/2-504 element left at Bobcat maneuvered on a sniper originally, the troops at Lion pushed out toward the bridge with the battalion scouts. There they took significant enemy fire." B Company was now split between the northern and western portions of the objective, and the B Company troopers who landed on LZ Lion were becoming intermixed with A Company.

179

As the skirmishing continued around Panama Viejo, Colonel Axson decided to leave the B Company platoon where it landed and place it under the control of Captain Defleuri until the platoon could link up with B Company. When Major Chase heard this decision over the battalion command radio, he told Captain Ramsdell to break contact and move east to seal off the northern portion of the objective. He then told Captain Phelps to move his troops to the east out of the kunna grass and toward the objective.

While these units were moving, the battalion scouts ran into a number of PDF and UESAT forces north and west of the objective, trying to disrupt the U.S. air assault. A Company on the west used the platoon from B Company to secure its western flank while it maneuvered toward the main barracks building at Panama Viejo. B Company linked up with the battalion mortar platoon and moved to the east until it crossed the road leading north out of Viejo.

After repeated attempts to call out any PDF still remaining in the headquarters building, Colonel Axson ordered Captain Defleuri to seize the building. While Colonel Axson directed A Company toward the main headquarters building, Major Chase sent B Company into a position behind C Company, where they could support C Company as well as fire on the main barracks building if necessary. Once A Company had achieved a foothold in the headquarters building, Major Chase linked up with the main portion of the assault CP. Still not hearing from D Company, Colonel Axson moved C Company into Panama Viejo and ordered them to commence clearing the remaining buildings.

Unknown to Axson and his men, at about 2300 on the night of the nineteenth, eighty of the PDF force that had been in the Panama Viejo barracks got out of their uniforms and into civilian clothes, took their weapons, and headed north out of the area to defend fixed sites nearby. At about 0600 on the morning of the twentieth, having gotten word of the parachute landings at Torrijos and Río Hato, many of the rest of the Panama Viejo PDF garrison changed into civilian clothes and, with their weapons at hand, occupied more of the "civilian" buildings around the area. By the time 2-504 arrived, about eighteen soldiers of the PDF were still in the barracks and some twenty-five were dug in around the compound. It was this group and those in nearby buildings close to the compound who greeted the first 2-504 helicopters on both LZs with intense small-arms, mortar, and machine-gun fire.

The PDF had obviously vacated their barracks in some haste. When A Company went into the barracks to search it, they found a mess hall with half-eaten breakfasts on the tables and a gun room in shambles. On the second floor were the troops' living quarters. In each wall locker were personal weapons such as guns, knives, and steel knuckles.[26]

For the next forty-five minutes, the troops of the 2d of the 504th continued to receive a large amount of harassing fire from small arms and AK-47's from PDF on the dikes near the main barracks. An AH-64 Apache took the ZPU-4, on the road to the north of the barracks, under fire and knocked it out. Some civilians reported to Captain Ramsdell's men that a PDF tank was down the road to the north. When Ramsdell's men found it, one of his AT-4 missile gunners got into position and took aim at the V-300 armored vehicle, not a

180

tank. As soon as the PDF crew saw the gunner take up firing position, they left running. The AT-4 round destroyed any utility the V-300 might have had.

While Ramsdell's company was landing on LZ Bobcat, they were fired on by PDF from the police station. Some of the helicopters took hits. Ramsdell sent a platoon to knock out the police station. The PDF in the police station, according to Ramsdell, "did engage in a small-arms firefight for several minutes before they fled."

By noon, most of the PDF had left the area. But in the afternoon, a number of PDF soldiers came down the main road to the barracks in civilian clothes in their automobiles—some BMWs and Mercedes—apparently reporting to work and seemingly unaware of the landing of 2/504. Some of the PDF carried Israeli Uzis, others AK-47's, some even LAWs. The carloads of PDF drove up to the fighting positions of the 2/504 blazing away with their assorted weapons. The battalion stopped or knocked out nine such impromptu fighting vehicles— hardly Bradleys, but perhaps "Noriegas." A 2/504 sniper stopped one car. In another encounter, Apaches from the 82d destroyed three V-300's. Intermittent sniper fire continued throughout the day, and three PDF mortar rounds landed harmlessly in the area occupied by the 2/504. By dusk, the battalion had established a perimeter around the area that was, by then, relatively quiet. But before that calm settled over the area, two men would be killed: Pfc. Martin D. Denson, twenty-one, of B Company, 1/504, and Spc. Alejandro I. Manriquelozano, thirty, of D Company, 2/504.

Throughout the day, a few diehard snipers had continued to take random "potshots" at the troopers in the area. One of them made his way to the top of a crane about three hundred meters from Ramsdell's position. One of Ramsdell's men took it under fire with an AT-4, wrecking the crane. Then some ten PDF snipers in "Ghille" suits, somewhat like strips of rags over their clothes and hats, fired sniper rounds from five hundred to eight hundred meters away. None found a mark. By late afternoon the main force of the PDF had melted into the civilian population. For a short time thereafter, they and the Digbats resorted to spasmodic and generally worthless hit-and-run guerrilla tactics on the various positions occupied by Ramsdell's men.[27]

Axson's troopers captured one fully loaded and operational ZPU-4 in the area near the barracks. They found some expended shell casings, but it was unclear whether this weapon was fired against the 2-504 in an antipersonnel or an antiair role. The PDF had hidden two V-200's and several 2½-ton trucks in a junkyard near the city. Apaches destroyed this miniature motor pool with 30mm AWS and Hellfire missiles.

At various times, Panamanian anti-Noriega civilians reported to Axson's men that Noriega was "here" or "there" in the city. One such report unearthed Colonel Mina, Noriega's secretary of economics. On 27 December, Axson's men picked up Mina, searched his house, and found there some $267,000 in U.S. currency.

At 0910 on D-day, a convoy of five vehicles and two M551 Sheridan tanks with some sixty troopers from Axson's D Company attempted to move out of the Torrijos Airport airhead area along Highway 1 to link up with the rest of the battalion near Panama Viejo. Forty PDF men armed with automatic weapons and RPG-18's assaulted the convoy at a bridge over a small canal near the Torrijos international terminal. The bridge was blocked with two burned-out automobiles. The D Company commander dismounted his men and started an intense firefight with the Panamanians.

Sfc. Gene G. Wolf was the platoon sergeant of the 1st Platoon of D Company. The company commander assigned the 1st Platoon to clear the roadblock. After taking out the roadblock, the platoon came under heavy fire from automatic weapons in a two-story building two hundred meters west of the bridge. The platoon maneuvered around the building but was pinned down by the fire, and one trooper, Spc. Alejandro J. Mannique-Lozano, D/2-504, was killed. To eliminate the fire, the platoon leader, 1st Lt. Steve Hayden, had his men lay down a base of fire, and Sergeant Wolf moved close to the building. He fired a LAW into the machine gun position and wiped it out. Then Wolf and Lieutenant Hayden entered the building. The entire platoon followed and cleared it. Eleven PDF were killed in the building while fighting in close quarters room to room. Two PDF were killed by soldiers around the back of the building. "The actions of Lieutenant Hayden and Sfc. Wolf were heroic," wrote one of Colonel Axson's staff officers. "The two paratroopers were later awarded Bronze Stars for valor medals by General Johnson. Incidentally, Sergeant Wolf had been selected earlier in the year as the 82d Airborne Division NCO of the Year. He sure lived up to the honor."[28]

Fighting continued in the area of the roadblock. The company commander requested help from the battalion executive officer, Maj. Rick Ballard, who was still in the Torrijos airhead. He sent another M551 and twenty men to help D Company. With the added help, Capt. Greg L. Sawyer and his men repulsed the PDF, killing three more of them and wounding an unconfirmed number. Captain Sawyer remounted his men to continue his move to Panama Viejo. Colonel Nix, however, ordered Sawyer to return to Torrijos and link up with another convoy from the 1/504.

At 1155, Colonel Axson reported to Colonel Nix that he had secured his objective at Panama Viejo in spite of continuing harassment from random snipers and PDF who drove by shooting wildly from their civilian cars. The PDF also lobbed mortar rounds from a wood line near the barracks throughout the day. Axson directed Apache helicopters to the enemy mortar sites and eventually took the positions under fire and suppressed them.[29]

Panama Viejo was not out of the hands of the PDF. Axson's men consolidated on the objective and settled in to "stabilize" the area and its environs.

19 | The Marriott Incident

Freeing hostages held in a plush hotel in the middle of a large city was not exactly the type of mission for which the 82d Airborne Division had spent an inordinate amount of training time. But at 1807 on the evening of the twentieth, General Stiner's headquarters notified General Johnson that possibly the PDF had seized twenty-nine U.S. hostages at the Marriott Hotel in downtown Panama City and that he had the mission of securing the hotel and freeing the hostages. General Johnson knew his troopers were flexible and could handle this unexpected mission. He passed the task on to Colonel Nix, who, in turn, passed it to Colonel Axson and the 2-504.

Initially, at 1700 hours, Colonel Nix had told Colonel Axson to be prepared to conduct a company-size air assault on Paitilla Airport, where earlier four Navy SEALs had been killed. Axson's commanders were continuing to prepare positions in and around Panama Viejo as well as patrolling aggressively to set up a safe zone in the built-up areas surrounding the former PDF headquarters. Axson knew of the aborted attempt by D Company to reach Panama Viejo and that D Company would be linking up beginning at first light on the twenty-first. When Axson received a radio message that Colonel Nix was inbound with a change of plans, the 2-504 staff was making plans for the mission to Paitilla. At 2020 hours, Colonel Nix arrived with his assistant brigade S-3, Capt. Chuck Durr, and told Colonel Axson that his new mission was to rescue twenty-nine hostages from the Marriott Hotel by seizing the Marriott not later than midnight—tonight.

The origin of the mission to free the "hostages" in the Marriott is somewhat muddled. The fact is that an Eastern Airlines pilot, Capt. Jay Skinner, a guest at the Marriott, aware of the shooting and the miniwar zone around the hotel, called, via commercial phone, his corporate headquarters in Miami. The pilot summarized the situation at the time, stating that the PDF had taken hostages from the hotel at gunpoint to another location in town. The hostages were

183

lectured and threatened, he said. Later the PDF soldiers seemed nervous when they brought the hostages back to the hotel. The PDF told the hostages to stay in the hotel. The PDF then "posted" the hotel grounds with soldiers. From Miami, an Eastern Airlines official called a staffer at the White House and passed the message about the deteriorating situation at the Marriott.

Mr. Skinner later said that because the PDF had not cut the phone service and could not watch all the phones at once, he was able to use a phone to relay facts to his corporate headquarters almost at will.

As the situation developed, the U.S. forces came up with the mission knowing that there was always the possibility that hostages were being held in other areas of the large hotel and that substantial problems could develop if the PDF decided to fight and hold the hostages at all costs.[1]

After Colonel Axson got the Marriott mission from Colonel Nix, Colonel Axson and his staff made a hasty mission analysis: How are we going to do this job? He postponed moving D Company until the next morning and decided to concentrate on getting the Marriott Hotel under control—and then plan for the evacuation of the hostages to Tocumen Airport. During this brief planning session, Axson peered at the map to locate the Marriott Hotel. Thinking out loud, he said to his Battalion S-2, Lt. Bob Cejka, "You're the intelligence officer. Where is the Marriott?"

"There it is, sir," responded Cejka, pointing across the bay to the well-illuminated marquis on top of the Marriott Hotel. Major Chase recommended to Colonel Axson that he send B Company on the mission along with a battalion command and control element. Then, when the battalion executive officer arrived at Viejo in the morning, arrangements could be made for the evacuation and processing of the hostages.

Axson's scheme called for a rifle company, with its engineer squad, to move by foot along the shortest and fastest route to the hotel. The force would leave its rucksacks at Viejo but carry its special-purpose equipment, such as night-vision goggles. B Company would also leave behind its 60mm mortar section, since it would slow the advance, and these small mortars would have minimal effect in such an operation. The battalion command post moving with B Company would include the commanding officer; the S-3; the S-2; the fire support officer, Capt. Glen Goldman; the Air Force tactical air controller, Capt. John Wittington; and the battalion's surgeon, Capt. John Marriott (no relation to the founder of the hotel chain). In support of this operation would be a commandeered white civilian van that would trail the walking formation to act as an ambulance.

At this point someone reminded Colonel Axson that Capt. Chuck Durr, who had come with Colonel Nix to Viejo, had left an assignment in Panama only six months earlier. Durr, when asked by Axson, said that he was still very familiar with the road network between Viejo and the Marriott. Intelligence reports indicated that there were several pockets of resistance and ambushes already set up by the PDF along the route to the Marriott. Colonel Axson realized that to maintain the speed of the attack and clear the hotel by midnight, he would have to avoid the enemy and perhaps change his route of approach. Colonel Axson immediately drafted Captain Durr and told him to guide the lead platoon of B

Company on the march. Captain Durr was as good as his word: Repeatedly on the march, he changed the route to avoid ambushes and traps.[2]

Major Chase assembled the company commanders at 2130 at Viejo and put out a brief but detailed oral operations order. He pointed out that the operation had to commence at 2215 to have sufficient time for B Company to move through the city and seize the hotel by midnight. He pointed out the route. He had already numbered the key buildings to provide a reference for the AC130 gunship that would overfly the operation. He gave copies of the reference map to Axson, the Air Force liaison officer, and Durr. Speed was of the essence, he pointed out more than once. Speed and the AC-130 overhead would provide the security for the mission. He also said that he would coordinate with the AC-130 by radio to conduct a reconnaissance of the route ahead of the advancing troops.

Back at his company area, because of the shortage of time before moving out, Captain Phelps had time to brief only the lead platoon on the route, tell the men what gear to carry, and set up the movement formation. Phelps selected the 1st Platoon to lead the way because its leader, 2d Lt. Kevin Stoddard, was "the most experienced platoon leader I had," said Phelps. Then it was time to move out. Any unexpected actions at the Marriott would have to be based on the soldiers' training and the response of the chain of command.

Axson left Ramsdell in charge of the perimeter at Panama Viejo and gave him the mission of linking up with D Company and the battalion executive officer, Major Ballard, the next morning. Axson told him to brief Major Ballard on the situation and to tell Ballard to prepare to receive the hostages and process them to Tocumen in accord with the battalion's noncombatant-processing SOPs. At 2215, B Company and the Battalion CP group left on the 2½-mile march (almost a run) to the Marriott.

Just as the column left the perimeter, it started marching past an auto repair shop on the right side of the street. The shop's lights lit up a large area about 150 meters from the battalion's perimeter at Viejo. Captain Durr, at the head of the column, decided on the spur of the moment to shoot out the lights. With his first shot, he sprung a PDF ambush that was waiting for U.S. vehicles to leave the Viejo compound. The result: a firefight. There was one PDF casualty, and the others fled into buildings along the route of march. Colonel Axson got the column moving forward again, "this time with a sense of urgency that only a shot of adrenaline can provide," wrote one of his staff officers.

Down the road another five hundred meters, the 1st Platoon of B Company heard what sounded like a large tractor trailer truck grinding through its gears. Although no one saw the vehicle, the noise made it clear that the truck was moving toward the column at high speed. Suddenly, from a side street, a truck the size of a UPS delivery truck roared into the column between the 1st and 2d platoons. The truck's aluminum sides had been cut open, and five Panamanians were in the rear firing at the advancing troopers with a variety of automatic weapons, some mounted on tripods bolted to the floor of the Tinkertoy APC. In the cab sat a driver and a passenger who, not to be outdone by the cowboys in the rear, was firing a pistol and throwing hand grenades wildly out the passenger side of the cab.

By this time, late on the evening of D-day, the battalion's troopers had been through a long preparation period at Bragg, a six-hour flight to Panama, a night parachute assault, and an opposed daylight helicopter landing; and on the ground, they had withstood snipers, drive-by shootings, mortar attacks, and sustained automatic-weapon firings. Now they were on their way, on foot, some thirty-six sleepless hours after their alert at Bragg, to rescue American hostages, and they were being heckled by this unexpected attack.

The B Company troops reacted swiftly with an "immediate action drill" and returned fire. The truck turned left and continued between the column of soldiers on either side of the road. Many of Phelps's men found themselves literally with their backs to the wall, a seawall next to the street. One trooper elected to jump over the dark wall for cover. Unfortunately, from the top of the wall to the mud flats below was a twenty-foot drop. The other troopers kept up a large volume of fire when the truck had turned so that they could see into the rear of the truck. The trooper who leapt over the wall was slightly injured and was missing for some time until he made his way back to the company— embarrassed and disheveled.

Spc. Walter Randall ("a super troop," according to Captain Phelps) was hit in the bicep as the truck passed the 1st Platoon. The truck roared on through the gauntlet of fire toward the company command element. As it passed by the 2d Platoon, Major Chase was hit in the face and his radio telephone operator was hit in the leg as they returned fire. A Spanish interpreter working with the battalion was blown over the seawall by a shotgun blast. The entire column, in turn, raked the truck with their weapons. "It was like a cone of fire," said Major Chase.[3]

Within the confusion of this mad, thirty-second engagement stood Specialist Harrod, an M-203 grenadier from the 3d Platoon. As the truck made its turn onto the main street, Harrod stepped into the middle of the street. With the truck headed directly toward him, he fired his rifle grenade at the cab of the truck. The round blew off the right arm of the cab's passenger, throwing it free of the truck and landing on the street below. The truck did not slow down but kept moving at a high rate of speed. With little emotion other than saying, "Shit, I'll get him with the next round," Harrod reloaded him M-203. Dropping to one knee, he took aim and fired again. This round hit the driver in the face. The truck veered off the street and crashed into a local café about twenty meters from where Colonel Axson had been watching the action.

The night air became still and quiet as the troopers hurriedly searched the truck's wreckage for survivors. There were none. Colonel Axson broke the silence when he said to Harrod, "Good shot, Harrod. You got huge steel balls, or what?"

The wounded were quickly brought to the vicinity of the battalion S-3, who handed Colonel Axson his map with the AC-130 checkpoints on it before he, too, was loaded, along with the other B Company wounded, into the makeshift ambulance. The rest of B Company—by now moving at the "airborne shuffle" pace—sped on toward the Marriott.

Throughout the remainder of the march, the AC-130 gunship cruised overhead, giving detailed intelligence to Axson, through his Air Force ground liaison officer, using the numbered building reference system that Chase had developed. Colonel Axson was well aware of the capability of the AC-130 with its advanced optics and weapons system. His extensive work with the aircraft in Grenada would prove invaluable to the success of the remainder of the mission.

Now, some fifteen minutes after the fight with the truck, the Air Force LNO received a message that the first bridge crossing was manned by eleven PDF soldiers. When Axson heard this, he told Durr to change the route and avoid the bridge. Durr turned north immediately and led the column quickly and quietly down another route. As they moved, Axson mentioned that he could still hear small-arms fire on the road to the rear. He said that he didn't know what was happening back there.[4]

The makeshift ambulance had been left behind with one of the company medics to evacuate the wounded. Sergeant Lucas, a member of the assault CP and a Vietnam veteran with thirty-six confirmed kills as a Marine sniper, volunteered to take command of the ambulance, get it back to Panama Viejo, and then return it to B Company before they got to the Marriott. On the way back to Viejo, Lucas and the ambulance met only sporadic fire from buildings along the way. The trip back was another story.

Spc. Richard Lucas, a small clerk-typist and RTO for the battalion S-3, was the driver of the ambulance. "Radar O'Reilly," one officer described him, but he did not hesitate to volunteer to drive the ambulance when the S-3 told him he was going to be left at Viejo to monitor the brigade radio net. His passenger and guide initially was a volunteer from the scout platoon, Specialist Juarez. He moved to the rear of the ambulance when Sergeant Lucas took charge. When Sergeant Lucas briefed Colonel Nix in Viejo that he intended to regain contact with Colonel Axson, he could see the Marriott Hotel sign across the bay and knew he had some catching up to do.[5]

Sergeant Lucas left the Viejo perimeter knowing the route he had to take. He told the ambulance driver (the other Lucas) to move out at breakneck speed—not only to catch the column but also to flash past any enemy ambushes before they could put effective fire on the ambulance. Unfortunately, he did not know that B Company had turned away from the possible ambush at the bridge and that it still might be manned.

When he hit the bridge, he sprung the ambush. The PDF fire blew out all the windows of the van. Both Sergeant Lucas and Specialist Juarez were able to return fire. As they left the ambush site, Juarez was wounded in the leg. In addition, Sergeant Lucas realized that they were being followed closely by another vehicle. It closed on the ambulance and started a running gun battle for several blocks. During the exchange of fire, Sergeant Lucas was firing across Juarez's front and into the Panamanian vehicle. Whenever the pursuing vehicle would slow enough for him to shoot, Juarez fired. This running street battle, Mafia movie style, continued until Specialist Lucas turned sharply to the left, down a side street.

Sergeant Lucas decided to return to Viejo to get Juarez attended to and to get himself a new set of glasses as well as a resupply of ammunition. During the gun battle, both lenses of Specialist Lucas's glasses were shattered, but the frames remained intact. Specialist Juarez wondered later why Lucas kept swerving off the road. Without his glasses, it turned out, Specialist Lucas was as good as blind.

Sergeant Lucas got the ambulance back to the Viejo perimeter and into the area of the headquarters building—now well set up as an aid station and resupply point. When he tried to leave again to rejoin the column, Colonel Nix stopped him and ordered him to stay at Viejo because Axson and B Company were about to enter the Marriott.

Ten minutes after Lucas and the ambulance activated the bridge ambush, the AC-130 reported to Colonel Axson that four snipers were on top of building seven. Axson asked the AC-130 to repeat the building number. Again the AF LNO confirmed it was building seven, which happened to be across the street from where Axson was standing. As the command group looked across the street, several rifle barrels disappeared from the top of the building. Axson decided that they were waiting for his small group to pass the building so they could take the rear of the formation under fire. At this point the first two platoons of B Company had already turned the corner, heading for the Marriott. Axson told the AC-130 to engage the snipers. The ALO asked Colonel Axson, "Say again?" Axson said, "Tell them to shoot 40mm and destroy the snipers on the roof." The AC-130 came back and said, "Roger, move over eight feet." B Company momentarily stopped their movement, and as soon as the troopers hit the sidewalk, the AC-130 sprayed the roof of building seven with 40mm fire—effectively putting an end to that threat.

The AC-130 continued to report enemy on rooftops with the next sighting on the roof of the Marriott. Axson told the AC-130 not to shoot the Marriott, that there were hostages somewhere in the building, and that he would take care of them in a few minutes. Ten minutes later, B Company unlocked the front door of the Marriott Hotel after shooting a hole in one of the large windows beside the door.

Captain Phelps remembers blasting open the door of the Marriott. "I laugh about it now and even found it humorous then," he remembers, "that the two front double doors were open the entire time. Yet we tried to shoot them down/open because we could not open them. We were pushing them toward the hotel and away from us. To open them, we merely needed to pull them toward us."

Once inside the hotel, Captain Phelps had one platoon secure the entrances. He ordered the remaining two platoons to clear the fifteen-floor building systematically—a standard building clearing drill. He assigned Lt. Maurice Heising and his platoon the specific task of moving to Room 1015, where the hostages were allegedly being held. Captain Durr went to the hotel switchboard and started calling each room. For everyone who answered the phone, the message was the same: "The Marriott Hotel is now under the control of U.S. Army paratroopers. We will be on your floor shortly. Unlock the door, prop it open with a pillow, and lay down on the floor face down. Do you have any questions?"

Every room was searched, and "hostages" were found everywhere. Twenty-eight hostages were found in one of the hotel elevators. Phelps's men moved any guests to a collection point in a windowless room behind the front desk. As the hostage count came to 80, Colonel Axson had the hotel disco opened by using two M-203 rounds. All the hostages were brought there for safekeeping. The final count was 106 people, who represented about every nation of the free world, as well as a group of hotel employees who feared for their lives if they would have been released.

While the building was being cleared, Lieutenant Cejka, the battalion intelligence officer, began interrogating the guests and dividing them into groups: confirmed U.S. citizens, people with valid passports and visas, and others. In the meantime, Capt. John Marriott, the battalion surgeon, tended to one soldier who was injured during the AC-130 mission on building seven, and another soldier who was injured during the initial assault on the hotel entrance. Later the surgeon treated one of the hostages who had gone into cardiac arrest.

Communications inside the building were less than ideal. Only radios on the fifteenth floor could contact the rest of the battalion. Axson set up the assault CP on that floor, while Phelps set up his CP in the offices in the lobby on the ground floor. When the building was cleared at 2330, Colonel Axson attempted unsuccessfully to contact his boss, Colonel Nix. He decided then to call the Fort Clayton EOC on a commercial phone. When he finally got through to the 82d Airborne Division CP, General "Smokin' Joe" Kinser, the assistant division commander, was on the line.

"Harry, where are you?"

"Sir, I'm in the lobby of the Marriott Hotel."

"Well, we thought that was a bridge too far. . . . What do you need?"

"Sir, we could use some claymores, LAWs, sniper match, and M-16 ammo. . . . We also need some medical supplies. I'll put my doc on the phone to give your folks the specifics. Also need transportation for about 106 hostages back to Tocumen."

"Okay, we'll get you the supplies . . . probably have to sling-load it to you, since the sniper fires have been pretty intense in your area . . . can't risk setting an aircraft down unless you have some critically wounded."

"No medical problems that won't keep until tomorrow. Sir, we'll take anything you can give us."

"What about chow, Harry?"

"Sir, don't need any chow. We're staying at the Marriott."

"Right, we'll get those hostages off your hands in the morning. Put the doc on and keep this line open."

"Wilco, sir. Here's the surgeon."[6]

Major Ballard flew in the supplies from Tocumen within a few hours. While the 2-504 was waiting for ground transportation to evacuate the civilians, numerous PDF "drive-bys" fired automatic weapons at the hotel. PDF or Digbats fired sporadically from nearby rooftops at the hotel windows and doors. At 1000 hours on 21 December, the evacuation force, led by Capt. Greg Sawyer and consisting of four .50-caliber mounted HMMWVs, one Sheridan tank, two cargo trucks from 1st Brigade, and two large civilian "Marriott" trucks from the airport, arrived on the scene. The force carried with its flak vests for all the hostages, and intelligence personnel with MPs to handle the hostages once they left the hotel. There was a short exchange of gunfire between Captain Sawyer's forces and lone gunmen on the rooftops both as the force approached the hotel and during the loading of the hostages into the transportation. Only one Panamanian civilian was hit during the exchanges. The gunfire actually sped up the loading process.

While Captain Sawyer was loading the hostages in the varied vehicles, he briefed Colonel Axson that Major Ballard was at Viejo and that the brigade CP was moving next to the battalion's main CP in the vicinity of the ruins at Viejo. By 1200 hours on 21 December, all the hostages were safely at Tocumen Airfield. Captain Phelps and his company stayed at the Marriott for the next few days to secure the hotel's valuables and maintain a military presence in the area. From this location, Colonel Axson could direct B Company's actions as the search for Noriega went on.

Captain Phelps and his company were still at the Marriott on Christmas Eve. "That evening," wrote Captain Phelps later, "three Panamanian special agents requested U.S. troops to help them capture Noriega. One of the men wore a hood. Another man said that this man was Noriega's personal bodyguard. He stated that the bodyguard had left Noriega just a few hours before and that he was at the home of a wealthy friend a mile or so away. He asked that U.S. soldiers isolate the objective (the house), and, if need be, use forced-entry techniques in gaining entry.

"I selected Lieutenant Helm and the third platoon for the mission. First, a select few soldiers did a recon in civilian clothing. (The clothing was taken from the luggage left by the hostages.) The B Company first sergeant called the battalion headquarters, explained the situation to Major Chase, and requested assistance. Twenty minutes later the battalion command group arrived at the Marriott.

"Major Chase immediately wrote up a plan, got it approved by Colonel Axson, and notified brigade headquarters.

"Before the actual movement of troops and in order to reduce the chance of fratricide, the Panamanians were put in military BDUs so they would not be mistaken. This was humorous, as the soldiers who turned over their clothing were left only in their underwear in the hotel lobby.

"Upon our arrival, a neighbor reported that a helicopter just departed, and we believe it was with Noriega. The homeowners denied everything. The ex-bodyguard took us to the guest room where he claims Noriega stayed.

"Later we identified the homeowner as a man wanted on an indictment by the United States. We apprehended him and turned him over to the military police.

"While at the home, we saw that one of the Panamanian men had a bandaged bullet wound. A car in the garage had bullet holes and was identified by Specialist Boaz, B/2-504, as a vehicle which participated in a drive-by shooting at the Marriott shortly after B Company secured it."[7]

Before that incident, the U.S. forces were, of course, still searching for Noriega. At 0500 on the twenty-first, Axson tasked Ramsdell with the mission of taking a platoon to search Noriega's golf house in the north-central part of the city. The golf house was one of Noriega's many residences in and out of the city. Ramsdell appropriated a couple of Panama civilian trucks, hot-wired them, and sent Lt. Louis Ortiz and his 3d Platoon to secure and guard the golf house.

The golf house was in an area of other large homes of well-to-do Panamanians who were in no way connected to any of Noriega's schemes. One of the owners told a U.S. officer, "We have felt like prisoners. You have released us from prison and we will always be grateful."[8]

The golf house was actually a compound of several houses. One, called the Delta, was apparently Noriega's personal residence, where his wife and daughters lived. It was about four thousand square feet in size and was surrounded by a concrete wall ten feet high. In it the platoon found three safes containing some $4 million to $5 million U.S. dollars and priceless works of art—but no drugs. Some Christmas presents were lying on the tables. In the rather extensive library, Ortiz and his men found one book of some interest: William Casey's *The American Revolution.* Inside the front cover of the book was a personal inscription that read: "To Manuel, Thanks for cleaning up a troubled region." Signed Bill Casey.

One room was a voodoo room; another resembled a Catholic chapel; still another was a weight and workout room. The compound also held three smaller houses for Noriega's guards. Ortiz's platoon moved into the main house and stayed there until time to return to Fort Bragg.

"Noriega is a junk collector," said Lieutenant Ortiz after spending four days in the house. "Using drug money, he collected a lot of expensive junk. And yet, at the same time, he has all these Christian icons and hides out with the Pope. As a general, I don't think he ever actually led his troops. He had, more or less, an army built up around protecting what he had. If you look around the house, at the way the house was built, you notice it wasn't built to be defended from attack. It was built to keep burglars out; that's about it."

Sgt. Gordon Pargellis was a weapons squad leader in the 2d Platoon. He remarked later that almost everything in the house was personalized by Noriega. His name was on every pen, knife, every plaque. "There's this desk plaque upstairs, engraved with a self-assessment of himself," Pargellis said later. "It says he's intelligent, not worried about himself. . . . I think he's really an insecure person who discovered he had a lot of charisma."

On a tip from one of the neighbors in the area, Ortiz's men found a large weapons cache not far from the golf house. Despite the fact that it was well stocked with assault rifles and mortars, there was no resistance to Ortiz's seizure of the cache and its contents.[9]

The Marriott and the golf house complex were now secure. But Noriega was still at large.

20 | Tinajitas

The Tinajitas Army Garrison was the home of the PDF 1st Infantry Company. Prior to the U.S. attack, the 1st Infantry Company was something of an enigma to the Southern Command because, during the 3 October coup attempt, it stayed in its barracks and did not rush to Noriega's rescue. The company may have been dormant during that brief interruption in Noriega's reign of power and terror, but when the helicopters carrying the 1st Battalion of the 504th descended on it, its reaction was far from passive.

The Tinajitas barracks, and the objective of 1-504, sits atop a five-hundred-meter hill whose approaches were limited by civilian buildings in close proximity. The barracks overlooked the slums of San Miguelito, an area about six kilometers to the northeast of the heart of Panama City and about nine kilometers due west of Torrijos Airport. Prior U.S. intelligence had determined that the 1st Infantry Company had 184 men armed with four 120mm mortars, six 81mm mortars, three 60mm mortars, and one ZPU-4 AAA weapon.

At 0800 on the morning of the twentieth, after it had assembled on PZ Center after parachuting onto Torrijos, the 1/504 took off in three helicopter lifts and landed on two LZs that were on a ridge line about seven hundred meters from the hilltop barracks. Before the arrival of the troop-carrying helicopters, two AH-64 Apaches and one OH-58C Kiowa had been overwatching the area. They approached San Miguelito from the northwest and overflew the objective. From that direction, they received no ground fire. But when they turned and headed back over the area from the southeast to support the air assault, all three aircraft took heavy and effective ground fire from a built-up area in the northern part of San Miguelito. To avoid collateral damage in the village, the team of attack helicopters did not return fire and flew to and made emergency landings at Howard Air Force Base.

Before they left the area, they gave a "target handoff to the next team which was simultaneously arriving on station," according to the division's after-action

192

report. "The lead scout passed the enemy information to the air assault TF commander on the air assault FM net, who acknowledged while the flight was in the PZ at Tocumen." While the assault helicopters were bringing in the 1-504, one of the attack helicopters finally located, in a hilly area in northern San Miguelito, a PDF battle position of eleven soldiers armed with automatic weapons. CW-2 Flankey, flying the lead scout helicopter, an AH-64 Apache, requested and received permission to engage the target. He and his team made contact with the group with its laser range finder. They neutralized the enemy position with salvos from their 30mm cannons from a distance of some twenty-eight hundred meters. Subsequently, the 1/504 found ten PDF dead. A helicopter pilot saw one of the PDF running away.

At 0830, the first lift landed on LZ Leopard aboard five UH-60 Black Hawks and, at 0840, onto LZ Jaguar with one Black Hawk. The second and third lifts, each with six Black Hawks, landed on Leopard. The helicopter flight path had been from Torrijos to Panama City to a point near Panama Viejo and then north to San Miguelito. The 1-504 S-2 said later that the people in the city came out on rooftops to wave at them, but when they crossed over Highway 1 into the area of San Miguelito, people came out on the rooftops to shoot at them.

Once the first air assault helicopters had landed, it became obvious that the PDF 1st Infantry Company had had advance information of the U.S. attack. A stay-behind element of the PDF had surrounded LZ Leopard and engaged the helicopters and the emerging paratroopers with intense automatic-weapons fire and 81mm mortars. Even before the first lift touched down, the PDF took them under fire in the air from a number of positions in buildings to the west and southeast of the LZ, a definitely "hot" LZ. After they landed and were deploying into their attack formation, they came under heavy fire not only from the hilltop, which was covered with elephant grass, but also from the barrio around it.[1]

"The LZ at Tinajitas turned out to be the 'hottest' of all," Lieutenant Kutschera recalled. "Mr. Mann and I were made flight lead of a flight of three when we reorganized after losing the two damaged aircraft. As we flew over the start point of the route to the LZ, we could hear the radio traffic of the two flights preceding us, though they were too far ahead for us to see them. The first flight and then the second reported taking and returning fire from both sides as they approached the LZ.

"Suddenly the realization that we were in combat was brought home to everyone in A Company when CW-2 Vandenhueval, the PIC flying with Captain Muir, said on the radio that Captain Muir had been shot in the head and he was returning to Howard Air Force Base for medical aid. There was a moment of stunned silence on the radio as the message sunk in, then the necessity of completing the mission and getting out of the LZ reclaimed everyone's attention. About a minute later First Lieutenant Healy, one of my fellow platoon leaders and now acting company commander, reported as he took off from the LZ that his door gunner had been shot and he would return to the PZ as briefed to get medical aid from the medics there. We figured out later from the blood stains and holes in the floors of a couple of aircraft that some of

193

the infantry had been wounded on the approach also, but they had either gotten or been taken off the aircraft at the LZ and stayed with their units.

"By this time I was within three kilometers of the LZ and not looking forward to what I was flying into. I found out later that as the second flight cleared the LZ, a Cobra fired on the area where most of the firing was coming from and the volume of fire decreased somewhat. Whatever the reason, only one of the aircraft in my flight was hit as we flew in low over the treetops and landed in the ten-foot-tall grass in the LZ, paused about ten seconds for the troops to get out, and took off on the steep climb over the two-hundred-foot high-tension wires on top of the hill on the departure end of the LZ. Whoever planned that LZ gave the PDF an easy shot at us as we departed the area. We couldn't go under the wires because of a shorter set running alongside the tall set.

"It was a subdued group of aviators who shut down back at the PZ to regroup and wait for the rest of the 82d to get into PZ posture. . . ."[2]

Spc. Andrew "Slats" Slatniske of B Company said later, "It was the longest seven hundred meters I ever did—up that hill in that elephant grass. It may have been seven hundred meters on the map, but it was about three thousand meters the way we had to go."

S Sgt. Joe Sedach, Slatniske's platoon sergeant, said, "The soldiers fought just the way they practiced back at Fort Bragg, but with a difference: Usually the 'live fires' we had at Fort Bragg are only one way." He added that if the PDF mortar crews had been better, "It could have been very bloody." He said that the paratroopers kept moving, so the PDF mortar crews kept having to adjust the fall of their shells.[3]

Lt. Col. Renard Marable was the commanding officer of 1-504. His plan of attack was to advance in three directions on the garrison—"One company advanced from the south of the garrison, one from the far east, and one from the far west," said the division's after-action report.

> The task force seized the hilltop next to the Tinajitas Garrison and attempted to gain line of sight with the enemy company. After two hours, two companies reached the top of the hill and they discovered that the 1st Infantry Company had abandoned the garrison. The battalion continued to receive sporadic sniper fire from all directions of the hilltop. This fire was from the slum areas that surrounded the area. The unit observed that the 1st Company abandoned Tinajitas in a very orderly manner and no evidence of a hurried withdrawal. 1-504 found three 120mm mortars set up in position in the garrison. Two of the tubes had hung rounds in them and were pointed toward Fort Clayton. The area was littered with mortar rounds that were apparently being prepared for firing.[4]

The 1-504 did not escape unscathed. Pfc. Jerry Scott Daves, twenty, was an infantryman assigned to B Company. He had been wounded from the PDF fire earlier, but he was killed by a mortar shell while a medic was working on his first wound. The medic was wounded. Pfc. Martin Denson, from B Company, was shot as he stepped off a helicopter and was later killed by mortar fire.

In spite of the superb physical condition of the paratroopers, a number of

194

them fell victim to heat exhaustion during the attack up the hill, so steep that the paratroopers often fell to their hands and knees to climb through the thick and tall elephant grass. Heat, lack of water, and fatigue slowed the troops, yet the "Red Devils" of the 1/504 continued their advance. "The weather made a big difference," Sergeant Sedace said. "It was really hot compared to North Carolina," remembering the ice storm that had delayed the 82d's departure. Eventually their physical conditioning and aggressiveness pulled them through. They also knew that they had to keep moving to frustrate the PDF mortar gunners.[5]

"One of the interesting stories to come out of the assault on Tinajitas come not from the 82d, but from the UH-60 lift unit," reported a SOUTHCOM spokesman after the operation.

Whether or not female soldiers ever faced death in ground combat may be debated, but bullet holes in helicopters flown by female pilots cannot be denied. Both the #1 and #2 aircraft on the "hot" LZ at Tinajitas were piloted and commanded by female aviators. The debate concerning assignment policies for women is ongoing and will continue. However, the simple truth of the matter is that these women were assigned to units that had a mission to complete. The units completed their mission. No thought was given to precedent setting or the reality of women in combat. The men—and the women—of the units were too busy doing their jobs to concern themselves with either precedents or their impact on history.

In the aviation brigade of the 7th Infantry Division there were twenty females, of whom four were pilots, one was a crew chief, three were in aircraft maintenance, and one was the brigade communications officer.[6]

At 1433, Colonel Marable reported to the division CP that he had secured objective Tinajitas. Some additional firing went on during the afternoon, but by nightfall of the twentieth, the 1/504 had completed their physically demanding mission. The following morning, combat patrols eliminated remnants of the PDF still "sniping" at them from nearby buildings. Marable's battalion at Tinajitas was geographically isolated from the rest of the brigade and consequently found itself in an unexpected and unusual position. The civilians expected them to perform the government functions that were now in a state of chaos. The 1/504 reacted with style. The battalion's medics started health care programs while the rifle companies moved out to help workers restore the electrical power plant and distribute MREs to the needy.

The distribution of food to the poor from the slums of San Miguelito was a major undertaking for the battalion. More than ten thousand people were in line even before the trucks carrying the MREs for them arrived. When the flatbed trucks carrying more than fifteen thousand MREs did arrive in the area, they were greeted with loud cheers from the people. Marable's initial estimate was that he would be able to distribute two meals per day, per person, and in keeping with the gallantry of the American soldier, the "Red Devils" escorted pregnant women to the front of the lines and fed them first.

"It's amazing to see all these people," said Capt. Bart Physioc, the battalion chaplain. "Last week there was no one on the streets. They were hiding. Then we got here. We gave them liberty, then peace. Now, we're doing what we can to feed them. And they're so patient. They wait—and the line must be a mile or more long—then they come in and take what little we have to give them and leave with a smile. It just makes me feel good."

Second Lt. Eloy Mazo, an officer in the battalion's S-2 section, saw another side of the picture. "Being able to speak Spanish, you get an inside look into these people's lives," he reflected. "You get to know what's actually going on. These people are very, very poor and right now, very happy. They lead simple lives. If they have shelter and food, they're happy. Everyone who can walk in here is going to get an MRE."[7]

The actions of the battalion won the trust of the people, that, in turn, over the next few weeks, led directly to successful programs to recover weapons and persuade former PDF soldiers to turn themselves in.

21 | 7th Infantry Division (Light)

Because the units of the 7th Division did not parachute into Panama on D-day and because the only ground element of the 7th engaged in operations on D-day was on the Atlantic side of the canal, the division's major role in Operation Just Cause has been somewhat obscure and underreported. In reality, the 7th Infantry Division supplied more soldiers and equipment to the operation than any other comparable unit. By D+3, almost the entire division had deployed to Panama from Fort Ord, California.

Col. David Hale, commander of the 1st Brigade of the 7th, had deployed his brigade to Panama on 12 May 1989 as the Army element in Operation Nimrod Dancer. The brigade's headquarters, the 1st and 2d battalions of the 9th Infantry, the 2d Battalion of the 8th Field Artillery, and the forward area support team had moved into and occupied Fort Sherman near Colón on the Atlantic side of the canal. The brigade then began a series of "force projections" that permanently placed infantry forces in close proximity to the PDF's naval infantry at Coco Solo, the 8th Infantry Company at Fort Espinar, and the Colón Bottleneck. The brigade prepared and rehearsed detailed plans for its part in ensuring freedom of transit through the Panama Canal, the freedom to exercise treaty rights, and the possible overthrow of Noriega as part of Sand Flea exercises. On 16 October, the 3d Brigade relieved the 1st Brigade in place, and the 1st Brigade returned to Fort Ord.

The 7th's 2d Brigade, commanded by Col. Linwood Burney, was the 7th's ready brigade on 19 December. At 0749 on the nineteenth, Maj. General Carmen J. Cavezza, the 7th Division's commander, received the alert from the Joint Chiefs of Staffs' office to execute Blue Spoon and immediately triggered the notification system down his chain of command. He set "N-hour" for the 7th Infantry Division at 0900 on the nineteenth. Colonel Burney alerted his battalions in turn. At 1930 on the evening of the nineteenth, Lt. Col. Robert Cronin and his 5th of the 21st Infantry left Fort Ord for the trip to Travis Air

197

Force Base, 150 miles northeast of Fort Ord. The battalion's strength was 32 officers, one warrant officer, and 383 men. The first elements of the battalion arrived at Travis at 2158 hours.

At 0237 hours on the twentieth, the division's tactical CP—General Cavezza plus a scaled-down operational staff—left Travis, followed at 0310 hours by the 5th of the 21st, and at 0318 by the 2d Brigade's tactical CP. Lt. Col. Alan Rock's 2d Battalion of the 27th Infantry left Travis at 0615 hours. At 0123 hours on the twenty-first, another 2,104 troops, 95 vehicles, 16 trailers, and 56 supply pallets left Travis aboard 10 C-5's and 21 C-141's.

The 5/21st began arriving at Tocumen at 1515 hours on D-day and immediately assisted in securing the airfield. At about the same time, General Cavezza and his tactical CP arrived at Albrook Air Force Base and established a command post. Shortly thereafter, the 2/27th arrived at Tocumen. On arrival, the 2d Brigade came under the direct control of Task Force South, General Stiner's command.[1]

On the twenty-first, General Stiner assigned Colonel Burney an AO (area of operations) ranging west from the Panama Canal to the Costa Rican border. The primary objectives in the area included neutralizing the PDF in the area, securing key sites and facilities, protecting U.S. lives and property, restoring law and order, and demonstrating support for the emerging Panamanian government.

Colonel Burney began operations by directing Colonel Cronin and his 5th of the 21st Infantry to air-assault into the town of Coclecito on the 22d while the other two battalions of the 1st Brigade, 2/27th and 3/27th, relieved the 2/75th and 3/75th Rangers in Rio Hato. The 2d Brigade staged out of Rio Hato to continue a two-phased operation in the west. The first phase had B Company, 3/27th Infantry, air-assault into Las Tablas and secure the area. B Company captured two hundred prisoners. During the second phase, the 2d Brigade moved to the city of David in the western part of Panama to conduct stability operations until relieved by the 2d and 3d battalions, 7th Special Forces Group. On 8 January, after being relieved in the west, the 2d Brigade moved east to join the 1st Brigade in Panama City and relieve the 82d Airborne Division. On 13 January, the 2d Brigade assumed total responsibility for the city. During this phase, the 2d of the 27th Infantry returned to David by order of General Stiner to demonstrate the ability to reenter swiftly any area and show U.S. support for the new government.

The 2d Brigade expanded operations in the east toward the Colombian border from 24 January to 6 February. Primary objectives were to show a strong U.S. presence, support the new Endara government, and neutralize any remaining PDF elements.[2]

On 22 December, D+2, at 0900, Colonel Hale began deployment of his 1st Brigade from Fort Ord to Howard Air Force Base, Panama. On arrival, his brigade was attached to General Johnson's 82d Airborne Division, Task Force Pacific. General Johnson gave Colonel Hale the mission of clearing and securing a major portion of Panama City. By 24 December the brigade was establishing control of an area encompassing six-hundred-thousand residents. Over the next week, the brigade had some twenty-one separate engagements with elements of the PDF and Digbats while clearing and securing its AO. On 6 January the brigade relieved the 82d Airborne Division of security of the Papal Nunciatura. On 10 January the brigade reverted back to General Cavezza's control and expanded its AO in Panama City to control that area formerly held by the departing 82d Airborne Division. Subsequently the brigade transferred its AO to the 2d Brigade and combined U.S. MP/Fuerza Pública de Panama (FPP) control and deployed back to Fort Ord on 17 January.[3]

Lt. Col. William J. Leszczynski, Jr., thirty-nine, West Point Class of 1972, commanded the 3d Battalion of the 9th Infantry, part of the 1st Brigade. He had received his alert on the nineteenth. His first aircraft, a C-141B, was "wheels up" from Monterey Airport at 0130 on the twenty-third. The battalion used eight C-141's and landed at Howard at approximately 1200 hours the same day.

"We moved into an assembly area on the western side of the Panama Canal, a couple of miles from the Miraflores swing bridge," he wrote later. "At 232100 December, I linked up with Colonel Mike Snell, commander of the 193d Infantry Brigade, and he took me on a recon of the area so I could get the 'lay of the land' of the sector. (Note: Lesson 'Relearned': Nothing is better than a personal recon by commanders.) The next morning at 240700 December, the company commanders were taken on a recon of the sector's key sites. Later that day, we moved into the sector."

Less than twelve hours after his battalion touched down, Colonel Leszczynski had started to deploy his men in some sixty squad-size elements and individual snipers throughout his area of responsibility in Panama City and had moved part of his battalion to secure such key sites in the city as the Cuban, Nicaraguan, and Libyan embassies; TV Channel 4; and the Panamanian Ministries of Treasury, Health, and Foreign Affairs. The latter building was especially important because it was the temporary headquarters of the new Endara government. Lt. Col. Thomas Plant and his 1st of the 9th Infantry and Lt. Col. Charles Swannack and his 2d of the 9th Infantry had arrived at Howard within the same time frame on the twenty-third.[4]

On the sixteenth of October, when Col. Keith Kellogg's 3d Brigade of the 7th had assumed responsibility for all U.S. forces in the vicinity of Colón from the 1st Brigade, it also had become Task Force Atlantic. The task force spent the time in "hard training and planning, and in intense mission analysis, preparation, and rehearsals." Every three weeks, battalions rotated to the Jungle Operations Training Center and became familiar with Op Plan 90-2. Units conducted Sand Flea exercises primarily to exercise "U.S. freedom of movement rights" under the Panama Canal treaties and to rehearse contingency plans. The brigade conducted "freedom of movement" convoys twice weekly from Fort Sherman to Fort Clayton or from Howard Air Force Base and back to Colón.

By 0600 on D-day, Task Force Atlantic had cleared Coco Solo and Fort Espinar and had secured Madden Dam, neutralized the Cerro Tigre logistics site, cleared and defended the town of Gamboa, and seized Renacer Prison. The cadre of the Jungle Operations Training Center had secured the Gatun Locks and Fort Sherman.[5]

Colonel Leszczynski's experiences in Panama City were typical of those of the commanders whose units operated within the urban area. "Basically, when we went into Panama City," he wrote, "we conducted a linkup with elements of the 193d Infantry and relieved them. We were given a sector, and a number of key sites were located in the sector and needed to be secured/protected.

"We later took over the security of the American embassy and held this mission until we left for Howard Air Force Base for our redeployment to Fort Ord.

"Additionally we conducted active patrolling the entire time in Panama, with patrols going virtually twenty-four hours a day. We also ran checkpoints and roadblocks to capture any Panamanian Defense Force personnel, Dignity Battalion personnel, and personnel on the 'most wanted list.'

"Immediately after occupying our sector, we began to acquire intelligence and followed up on intel leads. We raided a local Communist Party headquarters and captured a number of documents, including the May election results. We also raided a DENI station and captured over fifty weapons (rifles, shotguns, handguns), assorted ammunition, small quantity of drugs, and three individuals. Additionally, the DENI station contained a roomful of records.

"There were a number of firefights. Most of them were small (squad/squad($-$)). Our biggest problem (and my biggest concern) was the sniper activity. The first week we were in our sector the streets came alive at night. The major road which runs by the American embassy, Balboa Avenue, was the boundary (eastern) of my sector and ran right by my initial CP. It was 'affectionately' knowns as 'sniper alley' and our vehicles were always being fired at from the vicinity of San Tomas Hospital, which we cleared/secured on 27 December.

"Probably the most significant firefight occurred on Christmas. A platoon ($-$) from C/3-9 was sent to reinforce a small element that was securing the DENI station, which had been raided earlier in the day. As the platoon ($-$) was crossing a street, it was engaged by two men firing automatic weapons from a nearby bank. The platoon ($-$) immediately hit the ground, found cover, and returned fire, killing one of the individuals and setting the bank on fire. The other individual escaped.

"I suspect the individuals we were up against were probably Dignity Battalion personnel still operating in the area. I think we killed five personnel total. They were not wearing uniforms.

"My soldiers did anything they were asked to do. For a number of my soldiers (new), the first time they *ever fired,* except for weapons qualification, was when they fired their weapons in Panama. They guarded embassies/secured key facilities twenty-four hours a day; *not very* exciting; pretty boring. They ran patrols twenty-four hours a day, seven days a week through some of the poorest and most crime-ridden areas of Panama City (Curundu). They never fired on a target unless the target was *positively* identified as being hostile. They always stayed in the proper uniform (which included flak jackets and Kevlar helmets) and camouflage. They cleared numerous buildings room by room. At the end of the mission (beginning 5 January) they helped train the new PPF (Panama Police Force), a mission which we continued until we left the sector and went to Howard Air Force Base.

"When we cleared San Tomás Hospital on 27 December, they searched operating rooms, maternity wards, the children's hospital, and *even* the caskets that were coming into and leaving the morgue with the dead bodies inside. This was not an easy task, but my soldiers did it without hesitation.

"When we cleared San Tomás Hospital on 27 December, the entire situation was very confusing. San Tomás is a large hospital complex with a large number of buildings. One of the buildings was the military hospital, which was known to contain over twenty patients, including some UESAT personnel. We had been receiving sniper fire from inside the hospital grounds and, needless to say, I was a little apprehensive and expected some fighting when we went inside.

"Our basic plan was to cordon off the buildings to prevent any PDF who may have still been inside from leaving and to use some loudspeaker teams to encourage any PDF to surrender.

"My plan was put together very quickly and I issued the plan to the B Company commander at 270700 December. When we went inside the hospital at approximately 1100 hours, we found a much different situation than we expected. The hospital was loaded with civilians (doctors, nurses, patients, workers, etc., etc.) and it was very confusing for the soldiers who had expected there would be some fighting, especially in the vicinity of the military hospital.

"The soldiers quickly changed focus and took charge, dealing with the civilian personnel firmly but professionally. There was not a single incident and we had soldiers in virtually every part of the hospital as we searched and cleared the complex. We even had soldiers clear the operating room. I can guarantee that there is nothing in any publication that tells a soldier how to clear a hospital.

"During building-clearing operations, a particular technique is always used to clear rooms. Demolitions are used (if necessary) to blow open the door. Once the door is opened, the first man enters the room and is immediately followed in by a second man—crisscrossing. We practiced this procedure a number of times during training and used the same technique for our room-clearing. Soldiers didn't even need to talk.

"At the American embassy (which we took over from the 3d Ranger Battalion) we were responsible for the 'outside' security. . . . The American embassy had been attacked by RPG-7's on D-day. Our mission at the other embassies was to prevent personnel on the most wanted list from entering or leaving. We stopped all personnel and vehicles entering or leaving. We searched the vehicles to ensure none of the most wanted people were inside. We were also looking for weapons and contraband."

"Our company helped secure the outside of the Cuban and Libyan embassies," said Cpl. William Stansberry, a team leader in A Company of the 3d Battalion, 9th Infantry. "Before General Noriega turned himself in to the papal nuncio, it had been rumored that he might seek asylum at the Cuban embassy, so we doubled our security there. On Christmas Day, a Panamanian vehicle tried to break through our barricades without any success. It was a scary moment, as we had received some sporadic sniper fire from the area."

"Our unit helped secure the Channel 4 TV station so that the Panamanian people could be informed on what was happening with the new government and the American forces," said S. Sgt. John Carter, a squad leader with B Company of the 3d of the 9th. "We set up barricades with the help of the Panamanian people."

"We were prepared for the search and patrol missions, but not the police role," said Command Sgt. Maj. Thurman Beaver of the 3d of the 9th. "Our soldiers were looking for aggressive action and didn't want to be policemen, but they accepted that role when it came. Our troops were very disciplined during their missions and didn't fire their weapons at animals, each other, or even at armed Panamanian shopkeepers, who were protecting their property from looters, especially during the first few days of Operation Just Cause. I'm proud of everybody in this battalion."[6]

Many newspapers reported and numerous TV shots depicted the widespread fires and destruction of neighborhoods in Panama City, especially in the Chorillo district, where Noriega's headquarters was located, and blamed the U.S. forces, either directly or by implication, for the devastation. Inevitably there were some fires started by U.S. gunships, artillery, and mortar fire. But the U.S. commanders insisted that their troops be careful with their fires and shoot only at known enemy targets to avoid unnecessary "collateral" damage. Roberto Eisenmann, the publisher and editor in chief of *La Prensa,* said in an interview in the April 1990 issue of *The American Legion,* "In Chorillo, where most of the damage occurred, there was extensive testimony from eyewitnesses indicating that most of the destruction was because of fires set by Noriega's troops. Many 'Dignity Battalion' members were seen throwing gasoline on buildings and then firing grenades into the area."

General Stiner insisted that all firing be held to the minimum essential and that a field-grade officer approve artillery targets and air strikes. The troops followed that guidance and sought to limit damage. In one instance, a young private first class from the 193d, a gunner on a Sheridan tank firing his tank gun at the corner of the Comandancia, moved his tank from one location to another. An officer asked him why he had moved. The young soldier said, "From here I have a better shot at the building, and I've got less chance of hitting those civilian buildings over there."[7]

*   *   *

On 18 December, two days before the beginning of hostilities, Col. Douglas Terrell deployed the tactical command post of his 7th Aviation Brigade from Fort Ord to Panama. Once there, the TAC assumed command and control over Task Force Hawk, a unit that had been organized to support Nimrod Dancer. He then formed Task Force Aviation, comprised of the 1st Battalion of the 228th Aviation, elements of the 82d's aviation brigade, and his own aviation brigade from the 7th. He then organized Task Force Aviation into four subordinate elements: Task Force Hawk, Task Force 1-228, Team Wolf, and later Team Candor.[8]

Combat operations began for Task Force Aviation with simultaneous battalion and company air assaults, flown by pilots with night-vision goggles (NVGs), in support of Task Force Bayonet to Fort Amador and Task Force Atlantic to Renacer Prison, Gamboa, and Cerro Tigre. Attack helicopters engaged targets at Río Hato, La Comandancia, Fort Cimarron, Panama Viejo, and Torrijos

Airport. After daylight, Task Force Aviation flew air assaults into Panama Viejo, Tinajitas, and Ft. Cimarron in support of Task Force Pacific. Upon completion of these missions, Task Force South took over command of all aviation assets.

Task Force Aviation conducted resupply, command and control, reconnaissance missions, and support for the hostage rescue forces at the Marriott Hotel. On D+2 the AO expanded, with the air assault of the 5th Battalion, 21st Infantry into Coclecito in the west. Elements of Task Force Aviation also flew recce missions in Colón, on the Atlantic side.

On D+5, General Cavezza's TAC requested and was given air assets to support the 2d Brigade's operations in the west. TF Condor was formed and consisted of UH-60 Black Hawks, AH-1 Cobras, and OH-58 Kiowas. This support of the 2d Brigade in the west consisted mainly of air assaults and recce missions. As the 2d Brigade turned over the AO to Special Forces, Task Force Condor began a phased recovery from David through Rio Hato to Fort Kobbe. Task Force Aviation redeployed all augmentation forces and reduced Task Force Hawk to Team Hawk.

Lieutenant Kutschera summed up the operations of her 7th Division helicopter unit this way: "We continued to fly missions throughout Panama. . . . I spent Christmas Eve laggering at Rio Hato waiting to take troops to a new area just before dawn. On 27 December we deployed to David near the Costa Rican border to support operations throughout the mountains of western Panama. We returned to Fort Kobbe about 4 January and the next day we deployed to Fort Sherman on the Atlantic end of the canal with two other aircraft to support missions in that area for about a week. Captain Muir rejoined us on 15 January after convalescing in the States, and cheerfully accepted all the ribbing about being the hardest-headed commander in the Army. On 23 January I flew recon to La Palma on the eastern side of Panama not far from the Colombian border and in February we deployed the company to nearby Sante Fe for about a week to support 7th ID (Light) operations there. . . .

"B Company had returned to the States the first week in January . . . we finished our normal rotation. . . .

"Life at Fort Ord has gotten almost soft. We now get weekends off consistently and I even managed to get enough training time in to complete the Big Sur Marathon. I've also taken up sky diving and in the past year have managed to make 150 freefall jumps."[9]

Lieutenant Kutschera seems to suggest that some women, at least, are ready for combat.

III | FINISHING THE JOB

22 | Follow-on Operations

Prior to the operation, the SOUTHCOM intelligence picture depicted Fort Cimarron, the home of the elite Battalion 2000, the outfit that had come rapidly to the aid of Noriega during the 3 October coup, as one of the most difficult objectives that the 82d Airborne Division would have to neutralize. According to best estimates, Battalion 2000 had three companies at Fort Cimarron along with eight V-300 armored cars, fourteen mortars of assorted calibers, four 107mm rocket launchers, and perhaps three large 120mm mortars. It could be a formidable force if it were dug in a strong defensive position. But fortunately that was not to be the case.

At 1205 on the twentieth, Lt. Col. John R. Vines led his 4/325 on an air assault into the Fort Cimarron area from its PZ at the northern end of Torrijos. The first lift of eleven Black Hawks, escorted by two Cobras, landed part of A Company on LZ Cougar and part of B Company on LZ Tiger. The second lift repeated the first.

Once on the ground, B Company conducted an aggressive patrol south and west of the area to determine enemy positions. The company found scattered PDF soldiers at Paso Blanco and Naranjal. The battalion's scout platoon screened to Paso Blanco and found some additional enemy troops in civilian clothes. The result of the encounter was a firefight in which five enemy were killed. The firefight went on into the evening.

A Company went to the west of the Fort Cimarron airfield into an overwatch position. They were not unobserved. Some enemy troops in the Battalion 2000 barracks fired on them. A Company reacted according to a very positive plan. The company commander first directed his Psyops team to warn the troops in the barracks that if they did not "lay down their arms" he would call in an air strike. The warning went unheeded, so the commander did as promised: He called in an AC-130 to suppress the fire from the barracks. The AC-130 stayed on station from 2100 to 0100 the next morning, firing almost continuously at the area. The barracks was "neutralized."

At 0730 the next morning, Colonel Vines reported to the division tactical CP that he had secured Fort Cimarron. Vines moved a task force into the garrison area and found the barracks deserted. Throughout the twenty-first, the battalion searched the area and set up a perimeter for an expected counterattack that night. During the evening, Battalion 2000 troops did attempt to probe the position to the south near Naranjal, but they were repulsed by the paratroopers. During the twenty-first, the 4/325 cleared the area and found an arms room in each of the company areas. But the small PDF probes were the extent of the enemy action at Fort Cimarron.

This was a surprise to the 4/325. Subsequent to the operation, Battalion S-2 learned that, starting in early December, Battalion 2000 troops had routinely displaced from their barracks area during the night to a position about three kilometers north of the barracks. But they did not make any attempt to counterattack the 4/325 with any large force from the remote position.

After the battle with the remnants of the Battalion 2000, patrols from the 4/325 found that thirteen PDF had been killed, ten vehicles destroyed, and three 120mm mortars were unharmed. A and B companies consolidated their positions and awaited the linkup with the remainder of the battalion.

On the twenty-second, at about 1750, the 4/325 less B Company, which remained at Fort Cimarron, but with A Company of 3/505, which had been in reserve at Torrijos, air-assaulted into Punta Paitilla Airfield in Panama City "to secure that area for future extraction operations." Colonel Nix also gave the battalion the responsibility for the security of the district containing the Papal Nunciatura.[1]

The first night the battalion was in Paitilla, Pvt. James Allen Tabor, eighteen, a .50-caliber machine gunner assigned to Headquarters Company, was shot and killed when his patrol moved toward the main part of Panama City. Spc. Glenn Lame of A Company said, "The first night, we started out the gate (of Paitilla) on patrol and started taking sniper fire immediately. Lame also had some kind remarks for the ability of the Hummvee to run on flat tires. "They really run on flat tires, just like they are advertised. We had one come in running on the rim, not the rubber. It just came right in."

Pvt. Tony Moore, a member of a forward observer party from C Battery, 3d Battalion, 319th Field Artillery, who was with A Company 4/325, said his worst moment came when his sergeant and lieutenant adjusted artillery fire by sound. "That was a bit hairy," he claimed. "Other than that, it has been pretty quiet around here."[2]

Another episode that received some press coverage was the "Smithsonian rescue." The Smithsonians were a group of five Americans, four Panamanians, one Venezuelan, and one Pole. The Americans included Dr. Nancy Knowlton and her four-year-old daughter, Rebecca; Preston Hardison, graduate student at the University of Washington; Steve Travers, a research assistant to Eric Fischer, deputy director of the Smithsonian Tropical Research Institute; and Greg Summers, a research assistant and student at the University of Washington.

The group had been conducting research on "Smithsonian Tupu" Island in the San Blas group on the Atlantic side of the canal. The PDF "captured" them by dispatching a twenty-foot patrol boat and crew to the island, forcibly loading them up, and transporting them as far as Carti Airstrip on the mainland. Two Smithsonian Boston whalers followed the PDF boat. From Carti Airstrip, the PDF marched the Smithsonians overland some twenty-one kilometers to the Cuna Indian Research Station at Nasugrande. Apparently during the land march, the PDF lost interest in the whole project and faded away. For two days the group stayed in a remote schoolhouse between the towns of Carti and Llana. "Rescue" came when the party was able to contact U.S. forces and arrange to be picked up by helicopter on 22 December.[3]

As December faded into New Year's Day, the U.S. forces spread out around the countryside, intent on returning the country to its legally elected administration and assuring the Panamanians that Noriega and his thugs were no longer in power. General Thurman still had one more objective to achieve: finding and arresting Noriega.

The D-day operations were a success from a number of standpoints. At a breakfast-hour briefing on the morning of D-day, Gen. Colin Powell said that Noriega was "not running anything, because we own all of the bases he owned eight hours ago." At the end of the operation, Lt. Gen. Tom Kelly, General Powell's director of operations, said, "It is among the most professionally executed operations that I have seen in thirty-three years of military status. . . . It looks like the organized resistance is a thing of the past. . . . We have a concern that they have gone off into the jungle. There is every chance that we will go after them." And "go after them" they did.

On D-day, thousands of American troops from the United States and Panama had converged from widely scattered bases in the United States and Panama to defeat a spread-out, in-place force with "rapid and overwhelming combat power." By the end of D+2, over twenty-seven thousand U.S. troops were in Panama, under the operational control of one headquarters and had accomplished over twenty-seven separate missions in various spread-out locations. Two hundred forty-five U.S. Air Force airframes supported the U.S. forces on D-day as transports for paratroopers and heavy equipment, as transports for air-landed troops primarily from the 7th Infantry Division, as gunships, as airborne command and control ships, or as air warning platforms. It had been a massive, rapidly executed undertaking both in the planning phase and in the operation itself.

With the end of D-day and the defeat of the majority of the PDF units, there remained a less spectacular but perhaps far more important phase yet to be executed: the stabilization of the Panamanian people and their institutions, the "going after" and capturing of former PDF and Digbat leaders (including El Jefe himself—Noriega); the provision of humanitarian relief and assistance; the restoration of basic services to include, most especially, law and order; and the insuring of the security of U.S. citizens and key facilities.

By the end of D-day, no major PDF unit had mounted a counterattack. But Panama "remained a very lethal environment for U.S. forces," according to a Southern Command spokesman. "Sunset found every objective secured. . . . The Blue Spoon operations order had been executed nearly flawlessly."[4] Now it

209

was time for follow-on operations. As General Johnson, commander of the 82d Airborne Division, reviewed the situation, members of his Task Force Pacific occupied key locations at the eastern end of Panama City.

On D+1, the twenty-first of December, sniping and drive-by attacks, similar to what the 2d of the 504th had endured, persisted throughout the city. By that morning, B Company of the 2-504th had rescued twenty-nine civilians who had been trapped in the Marriott Hotel and feared of being taken hostage. Additionally, eleven employees and family members of the Smithsonian Institution were rescued from near the continental divide east of Panama City. Other elements began moving into the city to assert a U.S. presence. As PDF members, or more commonly, Dignity Battalion members were encountered, they were captured and moved to detention centers. On D+2, the highly publicized "attack on Quarry Heights" occurred. Although the media indicated the attack was aimed at the Southern Command's home base, the attack actually disrupted activation activities of the new Public Forces at the bottom of Ancon Hill.

During the first couple of days after the operation began, anarchists had reigned in the streets of Panama City. Vandals set a supermarket warehouse on fire. Thugs stole cars and then abandoned them after turning them upside down. Digbats roamed the streets, rattling off bursts of automatic-weapons fire at random. "You could see the fires and the Molotov cocktails," reported Sgt. Jeffrey Newport of Springfield, Massachusetts. "You could hear the screams. It was amazing what they were doing to themselves."

The president of the Panamanian Chamber of Commerce, Alfredo Maduro, put losses by looting at $50 million to $1 billion.

Melquiades Dominguez was a security guard at an American-owned electronics warehouse in Panama City. For five days he was a one-man police force, using a 12-gauge shotgun to try to drive off a mob of thieves and hoodlums who ransacked his warehouse and terrorized the civilians in the area. One night he stood atop his warehouse and watched thieves across the street loot the Superior Products warehouse and litter the area with crates from stolen refrigerators, TV sets, and shoes. Felix Larringa was an insurance salesman. He watched helplessly from his apartment balcony as marauding bands on the street below him ripped off all the cars from a Hertz parking lot and blasted the door of a jewelry store.

"Small bands of armed thugs wandered through the barrio," wrote one reporter, "raping, stealing, and murdering at will . . . a man got out of his car, walked to another parked beside it, drew a gun, and killed the driver."

"Have you ever seen a BMW going down the street on a forklift?" asked Lt. Col. Johnny Brooks, whose men tried to stop the theft.

A number of concerned citizens tried to generate some order out of the chaos created in the policeless city swarming with violent, unruly, armed mobs. Some residents dragged abandoned cars, stones, poles, and old refrigerators into their areas to block the roaming looters. The residents developed shifts "to man the barricades." Mr. Larringa said, "We had no choice. We were our own security."[5]

In early January, Gen. Ed Scholes, the chief of staff of XVIII Airborne Corps, took Gen. Carl Vuono, the Army's chief of staff, on a tour of some areas in

Panama City. In one section, where some wealthy Panamanian civilians—doctors, business owners, other professionals—lived, they were greeted warmly. One of the homeowners in the area said, "We feel as if we have been released from prison. In our own country, we feel like prisoners." The people in the area had showered the American soldiers with soft drinks and food.[6]

After a couple of days, the situation in Panama City gradually returned to some sort of normalcy as U.S. soldiers spread out through the city and patrolled the streets, generated a sense of calm and order, and filled in the wide gap in the police ranks left by the surrender and desertion of the PDF who had formerly doubled as the civilian police force.

"We're trying to establish a police force as opposed to a paramilitary organization like the old PDF," said Col. Larry Brede, the commanding officer of Fort Bragg's 16th Military Police Brigade. Colonel Brede had command and control of some eleven hundred MPs who came to Panama at various times during the crisis from posts across the United States. In an effort to change the way the Panamanian people think of their police forces, the Southern Command has brought into Panama eleven thousand sets of green, Vietnam-style jungle fatigues from Fort Bragg for the reconstituted police force. Colonel Brede said that this change in uniform was an attempt "to remove the taint" of the PDF's old blue uniform. He added, "I don't want this new organization to be the old PDF in new uniforms."

When his MPs checked some of the PDF's old police stations in and around Panama City, they found cattle prods and rubber hoses among other devices used to coerce and control the populace. The devices were mute testimony as to why the people feared the Noriega regime.

The MPs from the various units under Colonel Brede's command performed many more duties than just trying to control traffic and prevent looting. They enforced basic laws and operated "detainee" camps for looters, former prisoners, and PDF members. They are "detainees" rather than POWs because, while Noriega declared war on the United States, the United States did not declare war on Noriega. "We're transitioning from pure combat to nation-building," Colonel Brede explained. "We will stay here longer than everyone else."

In the days following the operation, the MPs had processed over 4,000 Panamanian prisoners at a converted rifle range north of Panama City on the Panama Canal. They used 105 tents and 780 rolls of concertina wire to transform the range into a semblance of a detention camp. By the middle of January 1990, less than 1,000 "detainees" remained in the camp. Capt. Kerry Skelton, commander of the 65th MP Company from Fort Bragg, said, "For a couple of days, this place was wall-to-wall people coming through as fast as they could. . . . Some of them were people who performed patrols with my MPs four months ago. We had MPs that worked with PDF members they recognized. They very well may work together again in the future."

"We've got them under control," said Sgt. Michael Hare, a member of Skelton's company. "We take them for chow and showers."

In the operation of the camp, the 65th MP Company was augmented by fifty-six MPs from Fort Lee, Virginia, thirty from the Missouri National Guard, and the 519th Military Intelligence Battalion.

Some of the Fort Bragg MPs have spent so much time away from their home base, in places such as St. Croix and Panama, that they consider a return to Bragg "R&R." "The demand for bilingual soldiers is tremendous," said Colonel Brede. He added that he has an Hispanic mechanic whose Spanish is more valuable than his MOS.[7]

SOUTHCOM's goal was to reconstitute the Panamanian police force. The MPs, of course, work along U.S. lines in their methods to reestablish law and order. "We're trying to show that if people are arrested and taken to the police station, they're not going to get beaten with a hose," Colonel Brede explained. "When we are down there alone, people cheer and clap and want autographs and to take pictures. When we're with Panamanians, people tend to get sullen and see our association with the old regime. We're trying to diffuse that."

But in spite of the whooping and hollering, the celebrations and the pot-banging on the street corners, there was still chaos and anarchy in many parts of the nation, especially in Panama City itself. Because many foreign countries wanted to evacuate their citizens, the United States had to open an airport to receive relief supplies and to permit the resumption of some sort of routine air travel. Commercial flights out of Tocumen were resumed on 30 December.

The needs of the Panamanians in Chorillo were most urgent. Their homes and businesses had been burned, in most cases by the looting and ravaging Digbats, but in some cases by battle. The people of the district fled into Balboa. In the Balboa High School athletic stadium they found a refuge where Maj. Michael Lewis and his D Company of the 96th Civil Affairs Battalion had established a "displaced persons" camp. After it had been in operation a few days, the makeshift camp received high marks from Panama's surgeon general and the International Red Cross. The Chorillo mayor acted as camp mayor, and the camp residents had set up their own administrative systems. At the camp, Major Lewis and his men processed and screened almost eleven thousand Panamanians; his camp had an average population of thirty-five hundred at any one time.

"It's a daily battle to control sanitation and health," Major Lewis said, "but we're winning the battle. They have no discipline problems or control problems. They're poor people and probably didn't have much before the fire. A lot of people may be living better now than they were before."[8]

When the humanitarian assistance program was under way about three days after the operation began, there were thirteen military distribution sites (they were closed out on 3 January), at which the U.S. forces in each of the task force areas distributed, to long lines of Panamanians, 75,000 cases of MREs and 1,120,000 pounds of bulk food, including baby food, liquid and dry milk, and dried beans.

In the field of medical assistance, during and just after the operation, the U.S. forces found a paucity of medical supplies in the Panamanian hospitals. As a consequence, the U.S. forces shipped in some 615,920 pounds of medical supplies and treated over 15,000 civilian sick and wounded at fixed and improvised hospitals and aid stations. But the tragedy of the situation was that, during the operation, the U.S. forces found a large PDF warehouse in the

212

Balboa engineering complex where the PDF warehouseman had hoarded over 150,000 pounds of medical supplies. He had been in the habit of demanding bribes before he would distribute any of his wares to legitimate customers. Such was the legacy of Noriega.

Besides the effects on the nation of the political instability caused by Noriega's harsh regime, the prewar U.S. economic sanctions, and the battles of Just Cause, the Panamanian economy had been battered by a deepening recession. A depositor run on the banks prior to the operation had caused bank deposits to drop from $40 billion to $15 billion.

"To keep from having to do this again in five to ten years, it's important to create a strong infrastructure and conclude this conflict on favorable terms to our national interest—a stable, democratic government in Panama," said Lt. Col. Dwayne Aaron, civil-military operations officer for the joint task force and assistant chief of staff for civil-military operations of XVIII Airborne Corps.

"The way this place was organized before, Noriega ran it all and the PDF was in charge," said Lt. Col. Michael P. Peters, 96th Civil Affairs Battalion commander. "You had civilians in nominal charge, but the military was the real authority in the country. They worked independently from the civilian government. The military was so in charge the civilian sector had atrophied. You didn't have a loyal opposition to take its place."

Capt. Ken Carter is the principal adviser to the government of Colón Province, on the Caribbean coast. "He's helping them do everything from collect the garbage to setting up the police force," said Colonel Peters. He added that Capt. Dave Heckert is working with officials in the town of David, on the western coast. These two captains are examples of the civil-affairs world that grew throughout Panama in the days after the demise of the PDF.

The 96th Civil Affairs Battalion is part of the 1st Special Operations Command at Fort Bragg and is the Army's only active-duty civil-affairs unit. About 97 percent of the Army's civil-affairs personnel are in the reserves. Colonel Peters said that it is the reservists, with their in-depth expertise—from air traffic control to banking to police administration to law to medical support—who will provide the long-term care and monitor the various programs set up by the active-duty combat forces and civil-affairs teams. For the first time in its history, the 96th Civil Affairs Battalion deployed in its entirety. In the first stage of the operation, civil-affairs officers and men parachuted into Rio Hato with the Rangers to assist in dealing with civilians from the beginning of the operation. "Commanders here have been made believers in how valuable civil affairs can be," Colonel Aaron said. "Battlefields are not clean. The real world is full of civilians and they're always in the wrong place at the wrong time."

"The challenge is to build a security force that is competent and yet has credibility with the people and understands its role in society and is responsible to the civilian leadership," said Colonel Peters. "If we get the military too efficient too fast and the civilian structure doesn't mature, you'll be in the same situation you were in before."[9]

During the operation and immediately thereafter, the U.S. forces collected over 52,000 weapons from the Noriega regime. They also picked up 28 armored vehicles, 7 ships, almost $8 million, 600 tons of ammunition, almost 14,000 canisters of chemicals (type CS/CN), and 417 kilograms of drugs valued at about $6.8 million.

But by the morning of Christmas Day, Noriega was still at large. The thinking in the Pentagon and in SOUTHCOM prior to the operation had been that Noriega would "take to the woods" with any of his PDF forces who could escape the U.S. forces and fight a guerrilla war à la Robin Hood.

In his office on the twenty-third, General Powell had said, "We will destroy his Robin Hood image."

23 | Winning the West and Noriega's Surrender

But now it was the time to "win the West."[1]

Lt. Col. Luís A. Del Cid was a close Noriega associate who, like Noriega, was wanted by the United States on drug charges. Del Cid was the Noriega-appointed "boss" of the PDF military operations in Panama's western frontier who ran the operation from his headquarters in David, the capital of Chiriquí Province, the area that was the Panamanian version of the "Wild West." The D-day attacks triggered Del Cid's long-standing, Noriega-approved plans to fade into the jungle with a ragtag band of PDF regulars and criminals he had released from jails and continue armed resistance against the Americans.

Maj. Gilberto Pérez was the Spanish-speaking commander of A Company, 1st Battalion, 7th Special Forces Group. His Special Forces unit was "oriented" toward Latin America, and he was well steeped in the history of Panama, its institutions, its military forces, and its culture. On the twenty-second of December he received a warning order through his chain of command to "pacify the districts of Herrera, Coclé, Los Santos, and Veraguas," all provinces to the west of Panama City. His mission was to operate with the 75th Rangers and elements of Colonel Burney's 2d Brigade of the 7th Infantry Division (Light) to cause the commanders of scattered PDF *cuartels* throughout western Panama to surrender their arms and men with as few casualties as possible on both sides. As soon as he received the mission, Major Pérez contacted Colonel Burney at Albrook Air Force Base, sketched the outline of a plan, and then flew his Special Forces company to Río Hato to begin the detailed planning.

From his knowledge of the terrain and military forces of Panama, Pérez was aware that a *cuartel* was the generic term used throughout Latin America for a military base of any kind. Frequently a *cuartel* is an area the size of some four to six city blocks surrounded by a solid wall of varying height and thickness. Perez also knew that the *cuartels* were manned by PDF forces whose size and dedication to El Jefe were not constants.

215

To accomplish his mission over the wide area he had been assigned, Pérez developed a two-phased concept, later referred to as the "Ma Bell approach."[2] In phase one, he planned to insert Special Forces teams into the towns of Santiago, Chitré, and Las Tablas. He selected the airfield in each town as the initial landing zone for his men. An AC-130 Specter gunship would be available in the air to provide close air support. He had arranged with Colonel Kernan and Colonel Burney to have one of their infantry or Ranger battalions standing by with helicopter lift as a quick reaction force should he encounter any resistance his small forces of Green Berets could not handle.

Once he and his team were in place at the town's airfield, Pérez planned to telephone the commander of the local *cuartel* and ask him to meet him at the airfield. When he appeared, Pérez would then tell him that he had an infantry or Ranger battalion standing by and that he wanted the commander to surrender his *cuartel*. There were three terms to the surrender, Pérez would tell the local commander: One, the surrender would be unconditional; two, all weapons would be placed in the *cuartel*'s guard room; and three, all of the PDF in the *cuartel* would assemble on the *cuartel*'s parade ground. Then Major Pérez would "invite" the commander to fly with him over the parade ground to ensure that all of the terms of the surrender had been met. If Pérez detected any hesitancy or reluctance by the commander to comply, Pérez would have the AC-130 fire a few inhibiting 105mm rounds into an unoccupied open part of the *cuartel*. Pérez felt that it was essential to use all available means to gain a peaceful surrender with minimum casualties on either side. That was phase one of the "Ma Bell approach."

In phase two, Pérez and some of his Special Forces would move into the *cuartel* to search the area and to process the PDF soldiers. At the same time, a backup 7th Infantry Division or Ranger company would move into the town to establish law and order. The company's mission would be to prevent looting and reprisals that the citizens might be inclined to take against the surrendering PDF, whose past transgressions of varying degrees against the civilian population might have warranted considerable revenge and retribution.

At 1400 hours on the twenty-third, Pérez launched his first mission. He and his Special Forces flew into the town of Santiago in the province of Veraguas in helicopters from Task Force Hawk of the 7th ID and 617th Aviation Company. As soon as his helicopter set down, Pérez and his team captured three PDF who were at the field. Then Pérez tried to contact the local *cuartel* commander but could not find him. Pérez then decided to fly to the *cuartel* with five of his men. When he got there, he found that the PDF were prepared to surrender and were already assembling on the parade field. One dissatisfied PDF took a shot at the helicopter as it was landing but did no damage. Pérez's men quickly took the misguided youth under control. Pérez then called forward the rest of his SF Company and searched and cleared the *cuartel*. He also brought in Captain Stone and his 7th ID Company and gave him command of the *cuartel*. Pérez left behind with Stone a small Spanish-speaking SF detachment to assist Stone in his work with the local community. Pérez gave Stone four missions: One, gather intelligence on the weapons caches of the PDF and the Digbats who had not yet

216

surrendered; two, assist the local civilian community leaders in gaining control of the town; three, assess the condition of the local infrastructure—hospital, public utilities, law and order, and establish priorities for follow-on civil-military operations; and four, conduct joint Panamanian-U.S. patrols throughout Santiago. For the next few days, Stone and his company followed the instructions carefully, with the resultant restoration of order in Santiago.

At 0630 on the twenty-fourth, Pérez launched his second mission, this one into the town of Chitré, in the province of Herrera. At the airport, he and his men captured one PDF soldier. Pérez then phased into his plan and telephoned the *cuartel* commander, who surrendered his force without any resistance. Colonel Burney's troops followed and accomplished, without serious incidents, the same missions that Stone had accomplished in Santiago.

At 0900 on Christmas Day, Pérez and his team flew into Las Tablas, the capital of Los Santos Province, on a Panamanian peninsula that juts into the Pacific Ocean about due south of the Pacific end of the canal. He landed in an open field and immediately went to a nearby house and telephoned the local commander, who surrendered with no difficulty. Pérez and his small team entered the *cuartel*. When they had finished checking and securing the area, Pérez noticed that a large number of civilians had gathered outside the wall. Pérez made a quick decision. He ordered the PDF to assemble on the parade ground with his own troops lined up beside them. Then Pérez called the combined force to attention, ordered "present arms," and had the Panamanian flag raised on the *cuartel's* flagpole. With this small but symbolic ceremony, Pérez demonstrated that the United States was not a conqueror but a liberator. His impromptu ritual gained the support of the civilians for the follow-on U.S. efforts in the area. An ancillary result was a steady flow of valuable intelligence from the civilian populace.

Meanwhile, at 1000 on Christmas Day, Lt. Col. Joseph Hunt and his 3d Battalion of the 75th Rangers had air-assaulted into Malek Airfield in the town of David, the capital of Chiriquí Province, which abuts the eastern boundary of Costa Rica. David is about fifty miles from the border. Hunt's mission was to seize the airfield for use by follow-on forces, to accept the surrender of PDF forces in the area, and to locate and secure cache sites. By 1100, Hunt's men had secured the airfield. Five hours later, Hunt moved one company into the city of David and began searching for and securing suspected cache sites.

Lt. Col. Robert Cronin and his 5th of the 21st Infantry from the 7th ID arrived at Río Hato on 21 December and relieved the 3d Battalion of the 75th Rangers. In the early morning hours of the twenty-third, the 5th of the 21st took over control of the 6th Zone Police headquarters in Penonomé, about 62 miles southwest of Panama City, from the 3d of the 75th. Capt. John Fieder commanded B Company of the 5th of the 21st Infantry. He said that his mission at Penonomé was multipurpose: to relieve the Rangers, to secure the PDF who were surrendering themselves, and to gather and secure arms and equipment from the PDF and the Digbats.

Inside the prison at Penonomé, Fieder's men found a small cache of weapons, including the ubiquitous and rugged AK-47, some ammunition, and some

Molotov cocktails. The 5th of the 21st debriefed the detainees, fed them, and separated them into three groups according to rank. Civilians gave the gate guards leads on the location of other PDF members and arms caches.

On the night of the twenty-sixth, the 5th of the 21st flew out of Río Hato aboard C-130s and arrived at Malek Airfield in David early the following morning. Within an hour of landing, the battalion was in the process of relieving the Rangers in David. One platoon finished securing the airfield, while another platoon moved to a nearby rock quarry to confiscate a reported weapons cache. A third platoon helicoptered to an area in David secured by the Rangers. When the platoon landed in the helicopters, it was surrounded by about a hundred Panamanians trying to "get a good look at the machine and the passengers. As the crowd formed around the aircraft, the Light fighters slipped into the city streets on the way to relieve the Rangers." The citizens were definitely friendly and welcoming.

Colonel Cronin became the commander of the district. Major Pérez served as his adviser and interpreter. During the next few days, Cronin and his men visited all the *cuartels* and towns in the region. They established liaison with the newly appointed Panamanian commanders of the *cuartels* and the governors and mayors throughout the district. Colonel Burney and the entire 2d Brigade operated throughout the central and western portions of Panama and provided support to the governments in Río Hato, Santiago, and David. Their efforts paid off in a number of ways. One was very important: Major Pérez and his team accepted the surrender of Del Cid.

The surrender of Del Cid was accomplished more easily than Pérez and his men had at first thought possible. On Thursday, the twenty-first, Del Cid had had second thoughts about fighting from the jungle with his motley crew of renegades. He contacted some Catholic priests in his area and through them arranged to talk to Gen. Marc Cisneros, the Spanish-speaking commander of the Army's forces in Southern Command, who was acting as General Stiner's deputy. They agreed on the phone to the unconditional terms of the surrender and, by Friday, a white flag flew over Del Cid's camouflaged jungle headquarters. This somewhat unexpected action negated the need for an American foray into the jungle and saved the lives of many men on both sides of the battle.

Another payoff: Lieutenant Colonel Cronin and Major Pérez convinced the governors in the area to permit the new Panamanian security forces to carry weapons and thus begin to take over the role of maintaining law and order. They also established a program to train the security forces to deal with the population as a "protecting police force and not a dominating military force."

Major Pérez was still not satisfied with the pace of the pacification and felt that there were not enough U.S. forces present to bring peace to the region. From one of the outlying areas, he flew to David and convinced Colonel Burney to redeploy a battalion to Río Hato to conduct "reconnaissance in force operations" throughout the region. These incursions into the areas outside the towns resulted in the capture of several weapons caches and a number of former PDF soldiers and Dignity Battalion troops. Major Pérez continued to conduct strike operations in the same successful way that he had in Santiago, Chitré, and

Las Tablas. In one location, his Special Forces team captured 180 members of the Macho de Monte.

He also used his Psyops men and their equipment and techniques to great advantage. One communiqué, read over the local radio, urged Digbat members in Chiriquí to turn in their weapons. Within an hour, a large number of them were lined up ready to surrender their weapons in exchange for a bounty of $150 promised by the United States.

In addition to Del Cid, four other regional commanders formerly intensely loyal to Noriega and beholden to him for their positions, pledged loyalty to the new president, Endara, by the end of the week and were allowed by the U.S. commanders in the area to retain their posts—at least temporarily.

On Saturday, the twenty-third, the reign of looters and thieves in La Chorrera, about twenty miles west of the canal, came to an abrupt halt. A unit from the 7th ID moved into the empty PDF headquarters and quickly restored order to the area. The PDF headquarters had sustained surprisingly little damage during the earlier fighting. By dawn on Saturday, groups of Panamanian civilians were forming outside the headquarters, and by midmorning the crowd had swelled to thousands, ready to thank the United States for the intervention of its armed forces. People hollered, flashed peace signs, and waved at the soldiers. Women and young girls hugged and kissed the grinning and embarrassed soldiers.

Noriega's grip was loosened. But he was still "AWOL" as far as the U.S. troops were concerned.

* * *

Max Thurman had had four objectives to achieve during Just Cause: Protect American lives, safeguard the integrity of the Panama Canal, restore democracy in Panama, and capture Noriega. On Christmas morning he had accomplished only three quarters of his missions; Noriega was still loose.

In the early developmental stages of Blue Spoon, the planners at the Pentagon and in SOUTHCOM had allocated Special Forces teams to trail Noriega, totally surreptitiously, and to capture him when the National Command Authority made that decision. The tracking began weeks ahead of the actual D-day for Just Cause. General Thurman said later that the teams knew of Noriega's whereabouts 80 percent of the time.

One spokesman for the U.S. Special Operations Command, Gen. Jim Lindsay's outfit, said in a wrap-up of the operation:

> An additional force that can only be mentioned in passing is Task Force Blue and Task Force Green. These forces, supported by quick-reaction helicopters and AC-130 gunships, had the difficult task of capturing the elusive Noriega. Our intelligence efforts greatly narrowed the possibilities for his location and allowed this force to apply pressure to him commencing at H-hour. This pressure never let up, with our force systematically pursuing each substantive lead. This effectively denied Noriega a place to hide and prevented his escape from Panama.[3]

Noriega had a series of plush apartments, condos, and beach houses scattered throughout Panama. One of them, the Farallon beach house, was on the shore of the Gulf of Panama near Río Hato. At H + 2 hours, Buck Kernan dispatched a team from his 2d Battalion, which had jumped onto Río Hato, to investigate the beach house. The team found a palatial, beautifully furnished house—without Noriega.

Noriega's other homes and offices were equally luxurious. One office, at Fort Amador, was windowless and drab on the outside but well appointed on the inside. "Noriega was a conditioned drinker," according to a SOUTHCOM speaker,

and well-stocked bars were centerpieces of each of his various residences. The beach house at Río Hato reportedly had a bar in every major room. As the fine furnishings attest, Noriega liked the good life. His corruption and drug money allowed him to indulge in expensive furniture and pieces of artwork. He enjoyed all this while his country's economy went to ruin.

True to his image of machismo, Noriega was also a womanizer. Despite the jealousy of his wife, Felicidad, Noriega kept several women. His favorite apparently was Vicky Amado—the person he called first in this office during the October coup attempt. Another mistress was identified in Santiago and, of course, he had planned to spend the night with a temporary liaison the night of the invasion.

Despite Noriega's devotion to his daughters and his propensity for high living, dark hints of depravity are evident. TVs and VCRs with pornographic tapes still seated, were found in several of his homes. Rumors had circulated of Brazilian witches. A set of quarters on the causeway at Fort Amador yielded proof of the rumors.[4]

From H-hour on, General Thurman had kept General Powell informed of the details of the search for Noriega. Just before midnight on the nineteenth, General Powell went to the Crisis Situation Room in the Pentagon's National Military Command Center (NMCC). There he had direct communications with General Thurman in Panama. Throughout the early-morning hours he kept track of what was happening, especially of Noriega's whereabouts and the rescue of Kurt Muse. The news from Thurman was good and bad: Good—the drops at Torrijos and Río Hato were going well; the initial assaults by the in-country forces were proceeding generally as planned; the Comandancia was in flames; the PDF were surrendering in droves; bad: three SEALs had been killed at Paitilla Airport; the Muse helicopter had crashed; Noriega was still at large.

General Thurman told General Powell that the Rangers who jumped on Tocumen had almost captured Noriega in the Officers' Club at Tocumen. But when Noriega heard the aircraft and saw the parachutes, he jumped into his clothes and ran to his ever-present getaway car. He roared away from Tocumen and headed for Panama City where, for the next few days, he moved from one hideout to another, collecting IOUs from his various cronies.[5]

In its frustration, the U.S. administration put a $1 million bounty on Noriega's head, hoping to encourage a PDF trooper or some member of the opposition to put the finger on the dictator. General Powell, by now referring to Noriega as "a dope-sniffing, voodoo-loving thug," was becoming increasingly vexed that, with the success of the military operation in Panama, neither the troops spreading throughout the countryside nor the Special Forces who had been targeted on Noriega had been able to find him.

But the relentless tracking had an effect. At about 1530 on Christmas Eve, a car drove up to the residence of the Vatican's representative in Panama, the papal nuncio, Monsignor Sebastian Laboa. Out of the car emerged General Noriega, wearing a T-shirt and shouldering two AK-47's. Noriega went inside the nunciatore and requested political asylum.

Prior to Noriega's arrival at the nunciatore, the U.S. forces had been overwatching other embassies in the hopes that Noriega might seek asylum in one of them, particularly the Cuban embassy. His selection of the papal nuncio's quarters had a double deterrent: It was both an embassy and church property.

But both Max Thurman and Carl Stiner reviewed the methods by which they might get Noriega out of the nunciatore. Monsignor Laboa met with Max Thurman and Stiner and told them that if shooting started in the nunciatore, they were authorized to make an assault to rescue as many people as possible. Stiner got on the hot line to Kelly in the Pentagon and asked for new rules of engagement that would comply with Monsignor Laboa's statement. Kelly went to Powell and Cheney and got the rules changed. Throughout the time that Noriega was holed up in the nunciatore, Thurman was frequently on the hot line to the Pentagon discussing the "what ifs." What if a hostage is taken? What if there was shooting in the nunciatore? By this time, over a hundred U.S. soldiers surrounded the nunciatore.

On 27 December, Max Thurman ordered loudspeakers placed in a parking lot next to the nunciatore and blasted the building with rock music. The noise was not specifically intended to force Noriega out of the building, as some Panamanians reasoned; rather, it was to prevent eavesdropping on SOUTHCOM's negotiations with the papal nuncio. Some of the rock numbers included "I Fought the Law," "Voodoo Child," and "You're No Good." Reporters could hear the music from the twelfth floor of a nearby hotel, and people walking the streets could hear the music for blocks.[6]

By the twenty-seventh, the Panama Canal was returning to normal operations, and officials said that they hoped to go into a twenty-four-hour-a-day operation to clear up a backlog of some 125 ships.

In Rome, Vatican spokesman Joaquín Navarro said that there was no legal way for the Holy See to turn Noriega over to the United States because the Vatican and the United States had no extradition treaty. He added that the Vatican was studying the case in its "judicial, diplomatic, and humanitarian, and therefore ethical considerations." At one point General Thurman tried curbside diplomacy, talking to Monsignor Laboa outside the embassy. General Thurman did not neglect the military side: He had the embassy tightly surrounded with troops and ordered helicopters and AC-130's to patrol the sky overhead constantly. U.S. troops shot out the street lights with pellet guns

(M-16's would have endangered nearby Panamanian civilians), erected concertina wire around the area, blocked the streets in the area with APCs, and mowed the grass outside the embassy compound to improve the view. Noriega appeared not to notice.[7]

During the ten days Noriega stayed in the nunciatore, the U.S. administration became more and more concerned and even felt that the standoff might continue indefinitely. President Bush said that if the Vatican refused to turn over Noriega, "that complicates things." To preclude other countries from granting Noriega asylum, the U.S. Justice Department filed papers in four countries to freeze bank accounts in which Noriega was thought to have stashed more than $10 million in "illegal drug money." Cuba and the Dominican Republic, where one of Noriega's daughters lives, had been mentioned as possible havens. But the Dominican foreign minister, Joaquín Ricardo, said that his country had an extradition treaty with the United States and that Noriega could be extradited if he went there.

During Noriega's incarceration, President Bush seemed to have left open the possibility that Noriega could be tried in Panama. He mentioned that Noriega might regain power if left in Panama "unless he were in total custody and sentenced to the prison sentence he deserves."

In a little-noticed footnote to the events of the twenty-seventh was the item that Vicky Amado, Noriega's longtime mistress, had been arrested along with hundreds of PDF soldiers. And Benjamin Colomarco, the head of Noriega's Dignity Battalions, surrendered on 11 January 1990 and was in U.S. custody.

Life inside the Vatican embassy had not been pleasant for the deposed dictator. Monsignor José Sebastian Laboa, the papal nuncio, who had once served in the Vatican as the "devil's advocate," taking the negative side when the Vatican examined the veracity of miracles, tried various means of pressure to force Noriega to surrender to the U.S. authorities. In the white stucco embassy, Laboa assigned Noriega a white room decorated only with a broken TV set and a crucifix. The one window was opaque. Initially Laboa shut down the air conditioning, resulting in an almost unbearably hot and humid room. He allowed Noriega only one alcoholic drink—a beer—during his entire ten-day stay.

Among other means of pressuring Noriega, Laboa arranged for two diplomats to hold a stage-whispered conversation outside Noriega's door, during which the diplomats discussed the fate of deposed Nicaraguan dictator Somoza, who died in exile in an ambush in Paraguay. The monsignor told Noriega that he had authorized the U.S. Army to "storm the embassy if a hostage situation arose." The priests in the embassy reminded him that he was an unwelcome guest and provided only minimal hospitality. He was given nothing special, said embassy spokesman José Cubillas. "He was a vegetarian but did not get vegetarian meals." He also mentioned that for most of the time Noriega had carried on very few conversations.[8]

Monsignor Laboa kept up the psychological pressure. He told Noriega, "You could be lynched like Mussolini and exposed in a plaza as the laughingstock of the people. That would be less than a dignified end for you." He also told him that the Panamanian bishops had written to Pope John Paul II and that the pope had agreed with the bishops that Noriega was a common criminal and ineligible for political asylum.

But then Monsignor Laboa became more conciliatory. He turned on the air conditioning in Noriega's room and invited him to eat the New Year's Eve dinner with embassy personnel and some Noriega cronies who had also sought sanctuary. At the dinner, Noriega and embassy personnel sat at a large table and ate pasta. Monsignor Laboa said that the conversation was strained because no one wanted to discuss the circumstances of Noriega's presence. After dinner, they all attended Mass in the embassy's chapel, with Noriega sitting in the last pew by himself.

During the four days that the U.S. Psyops team pummeled the nunciatore with loud rock music, Noriega, an opera lover, could hear the blasting music that pounded his ears. And he also heard news over the loudspeakers—that his top aides were surrendering to the U.S. forces and that his millions of dollars in foreign banks were being frozen. For a time he had access to a phone, but it was pulled to prevent his manipulation of his fortune. The last day of his stay in the nunciatore was perhaps his worst: Twenty thousand people filled the streets shouting "Assassin!," "No More!," and "Out of the nunciatore!" Panamanians hung him in effigy. The figure was in full military uniform, and the face was a pineapple—reminiscent of Noriega's pockmarked face. Often during his ten-day stay, to show their contempt and hatred for the man, Panamanians smashed pineapples to pulp in the streets. In a poll taken during the first week of January 1990 by CBS News and a Washington research firm, 92 percent of Panamanians interviewed approved of the "invasion."

One of Noriega's last conversations before his surrender was with Vicky Amado. General Thurman's office had tried to get her to convince Noriega to come out. But she didn't. During that ten-minute conversation, she told him, in effect, "The decision is in your hands."

Monsignor Laboa's last words to Noriega were, "You have to decide." Noriega, increasingly withdrawn and silent, finally said, "That solution of yours is best."

Before Noriega walked out of the nunciatore, he had made three requests of the United States: that he be allowed to make a few phone calls, that his decision to leave be kept secret until the actual time of his arrest, and that he be permitted to wear his uniform. The administration had earlier given assurances to Noriega that he would receive a fair trial and that he would not be tried on a federal drug kingpin statute that carries the death penalty. Because the administration did not deal directly with Noriega, all communications were through the Vatican nuncio. Because Noriega did not have a uniform with him, General Thurman's headquarters delivered one to the embassy.

At 2044 on the evening of 3 January 1990, General Noriega, accompanied by Father Villanueva, walked the twenty yards from the Vatican embassy front door to Avenida Balboa and surrendered to Delta Force troops outside the embassy gate. He was escorted across the street to the elementary school that the U.S. Special Operations troopers used as a headquarters. Noriega carried a Bible and a toothbrush. One senior U.S. official on hand said that Noriega "really looked like a whipped and beaten little man." Noriega was immediately handcuffed. "I will pray for you every day," said Father Villanueva, the parish priest who had been helpful in getting Noriega to give himself up. *"Gracias,"* said a visibly shaken, fully uniformed Noriega.

General Thurman said later that U.S. officials had only a few minutes' warning that Noriega would leave the embassy. He said that Gen. Henry Cisneros received a telephone call at his CP across the street asking him to "report to the gate." No Panamanian officials were present, but the Endara government was aware of what was going on.[9]

Noriega was escorted to a UH-60 Black Hawk helicopter waiting on the soccer field behind the school building and flown to Howard Air Force Base, where the helicopter landed on the tarmac in front of the small field medical hospital set up there. Noriega was escorted from the helicopter to a waiting MC-130 Talon aircraft, engines running, and was turned over to the DEA agents and U.S. marshals waiting aboard. It was 2131, just forty-one minutes from the time he had left the nunciatore. He was on his way to the U.S. District Court in Miami on federal drug trafficking charges.

Once inside the plane, the agent in chief told him to undress completely. At the time, he was wearing a dress uniform without hat. Underneath, he wore a white T-shirt and two pairs of underwear—one set of white boxer shorts over a set of bright red Jockey undershorts. Two Special Operations physicians then gave him a complete physical examination, asked him for pertinent medical history, and found that he had no physical complaints besides being tired and thirsty.

After the physical, the agents gave him brown Army boxer shorts, a brown T-shirt, a green Army aviator coverall-type flight suit, Army green socks, and hospital patient slippers. After he dressed in that outfit, he was handcuffed and manacled by U.S. marshals, and seated and strapped into the nylon jump seats set up in the forward part of the aircraft just behind the radio and navigational consoles. DEA agents photographed him and asked him a number of questions after formally placing him under arrest and reading him his Miranda rights—in Spanish. One special operations physician stayed aboard for the 5½-hour flight to Florida.

During the flight, Noriega appeared anxious and very tired; the only time he smiled was when a DEA agent told him that the physician stayed aboard to take care of him on the flight. He slept for nearly four hours sitting upright after agents gave him more water and told him what to expect on landing in Florida.

An hour before touchdown, Noriega asked permission to get dressed again in his military uniform. The U.S. marshals found the uniform in the luggage but discovered that they did not have a key to open the handcuffs. They finally broke the chain connecting the two cuffs. Noriega dressed in his uniform. The marshals again manacled him and put him into another set of handcuffs (with the separated cuffs from the first set still on his wrists). Once again he sat down, and the marshals strapped him to the seat. After the plane landed at Homestead Air Force Base in southern Florida, DEA and other U.S. officials interviewed him in the back of the plane. Then he was led to one of a caravan of black limousines that took him to a nearby taxiway, where a small government Learjet was waiting to fly him to Miami International Airport. From there he was transported to the jail in downtown Miami.[10]

As word of Noriega's departure from the nunciatore and his surrender to the U.S. officials spread across Panama City, horns honked; fireworks shot into the black sky; and people laughed, yelled, and raced up and down the streets, waving U.S. and Panamanian flags. Hundreds of cars jammed Fiftieth Street, near the center of what had been a thriving international financial center.

Max Thurman had accomplished the last of his missions.

24 | The New Military

The post-Vietnam doldrums were over. The military forces of the United States—all volunteers—had proved, in combat, that they were highly trained, superbly equipped with the latest and best arms and equipment available to any nation's military, that they were disciplined and dedicated professionals who knew their business—the business of war.

Gen. Edward Meyer, Army Chief of Staff from 1979 to 1983, said that Operation Just Cause "was probably the best-conceived military operation since World War II." A senior Pentagon officer said that "the Panama invasion was a test of manhood."

Dan Rather, in a CBS Radio news analysis and commentary on 28 December 1989, said,

> The men and women of the United States armed forces have done a superb job. They have performed efficiently and professionally. . . . The men and women of the armed forces of the United States were given a mission by their commander in chief. They had their orders. They were given a job to do, and they did it well. In the words of Tennyson's poetry, "Theirs was not to reason why, theirs was but to do or die." They did and some of them died.
>
> It is easy to blow bugles, have the band play marches and wave flags. It is hard to storm the beaches, hit the silk, and blow the barracks. Very hard and very dangerous.
>
> Before the smoke clears in Panama, before the politicians and the propagandists complete weaving their self-serving spells, it would be well for the rest of us to note and ponder the brave, efficient, professional service our citizen-warriors have given our country in the streets and jungles of Panama.[1]

Will and Ariel Durant have written that "War is a constant of history. In the last 3,451 years of recorded history, only 268 years have seen no war." In the

215 years of its history, the United States has been involved in 11 major wars and over 171 battles. The U.S. armed forces have lost over 650,000 men and women in battle and have had nearly 2½ million wounded. Since World War II, worldwide, there have been almost 400 revolts, coups, and small wars, and 69 major wars, including Afghanistan, Iran-Iraq, the Falklands, the Yom Kippur War, and the Vietnamese invasion of Kampuchea.

Since World War II, the United States has been involved in six major engagements, including Korea, Vietnam, Panama, and the Gulf War, and has resorted to the use of or the threat of the use of force for political effect some 219 times. These include the air attack on Libya, the stationing of forces in the Sinai, the *Mayaguez* affair, and the dispatch of Marines to Lebanon.

The road back from the victories of World War II has been long, difficult, and circuitous. The Korean War started with a weak, undisciplined Army used to the easy life of occupation duty. By the end of the Korean stalemate, the Army had regained some stamina, discipline, and esprit. But the politically designed end of the war—an armistice—left the Army with a feeling of frustration and skeptical of the worth of its sacrifices and losses.

Vietnam started out with a will and a determination—"Ask not what the country can do for you" enthusiasm. It ended with another political solution and a military establishment shot through with defeatism, marginal discipline, an "anything goes" philosophy, and barely functioning as a fighting machine.

On 20 November 1970, a group of Green Berets led by the stalwart and battle-experienced Col. "Bull" Simons raided the Son Tay Vietnamese camp allegedly holding American prisoners of war. The raid was carried out with surprise, skill, and courage by a singularly well-trained, disciplined, well-led group of volunteers. Unfortunately, the North Vietnamese had moved the U.S. POWs, and the raiders found the Son Tay camp empty.[2]

In April 1980, the United States launched an airborne raid to rescue the U.S. embassy personnel held hostage by Iran. On the night of 24 April, the plan began to disintegrate in Desert One—a blinding dust storm made helicopter navigation difficult, the Marine helicopters arrived late, a fiery accident in the desert cost eight American lives, and eventually there were not enough helicopters to complete the mission successfully. Col. Charlie Beckwith decided then and there to abandon the rescue attempt.

In 1983, commanders in Lebanon failed to build a barricade that could have prevented just one explosive-laden truck from crashing into a Marine barracks and snuffing out the lives of 241 Marines. As a result, the United States was forced to pull out.

In 1983, the United States invaded Grenada, an ultimately successful operation against a motley crew of 680 Cuban construction workers, of whom only 50 or so were soldiers. But the operation was fraught with difficulties—19 Americans died and 152 were wounded, communications between services did not work, and the command structure was multiheaded and ill-defined. In addition, the tactical plan was fraught with difficulties—no surprise, piecemeal commitment of forces, little maneuverability, no unity of command.

The Grenada strike was thrown together rapidly just a couple of days before the assault. Vice Adm. (Ret.) Joseph Metcalf III, who commanded the Grenada task force, said: "In Panama they had a lot of time to prepare, and they did a hell of a job; they were able to tailor things a lot better."[3]

Operation Just Cause in Panama was different. The work, the training, the revitalization of the U.S. armed forces during the eighties was evident. TV shots of the troops in action in Panama showed soldiers properly clad in their uniforms, wearing helmets, and handling their weapons expertly. But that was only part of the metamorphosis of the post-Vietnamese U.S. military establishment. The men and women who fought in Panama were all volunteers. Almost all of them had at least a high school education. Recruiters could be "choosy" about whom they would select for enlistment. The military's leaders had reinstated discipline in the ranks. NCOs and officers were well trained in their specialties. Training was not a hit-or-miss proposition. The National Training Centers at Fort Irwin, California, and Fort Chaffee, Arkansas, forged men into units who knew how to fight the AirLand battle specified in *FM 25-100*.

Just Cause was one of the largest and most sophisticated joint airborne and ground contingency operations in modern history. (The 1982 British invasion of the Falklands is by far the longest. It was, for the most part, a British Navy, Marines, and Army operation.) Just Cause represented integrated planning and execution among joint forces—Army, Navy, Marines, Air Force. It demonstrated that the mixing of special forces and conventional forces was not only possible but also enhanced the success of the operation. It showed the practicability of the use of joint communications-electronics operating instructions. It validated the necessity for small-unit drills and training in urban terrain. It proved that troops fight to the standards to which they are trained. It showed that night operations have a great advantage, and that night-vision devices are essential for night air assaults. It proved that live fire exercises are imperative for soldier confidence, fire control, and fire distribution. It certified the worth of the AH-64 Apache on night operations and the Hellfire missile as a "surgical weapon." It proved the value of using Psyops and electronic warfare and the necessity of training Psyops troopers with conventional forces. And it proved that U.S. military planners could tailor and package a force of paratroopers, special forces, light infantry, mechanized infantry, marines, sailors, airmen, psyops units, military police, and civil affairs units to the task immediately at hand. It proved that obedience to the oft-repeated but oft-ignored principles of war—surprise, mass, objective, unity of command, maneuver, offensive, and economy of force—paves the way for success in battle.

The commander in chief of the U.S. armed forces, the president of the United States, gave his military forces a job to do and then let them do it without second-guessing or "tying one hand behind their backs." President Bush did not pore over maps and select targets for air strikes the way President Johnson did during the Vietnam War. President Bush was not in direct communication with the commander in the field to give suggestions or orders, as President Carter allegedly was. And the Pentagon let the field commanders fight the battles. General Powell was upset, for example, that the forces in the field could not find Noriega immediately after H-hour. But he let the plan unfold and permitted Max Thurman to "run the show." General Stiner had full command in the field. Every "trooper who carried a gun" was under his command. He was the sole commander, even though the commanding general of Fleet Marine Forces, Atlantic, did want General Stiner to use more Marines and to set up a separate Marine headquarters for the operation.

A spokesman for SOUTHCOM said,

> Operation Just Cause was the largest use of strategic air assets to introduce tactical forces directly into combat in the history of the U.S. military. In the initial operations, it delivered the equivalent of a division minus onto tactical drop zones and had delivered an entire division within the first thirty-six hours. Strength figures peaked out at just over twenty-seven thousand soldiers, sailors, airmen, and marines. Enemy personnel losses are difficult to categorize due to the use of the paramilitary Dignity Battalions and the proclivity of many of the uniformed PDF to become nonuniformed as soon as possible after hostilities initiated.[4]

The operation was not without its costs. Twenty-three U.S. servicemen were killed and 324 wounded. The reported enemy losses were 314 killed in action and 124 wounded. The estimated civilian casualties were 202 killed and 1,508 wounded. The exact figures will never be known.[5]

General Thurman went to extraordinary measures to determine the number and type of civilian casualties. For a month after the surrender of Noriega, General Thurman's teams of experts went to morgues, hospitals, churches, schools, and even cemeteries to try to track accurately the civilian casualties. His teams worked closely with the Panamanian Red Cross. The Panamanians also did substantial research on casualties and actually came up with figures less than Thurman's teams. General Thurman assigned his civil affairs/military government units to assist the government of Panama "in any way possible."[6]

There were, of course, difficulties. General Stiner alleged at a Washington meeting with defense writers on 26 February 1990 that, while he had "no direct knowledge" but "had heard" of them, he cited three "possibilities" that the operation had been compromised. One was that "A call went from someone in the State Department to a friend of his who was a member of the Panama Canal Commission that said, 'Tonight is the night. One o'clock in the morning is the time.' This individual (in Panama) began to call around to his buddies . . . and word spread.

"The second thing that I heard, and this is being looked at at the National Security Agency level, was that there was a burst broadcast [a message sent out in less than a second and decoded at the other end] that went out of Cuba to the south toward Nicaragua and Panama. I don't know what that said, and I don't know if anybody knows what that said, but I heard it.

"There was speculation (about the U.S. military action) on the evening news at 2200 that night (19 December) . . . that the 82d Airborne had left Fort Bragg and it is expected that they headed to Panama."

A few days later, chief Pentagon spokesman Pete Williams released a statement saying General Stiner was wrong in just about everything he said to reporters about how leaks had "compromised" the operation.

The Army's commanders in the field also recognized some faults. They saw the need for better equipment to prevent fratricide—"antifratricide equipment," they call it. At Río Hato, for example, during the hours of darkness, a "Little Bird," a Hughes 500 helicopter, fired on a squad of men moving forward along the ground in the same area where it was strafing. Two men were killed. In another case, the Specter firing near the Comandancia on D-day wounded a number of men assaulting the building.

There were some difficulties on the ground in Panama during the operation. For example, a number of paratroopers and some of the 82d's heavy-drop equipment missed their designated DZs. And, of course, the miserable weather at Pope Air Force Base postponed the arrival of the 82d's paratroopers at the scheduled time, causing a delay in the start of their ongoing missions.

Civilians were killed and civilian areas damaged. But the media seem to have exaggerated the extent of the deaths and the damage. CBS's *60 Minutes* in the summer of 1990 quoted sources that as many as four thousand civilians may have been killed. Sgt. Lewis A. Matson, who was present in the area after the cessation of hostilities and who took many photos for the Department of the Army, wrote that CBS's claim "is ridiculous. American soldiers would have been involved in the burial of these bodies or the elimination of these bodies. American soldiers have been unable to hide such facts."

Sergeant Matson also wrote, "As the fight for the Comandancia began, PDF soldiers took refuge in El Chorillo, the dense neighborhood of makeshift housing, cardboard boxes, all around several high-rise buildings adjacent to the Comandancia. Vulnerable from all sides, American soldiers fired back when fired upon, and while capturing the Comandancia, the neighborhood was set on fire. By whom? There's no saying. It could have been the PDF themselves. So the fight to take the Comandancia resulted in the destruction of one neighborhood, and at that the high-rises are still standing. . . . But that's it—no other large-scale destruction took place in Panama during the invasion. . . . Any destruction downtown was brought on by the Panamanians themselves. Americans didn't loot Panama City—the Panamanians did."

I. Roberto Eisenmann, Jr., is the crusading publisher of *La Prensa,* a Panamanian newspaper that in February 1988 was forced to shut down when some of Noriega's "thugs" wrecked its offices. He is now back on the job running the paper. In an interview published in the April 1990 issue of *American Legion Magazine,* he was asked about the charge that U.S. troops caused extensive damage and destroyed entire civilian neighborhoods, especially in the Chorillo district of Panama City.

"In Chorillo," he said, "where most of the damage occurred, there was extensive testimony from eyewitnesses indicating that most of the destruction was because of fires set by Noriega troops. Many 'Dignity Battalion' members were seen throwing gasoline on buildings and then firing grenades in the area."

To underscore the fact that the Panamanians did in fact do some destruction themselves, no one less than President Endara himself took a sledgehammer to the wall of the Comandancia on Thursday, 11 January 1990. The Panamanians who were watching President Endara grit his teeth and swing the sledgehammer shouted "Harder! Harder!" Vice President Ricardo Arias Calderon, who accompanied Endara to the symbolic destruction of Noriega's old headquarters, said, "The demolition indicates in concrete terms to our people that Noriega's regime is over." Endara said, "For us, it is the end of an era of militarism."

The Comandancia, a bullet-scarred, four-story building, was razed and replaced by housing for families who were left homeless by Just Cause, government officials said.

"The invasion forces targeted with unprecedented accuracy the PDF and their locations," continued Sergeant Matson. "On the night of 19 December, the DNI . . . located in a heavily populated residential area of Balboa about a mile north of the Comandancia was targeted by Air Force gunships. The internal walls of the DNI were completely destroyed; however, the external walls were left standing as were the palm trees on the front lawn. Across the street from the DNI is a three-story 'Young Men's Christian Association' building. The YMCA received not a single piece of shrapnel."[7]

Some armchair tacticians, with twenty-twenty hindsight and little knowledge of military tactics or capabilities, questioned the advisability of dropping, instead of airlanding, the 82d's paratroopers on airfields that the Rangers had already secured. But to the commander of the 82d, Maj. Gen. James Johnson, there was no question about his method for introducing the 82d into Panama. "Given the choice, I can tell you on my watch we will always airdrop," he said when questioned about the drop versus airland issue. As far as he knew when he left Fort Bragg, the airfield was probably "hot," and it was not until about 0530 on 20 December that the Rangers told him the field was secure. And, he added, "It's usually faster and safer—given the possibility that the enemy can launch a surprise attack on taxiing planes—to parachute."[8]

As the division chief of staff, Col. G. A. Crocker, said after the operation, "The 82d Airborne Division combat parachute assault into Torrijos was a large success. The assault rapidly introduced a fully capable combined arms brigade task force into a combat environment with accuracy and minimum injuries. The operation validated joint Army/Air Force doctrine and training."

By and large it was a winner, an operation executed as planned with vigor, daring, and success. The Vietnam doldrums were over. The president of the United States could order his military forces into combat and within fifty-three hours the lead elements of the attacking force would be in action. Execution of contingency plans was not only a possibility but also, proven in Panama, a certainty. The next display of U.S. armed might, about a year later, would be a roaring, TV-centered, hero-worshiping, chest-thumping, flag-waving, parade-making, military success. Desert camouflage fatigues became a fashion.

The Gulf War was yet to come, however, when 1,924 XVIII Airborne Corps and 82d Airborne Division paratroopers, led by General Stiner and General Johnson, parachuted back onto Sicily DZ at Fort Bragg at 0800 on 12 January 1990 on their return from Panama. They dropped from eight hundred feet from twenty C-141 Starlifters. Gen. Carl E. Vuono, the Army chief of staff and a former member of the 82d himself, was on the DZ to greet the troopers, who formed into five columns and marched toward the stands where over five thousand families, soldiers, and friends awaited them. The jump was symbolic and represented the other men and women who had made the Panama operation such a success. General Vuono congratulated the soldiers on their "unqualified success." For the 82d soldiers, the battle was over. But for many of the troops still in Panama, there was the problem of nation-building still to be done. As General Stiner told the troops in formation on Sicily Drop Zone just after the drop, "The mission in Panama was a difficult one. We were literally to decapitate a government and then shake hands with the same people who we fought the night before and say, 'We want to help you now.'"

General Stiner had full praise for his troops. "You would have been very proud of your soldiers," he told the assembled crowd on the edge of the DZ. "They're dedicated and motivated by all the things the American flag stands for, the very flags you were waving. Everyone knew there would be danger, but not a single one hesitated to go or enter battle time and time again. They were well trained for the mission, and they fought the way they trained."[9]

The Panama operation proved that the military forces of the United States had turned a corner. The military technology developments and the buildup of the volunteer forces in the eighties, the dedication of the leaders from corporal to chairman of the Joint Chiefs of Staff, and the resurgence of the U.S. military were now realities. Resort to war is a difficult decision for a president to make. And as any combat-tested soldier knows and believes, the resort to war should be the last and only solution to the salvation or the protection of the nation's interests. "War is still hell," and no one knows that better than a soldier who has fought in one.

One can debate the wisdom of Just Cause as a solution to the problems of the United States with Noriega. One cannot debate that when the military forces of the United States were given a mission, they accomplished it with new fervor, dedication, self-confidence, and professionalism. Today's U.S. military forces are without doubt the best the country has ever built.

The U.S. military was now a force capable of carrying out the will of the commander in chief. Just Cause proved it; Desert Shield and Desert Storm would further validate it.

Notes

1. Noriega's Rise to Power

1. John Dinges, *Our Man in Panama* (New York: Random House, 1990), p. 31. Dinges's book covers the career of Noriega in detail.
2. *Current Biography Yearbook 1988,* pp. 428–31, contains a concise biographical sketch of Noriega, including his relationship with Torrijos.
3. Frederick Kempe, *Divorcing the Dictator* (New York: G. P. Putnam's Sons, 1990). Extracts of this book appeared in "The Noriega Files," *Newsweek* (15 January 1990). The book covers minor parts of Noriega's career in enough detail to paint an accurate portrait of Noriega and his "peculiar" personality.
4. *Current Biography Yearbook 1988,* pp. 428–31.
5. *Facts On File* contains a number of references to Noriega's drug deals.
6. *Current Biography Yearbook 1988,* pp. 428–31.
7. Ibid.
8. Sally Quinn, interview of Noriega published in *Washington Post* (8 March 1978).
9. Kempe, *Divorcing the Dictator.*
10. Dinges, *Our Man in Panama,* p. 118.
11. Oliver L. North, *Under Fire: An American Story* (New York: HarperCollins 1991), p. 226.
12. Kempe, *Divorcing the Dictator.* As quoted in *Newsweek,* "The Noriega Files," Jan. 15, 1990, pp. 23–24.
13. *New York Times* (12 June 1986).
14. Spadafora's career and assassination are covered in some detail in Dinges's *Our Man in Panama.* They are also covered in Georges Fauriol, *Security in the Americas,* pp. 223–24.
15. *Current Biography Yearbook 1988,* p. 430.
16. *New York Times* interview with José I. Blandon (26 November 1988).
17. *Insight* (8 January 1990), p. 27.
18. U.S. Southern Command briefing.

2. 1989: The Climactic Year

1. *Facts On File* (12 May 1989) covers the 7 May elections and the irregularities and fraud underscored by President Bush, who called on Noriega to resign. Former President Carter later told reporters that he did not advise any hasty moves by the United States such as abrogating the Panama Canal treaties, or taking military action.

2. *Insight* (8 January 1990), photo on p. 27.
3. *Facts On File* (12 May 1989).
4. *Insight,* p. 28.
5. U.S. Southern Command briefing.
6. Lt. Col. Dave Huntoon reviewed and amended this paragraph.
7. U.S. Southern Command briefing.
8. *Facts On File* (12 May 1989).
9. Col. C. E. Richardson, the commander of the Marines in Panama at the time of Just Cause, sent me six letters covering the part played by the Marines before and during the operation.
10. *Facts On File* (8 September 1989), pp. 650–51.
11. *Time* (27 February 1989), p. 45.

3. A Tightening Noose

1. *Army Times* (6 August 1990) ran a cover story by Margaret Roth and an editorial on General Maxwell Thurman. Both pieces summed up the career of a dedicated, unusually hardworking, self-disciplined Army officer and his modus operandi. I know both Generals Thurman and can vouch, in general, for the authenticity of the cover story. Newsweek (16 July 1990) also ran a piece on the career and personality of Gen. Maxwell Thurman. Bob Woodward also discusses General Thurman in *The Commanders* (New York: Simon & Schuster, 1991).
2. Personal knowledge.
3. *Army Times* (6 August 1990).
4. *Register of Graduates,* USMA, 1991, p. 479. The *Register* contains biographical data on all West Point graduates.
5. *Facts On File* (6 October 1989), p. 734.
6. USSOCOM briefing. Dinges also covers the coup in *Our Man in Panama,* pp. 304–5.
7. *Facts On File* (6 October 1989) covers the failed coup in some detail.
8. Woodward explains Thurman's reaction to the Giroldi coup attempt.
9. Woodward, *The Commanders,* pp. 121–22.
10. *U.S. News & World Report* (30 July 1990).
11. *Facts On File* (6 October 1989), p. 734.
12. USSOCOM briefing.

4. The Planning Phase

1. Interviews with Maj. Gen. (then Brig. Gen.) Ed Scholes, XVIII Airborne Corps chief of staff on Operation Just Cause.
2. Interview with Brig. Gen. (then Col.) Thomas Needham, XVIII Airborne Corps G-3 on Operation Just Cause.
3. Interview with Lt. Col. (then Maj.) Dave Huntoon.
4. USSOCOM briefing.
5. Personal knowledge and General Stiner's biographical sketch.
6. Oliver L. North, *Under Fire: An American Story* (New York: HarperCollins 1991), p. 211.
7. JTF SOUTH command briefing.
8. Discussions with Col. (then Lt. Col.) Dan K. McNeill, then the G-3 of the 82d Airborne Division.
9. When Lt. Col. Dave Huntoon reviewed this section, he included this paragraph.
10. Report of General Stiner's preparations and movements have been verified by XVIII Airborne Corps staff officers.
11. *Facts On File* (22 December 1989), p. 941.
12. Woodward, *The Commanders,* pp. 158–59.
13. *Facts On File* (22 December 1989), p. 942.
14. Frederick Kempe, "The Noriega Files," *Newsweek* (15 January 1990).
15. Joint Chiefs of Staff briefing following Just Cause.

234

16. Joint Chiefs of Staff briefing notes.
17. USSOCOM briefing.
18. Kempe, "The Noriega Files."
19. Douglas Waller, writing in *Newsweek* (17 June 1989).
20. Lt. Col. Huntoon reviewed this entire section and added a number of comments.
21. XVIII Airborne Corps briefing notes.
22. USSOCOM briefing.
23. Lt. Col. Huntoon reviewed this entire section and added a number of comments.

5. The Decision

1. Bob Woodward, *The Commanders* (New York: Simon & Schuster, 1991), p. 85.
2. USSOCOM briefing.
3. Lt. Gen. Tom Kelly, Joint Chiefs of Staff chief of operations, furnished the chronology to the author.
4. This meeting is covered in some detail by Woodward in *The Commanders,* pp. 162–67.
5. Woodward relates in *The Commanders,* p. 173, that "Blue Spoon" became "Just Cause" during a telephone conversation between General Lindsay, the cigar-chomping, marathon-running, down-to-earth commander in chief of Special Operations Command, and General Kelly. After Jim Lindsay knew that "Blue Spoon" had been approved for implementation, he called Kelly on Sunday afternoon and said that "Blue Spoon" was a terrible name for the operation they were about to launch. "Do you want your grandchildren to say you were in some war called 'Blue Spoon'? he asked the ex-tanker Tom Kelly. Apparently not, because Kelly took immediate steps to change the name. He asked his deputy for current operations, Joe Lopez, "How about calling it 'Just Action'?" Lopez said, "How about 'Just Cause'?" Kelly thought that was a much better idea and then took whatever steps were necessary to get the name changed.
6. Lt. Gen. Tom Kelly and one of his officers, Maj. Raymond Melnyk, reviewed and amended this entire chapter and made necessary corrections.

6. Alerts

1. Lt. Gen. (then Maj. Gen.) Wayne Downing reviewed this entire section and made a number of comments and additions.
2. Letter from Lieutenant Colonel Maestas, undated.
3. Letter from Sergeant Spano, undated.
4. Letter from Private First Class Bunch, undated.
5. Discussions with Major General Scholes at Fort Bragg.
6. Lt. Col. Dave Huntoon and other members of the XVIII Airborne Corps staff have reviewed and commented on this section.
7. Discussions with 82d Airborne Division staff officers at Fort Bragg.
8. Lt. Col. Gerald L. (Jay) Behnke escorted the author through the PHA and explained the functions of the various buildings and elements of the PHA.
9. 82d Airborne Division briefing notes.
10. Letter from Maj. Steven Hill, chief of public affairs, 7th Infantry Division (Light) (6 September 1990).
11. *Salinas Californian* (20 December 1989).
12. *San Francisco Examiner* (21 December 1989).
13. Discussions with Maj. Gen. Ed Scholes at Fort Bragg.

7. Initial Deployments

1. U.S. Southern Command briefing.
2. Interview with General Downing; he also reviewed this section of the book and made some changes and additions.
3. Letter and comments from Colonel Snell detailing the part played by Task Force Bayonet.

4. Letter from Colonel Richardson.
5. Article in *Marine Corps Gazette* (September 1990) by Capt. Stephen J. Linder.
6. Article in *Marine Corps Gazette* (September 1990) by Capt. G. H. Gaskins and 1st Lt. Brian C. Colebaugh.
7. Article in *Marine Corps Gazette* (September 1990) by Lt. Kenneth M. DeTreux.
8. Letter from Colonel Richardson including his Just Cause narrative.
9. General Downing reviewed and commented on this section dealing with the initial deployments.

8. The Attacks Begin

1. Letter from Maj. Kevin M. Higgins. He reviewed the Pacora River Bridge section of the book and inserted some eighteen comments, corrections, and explanations.
2. Interview with Capt. Stuart Bradin in Beaufort, South Carolina. He provided most of the details of the operation later verified by Major Higgins.
3. U.S. Special Operations Command briefing.
4. Ibid.

9. Task Force White

1. Joint Special Operations Command briefing
2. *The Warriors: Operation Just Cause,* published by U.S. Southern Command, a series of articles about various elements of the forces engaged in Just Cause. One article, "TV Whiskey, Balboa Harbor PDF Patrol Boat Operation," covers this section of the book.
3. *Time* (1 January 1990).

10. The Rescue of Kurt Muse

1. XVIII Airborne Corps staff officers have reviewed this section and made some changes and additions. I also had some knowledge of the Son Tay raid because the men on that operation were all selected by Colonel Simon from my command—the Special Warfare Center at Fort Bragg.
2. Bob Woodward, *The Commanders* (New York: Simon & Schuster, 1991), p. 183.
3. The rescue of Kurt Muse, as described in this book, is based, with permission, in large part on a magazine article, "Danger in the Air," by Neil C. Livingstone and published in the *Washingtonian* issue of June 1990. The quotations are from that article, which is copyrighted by the *Washingtonian*. The entire section on the rescue of Kurt Muse was reviewed by officers in the Special Operations Command at Fort Bragg.

11. The Comandancia

1. Colonel Snell's summary of Operation Just Cause.
2. Letter dated 12 February 1991 and summary of Operation Just Cause from Lt. Col. James W. Reed Commanding Officer of the 4th Battalion (Mechanized), 6th Infantry, 5th Infantry Division, Fort Polk, La.
3. *The Guardian,* Fort Polk, La. (5 January 1990), p. 2.
4. Colonel Reed's letter of 12 February 1991 gives a complete description of his battalion's operations.
5. David Harris, Reuters Information Services.
6. Recommendation for posthumous award of Silver Star for E-4 Ivan D. Perez from his commander, Colonel Reed, 4th Battalion, 6th Infantry, dated 20 January 1990; also letter from Colonel Reed dated 12 February 1991.
7. *The Guardian,* Fort Polk, La. (5 January 1990), p. 10.
8. Recommendation for award of the Silver Star from Colonel Reed, Commanding Officer, 4th Battalion, 6th Infantry, and his 12 February 1991 letter.
9. "A Night at the Comandancia," pp. 18–19 of DA pamphlet, Command Information publication, *Soldiers in Panama.*

10. Colonel Reed's letter of 12 February 1991 and summary.
11. Interview with General Downing.
12. Colonel Reed's letter of 12 February 1991 and summary.
13. Letter and comments on the Comandancia final "takedown" from Maj. (then Capt.) Albert E. Dochnal.

12. Fort Amador and Balboa

1. Personal knowledge gained after almost thirty-six years of continuous active duty.
2. An article in DA pamphlet *Soldiers in Panama* titled "The Fight for Fort Amador," pp. 12–13.
3. Letter from Colonel Snell.
4. Article in *The Warriors*, USSOUTHCOM publication, "Reduction of PDF 5th Rifle Company."
5. Tab P of note 7 following.
6. Memo from Lt. Col. Bob Fitzgerald to Lt. Col. Dave Huntoon commenting on this chapter of the book and adding and correcting details.
7. Lt. Col. Bob Fitzgerald's after-action report is very detailed. Each of his company commander's reports is included. At Tabs A through S are missions, commander's intent, concept of the operation, chronologies, maps, organization charts, company rosters, and other reports. It is the most complete battalion after-action report on Just Cause that I have seen.
8. Letter from Lt. (now Capt.) Lisa M. Kutschera (23 May 1991).
9. U.S. Southern Command briefing.
10. *Soldiers* (the official U.S. Army magazine) (February 1990), pp. 38–39; "Operation Just Cause" by Donna Miles.
11. After-action reports by company commanders in the 5th Battalion, 87th Infantry.

13. Task Force Atlantic

1. U.S. Southern Command briefing.
2. Just Cause command briefing and after-action report and journals from the 82d Airborne Division and 7th Infantry Division (L) cover the general outline of this chapter.
3. Article in *Fort Ord Panorama: Operation Just Cause Perspective,* "4/17 Completes Five-Part Mission," by Bob Britton.
4. Article in DA pamphlet *Soldiers in Panama,* "Conquest at Coco Solo," pp. 25–27.
5. "4/17 Completes Five-Part Mission."

14. Madden Dam, Cerro Tigre, and Renacer Prison

1. Article in DA pamphlet *Soldiers in Panama,* "Raid at Renacer Prison."
2. *Fayetteville Observer* (3 January 1990), p. 44; article by Rich Browne.
3. *The Warriors,* "The Action at Renacer Prison," Tab A.

15. The Jump on Río Hato

1. Letter from Colonel Kernan (23 August 1990).
2. Letter from Lieutenant McCown (11 January 1990).
3. Memo from Pfc. Richard Fox (undated).
4. Memo from Spc. Steve Stadelman (undated).
5. 75th Ranger SOP.
6. Letter from Colonel Kernan (31 October 1990).
7. Letter from unidentified 75th Ranger.
8. 75th Ranger briefing notes.
9. Letter from Lt. Tim Nye (undated).
10. Letter from Pfc. Leon Erickson (undated).
11. Letter from Capt. John A. Davis (undated).

12. Letter from Lieutenant Dichairo (undated).
13. Letter from Maj. Clyde M. Newman (undated).
14. Letter from Lt. Jeffrey A. Bouais (undated).
15. Letter from Capt. William A. Doukas (undated).
16. U.S. Southern Command, briefing.
17. 75th Ranger command briefing.
18. Interview with General Downing at Fort Bragg.
19. Letter from Twenty-first Air Force historian, Clayton H. Snedeker (5 July 1990).
20. *Aviation Week & Space Technology* (1 January 1990); article by John D. Morrocco.
21. Letter from Capt. Philip D. Colahan (undated).
22. 75th Ranger command briefing.
23. Discussion with Colonel Kernan.
24. Interview with General Downing.
25. Letter from S. Sgt. Richard J. Hoerner (undated).
26. Letter from Specialist Kristops (undated).
27. Letter from Staff Sergeant Brackenbury (undated).
28. Letter from Capt. Steven G. Fogarty (undated).

16. Río Hato Takedown

1. Letter from 1st Sgt. Joseph L. Mattison (undated).
2. Letter from Capt. Jonathan L. Beegle (undated).
3. Interview with Capt. Raymond A. Thomas at Fort Bragg. At that time he was the aide de camp to General Downing.
4. Letter from Capt. David B. Haight (undated).
5. Letter from an unidentified soldier in the 75th Rangers.
6. Letter from Sgt. Greene (undated).
7. Letter from Spc. Michael A. Sonnenschein (undated).
8. Letter from Sgt. David R. Clifton (undated).
9. Letter from Lt. Brian M. Drinkwine (undated).
10. Letter from Capt. Mike Newcomb (undated).
11. 75th Ranger staff memo, "Summary of Ground Action at Río Hato—20–24 December 1990."

17. The Airport

1. 75th Ranger command briefing notes.
2. 75th Ranger memo, "Summary of Ground Action at Torrijos-Tocumen."
3. Ibid.
4. Ibid.
5. Ibid.
6. Interview with Col. Dan K. McNeill, 82d Airborne Division G-3, on Just Cause.
7. Capt. (now Maj.) Albert E. Dochnal reviewed this entire chapter and added his comments and corrections.
8. Interview with General Downing.
9. 75th Ranger after-action report.
10. 75th Ranger journal.

18. Task Force Pacific

1. Memo from chief of staff, 82d Airborne Division, to chief of staff, XVIII Airborne Corps.
2. Interview with Capt. Gary J. Ramsdell.
3. 82d Airborne Division historical summary.
4. Interview with and letter from Captain Ramsdell.
5. Chronology from the S-3 of the 2d Battalion, 504th Infantry.
6. Lt. Col. Harry Axson and his staff reviewed this entire chapter and added parts in which he

was personally involved. On 7 February 1992 he wrote, "This is the rewritten copy. My S-3 (Maj. Jon Chase) and I were able to reconstruct some more facts and details."

7. Interview with Captain Ramsdell.
8. Colonel Axson et al. review and additions.
9. Interview with Captain Ramsdell.
10. 82d Airborne Division historical summary.
11. Interview with Captain Ramsdell.
12. Letter from Capt. Steve Phelps.
13. 82d Airborne Division historical summary.
14. Joint "MAC/Army Hotwash," review of Operation Just Cause.
15. Colonel Axson et al. review and additions.
16. Letter from Captain Phelps.
17. Memo from chief of staff, 82d Airborne Division, to chief of staff, XVIII Airborne Corps.
18. 82d Airborne Division after-action summary.
19. Input from Colonel Axson and his staff, who reviewed and commented on this entire chapter.
20. *The Warriors,* "Days of Stars—Bronze, That Is."
21. Letter from Capt. (then 1st Lt.) Lisa M. Kutschera (23 May 1991).
22. Input from Colonel Axson et al.
23. Interview with Captain Ramsdell.
24. "Days of Stars."
25. Ibid.
26. Ibid.
27. Interview with Captain Ramsdell.
28. Input from Colonel Axson et al.
29. Ibid.

19. The Marriott Incident

1. Lieutenant Colonel Axson and his staff also reviewed this chapter and rewrote many portions of it. The comments about Mr. Skinner are Colonel Axson's input.
2. Ibid.
3. *The Warriors,* "Days of Stars—Bronze, That Is."
4. Colonel Axson et al. review and rewriting.
5. "Days of Stars."
6. Colonel Axson et al. review and rewriting.
7. Letter from Capt. Steven Phelps.
8. Interview with Maj. Gen. Ed Scholes.
9. Article in *Fort Bragg Paraglide* (28 December 1989), p. 2A.

20. Tinajitas

1. 82 Airborne Division after-action report.
2. Letter from Capt. Lisa M. Kutschera (23 May 1991).
3. *Fayetteville Observer* (11 January 1990), p. 1D. The *Observer* of 28 December 1989 also carried a description of the action at Tinajitas, on p. 3D.
4. 82d Airborne Division after-action report.
5. *Fayetteville Observer* (11 January 1990 and 28 December 1989).
6. U.S. Southern Command briefing.
7. 82d Airborne Division summary of Operation Just Cause, and 82d Airborne Division *Notebook.*

21. 7th Infantry Division (Light)

1. 7th Infantry Division (Light) chronology of events for Operation Just Cause.
2. Operation Just Cause retrospective (16 February 1990), p. 7.

3. 82d Airborne Division historical report.
4. Letter from Lt. Col. William Leszczynski (10 March 1990).
5. Operation Just Cause retrospective, p. 10.
6. Letter from Colonel Leszczynski.
7. Conversation with Colonel McNeill after the operation.
8. 7th Infantry Division (Light) chronology.
9. Letter from Capt. Lisa M. Kutschera (23 May 1991).

22. Follow-on Operations

1. 82d Airborne Division after-action report.
2. *Fayetteville Observer* (11 January 1990), p. 1D, "Panama Notebook" by Rich Browne.
3. Letter from Dr. Robert K. Wright, Jr., XVIII Airborne Corps historian (24 May 1991).
4. U.S. Southern Command, briefing.
5. *Fayetteville Observer* (28 December 1989), p. 3D; article by Douglas Jehland and Bob Secter.
6. Conversation with Maj. Gen. Ed Scholes.
7. *Fayetteville Observer* (10 January 1990), pp. 1–4A.
8. *Fayetteville Observer* (11 January 1990), p. 4A; article by Harry Cunningham.
9. *Fayetteville Observer* (10 January 1990), pp. 1–4A—a long article covering the part played by civil affairs units in the postfighting period in Panama.

23. Winning the West and Noriega's Surrender

1. DA pamphlet *Soldiers in Panama* covers this chapter in an article, "Winning the West." The same general subject is covered in more detail in *The Warriors*—also called "Winning the West."
2. I first heard about the "Ma Bell approach" during my interview with General Downing.
3. Special Operations Command briefing.
4. U.S. Southern Command briefing.
5. Bob Woodward, *The Commanders* (New York: Simon & Schuster, 1991), p. 186.
6. *Fayetteville Times* (28 December 1989), p. 1A.
7. Ibid.
8. *Fayetteville Times* (5 January 1990), pp. 1–4A.
9. *Fayetteville Times* (4 January 1990), p. 1A.
10. Memo from Maj. Gen. Ed Scholes (undated).

24. The New Military

1. Dan Rather, CBS Radio News analysis and commentary (28 December 1989).
2. Personal knowledge. The Special Forces soldiers selected by Col. Bull Simon for the Son Tay raid came from the Special Warfare Center of which I was the commander at the time.
3. *Time* (8 January 1990), p. 43.
4. U.S. Southern Command briefing.
5. Telephone call from Lt. Gen. Tom Kelly, Joint Chiefs of Staff operations chief.
6. Conversation with Maj. Gen. Ed Scholes.
7. Letter from Sgt. Lewis A. Matson (3 January 1992).
8. John Monk, "Did the 82d Look Before It Leaped?" *Savannah News Press* (4 February 1990).
9. *Fayetteville Observer* (12 January 1990), p. 2A.

Sources

Interviews

A number of officers who participated in Just Cause were generous with their time and granted me interviews in person or on the telephone. Among them were Lt. Col. Gerald L. Behnke (who also escorted me around the 82d's marshaling area); Capt. Stuart W. Bradin; Maj. Donald K. Bridges; Lt. Gen. Wayne A. Downing; Lt. Col. Michael Franks, USMC; Lt. Col. David Huntoon; Lt. Gen. Thomas W. Kelly; Brig. Gen. William F. (Buck) Kernan; Col. Dan K. McNeill; Brig. Gen. Thomas H. Needham; Cmdr. David Porter, USN (Ret.); Capt. Gary J. Ramsdell; Maj. Gen. Edison E. Scholes; Capt. Raymond A. Thomas; and Dr. Robert K. Wright.

Private Papers, Letters, and Personal Communications

A number of officers and soldiers, and others wrote about their personal and unit experiences on Just Cause. Among them were Maj. Dorian T. Anderson; Pfc. R. T. Anderson; Staff Sergeant Arta; Maj. Charles W. Barker; Maj. Craig D. Barta; Capt. Jonathan L. Beegle; S. Sgt. Kurt Boehm; 1st Lt. Jeffrey A. Bouais; Staff Sergeant Brackenbury; Maj. Donald K. Bridges; Lt. Col. Robert V. Bryant; Private First Class Bunch (a letter nineteen handwritten pages long); Spc. Steven L. Clark; Maj. Stan Clemons; Sgt. David R. Clifton; Capt. Philip D. Colchar; Ms. Mary Ellen Condon-Rall; Capt. George R. Copeland; Capt. Edward B. Daly; Capt. John A. Davis; Sgt. Steven L. Denelsbeck; First Lieutenant Dichairo; Capt. (Dr.) William C. Doukas; 1st Lt. Brian Drinkwine; Pfc. Leon Erickson; Capt. Stephen G. Fogarty; Pfc. Richard Fox; Capt. (Chaplain) Peter J. Frederick; Lt. Col. Robert L. Granville; Lt. Col. James J.

241

Grazioplene; Sergeant Greene; Mr. George B. Grimes, PAO office, USSOCOM; S. Sgt. Frank A. Grippe; Capt. David B. Haight; Col. John W. Handy; Capt. Louis E. Herrera; Maj. Kevin M. Higgins; Maj. Steven R. Hill; S. Sgt. Richard J. Hoerner; Capt. Samuel H. Johnson; 1st Lt. Paul Kelly; Brig. Gen. William F. (Buck) Kernan; First Lieutenant King; Private First Class Kovac; Specialist Kristops; Capt. Lisa M. Kutschera; Lt. Col. William J. Leszczynski, Jr.; Gen. James J. Lindsay; Lt. Gen. Gary E. Luck; Lt. Col. Alan H. Maestas; Spc. Richard Malvarose; Col. Donald P. Maple; Spc. Paul Margeaf; Sgt. Lewis A. Matson; 1st Sgt. Joseph L. Mattison; 1st Lt. Kerry D. McCown; Specialist McKinnon; Brig. Gen. Charles W. McLain; Maj. Raymond Melnyk; Capt. John W. Metz; 1st Lt. Joseph A. Mullally; Capt. Mike Newcomb; Maj. Clyde M. Newman; 1st Lt. Tim Nye; Specialist Oler; Capt. Steven Phelps; Capt. Gary J. Ramsdell; Lt. Col. James W. Reed; Col. C. E. Richardson, USMC; Col. Peter J. Schoonmaker; Pfc. Paul Signonetti; Mr. Clayton H. Snedeker, Twenty-first Air Force historian; Col. Michael G. Snell; Specialist Sonnenschien; Col. Daniel E. Sowada; Sgt. Andrew A. Spano; Spc. Steve Stadelman; Pfc. William Stasburg; Maj. L. D. Walker; and Sergeant White.

Military Documents and Publications That Provided Many Facts and Background

After-action report, Southern Command Network
Capt. Donald K. Bridges, 75th Ranger Regiment summary of operations
Bulletin No. 90–9 (October 1990), *Operation Just Cause Lessons Learned* Volumes I, II, and III, U.S. Army Combined Arms Command, Fort Leavenworth, Kansas
Maj. Gen. Carmen J. Cavezza's biographical sketch
Chronology of events for Just Cause, 7th Infantry Division (Light)
Capt. Mark Conley, B Company, 5/87th Jungle Cats after-action report
Capt. Don Currie, C Company, 5/87th Panthers after-action report
DA *Field Manual 100-5* (September 1954)
Maj. J. M. Donivan, 4–6th Infantry, Citation for Army Commendation Medal
XVIII Airborne Corps Briefing Charts for JTF South
82d Airborne Division: Operation Just Cause briefing charts and notes; SOP for airborne operations; operational summary (23 December 1989–5 January 1990); memo, chief of staff
82d Airborne Division to chief of staff XVIII Airborne Corps (undated); historical summary (17 December 1989–12 January 1990)
Lt. Col. B. R. Fitzgerald, 1/508 unit history, Operation Just Cause
Capt. Bill Flynt, A Company, 5/87 Jaguars after-action report
Lt. Col. James J. Grazioplene, history of 3/73d armor and briefing charts. Also "Armor Support to Infantry in Contingency Operations"
Lt. Col. William H. Huff III, 5/87th Infantry after-action report
Joint Chiefs of Staff chronology entry log (16 December–20 December 1989)
Joint Special Operations Task Force (JSOTF) briefing charts

Just Cause briefing notes and charts; chronology of Panamanian crisis (February 1988–January 1990)
Just Cause "Hotwash Agenda" with comments
Brig. Gen. William F. Kernan, 75th Ranger Regiment, briefing charts and notes; biographical sketch; 75th Rangers SOP
Col. Dan K. McNeill, 82d Airborne Division G-3, on Just Cause: personal diary and notes
Maj. Raymond Melnyk, office of Joint Chiefs of Staff, information paper "Panama—Just Cause," JTFSOUTH (20 December 1989–13 January 1990)
Operation Just Cause, DA PIO releases, Section B
Operation Just Cause retrospective, *Fort Ord Panorama* (16 February 1990)
E-4 Ivan D. Pérez, 4/6th Infantry Battalion, citation for Silver Star
E-4 Roderick B. Ringstaff, 4/6th Infantry Battalion, citation for Silver Star
7th Infantry Division (Light), chronology log (12 December 1989–10 February 1990)
Soldiers (February 1990)
Col. Michael G. Snell, after-action report, 193d Brigade
Soldiers in Panama, chief, Public Affairs Command Information Division, U.S. Army
General Carl W. Stiner, career résumé
Task Force Bayonet overview of Operation Just Cause
U.S. Special Operations Command, briefing and charts for Just Cause
U.S. Southern Command, briefing and charts

Magazines That Have Been Quoted from or That Proved Useful for Background

American Legion Magazine (April and August 1990)
ARMY (February 1990)
ARMY TIMES (ten issues between 2 February 1990 and 29 October 1990)
AVIATION WEEK & SPACE TECHNOLOGY (1 January 1990)
Current Biography Yearbook 1988
Current History ("World Affairs Journal," December 1988)
Facts On File, Vol. 49, No. 2529, May 12, 1989; Vol. 49, No. 2550, Oct. 6, 1989; Vol. 49, No. 2561, Dec. 22, 1989.
Fort Ord Panorama (Operation Just Cause retrospective, 16 February 1990)
INSIGHT (29 January 1990)
Marine Corps Gazette (February 1990, September 1990)
Marine Magazine (January 1990)
Military Life Style (July–August 1990)
Newsweek (1 January 1990, 15 January 1990, 25 June 1990, 16 July 1990)
TIME (1 January 1990), 8 January 1990), 16 October 1990, 23 October 1990)
U.S. NEWS & WORLD REPORT (30 July 1990)

SOURCES

Published Sources from Which Facts or Quotations Have Been Taken

Dinges, John, *Our Man in Panama.* New York: Random House, 1990.
Donnelly, Thomas, Margaret Roth, and Caleb Baker. *Operation Just Cause.* Lexington Books, 1991.
Kempe, Frederick, *Divorcing the Dictator.* New York: G. P. Putnam's Sons, 1990.
North, Oliver L. *Under Fire: An American Story.* New York: Harper Collins, 1991.
Woodward, Bob. *The Commanders.* New York: Simon & Schuster, 1991.

Articles That Have Been Quoted from or That Proved Useful

Akers, Col. Frank, "The Warriors," a DA summary of Just Cause operations
"Did 82d Look Before It Leaped?," *Savannah News Press* (4 February 1990).
Fauriol, Georges, "Security in the Americas," National Defense University Press, Washington, D.C., 1989.
"Focus on Panama," a section of Marine Corps Gazetteer (September 1990) featuring articles by Marine officers who served in Panama during Just Cause. Included were Col. Robert P. Mauskapf, Maj. Earl W. Powers, Capt. Stephen J. Linder, Capt. John S. Dunn, Capt. Gerald H. Gaskins, 1st Lt. Brian C. Colebaugh, Capt. Richard R. Huizenga, and 1st Lt. Kenneth M. DeTreux.
Hammond, Capt. Kevin J., and Capt. Frank Sherman, "Sheridans in Panama," *Armor* (May/April 1990).
Livingstone, Neil C. "Danger in the Air," *The Washingtonian* (June 1990).
"Misuse of SEALs in Panama," Chicago *Tribune* (9 February 1990).
Quinn, Sally, "Interview with Noriega," *Washington Post* (8 March 1978).

Reviews and Comments

A number of officers reviewed pertinent portions of the text and made comments and corrections. Among them were: Lt. Col. Harry Axson; Capt. Stuart W. Bradin; Maj. Albert E. Dochnal; Lt. Gen. Wayne A. Downing; 1st Lt. Byron K. Echols; Maj. Kevin M. Higgins; Lt. Col. David Huntoon; Maj. Raymond Melnyk; Brig. Gen. Thomas Needham; Capt. Gary J. Ramsdell; and Maj. Gen. Edison E. Scholes.

Index

About the Author

Lt. Gen. Edward M. Flanagan, Jr., U.S. Army (Ret.), was born in Saugerties, New York, and graduated from West Point with the World War II class of January 1943. In World War II he served with the 11th Airborne Division in combat as a battery commander and division staff officer in the Philippines and later with the occupation forces in Hokkaido, Japan. During the Korean War he commanded the parachute artillery battalion of the 187th Airborne Regimental Combat Team. In Vietnam, he served in Chu Chi as assistant division commander of the 25th Infantry Division, in Saigon with the staff of MACV, and at Da Nang as the operations officer of the 3d Marine Amphibious Force. He commanded the 3d Armored Division Artillery in Germany, the JFK Center for Special Forces at Fort Bragg, the 1st Infantry Division at Fort Riley, Kansas, and the Sixth Army at the Presidio in San Francisco. He was the deputy commander of the Eighth Army in Korea. He served two tours in the Pentagon, first as a lieutenant colonel in the Army's Secretary of the General Staff and later as a lieutenant general as the Army comptroller. He is a master parachutist with one combat jump and an Army aviator. His military decorations include two Distinguished Service Medals, two Legions of Merit, a Bronze Star, two Air Medals, and nine battle stars. He has had published five books on military history and writes a monthly column and other articles for *Army* magazine. He and his wife, Peggie, have five children.